I0700155

Restless

A Death Dwellers MC Novel

By

Kathryn C. Kelly

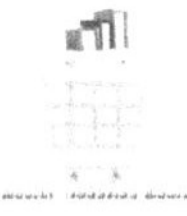

Restless by Kathryn C. Kelly
Published by Makin Groceries Media
24200 SW Freeway, Suite 402, #353
Rosenberg, TX 77471
www.katkelwriter.com
www.deathdwellersmc.com

© 2023 Kathryn C. Kelly
© 2023 Restless Cover Art Kathryn E. Ferdinand

Restless
A Death Dwellers MC Novel
By Kathryn C. Kelly

All rights reserved. This book or any portion thereof may not be reproduced or used in any manner whatsoever without the express written permission of the publisher except for the use of brief quotations in a book review.

Manufactured in the United States of America

This is a work of fiction. The characters, incidents and dialogue in this book are of the author's imagination and are not to be construed as real. Any resemblance to actual events or persons, living or dead, is completely coincidental.

ISBN: 979-8-88630-009-3 (ebook)
ISBN: 979-8-88630-010-9(paperback)
ISBN: 979-8-88630-012-3(hardcover)

Library of Congress Control Number: 2023923493

"Do Not Go Gentle Into That Good Night" By Dylan Thomas, from THE POEMS OF DYLAN THOMAS, copyright ©1952 by Dylan Thomas. Reprinted by permission of New Directions Publishing Corp.

DEDICATION

Lucian, welcome to the world, my love.

Kate, your covers are magnificent, and your observations are hilarious.
You gave me great one-liners.

Deborah Bays-Wolf, I don't know what I'd do without your hysterical
commentary. Thank you for being Johnnie's #1 fan. ::Evil laughter::

"I'm pregnant."

Since this morning's doctor's appointment, Kimber Caldwell had rehearsed how she'd inform her man that she was expecting. She tried writing a note, but after staring at a blank sheet of paper for an hour without finding the right words, she'd given up. Her brother, Cee Cee, suggested she buy an over-the-counter pregnancy test, pee on it, and leave the results on Joe's dinner plate.

Ew. Bleh. Blah.

Cee Cee could be such a fucking asshole. No wonder Joe hadn't talked to him in months.

She'd just hung up from sharing her news with Vivian Frank, when Joe walked in, smelling of smoke and motor oil after a long day at the auto shop.

Their place was small, three rooms that included a living room, kitchen, and bedroom, but it was the first bit of stability she'd had. Although Joe paid their bills, he'd added her name on the lease.

He was a good man. She was sure he'd be happy about the baby, unplanned though it was.

However, as he froze in the process of grabbing a cold beer from their refrigerator and his hand tightened on the handle, doubt assailed Kimber.

"What did you say?"

Shifting her weight, she wrung her hands together. "I'm pregnant," she said quietly.

Straightening, he turned and stared at her, his face unreadable. He was a tall man with broad shoulders and bulging muscles. He favored man buns for his golden blond hair, and the brilliance of his blue eyes had mesmerized her from the moment she met him.

"Are you sure?"

"My doctor confirmed it this morning."

He walked to her and stared at her. Kimber managed not to flinch. Joe had never lifted a hand to her, but she couldn't forget her father's abuse.

Her first cognitive memory was of her father's vileness to her and Cee Cee while their mother watched.

"Say something, Joe. If you don't want it, I can raise it alone—"

Joe interrupted her with a kiss. "No, babe. I want it! I...you're making me a father, Kimber, and I don't know what to say. I'm not good with words. Not like you. You're beautiful and smart." He kissed her again. "And mine," he said, wrapping his strong arms around her. "I love you so fucking much."

Kimber's heart melted and she clung to him. "I love you, too, Joe. So much. I can't imagine how my life would be if I hadn't gone to Cee Cee's club after his wedding to see Bash and tell my brother to get Celia."

Cee Cee usually wanted nothing to do with his girls. He was crazy fertile, but he only claimed the boys. However, Kimber was at the club about a year ago when Celia's mother brought the baby to Cee Cee to soften him. She was wasting her time, although she found out the hard way.

Kimber offered to babysit the girl. Her niece's mother, whose name she'd never learned, laughed in her face and said if Cee Cee didn't take the child, she'd throw her in a garbage can.

Wrinkling her nose, Kimber shoved aside the bloody aftermath of that threat.

"Sit down, babe," Joe said, bringing her back to the present and guiding her to their dinette chair. He knelt in front of her and took her hand in his, kissing the back of it. "My beautiful, beautiful Kimber. My love."

"Are you happy, Joe?"

He nodded. "I'm going to have to get more work. We can't stay here, sweetheart. You need a bigger house. When you start waddling—"

She swatted his arm and giggled. "Fucking asshole. I am not going to gain a lot of weight so you lose interest in me."

"Kimber, you gain as much weight as you need to for the baby. I won't ever desert you for stupid shit."

She believed him because she trusted him.

Standing, he swept her into his arms and carried her to the sofa. When he sat, he secured her on his lap, tucking her head underneath his chin.

"Maybe, I should visit Logan Donovan."

Not long ago, Cee Cee wanted Joe to watch Logan, but Joe resisted. He didn't like Logan. He was a power-hungry loose cannon, whom Joe bitterly regretted allowing to live.

"We need the money now, although I'd prefer if the Scorpions absorbed the Dwellers. Cee Cee could return to watch Logan himself and I'd ask to go to Richmond."

"What about K-P?"

Kimber liked Kaleb Paul Andrews. He was fair-minded and laid-back. She wished Vivian planned to marry him in a few months rather than Sharper Banks.

"K-P is my right hand, sweetheart. He'll go wherever I do."

She sighed. "I'll talk to Cee Cee again about the Scorpions and the Dwellers."

"I know, sweetheart. It isn't fair to K-P to bring him into the hornet's nest. He might think he can handle Logan, but sometimes I doubt I can. That's why I want Cee Cee to handle him. Rack was supposed to do the honors, but he is completely enamored of Logan."

"He would be," Kimber snorted. "He's a pig like Logan."

"Don't tax yourself, sweetheart. Work on your Great American Novel and become a world-famous author. I'll figure this out for us." He tightened his hold on her. "I'm going to lay the world at your feet, babe. Our kid won't ever know hunger or fear or homelessness. I promise you I'm going to make so much money you won't be able to spend it in ten lifetimes."

"You're so silly!" she said, laughing happily. "You won't have to work so hard once I become rich off my writing."

"That money will be yours to spoil yourself, babe. The millions I earn will be ours. I'll use half to spoil you like a man should his woman and the other half to take care of our family."

"Do you know how deep into the criminal underworld you'd have to traverse to earn the type of money you're discussing?" she said, grinning. "And I don't care about money. I want you safe. I want us to be together and happy. I want our ten children healthy."

Joe choked. "Ten...babe...ten..."

Clenching her jaw so she wouldn't roar in laughter at his worried tone, she nodded. "Nine girls and one boy to carry on the Foy name."

"Goddamn…" He heaved in a breath. "Ten? Yeah, fuck, Kimber. Ten children will be expensive as hell."

"I'm fucking with you, Joe," Kimber relented around peals of laughter. "I would like four. Two boys and two girls, but I'll be happy with how ever many babies we have."

"You're a little bitch for fucking with me like that," Joe said, chuckling.

She tipped her head back. "Ummm, kinky. I'm a little bitch when I fuck you."

He bent and covered her mouth with his. "Can we fuck?" he asked once they came up for air.

"Of course!" Kimber said breathlessly.

"Isn't your belly delicate? I don't want to hurt you…I'll let you take the lead."

Straddling him, Kimber placed her fingers over his mouth. "Shhh, it's okay, babe. I'm strong and healthy. Nothing is going to happen to me."

"It better not," Joe said gruffly. "I don't know what I'd do without you."

"Survive. Find another woman to love. Thrive. The same thing you told me to do if something happened to you."

Big hands gripping her ass cheeks, Joe leaned his head against the back of the sofa and ground his hard cock against her. She knew she should've changed into a dress! Her jeans were a hindrance.

"I smell like motor oil, Kim. I need to shower."

"It isn't as if we haven't fucked before with you smelling like motor oil, Joe."

"I have a surprise for you, though. It's late. I don't want it to arrive just as I sink into your pussy."

"What is it?"

"Something you've wanted for a while."

"A new computer?"

Joe winced. "I'm still saving for the one you want, babe."

"You should let me get a job—"

"I'm not stopping you, sweetheart. But I want to spoil you. I want to provide all your needs and give you the life you should've had growing up."

"Oh, Joe. Once Cee Cee got me away from our parents, my life wasn't particularly bad. I missed him so much, though."

She'd never known the exact story. She'd been a toddler and he'd been quite young, too. The sheet of paper with his name, birthdate, and last known address had survived shuffling between strangers after a hospital stay.

Sometimes, Kimber wondered if she imagined the name-calling and the pain that lived in her memory and haunted her dreams.

"I'm going to be a father," Joe said in wonder. "Cee Cee will be an uncle and Bash will be a cousin."

Kimber grinned. "You haven't seen either of them in over a year." They'd had a falling out, although she wasn't sure over what, but she suspected it had something to do with the Donovan girls. "Does it matter what they will be?"

"Not really. I do wonder about Donovan's grandsons sometimes. The older one is about fourteen or fifteen months now, so the other one would be eight or nine months."

"Cee Cee is such a fucking asshole," she grumbled. "He doesn't think our twisted fucking family tree isn't complicated enough. He knocked up two sisters, so his sons are brothers and cousins."

"I know, babe. We aren't helping matters, Kimber."

"We aren't related, Joe. Shocking, I know, considering we

seem to pull motherfuckers out of crayon boxes to make up our family tree."

He sniggered. "This is a clean slate for us, sweetheart," he said, sobering up and caressing her ass. "A new beginning. No more twisted family trees. I'll take more hours at the shop. Maybe, repair cars in my free time. Fuck Logan. I'll make it work. One day, I'll own my own repair shops. Just wait. You'll see. You'll be a lady of leisure when you're not writing. Our daughters will be spoiled little princesses, and our sons will one day rule the world."

Kimber smiled.

"Let's get married," he said suddenly. "We love each other. You're having my baby. Let's—"

"Absolutely not, Joe," Kimber said, so happy she could burst. "I want a big wedding. Maybe, not as big as Vivian's will be, but one to remember. Let's get engaged and six months after I give birth, we marry."

"Anything you want, sweetheart, as long as you agree to be my wife."

"I want nothing more than to have your name," she said dreamily as someone knocked on the door.

He patted her hip. "Your surprise."

Unable to contain her curiosity, Kimber scrambled off Joe's lap. When he stood, he pulled her to her feet and guided her to the door. Before he opened it, he placed himself in front of her. "Don't peek over my shoulder."

"I won't," she promised, trying and failing to think of what she was in store for.

"Hey, Joe." The sound of K-P's voice disappointed Kimber. "It was a long fucking flight."

"Are you okay, sweetheart? K-P's ugly mug didn't frighten you?"

Childish laughter greeted Kimber, and her heart rate

sped up.

"Noooo," the little voice said.

Kimber gasped. "Celia?" she whispered, forgetting her promise, stepping next to Joe and gazing down at her niece.

"Aunt Kimmie!"

Kimber knelt just as Celia launched her tiny body into her arms. Kimber thought she couldn't have loved Joe any more than she already did.

She was wrong.

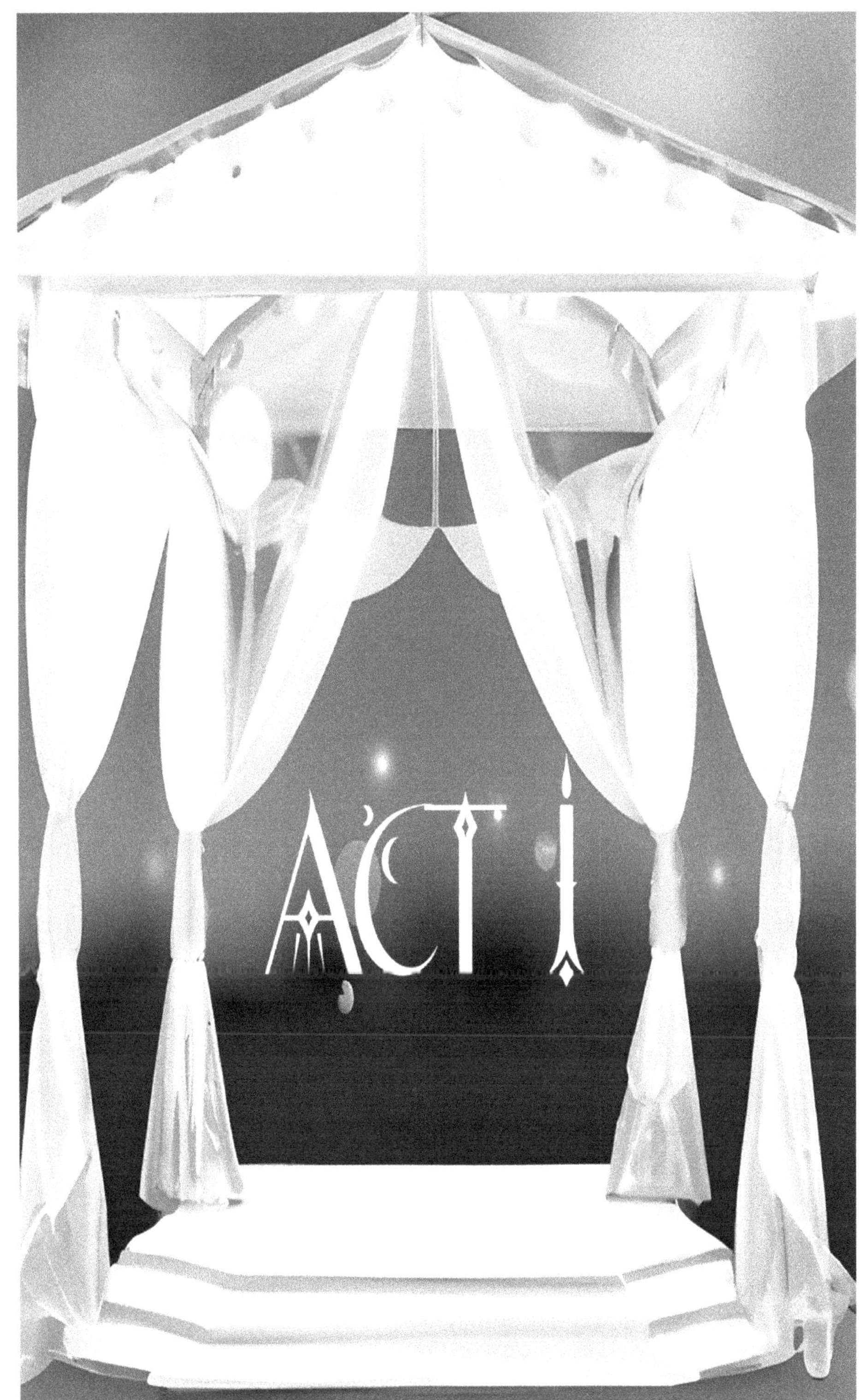

ACT I

Her orange and green wedding colors blended well together. While green represents life, hope, and anticipation, orange stands for joy and creativity, suggesting safety. *Warmth.*

Vivian Frank brushed off her pastel palette, focusing on each color's meaning rather than the vibrancy of the shades. The myriad orange roses, begonias, and tulips as well as green carnations, chrysanthemums and dahlias sweetened the air. Even though she sat in her bedroom, finishing her makeup and hiding her bruises, the scents wafted through the air vents.

Her lips trembling, she fingered her diamond choker. Until a week ago, her life had been like a fairytale as the only child of doting parents. She was their princess and never knew a day's struggle. She'd lived a charmed existence from the moment she was born. Today, on her 20th birthday—her wedding day—she should've looked forward to years of happiness.

Instead, she'd walked in on her soon-to-be husband in bed

with Logan Donovan. Naked, sweaty, and…and…

Tears rushed to her eyes. She sniffled.

"Vivian?"

Huffing a breath, she swiped at the escaping tear, not intending to respond to Joe Foy.

Her doorknob turned.

"Let me in, Viv."

"I'm here with him, Vivvie," Kimber Caldwell murmured.

Over the nearly two years since her engagement to Sharper, she'd become good friends with Kimber. Vivian needed a friend right now. Stumbling to her feet, she tripped forward and unlocked the knob.

The door opened and Kimber rushed in. She was so gorgeous with her wealth of black hair and green eyes. At six months pregnant, she'd gained a lot of weight but was never happier.

"Sit, babe," Joe said to Kimber, taking Vivian into his arms and hugging her. "Are you okay, Viv?"

More tears rolled down her cheeks. If she didn't pull herself together, she'd ruin her makeup. She shrugged.

"Come," Kimber murmured, wrapping her arms around Vivian and guiding her back to the vanity.

"Kimber—"

Placing a finger over Joe's mouth, she grinned and leaned in for his kiss. "I'm fine, babe. I'm not risking your son, you bossy motherfucker."

Joe snickered, slapping her ass when she turned away.

Kimber yanked several tissues from the box on the table and dabbed Vivian's cheeks. "You're only going through with the wedding to that fuckhead because you want your baby to have a name."

"You're expecting, babe?" Joe asked in surprise, cutting a fine figure in his tuxedo. He reminded her of a Viking with his height, icy blue eyes, and golden hair. "Have you gotten checked out?"

"I-I think the baby is fine," she said. "After Logan…when he…" She dissolved into tears again. "Until last night's rehearsal dinner, I stayed in bed."

Anger swept away Joe's kind expression and he kneeled next to her. "Does Sharper know?" The quiet tone contrasted with the burning fury in his eyes.

She shook her head.

"That motherfucker needs to know," Kimber snapped, adding as she stomped out of the room, "I need some cold cloths."

Alone with Joe, Vivian turned and sobbed on his shoulder, not understanding his words of comfort.

"Hey, Viv." Kaleb Paul's voice broke through her misery.

She laid her head on Joe's shoulder as Kimber rushed back in and placed a cold towel on her forehead.

"My offer still stands," Kaleb said, closer, though she couldn't see him since Kimber stood in her way. "Fuck Sharper. I'll marry you and raise your kid."

"No," Joe said flatly, shooting to his feet. "I can't protect you from *both* those motherfuckers."

"It isn't your fucking decision, Joe," Kaleb snapped. "Vivian's a good girl. If Sharper can't keep his cock out of Logan, he'll make her miserable."

"Shut up, fuckheads," Kimber ordered. "This is a free fucking country. If Vivian wants to marry motherfucking Sharper—"

"I don't want to marry anyone," Vivian admitted on a sob. "Not even you, Kaleb. You're a good man. Otherwise, I wouldn't have asked you to be the baby's godfather. But Joe's right. If you marry me, you'll be a target of both Logan and Sharper. I learned the hard way about getting on Logan's bad side."

Kaleb walked to her. His head full of hair, strong jaw, and kind eyes always drew her in. He was quiet strength whereas Joe was pure hellfire. In her head, she'd always believed Sharper drew from each of their characteristics, giving her the best of both worlds—a decent man interested in becoming a fire and brimstone minister.

"You don't have to marry today, babe," Kaleb whispered.

"I wish I'd fallen for you."

His smirk revealed deep dimples. "I can always kill Sharper."

Joe slapped the back of his head. "Shut the fuck up."

"K-P's right," Kimber said. She loved nicknames. She'd bestowed Kaleb with K-P; Joe with Boss; her brother, Sebastian, with Cee Cee, and her nephew with Bash. "Cee Cee, the asshole, throws fucking stones when he's loyal to his fucking brother and cousin."

That Wallace Bart was Cee Cee's half-brother and Sharper their cousin still blew Vivian's mind. Certainly, there were darker-skinned men. Her father for instance. But Sharper's appearance gave no indication he'd had a white mother, who'd been the sister of Cee Cee and Wally's father.

Cee Cee and Wally's mothers and father were killed in a drug deal gone bad. Sharper's mother, by then long single, took in her nephews before her criminal lifestyle caught up to her and the three boys ended up in foster care where they'd met Joe and Kaleb.

Jingling spurs accompanied by boot falls pounded toward her door and they all fell silent. Without invitation, Cee Cee walked into her bedroom. He halted, zeroing in on his younger sister, and smiling.

"Hey, babe," he greeted, holding out an arm and taking a drag on his cigarette.

Kimber sailed to him and stepped into his embrace. "Hey, asshole."

Blowing out smoke, he sniggered.

Vivian had never figured out Kimber and Cee Cee's real connection. He'd been in foster care for several years, so Vivian often wondered how they'd reconnected and whether they were full siblings or half. They were beautiful people and shared a strong resemblance. Unlike Wally and Cee Cee. Or Sharper and Cee Cee.

"Only invited guests are allowed on premises," Joe barked, "so get the fuck out, Cee Cee."

He dragged on his cigarette again, released more smoke, and smiled at the frown Kimber threw Joe.

"I'm invited, Joseph," he said calmly. "Kimber wanted me to see my girl."

Joe glared at Kimber. "Why didn't you tell me he was coming?"

"I told her not to," Cee Cee said coldly, flicking ashes on the hardwood floor.

"Hey, fuckhead," Kaleb growled. "Show some fucking manners." He pointed to the ashes. "This isn't a fucking yard."

"I haven't seen you in almost two fucking years, Kaleb Paul, and you still have that stick up your fucking ass," Cee Cee said, squeezing the tip of the cigarette between his fingers to extinguish it. His green gaze fell on Vivian. "Hey, girl."

"Hi, Sebastian," she said, never comfortable enough to call him by Kimber's designated nickname.

"I hear you ran afoul of Donovan."

Swallowing, Vivian nodded.

He pulled out a flask, opened it, and swigged. "I have him in a holding cell at a nearby house. He won't ever bother you again. I don't have regard for many cunts, but I love Kimber.

Bitch was in tears over your pain, and I took great fucking issue with that."

Kimber rolled her eyes. "I'm just overcome by your sentimentality."

Ignoring her, Cee Cee looked at Vivian again. "I have a long ride ahead back to Richmond, so you need to get a move on. Joe, Kaleb, and me are burying that motherfucker while everybody's engaged at your wedding ceremony."

Part One

Death, Be Not Proud

PROLOGUE

True love was a quixotic ideal, though a plausible desire.

For most, love was a fleeting euphoria that either imploded without warning or slipped away in drawn-out pain. And a love for the ages…? That elusive perfect love for imperfect people? That was an exclusive club where only a select few had a membership.

John "Johnnie" Donovan learned the hard way he'd been denied admission. He had loved and lost and loved again. And almost lost everything. His friends. His life.

His wife.

Kendall's suicide attempt sobered him. He'd sought perfection from imperfection. He'd based his own frustratingly imperfect relationship on someone else's impossibly perfect marriage.

She'd been discharged from medical care and put into a psychiatric facility. Unlike times past, Johnnie made sure she was as close as possible. After three months, she was released. He'd never been so relieved or grateful, yet she insisted on staying in a guestroom.

When their kids moved back in with them almost a year after Kendall's near death, Johnnie convinced her to return to the master bedroom. Upon her agreement, he'd thought she wanted to share a bed with him again.

She hadn't.

Instead, she'd sworn if he didn't move to a guestroom, she wouldn't return to the master suite. Mystified at why she resisted each one of his seduction attempts, he'd given her the master suite. As time progressed, they became each other's best friends. He awakened with her on his mind and fell asleep with her in his dreams.

They were like teenagers, sharing secrets and spending every waking moment together. Once Rory, Matilda, and JJ returned, Johnnie had never felt so complete.

And, yet, his sex life was non-existent. Kendall denied him access to her body.

Over the next six months, Kendall was slowly welcomed back into the fold of the other old ladies. Megan, as always, was the first to forgive. She, with the help of Roxanne, paved the way for the others.

For the first time ever, Johnnie knew what real happiness was. He *saw* how it looked on Kendall. She glowed and he floated. He'd never love anyone the way he loved her. Not even Megan, whom he'd loved with everything in him. She'd been his first love and he'd always hold a special place for her. Committing to help Kendall through her near fatal suicide attempt forced him away from constant contact with Megan. True, Rory, Matilda, and JJ lived with her and Christopher, but Johnnie knew they were in good hands and refused to use his children as an excuse to talk to his sister-in-law.

As his feelings for Megan faded into sweet memories, he realized how much he truly loved Kendall; *she* was his everything.

Exactly two years after she tried to end her life, she finally welcomed him into her arms again. The next day, Johnnie moved back into the master suite and slept by her side from that day to this one. There were exceptions, of course, such as club runs and business trips.

Kendall wasn't perfect, so she had her moments, but neither was he.

And so that notion of true love *was* a quixotic ideal. *Real, constant* love took work and care and time.

It took understanding and protection.

It was that last, *protection*, that saw Johnnie in the passenger seat of a Mercedes, driven by the club's attorney, Brooks Redding.

For most of the twelve-hour drive, Johnnie hadn't said much. Understanding the wisdom of remaining on Johnnie's good side, Brooks kept his mouth shut.

As he turned into the entrance of a wood and metal building, west of Salt Lake City, and paused at the gate, a shaggy motherfucker wearing a denim cut, indicated he roll his window down.

Swallowing, Brooks sidled a glance at Johnnie.

"Go ahead, Brooks. This is for Kendall."

"Suppose they kill us?" Brooks whispered.

The biker knocked on the window.

"If I have to die to save my wife, then I will."

Johnnie didn't intend to die, but it was a very real possibility. They were there without Christopher's— *anyone's*—knowledge. Death was a very real risk.

"Johnnie—"

"Open the fucking window," Johnnie and the enemy chorused.

Brooks swallowed again. Heaved in a breath. Finally, he pressed the button.

"Who the fuck are you and what the fuck do you want?" Shaggy Motherfucker demanded once the window was rolled down.

High fences surrounded the property, so Johnnie couldn't discern if an army of motherfuckers trained guns on them, ready to fire.

"Repeat your name."

"Brooks Redding."

"And the motherfucker in the passenger seat?"

Johnnie leaned forward, all the better to see fuckhead. "I'm Johnnie. Bash's little brother," he said blandly. "Outlaw's little brother." Only by six months. Asshole didn't need a fucking family history.

The gatekeeper leaned into the car and dropped his gaze to the patches on Johnnie's cut. Straightening, he backed away and opened the gate.

By the time Brooks pulled into the parking space another biker directed him to, Johnnie had lit a cigarette. Jamming it in the side of his mouth, he got out of the car and slammed the door shut. Standing for the first time in several hours felt good. His full leathers and steel-toed boots protected him from the January cold.

"It's a full house," Brooks said, suddenly at Johnnie's side, briefcase in hand, glancing around the parking lot in wide-eyed fear.

Puffing on his cigarette, Johnnie nodded. Chrome from several dozen bikes gleamed underneath the winter sun. Bikers walked between narrow pathways, keeping watch.

The biker who'd allowed them entry halted in front of

Johnnie. A patch proclaimed him 'Stone'.

"Always heard you were the smart one."

Stone hocked a wad of spit. Droplets brushed against Johnnie's cheek as it blew past him. Stone would pay for that fucking insult.

"Wearing your colors and showing up uninvited might be perceived as a threat."

Johnnie blew smoke into Stone's face. "Granting me access when *you* stopped me at the gate might be seen as treason."

"We come in peace," Brooks said with admirable force. "Bash should be expecting us."

Stone kept his icy gaze on Johnnie. "Bash is expecting *you*, lawyerman."

"Brooks values his head on his shoulders instead of beside him at the bottom of the ocean," Johnnie said, enjoying the hell out of his cigarette. "He came to me with his information. *I* greenlit his call to Bash."

The door opened and a tall, barrel-chested Black man stepped outside, but leaned against the door so it wouldn't close. He held a metal detector wand.

Knowing what he did, Johnnie supposed the man's strong resemblance to Mortician and Digger was expected. "Cleaner."

Cleaner scowled. "Bash saw you on camera," he grumbled, beckoning him over with the wand.

Still blocked by Stone, Johnnie nodded to Brooks.

"Unless he's suddenly grown balls, I already know he's unarmed," Cleaner said, allowing Brooks entry without checking him or his briefcase. "This is for you."

"Call your Chihuahua down and I'll come to you," Johnnie said, throwing his cigarette on the ground and stomping it. "But I'm not giving up my gun." Or his blade.

"Then you're not seeing Bash," Cleaner countered.

Johnnie laughed with genuine amusement. "You have at least forty members inside." *At the very least, if the parked bikes were any indication.* "I'm not a superhero, able to extricate myself from such uneven odds."

Stone reached for Johnnie's cut.

"I wouldn't do that if I were you," Johnnie warned.

"Let him through, Stone," Cleaner ordered.

"I'll be waiting for you," Stone said under his breath.

Johnnie smirked at the motherfucker, brushing past Cleaner without comment.

Inside, warmth and noise greeted Johnnie. *TNT* by AC/DC blasted from speakers hanging at the tops of the walls. Brooks waited near the door, sweat beading his brow. Women and bikers surrounded the lacquered bar and filled the chairs at the tables. Small American flags painted on the walls shared space with rendered scorpions. The stage on the opposite side contained a center pole.

As more bikers caught sight of Johnnie, silence rolled in, until he and Brooks stood with all eyes on them.

Brooks shifted his briefcase from one hand to the other. He trembled, still scarred by the violence he'd brought upon himself so many years ago. Yet, he'd gotten back into the club's good graces. More importantly, Kendall saw him as a father and Brooks treated her as one of his daughters. For that alone, Johnnie would protect him.

He placed a hand on Brooks's shoulder. "You're fine," he soothed. "The meeting will be over before you know it and we'll check into the hotel to get a hot shower and a good meal. Tomorrow night, we'll be at home with our wives."

Drawing in a deep breath, Brooks nodded. "We should've told Outlaw—"

At the sound of heavy footfalls accompanied by jingling

spurs, Johnnie blinked. Even before Bash came into view in the hallway that seemed to branch off, the familiarity of the spurs arrested Johnnie.

Christopher loved his spurs, too.

Though Bash had a bald head, a beard, and scarred and pockmarked skin, he shared both Christopher's green eyes and Cee Cee's maniacal light.

Bash paused in the doorway. Signs pointing toward the hall indicated bathrooms and a staircase lay in that direction.

Walking forward, he glanced from Brooks to Johnnie. "To what do I owe the pleasure, little brother?" He paused. Smiled. "Outlaw turned forty-nine a week ago. I thought the celebrations would still be underway."

The birthday party reminded Johnnie of old times, before all the pain and betrayal, especially on his part. He wanted to atone for his many mistakes.

Bygones were bygones. Happiness abounded amongst the brothers and their old ladies. His children—his nieces and nephews—knew nothing of the grief that had passed.

Johnnie *would* die before he allowed motherfucking Bash to undermine his family's joy. "Forty-nine isn't the milestone, so it was just a birthday party. I'm sure Christopher's fiftieth will go down in infamy."

"Big Joe's girl will pull out all the stops for her man." Bash transferred his glacial gaze to Brooks. "I told you not to open your fucking mouth until you spoke to me."

Brooks straightened. "I work for Outlaw, Mr. Caldwell," he said evenly.

"Will you die for him, too?" Bash questioned.

"Shut the fuck up," Johnnie said coldly, fed-up. "When you want Brooks on your payroll, he'll follow your orders. Otherwise, take it up with me or Christopher."

Grumbles floated to Johnnie. He was disrespecting a club

president on his own turf. He drew in a deep breath. "Let's have a seat and talk, Bash."

"We're in my fucking club, John Boy. I'll give the directives."

"Then direct," Johnnie said flatly. "Your song and dance bore me."

"I resent your tone, little brother."

"Remind me when I gave a fuck about what you resented, *big brother*."

Cleaner sidled next to Bash. "Shut your fucking mouth, boy," he said to Johnnie, then glanced at Bash. "I can take him and lawyerman to the pit."

Brooks gulped. "Wh-what, pray, is the pit?"

"Probably the equivalent to our meatshack," Johnnie said with a shrug.

"*What*?" Brooks shrieked, paling before dropping to the floor in a dead faint.

"He's shitting me, right?" Bash asked, while Cleaner rapidly blinked at Brooks's prone body and roars of laughter rose around them.

Sighing, Johnnie lit another cigarette. "Motherfucker's out cold," he announced after taking a few puffs. "A remnant of crossing Christopher."

Bash and Cleaner exchanged glances, before Bash cleared his throat and beckoned someone at the bar. He indicated the table closest to where Brooks lay on the dirty floor.

The two bikers and three women sitting at the table scrambled out of their chairs, careful to walk around the attorney who still gripped the briefcase.

Bending, Johnnie seized it out of Brooks's limp hand and sat it in one of the empty chairs. He rested his cigarette in the ashtray on the table. "I need a bucket of ice."

Bash lifted a brow.

"A bucket of ice," Johnnie repeated.

Before the order was carried out, Brooks moaned and lifted himself to a sitting position.

"Get the fuck up before I shoot you myself," Johnnie ordered.

"Oh my god." Brooks sniffled and staggered to his feet.

The lawyer wasn't cut out for the likes of Bash. Kendall was. The thought rocketed through Johnnie's brain, along with immediate regret. Had he handled certain situations better, his wife could've been one of the attorneys for the club.

It took so much heartache for Johnnie to realize she'd wanted his attention and devotion and sought it anyway she could. Instead of being the man she needed, he'd tried to turn her into the woman he thought he wanted.

"God. God. God." Tears pooled in Brooks's eyes and streamed down his cheeks. He stood, arms clutched around his waist, rocking back and forth. "It wasn't a dream."

"Shut the fuck up, Brooks," Johnnie gritted. Even if things had gone differently, Kendall couldn't have accompanied him on this mission. He was there to protect her, not endanger her further. "Watch *Better Call Saul* and take some fucking notes."

The bikers and their women laughed.

Bash sucked his teeth and pointed to a chair. "Sit."

Immediately, Brooks sat.

Once Johnnie took a seat, Cleaner stood guard in front of their table, though the place was still eerily quiet. With so many present, there should've been some noise.

A naked girl with flaming red hair on her head and her pussy, a small waist, and melon-sized tits brought an opened bottle of whiskey, two glasses, and a small bucket of beer. She was so fucking young, Johnnie felt sick. He doubted she'd reached her eighteenth birthday, yet.

She had the look and build of Kendall. In turn, it reminded him of his precious Matilda. By sleight of hand, she could've been in this girl's position.

Smiling at Johnnie, she sat the items on the table.

"Gabby, this is Johnnie, one of my brothers."

Gabby sidled closer. If he turned, her breasts would shove against his face.

"I'm not interested in your whore or your alcohol, motherfucker," Johnnie growled. "It's telling that you bring an open bottle to us while you chose beer for yourself."

"She's our best slut," Cleaner threw over his shoulder. "You insult us by turning down the pussy she's offering."

"You insult me by offering pussy," Johnnie retorted.

Bash grabbed the bottle of whiskey, poured a measure in both glasses, then downed the contents in each. "Satisfied?" he asked, holding the bottle out to Johnnie. "I'm not a novice. My attempt to poison you wouldn't be so obvious."

Johnnie accepted the bottle and poured whiskey for himself and Brooks. All the while, Gabby remained at his side. With each move he made, he brushed against her.

"Go away, Gabby," he ordered.

"No, she's here to do a job," Bash said calmly. He took a beer from the bucket, opened it, and drank. "If she doesn't perform, she's no longer needed."

Not liking the implication, Johnnie narrowed his eyes.

"What if we pay you her going rate?" Brooks asked, misunderstanding what the asshole meant. "You'll still have made the money you expected from us, and she'll have her job."

The amusement dancing in Bash's eyes chilled Johnnie. Declining Gabby's services wouldn't cost her job. It would forfeit her life.

Gripping the girl's arms, he got to his feet and backed her to the seat on the other side of him. Pity rose in him at the stark fear on Gabby's face. He smiled gently. Once he sat, he took her hand in his and kissed the back of it to buy time. Though he didn't appreciate the censure in Brooks's eyes, he ignored it and kept Gabby's hand in his. He'd want a motherfucker to find a way to save his daughter, too.

"I take it you've read everything I sent to Brooks," Bash started.

Gabby trembled. Johnnie drank. "I did."

At Bash's nod, Cleaner ambled behind Gabby's chair. Tension settled into Johnnie and he emptied his glass. Foregoing the pleasantries, he swiped the bottle and guzzled.

Snickering, Cleaner placed his hand on Gabby's throat.

"Mr. Banks, I'll pay you double her rate for the night," Brooks blurted.

"Double?" Cleaner ran a long finger over her chest, not commenting on the way Brooks addressed him. "But you don't know her asking price, lawyerman."

Brooks snapped his mouth shut.

"Take her now or else it won't be pretty, Johnnie," Cleaner swore.

Her death would be long, painful and gruesome.

Dropping her hand, Johnnie looked at Bash. "Let's conclude our business first, then I'll enjoy your gift."

"No!" Cleaner insisted. "I want you to fuck her *now*."

Bash finished his beer. "I'm a reasonable man," he said around a sour belch. "Let her suck your cock for the time being. Show good faith before we proceed."

"Otherwise, her tongue's useless," Cleaner said, drawing a knife out of his cut.

Gabby burst into tears as horror washed over Brooks's face.

Grabbing a handful of her hair and yanking her head back, Cleaner slid the knife from the corner of Gabby's mouth to the edge of her jaw, ignoring her struggles. It wasn't a deep cut, but it was long. Blood bubbled to the surface.

Johnnie's nostrils flared. Somehow, he ignored the sudden urge for gore and death. The scent of blood still held power over him.

Yet, there would be no saving this girl, now or later. If Johnnie allowed the travesty to continue, Gabby *would* suffer grave indignities and tremendous pain.

"Tell your fucking cousin to stand down," Johnnie snarled.

Bash grinned. "He's your cousin too, asswipe."

True. If Cee Cee Caldwell and Sharper Banks were first cousins, then their sons and daughters would be second cousins. Meaning, Cleaner wasn't only Mortician and Digger's half-brother but Johnnie and Christopher's cousin. Unbelievably, motherfucking Rack had been their uncle.

Gabby's blood still flowed. Her sobs reached Johnnie through a tunnel covered in red and scented with death.

His temples throbbed. "My mistake," he said softly. "Tell *our* cousin to stand down."

Bash nodded to Cleaner. A moment later, the motherfucker resumed his position in front of the table.

Brooks dug in his suit pocket and got a handkerchief. Sliding his chair closer to Gabby, he pressed the silk against her cheek.

"You're not here to nurse a cunt," Bash snapped. "I summoned you for advice on the OGs and Hoochie Mamas."

His hand trembling, Brooks glanced over his shoulder, keeping the handkerchief in place at Johnnie's nod.

"Do you even know what a hoochie mama is, Bash?" Johnnie said with a snicker.

"Do you, boy?" Cleaner demanded, glaring at Johnnie.

"Oh, indeed," Johnnie retorted. "But let's not get into who knows more slang. You summoned Brooks to set him up. Gabby wasn't for me. She was for Brooks. Alone, he'd have no choice but to obey. Even if he didn't get a hard cock under such distress, photographs would tell a different story."

Brooks went still, dropped his hand away from Gabby's cheek, and looked at Bash.

"Caught," Bash said with an unrepentant smile. "But that wasn't the only reason I wanted to meet with him."

"The other reason is Kendall," Brooks said quietly, handing Gabby the handkerchief and turning his full attention to Bash. "And Matilda."

"Which is why he came to me," Johnnie said coldly, a hair's breath from shooting the fuck out of Bash and damning the consequences. "You're playing fucking games with my wife and daughter over documents that have nothing to do with them and should never have seen the light of day. If I ever discover who sent them to you, I'm fucking killing them."

"I merely stated I might have to take your wife and daughter to get the attorney's cooperation," Bash said affably. "There was no call to arms."

Johnnie glared at him. "What the fuck do you want, Bash? You have no fucking reason to want the documents exposed. The original charter and bylaws benefit Christopher. The house where Kendall's sister died was sold years ago. The house Big Joe purchased for his daughter was gambled away by her stepfather. Christopher's house in Long Beach, along with mine, was blown up. As was Sharper's mansion and church. Roxanne still has the house K-P purchased for her, but that doesn't relate to you. *None* of it does, since Cee Cee had nothing to do with the Dwellers. He was a fucking Scorpion."

"He might've been a Scorpion, but without him the Dwellers wouldn't have gotten off the ground."

"Bullshit! Big Joe put blood, sweat, tears, and money into the fucking club," Johnnie countered. "Without *him*, the Dwellers wouldn't have gotten off the ground. Cee Cee was too busy ruining women to give a fuck about our club."

"Rack was a charter member, asshole," Bash yelled. "He was my uncle, which gives me a claim to the Death Dwellers."

Johnnie lifted a brow. "He had a fucking son, who's probably long dead by now. Wallace, Jr., would have claim to it. Not you."

An odd expression passed over Bash's face, so fleeting Johnnie couldn't decipher the meaning.

"Leave Kendall and Matilda out of your bullshit, Bash," he ordered. "I don't take kindly to my wife and daughter being threatened." He nodded to Brooks.

Obediently, the attorney opened the briefcase and took out a cashier's check, then handed it to Bash.

Those green eyes widened.

"I want you to rip the documents and forget you ever saw them."

Cleaner walked behind Bash and leaned forward, squinting as he looked over the check. His eyes widened, too.

Bash set the check in front of Brooks, then glowered at Johnnie.

"Big Joe put everything in *her* name."

Only in Bash's fucked-up reasoning did the actions of Megan's father relate to Kendall.

Johnnie gritted his teeth. When he left, he wanted his top priority to be finding the fuckhead who opened this can of worms. He had the awful feeling that would be the least of his worries.

"*Everything* goes to her. The building housing the club. The grounds. Some of the businesses. Everyfuckingthing Joseph Fucking Foy ever purchased he put in Meggie's name."

"None of which she knows about," Johnnie pointed out.

"Meggie is a kind, reasonable woman," Brooks said. "We can arrange a meeting—"

"No!" Bash interrupted. "Fuck no. Outlaw tracks her. I have to stay one step ahead of him. Somehow! If we move too quickly or too slowly, we're dead."

"Outlaw takes no prisoners," one of the bikers called.

Johnnie scrubbed a hand over his face. He was running out of fucking options.

When Brooks invited him to his office the day after Christmas and showed him all Bash sent, Johnnie decided to investigate the matter before he went to Christopher. At the time, Megan hadn't been a factor because Bash directed his threats to Kendall and Matilda. Now, she was.

Glancing at Gabby, Johnnie found her sitting quietly. She was pale and the handkerchief still pressed against her cheek was soaked in blood.

He looked at Bash again. "After involving Brooks in a situation he couldn't have easily extricated himself from, you intended to blackmail him into doing what exactly?"

"Convincing Outlaw to turn off her tracking and then bringing her to me."

"Her who? Meggie?" Brooks squeaked. "Not Meggie. Certainly not Meggie. No, it couldn't be Meggie. Never Meg—"

Bash shot to his feet, causing Cleaner to stumble back. "Say her name one more fucking time and I'm killing you."

Johnnie rose, wordlessly telling Brooks to remain seated, suddenly in perfect position to achieve what needed doing.

"Outlaw would rip me apart," Brooks pushed out, pale, sweaty, and on the verge of tears again.

"When she dies, it all goes back to the club," Cleaner said.

"Logan saw to that stipulation," Bash added. "K-P had a set of the documents. I think they were the originals but he refused to tell their location. Over the years, Cee Cee tried to talk him into giving up their whereabouts. Logan was afraid of Pa. K-P refused. We never knew why. Until the envelopes began arriving two months ago. He was protecting Meggie."

"She was Joe's daughter," Johnnie pointed out.

"He had a fucking daughter! Bailey. It was Pa who protected her from Logan. Made her off-limits. If Pa hadn't been killed, K-P wouldn't have been skinned. Logan would never have crossed Pa."

The argument wore on Johnnie. "Take the fucking check and leave my wife alone. If you know what the fuck's good for you, you won't fuck with Megan. She doesn't know—"

"Your bitch is best friends with that cunt," Bash snapped. "I don't give a fuck anymore who has to go down. I want my just due."

Images of Kendall ran through Johnnie's mind. The first time he saw her when she'd strutted into the clubhouse, hellbent on seducing Christopher. The night she reappeared, on the eve of Logan rising from the fucking dead, when she'd seemed so jumpy and out-of-sorts. Finding her beaten half to death in the midst of a miscarriage.

Hearing Roxanne's sobs when she'd called him and told him Kendall had coded.

Listening to her on the two-year mark of that dark day as she revealed the abortion she'd had because she'd been angry with him and so many other missteps she'd made because he'd been such a fucking unfeeling, *unseeing* jerk.

Maybe, his many transgressions brought him to this point.

Christopher and Megan shared an ethereal, mysterious type of love. The quixotic ideal and the plausible dream. It was timeless. Endless. If Christopher lost her, his life would be over.

Yet, it was *their* love. Mystical and magical, but theirs.

Johnnie's love for Kendall had been honed in fire and blood. It had been a battle hard fought and well won. The rough edges were refined to simple joy rooted in friendship. He didn't want to live without her. He couldn't imagine life without her.

"Leave Kendall alone. My life for hers. Kill me instead."

Brooks got to his feet, eyes wide. "Johnnie—"

Johnnie raised a hand, silencing the attorney. "And Brooks will send you the same amount I gifted you today, if you forget Megan exists. Your bloodlust will be soothed and your pockets lined. She might be Big Joe's daughter, but she's innocent. She had no say in her father's business dealings. He'd been dead a year when she arrived. Dead over two years when my wife first showed up." He drew in a deep breath, removed his watch and held it out to Brooks. When the attorney didn't take it, Johnnie laid the heavy gold piece on the table. "Torture me. Kill me. Dismember me. As long as you don't hurt Kendall. Allow Brooks to leave   "

"No! No!" Bash shook his head wildly. "If you turn up missing, Outlaw'll leave no fucking stone unturned...No!" He ran up on Johnnie, shoving him backwards, farther away from Gabby. "Fuck you, asshole! Outlaw's a madman. He killed Pa. No motherfucker could do that. Do you know how many attempts were made on Pa's life? He was invincible and feared. Christopher...*Outlaw* didn't give a fuck. If he can kill Pa..."

Swallowing, Bash scrubbed a hand over his face and trembled.

"He doesn't have to know it was you who took me out." Johnnie met Bash's gaze and didn't flinch. "Please. I'm begging you. Don't hurt my Kendall. I love her…she's my everything, Bash. Keep me hostage. Take a chunk out of me daily. Whatever. Just don't hurt Kendall."

"Suppose I say it's your bitch or Outlaw's?"

"Then I'd say you aren't as afraid of Christopher as you pretend," Johnnie snapped. "*Cee Cee* fucked with Megan. He might've lived if he'd left Christopher's woman alone."

"Fuck those hoochie mamas," Bash spat, the pendulum of his sanity swinging again. "All of them. Your bitch. Mortician's slut. Outlaw's cunt. Those young pussies your cumrags pushed out."

"My daughter is a perfect lady," Johnnie said tightly, imagining the warmth of Bash's blood sliding down his hands.

His daughter was young and carefree and bubbly. She'd danced with Kendall at Christopher's birthday party and Johnnie couldn't have been prouder of her. But if he had to hide her away in a convent to keep her safe, he would.

"Leave!" Bash ordered. "Get out."

"Brooks can alter the documents," Johnnie said. "Half of everything will be yours."

"No! The originals are still out there. I received copies."

"I'll hunt for the originals—"

"Until they're found, there can be no alterations, so I reject your alternative."

"It really sounds as if you just want a fucking problem, big brother."

Wildness crept into Bash's eyes. "I don't! I want what's owed me. That's it, Johnnie. I'll do whatever I must to get it, preferably without Outlaw's knowledge."

"I'll send money to you to keep Kendall and Matilda safe and I'll...I'll..." What? Johnnie wasn't sure. He was making up shit as he went along. "I-I'll drive Megan away and pay you for her life, too." It had worked for many years with Cee Cee and Logan. Johnnie would make it work, as well. "If...*when*...she goes, you let her live in peace."

As if she'd have any without Christopher. At least, she'd be alive.

Who was he kidding? Nothing could ever separate them. *Maybe*, though, he'd buy time.

"Money every month for your bitch and six months to drive Outlaw's cunt away."

"Fifty bands a month and a year to drive Megan away," Johnnie offered. Sliding a hand inside his cut, he backed away from Bash and wrapped his fingers around the handle of his blade.

"A hundred," Bash expectedly countered.

"And the year?" Johnnie asked.

"Done," Bash responded.

At Johnnie's nod, Bash indicated Gabby with a wave of his hand. Johnnie snatched the blade and threw it before Cleaner moved a muscle. It landed in Gabby's throat. She shuddered and gasped, gurgling.

Walking to her, Johnnie pulled the knife away, reveling in the spray of blood. He leaned over and slit her throat, hastening a death only minutes away, ending her life quickly rather than leaving her at the mercy of Cleaner and Bash.

He wiped the blood on his leathers, ignoring Brooks's screaming sobs. Maniacal laughter boomed over the attorney's hysterics.

"Kudos, little brother," Bash congratulated.

After stuffing his blade back into his pocket, Johnnie closed the briefcase and took it in hand. "Stone spat on me, an insult that won't go unanswered."

A moment of silence went by.

"I see," Bash said finally.

Snatching his watch from the table, Johnnie bared his teeth. "Excellent."

Cleaner snickered.

In response, Johnnie put his watch on, grabbed Brooks by the collar and dragged him away. In the parking lot, dusk was falling and the temperature had dropped.

He shoved Brooks into the passenger seat of the Mercedes, jogged around to the driver's side and slid in. Once he started the engine, he grabbed his Glock from the inside of his cut. At the gate, he waited until Stone opened it, before he rolled down the window, shot the motherfucker between the eyes and sped away.

CHAPTER 1

Harley

10 months later

Glaring at the photo of CJ grinning at his "lab partner", Harley Banks shoved her phone inside her blazer pocket. Leaves crunched, and she pressed her lips together to hold back her tears. Turning, she smiled at her costar in the school play.

"Wassup, Harley?" Nardo Grevenberg greeted and grinned, his dark eyes sweeping her with a look from head to toe.

She studied his full lips, once again struck by how gorgeous he was, resembling a young Michael B. Jordan. "Hey."

He glanced around the small ramshackle structure.

"It's an old picnic shelter," she said, nervous and guilty.

CJ brought her here on their one and only date. Three months ago, that night had been dark and chilly. Today, the first of December, was cloudy and cold.

A couple of times, she'd come here on her own, sneaking away from school. Until today, when she got a series of photos with CJ and Molly, Harley had considered the old shelter a sacred spot, meant only for her and CJ.

"Hey, ma, why you brought me here? I cut class to just stare at you? You a'ight but you not bumping enough for me to freeze my butt off."

"Right," she mumbled, drawing in a deep breath. Shoving the memory of the photos out of her head, she lowered her lashes. "We spend so much time together at rehearsals, I just thought we could get to know each other away from school."

He considered her, then picked up a handful of her braids and cascaded them over her shoulder. He twirled one around his finger. "I don't know, Harley. I don't want to face your old man. Ever again. *Never*."

Snapping her brows together, Harley stepped back, forcing Nardo to drop the braid he continued to play with. "What?"

She'd been so caught up in her feelings the week before Homecoming that she'd lied on CJ to manipulate her parents into agreeing to her movie date with Nardo. She hadn't counted on Mommie and Daddy bringing up her allegations at the weekly family get-together. The repercussions for her lies angered her further and she'd taken her wrath out on CJ.

Daddy was so outraged on CJ's behalf, Nardo barely came up in the conversation. She'd certainly never expected to discover her father confronted him.

"I'm so sorry, Nardo. I don't...my father is over-the-top in protecting me," she huffed, annoyed. "You're a child, so whatever threats he made to you is just hot air."

Cocking his head to the side, he studied her. "*I* might be beyond his wrath, but my father isn't. My pops isn't a bitch-ass motherfucker, ready to jump at another man's orders."

Harley giggled.

Nardo lifted a brow, and she slapped a hand over her mouth.

"I'm sorry. I've never heard you use profanities. You sounded funny."

He narrowed his eyes.

"I-I mean *it*, the *words*, s-sounded funny coming from you. You're always so buttoned-up."

He backed away from her. "Yeah, whatever, girl."

Harley ignored his look that bordered on insulting. She couldn't lose his friendship. He was the only one buffering her pain at CJ's betrayal. She wrapped her fingers around his wrist and pulled him closer, resting her head against his chest.

"Don't be mad at me, Nardo," she whispered, hurt to her core.

CJ promised her that Molly was only his lab partner, but he was a liar. The pictures Molly sent proved that he'd spent time with her at a mall, an amusement park, at the movies *and* at dinner. He was a backstabbing snake, playing Harley and making moves on his cousin's chick.

If that was the game he wanted to play, she'd play it better. Smarter. She'd string him along as he was stringing *her* along, while using Nardo…

No, while getting to know Nardo to use…

Nope…

She *wasn't* using Nardo.

"Are you slow, Harley?"

Nardo's annoyed voice broke into her jumbled thoughts.

"I beg your pardon?"

"I've been talking to you and you've been staring into space like you belong with the retards."

She gasped. "I can't believe…you're a disgusting asshole. That's a horrible thing to say."

"You know what's horrible, Harley? Your old man. He embarrassed my father and me, so I know what he does to you."

"Wh-what?"

"He intimidates you. No wonder you're always up in that white boy's grill."

"*What*?"

"No matter what your daddy says, you'll never be good enough for them. He's fronting and shit, just because he has some lame 'Enforcer' patch. Mortician?" Nardo flipped the bird. "Fuck you, bruh." He glanced over his shoulder. "My old man just got out the tank. In my house, thug life is some real shit."

Swallowing, Harley touched her hair. She'd broached the subject with CJ at this very spot. He'd been outraged, but maybe…?

God, what was wrong with her?

Fingers trembling, she caressed her cheek, her heart dropping at her bumpy skin.

Lips brushed over hers, and she jumped.

Nardo leaned back and swiped at the tears sliding down her cheeks, before tipping her chin up and covering her mouth with his again.

She'd only ever been kissed by CJ, but he was a liar and a cheat. He'd said her color and hair didn't matter to him, yet he was chasing Molly. Although she wouldn't like his attention on anyone other than her, he ignored Jaleena Davis, his date for Homecoming. He preferred Molly.

And what about Daddy? Nardo was right. Daddy *did* intimidate her with his stupid demands that she not date until she was forty. Maybe, like Nardo said, Daddy was reaching. He'd never attain the rank of Uncle Christopher or Uncle Johnnie.

In most clubs, the enforcer wasn't even an officer. They were regular members, with special status. Everything Daddy had was because of Uncle Christopher's grace. Maybe, that was why he was so determined to block her from growing up. As long as he had her to dangle in front of the president's son, he'd always have certain perks.

Even Uncle Digger had higher ranking. He also received special regard because his wife was Aunt Meggie's assistant.

Nardo pulled his lips away and glared at her. "You're not worth shit, Harley. You can't kiss. I'll bet you'll just lay there, and I'll have to do all the pumping."

Harley deflated. On the verge of tears, she glanced at her watch. She needed to get back, for Mommie's pickup. Turning, she grabbed her knapsack and started her trek back to school. Marching through the brambles, she was aware of Nardo's presence behind her.

Cresting the pedestrian walkway of Turn Creek Bridge, she halted so suddenly Nardo barreled into her and sent her sprawling. She landed on all fours. Her knee-highs were thick enough to protect her knees from skinning.

"Harley!" her little brother, Lou, called, running to her, and helping her to her feet. "You okay?"

He resembled their father more than she or their youngest brother, Kaleb, who shared their mother's green-brown eyes and thick, silky hair. Like Daddy, Lou was brown-skinned with light-brown eyes. Over the coming Winter Break, Mommie had intended to start his twists so he could grow dreads like Daddy, but with Aunt Meggie…

"What are you doing here, Nardo?" Lou demanded.

"I'm telling CJ!" Axel Caldwell announced, part of the group of boys now crowding her and Nardo. Axel looked Nardo up and down. "He's going to beat your fucking ass for touching his woman."

Ryder Caldwell folded his arms and exchanged glances with his other brother, Ransom. He was in the middle of those three heathens, younger than Ransom by a year and older than Axel by a year. Ryder was also the only blond of Uncle Christopher's sons. Separately, they were hell. Together, they were vile.

"We can fuck him up, bro, and throw his dead body over the bridge," Ryder said.

Behind her, Nardo stiffened.

"CJ doesn't own me," Harley snapped, glaring between his three brothers, collectively known as the Terrible Triplets, though they had different birthdates. "We're friends. He has Molly, anyway."

Rory Donovan lifted a brow. Since the tragedy on Thanksgiving night, they all seemed to have aged ten years.

"Molly is Ryan's chick," Mark JB, her biological cousin, said. "You're CJ's."

Although she still couldn't see him, she *felt* Nardo's glare. Perhaps, it was because of her cousin's condemnation. Or, maybe, he was jealous.

"Yo, fuckface, don't look at Harley like that," Ransom ordered. "We might have to pluck your fucking eyes out."

"I'd like to see a scrawny little motherfucker like you try," Nardo gritted, looming behind her like a bad omen.

Rory tossed his cigarette. "How about I cut your fucking head off and dance in your fucking blood?"

The light in Rory's eyes, and the oddness of his voice, chilled Harley. Rumors persisted that Uncle Johnnie took

Rory into the meatshack. At first, Harley couldn't believe Uncle Johnnie would disobey Uncle Christopher's direct order, but Rory's tone and the fervency in his eyes changed her mind.

Her brother and cousins smiled.

"Maybe, I'll just tell Uncle Mort and my dad," Mark JB said casually.

No matter the valid points Nardo brought up, Harley didn't want to involve her father and uncle.

"Enough!" she ordered. "Nardo and me are costars in the play, and we cut class to rehearse our lines, so shut up all of you."

Lou glanced at Nardo, who still stood behind Harley. "That true, bruh?" He glared at her. "My sister is stupid but she's not a fucking toy."

"Stupid?" Harley folded her arms, hurt at his description. "Really, Lucas?"

"I'm not falling for your bait, sister. You're not insulting me by calling me by my given name. As a matter of fact, it doesn't mean shit coming from you."

"When Mommie says it, you tremble in your fucking shoes, asswipe," she sniped.

"Yep. She my momma, sis. You not."

"Yo, don't front." Nardo stepped beside her. "Just because you drop a few letters from words, don't make you bad, bruh."

"Don't talk out of your fucking ass, Grevenberg," Lou grumbled. "You don't know shit about me, so I suggest you shut the fuck up before you find out."

Nardo settled an arm around Harley's shoulders, then leaned down and kissed her. Out of pure contrariness, she opened her mouth, allowing him to push his tongue in. She turned—

Without warning, Mark JB snatched her away from Nardo and she stumbled. Her cousin gripped her arms to save her from falling. Once she balanced herself, he released her.

The scorn on the boys' faces cut through her. She lifted her chin.

"We might have to add this motherfucker to the same hit list we have Willy and Wally on," Axel announced.

Mark JB slapped the side of his head. "Shut the fuck up, stupid. We got a stranger in our midst."

Lou eyed her. "A fucking traitor, too."

"Shut up!" Harley screeched, Axel's words settling in her head. "What hit list?"

"Don't hit me again, fuckwipe," Axel yelled to Mark JB, rubbing the side of his head, fury on his face.

"What hit list?" Harley demanded again.

"The one where we fuck up the Byrds for fucking with Mattie," Axel said sullenly, his look daring Mark JB to touch him again.

"I'd say Willard and Wallace deserve fucking up," a new voice inserted.

At the unexpected words, they all jumped and turned.

A tall man with a goatee, bald head, and green eyes stood behind them, smoking a cigarette. Something about him was familiar, though Harley was certain she'd never seen him before. He wore a leather duster, black shirt, and black jeans.

His cold gaze caught and held hers before Rory, Lou, Mark JB, and Ryder stepped in front of her.

"I'm not here to harm Harley, Rory," the man said.

"Who the fuck are you and how the fuck do you know my fucking name, motherfucker?" Rory demanded, sounding like a cross between his father and Uncle Christopher.

Insanity touched the stranger's laugh. "Axel, Ryder, Ransom, where's CJ?"

Axel and Ransom joined the other boys, creating a solid wall.

"You're lucky we'd get our asses beat for cutting class, fuck nose," Axel spat. "Otherwise, I'd tell Outlaw a strange motherfucker was harassing us."

"My name's Bash. I'm no longer a stranger."

"We still don't know your bitch-ass," Mark JB said.

"You look like a fucking serial killer," Ransom added.

"The way you looked at Harley was creepy," Lou said.

"A name doesn't make a fucking difference if we've never seen you before," Ryder contributed.

"You a biker?" Rory asked.

"A biker?" Bash echoed. "What makes you say that?"

"This isn't Mother Goose, motherfucker," Ransom said. "So you're not a fuckhead looking for Snow White. With a name like Bash, you're either a fucking elf or a biker."

"It's a dwarf, dummy," Axel said with disgust.

"Dwarf isn't PC," Ransom responded.

"Man, fuck PC," Mark JB said. "We have a Leatherface motherfucker to deal with. Be politically correct after."

"Don't ruin my motherfucking fairytales, dick breath," Axel ordered.

"Man, fuck off," Ryder said, waving his hand in disgust. "You're nothing but a bitch-ass baby if you still like fairytales. Where's your fucking pacifier?"

Axel stepped out of the lineup, allowing Bash a clear view of Harley. "Say that to my fucking face, Blondie."

"Dumb ass, get back in place. We have to hide Harley from this Texas Chainsaw Massacre motherfucker," Ryder said.

"You like fairytales, Little Outlaw?" Bash asked before Axel responded to his brother.

"Little Outlaw?" Axel said in disbelief. "Not us, Ass. I mean, *Bash*. That's CJ."

Bash ignored Axel. "What's your favorite fairytale?" he asked no one in particular.

"Mine's *The Juniper Tree*," Rory announced.

The what?

"Kind of dark for Johnnie's son," Bash said, a smile in his voice. "But I appreciate your bravado."

"I don't have a stepmother or box of apples for you to reach into, so I can decapitate you. I'll improvise. *Bash*," Rory added. "Mister Not-A-Fucking-Biker."

Bash pointed from Ryder to Rory. "You and your brother are hilarious."

"Ro's not my brother, stupid," Ryder said. "His brother couldn't attend our meeting. Be a decent fucking criminal and get your facts straight."

"I'm sorry to disappoint you, Ryder Donovan," Bash said gravely. "Johnnie is your father."

Stunned silence followed the announcement. Harley searched for something to say, but couldn't find the right words.

"Megan Caldwell isn't as boring as she seems," he continued. "She gave pussy to Johnnie and pushed his kid out of her cunt. She also killed a motherfucker to save Outlaw."

"You sure about that?" CJ demanded, creeping up on them much like Bash had.

For a moment, Bash stilled before a small smile creased the corners of his mouth and he half turned.

Like all the kids, including herself, CJ wore his school uniform. Besides Rory, CJ was the only one of them who wore motorcycle boots.

Thanks to Mattie's lies about Aunt Meggie shooting someone, Bash's announcement didn't surprise Harley or CJ, although the other boys shifted.

"Positive, CJ," Bash answered with mock sympathy.

He knew a lot about them.

"Uncle Johnnie would be fucking deader than dead, motherfucker," CJ growled, fierce and fearless.

"Bro, we got a stranger among us," Ryder said, nodding to Nardo.

For the first time, CJ caught sight of both Harley and Nardo. He glanced between them, though his look never changed. His disregard hurt.

"Leave, Grevenberg," he ordered in a hard voice.

"Harley invited me, Caldwell. Only *she* can uninvite me."

"I was right," Ryder said. "We got to throw his dead ass over this fucking bridge."

Bash's wild laughter cut through the tension.

"Harley, come here *now*," Nardo ordered.

CJ's suddenly pained expression satisfied Harley and she lifted her chin. Now he knew how *she* felt each time she was confronted with his and Molly's secret relationship. She smirked, then glanced at Nardo through her lashes.

"Harley, Aunt Bailey is running late," CJ said coldly. "Rebel texted me because she knew you were here and started to worry when you didn't show up at the time you told her." That said, he glanced at Bash again. "I don't know who the fuck you are, mister, but I'd hate to tell my dad you're fucking with us."

"Outlaw wouldn't give a fuck, boy," Bash said, grinning. "He's all wrapped up in his bitch."

A muscle ticking in his jaw, CJ glanced away. He looked sad, angry, and alone. Suddenly, Harley regretted her fit of jealousy. Dark circles ringed his eyes and his features were pulled down in fatigue.

Bash sniffed. "Sorry to hear about the baby twat she lost. Surprised she didn't give up the ghost."

Axel burst into tears.

"Cuz, c'mon," Mark JB said in a wobbly voice, embracing Axel since he was closest. "Fuck this dude."

"When's Momma coming home, Mark?" Axel sobbed.

"Mom's getting better every day, big head," CJ said gruffly.

"So's Jo," Ryder said, sniffling. "Whatever they did while they were telling Dad she'd died made her come back to life."

"Jo's so small," Ransom said in a trembling voice. "She has so many tubes in her."

"She's getting better every day, Ran," Lou said quietly. "Just like Aunt Meggie."

"You've caused enough shit for the day, Bash," Rory said tiredly. "Go."

A thoughtful look crossed CJ's face. "Bash?"

"You know him?" Rory demanded.

"I overheard Tabitha and Ryan talking during Thanksgiving dinner. They were discussing 'Bash', but I couldn't understand the words."

Rage crossed Bash's features, but he covered it with a phony smile. "I don't know a Tabitha or a Ryan."

"You're a fucking liar," CJ said without flinching, mere inches away from Bash.

CJ was beautiful and brave, and Harley nearly swooned at his feet. She'd never be good enough for him. She had acne and rules and a pathetic father. Daddy flipped out if she wore a short skirt. Uncle Chris was the real deal. He had genuine power. He'd rightfully disciplined Rebel when she was acting like an idiot. Deep down, Harley blamed Rebel for Aunt Meggie's condition. She'd been a mean, hateful bitch over her own brother. Adopted or not! Diesel was a grown-ass man to boot. Not only was Rebel a vile daughter, but she had slutty morals.

Daddy, meanwhile, was nothing but an abuser.

"What's Tabitha and Ryan's last names?" Bash asked.

"Fuck you, Bash," CJ replied. "You know who the fuck they are. If you know us, you know them. I don't know your game, but I'm giving you one fucking warning. Stay away from my brothers and my cousins, and stop spouting your fucking lies about my mom, and you'll live."

"What about Harley, Mattie, and Rebel?"

"Don't fuck with my sister and my cousin," CJ warned, low.

His blatant omission of Harley infuriated her.

"On second thought, how about I tell my uncles?" CJ smiled. "Uncle Johnnie, maybe? Spouting your fucking bullshit might get to Aunt Kendall and set her off. She has her moments, but we love her and we take issue with anyone who'll send her over the edge. What about Uncle Mort? The fucking enforcer, *Bash*. He designed our meatshack and is well-versed on the fucking tools. Even the autopsy table with the drain."

Liar.

"Do you know what my dad said once, cuz?" Rory asked, digging in his pocket for his pack of cigarettes and lighter. "If I want to feel a spray of blood," he continued once he'd took a drag, "I need to cut a motherfucker while his heart's still beating. I've been looking for a test subject." He peeked over his shoulder, studying Nardo before turning back to Bash. "Want to volunteer?"

Bash glanced between CJ and Rory, then he smiled. "Your fathers are reasonable—"

"If you fuck with my mom, my dad will shoot the fuck out of you," CJ interrupted, "and be done with it."

"We've seen him do it," Rory added.

At the meeting with the Scorched Devils.

Shifting his weight, Bash scratched his jaw. "Outlaw's

reputation precedes him. He's a fucking legend. Wouldn't want to get on his bad side."

"Then don't," CJ advised. "You breathe another day if you swear you'll leave my mom and us the fuck alone."

"A promise is all you require?"

"We're reasonable men," Ryder said. "Outlaw always says a liar is the worse motherfucker in the world. If you can't trust a man's word, he's not worth shit."

"Quite right," Bash agreed. Turning, he held out his hand to CJ.

Just as CJ accepted, the Terrible Triplets barreled into Bash, their momentum pushing him against the railing and sending him tumbling over.

At the loud splash, the three Caldwell brothers high-fived, guffawed with laughter, and took off running.

"You little motherfuckers!" Bash hollered. "I fucking owe you."

"I have to get to the hospital to see Mom and Jo," CJ said, not sparing Harley a glance as he turned and sauntered away.

CHAPTER 2

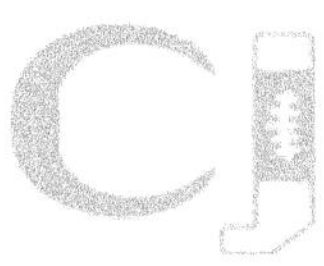

By the time CJ arrived back at Ridge Moore Charter School, he was ready to kill several motherfuckers. Instead, seeing Aunt Bailey's Escalade and Rebel and Mattie frantically texting, he had to do damage control on Harley's behalf.

Just as he spotted the SUV, his sister and cousin saw him crossing the parking lot and heading their way.

Aunt Bailey rolled down her window and waved at him. "CJ?"

"Did you find her?" Rebel asked, cutting him off, worry and fear in her eyes.

"Is Harley okay?" Mattie asked with just as much concern.

Since Aunt Bailey stood near, both his sister and cousin spoke under their breath.

"She isn't wired to cut class," Mattie continued. "She didn't give me much warning, so I couldn't intercept the signals. Uncle Mort probably already knows she cut. I told her she should talk to you before she went off with that idiot."

"What are you talking about, Mattie?" CJ asked. Harley didn't have to talk to him before she cut class with any idiot, Grevenberg included, even if CJ hadn't realized she'd cut until then. He'd thought she had time on her hands.

"Where's Harley?" Aunt Bailey demanded, suddenly right next to them.

Rebel and Mattie glanced at him, then flanked each of his sides.

Hands on her hips, Aunt Bailey lifted a brow. "Tell me *now*," she ordered.

"Too funny, Aunt Bailey." Mattie laughed nervously. "Now, as opposed to later."

"Hilarious, Auntie," Rebel said, her high-pitched giggle unnatural and annoying. "Tell me later." Another fucked-up giggle. "Tell me now."

"Now and Later," Rebel and Mattie chorused, snorting with false humor.

"Fuck my life," CJ mumbled.

"You know exactly where she is, CJ," Aunt Bailey accused. *Unfortunately.*

"Mommie!" Harley called, standing at the edge of the breezeway as if she'd just walked out of one of the buildings.

CJ didn't want to explore how she'd made it back on school grounds without anyone noticing.

Aunt Bailey gave Rebel, Mattie, and him severe looks, shoved some hair behind her ear, and returned to the Escalade, where Harley was waiting at the passenger side door.

"Where were you, young lady?" Aunt Bailey demanded, less than pleased.

Harley pursed her lips and looked from him to her

mother.

Swallowing, CJ averted his gaze, remembering the moment he'd realized she was on Turn Creek Bridge with Nardo Grevenberg. Her lips had seemed slightly swollen and pinker than normal, as if she'd been kissed.

"Is that true, CJ?" Aunt Bailey asked.

"Totally, Aunt Bailey," Rebel said, a smile plastered on her face.

"Yep, Harls, is telling the truth," Mattie agreed.

"Yeah, I am," Harley said primly and gave him a look that suggested he knew what the fuck she meant. "Tell Mommie, CJ."

"Tell her what, Harley?" he snapped. "I didn't hear what you said to corroborate."

She stiffened. "I told Mommie how you convinced me to go to Turn Creek Bridge. You needed me to listen to you because you're so worried about Aunt Meggie and Jo."

"Is that true, honey?" Aunt Bailey asked.

He didn't intend to allow Harley to use him as her scapegoat and he *especially* wouldn't allow her to twist his family's trauma to fit her fucking deviousness. Later, he'd set her straight. At the moment, he needed to break Ryan in two, then get to the hospital to see his mom and little sister.

"Yeah, Aunt Bailey," he gritted. "It's whatever."

"It's not whatever," Harley said, nastier than he'd ever heard her. "You owe me. *Molly* wouldn't cut today, so you asked me."

"Bro," Mattie said around a cough.

"What the fuck are you talking about, Harley?" CJ snarled, in spite of himself. "I don't ask Molly to cut with me."

"You do. You invite her on dates. You take her to lunch. You take her shopping."

Mattie rolled her eyes. "Uh, bro, Maman, Aunt Zoann and

me were with CJ when we took Molly shopping. You had rehearsals with Nardo."

"I was at the hospital with Momma," Rebel added, "so I couldn't go. Ryan, the dickhead, was busy with his fuckface friends."

"I gave money to buy Molly clothes, too," Aunt Bailey said tightly, staring at Harley with that look of displeasure all mothers perfect. "*CJ* went in place of Meggie because she couldn't go."

"A biker who knows how to dress a Barbie," Harley chortled, clapping. "Nice."

"Dude," Rebel said with a shake of her head.

"You're lying to me," Harley said, looking him in the eye to assert her charge. "She's more than your lab partner. I have a bunch of photos as proof."

"Stop, Harley," Aunt Bailey said angrily. "CJ is going through enough. If anyone's the liar, it's you."

Tears rushed to Harley's eyes. "That isn't true, Mommie," she said on a sob. "I'm not lying about anything."

No, she was lying about *everything*. Hurt to his core, CJ looked at Aunt Bailey. "She isn't lying, Aunt Bailey. I was with her. I needed a friend to talk to."

Not her. Not any longer. They'd made up at the club's annual Thanksgiving dinner and, days later, they were back to the same place they'd been ever since Molly was assigned as his lab partner.

"Get in the car, girls," Aunt Bailey instructed. Once they complied, she walked to CJ and hugged him. "I'm going to have a long talk with Harley, CJ. I don't know what's gotten into her."

He hadn't been sleeping the best lately because the house just wasn't the same without Mom. Rebel cried a lot. Her bedroom had been moved to the second floor to make room for Jo on the third floor. Often times, CJ heard Rebel in her old room, sobbing softly. Aunt Bunny and Lolly kept them well-fed, while Diesel was back in his old room, serving as the adult on premises at night. Aunt Ophelia, Uncle Stretch, and Uncle Cash looked after Gunner.

Everything was different, and CJ was scared it would never be the same again. He hadn't had the time to help Harley through her insecurities, but he was beginning to think no matter what he did, it wouldn't be enough. *He* couldn't fix her. Only she could work on herself. Yet, for now, he would protect her as best he could.

"Harley's upset, Aunt Bailey," he said, broken and lost. "Don't be too hard on her. I shouldn't have asked her to leave school."

"You didn't," Aunt Bailey said crisply. "You would never do such a thing, nephew."

"I cut class sometimes. Today was one of those days, and I needed Harley with me."

"Sweetheart, thank you for always protecting Harley, but when she didn't answer her phone, I called Lucas."

Fuck.

CJ thrust his fingers through his hair. "I was with—"

"No, you were at school until Rebel called you, then you went to Turn Creek Bridge, where Harley already was. *With Nardo.*"

CJ groaned. "Next, they'll intercept our texts."

"Don't give your daddy and your uncle ideas," Aunt Bailey said with a shake of her head.

"Wait. How'd he know Nardo was with her?"

"After her lies and schemes got them on a date, Lucas met with Nardo and his father."

"Oh, goddamn." He'd had a meeting with Uncle Mort once and didn't envy Nardo.

Aunt Bailey laughed.

"Harley didn't cut, Aunt. She'd never. She got permission to go." CJ rocked on his heels. "Something about a change of scenery to help along rehearsals." How he said that shit with a straight face, he didn't know.

At Aunt Bailey's skeptical look, he grinned.

"I swear, Auntie."

She lifted a brow. "Are you sure?"

"Positive. Harley is a good girl. She doesn't have it in her to cut."

The words hit the jackpot.

Aunt Bailey beamed at him, then hugged him again. "I didn't think she did either," she said with relief. "I knew she'd gotten permission. My baby is a sweet girl whose trusting nature can lead her to disaster. Her gullibility worries me."

CJ remained silent. Harley was no wilting flower.

"To keep the peace, she will blindly follow."

"Are you referring to the night she went to the movies with Nardo?"

"Yes," she hissed, and sniffed. She straightened her shoulders. "I have to get home." Her abrupt end to the conversation told CJ she still blamed him for Harley's behavior. "Do you need a ride?"

"I have my pussyped, Aunt." He wouldn't bother with Aunt Bailey or Harley's feelings about him for now. He had to find Ryan. "I'm headed to the hospital to check on Mom and Jo once I leave here."

A few minutes later, Aunt Bailey drove off with Harley, Rebel, and Mattie, allowing CJ to continue his trek to the football field. The Byrd brothers were supposed to return to school weeks ago but hadn't yet.

Practice was just wrapping up when CJ reached the field and spotted Ryan, talking to two wide receivers, Head Coach

Yancy, and the Athletic Director, Roger Marksum. Molly hovered in the background.

"Hey, CJ," she started, alerting the others to his presence.

"Caldwell, shouldn't you be at the hospital—"

CJ snatching Ryan by the jersey and punching the fuck out of him interrupted Coach Yancy.

"Who the fuck is Bash, motherfucker?" CJ snarled, in a blind rage, overcome with almost losing his mother and his little sister, and so betrayed by Harley he didn't know if he ever wanted to talk to her again.

Ryan swung at him, but CJ ducked and punched him again.

"Who?" he snarled, just as Yancy and Marksum dragged him away and the two wide receivers grabbed Ryan. "He knows our entire fucking family, asshole. Who is he?"

"Enough, Mr. Caldwell," Mr. Marksum warned, "before I suspend you."

Molly was staring at CJ, wide-eyed and frightened. She'd mentioned Bash, too. He hadn't forgotten. He just hadn't made the connection because the same night he'd overheard Tabitha and Ryan…

Bash was bad fucking news and Ryan, the prick, was somehow involved with him.

Ryan zeroed in on Molly's trembling and fury settled into his features. She started to cry.

"I'm letting you go, son," Coach Yancy told CJ. "We're giving you a pass because of all that you're going through, but don't let it happen again."

"It won't," CJ promised. And it wouldn't. He'd get to his motherfucking cousin on club grounds.

In the meantime, he had to save Molly from her own trauma.

"I have a meeting with Roger, CJ," Coach Yancy

continued. "I trust you not to fight. Understand?"

CJ nodded.

"Good."

"Mo?" CJ called, once the two men disappeared into the building.

"You call my girlfriend *Mo*?" Ryan asked in outrage.

CJ should've punched him in the fucking face instead of the stomach. Maybe, then, the fuckhead couldn't talk.

"It-it's his n-nickname, Ryan," Molly said around sniffles. "You said cunt is your term of endearment for me."

Stefan and Robby, two of the best wide receivers on the team, laughed, mortifying Molly a little more. Her shoulders sagging, she bowed her head.

"I need to talk to my bitch alone," Ryan announced, grabbing Molly's elbow and jerking her forward.

She stumbled. Instead of attempting to catch her, Ryan released his hold, allowing her to fall to the ground. Adding insult to injury, he stooped and flipped her short cheer skirt over her waist. She wore a leotard underneath, but it was still a foul move.

CJ hated how Stefan and Robby were laughing at Molly's expense, thanks to his fucking cousin. Gritting his teeth, he went to her, bent, and helped her to her feet. She leaned against him, shivers and sobs racking her.

"I'm going to fucking kill you, Ryan," CJ swore, removing his jacket and allowing Molly to put it on.

"That's fucking rich, CJ," Ryan said bitterly. "How should I treat a slut? It's obvious she's fucking you. Or, at the very least, sucking you. Otherwise, she wouldn't have told you about Ba—"

"Bash?" CJ said viciously. "She never told me a motherfucking thing about Bash. I didn't know she knew that motherfucker."

"You're a liar."

"I've been called a liar once too many times today, Ryan," CJ warned. "Say it again, motherfucker, and I'll smother you in your fucking sleep."

He wouldn't. First, he'd have to get past Hogzilla, then Uncle Val.

"How the fuck did you know about Bash if this cunt didn't tell you?" Ryan demanded. "You told him about Bash, right, Molly?"

"What if she had?" CJ said, before she could incriminate herself. Remembering their conversation from the first time he visited her house, he cleared his throat, determined not to feel like a jackass. "She doesn't trust me enough. Besides, mindreading is overrated."

Ryan frowned. "Fucking...*what*?"

CJ refused to look at Molly. Somehow, he managed to keep a straight face as he continued. "Bash was at Turn Creek Bridge, fuckbag."

Molly gasped.

If CJ announced little green Martians were creeping up on Ryan, his cousin wouldn't have reacted by dropping his mouth open and losing every ounce of color in his face.

CJ glared at Stefan and Robby. "Get the fuck," he ordered, "and don't say a motherfucking thing to no fucking body."

The boys scrambled away.

"CJ—"

"No, Ryan. I don't want to fucking hear it. I don't know what the fuck you're involved in. *Uninvolve* your motherfucking ass."

CJ had never seen such gravity on Ryan's face.

"He's bad news, Ry," he whispered. "Back away from whoever Bash is before you get caught up in a situation you can't get out of so easily."

Drawing in a deep breath, Ryan considered CJ for a moment, then glanced at Molly. "Says you, cuz? Just because you're a pussy ass bitch, hiding behind Outlaw don't mean I am."

"Look, asshole—"

"Have you ever killed, cousin?"

"Have you?" CJ demanded, already knowing the answer.

Ryan smirked at CJ and stepped closer, until they were nose-to-nose. "I'm a real man, beta boy. I fuck. I kill. I smoke."

"You're going to get your stupid ass killed," CJ uttered.

"I'm not you, cuck. You're a fucking wannabe, when really you're just a *neverbe*. You'll never be Outlaw or me or any biker. You'll never be happy without Aunt Meggie and Uncle Christopher as your crutch. You'll never be an alpha. You'll never be with Harley."

"My dad's worried about my mom," CJ spat, refusing to explore any of Ryan's allegations. "She and Jo needs his full attention right now, but if you don't set that motherfucker straight and tell him to back the fuck off, I'm telling Outlaw

about Bash and your affiliation."

Fear marched across Ryan's face. "You wouldn't dare." He swallowed. "The club...That would be seen as..."

Disloyalty. Betrayal. Treason.

Clenching his jaw, Ryan glared at CJ. "Fine," he finally said. "I'll handle it."

CHAPTER 3

Harley

For the entire ride home, Harley refused to talk and, instead, seethed in silence. She was livid and hurt at CJ's disregard and dismissal of her. Honestly, Harley wished they'd never made up on Thanksgiving Day. She wouldn't have had such high hopes that he'd ignore Molly unless it was for the project, as he'd led her to believe.

"No, I think he went to the hospital to see Momma and Jo."

Belatedly tuning into the conversation left Harley clueless about the context.

"It shocks me how he can act normal at school," Mattie muttered. "If Maman had almost died, along with my little sister, I'd be a fucking wreck."

Harley waited for her mother to chastise Matilda for the bad language, but she remained silent.

"Me, too," Rebel admitted on a sigh. "I *am* a nervous wreck. I'm so scared for Momma and Jo. If they were out of danger, they wouldn't still be in ICU…NICU in Jo's case. CJ is like Daddy, though. I know he's worried, but he knows how to get things done."

"He's also not suffering a case of pressing guilt," Mattie snarked.

"Fuck off, dummy," Rebel snapped, elbowing Mattie.

She grunted, and returned the favor, hitting Rebel's side.

"That's enough," Mommie said sternly, focused on the road.

"Mattie cursed, Aunt Bailey," Rebel grumped, "and you didn't ream her ass out."

"I'm not reaming your ass out because you cursed, honey. I'm reaming you *both* out for the elbowing. Stop before it turns into a fight."

"That isn't fair, Mommie!" Harley cried. "If I cussed, you'd ground me. By the way, Rebel," she went on before her mother responded, "stop pretending CJ is so concerned about Aunt Meggie and Baby Jo. He's been up Molly's ass for days!"

"Bro, Molly is CJ's *lab* partner," Mattie said with displeasure. "Control yourself. We already had *Rebel*."

"Yeah, Harls," Rebel said, surprisingly agreeable. "Don't let jealousy turn you into a miserable cunt. It isn't fun and it turns everyone against you."

"Shut up!" Harley snarled. "You were a cunt because you're an idiot. You want to fuck your brother and you didn't want a little sister. My behavior is nowhere close to yours and I resent the comparison, especially since you're making a joke of the havoc you caused."

A beat of silence went by before Rebel released an audible breath. "To you, it sounds as if I'm oversimplifying my behavior. In truth, I'm not, Harley. I was a beast, and that's the only reason I'm not climbing over the seat to fuck you up for your bitchy comments."

"You wouldn't dare. Mommie would slap you."

"Perhaps," Rebel said, dismissive. "But until you've been spanked by Outlaw, you won't know anything that comes after is child's play. Besides, your ass is on your shoulders because CJ is tired of your bullshit. *Dude*. Grow the fuck up. You cut class to go with fucking Nardo Grevenberg, a bigger dickhead than Ryan."

"You *did* cut class, Harley? And for *Nardo*?" Mommie demanded. "But I was told—"

She abruptly stopped. Judging by the sudden anger in her mother's voice and the tightening of her mouth, Harley was in big trouble.

"How dare you lie on me!" Unbuckling her seatbelt, Harley twisted around and glared at Rebel. "You fucking bitch!" she screamed, and would've lunged if Mommie hadn't yanked Harley by the collar and stopped her.

"Sit down, *now*!" Mommie ordered, swerving onto the dead-end street that led to the club at breakneck speed.

Luckily, Mommie still gripped Harley, Otherwise, she would've banged against the door, since she hadn't strapped herself in again.

Before Mommie punched in her code, the probate on duty opened the gate and waved her in. Rolling her window down, she said, "thanks," and drove on.

A couple minutes later, she stopped in front of the Caldwell home.

Rebel opened the door. "Harley, I know you're hurt because you're insecure about your place in CJ's life. My brother adores you. If you can't support him right now, then back off. He's dealing with enough. As *your* friend, your "cousin", *I'm* telling you not to make the same mistake I made just a few weeks ago. Instead of pitching a bitch fit, ask CJ how he's doing. At the moment, his problems outweigh yours, so shut the fuck up, grow the fuck up, and take the fucking advice you gave me." Without awaiting a response, she got out and slammed the door shut.

Tears rushed to Harley's eyes, and she shuddered. Her phone was a looming presence filled with the evidence of CJ's betrayal.

As Mommie started off, a gentle hand landed on Harley's shoulder. "It's okay, Harley," Mattie said. "Whatever set you off is probably a misunderstanding."

"It isn't," Harley spat, digging into her blazer pocket and yanking her phone out. She opened the incriminating messages. "Look."

Mattie snatched the phone. "Oh," she said a moment later.

"You'd go off the deep end, too," Harley charged. "I love him, and he's nothing but a cheater." Her voice broke.

"*You* rejected him," Mattie said with annoyance. "You need to check yourself, Harley."

"Shut up, Mattie!" she said, her voice thick and shaking. She swiped her wet cheeks. "I love him. He promised he'd wait for me. He. *Promised*!"

"Oh, baby," Mommie said, her anger dying. She started past their house as Mattie returned Harley's phone.

"I can walk home, Aunt Bailey," Mattie said. "Your house is the halfway point to mine."

Mommie slid the Escalade to a stop and glanced at Mattie through the rearview mirror. "Are you sure, baby?"

"Yeah. Hogzilla is probably penned for the night, so I'm good."

"You can come inside," Mommie offered, putting the SUV in reverse, swerving into the driveway and shifting to park.

She allowed the engine to idle. "Momma is cooking red beans and rice with pickle meat and French bread."

Mattie opened her door. "It's too unhealthy, Aunt Bailey, but I'll let Daddy and the boys know."

"Tell them she also has bread pudding and rum sauce for dessert."

"Maman loves Lolly's desserts. I'll tell her. If she doesn't call, I'll text you what she says."

Needing an ally and seizing upon her mother's softening, Harley handed Mommie the phone, already opened to the first photo of CJ and Molly. "Tell me I'm wrong." She sniffled, wishing she *was* wrong, but with such irrefutable proof, knew she wasn't. "CJ and Molly are more than lab partners."

After studying each photograph, Mommie handed Harley the phone. "Oh, baby, I'm so sorry."

"I've been right all along. You and Daddy ganged up on me because Aunt Meggie convinced you of CJ's innocence."

"You lied to us, sweetheart," Mommie said gently. "That's unacceptable."

"I know, and I'm so sorry. I've been so hurt. I know that isn't an excuse, but I love CJ so much and I can't think clearly, Mommie. Thanksgiving, he *promised* he would only spend time with Molly for their lab project and nothing more."

"Well, obviously he lied," Mommie agreed.

"No, CJ didn't," Mattie insisted.

"Shut up!" Harley snarled. "You can defend him as much as you wish. He hasn't hurt and betrayed you, and the evidence—"

"He hasn't done either to you," Mattie said in exasperation. "He's going through so much right now. Please don't do this to him."

"We aren't taking away his pain, Mattie," Mommie said briskly. From her tone, she was now solidly on Harley's side. "That's no excuse for his dishonesty and disrespect toward my daughter."

"He hasn't disrespected Harley," Mattie argued. "Nor has he lied to her, Aunt Bailey."

"It's commendable that you are defending him, sweetheart, but as a young lady, put yourself in Harley's position. You should revisit your loyalties."

"My loyalties are where they belong, Aunt. If I thought CJ was in the wrong, I would defend Harley, but—"

"That's enough, Matilda," Mommie said. "I'll allow you or no one else to malign Harley."

Silence fell, until Matilda huffed and said, "I think the boys are going to be late because of whatever extracurricular activities they're involved in. They may not be able to come to dinner."

"Don't you mean because they cut, too?" Harley said scathingly. She refused to be the only one in trouble.

"Oh?" Mattie asked innocently. "I wasn't aware."

"Liar!" Harley charged as the garage door opened, revealing Daddy and Pop.

"Get over yourself, Harley," Mattie said, rushing out of the Escalade and slamming her door shut. "Hey Uncle Mort. Pop," she acknowledged cheerfully.

Harley tuned out the hellos, although Mattie's happy giggle annoyed her. Once she walked off and disappeared around the side of the house, Pop opened Harley's door while Daddy did the same for Mommie.

"Hey, pretty girl," Daddy greeted.

"Hi, sweetheart," Pop said, drowning out Mommie's response.

Harley glared at him, grabbed her knapsack from the floor

and rushed out of the vehicle. She didn't bother responding or closing the door. She wanted to get to her room and cry. Mostly, she wanted to call CJ and demand answers, so she stomped by her grandfather and headed into the garage.

"Baby girl," Daddy called. "Roxanne finishing up dinner. Your momma said you had a bad day. Why don't me and you take a walk so we can talk about it?"

"No, thank you," Harley snapped, remembering Nardo's revelations about her father. She reached the door that led into the house. "You're as much a traitor as CJ."

"Harley!" Daddy said.

Ignoring him, she stormed down the small service hallway, hoping to sneak past the kitchen so she wouldn't have to see Lolly.

"Stop right now," he said.

"She's upset, Lucas," Mommie hissed. "Leave her be."

"I didn't do her anything, Bailey."

"Nor did I," Pop added with displeasure. "And she refused to acknowledge me."

"Stop! Both of you," Mommie said. "You won't gang up on my daughter."

"Gang up?" Daddy's eyes widened in surprise. "I'm not ganging up on my baby girl. I'm trying to make sense of shit, so I can help her."

"Help me?" Harley cried. "All you ever do is fuss!"

"Harley, baby—"

"Shut up, Lucas! You're not helping matters. You're making it worse for my daughter."

"Harley belong to me too, Bailey," Daddy said, the irritation rising in his eyes creeping into his voice. "I got a right to try to help her and have her show me more respect than she doing. I haven't done her anything."

Indecision tore across Mommie's face. Concerned that

she'd lose her only support, Harley tugged her mother's sleeve and recaptured her attention.

"CJ is so mean to me, Mommie."

Daddy snorted. "You were mean to him, too, baby. You lied on the boy. No, fuck, Harley, you *lied* to get your fucking way."

Harley wailed at her father's harshness.

Mommie drew herself up. "You have a lot of nerve throwing that in her face when she's so distraught. Leave Harley alone, Lucas! I mean it."

"What's going on out here?" Lolly asked, standing in the archway. She smiled at Harley. "Hey, sugar. How was school?"

"Not now, Momma," Mommie said briskly. "Harley has had a rough day. She even cut class. Because of CJ."

"CJ wasn't nowhere near Turn Creek River, Bailey," Daddy said with disapproval. "Harley and motherfucking Nardo was."

Of course, he would know. Stupidly keeping tabs on her as if that would stop her from doing whatever she wished. If he knew so much, then he didn't need *her* to tell him about Bash. A real gangster or spy would've had audio to hear hooked in on the tracking devices. Daddy was nothing but a joke.

"Don't blame CJ because Harley fucking cut class, Bailey."

"Don't blame *our* daughter for CJ's bad behavior, Lucas," Mommie snapped.

"Bad behavior?" Lolly echoed. "What the fuck are you talking about, Bailey? CJ doesn't need your censure. He's dealing with too much right now."

"Are you kidding me?" Mommie cried. She pointed to Harley. "Look at her little face. She's crushed, and you're taking *his* side."

"There's no sides, pretty girl," Daddy said, calmer. "This is some teenage drama that we don't need to be party to. But CJ not in the wrong here, Bailey. He not responsible for Harley cutting class. He wasn't even with her."

Lolly glared between Harley and Mommie. "I'm surprised at both of you. This is bullshit."

"Bullshit?" Mommie echoed. "Show them the photos, hunny bunny."

Gladly. Smug, Harley got her phone and pulled up the evidence, then handed the device to her mother. She held the phone out to Daddy. Though his face remained blank, he grunted at the end and passed the phone to Lolly. By now, Pop stood next to her, so they looked at the photos together before she gave Harley the phone back.

"You both owe Harley an apology," Mommie said tightly. "It's clear that Molly is more than CJ's lab partner."

"So?" Daddy said. "CJ going to be seventeen in a matter of months, and he definitely can't do with Harley what most fucking teenage boys *want* to do with girls."

Folding her arms, Mommie glared at Daddy. "It's the principle."

"It's the reality, baby," Daddy retorted.

"Harley, that boy asked you to go steady with him," Lolly reminded her, because she was mean and horrible. "*You* friend zoned him. Don't get your ass on your shoulders if he has a girlfriend."

"You're blaming Harley for CJ's lies, Mother, and I won't allow that."

Daddy snorted. "Roxanne not blaming Harley for nothing, Bailey. You fucking tripping, girl."

"No, Daddy, *you're* tripping," Harley screeched, rewarded by the shock on her father's face. "You're the reason I turned CJ down. You intimidate me with your stupid demands that I not marry until I'm forty and all your hollow threats." She swiped at the tears slipping down her cheeks. "You're nothing but a wannabe. Wannabe gangster. Wannabe officer. Well, you're neither. Even Uncle Digger holds a higher position." She glared at him, ignoring the hurt in his eyes and his clenching jaw. "You're the *enforcer*." She spat the word. "Of what? You just sit around all day, hoping to cull Uncle Christopher's favor, Uncle Toady. Well, guess what? Nardo's right about you. His father is a *real* gangster. He's spent time in prison and everything—"

"Harley, shut the fuck up," Lolly snarled, "before I beat your fucking ass—"

"You won't touch me!" she fumed. "You're mean and bitter—"

"All right, young lady, that's enough," Pop inserted.

Meanwhile, Daddy stood in silence just staring at her, while Mommie rubbed Harley's back.

"You can't tell me what to do, Pop," she said, lifting her chin. "You're not my real grandfather. You're nothing but a stale, white bread, out-of-touch, nepo baby and—"

Lolly lunged for Harley, snatching a handful of her hair. If Pop hadn't intervened and jerked Lolly away, she probably would've dragged Harley from one end of the house to the next.

"Get out of my house," Mommie ordered, shielding Harley with her body.

Harley peeped around her mother as Pop pulled Lolly toward the door that led to the garage.

"I don't ever have to come back to this motherfucker, Bailey," Lolly yelled, halting.

Though Pop tried to urge her out the door, she made herself deadweight and remained in the house.

"I'm so disappointed in you, Harley. The disrespect you

showed your daddy and Knox is bullshit. They deserve better. Even if CJ was fucking every bitch he saw, *these* two motherfuckers haven't done you a goddamn thing. The fact that you don't have fuck all to say about who the boy is with because you broke his goddamn heart makes your treatment of Mortician and Knox all the more fucked up. You owe them both an apology."

"Of course I do," Harley sobbed. "Their precious feelings are hurt, but what about my feelings?"

"Fuck your motherfucking feelings," Lolly snarled. "They're too fucked up to be important. I've never heard no fucking bullshit about a motherfucker not being a real gangster because he hasn't gone to prison. It just makes the motherfucker a smart gangster. Apparently, the apple don't fall far from the tree. Nardo's daddy is a stupid motherfucker and so is he."

"I hate you!" Harley screamed.

"I don't give a fuck," Lolly said. "I love you dearly, but I want to beat your ass for your fucking disrespect."

"Mother, get out," Mommie said in a trembly voice. "And don't come back until you have more sympathy for my sweet baby."

"Sweet baby, my ass. She's turned into the fucking devil." Lolly wrenched open the door and stomped off.

Pop didn't bother to say 'goodbye'. He slammed the door shut.

As Mommie hugged Harley and promised everything would work out, Daddy leaned against the wall and lit a cigarette.

"Bailey, you and me need to talk," he said once Mommie released Harley.

"Unless you tell me you're firmly on Harley's side, Lucas, I have nothing to say to you. The pictures speak for themselves. CJ is guilty.”

“He is, Daddy,” Harley said, calmer. Now that it was just her and her parents, she didn’t feel so attacked. “He promised he’d wait for me, until *I* was ready to go steady. I even told him he could get another girlfriend and he said he wouldn’t.”

Smoke pouring through his mouth and nostrils, Daddy took his cigarette in hand. “Harley, you always been my pride and joy,” he said quietly, sadder and more subdued than she’d ever seen him. He looked crushed. “Right now, you not being nice or fair.” He glanced at Mommie, then back at her. “CJ is older than you and Roxanne right. *You* turned him down. You can’t put a motherfucker on the shelf and keep him there until *you* ready. Suppose that never happens? He got a life to live, too. Having said that, the little motherfucker adore you. He wouldn’t do anything to hurt you. But have you even thought about what he’s going through? He idolize his old man, but he’d move heaven and earth for Meggie. He love her to bits and pieces and he almost lost her. He not having an easy time. Maybe, ease up on him for now. Be the friend he need, instead of turning on him at this crucial moment.”

“You’re still blaming Harley, Lucas.”

Daddy pinched the tip of his cigarette and headed for the door. “I’m not, Bailey.” He sounded tired and weary. “I’m just advising her to be his friend.” He left, quietly closing the door behind him. A moment later, his Harley rumbled to life, and he sped away.

Mommie stared at the door, then pasted a smile on her lips. “I guess it’s just you and I for dinner, hunny bunny. Wash up while I set our plates out.”

Debating on texting Mattie to inquire if she and Aunt Kendall would join them, Harley trudged to her bedroom.

She told herself her angry words to Daddy, Lolly, and Pop were justified, but in the silence of her room, she wasn't sure. Worse, the pain and disappointment in her father's eyes haunted her.

After changing from her school uniform and into a romper, she sat on her bed with her phone in hand. Instead of texting Mattie or Daddy, she sent one to CJ.

CHAPTER 4

"When will she grow the extra two hundred bones needed to survive?" Molly asked, staring at Jo through one of the windows of the Neonatal Intensive Care Unit of Hortensia General. Christmas decorations hung in the hallway and inside the NICU. Behind the nurse's station stood a small tree, surrounded by presents.

"She has all the bones she'll ever need and more, Molly," CJ said tiredly, staring at his newborn sister and hating all the tubes and IVs attached to her.

Though she was nearing two pounds, she still looked so small and fragile. Sometimes, CJ worried someone would awaken him and tell him he'd been dreaming, that his little sister and mother had, in fact, died. So far, that hadn't happened.

"She doesn't," Molly insisted. "Adults have ten thousand eight bones. Kids are born with eight thousand eight. She needs two hundred more. That's why her skin is so...so..."

Translucent?

CJ didn't have the energy to address his little sister's skin and he wished he'd left Molly with fuckbag, instead of pretending they had to work on their science project. "She'd need two thousand more bones, Mo. Babies are born with three hundred or some shit. Adults have less. A hundred ninety-six or two-hundred-six." He squeezed his temples. "I can't remember the number."

An instrumental rendition of *Rudolph the Red-Nosed Reindeer* piped through the hospital's loudspeakers.

CJ had never felt so disconnected from the holiday season. That fact added to his misery.

Molly pulled back the sleeve of the jacket he'd lent her to reveal her hand and laid it against his arm. "Your baby sister is fighting," she said quietly. "I can see how worried you are, but just say your prayers and He'll make her well for you."

Tears glistened in her blue-gray eyes and she smiled sadly.

CJ nodded, only realizing the moisture in his own eyes when she thumbed his cheeks. Evading her touch, he turned back to the glass. "I'm fine, bae."

She wiggled under his arm, settling it around her shoulders. "Ryan was really mean today. He shouldn't have said those things to you."

CJ hadn't felt so low on his sixteenth birthday, when Harley broke his heart.

The first time.

He couldn't allow her to continue treating him like shit. He'd stand at her side and help her through whatever, but she had to see him as a person, instead of an ideal. For their entire lives, their parents joked about becoming in-laws once CJ and Harley married. And that was all she saw him as—her future husband. She didn't even see him as a friend anymore.

He was a thing. A goal. She couldn't continue, *they* couldn't continue, that way. If she wanted Nardo, then CJ hoped her the best, but she couldn't use him to save her ass when she hadn't even checked on him and asked if he was okay.

"You're sending Harley photos again, aren't you, Molly?"

"Just the fun ones," Molly admitted with that frustratingly innocent way she had. "I've heard you invite her out and she turns you down more than she accepts. If she's jealous, she might think she'll lose you."

"Or she might turn to another guy," CJ snapped.

"If she does, she wasn't that into you, dummy," Molly sniffed. "Harls is smart, despite having a friend named Reb Elle because of some crusty Civil War dude."

"My sister's name is Rebel."

"Whatever. By another guy, you mean Nardo," she said, changing the subject.

"Fuck him." CJ huffed out a breath and turned away. "I need to see my mom." He stalked down the hall, to the other side of the floor, where a special wing had been set up on Outlaw's orders, so he could remain with Mom whenever she stayed.

CJ finally understood why it was on the same floor as NICU.

"You're late," Slipper greeted, when CJ reached the doors to his mom's wing. "We thought you'd snuck up the back staircase, but your old man started checking the cameras since you didn't answer his calls. He was about to send out the cavalry."

CJ must've forgotten to unmute his phone after class.

"Outlaw was going to send a search and rescue for you, boy."

Nodding to the other brothers guarding Mom's floor, CJ smiled and waited for the buzzer to click open the door. He placed his hand at the small of Molly's back and guided her toward his mother's room.

He halted at the door, afraid to turn the knob and walk in. Maybe, he'd step over the threshold and *would* wake up to the truth.

"Are we going in?" Molly whispered.

"Yes." He didn't move.

"When?"

"Right now."

"Are you sure?" she asked a moment later. "Or is it this right now, instead of that right now." Silence and then, "The door is pretty."

"It's just a door, Molly."

"I like Mo better. And it isn't just a door. Branches grow out of it."

CJ blinked and saw the garland that he brushed by every day. "That's not a branch. A fucking branch can't grow out of a fucking door."

"Yes, it can, silly," she retorted in exasperation. "A door is wood, and wood is made from trees. As long as you water the door branch every day, it grows."

CJ glanced at her, but she refused to look at him. Her profile belonged on a cameo; it was almost perfect. "You don't really believe that nonsense, do you?"

Clearing her throat, she pursed her lips. "Does it matter?" She turned to him but refused to meet his gaze. "My baby won't care."

"You're pregnant? Ryan's?"

"I don't know. I think it is, but it might be…it might be…"

"Bash's."

She nodded. "Yes."

"Do you want it?"

"If Ryan was still nice to me and it was his. But it wouldn't matter if he didn't take me away. If Daddy didn't beat it out of me, Bash and Cleaner would."

"Jesus Christ," CJ whispered. "Your parents are—"

"They're good, CJ," she said softly, and sniffled. "I love them. Mama told me if I'd lived a long time ago, I would've been as wise as the lady who turned and looked back at that city."

For as long as he remembered, his mother took him and his siblings to Mass at least once a month. She respected Dad's agnosticism, though he did attend occasionally, especially for special events. Rule's near zealotry turned CJ off from sermons. He did know some things, though, and it fucking appalled him that Molly's mother wanted to turn her daughter into a pillar of salt. He frowned. "That lady wasn't wise, Molly," he said with indignation. "She went against a direct order and suffered dearly."

Molly flinched. "No—"

"You need to get away from them."

"They love me."

"They're abusing you! They're allowing Bash to abuse you."

She shook her head. "Bash rises from the ground when he isn't on our shelf to see everything. He flies into Daddy's ear and tells him to be mean to me."

"My Dad will help you—"

"No! I don't want to leave Mama and Daddy. They are the only mama and daddy I've ever known. Mother Goose let them leave her shoe."

By the expression on her face, CJ knew she believed her

words.

"I love them. They're my parents."

He'd accomplish nothing by denigrating those fuckheads.

Molly bit her lip. "You come from a big family."

"Yes," he agreed, wary at the sudden hope in her eyes. "What does my family have to do with yours?"

"You want kids," she answered, placing her hand over her belly. "Harley told me."

Sighing, CJ stared at the door again. It was so silent on the other side. His mother was probably still drugged up and barely lucid, while his father sat in a chair close to her bed, staring at her. Whenever CJ visited, he never saw his father utilizing the second bed in the private room so Dad could spend the night in a semblance of comfort.

CJ felt emotionally overloaded. He was so scared he might still lose his mother and little sister. Harley's behavior concerned him, too. He wanted to have patience with her, but he wouldn't allow her unfair bullshit. The last thing he needed was Molly lying to Harley. As much as he empathized with Molly's situation, she couldn't complicate his life to ease her own. "I'll never forgive you if you tell Harley that I'm the father of your baby."

"I want you to be."

"I'm not, Molly, and *I* don't want to be. I am your friend, though. I'll find a way to help you, but you have to be my friend, too. I'm not excusing Harley's bullshit. However, *your* bullshit is adding fucking fuel to the fire. Stop it."

"*Now I lay me down to sleep, I pray the Lord my soul to keep. If I die before I wake, I pray the Lord my soul to take.*"

CJ frowned.

"That's my favorite prayer."

"It's fucking frightening."

"It's for children."

"It's about death."

"Nuh-uh! It's about sleeping and waking up with a new soul."

CJ scowled at her. Before he spoke, the door opened.

"Hey, boy," Dad said, stepping aside so CJ could enter. "I thought I heard you."

"Hi, Mr. Outlaw," Molly whispered, tiptoeing into the room like the fucking Grinch stealing toys in Whoville.

"What the fuck you doin', Molly?"

"Being stealthy," she murmured. "I don't want to wake Mrs. Outlaw."

Dad glared at CJ.

"Hi, Molly," Mom greeted, sounding more lucid than she had in days.

"Mrs. Outlaw!" Molly squealed, rushing to Mom and throwing her arms around her.

"Back the fuck up," Dad ordered, stomping to Molly and dragging her away from Mom.

CJ stared at his mother. She still had an IV with bags of medicine hanging from the pole, but that sickly pallor didn't color her skin and her two plaits were gone. Her hair was in a ponytail.

"Mom?"

She smiled at him. "Hey, potato."

"Is he French fries or boiled?" Molly asked.

Mom giggled. "He's everything, Molly. He had the chubbiest cheeks as a baby."

"Like a butter turkey?"

"A Butterball."

"Oh. So, all butter turkeys are boys?"

"Ummm, well—"

"Nope, ain't doin' this shit," Dad proclaimed. "You ain't usin' all your fuckin' energy explainin' shit and you ain't usin' all *my* fuckin' energy makin' me listen. Molly, sit the fuck down and shut the fuck up."

"Christopher," Mom said.

The wind taken out of her sails, Molly trudged to the window seat and sat. Bowing her head allowed her hair to partially hide her features.

Dad scrubbed a hand over his face. "Molly, lemme take you to the cafeteria."

She sniffled. "Are you going to be mean to me?"

"No, baby," Dad said on a sigh. "Ain't meanin' to be, but you ain't knowin' when to shut the fuck up and Megan still not all well."

Molly swiped at her cheeks. "I'll go if you answer one question."

"You hungry or not?" Dad demanded.

"It's the same question I texted CJ last night."

Oh, goddamn. "Uh, Mo—"

"One fuckin' question," Dad interrupted.

Panic settled into CJ, and he stared at Mom, widening his eyes in their special way of silent communication.

"Oh, um, Molly's really hungry, Christopher—"

"Who'd win? Twenty bodybuilders on steroids with plastic bats or one blood lusted Silverback?"

Dad transferred his filthy look from Molly to CJ, opened his mouth to speak, then stalked out of the room.

"I'd say the bodybuilders, hands down," Molly announced. "That gorilla wouldn't stand a chance against those plastic bats."

"Shut the fuck up, Molly, and come eat," Dad roared from the hallway.

"You're lucky I'm hungry, Mr. CJ's Dad," Molly huffed, stomping out of the room.

"I'm hungry, too, Dad," CJ called.

"Starve," Dad snapped.

CJ grinned. Waiting a moment to make sure Dad or Molly wouldn't return, he went to his mother and hugged her for the first time in days. He thought it would be easy, but she'd lost a lot of weight and felt as fragile as Jo looked.

Today, Mom's overriding smell of medicine and sweat didn't suppress the softer cherry blossom scent he always associated with her.

"You washed your hair."

"Your daddy helped me to shower."

Heat rose in CJ's cheeks. "Oh."

"He's helped me before. We're married."

"I know, Mom. It's...this was your first shower since...?"

"I was getting sponge baths, potato. I was too weak to shower."

"You kept your hair braided."

"Christopher plaited my hair. He combed it today."

Finally releasing his mom, he straightened and stared at her. "Dad knows how to comb your hair?"

"Hasn't he styled your sister's hair?"

"Yeah." He shoved his hands into his pockets. "Are you okay? I was so scared I'd lost you. I-I-I mean, *we'd...Dad* lost you."

"It's okay, son," she said. "I'm your mother, first and foremost."

"You're Dad's wife first and foremost."

"Yes," Mom said softly, her smile tender. "And I'd die to save your daddy, as long as none of you were at risk."

"I feel so stupid," he admitted. "Like a little baby, Mom. A beta boy."

"Omigod, you've had another run in with Ryan?"

It crossed CJ's mind to tell her about Bash, but he decided against worrying her or Dad. Right now, everyone's concern focused on his mother and baby sister. Well, everyone except Uncle Johnnie, who barely visited.

Could he trust that stupid motherfucker? CJ had as much faith in Uncle Johnnie as he had in Ryan, but someone needed to know if only to help Molly.

"What's on your mind, potato?" Mom asked.

A beep alerted him to an incoming text message.

Harley: I'm sorry. Please come and watch my rehearsals during lunch.

"CJ?"

"Huh? Uh, I'm fine, Mom."

Pulling a chair closer to her bedside, CJ shoved his phone in his pocket, sat down to small talk with his mom for the first time in days, and left Harley on read.

CHAPTER 5

Matilda

The next afternoon, Mattie puffed on her bud, inhaling the smoke and allowing it to linger for a moment before tipping her head back and blowing plumes. Sitting on the edge of the railing on the pedestrian walkway of Turn Creek Bridge, she allowed her feet to dangle.

The day was gray, the sky heavy with a snowy burden. Any minute, she expected flakes to fall. Below, Turn Creek meandered along, snaking through the weeds and brambles. Unlike Harley's disastrous foray from school, Mattie knew how to cut.

She'd slipped away during lunchtime, when other things preoccupied her brothers and cousins, namely Rory and CJ. Her brother was absent today and her cousin was wherever. Once she'd scoped out pertinent information, she'd set her plan in action by intercepting the signals feeding her location to Daddy, Uncle Stretch, and whoever else monitored their movements.

Mattie hoped Harley wised up and realized CJ's devotion to her. No, Mattie hoped Harley realized how nice CJ was. He had none of Ryan's dickheadness and bravado and none of Rory's weariness and hangups. CJ was just *sweet*. Sometimes, she regretted he was her first *and* second cousin, because, yeah, their family tree was more like overgrown and intertwined vines.

Giggling, she hit her bud again, then checked her watch. She'd head back in fifteen minutes since she didn't mind her art class. Not only was it the last of the day, painting relaxed her.

Some music would hit so hard right now.

Not wanting to drop her phone in the water, she swung one leg over, then turned and jumped the short distance to the concrete. As she pulled up her streaming service, she smoked. By the time she settled on a song, her bud had flickered out.

The first snowflake fluttered by, and she tipped her head back, allowing the iciness to batter her face. When she straightened, her surroundings swirled around her. She laughed again, not having a care in the world.

Aunt Meggie grew stronger each day. Jo had survived. Maman was calm again. Even Daddy wasn't preoccupied with Mattie being a lady. At school, Wallace Byrd had yet to return and Lumbly had resigned.

Life was good.

Grinning, she pulled up *Call Out My Name* by The Weeknd. She loved that song so much. Unfortunately, she'd never listen to it at home. Her parents liked Opera and Country. Without Aunt Meggie and Lolly, Mattie would have very stunted musical tastes.

The snow fell faster.

"Shit."

Mattie stumbled forward and pitched to the ground. The pain barely registered. Instead, she screamed with laughter.

"Hey, girl."

At the sound of the gravelly voice, she blinked. A tall man in a denim cut, leather duster, and leather chaps stood in front of her.

She blinked again. She'd know those eyes anywhere. Many people had green eyes, but only two people in the world had such burning intensity. She'd just seen CJ...*recently.* He wasn't bald. Her uncle stayed at the hospital with Aunt Meggie, so maybe he'd shaved his head and she hadn't been told. "Uncle Christopher, where's your hair?" She squinted. "When'd you grow a goatee?"

"I'm not Christopher, Matilda."

Her sudden alarm stole some of the fog in her head. The way he studied her mouth creeped her out. She'd seen those looks before and knew exactly what they meant.

She backed away, then halted. She needed to get around him and escape, not end up deeper in the woods. He could kill her and toss her body in the water.

She tried to read his patches, but with each movement his duster hid them from her view.

"I have to get back to school," she said, trying to walk around him.

He cut her off. "You go back when I say so."

Her heart banged against her chest. Fear ran fast and hot inside her. Somehow, she managed not to tremble. "What do you want, mister? If it's to get my father's attention by murdering me, kiss your fucking ass goodbye because *you* will die, too."

The only person she was certain of who'd actually killed

someone was Aunt Meggie, but Mattie wasn't stupid enough to admit there was a possibility Daddy had never murdered.

"I don't want to kill you, sweetheart."

"You'll *have* to kill me, asshole, since I'd rather die than fuck you."

Anger blanketed his face, and he reached out to grab her.

"Bitch-ass, fuck you," she snarled, jabbing her fingers into his eyes, then headbutting him with all her might. He screamed. Bone crunched and blood sprayed onto her face, but she didn't care.

Seizing her chance, Mattie ran down the incline as fast as she could.

As with all her other forays away from school, the incident was her secret. She'd been too unladylike to ever tell Daddy.

"Here you are, honey."

"Thanks, Aunt Kendall," CJ replied, following her into Uncle Johnnie's library. He halted when he spied his uncle behind his desk, shirtsleeves rolled up.

"Remind Rebel I'm taking her, Mattie, and Harley

Christmas shopping tomorrow," Aunt Kendall said.

"I will. Rebel isn't too excited because Mom and Dad haven't returned her debit card yet."

"I'll cover whatever she wants," Aunt Kendall promised. "I'm about to start dinner. Would you like to stay for a meal?"

CJ eyed her with suspicion. "What's on the menu?"

She smiled. "Kimchi and kelp noodles, beef heart topped with cottage cheese, and a kefir, quinoa, mango, and turmeric pudding for dessert."

"Uh, I'm not hungry," CJ said faintly. "Thanks, though." His stomach growled.

Lifting a brow, Aunt Kendall burst into laughter.

CJ adjusted his rucksack. Uncle Cash had picked him up this afternoon, since CJ overslept and had to hitch a ride with Aunt Bailey when she dropped the girls off this morning. Uncle Cash always came in through the back entrance since his house was closer via this route. Instead of going home and then having to walk through a snowy forest to Uncle Johnnie's, CJ had asked Uncle Cash to drop him off there.

"What's really for dinner, gorgeous?" Uncle Johnnie asked, not lifting his head from the documents he was reading.

"That *is* dinner, Johnnie. For me and Mattie. I'm cooking turkey lasagna for you and the boys."

"Turkey lasagna?" CJ and Uncle Johnnie chorused.

"Yes," she hissed. "It's a compromise."

"I'll have some, Mom," Rory announced, loping in and high-fiving CJ.

"Me, too, Aunt Kendall."

"Fine," Uncle Johnnie said tightly. "I'll have some, too."

"Mom, Mattie's acting all weird," JJ complained, walking

into the room. "Probably her time of month."

"Do *not* discuss a lady's business as if you have a right, son," Aunt Kendall chastised primly.

"I do," JJ said. "She turns evil."

Glaring at Uncle Johnnie, who shrugged, Aunt Kendall sniffed and sailed out of the room, slamming the door behind her.

"I agree," Uncle Johnnie whispered. "We have to know when to hide."

They all snickered.

"What are you reading, Dad?" Rory nodded to the stack of papers on the desk.

An oddly guilty look crossed Uncle Johnnie's face. "Nothing to concern you."

"But—"

"What brings you here, nephew?"

CJ's relationship with his uncle hadn't been the same since the night he'd walked into this house and found the entire family *naked*. He'd thought Uncle Johnnie was the go-to man about Bash because his uncle set himself apart from everyone else. He wanted to be Top Dog. Uncle Mort, Uncle Digger, Uncle Val...*any* of them would handle the situation but they'd also insist on telling Outlaw, when his main focus should be Mom. All CJ needed was Uncle Johnnie to shake the fuck out of Ryan and force him to do the right thing.

He also needed help with Molly's situation.

"CJ?"

On the other hand, Uncle Johnnie would probably look down on her. He treated his own daughter without an ounce of regard for her wellbeing.

"Uh, never mind. It's...I shouldn't have disturbed you."

Awkwardness settled between them.

Uncle Johnnie sighed. "Something's bothering you, CJ.

Talk to me. I won't pass judgment."

"It's a lot to unpack, uncle," CJ said quietly.

"Try me."

"I was at Turn Creek Bridge yesterday afternoon," he started, choosing his words with care so he wouldn't get his cousins in trouble.

"You cut class?"

"Not really. I left with fifteen minutes to go."

"You cut class."

"Dad, focus," Rory said with exasperation. "I cut class, too."

"*What*?"

"That's not important right now, man!" Rory flared.

"The fuck it isn't." He stared at the papers on his desk. It seemed as if he had the weight of the world on his shoulders. Then, his assholery returned, and he glared at CJ. "You're a bad influence on my son."

"CJ wasn't even with us at first and he isn't a bad influence on us," Rory argued.

Uncle Johnnie snatched the stack of papers from the desk, opened the drawer and threw them in, then slammed the drawer shut and locked it. He stalked to the liquor table, grabbed the decanter, and swigged from it.

"Never mind," CJ snapped, starting for the door. "Thanks for living up to my fucking expectations, Uncle."

"No, wait, CJ!" Rory called. "I think he's trying to tell you about Bash, Dad."

A moment of silence slid by before the sound of shattering glass made CJ spin around. Uncle Johnnie stood at the bar, ashen with shock. The decanter he'd held, filled with expensive whisky, was nothing but glass shards in pools of amber liquid.

"Bash?" he pushed out.

"You know that wretched motherfucker, Dad?" Rory demanded.

"Bash?" he repeated.

"He said horrible things about my mom, Uncle Johnnie," CJ said. "He said Ryder was your son and that Mom killed a man. We know only one of those things are true."

Wildness crept into his uncle's eyes, but he staggered back.

"I'm coming to you because Ryan is somehow involved with him, Uncle. And…and…Molly is pregnant." CJ hung his head. "Possibly by Bash," he whispered. "I don't know how to get her help and…and…Ryan's a fucking fuckbag. Most of the time I can't stand that stupid motherfucker, but if Aunt Zoann loves him the way Aunt Kendall loves her children and Mom loves us, it'll devastate her if he gets his dumb ass killed. Bash is evil and dangerous."

"He looks like Uncle Christopher, Dad," Rory said casually.

"Does he?" Uncle Johnnie sounded like a robot.

"You know him!" Rory accused again.

"I don't—"

Lying bitch. "There's no other reason for your reaction, Uncle."

He stiffened. "I won't have children questioning my judgment," he roared.

JJ jumped but rage blanketed Rory's face. "Go, J," he said. JJ left.

"You know him," Rory repeated.

"Shut the fuck up, Rory. I'm warning you."

"Don't be mad that we have more fucking sense than you, Dad," Rory retorted. "How do you know Bash?"

"I don't—"

"Another thing you're getting over on my dad?" CJ asked with derision, interrupting his uncle. He was in no mood to hear more of his fucking lies.

"How am I getting over on Christopher, CJ?"

"The way you play him to keep the peace? Now, you're cavorting with motherfuckers that doesn't mean any of us any good."

Uncle Johnnie stalked from behind the desk. "I resent that, you little motherfucker."

CJ shoved him away. "I don't give a fuck, Uncle. I came here because I needed you."

"Since when? Usually it's Mortician or Val. Even Digger."

"Can you fucking blame me? They'd tell Dad to protect him. You'd hold this shit in to manipulate him. But he's worried about Mom right now. He doesn't need Bash's distraction. I thought it was just about Molly and Ryan, but it's so much fucking deeper. Who the fuck is Bash?"

"I don't answer to a goddamn boy."

"Even if it'll protect the club, Dad?"

CJ gave Uncle Johnnie a chance to respond to Rory's question.

"Who is Bash, Uncle?" CJ demanded at his uncle's continued silence. "Answer to me or answer to my dad. I don't give a fuck. He needs somebody to protect him. Obviously, it isn't you. You can't even protect your own fucking wife and children."

Through the years, CJ had his fair share of ass beatings from his father. Usually, with a belt or a hand. 'Law had never raised his fists to CJ or any of his brothers, even Diesel. None of his uncles had. Even with all that had passed between CJ and Uncle Johnnie, he never would've expected the motherfucker to cold clock him and make him see stars.

"Dad, have you lost your fucking mind?" Rory demanded, rushing to CJ and preventing him from dropping to the ground. "You have a bad fucking habit of hitting Uncle

Christopher's son. One of these days, he's going to kill you."

"He's Megan son."

"That *Uncle Christopher* fathered!"

Uncle Johnnie ignored Rory. "Chances are high, he'll get you killed first."

"What—"

"Shut the fuck up. Go home, CJ, and don't come back. Your association is endangering my children."

"Are you crazy?" Rory said, still keeping a steadying hand on CJ's shoulder. "I think Bash was there for Harley, fuckhead. CJ wasn't even there when that motherfucker first appeared. It was *Harley.* He kept looking at her, like the fucking dickface motherfucker he is."

Horror washed over Uncle Johnnie's face. "Kendall!" he snarled.

"She's probably on the other side of the house, Dad. She can't hear you."

Rage twisting his features, Uncle Johnnie dug inside his suit jacket, producing his Glock, trembling so much he almost dropped the gun. He stared blindly around the room, until he focused on the mirror on the wall right beside where CJ and Rory stood.

The moment he lifted the gun, CJ shoved Rory to the floor and covered his body with his own. In the enclosed space, the gunshots were deafening. Glass and gilded wood flew in all directions. By the time the clip was empty, the wall was ruined, too.

Uncle Johnnie stared at the mess he'd created, breathing heavily, gun still clutched in his hand, now hanging at his side.

Aunt Kendall rushed in with Mattie hot on her heels. They stared at the man of the house, more unhinged than CJ had ever seen anyone. He staggered to his feet and helped Rory up. JJ halted in the doorway, tears running down his cheeks, holding a squirming and screaming Blade tightly.

"Kendall," Uncle Johnnie croaked. "CJ needs help with Molly. She's pregnant."

"Oh, um—"

"Not by him." That same frightening fury rose in Uncle Johnnie's face again. He started for the door. "Don't wait up for me."

"Johnnie?" Aunt Kendall ran behind him, fear widening her eyes. She grabbed his wrist, the huge diamond in her wedding set gleaming in the light. "What's going on? Talk to me."

His nostrils flared and he leaned his forehead against hers, deflating. "I love you, Kendall," he whispered. "So much."

Aunt Kendall hugged him. "I know, Johnnie. I know. I love you, too."

He kissed her as if he'd never see her again, then he walked to Mattie and hugged her with all the love a father should display, before rage gleamed in his eyes again.

He backed away, turned on his heel, and left without another word.

CHAPTER 6

CHRISTOPHER

"How is she?" Megan asked the moment Christopher passed the nurse on her way out, walked back into Megan's room and sat in the chair next to her bed.

"Tiny," Christopher said, nothing else coming to mind. He spent a lot of time in NICU, watching Jo and talking to her, wondering if she heard him. She was so small, he was afraid to hold her. During the rare times he gave in, he missed Megan's guidance more than anything. His girl was so weak, it made her uninterested in Jo. Nine days ago, she'd been strong enough to see their girl for the first time. All she did was cry and apologize for her failure to keep Jo inside her longer. Finally, he stopped her from going since it seemed to be affecting her recovery. "But she's getting stronger, baby."

Smiling, Megan nodded. "How are you?"

A fucking wreck. "Don't worry about me, Megan. I ain't the one in the fuckin' hospital bed."

She cocked her head to the side, grogginess setting in.

Christopher reminded himself she still felt pain, so they administered strong meds to relieve her. She was stable again. Her blood pressure had been stable for the past week. She didn't seem as swollen anymore and the fever from the infection she'd developed had broken. But seeing her eyes slip closed still sent panic through him. He couldn't forget the moment she'd collapsed, and he thought he'd lost her.

Initially, he'd blamed Rebel for acting like a miserable little cunt and spewing filth at her ma. When Doc Will delivered the news that Jo wouldn't survive and Megan might not either, Christopher's hatred toward Rebel ran unchecked. Then, it died. As had his love.

He'd felt absolutely nothing for her; once she'd been his princess. And, so, he'd walked away, intending to go to his Megan and order her to fight to survive. He hadn't given a fuck that Rebel was hysterical. Her pain vindicated his soul-crushing grief.

In tears, he'd stood in front of the elevator, awaiting its arrival, hearing Rebel's sobs. As much as he wanted to, he hadn't been able to turn his back on her. He'd gone back to her, his beautiful little princess who looked so much like her ma.

Seeing his boy trying to console his girl when he, too, was so devastated, almost broke Christopher. He'd wrapped both of them in his arms and cried with them. When CJ broke away and Rebel remained in Christopher's embrace, he continued consoling her.

More importantly, he'd forgiven her.

Later, it came to him that Megan hadn't consciously factored in his change of heart. He simply did what a father is supposed to do. Megan was imbedded in his very soul. She always saw the good in him and believed him the best daddy in the world. Deep down, she undoubtedly aided his decision regarding their girl. He prayed for the chance to tell her about his epiphany.

A curious thing happened between Doc Will's devastating news and Christopher's forgiveness of Rebel.

Jo took another turn. This one for the better. She was a micro preemie and not out of the woods, but while Doc Will was delivering her news, the baby's breathing and vital signs stabilized. She was fighting to live.

Both Jo and Megan remained in intensive care, however. He wanted Jo to survive. She was another little girl for him to love and protect. But it was Megan...*Megan*...he couldn't bear to lose.

He hated to leave her side. He hated to sleep. Keeping watch over her allowed him to be there if she needed him. If only to hold her hand or remind her she meant the world to him.

Usually, he waited until she slept before he visited the nursery. Today, she'd wanted him to see Jo, then report back to her before she fell asleep. It meant skipping the precious moments she was awake, but if it made her happy, he obliged.

His eyes drooped, then flew open and narrowed. He was certain Megan moved. Yet, she seemed positioned in the same spot, so maybe he'd imagined it.

He yawned, though he refused to sleep. Along with gallons of coffee, he took several cold showers a day to stay awake.

If Megan needed him, he *had* to be available.

Hunger pangs cramped his stomach. He tried to remember when he'd last eaten. Time escaped him, however. The hallway crawled with his brothers. They knew better than to disturb him, though. Unless he asked for a meal or coffee or anything, they left him to his own devices.

He hated hospital food, so it was never an option to eat the shit if he wasn't a patient. Even then, he preferred starvation.

His ringing phone annoyed him. Megan shifted, and his annoyance turned to fury. It was almost ten ofuckingclock at night.

Maybe, Mort? He'd called Christopher earlier and—

"Christopher?"

The phone stopped.

"It's okay, baby. Go back to sleep." He jerked the phone off the rolling cart next to him, intending to mute the volume. It started ringing again. She jerked, her brow wrinkling.

Brooks Redding's name flashed on the screen.

"Is that CJ?" she mumbled. "Are the kids okay?"

"You better have a good fuckin' reason for disturbin' Megan, motherfucker," he answered, staggering to his feet. "This Brooks, baby. I'm going right in the hallway. Don't go nowhere."

She smiled. "I'll be right here, waiting for you."

The words didn't comfort him. If he wasn't watching her, she might be there when he returned but not in the condition he expected.

He leaned over and kissed her, his pulse thumping at the base of his neck. "I love you, Megan. Don't go nowhere."

"I love you more, Christopher."

"Don't go nowhere," he repeated.

"I wouldn't dare leave you," she swore, and closed her eyes again.

For a moment, he stared at her, forgetting about Brooks. She looked so still. If not for the steady rise and fall of her chest and the consistency of her vital signs on the machine hooked to her, Christopher would panic.

"Outlaw?"

He didn't realize he still held the phone to his ear, until

he heard Brooks call his name. He turned, intending to leave, except he couldn't force himself to do so right now. He would, as he always did, to check on Jo.

Sighing, he returned to his seat, scrubbed a hand over his face, and said, "talk to me."

Brooks cleared his throat. "A situation arose a little while ago. Johnnie called me and thought it best I talk to you."

"I don't wanna hear it, Brooks. Johnnie the VP. Let him handle it."

"You're still the club president, Outlaw," Brooks said. "He wanted you to know that, uh, a few mon…er, *weeks* ago, uh B-Bash made contact."

The name turned over in Christopher's head. It took him a moment, but he realized who Brooks referred to. "Cee Cee's oldest?"

"One and the same."

Christopher rubbed his eyes. "So?"

"Uh, he would like to sit down with us and d-d-discuss the Scorched Devils."

Christopher tried, and failed, to connect the dots between the Scorpions and the Devils. As far as he remembered the Gnomes were the Devils' problem. Something wasn't adding up, but his brain was too tired and crowded with worry to figure out what. Or, for that matter, *care.*

"Why Bash wantin' to talk to us rather than to Derby, since he brought the Devils to us?"

"We intend to find that out, Outlaw."

"Does Bash want a stake in Dweller territory?"

"I-I'm not sure. J-Johnnie wants to iron out a peace agreement similar to what we have with the Gnomes, since Bash is a sworn enemy, he thought it best I inform you."

Megan turned on her side.

"Bash thought it best?"

"No, Outlaw. Johnnie."

"Yeah," Christopher agreed, only half comprehending the conversation.

"Johnnie has everything under control." Brooks cleared his throat. "There's quite a history between your father and grandfather."

News to Christopher. He'd always been told his grandfather hated him because Cee Cee stole Christopher's ma and raped her. It was also the reason Logan hated Christopher. His birth brought such shame to the sweet, kind, and gentle Patricia.

"Cee Cee Caldwell controlled Logan Donovan with money and threats."

It figured. No matter the reason, the information didn't surprise Christopher. Both Cee Cee and Logan were dirty motherfuckers.

"Apparently, er, Bash is afraid of you."

Christopher snickered.

"You killed Cee Cee."

If motherfuckers knew, they knew, but it wasn't shit Christopher broadcast. The knowledge could endanger Megan. Motherfuckers needed to shut the fuck up about that. "Accordin' to who?"

"Er, word around town. Whether it's accurate doesn't matter. Bash believes it and it gives the Dwellers the u-upperh-hand."

Vaguely, Christopher wondered why Brooks tripped over his words. "Why you tellin'…why are you tellin' me this now? You need me to meet with Bash?"

"Not at all. As long as Bash is aware that you know what's going on, he'll stay in line and keep to the bargain."

Megan was so fucking restless. Christopher wished he could climb beside her. He leaned forward. "Baby, you fine."

He squinted, vaguely recalling he'd worked hard to speak correctly. "Stop movin' so much."

"Christopher?"

"I'm here, Megan."

"Is everything okay?" Brooks asked.

"Fuck, I ain't...I don't know. She's tossin' and turnin'. Should I call the nurse?"

"Are her vital signs okay?"

Christopher glanced at the screen. They were still normal. "I-I think so, but fuck, Brooks, shit was normal the night she collapsed. How can I ever think she's fine going forward? I thought it before and almost lost her."

"Keep watch over her," Brooks said quietly. "I'm sorry to have disturbed you, but Johnnie, er, *I* thought it was important."

Christopher nodded, though Brooks couldn't see him. "You and John Boy handle it. I can't be bothered right now."

"We'll take care of everything," Brooks promised.

Megan shifted again. Christopher disconnected the call without another word.

CHAPTER 7

RORY

"Mom, you have to eat."

Instead of following Rory's orders, his mother blinked, the same response she'd had the past three times he'd encouraged her to try her food.

"Daddy will come home, Momma," Mattie said in a small voice. "He always does."

Still staring at Dad's empty chair, Mom started. "You called me 'momma', instead of '*maman*', Mattie?"

Rory frowned. That's what finally got a reaction from Mom?

"Oh, uh..." Looking from him to JJ and then to Mom, Mattie's throat worked. "I-I—"

Mom squinted at Mattie. "What happened to your head, darling?"

"Um, I took a fall during cheer practice."

She hadn't gone to practice today.

Rory lifted a brow at his little sister's lie, gritting his teeth when she scraped her fork tines over her dinner plate.

Leaning back in his chair, he folded his arms and glared at her.

"Do you think CJ made it home?" JJ asked, no longer in tears but...*affected.* "Or, maybe, he went with Dad since CJ left not two minutes after Dad walked out."

That was almost four hours ago. Somehow, Rory restored control. He'd ordered Mattie to bring Blade to Ella, promised JJ things were fine, and hugged his mother, comforting her as she'd sobbed as if her world was ending.

When his stomach growled, she'd ordered him to eat. Rory decided they all needed dinner. While JJ and Mattie warmed the food and plated their meals, Rory sat with their mother in the dining room. Watching her. Afraid to leave her alone. Wondering if he needed to hide the knives.

He'd never been so relieved to see his brother and sister when they arrived with the plates. Dad was *Dad,* and would take care of himself and eventually return, so Rory enjoyed his turkey lasagna. He'd need sustenance to take care of his mother. Thankfully, JJ emulated Rory, so he'd eaten, too. At almost eleven at night, Mattie took small bites; mostly, she pushed her food around on her plate.

Perhaps, it was because of Dad's stunt. *Or* it was because she had fucking slop on her plate. Jury was out on that shit. Mom, though, hadn't eaten. She'd barely moved. She'd sat in her armchair, at her end of the table, staring at Dad's spot. Her tears had dried up, replaced by fear and worry.

"Suppose he doesn't come home?" Mom whispered, her lips trembling.

Tears rushed to Mattie's eyes, but she blinked them away, refusing to allow them to fall. "You're a strong, independent woman, Momma. You're...*Maman.* Flawed and imperfect, but perfect to me."

Swiping at the tears sliding down her cheeks, Mom

nodded.

Rory wanted to add to what Mattie said. Words jammed in his head and stuck in his throat. As furious as Dad made him, he couldn't imagine a world without him. Mom was everything Mattie said, but Dad had learned to protect her and shield her. She'd learned to *allow* him to protect and shield her.

"What sent your father into such a rage, Rory?"

"Some Pale Rider motherfucker," Rory said in disgust. He needed to clean up the mess Dad made when he shot up that fucking mirror.

"P-Pale R-Rider?" Mattie squeaked.

"Yeah, it's an old Clint Eastwood classic and one of our favorite movies," JJ said. "One of the ones Dad doesn't allow you to watch, Mattie."

Mattie glanced at Mom. For the first time in hours, a semblance of normalcy returned when Mom gave the slightest shake of her head and placed a finger over her lips. Mattie gave a small nod.

Mom went back to staring at Dad's space. Worry settled over the room again. Like the rest of the house, the formal dining room featured expensive furniture, dramatic lighting and luxurious décor. The extravagance didn't take away tonight's trauma.

Rory, Mattie, and JJ glanced amongst each other.

"Ro said that mid motherfucker was wearing a duster like Preacher," JJ said into the overwhelming silence. "That's why he brought up Pale Rider."

"I-I s-s-see," Mattie responded.

Rory bet she fucking did. She'd seen the movie with Mom's approval. Mom and Mattie didn't need his judgment at the moment, so he'd focus on the positive. He applauded his little brother's efforts to bring their mother back to the present. It worked.

"Johnnie usually doesn't concern himself with mid-level anything," Mom said, staring at Rory, searching for answers.

Fuck. Rory didn't want to give away the real issue. He was certain Dad knew Bash. He was just as certain if the motherfucker was from a rival club, Dad would've spoken up. He wouldn't leave his family, the *entire* fucking club, exposed and vulnerable.

"He was following Harley," JJ volunteered when Rory remained silent, "although Ro, Lou, and Mark JB—"

Mom frowned. "This person was on school grounds?"

"Asshole," Rory mouthed to his little brother, who sat across the table, next to Mattie.

Lifting a brow, Mom looked at Rory, waiting for an explanation.

He sighed. "We were cutting class."

"*Cutting?*" Mom echoed. "Harley was cutting?"

"Me, too," Rory said slowly. He didn't want to rat Harley out because JJ had blabbed their secrets.

Mom pushed back from her seat and stood. Her plate remained untouched. She stumbled toward the door.

"Mom, don't tell on Harley!" Rory called, getting to his feet and intending to rush after her.

"Why would I do that, darling?" she asked, turning to him. The distant look in her eyes concerned him. She didn't seem completely present.

"She'll get in trouble with Uncle Mort and Aunt Bailey," Rory said.

"We track all of you," Mom responded, her smile dazed and her expression empty. "We know where you're at every hour of the day. We get alerts."

"C-can't we track Dad?" Mattie asked timidly.

Mom blinked in confusion. "Why do we need to do that,

darling?"

Mattie swallowed. "To find out where he's at, Momma," she
whispered.

"We know where he's at, Mattie." Mom backed away. "I must wash up for dinner. Johnnie will be home from work soon."

She left.

A moment of stunned silence went by.

"*What?*" Mattie finally gasped.

CHAPTER 8

Johnnie

"It's done, Johnnie."

Sitting in the stairwell of Hortensia General, Johnnie aimed his Glock at the dismal gray-green wall. It was after one in the morning, and he was still reeling from CJ's news.

He didn't know why he'd trusted Bash to take his money, then not stab him in the fucking back. After he'd walked away from his wife and kids, Johnnie disabled his tracker and drove around for hours, until he settled on a place to regroup and called Brooks.

Johnnie lowered the gun. "What did you tell him, Brooks?"

"Exactly what you told me to. We're working with Bash on behalf of the Scorched Devils. You intend to control him as Cee Cee Caldwell managed Logan Donovan."

The story sounded like the bullshit it was. His grip on the

Glock tightened. "Did he question you?"

"Outlaw isn't in the frame of mind for any of this. He's gone this long without knowing. I don't understand why you'd burden him with the details, *false* ones may I add, when he is so concerned about Meggie."

Snapping his brows together, Johnnie glowered at the ugly wall. "Are you fucking questioning me?"

"N-no, o-of course not, Johnnie. I'm merely wondering aloud how this lie will save us from Outlaw's wrath."

"It won't," Johnnie admitted. "I'm buying time until I figure out what to do about Bash. He takes my fucking money every month, yet he overlooked our gentleman's agreement and came to Hortensia."

"He isn't a gentleman."

Johnnie's nostrils flared and bleakness settled into him. "No. He admires Cee Cee so much, I thought he'd adhere to a scheme similar to Cee Cee's." Bowing his head, he closed his eyes and scratched his temple with the barrel of the gun. "I was wrong. Now, I'm out of time."

"Cee Cee was in the opposite position, Johnnie," Brooks reminded him. "I think Cee Cee had the money *and* the power."

If some of the documents were to be believed.

"I have the money, but Bash has the power," Johnnie admitted dully.

"We have to find a way to get the power."

"I know."

Without Christopher, Johnnie had no anchor. When he allowed it, Brooks offered advice, support, and encouragement to him, although he was so invaluable to Kendall and their children that Mattie referred to the attorney as 'Gramps' and his wife as 'Gram'.

"I will continue to try to make contact with him. So far, he hasn't answered. Cleaner won't confirm Bash's location. I can still call Riley and ask him—"

"No! Absolutely not. Christopher is distracted right now. Until Megan recovers. When it clicks, I'm as dead as Bash. As dead as you," he added drearily.

Brooks sucked in a breath. "We have tried to avert disaster. We haven't betrayed him or the club."

"Bash's primary target is Megan, Brooks," Johnnie reminded him. "He wants her eliminated."

"You were involved because he threatened Kendall and Mattie. Surely, Outlaw will understand that."

"He's unreasonable if it involves Megan. Kyler was killed partly because he left Christopher in jail, but mostly because he disrespected Megan."

"My poor son-in-law." Brooks's voice wobbled. "He was only doing as Charlotte instructed. As was I. We wanted her happy. She's my wife and was his mother-in-law."

"He still fucked over Megan." Johnnie leaned against the wall. He'd snuck up the rarely-used back staircase, built during the last renovation especially for club members trying to escape danger or law enforcement. "I wanted some of Bash's documents verified or disproved before I went to Christopher. Mainly, I wanted to extricate Kendall and Matilda from Bash's crosshairs. If he managed to escape Christopher's vengeance, he'd target them first to teach me a lesson."

Trembling at the thought of losing Kendall and Mattie, Johnnie couldn't fathom his next move.

"I've tried to find who sent the documents," Brooks said on a sigh. "I come up empty at every turn. Is it possible they're fabricated?"

"I've thought of that," Johnnie admitted. "But Bash has no reason to fuck with the club so drastically over bogus claims.

The Scorpions aren't as strong as they once were, especially after Christopher killed several of our half-brothers *and* Cee Cee. They aren't struggling either. We've both combed their financial records. If it was strictly about money and territory, he'd go after the club. He wants Megan because he claims she's the owner of the land and the buildings. Fuck, it would be easier if he was challenging the club."

"Johnnie, I love Kendall like she was my own daughter. I would give my life for any of my children. I'll do the same for Kendall." He sniffled. "I'll go to Outlaw and tell him I went behind his back to try to diffuse a situation involving Meggie. I'll tell him everything Bash confided to us and hand over all the documents to Outlaw. He'll kill Bash and eliminate the threat to Kendall, Mattie, and Meggie."

"Christopher will kill you, too," he said unnecessarily. Brooks said as much. "You're a fine man, Brooks. Kendall is lucky to have you, but I can't let you lay down your life in such a manner."

"I should never have told you. I should've gone to Salt Lake City on my own."

"Then you *would* be dead. Kendall and Charlotte would be heartbroken."

"I don't know what to do. Meggie isn't strong enough to leave. Not that she would, while Jo remains in the hospital. Once she recovers and Bash is on the move in Hortensia, she'll be on the move. If only she were still pregnant."

Johnnie stilled. Maybe, the key to solving his problems in the short-term was Megan. Deep down, he'd known all along what he needed to do. It was why he'd hidden in the stairwell.

"She would be entering her third trimester, wouldn't she?" Brooks rambled. "Outlaw wouldn't want her going many places. She was so gravely ill, I suppose she won't get pregnant again any time soon, if ever. Barring confession, finding a way to stop her from being out and about is our best chance to keep her safe and pray we find what we need to somehow stop Bash or go to Outlaw."

"I think I have a solution, Brooks. Get some sleep. I'll call you later today."

Disconnecting the call, Johnnie shoved the phone in the pocket of his dress shirt. He hadn't even changed from his suit, but he had a cut and jeans in the Navigator for emergencies. He returned his gun to the holster at his side and climbed the additional flight to the fifth floor, where he punched in his private code available only to a select few.

Getting onto a floor required the six digits; exiting didn't. It trapped whoever didn't belong in the hospital in the stairwell, leaving them vulnerable to retribution.

Slowly, he opened the door and peeped into the hallway. The overly bright fluorescent lights hurt his eyes after he'd lingered in the dim stairwell for so many hours. When his vision adjusted, he found the hallway empty. He stepped into a short hallway containing vending machines and an archway that led to a small waiting room, now darkened. He peeped in the hallway. The locked doors separating the ICU from the waiting areas and elevators were to his left. Right led to the rooms.

Without warning, the doors opened and Johnnie tucked himself in the shadow of the vending machine. A moment later, he heard Christopher's footsteps, quickly identifiable because of his spurs.

"She's sleepin'," Christopher said, passing the turnoff where Johnnie hid without pause.

"You look like you need some shut eye, Prez," Bishop said.

"I slept."

"The usual hour?" Potter asked as the doors closed and

their voices faded away.

Seizing the opportunity and unsure how long Christopher would be gone, Johnnie hurried to Megan's room, glad the nurse's station was unattended.

MEGGIE

"Wake up, Megan."

The harsh order came to Meggie from a distance. If hands hadn't grabbed her shoulders and shook her so roughly that it hurt her incision, she would've believed she was dreaming.

Eyelashes fluttering, she lifted her lids and blinked, surprised to see Johnnie's face so close to hers.

"Hey," she said, her brain fogged from medication, pain, and fatigue.

"Do you love Christopher?"

She struggled to comprehend his words. "What kind of question is that?"

"A legitimate one. Now answer me."

"Of course, I do! Are you mad?"

"Can you give him more children?"

Dizziness twirled around her, but she knew the answer immediately. "Even if I can, I don't want more children. I almost died, along with Jo. I'm grateful for the kids I have."

"Then that's a no."

Meggie licked her lips, wishing she was stronger or wishing Christopher walked in. "It's a definitive no, Johnnie. I left no room for doubt."

"Christopher won't be happy. He likes babies."

She swallowed. "I-I…that isn't true. I-I'm n-not sure, but I don't think he's left the hospital. If I were to get pregnant again, he'd die of worry."

"You stupid little cunt," Johnnie snarled. "You're so fucking selfish. He told me how disappointed he's been with your pregnancies. He's never been able to enjoy one of them because you're so fucking weak."

Pressing the button to lift the top half of her bed forced Johnnie back. She felt nauseated and overheated. "Christopher would never—"

Johnnie seized the controller with buttons for the bed, to call the nurse, and to work the TV. "Wouldn't he? Weeks after you met him, he asked you to have his baby. Do you think that's changed?"

"We have seven children, Johnnie," she said, her voice wavering. "Eight, if you count Patrick and nine with Diesel. Surely—"

"Leave him. I'll give you five million dollars to walk away."

She tried to snatch the controller from him, but he shoved her away and she fell against the pillows. He set it on the rollaway cart Christopher kept behind his chair when she wasn't eating.

"I'm not leaving my husband, Johnnie." Her pulse thumped, triggering an alarm.

He glared at her. "This isn't fucking over."

As the door opened, Meggie closed her eyes. She didn't want bloodshed or violence but she wanted Johnnie gone.

"Mrs. Caldwell?" the nurse greeted.

Meggie popped her eyes opened and glanced around. "You

made him leave?" she asked hopefully.

"Who, dear?" Her gaze fell on Meggie's wet cheeks and she frowned. "Oh, my dear. You've had a nightmare."

"No, I didn't! John—"

"Please remain silent while I recheck your pulse and blood pressure."

"But Johnnie—"

"Shhhhh. You're fine." She pressed a few buttons to measure Meggie's vital signs again.

"Where's Christopher?"

The older woman smiled. She had apple cheeks, salt-and-pepper hair, and a kind expression.

"He went to the nursery. As he usually does when you're—"

"Call him. I need to talk to him."

"But we don't want to alarm him."

"Please? Please," she whispered. "I...please."

"Okay. When I return, I'll call him."

"No, don't leave me until he comes back. Johnnie might return. Please."

The nurse laughed. "You're having nightmares. I'll get you a sedative, but I promise I'll call him before I administer it."

The moment the nurse left, Johnnie walked out of the private bathroom.

"Don't tell Christopher I was here," he ordered, his tone as cold as his eyes. "He doesn't want you to know and you'll hurt him further."

He didn't give her a chance to respond before he left.

When the nurse returned five minutes later, she held a cellphone to her ear. "Yes, Mr. Caldwell. She had a bad dream. Yes, sir. She's still awake. Hold on a minute." She handed the phone to Meggie.

"Baby, I'm on my way back to the room. I swear I ain't

leavin' your side again."

"Christopher, do you want more children?"

"What the fuck that mean, Megan? Ain't we got eight livin'?"

"Y-yes," she said, her voice trembling. "But Johnnie said—"

"Megan, Johnnie didn't say shit, baby. I haven't talked to that motherfucker in days."

The nurse smiled at her. She'd overheard Christopher's blare. "See? Just a bad dream."

"Megan, baby, you been so fuckin' drugged up, I'm surprised you ain't seein' Miss Piggy and Kermit the fuckin' Frog visitin' you. I want as many children as you want. We got a battalion of lil' motherfuckers, but if you want a fucking legion and you can survive, we can have more."

"Do *you* want more children?" she demanded, fogginess overtaking her. The nurse must have pushed the sedative into her IV. "Don't worry about what I want."

"It's your pussy, baby. How can I not worry if you want more lil' motherfuckers? Me? I'd worry your entire pregnancy, so no I don't want you to have any more of my kids."

"Do you wish I'd had easier pregnancies?" Her voice was fading but she found the strength to ask her questions. "If I could promise an enjoyable pregnancy, would you still say you didn't want more kids?"

"Megan, baby, I can't be more clear than to say I don't want no more kids. I don't think your body can take it and I ain't riskin' you. But I'm doin' whatever you want. Hear me? Now, get some rest. We can talk about this when you all better."

"Okay," she said, and sank into sleep.

CHAPTER 9

After tossing and turning the entire night, CJ knew he couldn't make it to school. There were less than two weeks left before Winter Break began and it couldn't come soon enough.

Rising early because he didn't want to run into anyone and offer explanations, he headed to the hospital to talk to his father. In between snatches of sleep, he'd debated if he should involve Outlaw. While Mom and Jo were in the hospital, his focus should be on them. Yet, Molly needed help. Going to Uncle Johnnie had been a stupid idea. CJ felt like kicking his own ass.

Honestly, what the fuck had he expected from that fuckhead?

If he went to any of his other uncles, Outlaw would find out anyway, so it was best to cut out *all* middlemen. Since the hospital doors didn't open until eight, and it wasn't seven yet, CJ called Slipper so hospital security would let him in. He also wanted to hang out with him until he was certain Outlaw was awake.

Slipper had been called away on an emergency; therefore, one of the younger members, Bishop, came down himself and opened the door for CJ.

"Fuck, bro, who gave you that fucking facer?" Bishop asked around a yawn.

"A shithead," CJ grumbled.

Bishop chuckled, leading CJ to the bank of elevators. "My brothers are little shits, too." He pressed the 'Up' arrow.

"Have any sisters?" CJ asked as they boarded.

"Nope," Bishop responded. "More's the pity. Girls are gentle. I'd prefer to be the only swinging dick amongst a gaggle of girls. Poor Reb. I feel sorry for her."

"Fuck, dude, my sister has the face of an angel, but the soul of fucking Beelzebub. She'll kick the shit out of you if you look at her wrong."

"Huh." Bishop thought for a moment, then nodded. "Bitch sounds like a wild one."

The elevator doors opened, and Bishop pressed the button to hold them until CJ walked off.

"*Rebel* is wild," he tossed out with meaning.

"Point taken, dude," Bishop said with a chuckle.

At the doors leading to the wing with his mother's room, CJ halted and glanced at his watch.

"Are you going in?"

"If things were normal and we were home, Mom would've been awake for at least an hour by now," CJ confessed. "I don't want to disturb her."

"CJ?" Dad called from behind him.

Startled, CJ turned, surprised to find his father dressed in scrubs and holding a mug of coffee.

"Dad?" He glanced over his shoulder at the double doors, then back at his father. "I-I thought..." A horrifying idea occurred to him. "Oh my God, Dad! Is Mom...Is Jo...fuck, I *was* dreaming, wasn't I? Wh-what happened?"

Suddenly, Dad was there, gripping his face between his hands and looking at him.

"Breathe, son," he said gently. "Just breathe. Your ma and lil' sister fine. I go spend time with her while your ma sleep at night. I tell her about you and the boys and Reb and Megan. That time for me. When I see her durin' the day, that time for Megan, 'til she go herself. Hear me, boy?"

CJ nodded, on the verge of losing his shit and feeling like a pussy.

"You good?"

"I don't know," CJ said after a moment.

"You on your way to school?" Dad asked, releasing his hold on CJ's cheeks, but laying his hands on his shoulders.

"I've been up half the fucking night. I'm taking today off."

No arguments, just acquiescence. "Got something to do with your black fuckin' eye?"

"N-not really." CJ studied his father. He had dark rings around eyes dull with fatigue. Like Mom, he'd lost weight and looked as if he carried the world on his shoulders.

Bowing his head, CJ stepped back, and Dad dropped his hands to his side. "Don't worry about me, Dad. Take care of Mom and Jo. They need you."

Dad turned away and snatched his coffee mug from the small table that sat between two chairs, one of which Bishop now occupied.

"You here for a reason, CJ," Dad said gruffly and sipped his coffee. "You ain't goin' to school for a reason."

"I'm worried about—"

"Ain't doubtin' that, but you here cuz you need me."

"You're taking care of Mom and Jo and protecting them. I'm taking care of you and everyone else and protecting *them*."

For a moment, Dad remained silent before he smiled, and pride gleamed in his eyes. He gave CJ a one-armed hug. "You do me proud, boy. But talk to me."

"Are you sure?"

"Your ma beat Death again. Your lil' sister won against that motherfucker, too."

"Death, be not proud," CJ said quietly. "Sooner or later, it takes us, Dad."

"As long as I go before your ma, it don't matter, CJ."

"Mom won't feel the same way."

Dad smiled and drank more coffee. "Megan'll fuck me up if she heard me say that shit."

"Mom's three feet four inches, Dad, and you're twelve feet ten inches. How can *that* shortie fuck you up?"

"Cuz she *my* shortie," Dad said, snickering. He finished the coffee and set the mug back on the table. "Megan gonna be wakin' up soon, so—"

"Oh, I'll go and come back to see Mom at the usual—"

"Ain't meant that, CJ. It just seem like you need to talk to me without your ma hearin'. And if I let you leave, knowin' you ain't goin' to school, and Megan find out, she ain't gonna be happy. She wanna see you before she see my ass."

"Nah, Dad. She'll save *my* ass before she saves yours, but she wants you to be the first person she sees when she opens her eyes and the last one she sees before she closes them at night."

"She love you lil' motherfuckers—"

"'Law, please. *Mom* told me that one time when you were away on a run, so take the win, dude. Your woman loves you."

Smiling, Dad nodded, his eyes suspiciously moist.

CJ leaned closer. "If you start crying in this motherfucker, I will, too, 'Law, so pull yourself together, man, before we end up as blubbering pussies."

"Whatcha wanna talk to me 'bout?" Dad asked after a swallow, slipping back into the way of talking he was most comfortable with, but he'd worked hard at correcting his speech.

When Diesel first went to college, their father enrolled in night school and obtained his GED. Sometimes, though, CJ missed the old version of his dad. It seemed as if he'd lost something of himself in trying to live up to…*Uncle Johnnie's* standards.

CJ snorted. "Has Uncle Johnnie always been a motherfucker?" he blurted, forgetting his father's cardinal rule of always respecting adults.

Bishop snickered, while Dad drew himself up and looked at CJ, his gaze touching on every inch of CJ's face. His eyes widened.

"Johnnie hit you?"

"He also shot the fucking mirror in his dining room and mangled the drywall. If someone had been walking in the hallway, they would've been fucked up."

Dad nodded. "Why?"

Because the motherfucker was insane.

However…

Dad still wasn't 'Law. *Outlaw.* Outlaw wouldn't have such a muted response to the news. CJ tested his theory. "Do you know Bash?"

"Where you heard that name from?"

CJ asked again, "Do you know him, Dad?"

"Motherfucker your uncle. He head the Scorpions." Dad shrugged. "What the fuck left of them."

"Aren't the Scorpions enemies of the Dwellers?"

"Dead fuckin' enemies."

"Orders are *on sight*," Bishop added.

Meaning either side were to fuck each other up *on sight*.

"Why Johnnie tellin' you 'bout…about one of Cee Cee's fuckhead sons?" Dad asked.

Because that motherfucker was a traitor and so was Ryan. Goddamn, that would mean death for both of them. Jesus. This was so fucking bad.

"Bishop, I need more coffee and bring a mug for CJ."

"You got it, Prez."

"Brooks called me last night and told me him and Johnnie workin' out a deal with motherfuckin' Bash on behalf of the Scorched Devils," Dad revealed once Bishop left them alone.

That motherfucker was covering his fucking tracks. If Bash's appearance was connected to the Scorched Devils, why stalk them? Why did Johnnie and Ryan know that motherfucker? Since CJ had no proof of any wrongdoing, he asked, "You're okay with that?"

"I ain't givin' a fuck right now, CJ."

"Have you lost your mind? I walked up on Bash at fucking Turn Creek Bridge, spouting shit about Mom and Uncle Johnnie. He told us Mom *killed* a motherfucker." Fuck, he hadn't had a chance to talk to Ryder, Ransom, and Axel and tell them to keep that shit to themselves. "I think he followed Harley."

"You told Mort?" Dad cocked his head to the side. "Wait, Harley was cuttin' class?"

"Fuck, stop Uncle Johnnieing my ass, Dad!"

"What the fuck that mean?"

"That you're focusing on the wrong fucking shit."

"Harley really cut class?" Dad grinned. "Mort must be so fuckin' proud."

"Aunt Bailey was pissed."

"Your ma don't like it either. You gotta teach Harley how to cut."

"Am I living in the fucking Twilight Zone?"

"Nope. Mort glad his baby girl a sweet lil' kid, but he don't want her to be a fuckin' square."

"No way! Uncle Mort feels that way?"

"Yeah, boy."

CJ eyed his father in suspicion. "You're fucking with me. Leading me on so I can incriminate myself."

"Ain't."

"Then you want me to tell on Harley."

"Nope. My ass just sayin' we know you lil' motherfuckers cut. If we ain't trackin' you everyfuckinwhere, we don't need to track you anywhere."

"But—"

"Take it up with Mortician, boy." Dad yawned. "I don't know what the motherfucker's thinkin'."

Not logically, because all their fathers had gone fucking insane. "Did he ever tell Harley he'll know when she cuts?"

"As far as I know, she never cut."

"She did yesterday."

"Then he must know."

CJ refused to believe Uncle Mort would accept Harley cutting class. Not because he felt as Uncle Johnnie. Uncle Mort was proud of Harley's studiousness and wanted her to foster that. "By the way, Harley isn't a sweet little kid. She's turning into...into...fuck, *Rebel* behind Diesel."

"Fuck, for real? At least you and her 'bout...about the same age."

"Not toward me! For some actor-motherfucker. Her co-star."

"Mort don't like that lil' motherfucker, son, so—"

"So nothing. Bash is a fucking threat. A real, true threat. He's dangerous."

"Brooks and Johnnie workin' it out. Brooks told me Johnnie got everything under control. He plans to control Bash like Cee Cee controlled Logan. With money and threats."

"Dad, listen to me—"

"Johnnie—"

"Isn't *you*, Dad. Uncle Johnnie isn't you."

"I offered to get involved, but Brooks said there's no need."

"You're the president, *Outlaw*. Your involvement is a given."

Dad shrugged. "He said as long as Bash knows my ass know, everything will be fine. Cee Cee was a vile motherfucker. Since my ass fucked him up, Bash ain't wantin' no attention from me."

"Dad, Molly's pregnant." CJ threw those words into the third dimension he currently dwelled in. Not only wasn't Dad *Outlaw*, but he also wasn't even a biker…

A *leader*.

"You fucked Ryan's girl?"

"No, Dad, the baby belongs to Ryan or Bash."

"Bash? Ain't Molly a kid?"

Hence the concern. "Exactly the fucking issue! She's turning seventeen in January."

Dad stared at CJ, his disconnect alarming. CJ had never seen his father so out-of-touch with his role as the club's president and general bad ass. He was standing there as if he were an ordinary man, a father with an on edge teenage son, and a husband with a wife who'd almost died recently.

Death, be not proud. Love, be not fickle.

Between his parents, love wasn't. It was that 'ever-fixed mark' Shakespeare wrote of in Sonnet 116. Nothing else mattered to his father right now, until Mom was home and well.

That was the type of love CJ wanted one day. Even though it was all-encompassing between Mom and Dad, it blanketed their entire family. Their parents loved him and his siblings, so he'd back off for now in regard to Bash. He'd go to Uncle Mort so Harley would be safe. However, Molly was his friend, too, and needed his help.

"Molly doesn't want the baby, Dad."

"Okay, son."

"Okay? What the fuck do you mean, *okay*?"

"Molly ain't wantin'…Molly don't want her kid."

"You're judging her."

"I ain't! Fuck, I'm not."

"You just said that she doesn't want her kid in a tone that suggested you're judging her."

"Ain't…isn't—"

"Stop fucking correcting yourself, Dad! I love you whether you say ain't or isn't."

"That's what Megan always say."

"Dad, focus. Please. You told me to talk to you. I need you to hear me. I don't need you to judge Molly."

"You wanna…do you *want to* fuck Molly?"

Thrusting his fingers through his hair, CJ gnashed his teeth together.

"Fuck, you do."

"No, Dad. I don't. I want to help her. She's my friend. You raised me and my brothers to protect girls. You raised us to respect girls. Molly. Needs. Help. Bash. Is. Hurting. Her."

"How can I protect her when I can't even protect your ma?"

"Mom was pregnant, Dad. *Pregnant*. You couldn't protect her from what happened to her."

"I coulda…could've…kept my cock outta…out of…"

"Don't you fucking dare," CJ growled, fed the fuck up. His father had lost his fucking mind and Uncle Johnnie was… *fuck, Uncle Johnnie.*

"Your ma been almost taken from me more than I been almost took from her, and she ain't a fuckin' biker."

"Hello? Dad?" CJ snapped his fingers. "She's not a biker. That's why she's an easy target."

"Megan an easy target for a lotta reasons."

"Dad—"

"I ain't gotta try and help fuck her up. If I hack my fuckin' cock off, it can't go in her and make babies."

"Get ahold of yourself, man! That's pretty fucking extreme."

"Ain't…" Dad huffed and rubbed his bloodshot eyes. "Isn't. I thought your ma was acceptin' that we might not have no more children. Maybe, it was just sedation. Cuz I left for a lil' while last night and when I came back she was in fuckin' tears. Ain't nothin' gonna stop her from her babies unless my cock gone."

"I don't want to hear that."

"It's the truth."

"I think you need help."

"A psycho camp?"

"What the fuck is that?"

"Where Kendall go."

"You're on the road to one."

"Fuck." Dad frowned. "For fuckin' real, boy?"

"For fuckin' *real* real, Dad. You've lost your fucking mind."

"You think I should leave your ma?"

"*WHAT*?"

"I ain't knowin' how else to keep her safe."

"If it makes you feel better, she'd have a target on her back regardless. She'll always be connected to *you*."

"Maybe, away from me she'll be safer."

"Don't you love Mom?"

"I worship your ma, boy. What the fuck kinda question is that?"

"The kind a psycho needs to hear when he's thinking about breaking my mother's heart," CJ snapped. "You'd destroy Mom."

"She'd be alive to be destroyed."

"This is the worst fucking time for you to have an existential crisis, dude."

"I gotta save her. As long as she with me, she at risk from bullets and babies."

Much like his father did earlier, CJ placed his hands on Dad's cheeks and stared into his eyes. "Dad, your wife is more fucking protected than some A-Listers. She's in no danger of being shot. And you two have *eight fucking children*. Nine, if you count Patrick. You don't need any more babies."

"I don't. She do."

"No, the fuck she doesn't!"

"She do."

Dropping his hands, CJ backed away and stared at his father. "Dad, tell Mom you don't want any more children."

"That'll break her fuckin' heart."

The fucking logic wasn't logic-ing. "But leaving her won't?"

Sadness crept into Dad's eyes, a feeling CJ identified with for so many different reasons.

"I thought she understood the risk," Dad whispered. "She don't. Or she don't care. If I force her to give up havin' babies, it'll break her heart," he repeated in a tone raw with fatigue.

CJ loved his mother and greatly admired her. She was the

backbone of their family. More than that, she loved his father with everything in her. In this instance, anger filled him at her selfishness. He liked living, so he wouldn't use those words as he tried to reason with his father. "Her heart will break?"

Dad nodded, yawned, and swayed.

"Like yours is breaking?" CJ pressed, concerned for his father's mental and physical state. "Mine? Reb's? My brothers'? If she ends up pregnant again, we're all going to be fucking zombies, worried she'll die. Is that fair to us or to you?"

"Life not fair."

"But Mom is."

"Your ma not perfect. She a spoiled lil' pain-in-the-ass motherfucker." He pointed to his temples. "She put all this fucking white in my hair."

"Mom is perfect, Dad. Everybody says so. She's like Pollyanna, flitting through life and looking after everyone."

"You know how Reb ain't able to understand we wouldn't ever stop loving her just because we had another girl? She couldn't appreciate her relationship was different, not lesser. All Megan know is taking care of motherfuckers that need her."

"What the fuck are you talking about?" CJ asked in frustration. "What does having twenty children have to do with that? *We* need her. The club needs her."

"I'm a grown motherfucker like the club members and their bitches, CJ. Gunner and, now, Jo, gonna need her in a different way, even from Axel, Ransom, and Ryder. Babies need your ma, like whiny Dinah needed her."

"What?"

"Your grandma grounded your ma for sayin' she wanted to be a homemaker. Then, she made Megan *her* ma. I know Megan and I know when she lookin' at Dinah picture sometime she feel like she failed her. She grieved for her and she grieved for Patrick. I know she feel like she failed him, too. When I got shot, not long after your ma came to the club, I told her I wanted a kid. She ain't wantin' to fail me like she think she failed her ma and our boy. It don't matter how much I tell her she *everyfuckinthing* to me, that wound inside her ain't healin' up."

"Then maybe she needs counseling."

Dad shrugged.

"Is that why you want to leave her?"

"I don't want to leave your ma, boy."

"But you just said…fuck, never mind. What the fuck do I know?"

"I just don't want your ma to die."

"Even Jesus died, Dad."

"For our sins. His death had a purpose."

CJ shifted. "Er, Rule's been praying for you?"

"Wilcunt been prayin' for us, too."

"Right. Uh, my point is *everyone* dies."

"He's not everyone. He's a Divine Being."

Dad was so out of it. "Oh, goddamn."

Dad scowled. "I been prayin'. For your ma and Jo."

"We all have. Father Wilkins said a special prayer for both of them."

"What the fuck the fat lil' motherfucker want now? Another trip to Monaco?"

"You sent the parish priest on a trip to Monaco?"

"Motherfucker more thug than priest. And, yeah, I promised a motherfucker I fucked up, his pieces would be prayed over."

"Uh, yeah, that entire statement is fucked up."

"Wilcunt agreed, only if I sent his ass to Monaco with fifty bands and all expenses paid.”

CJ huffed out a breath.

“How long you been awake?”

“Nearly all night. What about you?”

“Since your ma came here, I ain’t slept more than an hour here and there. Ain’t really had a full meal since Thanksgiving.”

“Mom’s been here two weeks, Dad.”

He looked at his watch. “It won’t be two weeks for another thirteen hours.”

CJ didn’t know how to respond to that, so he changed the subject. “Uncle Johnnie stormed out of the house last night. I haven’t talked to Mattie or Rory, so I don’t know if he’s come back. I went to ask him about Bash, and he went ballistic.”

“He hit you.”

Hadn’t that already been established? Instead of bringing that point up, CJ nodded. “Didn’t you stay up for days at a time? You still go on runs.”

“Twice a year, CJ, and my days of staying awake for a few nights long gone. Why?”

“Because you’re sleep deprived and malnourished. No wonder I can’t get through to you.”

“I heard everything. Johnnie hit you. Lost his motherfuckin’ mind and shot up that big, ugly mirror in the dinin’ room and left. Molly knocked up. Bash in Hortensia. You need to tell Mort. And Harley turning into Rebel.”

“You’ve heard me, but you aren’t processing anything.”

Scrubbing a hand over his face, Dad yawned. “What do you want me to process?”

“For now, *Molly*. Ryan’s a dickhead and Bash is a motherfucker. Her parents abuse her. She needs our help.”

“You want her to move in with us?”

"*NO!*"

"Then what the fuck I'm supposed to do? Fuck up Bash and her parents and put her on the street?"

"Dad!"

"I ain't understandin' how you think I can help her?"

"She's a girl! You always help girls."

"Your ma a girl."

Jesus Christ. "Molly doesn't want to leave her parents. She's afraid of them. She's afraid of Bash. I had to tell her she didn't trust me enough so they couldn't read her mind and discover she'd even mentioned them to me."

"That's fucking stupid."

"I was trying to protect her, the way *you* taught me."

"Your ma taught you, too."

CJ growled.

"How soon don't she want the baby, CJ?" Dad sighed, reached into the back pocket of his jeans and pulled out his billfold, thick with cash. "Now or later?"

"Dad!" CJ cried, appalled. "Since when do you put anything of importance in your back pocket instead of your cut?"

"Ain't nothin' but a thing."

"That's more than a fuckin' thing."

"Answer the fuckin' question."

"Now. She doesn't want the baby *now*. She's afraid of anyone finding out."

Dad emptied the billfold and handed CJ the stack of hundreds. "What happens after? If she still where Bash at or she still fucking with Ryan...?"

By then, his father would've gotten a good night's rest. CJ would see to that if he had to knock him the fuck out himself. "Isn't there some type of birth control that can be in place even if she can't remember?"

"Talk to your ma, she'd know." Scratching his jaw, Dad glanced away. "Fuck. She gotta get a lil' stronger first. All she been talkin' 'bout is all these fuckin' tests they runnin' and askin' me 'bout…*about* another baby."

"Where the fuck would she put another baby? We're out of fucking rooms."

Rage suffused his father's face, and CJ raised his hands.

"I'm sorry. I'm not disrespecting Mom."

"Aintcha fuckin' business cuz it ain't my business if your ma wantin' more babies, so, yeah, you disrespectin' her."

"Do *you* want another baby?"

"Ain't up to me."

"I disagree. It'll be your kid, too."

"As long as your ma ain't givin' in to that motherfucker, I ain't givin' a fuck."

"What motherfucker?"

"The grim fucking reaper. Who the fuck you think?"

"You're falling apart. Could you handle Mom being pregnant again?"

His father looked…*lost*. "I ain't ever thought nothin' could top findin' my Megan in that fuckin' hole in the ground. Or seein' her shot and that surprised look on her face." He closed his eyes. "So many fuckin' times. And I wonder if my penance for all the shit I did in my fuckin' life, losin' her. Then, I tell myself that's fuckin' insane. *She* ain't lost count of the motherfuckers she fucked up. Why she gotta be taken to pay for my fuckin' sins? This time, she wasn't doin' nothin' but bein' a ma and a wife."

An incoming text message perked him up. Once he read it, he gave CJ a half-smile.

"I can't be nothin' but your ma husband right now. My head and my heart here. If I go out there and try to be Outlaw, Ima fuck everything up, boy."

As Bishop appeared at the other end of the hallway, the doors behind CJ and his father clicked open.

Dad backed away. "Bein' a good leader is knowin' when to stop leadin'. C'mon, son. Your ma awake."

CHAPTER 10

Harley

Ridge Moore's theater department and auditorium had undergone a recent renovation and was completed around the same time as the Athletic Center. Before, Merriweather Hall housed the auditorium and several classrooms for general theatre. Now, two double-level wings flanked the auditorium and the school offered Theatre Arts, Technical Theatre or Theatre Production for grades nine through twelve. Arts and production were combined in one wing since they were so closely related.

The auditorium itself was a sea of blue seating in stacked rows. Spotlights gleamed onto the stage that featured an apron, a fly tower, a catwalk, and a crossover.

At least, Harley thought the department had those things. She was still learning the technical terms, so she might've gotten a few wrong.

She glanced out into the audience again, searching for CJ but only seeing Mommie and Lolly. The auditorium lights were also on, so Harley saw everyone clearly. Daddy had canceled at the last minute, yet that didn't matter. CJ's lies did.

Annoyance ripped through her.

"I'm not telling my name, bae," Nardo said. "I don't vibe with my name because you don't vibe with it, ma. I won't even write it. Save myself time from tearing it up."

He smiled as he finished his line.

Unamused, Harley glared at him and held her script up. "The lines are…

By a name
I know not how to tell thee who I am:
My name, dear saint, is hateful to myself,
Because it is an enemy to thee;
Had I it written, I would tear the word."

"Those are the original lines, Harley," he said, shaking his head. "I talked to Ms. Mendez. She likes my idea. It gives the play a more modern twist."

"I'll talk to her myself. We've been rehearsing for months and all of a sudden we're changing the entire script? No."

"It's not up to you, Harley," Nardo snapped. "Ms. Mendez said sometimes scripts are completely rewritten in the middle of filming. It'll be a good way to test how much we've been listening to her lessons."

"I'm here every single day. I have an 'A' in theatre—"

"The new script was in the room the girls will use for dressing the night of the production."

"I saw it," Harley admitted. "I just ignored it."

One of the auditorium doors opened, distracting her from the conversation. Her heart soared and she smiled, relief flowing through her. Instead of CJ, though, it was her brothers, Lou and Kaleb.

Her annoyance turned to anger.

"Just try it my way, Harley," Nardo suggested. He held the

revised script out to her.

She folded her arms, refusing to take the pages.

"Shaking his head, Nardo flipped to the page he'd been reading from.

"Romeo, oh Romeo," he said, pitifully attempting to mimic her voice. "You have mad rizz, so why be Romeo? Since you can't stop being a Montague, tell a sister how much you want her and I won't ever be a Capulet again."

"You're making a mockery of Romeo and Juliet," Harley seethed. "I'm going to read it as it's been read for centuries."

"No way, you're going so hard for a boring ass play, ma," Nardo said.

Harley scowled.

O Romeo, Romeo! wherefore art thou Romeo? was one of literature's most classic lines and a main reason Harley auditioned for the play. She hadn't been bitten by the acting bug, yet she was putting her heart and soul into the performance. They'd been rehearsing since September, and it was now December. The play was happening the last weekend of March, not long after Lolly's stupid Mardi Gras Ball. Set design was already in the planning stages. Set construction would begin after Winter Break. As the leading lady, she had every right to protest such a major change.

"If we make the play Urban Contemporary, the sets will have to be redesigned," she pointed out.

"Not necessarily, baby," Lolly called from the audience.

Maybe, if CJ hadn't lied to her, Harley would be more receptive to Nardo's stupidity and her grandmother's interference. Today, she was having none of it.

"No one asked you, Lolly!" she almost snarled.

"I'm telling you anyway," Lolly replied. "As one of the play's sponsors *and* your grandmother, I can pass my opinion."

Harley ignored the comment. "When is Ms. Mendez getting back from the office?"

"Harley, baby, what's bothering you?" Mommie asked. She was Harley's only friend.

The door opened again, and Harley held her breath.

"Hey, Harls," Rebel greeted, bouncing down the aisle and plopping next to Lolly, since Lou sat next to Mommie and Kaleb was perched on her lap. The little twit was nine and still wanted babying. "Sorry I'm late. I just finished eating."

Harley exhaled, on the verge of screaming and crying. After her invitation to CJ to watch her rehearsals, he'd left her on read and still hadn't answered her.

"CJ can't make it," Rebel continued. "He's—"

"A liar!" Harley yelled. "He promised he'd come and watch me."

"He did?" Rebel asked in surprise.

He hadn't, but no one could prove it. She hadn't done anything wrong. It was all on him! Sooner or later, more than just Mommie would defend Harley and realize how deeply CJ had betrayed her. "If it was Molly, he'd show up."

"Dude, chill," Rebel said kindly. "He's at the hospital with Momma and Daddy. He didn't come to school today."

Brushing past Nardo, Harley stomped down the steps on the right side of the stage and barreled to where Rebel sat in the first row. "You're covering for him."

"And you're losing it," Rebel responded. "CJ wanted to be here."

"If he wasn't with Molly, he would've texted me himself." She dug into her blazer pocket and came up with her cell phone. Securing the script under her arm, she scrolled through her messages, finding none from CJ. "Which he hasn't," she said in triumph.

"Let's go to the cafeteria, Harley," Mommie said,

indicating Kaleb stand with a tap on his shoulder. "You can calm down and cool off."

Harley ignored her mother. "You have no response to that, do you, Rebel?"

Rebel got to her feet, forcing Harley to step back. It hadn't occurred to her until that moment that she had two inches to grow before she caught up to Rebel's height.

"Has it ever occurred to you that my brother has more important things to worry about than your stupid play? Our mother is *just* now halfway back to normal after fourteen days. Our father is a walking zombie, and our little sister is still fighting for her life."

"Oh, so now you're claiming Jo." Hurt and betrayal cut deep into Harley. "You sure about that, Rebel? It wasn't so long ago you wanted your *little sister* and Aunt Meggie dead."

Rebel paled. For a moment, she stared at Harley before scooting past her and starting up the aisle.

"Hit a nerve, didn't I?" Harley screeched. "Run away."

Halting halfway to the door, Rebel turned. "I'm not running. I'm escaping before I punch the fuck out of you," she snarled. "You're throwing what I did in my face when you're turning into the same heartless cunt so shut the fuck up, dumb bitch."

Her words echoing in the silent auditorium, Rebel stalked away.

"Rebel, stop this instant!" Mommie called.

Rebel ignored her, banging the auditorium door open with unnecessary force.

"Excuse me—"

"Leave Rebel be, Bailey," Lolly ordered.

"Rebel shouldn't talk to Harley in that manner when she's clearly hurt and upset over—"

"Over nothing. There's no fucking reason Harley should be acting as she is." Ignoring Mommie's mouth falling open, Lolly looked at Harley. "If your ass is on your shoulders because you're waiting for CJ, that *is* a dumb bitch move, baby."

"*Mother*!" Mommie said with indignation as Harley gasped. "Bell's about to ring," she said to Lou and Kaleb when they snickered. "Get to class. You too, Nardo."

"Yes, ma'am, Miz Banks."

"It's *Doctor* Banks," Harley gritted.

"Sadity on top of everything else," Lolly said with disapproval.

"We do not allow criticism or negativity to enter our interactions with Harley, Mother," Mommie snapped, the moment it was just the three of them.

Lolly placed her hands on her hips. "Then maybe she needs her ass beat, Bailey. She's lost her goddamn mind. I never heard her talk to her daddy the way she spoke to him the other night. She damn near cussed out Knox. Now, she's stomping around, being nasty to everybody else."

"You aren't upset about Lucas. It's about Knox."

"It's not about either of those motherfuckers," Lolly shouted. "It's about this baby."

"You and I just started speaking again, Momma, after I extended an olive branch and apologized to you on my daughter's behalf as well as my own."

"Extended an...? Girl, fuck you. You're lucky I didn't fuck you and her up on *my* fucking behalf. You both owed me an apology. I set aside the fact that Harley has yet to apologize to me and came to see my princess rehearse, but you're on the same bullshit. No, you're on some next level bullshit."

"Enough, Mother. This isn't the time or the place. I don't need your attitude as well as Lucas's. When he *does* talk to me, he's cold and distant."

"If I was that boy, I wouldn't talk to either one of you bitches until you did some groveling," Lolly snapped.

Mommie gasped and pulled Harley closer. "How dare you? Harley's a child, and I'm *your* child. Your emotional abuse is unwarranted. You can't call us out of our names—"

"Bailey, fuck you. How's that for fucking emotional abuse? Allow me to give you some fucking advice—"

"I didn't ask for it, thank you," Mommie sniffed.

"Don't give a fuck. I'm giving it anyway before you fuck up your marriage any more than you already have."

"My marriage is fine!"

"The fuck it is. You just said your man isn't talking to you. That don't sound fine to me."

"Goodbye, Mother."

"For as long as I've known Mortician, I never saw him withdraw from no fucking body the way he did the other night. He got jokes and advice and is respected for both." Lolly glared at Harley, then transferred the look to Mommie. "You want to take Harley's side? Fine. You're entitled. But *your* daughter's words humiliated that boy, and you didn't open your fucking mouth to defend him."

Mommie blinked, startled. "Defend him? Lucas knows how much I admire him and look up to him."

"Words are easy, Bailey. The one time he needed you to *prove* what you claim, you fucking failed him. How the fuck would you feel if Harley suddenly attacked you, called you a sellout, a fraud, and a suck up, and Mortician didn't jump to your defense?"

"Lucas isn't that weak," Mommie said, but her voice wavered. "He knows his importance to the club and to *me*. As my husband. He's my best friend."

"On paper you're Dr. Bailey Banks, with a thriving private

practice." Lolly indicated Mommie's designer outfit. "When was the last time he even visited your office? Not since you moved into your own space and brought in associates. What? Two years?"

"Now, you're reaching. That's ridiculous. Lucas is welcomed any time he wishes to drop in."

"Fuck off with that. I've tried to "drop in", and that bitch you have for an assistant always says you're busy."

"I can't believe that! Velda is lovely. Meggie has stopped in and—"

"Because Kendall advised her not to wear her fucking cut, Bailey, so Meggie leaves it in the car. The week after the ribbon cutting, Zoann and Kendall stopped in. While Kendall was parking, Zoann went in. She was wearing her cut. Velda claimed you were in a meeting—"

"I remember that since it was the only time Zoann ever visited. She *visited*, Momma. So you must be wrong."

"She visited because Kendall came in and *wasn't* wearing her cut. She was in a designer suit. It wasn't until later, when I went in my cut to test that bitch of an assistant, that I realized she thinks you're too high and mighty to socialize with the likes of us. I bet my fucking fortune, Mortician hasn't set foot in your fucking office since you moved, and you haven't even noticed. He knew what the fuck was up when you got rid of Shanice."

"Lucas loves me," Mommie said firmly. "If what you're saying is true, it's because he knows how hard I've worked."

Lolly shook her head. "You don't even know if the boy has visited or not. No wonder Harley is so fucking selfish, ignoring what CJ is going through to act like a spoiled fucking brat, wanting to control that child's every fucking move."

Mommie drew herself up, dressed in a winter white suit

and stilettos. "I don't call my daughter names and will allow no one else to do so. Stop it this instant or else."

Lolly jerked and her eyes widened, then narrowed. "Or else, huh? Let me get my ass out of here before I fuck you and her up. How about *this* 'or else'? Fuck your fucking apology. It didn't mean shit, so stay the fuck out of my sight *or else*." Snatching her handbag and fur coat, she stormed out of the auditorium.

Mommie opened her arms and Harley fell against her mother's chest. "CJ promised!" she sobbed.

Knowing the beginning lent understanding to the journey.

Betrayal. Birth. Death. They were all wrapped up in what Logan Donovan wanted as his legacy.

In what *Sharper* wanted.

Lust, greed, and family ties entangled their past, but their futures were diverging. Sharper's children, eighteen-month-old Lucas, and the baby due in seven months, would be raised just as their mother had. With silver spoons and the world at their feet. Sharper planned to trot them out to show himself as the perfect father and family man.

But the club would always be his. The secret charter gave him majority ownership and he'd flaunt the document whenever Logan got out of line. The motherfucker wanted power, but he'd have it only through Sharper's grace.

"I first met Sharper when I gave a speech at his high school," his father-in-law, Milon Frank, said to the rapt congregation. The well-known businessman and philanthropist had the audience's full attention. "He was a fine, well-spoken young man with a bright future. Now, almost eight years later, he's being ordained as a minister and installed at this fine church."

Sharper had been licensed for several years. Then, the senior minister at Light of the World Church died suddenly and Sharper seized the opportunity to advance.

Next to him, Vivian shifted. She'd never lost the weight she'd put on during her first pregnancy and Sharper grew increasingly disgusted. It surprised him he'd gotten a hard cock and fucked her until he got her with child again. Sometimes, he regretted she hadn't fucking bled to death like Kimber had while giving birth.

After the cunt searched for Cee Cee, she'd had the fucking gall to die. Her death fucked with Cee Cee's head as much as it had Joe's, now a single father and a miserable fuckhead. Kaleb stayed in Joe's shadow but served as a sounding board and crutch.

Until Logan and Sharper's fallout, he'd sworn retribution against those three fuckheads. If Wally hadn't come across Logan, bound, gagged, and beaten in the closet of a house they were staying at and called Sharper, he wouldn't have known Cee Cee, Joe and Kaleb intended to kill him.

He hadn't known Logan raped Vivian. Sharper wondered why Logan allowed her to live.

"I'm proud to call Sharper Banks my son-in-law," Milon continued, "and the father of my grandchildren. Before Augusta's death a year ago, she expressed her pleasure in how well you treat our only child."

Cameras were flashing. By tomorrow, the ceremony would be front page news.

"Vivian, Sharper, please join me for a moment. Sorry, folks." Milon smiled. "We're going a little off script."

No one cared or dared speak up. Milon Frank did as he damned well pleased. Exactly what Sharper wanted for himself.

Logan fucking Donovan *believed* he had all the power, but that motherfucker was beside himself.

Vengeance was bred in Sharper's bones.

Fury pounding through him, he got to his feet and started forward. At the last minute, he remembered Vivian and helped her to her big fucking feet, tucking her hand into the crook of his arm and guiding her to her father.

"You and I have had long conversations, Sharper," Milon said when they reached him.

The way he'd intercepted Cee Cee, Joe, and Kaleb and begged for Logan's life pounded through Sharper.

"I have never known what it means to go to bed hungry and I've worked to make sure my little girl doesn't have to worry either."

Milon's words competed with the memory of Sharper's sobbing.

"*Her* grandchildren will be heirs to my fortune."

Sharper truly believed he'd been in love with Logan. Now, he loathed that motherfucker and wished to slit his fucking throat.

"You're a fine man, son."

He'd dance in that motherfucker's blood.

"Kind."

Maybe, hacking Logan into pieces was better. More satisfying.

"Compassionate."

Dry fucking every hole, then smothering him.

"Considerate."

Throwing his body from a mountaintop.

"Gentle."

Stomping his fucking head in and yanking his fucking teeth out of his filthy mouth.

"Loyal."

Literally stabbing that motherfucker in the back as he'd figuratively done to Sharper.

Bloodlust warmed his body and sweat beaded his brow.

"He's too overcome to speak, ladies and gentlemen," Milon announced with another jovial laugh.

Sharper blinked, swallowed. The images of Logan's broken and bloodied body melted away, and a set of keys came into focus.

"My congratulatory gift to you, son," Milon said. "You've worked your ass off to provide a good life for my daughter and grandson."

Greatly aided by his in-laws' huge wedding gift consisting of separate bank accounts for Sharper and Vivian. He'd been able to buy a decent house and hire a housekeeper, driver, and nanny. Appearances meant everything.

"You're moving up in the world and you need a place to reflect that," Milon said.

Sharper lifted a brow at his wife.

"Daddy signed over the titles to the estate we showed you a few months ago," Vivian said, her look as inscrutable as her tone.

She'd gotten good at hiding her feelings, although Sharper knew she hated him. Disgust gleamed in eyes once filled with love. That was why he used, abused, and humiliated her.

She wanted to leave, but no one knew the pictures he had of another woman licking her cat wasn't consensual. She'd agreed because he'd had a gun to Luke's little head. The fat slut liked her cunt eaten, so she'd lost herself in pleasure. If she walked, he'd leak those photos.

Milon held out a hand. "I'm so proud of you, boy."

"Thank you, sir," Sharper said with just the right amount of humility.

"I would ask you to say a few words—"

Sharper held up his hand, still holding Vivian tightly. "I couldn't, sir. Not until it is the appropriate time."

He pushed Logan's death to the back of his mind. As soon as she delivered, he'd get rid of Vivian. He didn't need her any longer. Her father had given him his own money and an estate that would become his solely upon her death.

As the service resumed and his ordination and installation drew closer, Sharper smiled and led her back to the two red and gold chairs.

"The house is in my name, Sharper," she said the moment they sat. "It was my mother's. I've drawn up a will. If anything happens to me, I've bequeathed it to my favorite charity. When Lucas and the new baby reach their majority, that'll change."

"Bitch," he said, low.

"Perhaps, but I'm the bitch laying the golden egg. As long as I stay alive, you live like a king."

Act II

Love was the most egregious of tragedies; even the truest never ended well. Love was blatant in its joys and sorrows, but a sneak in its inevitable outcome. Love could only end in one way—broken. Whether by death or detriment, love never lasted. Grief was always the consequence of love.

Love was like karma. And karma was a low-down, vindictive bitch that swooped in to wreak havoc at the most inopportune time.

Christmas, of all times, when Patricia Donovan Caldwell had to watch her daddy's vile treatment of her boy and his adoration of her nephew. It was a terrible sin to harm a little baby, so when she masterminded the plan to take care of Tess, she believed she removed her competition. She thought she'd regained Daddy's approval since he greenlit Patricia's idea and gave Simon the go ahead to implement the plot.

Towards the end, her sister developed pneumonia thanks to her weakened immune system from her days of little or no food. Delivering John, and a minute dose of cyanide, took care of the rest.

Patricia wouldn't ever have to worry about her husband taking her little sister to his bed again. It didn't matter that Tess hadn't wanted him and he'd forced his way there. Cee Cee was supposed to be Patricia's way out. Bad enough she had to compete with the club whores.

A high-pitched scream jerked her to attention. Straightening, she rubbed a hand over her rounded belly and made her way back inside. She adjusted the jacket sitting casually on her shoulders, her pumps clopping on the wooden floor.

The farmhouse she'd grown up in was unrecognizable. Cee Cee had kept his promise and paid for its renovation from the ground up. Not that Patricia cared much since he'd moved across the country. He called her occasionally, though, once a week, he spoke to the man he'd sent as her protector.

The more time passed without Cee Cee coming to claim her and Christopher, the angrier she grew. She'd called him when she went into labor to protect their son. Leaving did nothing but give Daddy's abuse free rein.

Somewhere inside of Patricia, she'd held a small hope that her father would grow to love her son once they spent time together.

That hadn't happened.

"Dirty, little idiot!"

She jumped at her father's roar, pressed her hand harder on her belly. The baby kicked.

"No, Grandda!" Christopher wailed.

Patricia swallowed.

"It's granddaddy, filthy beast."

"Mommie…No! No! No!"

Her son screamed; Patricia's lips trembled. She wanted

to rush into the living room, decorated with garland, holly berries, and mistletoe. Presents surrounded the tree, gifts for everyone except her son. He would be three years old in a few days, cognizant enough to feel left out.

Another loud thud reached her, like a body hitting the floor. Patricia flinched.

Cee Cee shouldn't have left them. She was his wife, Christopher his son. Many times, Cee Cee was cruel in bed—and out, for that matter. But she preferred him over her father, yet Cee Cee refused to adhere to her wishes.

Maybe, she was selfish for subjecting her son to Logan's whims. Daddy would never like Christopher, especially with John alive. Her father acted like a fool over that little chubby blond ball.

Daddy continued to yell; Christopher still screamed in agony.

A tear slipped down Patricia's cheek.

Cee Cee should've been with them.

It wasn't her fault that Daddy demanded she bring her family over for the holidays. Refusal was more dangerous than capitulation. If Cee Cee had stayed, she wouldn't have to subject her kids and her man to her father. Daddy wouldn't force her cooperation.

This was all Cee Cee's fault. And John's.

Over the past months, the status of the Donovans steadily grew in the community. Her daddy's MC was gaining power and popularity.

Christopher screamed again. The sound of the hit echoed through the festively decorated house. The warmth from several blazing fireplaces circulated the potpourri and filled the air with the scent of cinnamon and apples.

From the opposite end of the hall, Fred Sterling hurried toward the living room. He paused and frowned at her.

"She's asleep," he said, referring to Bev, their thirteen-month-old daughter.

Patricia nodded.

"Mommie, prease!" Christopher hollered.

Fred stiffened, threw her a dark look, and continued to the living room. He adored Christopher.

"Are you out of your fucking mind?" Fred's roar boomed.

Of average height with unremarkable features, he was a good, kind man. Cee Cee had chosen the perfect protector for her and Christopher. Unfortunately, Fred didn't like drinking or rough sex.

But she'd been faithful to him until he knocked her up a second time. Now, at least once a day, she fucked Rack or Sharper when he was in town.

She was a lady who knew how to be a slut. It was why they returned to her bed over and over again. She was classy and respectable, unlike those filthy club whores.

She also enjoyed the pity of the entire town as the unwilling victim of Cee Cee Caldwell's brutality. Their marriage was hush-hush. He refused to claim her? She saw to it that his reputation suffered.

A body thudded to the floor. A second child's wail rose into the chaos.

"Stop it this instant!" Mama yelled. "Fred, take that demon out of this house now. And if you ever hit my husband again, I'll kill you."

Fred stormed into the hallway, holding Christopher tight against him. Her boy was wailing, his little arm hanging limply.

"Logan broke Christopher's arm, Patricia!" Fred said, his face flushed in anger. He thundered past her, heading outside. "I'm telling Cee Cee," he threw over his shoulder.

"What?" She rushed after him, catching up as he hurried

down the porch steps. "You can't do that! He'll kill Daddy."

Ignoring her, Fred went to their Toyota Camry, opened the back door, and strapped Christopher into his car seat. Her boy continued to wail.

Fred slammed the door closed, then got behind the wheel.

"Fred—"

"Shut up, Pattie," he ordered. "How can you stand by and let Logan harm our son? Are you going to do the same for the baby you carry if it's a boy?"

"Mommie!" Christopher sobbed, holding his little arm. "Hurt, Mommie."

Patricia ignored him and placed a hand on her belly. "Of course I won't allow Daddy to hurt this baby, Fred. I haven't allowed him to touch Bev, have I?"

"Mommie!"

She leaned in, glimpsing her son's flushed little face and dark hair.

"See, boy, he's in the car."

Simon's voice traveled to her as he carried John down the steps and to the car. Unlike Christopher's thick, unkempt black hair, John's golden strands were pin neat. His three-piece suit contrasted with her son's jeans and T-shirt. John wore expensive baby shoes; Christopher went without.

"Kwistoffer!" John called, wiggling in Simon's arms and bawling as much as Christopher.

"Bring my grandson back to me!" Daddy ordered, standing just inside the door. "All of you get back inside. Dinner's about to be served. Except to that stupid dog."

Fred glared at Patricia as if she made her father say those words.

"Shut that demon up!"

"You made him cry, Daddy," Simon grouched, barely keeping hold of John as he turned and stomped back up the stairs. "You know the little twerp don't know how to shut the fuck up. Idiot."

"I've heard enough," Fred said in disgust, turning the key in the ignition. "I'm bringing him to the hospital."

"If you leave, you aren't welcome in my house ever again," Daddy called. "I gave you an order. Obey me or suffer."

"Make him back off, Pattie, or I will call Cee Cee," Fred warned, low.

He was serious. And Cee Cee would blaze into town because of Fred, meting out justice and demanding answers. She wouldn't be able to explain how her father expected every cent of the money Cee Cee sent every month for Christopher.

He might even take Fred from her. Either by death or reassignment, since Fred was a Scorpion brother. He was going against Cee Cee's direct order by not immediately calling him over Logan's behavior.

For her. Fred loved her.

But she loved her father. She admired his determination and his faithfulness. She loved his sense of right and wrong. If Cee Cee killed Logan, Patricia would be devastated.

Worse, Cee Cee still wouldn't settle down and be a father to Christopher or a husband to her.

She brushed her lips against Fred's. He was a bore, but she got him to do anything she pleased. Besides, she loved her son. It wasn't his fault he shared his father's black hair and green eyes. It wasn't his fault that his daddy paid to keep him alive but sent a man to watch her like she was a child.

"Mommie!" Christopher called again, his tears showing no signs of stopping. "Hurt!"

"Go, Fred," Patricia urged. "I'll take care of Daddy."

"I never want him to darken my door again, Pattie," Daddy said once Fred drove away with her distressed son and she reached the porch.

Just in time to see Simon hand John over to Daddy and then watch as he hugged the boy tenderly, despite his tears and calls for 'Kwistoffer'.

He was a little milk sap twat just as his mother had been.

Patricia pasted a smile on her face, ignoring Simon as he brushed past Daddy and walked into the house.

"Fred's my boyfriend, Daddy," she said calmly, huffing at John's continued noise and yanking him into her arms. She shook him. "Quiet!" she gritted.

She didn't see Daddy's fist before it crashed against her jaw. She staggered back. If she hadn't released John so Daddy had to catch him, she would've been hit again.

Sinking to her knees and holding her jaw, she sobbed. Daddy slapped her to the porch.

Marissa, Simon's wife, rushed outside and grabbed John. The child still hadn't shut his mouth. Without a word, she returned inside with the precious John cradled to her.

Daddy crouched next to Patricia, grabbed her throat, and dragged her to her feet. "If you look at my John wrong, I'll strangle you and bury you in the apple orchard with the others. Understand?"

Tears leaking from her eyes, she nodded.

"Christopher's birthday is in a few days. Bring him to me."

"Fred and I have plans for him," she pushed out.

She wouldn't willingly place her boy in her father's path any more than necessary. Christmas was the only time she'd suffer major repercussions if she didn't bring her child to pay homage to Daddy. Other than that, all bets were off.

He shoved her away. "You dare disobey me, Patricia?"

She crawled to the top step and sat, leaning her head against the banister. Despite the cold air, she was hot and nauseated. Her baby boy was suffering because of her anger towards Cee Cee.

"I want that stupid shithead here for his birthday."

She locked gazes with Daddy. "Cee Cee is a phone call away," she said coldly. "I'll give you Christmas with my son, but I'm warning you if you ever break another bone of his, hide your precious John."

She was so sorry she hadn't taken care of him before he tumbled into Daddy's life.

Burying his hands in her hair, Daddy twisted and dragged her to her feet. "If you ever hurt my little Johnnie, I'll throw Cee Cee's whelp in the trashcan and cover it tightly, then make your death excruciating." He shoved her away and started for the door.

"Then we're even, Daddy. If you ever hurt my Christopher, you'll find your little Johnnie floating in the Columbia. I'll tell Cee Cee you killed both boys."

Daddy glared at her and stalked into the house.

For now, she, Fred, and her kids were safe. Although her anger toward Cee Cee burned deep, she knew it was his protection that stayed her father's hand. She'd still have to keep a vigilant eye. Daddy was even more dangerous when he was angry. Fred was disobeying Cee Cee. And Patricia was caught in the middle.

She loved her father and Cee Cee, though neither deserved nor appreciated her. If she left, not only would Daddy hunt her down and make her suffer the consequences, but she'd miss him.

Christopher's little face came to mind, and her heart ached. Her sweet boy didn't deserve Daddy's abuse or Cee Cee's abandonment. Her son relied on her to keep him safe. Fred did what he could. He was Fred, though; a weakling caught between two powerful men.

Whether she liked it or not, she might eventually have

to gather her children and Fred and run away to keep her Christopher safe.

There was simply no rest for the weary.

Part Two
Sins
of the
Father

CHAPTER 11

REBEL

Later that afternoon, Rebel followed Potter off the hospital elevator onto the floor where her mother and little sister were. Usually, she visited Jo before seeing her mom, but earlier CJ texted Rebel and told her Momma had been asking about her and Daddy was in a bad way. Her brother had skipped school today but was now at home working on his science project.

Since she wanted to fuck up Harley and wasn't happy that Aunt Bailey was giving Harley a major pass for her behavior, Rebel had texted Potter and asked him to pick her up from school to bring her to the hospital. He'd agreed, not that he could decline, if he wasn't on more important club business.

As Outlaw's daughter, few things ranked above Rebel's requests. Dweller brothers milled about the floor, greeting Potter and Rebel as he led her to the locked doors of her mother's unit. By the time she reached them, Bishop was on his feet and the doors gaped open.

He smiled at her. "Hey, Reb."

Tall and handsome, he had dusky skin, dark eyes, full lips, and a short Afro. Slipping hair behind her ear, she grinned. "Shop."

"Yo, Reb, if we wanted to call this motherfucker Shop, that would've been the road name we gave him," his friend, Fuse, said.

Rebel rolled her eyes. Fuse was always fucking with her. "Whatever, asshole."

The guys snickered, but immediately sobered when they spotted her father walking with Diesel and Tabitha from toward Momma's room.

Tabitha sailed to Rebel and smiled. "Well, if it isn't Little Rebel," she cooed as Diesel and Daddy flanked her.

Gritting her teeth, Rebel ignored the urge to call that bitch a cunt. It would be misinterpreted as lingering hostility and seen as a step backward. While she still wanted to marry Diesel and loved him as no one else ever could, she'd learned her lesson from her mother's medical crisis. If Momma had died, Rebel wouldn't have ever forgiven herself. It was what she'd tried to impart to Harley on their ride home.

Diesel kissed Rebel's cheek and the scent of his cologne went to her head. He was dressed in suit and tie, a hotshot young lawyer from head to toe. "Hey, sweetheart."

"Hey, doofus." Smiling at the guffaws, including Diesel's, Rebel nodded to Tabitha, then looked at her father. She snapped her brows together. CJ had also alerted her to their father's condition. Reading a text that Daddy looked like a body just risen from the grave and seeing him couldn't compare. "Hey, Daddy."

"Reb." Rubbing the back of his neck, he yawned. "Bishop, I need another cup of coffee. Megan wanna watch some bitch ass romance and I gotta stay awake."

"You got it, Prez."

"No, Bishop!" Rebel cried. "Don't get him another cup of coffee until he goes to sleep."

Daddy frowned. "I slept already."

"An hour, Uncle Chris," Diesel said on a snort.

"Ain't needin' much else. Ain't never need a lotta sleep." He yawned again. "Bishop, the coffee."

"Bishop, if you get him one more fucking cup of coffee, I'm fucking you up," Rebel snapped. "What the fuck is wrong with you? He looks like the Walking fucking Dead."

"And if you ain't gettin' me coffee, Ima fuck you up, Bishop."

Rebel scooted in front of Bishop, blocking his exit. Before he thought to go around her, she grabbed his hand and held it. "CJ says Momma has been asking for me, Daddy."

"You touchin' my girl, Bishop. If you ain't lettin' her go, Ima chop your fuckin' hand off."

Gulping, Bishop tried to yank his hand away, but Rebel tightened her grip.

"Poor Aunt Meggie," Tabitha said with a sad shake of her head. "If she was my mother, I wouldn't leave her side so she wouldn't have to ask for me."

"Yo, bitch," Rebel said, losing her patience. "I didn't ask for your fucking advice. And, if she was your mother, you'd want to fucking pull your weight at home to help Bunny with the house and kids, so shut the fuck up, kiss my fucking ass, and don't offer what I haven't fucking requested." In the pin drop silence that followed, she glared at her father. "As for you, Daddy, if you have another cup of coffee, I'm telling Momma that you haven't been sleeping, you haven't been eating, and you've been surviving on coffee. Then, I'm calling Lolly." She held up her and Bishop's entwined hands. "Your choice. I'll let him go if you tell him to get you a sandwich and a beer—"

"This a hospital, baby," Daddy interrupted, as out of it as

CJ claimed. Otherwise, he would've handed her and Bishop their asses on a platter for defying him. "Ain't serving no beer."

"Uncle Chris, the cabin is still a viable option," Tabitha said, throwing Rebel a look of dislike.

"Right back at you, bitch," Rebel snapped. "What cabin are you referring to? One filled with bear traps and noxious fumes?"

Diesel huffed a breath. "Rebel, enough. Tabitha offered Uncle Chris the use of her family's cabin so he could rest. She even suggested Aunt Meggie go there to finish recovering."

"The solitude might do her good," Tabitha said. "She'd be alone and isolated."

Daddy yawned again and Diesel patted Tabitha's back. Only Rebel took issue with her choice of words. Why, she wasn't sure.

"Why would you want Momma alone and isolated?"

"For time to recover," Tabitha said. "What do you think I meant?"

"She feel bein' alone might benefit your ma."

"And what do you feel, Daddy?"

He shrugged. "Ain't sure, baby."

Alarmed, Rebel sighed and released Bishop's hand.

"Uncle Chris, I think taking Aunt Meggie on a vacation once Jo is released might be just what you both need," Diesel suggested.

"But it would help if Aunt Meggie was…" Tabitha's voice trailed off at Diesel's raised eyebrow.

Swaying, Daddy blinked, and Rebel worried he'd collapse at any moment.

"I'll get you some food, Daddy," she said. "Why don't you go back to Momma's room and…uh…see if she wants something special to eat?"

"Okay, baby."

"Why don't I go with you, Uncle Chris?" Tabitha offered, an unexpected boon since Rebel hadn't known how she'd get rid of her. "I can talk to Aunt Meggie about the cabin."

He grunted, then turned and walked in the same direction he'd come with Tabitha hot on his heels.

"Okay, sweetheart," Diesel said once Daddy and Tabitha were out of view, "what are you scheming?"

"First, Diesel, tell that bitch to back off. And tell her to shut the fuck up about sending my mother away, alone in the fucking woods. That's horror movie vibes, dickhead."

"Aunt Meggie wouldn't go without Uncle Chris, so I don't have to say anything. Tabitha is just trying to be helpful, so stop with your overactive imagination."

Rebel scowled but abandoned the conversation. "Potter?" she called.

"Yo?"

"Get Daddy a roast beef sandwich with some fries and a Coke. Crush a Xanax or two and add to the drink."

There were at least twenty brothers in her immediate vicinity. The same silence that befell them when her father first appeared overtook them now.

"You want to drug Uncle Chris?" Diesel asked incredulously.

Unrepentant, Rebel nodded. "He needs to fucking sleep."

"And I need to breathe," Potter retorted. "He'll fucking kill me."

"Fine. Give me the pills and I'll do it myself."

"Do what?" Uncle Mort's voice rose above the sudden chatter.

The guys parted to reveal her uncle.

Seeing his haggard appearance made Rebel wonder what anomaly was going on. It was as if a portal to another dimension had opened and driven her father and uncles insane.

Goddamn, but old age was proving rough for them.

Out of everyone, Uncle Mort was always the coolest and chillest, and that included her father. She understood Daddy was diving off the deep end because of his worry over Momma, but she'd never seen Uncle Mort look so sad and tired. If Rebel still received an allowance, she'd bet a year's worth of the money that Uncle Mort's condition had something to do with that raggedy Harley.

Rebel knew raggedy. She'd been afflicted with it herself. In hindsight, she remembered her mother's hurt and her father's anger. Not for the first time, she wondered if she was the reason Momma and Jo had almost been taken from her.

She shoved her hands in her pockets and shifted her weight. "Daddy hasn't slept, Uncle Mort. I wanted Potter to put Xanax in his Coke, but he's afraid Daddy might fuck him up, so I told him to give me the pills and I'll do it myself."

"You a ruthless little motherfucker, huh, baby?" Uncle Mort said with a fond grin. He scrubbed a hand over his face. "CJ asked me to come and check on Outlaw. He that bad off?"

"Mort, I'm not sure how Outlaw is still alive," Bishop admitted woefully. "The first two days after Meggie got here, he didn't sleep at all. Since then, he's slept an hour or two. When he's not in her room, he's in the nursery. He must drink a gallon of coffee a day."

"Did you ever think to open your fucking mouth and tell someone what was going on?" Rebel demanded.

Bishop scowled at her. "Motherfuckers got eyes, Rebel."

"First, don't talk to me like that. I'll fuck you up. Second, motherfuckers' eyes were focused on my mother and little sister, asshole. You're here to protect my parents. The fucking president of the fucking club." Rebel glared at him. "Your fucking eyes are supposed to see what he needs."

"You're a child, Reb," Bishop complained. "I'm ten years older than you. You're supposed to respect me."

"Wah, wah, bitch. Whine to somebody else because I don't give a fuck."

"Rebel—"

"Shut the fuck up, Bishop," Uncle Mort said. "Reb's right. You should've called me, John Boy, Val, or Ghost."

"Digger's the SAA, Mort," Bishop argued. "He should be here watching Prez, instead of playing nursemaid and chauffeur to the children."

"Get the fuck out my goddamn face," Uncle Mort growled. "You don't have shit to say about what Digger doing."

"I don't mean no harm," Bishop said, backtracking. "Shit just feel sideways. I've never seen Prez...fuck, I don't even think he visits the baby because he wants to see her. He goes to the nursery because he gets tired of staring at Meggie. I know that's crazy because he's a father and he loves his kids—"

"He adores us," Rebel cut in, "but Momma is his world. If there's a choice between saving us and her, it's her hands down. Now, stop talking. This isn't about you. This is about my father."

"You don't have a dick, Rebel," Bishop grouched. "You're supposed to be soft and gentle."

"Bishop—"

"You're a sexist idiot," she said, interrupting Diesel. "I didn't come for any of this. I came to see my mother, which I have yet to do. Uncle Mort, can you tell Potter to get me the pills, so—"

"I'm not letting you drug your old man, Reb," Uncle Mort said.

She wanted to punch away Bishop's smug look.

"Go talk to Meggie," Uncle Mort continued. "Diesel, bring Outlaw to the nursery." He dug in his cut and pulled out his billfold. He handed Potter five one-hundred-dollar bills. "Meet me in Meggie room with the sleeping pill. We're going to feed him and then make him sleep."

Instead of poking her tongue at Bishop, she gave Uncle Mort a quick hug. "I'm hungry, too. Can I have a sandwich?"

"I'll bring something for all of us," Uncle Mort promised. "Maybe, soup for your momma."

Rebel wrinkled her nose. "Tabitha's here, too."

"I'm going to send her home when I get Uncle Chris," Diesel said.

Relief swamped Rebel and she smiled. "Bet."

Diesel nodded.

"We're all clear on what we're supposed to do?" she pressed.

"You handle your business, sweetheart, and we'll handle ours," Diesel promised.

Relieved, Rebel turned to head down the hall to her mother's room, but Uncle Mort's voice stopped her.

"You saw Harley today, Reb?"

That was an odd question. Licking her lips, she faced her uncle again. The area was still full of brothers, so she wouldn't pry nor would she reveal how angry she was at Harley, though curiosity still ate at Rebel. "At school. I went to watch her rehearse."

"You mad at her."

Rebel shrugged. "I tried to tell her not to travel down my road, but she won't listen. I was never the levelheaded peacekeeper. Harley has always been kind and calm. She was our voice of reason. But she's being so unfair to my brother. He doesn't deserve her behavior."

Pain flickered in his eyes, and he glanced away. A moment passed before he smiled at her. "Go and see your momma."

"I'll be happy to beat her ass for you, Uncle Mort. We're both teenagers, so it would be equal."

"I don't want you fighting Harley or nobody else," he said.

"Uncle Mort, Mattie acts like a pristine lady because she doesn't want Uncle Johnnie's wrath. She's spoiled and can be pretentious and devious, but between me, Harley, and Mattie, she's the best of us. She'd never disrespect her parents the way I did mine. The way I think Harley did to you. My dad…" Rebel swallowed, and for the first time since that horrible day when her mother collapsed, wanted to cry. "Daddy loves me, but he rightfully beat my ass. None of us expected Harley to turn into such a spoiled brat, least of all you. Whatever she said to you…just talk to Aunt Bailey, she'll straighten Harley out. Even if she's unfairly coddling Harley, she'll never allow her to malign you."

He bowed his head, then turned and started off without another word.

"Uncle Mort?"

He paused. "Yeah, baby?"

"You're a great uncle and an awesome father. We're lucky to have you."

"Thanks, Reb." He walked off.

Making a mental note to get to the bottom of Uncle Mort's strange behavior, Rebel walked down the corridor towards her mother's room. She felt Diesel's presence behind her, yet she remained silent. The emotional toll of the past few days wore on her. Perhaps, that was the reason everyone was so out of sorts and on edge.

Daddy was on the verge of collapse and Momma was in the hospital. The rebellious demon that had invaded Rebel overtook Harley; everything was going to shit.

Despite the warm colors in the hospital, it was still a hospital with a faint antiseptic smell that Rebel hated.

As she reached the door, Tabitha stepped into the hallway. "You probably shouldn't disturb your mommy and daddy, Little Rebel. They're watching a movie."

"Tabitha, enough with the condescension," Diesel warned from behind Rebel.

His wife cackled. "No condescension, my love. I was offering sisterly advice."

"Bitch, I have one sister, too young to offer advice. Not only don't I consider you a sister, I don't consider you a part of my family."

"Then, you must not consider Diesel a part of your family, honey," Tabitha retorted.

"Rebel, shut your fucking mouth," Diesel warned before she could blast his bitch. "Tabitha, get the fuck out of here. There's enough fucking bullshit without you rehashing old shit."

"Diesel is a part of my family," Rebel said, ignoring his orders. "You aren't. That clear enough for you, dumb bitch?"

Tabitha raised her hand to strike Rebel, but Diesel jerked her away.

"Hit me, Tabitha," Rebel snarled. "I fucking dare you. We'd fucking fight up and down this motherfucker—"

The door to her mother's room opened. "What the fuck… Reb, whatcha doin' here?"

Rebel stalked past her father. "I'm finally coming to see Momma, and Diesel is here to take you to the nursery, so… Momma." She froze.

"Hi, my love," Momma said, sitting in a chair between the two beds. It was a good angle to watch the TV without obstruction, though, at the moment, the screen was dark. She was still pale and hooked up to monitors and IVs, but she wasn't lying down, barely lucid or completely sedated.

"Momma." All at once, every mean, horrible word she'd spoken to her mother rushed back to Rebel, and she burst into tears. "I'm so sorry," she cried. "I'm so, so sorry. I never meant what I said. Forgive me, please. I'm so sorry."

Her mother had been so horribly ill, she hadn't had a chance to apologize to her. She wasn't sure she'd even properly apologized to her father. All she knew was that he'd forgiven her.

"Come here, Rebel." Momma opened her arms. "All's forgiven, darling."

Sobbing, she ran to her mother and knelt in front of her before hugging her neck and leaning against her shoulder. When Momma wrapped Rebel in her arms, it was one of the best feelings of Rebel's life.

"I would never have forgiven myself if I'd lost you and Jo."

Momma threaded her fingers through Rebel's hair. "What happened to me wasn't your fault, Rebel."

"The stress I caused—"

"Shhhhh. None of it. It was a combination of factors that culminated in that moment."

"I don't know if I can ever make up for my behavior."

"There's no making up, Rebel," Momma said fiercely. "I think you've suffered enough these past weeks. We learn from it and move on."

"I love you so much, Momma, and Jo's beautiful. Have you seen her yet?"

"Tomorrow," Momma said wistfully.

Rebel straightened and glanced toward where she'd last seen her father. "Daddy, Uncle Mort—"

"Christopher left when you first spotted me, honey. I think he wanted to give us privacy."

"Uncle Mort's going to bring us food so we can all eat in

here."

"Roxy said she cooked red beans and rice, along with bread pudding and rum sauce yesterday. I wonder if he's bringing leftovers."

"No, it's sandwiches. Soup for you."

Momma wrinkled her nose.

"Megan Caldwell, you've been surviving on IVs. Solids will have to be reintroduced slowly."

"I know," Momma said on a sigh. "Maybe, your daddy will give me a small bite of his sandwich."

"Perhaps, but he needs to eat."

Momma nodded. "He has lost a lot of weight."

"He hasn't really been eating or sleeping, Momma." Rebel explained her plan. "I think Uncle Mort wants to prepare the drink in here, which is why Diesel has to keep Daddy in the nursery."

"Does he really need drugging?"

"Yes, Momma. He has so much caffeine in his system, I'm not sure it'll work, but he's going to collapse. This is required intervention."

"Fine," Momma grumbled. "As long as it helps Christopher and not harm him."

"It will." Rebel was certain a good night's rest would help her father see clearer, especially in regard to fucking Tabitha. "What's the next step? When can you and Jo come home?"

"I should be home in the next week or so. Jo will have to stay longer."

"Then what?"

Sadness dulled her mother's eyes. "I'll have an appointment.
At which time, Jordan will offer her recommendations."

"What does that mean?"

Momma's face crumpled. "She'll probably recommend a hysterectomy."

"You don't want a hysterectomy? You have eight children. We need and love you. Wouldn't a hysterectomy be the wisest choice to keep you with us?"

Tears brimming in her eyes, she smiled and nodded. "Of course, I want to do whatever will keep me here with my Christopher and our beautiful children, Reb. I love him so much and I just want him to be happy."

"You don't think he'll be happy if you can't give him more children?"

Before Momma responded, the door opened. At seeing Uncle Johnnie, Rebel's smile died.

"Go away," Momma said on a groan.

Rebel jumped to her feet. Daddy resembled a zombie. Uncle Mort looked drawn and defeated. But Uncle Johnnie had alarming wildness in his eyes.

"I need to talk to your mother alone, Rebel," he said. "Get out."

"Does Daddy know you're here?"

"No," Momma said tiredly. "He's been hiding in one of the staircases since yesterday. Somehow, he knows when your father leaves."

"She doesn't need an explanation."

"Johnnie, please just go."

"You heard her, Uncle Johnnie. Leave."

He glowered at her, his day-old stubble giving him a criminal air. He was fucking unhinged. He stepped farther into the room, so Rebel planted herself in front of her mother.

"This is between your mother and me, Rebel. I'm telling you one last time to go."

"Or what, fuckhead?" Rebel snapped. "If you're suicidal,

jump out the fucking window. If you put your fucking hands on me, you're dead. To save the environment, I won't allow a bullet to be wasted."

"You're a disrespectful little cunt," he snarled.

"And you're just a fucking cunt, Uncle, so we're even."

He glowered at her. Hands on hips, she glared at him.

"You're no lady and never will be."

"Good, fuck face. I don't want to be."

"Didn't Christopher say you have to respect adults?"

"When I see an adult, I'll respect them."

Behind her, her mother struggled to her feet. Horrified, Rebel turned and wrapped an arm around Momma to keep her steady.

"Get out, Johnnie. I won't have you disrespect my daughter. I've heard you loud and clear. You want me to leave. Christopher likes babies, and I'm too old and used up to give him anymore. I'm not leaving my husband even if you offered me fifty million dollars."

"The one fucking thing you're supposedly good at, popping out his children, and you've failed. He wants to leave a legacy."

"Why are you doing this to me?" Momma asked, her sniffles horrifying Rebel. "I can't leave...Please, stop torturing me. I'm not getting a hysterectomy. Okay? No matter what Jordan says. I'll give Christopher as many babies as he wants."

"What? Momma..." Rebel snatched her phone from her pocket, but before she dialed the door opened again and Uncle Mort walked in, carrying a bag in one hand and a cupholder with four drinks in the other.

He looked from Momma to Uncle Johnnie and leaned against the door to keep it open. "Don't say a fucking word. Just leave, Johnnie. I don't know what the fuck is possessing you, motherfucker, but Red losing her shit because your bitch-ass disappeared. Now, you here fucking with Meggie? If you not gone by the time my hands free, I'm shooting your fucking ass off and putting you out your goddamn misery."

For a moment, Uncle Johnnie seemed as if he'd argue. Then, Uncle Mort headed for the bed table. In the minute it took him to set the bag and cupholder down, Uncle Johnnie rushed out of the room without another word.

The encounter left Rebel shaken and her mother in tears. Anger blanketed Uncle Mort's face, although he was gentle as he helped Momma back to her bed and instructed Rebel to call the nurse then go to the nursery and get Diesel and Daddy.

When she returned with her father and Diesel in tow, Momma was asleep. Rebel suspected the nurse had sedated her. Still, it broke her heart as the scene played out.

"Megan, I took a couple pictures of Jo," Daddy said as he followed Rebel into the room and nodded to Uncle Mort, who sat in the chair Momma had vacated. Seeing Momma's closed eyes and still form wiped away Daddy's smile. "Megan?"

She didn't answer.

Diesel walked to the foot of the bed.

"Megan?" Daddy called again, his gaze snapping from the monitors to her. Her vital signs were steady and strong. "Baby?" He leaned down and kissed her lips.

"She started having a lot of pain, Prez," Uncle Mort said. It seemed he needed a few moments to control his anger toward Uncle Johnnie. For whatever reason, he wasn't revealing the truth. "I called her nurse and she gave her a sedative."

Daddy had gone pale. He nodded, then sat in the seat he rarely left, close to her side, between her bed and the door.

"I'll just wait for her to wake up."

Uncle Mort handed Diesel a white Styrofoam cup.

"We have a roast beef sandwich and a Coke, Uncle Chris."

"I'm not hungry—"

"Momma told me she's worried you're losing weight and was happy Uncle Mort was bringing you a sandwich," Rebel said. "She was going to steal a piece. When she wakes up, you can tell her that you ate."

He dragged his worried gaze away from Momma. "She… she's worried?"

"Daddy, don't do that. We don't care how you talk, and I will fucking scream if you correct every other word."

"I ain't…I don't want Megan worryin'," he said in a distant, distracted way that suggested he was a step away from going mad. "Where the fuck the sandwich?"

Rebel snatched the drink from Diesel and placed a straw in it, then held it close to her father's lips. "Have a sip first."

He followed her instructions. "Motherfucker kinda bitter."

"Here, Prez." Uncle Mort gave Daddy the sandwich and a couple napkins. "Take a few bites."

"Soda has caffeine and fructose," Diesel offered. "If you drink this, it'll help you stay awake as well as the buckets of coffee."

Daddy ate in silence, barely focusing on the sandwich, too busy staring at Momma as she slept. Once he finished the food, Uncle Mort took the wrapper and used napkins and discarded both in the trashcan.

"Momma's fine, Daddy," Rebel whispered, and hugged him, careful not to drop the cup. She kissed his cheek and smiled when he wrapped his arms around her. "Have more Coke," she said, stepping away from him and handing him the drink.

Halfway through, he yawned, and his eyes drooped. If

Rebel hadn't been standing near, he would've toppled to the floor.

She grabbed his shoulders while Diesel snatched the cup and set it on the rolling tray table.

"Either he's more tired than I thought or you gave him more than Xanax, Uncle," Diesel said. Crouching, he placed an arm around Daddy and hoisted him up.

Uncle Mort rushed to Daddy's other side. Together, they got her father to the other bed. Once he was laying down, Rebel removed his boots and covered him with the blankets piled at the foot.

She kissed his cheek again. "I love you, Daddy. Sweet dreams."

CHAPTER 12

RORY

Rory stared out of his window, the evening sun casting long shadows across the floor. His bedroom was on the northeast side of the house. He was campaigning to have his bank of windows turned into French doors that led onto a terrace. In the early morning, especially on weekends when he wasn't rushing to dress for school, he could go outside and watch the sun rise, its reflection glimmering off the stream. So far, his parents had declined his pleas. Their house sat alone in the meadow, close to the cave that sat near the stream. Not only that but the back entrance was unmanned, though the location was hard to discern without knowing exactly where to look.

Still, odder things had happened. If the club was ever breached via the back entrance, a second-floor terrace with French doors invited disaster.

Sighing, Rory shoved his hands into his pockets and

pressed his nose against the glass pane. Dad had been gone for over twenty-four hours. He hadn't called Mom or texted Rory, Mattie, or JJ.

Mom hadn't gone into the office today, so Rory hadn't gone to school. He was afraid to leave her alone. She looked devastated, and Rory felt like slitting his father from gullet to groin for torturing his mother.

To think, he'd believed Bash such a problem, he'd skipped class the day after the motherfucker found them at that bridge. Rory had stolen one of his father's guns, intending to shoot that asshole and be done with it. In Rory's head, it was perfect: Bash greeting him; Rory drawing his weapon and emptying the magazine into the fuckhead; Bash's face disappearing in a cloud of blood and bone; Rory dragging him into the brush and dismembering him, then leaving his body parts for scavengers.

For a minute, his vision blurred, and his breath shortened. Dad's face replaced Bash's. Horrified, Rory jerked himself back to the present.

Fueled by concern for his father's safety, Rory's fury toward Dad knew no bounds. He agreed with CJ: Dad knew Bash. Otherwise, the motherfucker wouldn't have gone off the deep end. Bash was bad news and needed dealing with.

Of that, Rory had no doubt. He'd presented himself as a stock villain, yet, deep down Rory believed Bash's presence was personal. Bash sounded like a road name.

An idea hit Rory. Turning away from the window, he went to his nightstand and picked up his phone.

Still no messages from Dad.

Fuckhead.

He Googled motorcycle clubs, and opened the first link that listed them by state. He didn't have time to click the hyperlinks to each club's website to find a president's name.

The Death Dweller listing didn't include a website. Shocking, but whatever.

The next website that he was directed to focused on the clubs' histories and their level of illegality. Still, no president's name.

However, the Death Dweller information raised alarms.

The Death Dweller Motorcycle Club was founded by Logan Donovan and Sharper Banks. Of its ten charter members of particular note are the aforementioned Logan Donovan and Sharper Banks, as well as Sebastian Caldwell and Wallace Bart, all dead now. Joe Foy, also known as Boss and Big Joe, became a member several years later along with his brother, Kaleb Paul Andrews. The original charter, long hidden, from the membership, listed Boss as president in perpetuity, though bi-annual elections were regularly held. Court records also call into question the club's ownership.

Rory's eyes bugged, and he reread the paragraph twice, then checked the input date of the information. It was yesterday.

He read again.

What did the writer mean by stating Kaleb Paul Andrews was Big Joe's brother? Club members called each other brother, but Rory doubted the words alluded to that. He hadn't referred to any of the others as brothers. No, he meant Joe Foy, Aunt Meggie's father, and Kaleb Paul Andrews, Aunt Bailey's father, shared family ties. They were related, which made Aunt Meggie and Aunt Bailey—

Fuck him.

He stumbled back and almost dropped his phone.

Aunt Meggie and Aunt Bailey were cousins, and they had no fucking idea.

Fuck, he needed to tell CJ and Harley. Posthaste.

Otherwise, they might end up with blue fucking babies as second cousins. On the other hand, Harley and CJ weren't as close as they once were, so maybe there was nothing to worry about.

Swallowing, Rory looked at the date again.

Law enforcement, writers, rival clubs, and motorcycle enthusiasts looked up these sites. Most people didn't bother because MCs, especially one percenters, operated on the fringes of society.

As long as Aunt Meggie was in the hospital, Uncle Chris wouldn't stumble across this information on his own. Someone, though, wanted him to find out; otherwise, they wouldn't have put this out into the world.

Rory drew in another breath, suddenly livid. This underhandedness had his father's stupidity written everywhere. When Dad walked out, he'd either added this information himself, paid someone to do it, or contacted the site's webmaster.

Because of Bash. There was no other reason Rory could think of for any of the goings-on over the last day.

Bash.

His mind whirling with solutions before what he'd read became a problem, Rory remembered he needed to find out about Bash.

Fingers trembling, he went to the next site that came up in the search results. It disappointed him that it was just a table with the MC name, the name of the founder, the place and year it was founded, and a note for each club. It wasn't a comprehensive list by any means. Here, the founder of the Death Dwellers was listed as Logan Donovan. Sharper Banks's name wasn't anywhere…

Sharper Banks.

Wasn't Uncle Mort and Uncle Digger's father named

Sharper Banks? Hadn't he been a respected and wealthy minister?

Rory stumbled to his bed and plopped on the edge. What tomfoolery was this? For a moment, he stared at his phone, the words onscreen blurring and merging together, as he tried to place all the puzzle pieces.

Dad would know, but he'd left because of...

Right. Bash.

Intending to close the site and go to the next one in the results, he scanned the MCs again. His gaze caught on the name Cee Cee Caldwell. He'd founded the American Scorpions several years before the formation of the Death Dwellers.

Cee Cee Caldwell was Rory's grandfather.

The location of the club's founding is a subject of intense debate. Some suggest the club was founded in Hortensia, WA, and later moved to Richmond, VA, to make room for the rise of the Death Dwellers. Others insist the American Scorpions' original charter was in Portland, OR.

Nostrils flaring, Rory clicked the hyperlinked American Scorpions. Immediately, a new page opened onto the club's website. He flipflopped between choosing the 'Free Birds' menu option or the 'Officers'. One might answer if Cee Cee and Sebastion were one and the same. Road names were given for a reason: anonymity. Sir names shouldn't be used for that purpose. On the other hand, that other website had Christian names and family names, but no road names.

Cee Cee was dead. Whether he was Sebastian didn't matter. Bash was very much alive and looked at lot like Uncle Christopher. He was the immediate threat.

He opened the page for the officers. The first picture he saw was Bash's. He was the club's president.

What the fuck was Dad up to? Was he betraying the Dwellers? That meant automatic death. As angry as he was with his father—as much as he felt like slicing him—the thought of Dad's death crushed Rory. Mom had come to truly love and accept Dad, which meant she'd come to love and accept Rory.

Kendall Miller Donovan was a strange dichotomy. On the surface, she was strong and dominant. Underneath, she was as fragile as handblown glass. Both sides of her was a schemer in Rory's eyes, yet Dad was her safe haven. He'd sworn to lay down his life—all their lives—to save Mom, and now that motherfucker was in cahoots with Bash?

Anger vibrating through him, Rory gritted his teeth and clicked on the 'Free Birds' page. It opened onto a huge photo of a man that looked uncannily like Uncle Christopher. And Bash. Except Uncle Christopher's green eyes were warmer, not maniacal like Cee Cee's or soulless like Bash's. Uncle Christopher didn't have Bash's pockmarked skin or Cee Cee's harshness. Uncle Christopher was handsome; the other two were frightening.

At the top of the photograph were: Founder and President-for-Life. At the bottom of the picture was the date of his birth and presumed date of death. Underneath that was a name: Sebastian "Cee Cee" Caldwell.

Holy fuck.

The Scorpions and Dwellers were mortal enemies, however, Cee Cee was listed as the founder of one club and a charter member of the other. Bash had come to Hortensia for a fucking reason, and Rory bet it had something to do with Cee Cee's involvement with the Dwellers. He'd even hazard to guess
that Dad knew that reason.

Glancing at the clock on the wall above the door that led

to his private bathroom, Rory jumped to his feet and sent a quick text to Ryan. CJ already had too many problems, otherwise he would've been Rory's first choice.

Get your ass to the cave. Now!

He didn't wait for a response, instead hurrying out of his room. Downstairs, he found his mother sitting on the floor in the foyer. Her back was against the wall and her knees were drawn up to her chest. Her pale skin and reddened eyes gave her a tragic air.

All the many times she'd made him sit in a darkened foyer for one infraction or another flashed through Rory's head, and a moment of triumph surged inside him. Then, he shoved aside his glee, reminding himself he categorized his life in before and after terms. Before Mom's suicide attempt and after.

He went to her and kneeled in front of her. "Mom," he whispered.

"Your father's dead," she said blankly.

For a moment, Rory thought she'd gotten confirmation and he recoiled. His mother was too calm, nor were any of the other members here to give condolences.

"No, Mom—"

She sniffled, tears streaming down her cheeks. "I talked to Brooks," she sobbed. "He wouldn't give me any details, but Johnnie is embroiled in a club matter that he hasn't told your Uncle Christopher about. After Meggie was out of immediate danger, your dad had Brooks call your uncle and offer a minimal account of whatever is going on." She swiped at her cheeks. "Brooks won't tell me. He's afraid for himself and afraid for Johnnie. He told me Outlaw is so distracted, the issue went over his head, and he said to keep him posted.

I begged Brooks for more details," she said tearfully. "All he said was he thinks Johnnie went to deal with the problem alone, but if we tell anyone he might get into trouble, be seen as a traitor, or both by the club, so we have to wait until he comes home, dead or alive."

She leaned her head against her knees and wailed, her shoulders shaking with the force of her tears.

Rory brushed his fingers over her hair. "Mom, Dad's smart." He was a motherfucking idiot. "I'm sure he knows better than to face any threat without the backing of the club, if it has to do with the club." Ha! Just as there was a reason behind his disappearance, there was a reason for keeping his dealings with Bash from the club. "He can't strike a rival club without repercussions. Brothers would wonder why we were being targeted. Dad knows he'd start a war."

The Scorpions were Dweller enemies; therefore, hostilities between the two clubs already existed. So, yes, it was a possibility that Dad felt as if he had nothing to lose if…what?

Mom lifted her head, and Rory dropped his hand from her hair.

"I asked Brooks to call me the moment he hears from your father, but it's been hours."

How long had Rory been in his room? Fuck, he hadn't been doing a very good job of watching over his mother. She could've slit her wrists and bled out; or OD'd on her pills and faded away.

He hugged her tightly, so grateful she was still breathing that he trembled. "I love you, Mom. Everything's going to be all right."

She shuddered against him.

A beep indicated an incoming message, and he disentangled himself.

Ryan: I'm here, fuckhead. You have five minutes before I bounce.

Scowling, Rory stood, then helped his mother to her feet. It pleased him that he was almost eye level with her. "I'm going talk to Ryan about something, then I'll get JJ, so we can cook for you and Mattie."

She nodded, instead of demanding to know why he'd meet with Ryan. "I'll call Brooks—"

Rory headed to the door. "No, Mom. I'll call him myself. It's club business, and you know Dad doesn't want you involved."

"I'll call Mort," she said in a small voice.

"Uncle Mort is a good choice. Or Lolly. Or Aunt Meg… Never mind," he mumbled, and rushed out the door. He didn't want dumb ass to leave, and he didn't want to put his fucking foot in his mouth again.

Rory walked the short distance to the cave and found Ryan inside. Daylight was fading away and casting long shadows into the rocky space. Rory used the flashlight on his phone to beam onto his cousin.

"Who the fuck is Bash?"

Ryan's belligerence turned wary.

"Look, fuckhead, I think the entire club is at risk. My dad knows who that motherfucker is, and so do you."

"You can't prove it," Ryan finally spat. "And if you try to, I'll reveal the information you just gave to me. Uncle Johnnie knows Bash as well."

"I don't give a fuck about you, motherfucker," Rory snapped. It shocked him to see hurt flicker across Ryan's face, gone too quick for Rory to experience true remorse. He opened the website with the incriminating information, then handed his phone to Ryan. "Get this shit off the fucking site," he said, watching the motherfucker closely as he read. "Erase it from the Internet."

"Goddamn," Ryan whispered, returning Rory's phone. He closed his eyes. "Goddamn, goddamn, goddamn. This is so fucking bad."

Rory thought about his father's library and the big desk with the locked drawer. As soon as he saw to his Mom and called Brooks, he'd find a way to get into that desk. Maybe, the answer to this puzzle was inside. Meanwhile, he wanted to shake his cousin until his teeth rattled.

"Do you care to fucking elaborate?"

"Bash and Uncle Johnnie are brothers—"

"I figured as much, asshole. I don't need bones. I need meat. The fucking crux of the situation."

"I'll take the information down, but a digital footprint is almost impossible to completely erase, Rory."

"This is an obscure website with only a few hundred visitors in the two years it's been up, so—"

"So how the fuck do you know about it?"

"My dad, who I'm sure wrote the fucking information."

The shadows bounced around them, making it nearly impossible to see Ryan's expression. He released an audible sigh.

"What does Bash want? How do you know him? Why is my dad involved with him?"

"I met him through friends."

"You have those?"

"Fuck you, Rice Krispy face."

Burn.

Rory wouldn't show how much the words affected him. "All right, Mighty Mouse Body. We can trade insults all night. Unfortunately, I don't have time. I have to see to my mom."

"Why should I help you?"

"Helping me protects the fucking club, Ryan. What's

wrong with you? It protects our mothers and our fathers—"

"My mother's a cunt and my father's a beta boy."

"And you're a fucking idiot, so you fit in. My father—"

"Is probably safe, Rory. Uncle Johnnie has been paying Bash to lay low, with extra thrown in, to keep Kendall and Matilda safe, while he sorts out the real matter with Brooks."

"And you know this how?"

"I talk to Bash, from time to time. He's been taking 50Gs a month from Uncle Johnnie. I guess he's bored, so he decided to ignore the payments and come to Hortensia to fuck with Outlaw's children. He's Christopher's brother, too."

"First, you're a disrespectful assface. Second, if he's Dad's brother, then I fucking know his relation to Outlaw. And why fuck with the cousins?"

"He can't very well fuck with your mom and sister, since your father is paying him to keep them safe."

"I'm so fucking confused."

"Your usual frame of mind, cuck."

"None of this makes sense, asshole-fuckbrain. Why does my father have to pay Bash to keep my mother and sister safe? What's the ultimate fucking goal?"

"To send Meggie away. She's tied into the club's ownership, thanks to her father. She doesn't know anything about it. There was a big meeting almost a year ago. It was only supposed to be Brooks Redding at the Scorps' mother chapter, but the attorney went to your dad when Bash threatened your mother. Uncle Johnnie thought he could handle the situation without going to Outlaw. He thought— stupidly—that Bash had a smidgeon of honor. See, Cee Cee paid our great grandfather and Sharper Banks to keep Outlaw, Big Joe, and K-P alive. Later, Big Joe did the same with his bitch and his cum squirt. He was also a cold ass leader and made oodles of money for the club. From what I understand Cee Cee supplemented Big Joe's funds and paid for Bailey, her ignorant mama, and Mortician and Digger. Great Grandfather wanted to rid the world of refuse, but Cee Cee had an odd bond with Big Joe. Of course, the stupid motherfucker put everything in his daughter's name, leaving her as vulnerable as a duck in a hunter's scope."

If Ryan had punched him in his fucking face, Rory wouldn't have been as gob smacked. "What?"

"It's an intense and twisty tale."

"Aunt Meggie owns the club?"

"The buildings and the grounds," Ryan corrected. "Bash thinks she's standing in the way of his claim to part of Dweller revenue."

"But she doesn't know! Has he ever thought to just tell her? Better yet, go to Uncle Christopher." Which was exactly what his father and Brooks should've done. Those two dumb asses.

"Bash pisses himself at the thought of facing Outlaw. He figures anybody who could take down their old man isn't a motherfucker to fuck with. Outlaw fucking shoots first and asks questions later. Even if Bash got Outlaw to a meeting and planned an ambush, Bash is convinced Outlaw would take down a few motherfuckers with him."

"Bash can't be that afraid of Outlaw if he's decided to fuck with his children."

"Bash is warped in the brain, so who the fuck knows what his reasons are. I think he's trying to force your father's hand. Bash has a massive amount of documents, but they are all copies. For some reason, he thinks Johnnie has obtained the originals and he's furious."

"Why would he think that?"

"I think he has an inside source."

"Yeah, fuckhead. You."

Ryan snorted. "Not me, idiot."

Was it Rory's imagination or did Ryan sound regretful?

"Bash was the one who showed me the documents. I wouldn't even know where to begin to find originals or prove their authenticity."

"Someone in the club is a mole."

"Someone close to the officers is a mole," Ryan corrected.

"Again, you."

"I've already told you I'm not."

A mole wouldn't admit to being a fucking mole. Still… "You know this shit and have kept it to yourself."

"Okay, son of the pot."

"You do make a fine kettle, asshole. Full of steam and hot air."

"Very fucking funny."

"Do you hear me laughing?" Except for Ryan's flashlight, pointed toward the ground, it was pitch black in the cave with rapidly dropping temperatures.

"Do you know where my dad is?"

"Nope. He doesn't know I'm acquainted with Bash. I assume he's near Hortensia General."

Alarm raced through Rory. "He's injured."

"No, stupid. The club supports the hospital. Bash said Cee Cee started that practice. There are back stairwells for members to escape."

"He's trying to escape?" Rory asked, clueless.

Ryan huffed. "You must promise me you won't tell anyone all I've revealed. You can talk to Brooks. He knows."

"What do stairwells have to do with my father?"

"Promise me, Rory. Johnnie, Brooks, and me will be killed. If not by Bash, then by Outlaw."

Then, Mom, Aunt Zoann and Uncle Val, and Charlotte Redding would be left devastated. The weight of knowledge pressed in on Rory, and he almost ran away.

"You can't even tell motherfucking CJ."

CJ would be a sounding board.

Ryan grabbed a handful of Rory's shirt. "Promise me, cuck."

The air around Rory felt heavy and thick. An odd premonition of death and destruction hit him, and his nostrils flared. "I promise."

"Your dad is probably urging Meggie to leave Outlaw. Maybe, offering to pay her off if she disappears and can't ever be found."

"Dad wouldn't do that. If Aunt Meggie left, it would destroy Uncle Christopher."

"She's leaving one way or the other." Ryan released him, and Rory stumbled back. "Let's see how high and mighty CJ is then. If Johnnie doesn't convince Meggie to vanish, Bash plans to kill her."

CHAPTER 13

CJ

Unlike CJ's other visits to the house Molly lived in, his mother hadn't brought him. He'd rode his pussyped over. He wouldn't have a meal later with his family. While Mom was in the hospital, all bets were off. Aunt Bunny saw to their breakfast and made sure the house was clean and food was stocked. Uncle Digger chauffeured the younger kids to school. Diesel stayed on premises at night. Aunt Fee had moved Gunner to her place. Lolly and Aunt Zoann sent over food. Aunt Kendall had checked in with them, but with Uncle Johnnie still missing, she barely saw to her own children. Once Aunt Bailey turned against him thanks to Harley, she ignored not only CJ but Rebel and their brothers.

For a little while after he arrived at Molly's house, it felt like a refuge. Her wild statements and how deeply she sometimes lacked logic were familiar to him. They had settled on making a cardboard hydraulic claw.

Admittedly, he was doing most of the building because it required some engineering skills. Luckily, he understood some mechanics thanks to years of working on bikes with his father.

"I still think my last idea was the best one," she complained, sitting on her bed and leaning against the wall, her hand resting on her belly.

She still wasn't showing, and he had yet to tell her not only had Dad given him money to help her but a contact too.

"We should've tried it."

He lifted his head before he settled the longest piece of cardboard into place. This was their third attempt at the build. The first one Molly cut in half to see what was inside. The second one she fucked up with water.

"Where the fuck would I have gotten chickens to test your theory they'd survive electrocutions?"

"Duh. The chicken store."

"A farm?"

"No, silly," she said with a little sniff. "The chicken store. Where they sell all types of chickens. Even designer ones."

What the hell was a designer chicken?

Fuck, who knew if they really had chicken stores? He returned to the project, proud of their accomplishments. It was almost finished. Then, they could start using it to test what it could and couldn't lift in terms of weight and height.

"I've been thinking."

Never a good sign, but whatever. "About what, Mo?"

"You and me. Us."

Definitely not a good sign.

"I want to be your girlfriend."

"You're Ryan's girlfriend. Maybe, pregnant by him. You can't be my girlfriend."

"I thought I couldn't be your girlfriend because of Harley."

"Her, too," he agreed, to keep shit simple, even if he spouted a bunch of fucking excuses.

His relationship with Harley was complicated, and his feelings were diminishing. Explaining the details to Molly took patience. He wanted to focus on their project.

"I like you so much, though. You're nice to me. Ryan doesn't care that I love him."

CJ grunted. Ryan was a dickhead. "I'll talk to him, bae. If he hurts you again, I'll fuck him up."

This claw was ricketier than the first. The cardboard wasn't as thick, a decision CJ regretted.

"Can I ask you another question?"

"Ask as many as you want, Mo," he said, wondering if they, he, should do a fourth build.

"How do you and Reb Elle have so many nice clothes? When those other ladies took me shopping, they said I could buy whatever I wanted. Then I saw the price tags and I was scared they'd holler at me. There was one T-shirt I loved, and it cost twenty whole dollars."

Pushing the folding chair back from the small table he'd bought her to set up their project, he stood and walked to her, sitting on the side of her bed. Her blue-gray eyes were wide and earnest. She wore her hair in a high ponytail. Her breasts pressed against her tank top, though CJ studiously ignored her hardened nipples.

"They took you shopping to buy whatever you wanted," he told her. He snatched his cigarette from behind his ear. Once he lit it and took a drag, he continued, accepting the ashtray she hid under her bed especially for him. "They wouldn't yell at you, especially over a $20 shirt."

She got her phone from under her pillow, typed something, then handed it to him. "That's the shirt."

It was black with the words, Birthday Girl, written in rose

gold rhinestones.

He really, truly hated to bring up her birthdate. It was February 29th. Instead of helping her celebrate on the 28th or the 1st of March between leap years, her mother had convinced her there were thirty-two days in February. Deep down, he knew she'd find a way to repeat her date of death: February 32, 2199.

Jamming the cigarette in the corner of his mouth, he stood and dug in his back pocket for his wallet, then took out his debit card.

"Go for it," he told her as he sat and handed her the card.

Her eyes widened. "Really?" she whispered.

He nodded.

"I told Ryan and showed him the shirt, and he said I was very expensive. He'd bought me French fries because I crave those a lot. He said I broke his bank."

Stingy asshole.

CJ didn't know how much allowance Ryan received, but he knew fucking fries wouldn't break that cheap motherfucker. "He doesn't have a sister, Mo. He's unfamiliar with the things girls like."

She scooted next to him to make the purchase then gave him his card.

"I'll wear my shirt on February 32nd, so Mama and Daddy will remember my birthday."

Fuck! CJ's heart broke for her. Not wanting her to feel even worse, he returned his card to his wallet and finished his cigarette in silence. He hadn't brought any napkins to remove the evidence of his smoking.

He sighed.

"Give it to me. I'll be careful not to spill the ashes," she promised.

Once the ashtray was tucked away, he stood, intending to

return to their project.

"How can you afford expensive things? The shirt you bought me, for instance."

"My mom is good at investing money. She understands what to purchase during bull markets and when to start divesting if she suspects a bear market."

"I never met a bear dealer before." She frowned. "Or does she own a zoo?"

Generally, CJ took Molly's observations in stride, but he was so startled by her words, he couldn't hold in his laughter. When her face crumpled, he sobered slightly. He didn't want to hurt her feelings, but Jesus.

"My mom doesn't sell bears, nor does she own a fucking zoo."

"A ranch?"

"No." With effort, he swallowed the guffaws dying to erupt. "She deals with the stock market."

She gave him a blank look. "Bull and bear stocks? She puts their feet in jail?"

"No, Molly! No! It forecasts the economy. A bull market means a strong economy. A bear market means a recession might happen. It has nothing to do with the devices to restrain your feet to punish or humiliate you. How the fuck do you know about that but not about stock markets?"

"Willard mentioned them once."

CJ gave her a dark look. "Don't mention that motherfucker to me."

"He's meaner than Ryan."

He stood. "I'm going to have to leave soon, but I wanted to let you know that my dad—"

Before he finished, Molly's bedroom door flew open. A rail thin woman who shared Molly's eye and hair color swayed on her booted feet. The military boots were notable since she was completely fucking naked otherwise.

"Mama!"

Mrs. Harris staggered into the room, the scent of alcohol and sweat wafting from her.

Molly stumbled from her bed and hurried to her mother. "When did you get home?"

"I've been home, girl," she said around an oniony belch. She looked CJ up and down and squinted. "Do I know you?" She farted.

The shame on Molly's face touched CJ. Determined not to wrinkle his nose, he shook his head. "No, ma'am," he said politely. "I'm CJ Caldwell, Molly's lab partner."

She swayed again, studied him, and nodded. "I think Ryan..." She cocked her head to the side and blinked. "Do you know a Ryan, Molly?"

"Yes, Mama," she said quietly. "He's CJ's cousin. He bought me the French fries I shared with you."

Her smile revealed jagged teeth. "You didn't tell your daddy."

"He didn't get angry with us, did he?" Molly said.

Mrs. Harris farted again. "CJ, right?"

"Yes, ma'am."

"My girl and me like French fries. You can fuck me in the ass if you buy us each a small fry."

Fuck, lady, have some standards. "I'll buy you both a meal without any payment."

"I'm too old for a young stud like you, huh, kid? I'll leave the room, so Molly can suck your cock." She shrugged. "Ryan makes her do it all the time. As long as he doesn't fuck her pussy, we'll be fine. Her daddy'll blame me."

Tears rushed to Molly's eyes, and she looked at her toes. It gave CJ the moment he needed to control his anger. He wasn't sure if he wanted to fuck up Ryan first or Tom Harris.

Deputy fucking Dog.

Coin toss time, since both motherfuckers were awful and needed a beat down ASAP.

Mrs. Harris stumbled back. Molly wrapped her arms around her belly. Footsteps pounded in the direction of Molly's bedroom. She stiffened, while uneasiness covered her mother's face. A moment later, Deputy Harris walked into Molly's bedroom.

CJ's gaze clashed with Molly's father's.

"If it isn't Outlaw's son."

The motherfucker wanted a reason to either shoot or beat the fuck out of CJ. Hostility radiated from him.

CJ nodded. "Sir."

Deputy Harris settled a big hand on Mrs. Harris's bony shoulder and she jumped. Snickering, he leaned in and kissed her cheek. "When did you get home, babe?"

"A little while ago."

"Any reason your clothes are scattered from the outside porch to the fucking kitchen door?"

She sucked on her teeth. "I was hot," she said, another fart escaping.

Jesus.

Molly cringed, sidling behind CJ. "I'm s-sorry," she whispered.

"Sorry, huh, Molly?" her father demanded. "Who are you apologizing to? Me or Outlaw's son?"

She sniffled.

These were the motherfuckers she wanted to stay with? Her mother was an abused, malnourished drug addict, a foot away from the grave, while her father was a fucking bullying fuckhead, hiding behind a badge and a gun.

"How's the project coming along, Molls?" Deputy Harris asked, strolling to the little table where all of CJ's hard work sat.

Before the motherfucker starting ripping apart the cardboard pieces, CJ knew what he intended and balled his fists at his sides to keep from throwing a punch. Each piece he tore, he threw at CJ's feet. When the hydraulic claw was completely destroyed, he smiled.

"Guess not that good," he said, and walked out of the room, leaving Molly in tears and CJ so fucking mad he was glad he wasn't armed because he would've shot that motherfucker.

CJ turned to Molly.

Raising her arms above her head, she cried out in fear. "Don't hit me."

He wouldn't dignify her words with a response, although she probably needed comfort right now, but so did he.

His entire fucking world was falling the fuck apart. A fucking fuckhead destroyed the one thing that was finally going right.

He backed away from her and right into her mother. She looked like a bag of bones covered by skin. She felt like a skeleton. Another bit of gas exploded from her, louder and smellier than the others.

"I'm hungry," she said, her breath as foul as her farts.

"Nora!" Tom Harris called.

CJ didn't trust he'd escape with his life if he had another run in with Molly's father. He wished he could help her and her mother, but he didn't know how.

"I'll have food sent over," he promised.

"For Daddy, too," Molly called, a plea.

He didn't want to spend his fucking money on that motherfucker. However, he knew if he didn't, Molly and her mother would either have to give him the lion's share or go without.

"Fine," he grumbled, and stalked to the front door, careful not to step on Mrs. Harris's threadbare skirt, shirt, bra, and panties, and grateful when he rode away and left that house in the distance.

CHAPTER 14

Harley

The next evening, Harley sat in the dining nook of her family's kitchen. The table stood in front of a curving booth, with Daddy's chair at the head, and four chairs on the opposite side. Whether seated in the booth or in a chair, outside was visible with a panoramic view of the back gardens and the walkway that led to Lolly and Pop's house.

At least twice a week, her grandparents dined with them. Once a week had been the family dinner at Aunt Meggie and Uncle Christopher's, impossible while she was still in the hospital. Usually, there was laughter and jokes and warmth.

Tonight was the first time Daddy had sat down to eat a meal with them since the big blowup three days before. Though he was talking to Lou and Kaleb, Daddy didn't have much to say to either Harley or Mommie.

Although her mother kept her expression closed, Harley

was both hurt and angry at her father's treatment. He was as bad as CJ, who hadn't been at school again today, although she overheard Jaleena Davis tell one of her friends that he'd texted her and asked if she could collect homework for him.

"The stew is good, Momma," Kaleb said. He'd inherited most of Mommie's genes, with greenish-brown eyes, cream-colored skin, and silky dark hair. "You haven't cooked a homemade meal in a long time."

Mommie winced and shifted in her seat. "Is the lamb tender, Lucas?"

"It's fine, Bailey. The lamb's still a little chewier than the beef, but it's cool, baby."

"I don't prefer one or the other," Lou said, copying their father's mannerisms because why not? He was the one who looked most like Daddy, so it stood to reason he'd mimic him, too.

"What about you, hunny bunny?" Mommie pasted a smile on her lips and met Harley's eyes. "Are you enjoying the food?"

Harley mixed gravy and rice, then shoved the food to the other side of her plate. She shrugged. "It's delicious."

Lou shook his head. "Have you even taken a mouthful?"

She shrugged again.

"Eat, sweet girl," Mommie encouraged, and smiled at Daddy. "Tell her Lucas."

"You got it covered, Bailey."

Her face crumpling, Mommie swallowed.

Though Harley didn't eat much, everyone else finished their meal in silence. Since it was Saturday, the boys left the table and headed to their music room.

"Nardo invited me out to the movies tomorrow," Harley announced. She smiled at her father. "I told him I'd ask you and Mommie."

Shoving his chair back, Daddy rose to his feet. "That's between you and Bailey, Harley." He bent and brushed his lips over Mommie's lips. "Boy having a poker match at his club," he said, referring to the president of the Night Flyers, one of the bigger Black MCs in the area. "I bought a seat at the table, so don't wait up for me."

Tears rushed to Mommie's eyes, and regret washed over Daddy's face but he backed away.

"Seriously, Daddy?" Harley screeched, jumping to her feet, and rushing to block her father's exit. "You're butt hurt that Mommie defended me over that backstabber so you're ruining your marriage?"

"Harley, thank you for defending me, but this is between your father and I."

"You're making overtures, Mommie! Daddy is ignoring each one." Folding her arms, she lifted her chin. Memories of how the waitress, Symphony, flirted with Daddy flashed through Harley's mind. "Or are you taking CJ's side because you're like him? He's cheating with Molly and Jaleena, and you're cheating with Symphony?"

A smorgasbord of emotions marched across her father's face: anger, hurt, disgust.

Mommie rushed over. Instead of outrage directed at Daddy, she glared at Harley.

"I said enough, Harley. If I didn't know about the incident you referred to, it could've caused even more damage."

"He's the reason for the damage," she said, pointing to her father. "He's not talking to you because you defended me."

"Harley," Daddy growled, but Mommie cut him off.

"He's not talking to me because I wrongly didn't defend him against your accusations. I allowed him to feel inferior and unworthy." Although she was looking at Harley, Mommie was speaking to Daddy. "He's my best friend."

Daddy snorted and mystifying shame crossed Mommie's face.

"I'm so sorry, Lucas. It never occurred to me that I was cutting you out of my professional life."

"It's okay, Bailey," Daddy said with a sad sigh. "You worked your ass off to get your own practice. You've written in academic journals, given expert testimony and consultation. You have four associates under you. You don't want me around, tarnishing your image in my cut, dreads, and jeans. It's cool, pretty girl. That's why I didn't pressure you. When you got rid of Shanice, I saw which way the tide was turning. She didn't fit your aesthetic at the office and neither do I."

"That isn't true! I love you. I'm proud to be your wife."

"I don't doubt your love for me, Bailey. It's your respect for me that's questionable."

"Lucas—"

Daddy shook his head. "No, pretty girl. You don't have to deny it. No matter which side your loyalties lay in this situation between Harley and CJ, when she called me a worthless piece of shit, your silence cosigned her sentiment."

Harley gasped. "I never called you a worthless piece of shit."

"It wouldn't have hurt as much if you had, Harley." Daddy looked at Mommie again. "That's when I started thinking about our life since you moved your practice to Portland."

"And you called Momma," Mommie said in a small, tearful voice.

"Prez not fit to talk to a goldfish. Digger overwhelmed with helping Bunny out. Kendall catatonic because Johnnie a fuckhead." Daddy rubbed the back of his neck. "He stormed out. I think he staying near Hortensia General. I just don't know why."

"What?"

"Don't sweat it, Bailey. Club business." He bowed his head. "And Meggie don't need to listen to my problems. I only had Roxanne."

"Lucas, I love you so much."

"I love you, too, Bailey. You my everything, but I just don't think I'm enough—"

"No!"

"Hey."

CJ's voice cut into the tension. Daddy looked up as Mommie and Harley turned. He wore jeans, a T-shirt, and motorcycle boots. He was tall and so beautiful, Harley nearly swooned. Instead, her jealousy flared at his near perfection.

"Hey, kid," Daddy greeted, brushing past Harley and Mommie. He paused to shake CJ's hand.

Mommie ignored CJ. Maybe, it was because she focused on Daddy, though Harley doubted it.

"Lucas, please," Mommie said. "Wait. Let's talk in private."

Daddy turned and kissed Mommie's cheek. "We can talk tomorrow—"

At the panic on her mother's face, Harley turned to CJ. "Please," she mouthed, unsure what he might do to stop this disaster in the making.

"Uh, I came to talk to Harley, but I need to discuss something with you afterwards, Uncle Mort."

"Tomorrow—"

"It's really important."

"I paid five grand to sit at Boy's fucking poker table, boy," Daddy growled, sounding more like himself. "I was going to win my fucking money back."

"Or lose more," CJ said, grinning. "Then, you'd be in the same ICU as mom, you fucking tightwad."

Tension seeped from Daddy's shoulders, and he snickered, then looked at Mommie, his gaze softer. "We can go to the den and talk."

Within moments, Daddy guided Mommie down the hallway.

"Key or code?" Harley asked, folding her arms.

"Neither. Lou and Kaleb were outside and they let me in."

Harley frowned. "That's strange. They said they were going to the music room."

"You would've heard some noise," CJ countered.

"What brings you here?" she asked, walking back into the kitchen and heading to the dining nook, where she sat.

CJ followed her. "We need to talk, bae."

"About what, CJ? Unless you've come to apologize for all your lies—"

"Didn't you just ask me for help? Now that I've given it, you're back to accusing me?"

"Your help is the least you can do. Besides, I didn't make you comply. You did it of your own free will. Now, apologize and swear you'll tell me the truth from this moment forward."

"I'm not apologizing for something I haven't fucking done, Harley."

"I have pictures as proof. And you know they speak a thousand words."

"Or a thousand lies," he retorted.

"What? Were you photoshopped into the pictures?"

"No, Harley. I was with Molly."

Pain sliced through Harley, and tears rushed to her eyes. "Get out."

"I'm tired of defending myself to you. If I wanted Molly, I'd tell you."

"I doubt that," she flared. "You're using the excuse of a lab project to cheat on me."

"I can't cheat on you, if we aren't together," he snapped.

"I'm not ready, but you promised to wait until I was, so you are cheating. And you're lucky I didn't get in trouble for cutting or else I'd be even madder at you."

"I don't give a fuck if you are mad at me."

Harley's mouth fell open.

"I didn't tell you to go to the creek with Nardo Grevenberg. You chose to do so of your own free will, so fuck off with your misplaced blame. I don't give a fuck if you would've gotten in trouble. Your decision. Your consequences."

"Motherfucker," she whispered, low. His words humiliated her.

"Am I?" CJ shook his head. "Maybe to you, but not to—"

"Jaleena?" she fired. "Yeah, because I know about her, too. You asked her to pick up homework for you when Rebel could've done it."

CJ stiffened.

"Go ahead. Try to defend that!"

"Again, there's nothing to defend. My sister is as worried about Mom and Jo as I am. She needs somebody to collect her fucking work, Harley. Instead of your accusations, you could pick up the fucking phone and text me or call me. You could ask if I need something. A candy bar. An ear to listen. A fucking walk. But you don't because you don't see me as a fucking person. You see me as an ideal. You've listened to the adults around us say we're going to marry, for your entire life. In your head, that's what you've decided. CJ and Harley belong together, so I'm marrying him. I'm no longer your friend or just a guy. I'm a goal."

"You're pathetic and overly dramatic," she seethed, "victimizing yourself when, clearly, I'm the victim, and you're soundly in the wrong. You can't defend the indefensible."

"I'm pathetic, overly dramatic, and a victim? What are you? You're stomping around like a jealous maniac after you turned me down when I asked you to go steady. I wanted nothing more from you than to call you my girlfriend."

"You kissed me. That just proves you're a liar."

Something flashed across his face, but Harley didn't care. She was too outraged to recognize the unnamed emotion in his expression.

"Weeks later, you kissed me," he reminded her.

"You're horrible for bringing that up," she said on an indignant gasp. "I was overwrought and wanted to show you how much I missed you."

"Don't blame your actions on me, Harley," he snarled, more furious than she'd seen him in a while. "You sent me a fucking text and I came with no expectations. I came because you asked me to. Grow the fuck up. Look in the fucking mirror and ask yourself what you want. First, you refused me because you said you didn't want to ruin our friendship if we didn't work out. Then, you told me it was because you weren't ready. Then, you said it was because your body wasn't developed, and you weren't getting periods yet."

Harley restrained herself from lunging across the table and slapping him. "You're a disrespectful asshole. How dare you use my medical condition against me and break my confidence to boot!"

His look turned severe as if she were the one in the wrong. She allowed a tense pause, expecting an apology. He remained silent.

"Tell me the truth now. How many times have you slept with Molly?"

"None."

"How many times have you slept with Jaleena?"

"Not once, Harley."

"I don't believe you."

CJ snapped his mouth shut, and she smiled, triumphant.

"I have proof that you're closer to Molly than you're admitting," she said with self-righteous smugness. "If you just tell me the truth and leave her alone, I will find a way to forgive you."

"I'm done." CJ got to his feet, his gaze sad and his face drawn. "Since Mom went into the hospital, the world seems upside down. It's almost like Death is punishing us because she and Jo beat him and survived. I miss you so much, Harley. I do love you, but I can't be your friend if you're going to use me as a cover or refuse to understand that I have fucking feelings, too. In our entire lives, I've never lied to you, so your fucking jealousy is bullshit and a fucking excuse for bad behavior. Molly is my friend. Jaleena is my friend. I have absolutely no interest in fucking either one of them."

"They want to fuck you!"

"How the fuck is that my problem?" he shouted.

Harley gasped.

"I can't control how the fuck those girls feel. They know my feelings, and where my loyalties were."

Were? Were alarmed Harley. Were meant past tense. She jumped to her feet.

"You're the reason my parents are fighting."

"No. I'm not," he retorted. "I don't even know what the fuck they're arguing over."

"Because Daddy defended you, and I told him what Nardo made me realize."

"Which is?"

"That Daddy isn't a real gangster. What does he do all day, except try to suck up to your father? I told him he's an Uncle Toady. A suck up and a sellout. Because Mommie didn't defend him, a grown man, he's butt hurt."

"I would be, too," CJ said flatly. He glared at her.

"Obviously, you've felt this way about Uncle Mort if you said—"

"I did not." Harley stomped her bare foot. Though she felt like a spoiled toddler, it got CJ's attention, and he widened his eyes. "Nardo pointed it out," she said loftily. "Daddy invited him and his father to lunch and embarrassed me and himself. Nardo's father went to prison and everything. He's a real G."

"And you're a fucking dummy."

"I refuse to allow you to call me out of my name."

"I called you a dummy. Definitely not out of your name if you feel like Uncle Mort hasn't proven his worth because he hasn't gone to fucking prison. What the fuck is wrong with you?"

"He had no right to threaten Nardo and his father—"

"Fuck, if you were my daughter and you said that shit to me, I'd kill both those motherfuckers on GP."

"There you go again, asshole. Daddy is a wannabe gangster, so he definitely isn't the big bad killer that he makes himself to be."

"Uncle Mort is a fucking killer, Harley," CJ barked. "My father is a killer. Uncle Val. Uncle Digger. Uncle Cash. Not so much Uncle Stretch, although he has killed. And don't even get me started on Uncle Johnnie."

"No—"

CJ cocked his head to the side. "Why's that so hard to believe? You know what happened to Cole at the Scorched Devils meeting."

Confusion muddled Harley's thoughts. Nardo's reasoning seemed so logical.

"As the enforcer, it suggests Daddy has killed or beaten a lot of people. At some point, he would've gotten caught."

"Only if he was a stupid motherfucker and slipped up," CJ

pointed out.

"But—"

"There's no buts, Harley. What you said to Uncle Mort is shameful. Frankly, if my mother ever heard any of us disparaged Outlaw in such a way, she'd be madder than a motherfucker."

Aunt Meggie had been madder than a motherfucker when Rebel scorned Uncle Christopher. She hadn't even tried to talk him out of spanking Rebel.

Despair hit the center of Harley's chest.

"Neither is Uncle Mort a sellout. He has personally sponsored many upgrades and renovations to the club, Harley. He and my dad are best friends. My father holds yours in the highest esteem."

"Daddy isn't even an officer—"

"In the Dwellers, he is."

"In other clubs he wouldn't be. Uncle Digger ranks higher. His position is just after the vice-president's."

CJ shook his head. "If this is the effect Grevenberg is having on you, I might fuck that motherfucker up. You've turned harsh and belittling."

Harley flinched, the words cutting through her. "He's my friend," she parroted.

Instead of responding, CJ started for the door, stopping when he walked into the hallway. "My dad, the entire club, wanted Uncle Mort to be sergeant-at-arms. In my eyes, the only other man fiercer and more loyal is my dad. Loyal, Harley. Uncle Mort chose loyalty to his kid brother over rank in the club. He removed his name and convinced the brothers to vote Uncle Digger into the position everyone wanted him to have."

Harley's heart beat in a painful rhythm. CJ sounded done with her and disappointed in her. She'd also been horrendous to her father, unfair, judgmental, and condescending. She felt lower than she ever had.

"Loyal, Harley," CJ repeated, his green eyes taking in every inch of her face. "Maybe, you should look up the definition of that word."

He left.

When her mother walked into the kitchen, minutes later, Harley hadn't returned to her seat. She continued staring at the place where she'd last seen CJ, his words rolling through her head.

"Harley?" Mommie called in a trembly voice, touching Harley's shoulder.

The faint sound of motorcycle pipes cut into her despair.

"Daddy left anyway?" she whispered, the first tears slipping down her cheeks.

Mommie nodded. "I've hurt him terribly," she sniffled. "It didn't...I didn't...in all the months, years...it never dawned on me." She swiped her cheeks and glanced around the kitchen, then gazed at Harley again, a question in her eyes.

"CJ left," Harley said miserably.

"Oh, sweet girl."

Together, they burst into tears and clung to each other, sobbing out the misery they'd brought on themselves.

CHAPTER 15

CJ

Stepping into the entrance hall out of the miserably cold weather, CJ leaned against the door. Because his mother loved Christmas so much, she always began decorating the Sunday before Thanksgiving. Tree trimming was an event that she saved for the week after Turkey Day, simply because of the number of trees: one in the entrance hall, another in the den, one in the second-floor hallway and another on the third. Then, there was the club's tree, where she invited all the members and their families, and the old ladies all pitched in to bring food.

Outside, brothers turned the Caldwell grounds into a lighted Winter Wonderland. In recent years, other family members who had houses in the exclusive enclave followed suit. CJ was sure their valley twinkled so brightly during this time of year that it could be spotted from the ISS during flyovers.

But, now, the outside decorations remained dark and

silent. No presents lay underneath any of the barren trees. His parents had missed their annual Black Friday date that went back to the first year they'd met. Before they were a real couple.

Often, he wondered how the love Mom and Dad had for each other burned so brightly, even now, almost eighteen years later.

Moving away from the door, CJ flicked on the overhead light and walked to the tall Scots pine. It was bright green, thick and full, but joyless. There were no strings of lights, no ornaments. No anything. It was just a tree. Waiting.

Waiting for beautification. Waiting for joy.

Waiting for Mom.

As he'd told Harley, the world seemed upside down. Mom wasn't around to preside over their family with Lolly's help while Dad ran the club, with his officers at his side, most especially Uncle Mort.

CJ never expected a day would come when Harley would be so fucking delusional and disrespectful. Never mind her refusal to believe CJ, her behavior toward Uncle Mort was infuriating. CJ was almost certain her bitchiness had trickled down—up?—and bruised her parents' relationship. Something else he never would've thought possible—a fracture in Uncle Mort and Aunt Bailey's marriage.

When CJ saw Harley's panic at Uncle Mort's imminent departure, he'd made up a story that he needed to talk to Uncle Mort. Things were so bad, though, he'd left anyway, without tracking down CJ to inquire about the urgency of CJ's matter. Maybe, he'd forgotten. He looked so defeated. Or, maybe, he'd known all along CJ was a lying motherfucker. Uncle Mort had an amazing bullshit detector.

The silence of his surroundings didn't help CJ's melancholy mood. Axel, Ryder, Ransom, and Gunner were with some of the aunts, uncles, and cousins in Portland at a holiday event, while Diesel took Tabitha to a Christmas party.

"CJ?"

"Hey, Reb." He didn't turn away from the tree. Somehow, Harley had broken his heart. Again. He wanted her to be the girl he'd grown up with. He wanted her to be his friend. "What's up?"

"I can ask you the same thing," she said slowly. "You're staring at a fucking undecorated tree as if it holds the answers to life's mysteries."

He tested one of the stiff branches. "Something should."

"Oh."

The silence stretched for so long, he thought she'd left him alone, until she came next to him and touched his arm. He looked down at her. She wore a troubled expression.

"What's wrong? Is Mom okay?"

"Where've you been?" she asked, instead of answering him.

"I spent part of the day working on me project," he said glumly, deciding not to detail Tom Harris's destruction. Just as football might be a lost cause, passing Billson's class seemed even more unlikely. "I'll probably have to go to summer school," he muttered.

At Rebel's snicker, CJ grinned.

"What's up, Reb? Talk to me."

Dropping her hand from his arm, she gazed at him through her lashes. CJ groaned under his breath. Very soon, he would have to fuck up more than a few motherfuckers thanks to Rebel discovering her girlness. Now, he had another little sister to worry about.

"You went to Molly's?"

Fuck, no. After yesterday's visit, he hated the thought

of returning to that house, so he'd worked alone on their project in his bedroom. But she'd appreciated the food he'd sent to her house. "I stopped at the hospital to see Mom and Jo. Dad was asleep. Mom said he'd awakened for about an hour, then fell into lala land again." In retrospect, CJ could've asked Uncle Mort just how strong the fucking sedative was, but it hadn't crossed his mind. He looked at the tree again. "Then, I went to talk to Harley."

"Oh. That bitch."

"She isn't a bitch, Rebel."

"Okay. Sorry. That fucking bitch. Better?"

CJ scowled at her profile. "No."

"I can think of worse."

"Never mind. Stick to what you have."

"I thought so." Rebel squeezed between him and the tree, forcing him to back up. She glared up at him. "Well, what did she say?"

"You don't even know why I went to see her."

"I don't need the reason. The result is written all over your face. She hurt you. Again."

"She doesn't believe I haven't slept with Molly," he said dismally.

"If I were you, I'd fuck Molly just to get back at Harley."

"Yeah, because you're fucking vicious."

"Quite petty," she agreed cheerfully. "If she's accusing you, why not make it a fact?"

"What the fuck will that help, Rebel?"

"God, you're so fucking nice! You have the best of both Momma and Daddy, while I have their worst traits. Spoiled like Momma and violent like Daddy," she said glumly.

He bent and kissed her cheek. "You're perfect in my eyes now that you're thinking clearly again."

She thumped his chest. "Perfection is overvalued, doofus."

"True," he agreed, not up for a debate.

"Awww, CJ, don't let that fucking bitch get to you. She'll come around. Make her fucking grovel or I'll never forgive you. I think she hurt Uncle Mort. I don't know how." She told CJ about her encounter with their uncle. "I can beat her ass. I offered my services to Uncle Mort, free of charge, but he declined. I need money, so I'll charge you, but give you a discount as a family member."

She was serious. CJ glared at her.

She shrugged, unapologetic.

"She also accused me of fucking Jaleena, too."

"Jaleena?" Rebel blinked, then frowned. "Didn't see that coming. Jaleena is gorgeous, but I fucking swear there's a spark between her and Mattie."

Fuck, CJ hadn't seen that coming. "She offered to fuck me at Homecoming."

"So? She might be bi."

CJ pursed his lips. "True, but it doesn't matter. I turned her down, even though my cock was about to burst through my pants."

Rebel scowled. "TMI, stupid. I could've gone the rest of my fucking days without hearing about your cock."

"Sorry," CJ mumbled. "I just feel…lost. Like I'm freefalling without a safety net. The most I had to worry about just eight months ago was passing Lumbly's class to stay on the team. I had Mom and Dad to talk to. I saw Harley at least once a day and talked to her all day. Rory was always around or calling me. Something changed after the Scorched Devils meeting. Then, after my birthday, a major shift happened in our lives. Everything's falling apart, Rebel."

He hung his head.

"Hey," Rebel whispered, laying her palm against his cheek. "A lot of responsibility has shifted to you and I since Momma went into the hospital, yet you don't complain, and you hold us together."

"I'm not doing anything, Reb. Lolly, Pop, and our aunts and uncles—"

"True. Aunt Fee, Uncle Stretch, and Uncle Cash are keeping Gunner. Lolly, Aunt Zoann, and Aunt Bunny call me a million times a day. Aunt Kendall had, but I haven't heard from her in a couple of days, although I think I understand why."

"What—"

"My point is, brother, our brothers and I, take our strength and inspiration from you. I swear I feel as if I've aged twenty years in two short weeks."

"Two weeks, four days, and—" He glanced at his watch— "Twenty-three hours."

Dropping her hand, she giggled. "You sound like Daddy."

He nodded. "I got it from him." Drawing her into his arms, he hugged her tightly. "Thank you, Rebel. I miss Mom and Dad—" Harley— "so much. I'm trying to hold everything together, like him, but I feel so fucking lost."

"Because you don't pray," Rule announced, directly behind them.

Rebel yelped and CJ jerked, startled by his presence. He hadn't heard his brother approach.

"Dickhead," Rebel yelled to her twin. "You scared the fuck out of me."

As a young child, Rule's hair had been as black as their father's and his eyes as green. Over time, his eyes changed to a pale green and a dark brown tinted his hair whenever he stood near light.

Now, those pale green eyes narrowed. "Your vile language crumples the blanket of protection my prayers offer."

"I'm Jesus-ed out, Rule," Rebel snarled.

"You're shameful," he said with disgust. Tears rushed to his eyes, but he swallowed. "Mom would be home by now if you helped me to pray." He glared at the tree. "It would be pretty because Dad would've gotten the decorations out and we would've had cider and egg nog and cookies that Mom prepared." He sniffled. "But you scoff at me, and ruin...you should pray."

Rebel held her glare a moment longer, before her face crumpled and her shoulders slumped. "I do, Rule. Pray, I mean. I've never...I was so scared. And...and..."

Her voice trailed off before she and Rule looked at CJ, searching for answers.

"It feels as if Mom will never come home and Dad will never be the same," he said. Not as long as she insisted on having more babies, but he kept that to himself. Resentment wouldn't help matters.

"Sometimes, I'm scared I'm dreaming," Rebel admitted, "and I'll wake up—"

"And Mom and Jo will be dead," CJ put in, because he knew that feeling all too well.

"Yes," Rebel whispered in a raw, broken voice. "I just want them home. As long as they're in the hospital—"

"If you really do pray, sister," Rule hissed, "then your lack of faith is negating your prayers. If you pray, don't worry. If you worry, don't pray."

"You are such a fucking asshole," Rebel said into the silence. "Zealotry can get you badly hurt or killed. By me," she added darkly.

"I feel most at home with my bible and art in a quiet place. I have a calling, Rebel."

"You have the fucking calling. I don't. I have long discussions with you about religion and spirituality—"

"Yet, you still behave with belligerence and a lack of

charity."

Rebel growled, her face flushing to devil red. Time for an intervention.

"Shut up. Both of you," CJ ordered. "Politics and religion are two subjects that shouldn't be discussed, especially with such strongly opposing viewpoints."

Drawing himself up, Rule palmed away his tears and backed away. More than likely, he'd return to his room and open his bible, stewing in worry and fear.

CJ wanted nothing more than to go to his own room and lick his wounds, before diving into the science project again and trying to make sense of Molly's notes. Or texting Uncle Mort to check on him. Or calling Mom, then Aunt Kendall, and check on them. Hopefully, Outlaw was still asleep. If he called Mom, he'd discover if Outlaw was awake or not.

Yet, he couldn't do any of that. Rule and Rebel were frightened.

He dug into his back pocket and got his debit card, then handed it to Rebel.

"You have an hour to buy whatever you please." His card was connected to his mother's bank account.

She snatched the card. "Gifts, right?" she said with a sigh.

"Whatever, Rebel. Gifts. Clothes and shoes for yourself. Makeup. I don't care."

"Daddy might be mad."

CJ doubted it. They could empty the bank accounts, and it wouldn't register with Outlaw. "He'll survive, but I promise you I'll take the heat for any fallout."

"Spare the rod, spoil the child," Rule said scornfully.

"Rebel isn't my child, you pompous little asshole," CJ snapped.

Rule's lips trembled.

"Fuck, I'm sorry, Rule," CJ said in frustration. "Just stop

being so prayerful tonight. It isn't helping."

"I'm always prayerful. I walk in prayer."

"You're going to fucking bleed in prayer if you keep it up," Rebel sneered.

"One more fucking word, Rebel, and I'm taking my goddamn card back. You're not helping matters either."

Throwing them a sullen look, Rebel flattened her mouth into a thin line and shoved the debit card into her pocket.

"You still have aspirations of being a priest?"

"Yeah, CJ. I have a calling."

"One dick suck from a club girl will change that."

Scowling, CJ yanked Rebel to him and placed his hand over her mouth. Pinned against him, she couldn't move. She made unintelligible sounds against his palm, but he refused to let her go until he finished with Rule.

"Can I ask why you're so set on becoming a priest?"

Rule opened his mouth, then snapped it shut. There was a reason, other than it was his calling. CJ saw it in his brother's eyes, but Rule didn't intend to reveal the truth.

"A truce? You don't harass Rebel about her praying, or lack of, and she won't disparage your spirituality."

After thinking about CJ's offer for a moment, Rule nodded. "Agreed."

"While Rebel is shopping, I'm going to the attic for decorations."

Rebel fell silent; interest lit Rule's eyes.

"We've all helped Mom prepare cookies for our tree trimmings. While I'm lugging shit to the foyer, you make the cookies, Rule. We don't have egg nog and I'm not sure if we have ingredients for the cider, but we can have milk."

A glimmer of happiness crossed Rule's face. Even Rebel relaxed against CJ.

"C-can we put the lights on outside?" Rule asked

tentatively.

"Dad uses a dedicated switch and I'm not sure its location," CJ said with regret.

Rebel jerked his hand away. "Can we spike our milk?"

"Not mine," Rule said automatically.

"Priests drink. Jesus turned water into wine," CJ pointed out.

"Wine, CJ, not hard liquor."

Rebel swept her blonde hair over a shoulder. "Just pretend He turned water into whisky."

Mouth agape, Rule drew himself up, pinned her with a hard stare, and stomped away. Instead of continuing to the staircase, he turned right and disappeared down the east hallway that would bring him to the kitchen.

"Did you have to, Reb?"

"Yep."

"I can still request my card back."

"But you won't. It'll make me cry."

"Crocodile tears."

"The best kind. Designed for guilt."

"You're incorrigible."

"I disagree. There's hope for my spoiled pettiness. For now, deal with it."

"Goddamn." Not having a response, CJ headed toward the west hallway and the back staircase that, to him, was the quickest route to the attic, though Dad disagreed. He paused and turned back to his sister. "Did you have something to tell me?"

Rebel licked her lips, glanced away, and thought for a moment. "No," she said finally, smiling at him. Her eyes were troubled. "It's not important."

"Are you sure?"

She nodded. "Positive."

CJ didn't believe her, but he was on emotional overload, so he dropped the subject.

"CJ?"

Sighing, he faced her again and lifted a brow.

"Thank you," she said, blushing. She looked so sad. "Truly. You're an amazing big brother and I'm so lucky to have you. I-I love you."

"I love you too, Rebel," he said sincerely. He grinned. "You're a fucking pain in the ass, but I wouldn't have you any other way."

Her smile was small. "She's coming back to us, isn't she? Dad's coming back to us?"

He nodded. "Yeah, sweetheart."

"I-I want to get these matching pajamas I saw for Momma, me and Jo. They're pink and frilly. Momma likes pink. Do you...do you think that'll be okay?"

Sometimes, he forgot Rebel wouldn't turn fifteen for a few more months. They'd grown up in unusual circumstances, with childhoods where they witnessed and heard a lot of adult activity. Sex, drugs, alcohol, profanity, and death. Yet, somehow they'd still been buffeted. Until these past weeks.

Just when he felt as if the last of their innocence was irrevocably destroyed, his little sister stood in front of him with tears in her eyes, ringing her hands, and shifting from foot to foot. She looked like a sweet, frightened child, and all CJ wanted to do was protect her.

"Mom will absolutely love those pajamas, Reb," he said truthfully.

"I'm going to be the best big sister in the world to Jo," she swore fiercely. "I'm going to teach her how to fight and curse and—"

CJ's laughter interrupted her, and she giggled, her expression easing.

"Can I keep your card all night? I have a recipe for spiked milk that I want to make. If I do it right, Rule won't know. If I only have an hour to shop, I can't try my recipe."

If it kept her from falling into a deep depression, she could keep his card the entire weekend. "Fine, Rebel. I expect to have money left."

She blinked. "Won't it trigger a deposit from Momma's account when the balance drops to a certain amount?"

CJ folded his arms.

"Fine!"

"By the way, fix your spiked milk, but give Rule a fucking choice. He doesn't drink. We don't need him blowing chunks."

"Good idea."

"I'll be back with a load," he said, starting off again.

"Get the ladder first, dummy," she called.

"It takes a fucking dummy to know one," he retorted.

She cackled. "Ha!"

Grinning, CJ continued down the hallway, relieved to hear his sister's brashness return.

CHAPTER 16

"Booyah!" Digger laid his four of a kind hand on the table, eliciting groans from Mortician, Boy, Mouse, Derby, and Dez.

After hours of playing amid very unfaithful luck, Digger won the all-in round, amounting to thousands of dollars that included not only the eight buy-in fees but the money they'd bet.

"One more round," Digger said, standing and making a production of sliding his stacks of chips in front of him.

"Fuck off, fool," Mortician grumbled, scowling at his empty glass. "You've taken enough of my fucking money."

He picked up his glass and tipped his head as far back as possible, hoping for a last drop of vodka.

"I'm out, too," Boy said, lifting his hand to summon one of the naked girls milling about. He was the long-time president of the Night Flyers, one of the biggest Black MCs in the area and an ally of the Death Dwellers.

The private room on the second floor of his club

resembled a mini casino with a curved bar that stocked only the best liquor, two slot machines, a roulette wheel, and two poker tables. Boy only allowed a select few to enjoy this room; the privilege always came with a hefty price tag.

A gorgeous woman with wild hair, big tits, a small waist, shaved pussy, delicious ass, and long legs stepped between Boy and Derby. She had a sandy brown complexion that glistened with vanilla-scented oil.

"Another round for the table, Pepper," Boy said, wrapping an arm around her waist.

Dez and Derby, president of the Scorched Devils and Burning Hounds respectively, stared at her. Smiling, she licked her lips.

"Hey, Dez," she cooed.

The Devil's leader flushed. He had a ruddy complexion and red hair. He was rather a soft-spoken man who sought the protection of the Dwellers. "Hey, babe."

She nodded to Derby. "How's Serina?"

Digger frowned. "She the bitch with the brother Outlaw fucked up?"

"One and the same," Derby said.

"Who her baby daddy?" Digger asked. "You or your son?"

"I'm the grandfather," Derby responded with a grin.

Boy tweaked one of Pepper's nipples. "The drinks and then cock sucks all around."

"Yes, sir," she murmured, turned on her stilettos and sailed off.

"Fuck, it's a good thing the other two motherfuckers folded and jetted," Digger said. "She'd have a lot of dicks to get off."

"She's a pro," Mouse, the Night Flyer's enforcer, said. He had a strong resemblance to Mighty Mouse, hence the road name. "I've seen her suck off ten motherfuckers."

Mortician lifted a brow at his brother. "You get your cock

sucked when you come to poker night?" he asked, shocked.

"Fuck, no! I don't cheat on Bunny. That still leaves four dicks to suck." Digger gave Mortician a sly look. "Or is it five?"

"Fuck you. Fuck off. You know I love Bailey."

"Pepper has a mouth like a suction cup," Derby offered. "A cock suck won't hurt."

"Where Gypsy?" Mort asked with sarcasm. "Sucking dick usually lead to fucking dick."

"You here for a reason, bruh," Digger said, shaking his head. "You rarely buy a seat at the poker table. The last time you came, Outlaw, Johnnie, Val, and Cash was here."

"As far as I recall, you only come when Outlaw does," Boy added as Pepper returned, carrying a tray crowded with an assortment of alcohol.

"Boy, Paco wants to know if the cards are finished?" she said, handing out the bottles.

"What do you say, fellas?" Boy asked, opening his gin and sipping. "Another round? All or nothing."

"I'm done," Mort said.

No one wanted another round, so Boy ordered everyone else but Pepper to clear out, bringing a screeching silence to the room once the background music ended and the other girls departed, laughing and rowdy. The bartender and poker dealer followed behind, leaving only Mort and the rest of them at the table.

"I know Outlaw bought in," Boy continued, "but he forfeited his money because he refuses to leave Meggie's side."

"Who's first?" Pepper asked, glancing at each of them, her gaze training on Mortician. "You, Mort? You're not a regular, so anything you want is on the house."

Mouse stood. "Come on, baby. My nuts are about to

explode, watching your ass cheeks bounce."

"Sucks are free," Boy said. "Fucks are five hundred, payable upfront."

"Goddamn, he don't even get a discount as a member?" Digger asked, opening his pint of vodka and sipping.

"It's part of the Bitch Fund," Boy answered, while Mouse dug inside his cut and came up with a handful of bills. "I was tired of Danicka bitching and complaining about the bitches I fucked. I don't like complications. I promised her I'd pay the girls every month."

"Fuck, how the fuck that make sense, bro?" Dez asked.

Mouse handed Boy six bills. "I'm a little short, but I'm good."

Boy counted the money. Recounted. And counted again. "This is $10, motherfucker," he growled.

"My bitch came over before the game, Boy," Mouse said. "She needed money for my daughter."

Derby slid five $100 bills to Boy. "I'll spot him."

Boy nodded. Mouse grabbed Pepper's hand and pulled her toward the door. Her giggles trailed behind them.

"Goddamn, that bitch is gorgeous," Digger said with a sigh. "My cock harder than a motherfucker." He smirked at Mort. "What about yours, bruh?"

Mortician would admit to nothing. As frayed as his marriage was, acknowledging his stiff dick over another woman made the situation ten times worse.

His heart hurt. For months, he'd allowed Bailey to do her own thing. He'd considered it just a phase. People grew and couples evolved. Stagnation was the death of relationships and sanity.

But Bailey allowing Harley, his pride and joy, to mock and belittle him without coming to his defense, spoke more than Mort wanted to know.

He hadn't planned to attend the game. As a general rule, he stayed in his own lane. Politicking wasn't part of his job as the enforcer. He could bullshit with the best of them. However, he didn't want to open his fucking mouth and inadvertently contradict what Outlaw might've said.

"Mort, hey, brother."

The seriousness of Digger's tone got Mort's attention.

"The demon that possessed Reb jumped into Harley. Just beat her ass, lock her in her room until she de-demonized, and be done with it."

Mort stared at his unopened bottle. "It's not that easy, Digger." Not with Bailey against him, too. "Besides, when Outlaw beat Reb, it didn't help. She straightened up when Meggie almost died."

"That was just luck," Digger said. "Meggie always almost dying from one fucking thing or another. Sooner or later, Death will win and fuck her up."

"What the fuck—"

"Digger's right, Mort," Derby said, lighting a cigarette and puffing. He held it and continued talking. "None of her fucking pregnancies have been easy, yet she keeps popping kids out her pussy. She must have a fucking death wish or she's just a stupid little cunt."

Dez choked and his eyes widened. "Outlaw killed Cole because of the names he called Meggie. Suppose this conversation gets back to him?"

"It won't," Boy declared, eyeing Mort.

It wasn't necessary to suspect Digger would betray them since he was the motherfucker who'd started this bullshit.

"It won't, if you all shut the fuck up," Mort snapped. "Meggie never did none of you motherfuckers nothing." He glared at Derby. "She don't like your bitch ass because Gypsy her friend and you constantly fuck over her, son."

"My cock, my woman," Derby gritted. "If Meggie kept her fucking trap shut, Gypsy never would've left me. How many fucking years have I fucked other sluts? How many other kids do I have that Gypsy didn't push out her cunt? Meggie got into her head and fucked my shit up."

Mort opened his mouth to defend Meggie. Not only because she was his president's old lady, but because he genuinely cared about her.

"Nothing you can say, Mort," Digger said. "One of Outlaw cardinal rules is to not involve himself in the business of other motherfuckers and their bitches. Meggie always involve herself."

"They're right, Mort," Boy added. "She causes anarchy amongst our bitches."

"Your fucking dicks the cause of the fucking anarchy," Mort said, his anger rising. Generally, he didn't allow much to bother him. If he didn't care about a motherfucker, it just wasn't worth expending energy to argue. Besides, he knew how to get his point across without a lot of fuss. But this talk bordered on fucking treason. "If you got a problem with Meggie, talk to her. I'm not fucking listening anymore."

"I thought you loved me, Mort." Digger drank more vodka. "If we go to Meggie and tell her how we really feel, Outlaw will kill us."

"Them?" Mort pointed from Boy to Derby to Dez. "Yeah, he'd fuck them up. You? He'd order me to fuck you up to prove where my loyalties lay."

He hated to think about that dark time when just such a scenario had arisen.

"Then I'm good," Digger boasted. "You'd let me go just like before."

Mort slapped the side of Digger's head. "Fuck you, motherfucker. I swore if you ever put me in that position again, I would fucking kill you. The only fucking reason you lived is because Outlaw know how much you mean to me."

"Really? You could've fooled me. He beat me half to fucking death."

"He had to," Boy said. "You went fucking AWOL."

"The club was hit hard," Derby reminded them. "And you were spotted amongst the enemies. Then, you took his boy. If he hadn't have meted out a severe punishment, one of your brothers would've."

"It also would've weakened Outlaw," Mortician said.

"Like Meggie?" Digger asked in disgust. "We haven't resolved the vulnerability of Dez's club yet. He could search for another club's help. The Gnomes, for instance."

"Although I agree with you, Digger, Dez knows better." Derby lifted a brow at Dez, satisfied when he nodded. "The Gnomes and the Dwellers have a peace agreement, but they still aren't allies. If Dez turns to them, he's fucked and so am I."

"I wish it would resolve itself sooner rather than later," Dez admitted. "Things are ramping up. I've lost two of my brothers."

He picked up his cellphone and, a few moments later, handed it to Mort. A photo showed a deader-than-dead motherfucker with his feet in stocks, and his bullet-riddled head clamped in a pillory.

"Fuck, this some Medieval type shit," Mort said, showing the photo to Digger, then giving it to Boy.

"Like the ghost of motherfucking Rack haunting us," Digger said.

"Rack?" Dez queried.

"A Freebird," Mort said quickly.

So far, Dez was loyal, but if he wasn't helped soon, desperation might change that.

"I ran across Wally, Jr., recently," Derby revealed.

Mort thought that motherfucker long-ago fucked-up. He hadn't ever met him, though Rack mentioned his son from time-to-time. Until he didn't. "No shit?"

"What he been up to?" Digger asked.

Derby shrugged. "Still a beady-eyed, slippery motherfucker. Couldn't pin him down for shit. What part of his brain alcohol didn't pickle, drugs fucking fried."

Beautiful by Christina Aguilera peeled through the room. Red was calling.

Motherfucking Johnnie.

He wished Prez was around. He'd get motherfuckers in order.

Sighing, Mort answered the call, ignoring the disappointment that he hadn't heard Bailey's ringtone: Just The Way You Are by Bruno Mars.

"M-Mort?" Red hiccupped.

"What up, baby?"

A motherfucking lot.

"J-Johnnie…" She sniffled. "He…he…he still isn't h-h-home."

He was too busy lost in motherfuckery. After he found Johnnie in Meggie's room, he'd hit up Stretch, ordering him to check the hospital cameras.

"D-do you think he's dead?" A sob escaped her. "I love him. I don't know what I'd do without him."

"He fine, Red," Mort soothed. Motherfucker deserved shoving over the railing of the stairwell. Maybe, if he fell on his fucking head, it would knock sense into him.

Johnnie refused to tell Mort why the fuck he was lurking in the shadows of the hospital. Meggie wanted to tell Outlaw. Mort didn't blame her. He wanted to tell Prez. Except he wasn't sure of the fallout. Shit was heading south without the fucking complication of having Johnnie as an open enemy if Outlaw didn't fuck him up or Outlaw being more fucked up if he fucked Johnnie up.

"You think he's dead too!" Red's voice blared through the phone. "You grunted when I asked again."

He hadn't fucking heard her. "Red—"

Her sobs tore through him, cutting out when another call came through. "Kendall, baby, calm down. Roxanne calling right now." Probably to ask where the fuck he was at. Maybe, Bailey did care about his whereabouts. She had her pride, too, and he'd walked out because he was trying to talk about them and she wanted him to understand Harley's point-of-view. "I'm going to tell her to call you."

"But—"

He disconnected the call, anxious to hear what Bailey had to say. But Roxanne had already hung up. Just as he pulled up his keypad, Tina's Proud Mary blasted.

"Hey, Roxanne," he answered, ignoring the amusement of the men at the table. "Everything okay?"

"Where the fuck you at, boy?" she demanded.

"At a poker game," he said cautiously.

Silence and then, "Things that bad that you tempting your dick around naked women, baby?"

He couldn't stand the suspense. "What did Bailey tell you?"

"Answer my fucking question, Mortician."

"Fuck, man. I'm not cheating on Bailey. You know me fucking better than that."

"If you are, I'm driving there and kicking the shit out of you. Goddamn, never mind. I have to save my strength to beat that bitch I gave birth to."

Mortician stiffened. She was talking loud enough to be overheard and the other men snickered.

"Put me on speaker."

"No."

"I'm not asking your fucking ass, boy."

"Mortician, please, just do it," Knox called in the background.

Scowling, Mort threw his phone down and pressed the appropriate button. "By the way, Roxanne, I don't appreciate you threatening Bailey. She a grown fucking woman. Don't you lay your hands on her."

"Boy?" she called, ignoring Mort.

Boy straightened. "Hello, Roxy."

"Fuck off. If you lead my son-in-law down the path of rack-and-ruin because his wife being a stupid fucking heifer, I'm hacking your fucking cock off."

"No, you aren't!" Knox barked. "That would require you touching his cock. That's cheating."

"Baby, your priorities fucked up," Roxanne retorted, "but okay. You'll have to do it."

"I'm not touching another man's cock!"

"We'll talk after, Knox. You heard me, Boy?"

"Knox is right," Boy said with amusement. "Not only would one of you have to touch it, you'd have to catch me."

"Fine, I'll shoot your cock off. Better?"

"More practical," Boy grumbled, "but definitely not better."

"Take what the fuck it is, motherfucker. As long as we know where we stand." Ice cubes clinked together. "Digger?"

Digger shifted, though he kept his mouth shut.

"I know you there, because Bunny called, wondering where the fuck you're at."

"Wait, Bunny called you, not Bailey?" Mort asked. Even he heard his disappointment. He snatched his pint, opened it, and drained half the contents. "I probably shouldn't have left.”

"I would've left that bitch, too," Roxanne said. "Bailey's lost her fucking mind."

"She protecting Harley."

"Another cow who's lost her mind," Roxanne said.

Mort sighed. "Don't be so hard on them."

"Don't be so soft on them, and I'll be as hard as I want to be on those two bitches. I get Bailey's in Mama Bear mode. If she wants to side with Harley, even if they're both wrong, that's her prerogative. She gave birth to the child. But she can't tell other motherfuckers how to feel. She can't excuse Harley's behavior toward CJ when the boy needs all our support to hold shit together. We stand together, Mortician. You need to find Nardo Grevenberg and beat the fuck out of him, then bury his fucking daddy. Stupid is trickling down to my family."

"I love you, Roxy," Derby called, chuckling.

"Fuck the fuck off, Derby," she ordered. "I don't love your ass."

"Just don't want to get on your bad side, babe," he replied."

"Not if you're ordering hits," Boy said, his eyes twinkling.

"Nardo a kid and his old man not a club enemy, Roxanne," Mort said tiredly.

"Nardo's a little motherfucker and his old man's a stupid motherfucker," she said. "You'd do the world a favor."

"It's not on these Grevenberg people, love," Knox told her. "It's on Bailey and Harley."

Roxanne grunted. Long ago, she'd drawn a line between Knox and her children, even though she'd stepped in as a maternal figure to his son after the murder of his ex-wife.

"She wanted to talk earlier tonight, Roxanne," Mort admitted, tired. Wasn't it enough that Meggie was in the hospital? Now, Kendall was inconsolable, Roxanne was on a warpath, and Bailey had deserted him. "I left. I didn't want an argument and I can't reason with her. She don't understand why I'm so hurt over her silence at Harley's words."

"Bailey don't have common sense if she don't understand how you felt at Harley's disrespect. Or how her fucking silence cosigned Harley's words."

"What the fuck they said, Mort?" Digger asked, his brows drawn together.

"Too fucking much," Roxanne inserted. "Mortician, you're a good husband and a good father. If Bailey wanted a motherfucker in a suit to go with her cushy position, she should've found a motherfucker in a suit."

She had, but Mort ran him away.

"You're the best thing that ever happened to that sadity heifer, baby. A rough rider with a lot of money to bring her down a peg and spoil the fuck out of her."

Mort snickered at her description.

"Since I ride, am I a rough rider, sweetheart?" Knox asked.

"Boy, get away," Roxanne said, sounding like a fucking girl. "You're making me blush."

"I can make you scream."

"Uh, images," Digger complained. "Please hang the fuck up. You like my momma, Roxanne. I don't want to imagine you fucking."

Boy frowned. "Jesus."

Hearing Bailey hadn't contacted Roxanne worsened Mort's mood. "On that note, call Red. She really having a bad time."

"Tomorrow," Knox said.

"Tonight," Mortician stressed.

"I'll call her," Roxanne promised, as good as her word. "I

wish I was a member of the club. I'd vote to make you vice-president. Johnnie's too fucking unstable for the position." She hung up.

"That was intense," Dez remarked. "Who is she?"

"Mort's mother-in-law," Derby volunteered, before Mort decided if he wanted to share the information. "That bitch is gorgeous. Even in her late 50s."

"Ever do something so she'll have to spank you, Mort?" Boy asked.

"Shut up, both of you," Mort ordered, ignoring the snickers, including Digger's. "Such supreme disrespect to my mama-in-law won't be tolerated." He glared at Digger, happy when the motherfucker snapped his mouth shut.

"We're not disrespecting her, Mort," Derby denied. "Fuck, I'd have her at my side quicker than I'd have some of my fucking pussy-faced brothers."

"Enough about Roxanne, bruh," Digger said. "What the fuck did Harley say to you? Tell us, then we'll tell you if you or Bailey is right."

"What the fuck difference does it make, son? Roxanne opinion not good enough?"

Derby waved his hand in disgust. "Cunts stick together, brother. She's saying all that right now because Bailey must've angered her, too. Otherwise, she'd be down your ass to forgive and forget."

"Actually, Roxanne fair-minded." Digger beat Mortician to the announcement. "Whether she mad at Bailey or not, if she think Mort right, she taking his side."

"Fuck, I wish she was my mother-in-law," Boy said.

"I met your in-laws, fool," Mortician said. They owned a wedding shop that Mortician used during his church wedding to Bailey. "They good people."

"Danicka is always right. No matter what."

"Yeah, asshole, to them," Derby pointed out. "To you, she's a fucking idiot. Gypsy never would've given me a pass to fuck whores because I set up a fucking Bitch Fund."

"Yeah, bruh, how do that shit work?" Digger asked. "Whether you giving them money or not, you still sticking your cock in other bitches."

"She gets half the cut," Boy admitted.

"You paying your bitch to look the other way when you fuck other bitches and that's fine with her?" Digger asked in astonishment.

"As long as I confine it to special occasions. Casino night, my birthday, Christmas, New Year's."

"Valentine's Day?" Digger asked.

"Definitely not! She threatened to burn my fucking house down while I slept."

They all laughed.

"Come on, Mort, confess," Digger said, once the funny moment passed.

Mort shrugged.

Derby lit another cigarette. Mort realized he hadn't paid attention to notice when the motherfucker finished the last one.

Silently, he smoked, studying Mort like a specimen under a microscope.

He tamped ashes. "Did I ever tell you about Oscar, my oldest kid?"

"How many other kids do you have, Derby?" Dez asked, eyes wide with awe. "I got two with my old lady. Both girls. We've been trying and trying for another one. Either my cum is defective or her eggs?"

"You do know there are tests for that shit, huh, bruh?" Digger asked, finishing his vodka and eyeing Mort's.

"I will break your fucking fingers if you touch my shit,

son," Mort warned.

"Fuck, that hostility uncalled for, Mort," Digger said. "But back to Derby's son. What about the motherfucker?"

"He's gay," Derby announced, shocking the fuck out of everyone. "Outlaw knows. He had a situation he seemed on the fence about, so I told him about Oscar."

Mort would bet that "situation" had to do with his sister, Ophelia, and her relationship with her motherfuckers, Cash and Stretch.

"Oscar's sexual preference never mattered to me. That's my boy, and I love him. His mother isn't as forgiving. When she found out, she called him every name under the sun. I stood there like a dumbass, instead of jumping to his defense. My silence hurt the fuck out of him. He swore I felt the same way. Otherwise, I would've stopped her or called her out or reminded her what a good son he's always been. It put the worst fucking strain on our relationship. We almost didn't recover."

Clenching his jaw, Mort nodded and glanced away. Harley believed him little more than a weak ass kisser. At any point, Bailey could've corrected her. Or, better, stopped her.

"Kids divide and conquer, Mort," Boy told him. "Even if you and Bailey disagree, in front of your children show a united front."

He'd said as much to her earlier. Bailey hadn't agreed. She wanted him to say Harley was right, period. How their daughter saw him didn't bother her because, according to Bailey, she didn't believe Harley truly felt that way. She was hurt he took CJ's side instead of hers.

The disintegration of his marriage was happening in slow degrees, yet the result would still be divorce. He didn't want that. He adored Bailey. However, it took two to make a relationship work. If Bailey had already checked out, then all was lost.

CHAPTER 17

MEGGIE

Violent shaking disturbed Meggie's sedated sleep. She forced her lids open. A blurry figure leaned over her.

"Megan?"

"Johnnie?" she whispered, sleepiness and thirstiness rasping her voice.

She closed her eyes again.

"You have to leave, sweetheart."

He sounded gentle, almost kind, like her old friend.

She struggled to comprehend, twisting and turning in the confines of the hospital bed. "I can't leave," she mumbled. "I love Christopher."

"Megan, look at me! Open your eyes."

When she didn't comply, he shook her again.

"Go away," she cried, some of the sleep clearing from her head.

Johnnie turned on the fluorescent light directly over her bed, and she blinked. The sudden brightness hurt her eyes.

"You can't stay. You know you want more children, but you're putting it all on Christopher. Remember what I told you earlier tonight? You'll be too unhappy if you can't have kids. That'll make him miserable."

Confusion fogged Meggie's brain. The words penetrated, and she shook her head, still so tired she could happily sleep for the next few hours. The incision ached; the pain, more than anything, was clearing away her fatigue.

Leaning over, Johnnie kissed her forehead, stared into her eyes, then stroked her cheek with more tenderness toward her than he'd exhibited in years. But his eyes were cold and flat, lacking humanity.

"Johnnie," she said quietly, fear sipping into her.

Images of his strangulation flashed in her mind, and she shrunk back. If he attacked her, she was too weak to fend him off. By the time a nurse checked on her, it could be too late.

This time, he blinked. His nostrils flared. "Sleep," he told her, and pulled away. A moment later, he flicked off the light and threw the room back into darkness.

When he opened the door to let himself out, light from the hallway slivered in.

Meggie sank back into sleep, relieved he left so quickly.

She wasn't sure how much time passed before the ringing of her cellphone startled her awake. Sighing, she grabbed it from where it lay beside her hip, frowning at Bailey's name.

"Hey," she answered groggily.

"Meggie?"

"Is everything okay?" She could ask herself the same thing. Hadn't Johnnie been in her room? "What time is it?"

"2:30AM."

Undoubtedly, Christopher was with Jo, so Meggie was certain Johnnie had been at her bedside. She found the remote and pressed the up arrow to raise her upper body. "Has someone been hurt?"

Of course, someone had! Why else would Bailey call Meggie at such an hour?

"It's CJ," Bailey said sharply.

Meggie gasped, and it felt as if her stomach bottomed out. "Wh-what? Does Christopher…I-I have to call my husband," she cried, tears pouring down her cheeks, her heart breaking into a thousand little pieces. She and Jo had survived, but she'd lost her beloved son. Her potato. "What happened?" she sobbed.

"Now that I have your attention, you'll understand how heartbroken I am at the pain your son is causing my daughter. At the pain your son is inflicting on my marriage. He's the reason Lucas hasn't come home tonight."

It took a moment for Meggie's grief-stricken brain to process that CJ was fine. Bailey's issue was because of Meggie's son.

"What—"

"You want to support your son. I want to support my daughter. I expect Lucas to do the same. Because CJ broke Harley's heart—there's proof by the way—my family is falling apart. Lucas sides with CJ. He's hurt because of what Harley said to him. Again, because of your son."

"What did Harley say to Mortician?" Meggie asked, still not completely recovered from thinking her son had been hurt or killed.

As Meggie listened to Bailey recount Harley's vicious words, her sleep evaporated, and her anger grew. There were so many different reasons she needed to get home. Foremost was her husband's sanity and physical well-being. He'd had to be drugged to even sleep.

They'd made progress, but while she remained in the hospital, he'd worry. Her kids needed her, too. Then, there was the Gypsy issue that she'd had to neglect after involving

Stretch.

Also, there was Johnnie to deal with.

And she didn't even want to think about the confusing call she'd received from Brooks.

There were also her business obligations. Apparently, now, she had to contend with Bailey blaming CJ for Harley's bad behavior as well as her own.

"My son was nowhere around when your daughter said those things to her daddy," Meggie started. "Furthermore, even if he had been, he didn't put those words in her mouth."

"She said them because of the pictures she received showing him and Molly Harris together."

"And? Molly's his friend. Much more so than Harley. For months, she's lied and schemed."

Bailey gasped. "How dare you!"

"How dare me? How dare you! It's the middle of the night, Bailey. You knew exactly what you were doing by frightening me half out of my mind. CJ had absolutely nothing to do with what Harley said to Mortician, or what you didn't say to him."

"What are you implying?"

"I'm not playing this game with you."

Of all the people Meggie expected nastiness from, Bailey was the most shocking. She had always been so kind, calm, and affable. But when she relocated her office and acquired associates, all with Mortician's money, she'd changed. At first, everyone attributed it to her increased workload and her higher visibility.

Slowly, accomplishments she once celebrated with her family and the club moved to expensive dinners in exclusive restaurants. She still participated in the family gatherings and remained a regular fixture at the club. Yet, she was different.

More than once, Meggie had to order a few gossiping old ladies to keep speculations to themselves when she'd overheard them talking about the possibility that Bailey was cheating.

"What do you intend to do about your son?"

"Not a thing, Bailey. My son is almost seventeen years old. Harley's too young and immature for him. They are at different stages in their lives."

"I'll forget you said that. My daughter is a very intelligent, mature young lady."

"Don't bother forgetting," Meggie retorted, fed up and in pain. "I want you to remember since I intend to tell CJ to stay away from your daughter."

"Don't you dare!" Bailey fumed. "That would crush Harley."

"Your daughter, your concern. CJ is my son, who you unfairly pin blame on for something that's your fault. You should never have allowed Harley to speak to her—"

"Stop right there, Meggie, before our friendship is damaged because you malign my baby girl."

"You're right, Bailey," Meggie agreed. They had been friends for years. "I urge you to remember that sentiment before you open your mouth and say anything about CJ."

"He promised he'd be there for Harley. He'd wait until she was ready to go steady. He promised, Meggie. She's a young girl with stars in her eyes and CJ has crushed her soul. No one understands that. I tried talking to Lucas before he left. He refused to hear what I was saying. It broke my heart, too. Now, he hasn't come home."

"He went to the poker game at the Night Flyers," Meggie said, attempting to ease Bailey's fear.

When Bunny called earlier, she'd told Meggie both Mort and Digger went. Christopher had also planned to go. She wished he had to take a break from his fear and worry. "Those games go well into the morning."

"I don't care anymore. He took your son's side and walked out, leaving me in tears. CJ visited Harley and left her in tears. They don't deserve us."

"Why'd you call me again?" They were getting nowhere. "You must be mad if you think I'll allow you to malign my son. The best thing you, me, Mortician, and Christopher can do is back off and let CJ and Harley work this out. We shouldn't allow their childish drama to affect our friendships or our marriages."

"I'm the psychologist, Meggie, not you."

"Then act like you have a psychology degree, Bailey."

"I do. I understand how important it is to not only believe my daughter but protect and defend her. She is a minor and still developing."

"What happened to her maturity?" Meggie asked peevishly.

Bailey ignored her. "I understand the importance of a father's support. Lucas's behavior will have a lasting effect on Harley's self-esteem. He has chosen to side with CJ—"

"From what you told me, neither of you gave Mortician the chance to take anyone's side before Harley called him a stupid butt kisser."

"She would never! I resent you putting such ugly words in my daughter's mouth, Meggie."

"I don't care what you resent, Bailey. Hang up and go over the conversation, then you decide what your daughter said to your husband. As for the rest of it, I will talk to CJ—"

"Don't you dare bar him from seeing Harley."

"I dare anything I please with my son. The only reason I won't is because of CJ. Not you and certainly not Harley. Take her side, Bailey. You're her mother. I expect no less.

But what you won't do is blame my son for the state of your marriage. Look in the mirror to find the person at fault. Now, anything else?"

"I don't even know why I tried with you." Tears thickened Bailey's voice. "You're raising a spoiled, arrogant cheater. I never thought I'd see the day when CJ has so thoroughly disappointed me and hurt Harley. He's hurt me too by driving a wedge between Lucas and me."

"Are you through?"

"What else can I say? You refuse to help me."

"You'd need to remove your blinders for my help to work. First? CJ is also a minor and still developing. No matter what Christopher and I were going through, I'd never pin the failings of my marriage on him. I'm warning you for the last time back off my son."

"Or what?"

Meggie wasn't sure. Bailey had been an integral part of the club for so long. Until recently, she was a close friend. Not only that, but she was also the wife of Christopher's best friend and Roxy's daughter. It was such a complicated situation.

If Harley calmed down a little, Meggie was certain Bailey would settle. She'd see the problems in her own marriage and save it before it was too late. If she still wanted to be married, that was. Meggie found it telling that Bailey wasn't expressing worry about Mortician's safety or concern that he might have fallen into the arms of another woman.

Of course, it could be because Bailey trusted her husband as implicitly as Meggie did Christopher. But Mortician didn't usually go to the poker games. As far as she knew, he hadn't been a scheduled participant at the table when Christopher sent in his fee, so it must've been a last-minute invite to replace her husband's vacant seat.

Under ordinary circumstances, Mortician never would've gone.

"You can't think of anything, right, Meggie?"

"Why don't you test me and find out, Bailey?"

Bailey hung up.

Groaning, Meggie sank deeper into the uncomfortable bed and closed her eyes. She willed sleep to overtake her again, but she knew it wouldn't, not with so many emotions running through her.

Bailey's charges against CJ infuriated Meggie, but she was also concerned about Mortician. She wasn't sure who else was at the poker table, though she knew Digger was supposed to go, too.

She sighed. She also needed Mortician's advice on Brooks.

It was time for her to check herself out. There was no getting around it.

Since she wouldn't get back to sleep anytime soon and Christopher wasn't expected to return to the room for several hours, Meggie dialed Mortician's number.

CHRISTOPHER

Jo had reached a milestone, and Christopher needed a smoke.

His newest girl's gestational age was 28 weeks old. Since she'd been born a little over two weeks ago, far earlier than her due date, her milestones were measured as if she remained inside her ma.

She was still so tiny, but she was finally over 1000 grams. She was 2.30 pounds and just under fourteen inches.

Axel had been a micro preemie too, born at 25 weeks and Megan had been deathly ill as well. There'd been so much other shit going on that dark day. No, for fucking weeks.

Sometimes, he still thought about Johnnie's gut-wrenching screams when Roxanne called and told him Kendall overdosed and might not survive. Christopher had been on the way to drive him to the parking lot, then CJ came in and said Megan hadn't gotten home. A few minutes later, his girl arrived. They'd argued and she'd collapsed.

She hadn't looked well and it still came as a shock. This time...

This fucking time...

Jesus, how could he ever breathe easy again?

Jo moved, drawing Christopher's attention back to the tiny child. She would be fine. He'd remind CJ to call her Squiggles like he'd intended and Jo would continue to grow stronger.

When Megan recovered completely, she'd be so fucking happy and relieved. He was, too. He just needed one motherfucking nicotine hit. But he didn't want to smell like smoke when he came into NICU and held his baby girl. Despite the amount of time he spent in the rocking chair near her incubator, Christopher was only allowed to hold her a few minutes each day. Her temperature or blood pressure destabilizing suspended that privilege. It also frightened the fuck out of him. He only gave Megan good reports. She needed to recover and he'd minimize any threat to that.

"Mr. Caldwell?" Torie's voice broke into his contemplation. When Jo first arrived, the head nurse was on the day shift. Last week, she'd rotated to night duty. She was a gorgeous woman with caramel skin, brown eyes, and a sharp wit. She smiled at him. "How are you?"

He scrubbed a hand over his face, exhausted. He shrugged. "Waitin' for Megan to be well enough to leave."

"I understand." She scanned her badge, then the tag on Jo's incubator before sliding the top back and scanning the baby's foot band. Jo still had so many tubes and wires. "The good news is we are steadily decreasing the amount of humidity and Jo is responding."

Christopher nodded. Torie checked the baby as she, or whichever nurse was available, did every several hours. They were very proficient at their jobs, especially Torie. He'd see to it she received a substantial raise. Once she finished, she closed the transparent lid and turned to him.

"Would you like a cup of coffee?"

"A smoke would work fuckin' wonders for my ass, babe."

Giggling, she lowered her lashes. "If you want to sneak away and have a ciggy, I won't tell. You deserve it. A devoted dad like you should have a little pleasure in his life."

He smiled, staring at Jo. The past few days had shattered him, leaving him lost and anchorless. Though he spent time with his children every day and made himself available to them, Megan was always the primary caregiver. The only child he'd named was Axel. Even then, he followed her lead. But with Jo, he spent hours each day with her. He was the first to hold her. The first to talk to her. The first to celebrate her stabilization.

Torie placed a hand on his shoulder, and he glanced up at her. "She's improving every day."

He thought she meant Megan, until she elaborated.

"She may need glasses, but tests are showing she doesn't have brain damage or heart defects."

"I know." He sighed, his head pounding. "Megan'll be so relieved."

"I'm sure she will." Torie hadn't removed her hand. "I promise I won't tell her if you sneak a cigarette."

"Thanks for the offer, babe, but Megan not like that."

Her smile widened and she met his gaze. "It's the least I can do. You lent me gas money."

"Don't look like I lent the motherfucker to you, Torie," he said with amusement. "You ain't repayed me."

"I will!" she swore.

"Forget it. It was only $20."

"Are you sure?"

"Positive." Twenty fucking dollars wouldn't make or break him.

Suddenly, she dropped her hand and twirled. "Do you like my scrubs?"

He lifted a brow.

"You complimented my Minnie Mouse scrubs," she reminded him.

He'd only noticed because Megan always liked Mickey Mouse's woman.

Torie thrust her tits out, almost in his face. "When I saw Rudolph and Santa, I thought of you." She stepped back, turned out, then posed, poking her curvy ass toward him.

His cock stirred and he recoiled, jumping to his feet.

Until that moment, he'd missed all Torie's cues. Fuck, he might've even accidentally encouraged her flirting. He didn't know, couldn't even remember most of their interactions outside of their discussions about Jo and the concern Torie showed her and him.

Usually, he kept his guard up. He wanted a clear boundary

of where he stood. "I love my wife," he said, so Torie would mistake nothing else. "Megan the most important thing in the world to me."

"But—"

"I ain't…I didn't mean to make you think I was open to something on the side."

Her gaze lowered to his erection, and he gritted his teeth.

"I'm a fuckin' man, babe, not a monk. Ain't nothin' I want from another woman."

"I look forward to seeing you," she admitted. "You make me laugh. I've been divorced for six months and I thought I never wanted another man. You take time to listen to me. You complimented my scrubs."

"Megan taught me how to be a good husband," he told her quietly. "She taught me how to be a good father."

Torie smiled, but when he didn't offer one in return, it faded. "You seem like such a man's man. It is hard to believe you'd allow a woman to teach you anything. I tried teaching Cleotis. It led to more hostility. A part of me believed you visited so regularly and stayed so long to see me."

"It was. You take time explainin' shit to me and reassurin' me about Jo."

Her face crumpled and her shoulders sagged. In the stillness of the early morning, Jo's machines and monitors broke the silence. At first, the sounds tortured Christopher. He didn't know if they'd suddenly stop because she'd faded away. In the first forty-eight hours after the emergency, he'd almost lost his mind because when he was with Megan, he was doubly scared.

If he lost Jo, he'd grieve. If he lost Megan, he'd die.

"I'm here cuz Megan can't be, Torie. I'm in the hospital because Megan can't leave. It's all her."

"And your daughter?"

"Megan expect me to be a good father. If she asked me for the moon, I'm gonna find a way to get it for her."

"You seem so alone."

"Not alone. Broken. Until my wife's better and at home, half of me missing."

Licking her lips, she nodded. "That's a beautiful sentiment."

"It's how the fuck I feel. Megan—"

Butterfly Kisses started, Rebel's ringtone. Jo jerked, so Christopher didn't waste time answering his phone.

"Daddy?"

She sounded wide the fuck awake.

He turned from Torie and walked to the window, staring at the deserted hallway. "You can't sleep, baby?"

"I have something to tell you."

Not liking her ominous tone, Christopher straightened. "Talk."

"Have you talked to Uncle Mort?"

A couple of times since the motherfucker helped drug him. "Why?" There was a fucking reason she asked that question.

"It's a yes or no question, Daddy," she said with impatience.

"I know exactly what the fuck it is, Rebel. Until you tell my ass why the fuck you want to know if I talked to Mort, I ain't answerin'."

She sniffed.

"It's after two in the fuckin' mornin', baby. I don't feel like playin' twenty fuckin' questions."

"Sorry."

"It's okay—"

"I'm not apologizing for the reason you think I am. I'm apologizing because I have another question. No, at least two more."

"Reb—"

"How old do I have to be to kill one of my uncles?"

"What the fuck you asked…you wanna kill Mort?"

"Nope. I love Uncle Mort. I want to kill Uncle Johnnie. I need you permission."

Christopher squinted, a buzzing starting in his head. Rebel's question coinciding with Megan's sudden insistence that Johnnie was creeping around wasn't a fucking accident.

"You ain't got the motherfucker, Rebel," he snapped. He wouldn't allow his girl to murder a motherfucker that Christopher needed to fuck up. "He's your uncle and an adult."

"He's a fuckhead, Daddy. Your sons might buy into the bullshit that all adults need respect. I don't. If a motherfucker doesn't respect me, then fuck them."

He was too exhausted to chastise her.

"Is there a back stairwell at the hospital?"

Christopher snapped his brows together.

"There is, huh? Never mind. Your shocked silence tells all. In case you aren't aware, Uncle Johnnie stormed out of his house. Aunt Kendall is a wreck."

"CJ mentioned Johnnie left."

"You're lucky CJ isn't me because that motherfucker would be dead."

Christopher was trying to put together what Rebel was telling him. Because it sounded as if… "Johnnie comes in the hospital through the private stairwell? And Mort know?"

"He's hiding out in the private stairwell, and Uncle Mort isn't really sure. He just found that sack of shit in Momma's room and threatened to fuck him up. We were more focused on you resting."

"If Mort not sure where Johnnie at, how the fuck you know?" Christopher demanded.

He wished he had his head on straight. Sometimes, he missed the drama and excitement of the club. However, such a life risked Megan more than anyone else. On the one hand, it was good motherfuckers knew who the most important person in his life was. It kept his children safe. On the other hand, she was the go-to fucking target.

His instincts felt rusty. Perhaps, it was just stress and fatigue. More than likely, though, he'd never be the same prez he once was.

"Rebel?"

"There are cameras," she admitted with a sigh.

"Stretch givin' you reconnaissance information?"

She hesitated.

"Fuck, Reb. You ain't hackin' shit, are you?" She wasn't as good as Mattie, but his girl was still bad ass at her hacking abilities.

"I'm worried about Momma. CJ and Uncle Mort don't want to stress you out more. I needed concrete proof before I came to you. When you leave Momma's room, Uncle Johnnie goes in within five or ten minutes, depending on if a nurse or doctor is with her. I bet he's using the camera to monitor the situation. By the way, Momma's room should be directly across from the nurse's station or a couple of the guys should be stationed outside her door or both."

Christopher walked out of the nursery, without reminding the baby he'd return soon. He stormed down the hallway, ignoring Potter, Slipper, Orange, Bishop, Hunt, Huck, Billy, Eric, and Pike when they all jumped to their feet.

"Hold on, Reb. Slipper, I'm going to call Stretch and have him do a sweep of the building. Take Orange and do a walkthrough of all the stairwells. Potter, Billy, Huck and Eric, guard all the entrances and exits to the floor. Pike, don't let a motherfucker pass these fuckin' doors if they ain't got the proper credentials. Bishop and Hunt, come the fuck with me."

He punched in the code and the double doors swung open.

"Stand outside Megan's door," he ordered as he passed the room, stalking toward the private access door, intended for club use during extreme emergencies to evade capture. He punched in his pin and shoved through the doors.

Johnnie startled awake.

Christopher barely registered drawing his SIG at the same time Johnnie pulled his G20. Their gazes met and clashed. His hesitation might've gotten him killed had he faced off with any other motherfucker. In the time it took Christopher to assess the threat, Johnnie lowered his gun, set it on the floor, and stood.

Drawing in a deep breath, Christopher shoved his .9mm back into his cut.

"I can explain, Christopher."

Rebel snorted, the sound loud in his ear.

"Ain't interested in your explanations, Johnnie. You fuckin' with Megan."

He stiffened. "I am not! She must be hallucinating. She—"

Growling, Christopher punched the motherfucker in the eye and he crashed against the wall. If it had been a different angle, he would've tumbled over the railing.

"Christopher—"

Not wanting to hear Johnnie right now, Christopher snatched a handful of the motherfucker's T-shirt and slammed him. His head banged the concrete, knocking the motherfucker the fuck out.

"I'm going check on your ma, baby," he told Rebel because he hadn't hung up and he was certain she hadn't.

"Okay, Daddy," she said. "Don't forget to get some sleep. I

love you."
    "I love you, too, Reb."

CHAPTER 18

MORTICIAN

It wasn't unusual for one of their women after the other to call Mort in a matter of hours. He was their sounding board, although he was closest to Red and Meggie. Yet, she hadn't called in days because she'd been so ill, so when *Run the World (Girls)* started, it startled him.

"Meggie girl, you okay?"

"I need to talk to you," she said tiredly.

Mort sat the phone on the table and put her on speakerphone. He needed to drink. He couldn't handle one more problem. From the tone of her voice, he knew she'd hit him with another one.

"Where Prez?" he said, after taking a healthy sip from his pint.

"With Jo."

"What up, Meggie?"

"First, I want a hysterectomy. I'm tired of having babies."

Derby lifted a brow at him.

Mort didn't have the energy to pick up his phone. "That's not up to me, baby," he said gently. "Talk to Prez."

"He said he wants what I want, though he told me he doesn't want more children. It'll risk my health."

She went silent; Mort waited.

"Does he want more children? Despite what Christopher told me, Johnnie swears otherwise."

Mort squeezed the bridge of his nose. "Meggie, don't let that stupid motherfucker get in your head," he snarled, harsher than he'd ever spoken to her. "You love Outlaw. Johnnie got nothing to fucking say."

"He's his brother."

"He's a fucking moron. Kendall half out of her mind because he's disappeared. I'm keeping it to myself that motherfucker in the private stairwell because Outlaw not Outlaw. You know why? Because he worried about you, Meggie. If you want a hysterectomy, what the fuck is the problem? Fuck Prez. Fuck Johnnie. They don't have to stress their bodies and carry the fucking babies."

When she sniffled, Mort realized how he'd endangered his life by yelling and speaking to her as he did. He emptied his bottle.

"How long Prez going to be gone?" he asked.

Tears greeted his question.

"Fuck. Meggie, don't cry."

"I just want Johnnie to leave me alone, Mortician. You asked me not to tell Christopher. Johnnie's ordered me not to. I'm just so tired."

"Me, too, Meggie," Mort said softly. In more ways than one. "But I'm going to get that motherfucker to leave. All this shit got to be addressed, baby. First, you got to get well and get your head on straight. It's the only way Prez can be Prez."

"I know. Johnnie keeps saying Christopher wants more

kids. Tonight, he told me deep down I want more too, and I'm selfish not to recognize that. He's gaslighting me."

"I'll get him to stop," he swore. "We need you well. We don't need you stressed."

"How are you?" she asked, sounding as sad and lost as Kendall but for a different reason, though it was because of the same motherfucker. "Bailey called me. She actually woke me up. She's blaming CJ for the argument you had with her and Harley."

Mort winced. "I'm sorry, Meggie. That was uncalled for."

"Whatever it was is debatable. What isn't is the blame she's placing on my son for Harley calling you Uncle Toady and not a real gangster because you've never been locked up."

At the sudden shock swirling around the table, Mort had never felt so humiliated. Though he and Bailey rarely had serious arguments, he kept shit to himself when they did.

"CJ was nowhere, not even near your house, when those words came out of Harley's mouth."

"Meggie—"

She sniffled. "Don't Meggie me, Mortician. Johnnie creeps in and out of my room just when Christopher leaves. Ryder, Ransom, and Axel are out of control. Christopher is a zombie. Kendall is hysterical. CJ hasn't been to school in days. I refuse, refuse, to add Harley's bad behavior and Bailey's acceptance of it, to that list."

"Not much you can do from a hospital bed, girl."

Digger's words revealed Mort had Meggie on speakerphone.

"I can tell Christopher Bailey called me in the middle of the night because your brother isn't home," she said evenly. "Not to mention her making me believe CJ had died!"

Digger swallowed, while Mort was shocked into silence.

No one wanted Outlaw involved. True, he wasn't himself and might not do a fucking thing at the moment. When shit returned to normal though?

"Meggie, don't disturb Prez with this," Mort said, glaring at his big-mouthed brother.

"Tomorrow, I'm telling my doctor I want to be released," Meggie announced, not revealing whether she'd keep shit to herself. "I'll be away from Johnnie in my own house, and we can get some normalcy back."

"Don't leave the hospital before it's time," Mortician said. "It won't help if you relapse and end up back there."

"Yeah, girl, that'll fuck Outlaw up more than this shit already did," Digger told her.

Mortician scowled at his brother, wanting him to shut the fuck up. His commentary wasn't helping.

"Everything is stable," she said. "I can continue healing from the surgery at home."

"Stay in the fucking hospital, Meggie," Digger said harshly. "You've fucked Prez up enough. He never been the same since you got kidnapped."

"As if that was my fault," she said.

"Wasn't it? You so fucking busy. If you hadn't wanted that fucking Valentine's Day Ball, your ass wouldn't have got taken by Mystic and thrown in the fucking hole. At one time, my prez would've told any motherfucker that didn't agree with what he wanted to do to fuck off. Now, he all about goddamn peace. He don't even fucking fight when Johnnie open his fucking mouth and put it to the vote."

"Digger, if you don't shut the fuck up, I'm not saying anything if Meggie tell Prez what the fuck you're saying," Mortician warned. He hated that almost everything was the truth. Still, Meggie was dealing with enough and Digger didn't have the best delivery.

"Don't have nothing to say to that, huh, Meggie?" Digger spat.

Mortician wanted to wipe away Derby's smugness.

"Are you finished?" Meggie asked dismally.

"Does it matter? Prez still fucked up in the head," Digger said crossly. "He half-assing at the club, leaving the Scorched Devils hanging in the balance."

"What do you want me to do?"

"Get better," Digger replied. "Stay better. Don't get fucking kidnapped."

"That was almost eleven years ago, Digger—"

"And yet it fucking haunts him to this motherfucking day, Meggie. Now we have to add another pregnancy where you just fucking collapsed. I thought you had the fucking sense to not get pregnant after what happened with Axel. Tell Prez to stay off you if you can't remember your fucking birth control."

"Why don't you tell him?" she asked. "Let's see how that works out for you, then we can talk."

Digger glowered. "Very fucking funny. I wouldn't be alive to talk."

"It must not matter to you since you have more than enough to say to me now. I can't make a baby on my own—"

"Exactly my fucking point, girl."

"Tell it to Christopher. Buy condoms for him."

"You out your motherfucking mind? It's not my business to tell that man to cover his cock."

"Finally, we agree. None of it is your business. But if you want to make it so, call Christopher and tell him exactly what you told me. Word for word."

Frowning, Digger went still. "I thought you liked me."

"I can say the same thing. I thought you liked me."

"I do. I'm just frustrated—"

"Shut up, Johnnie Jr. If you liked me, you'd talk to me like we both have sense."

"Did you just call me fucking Johnnie?"

"I'm done with you, Digger. Mortician, I'll call you—"

"Running away from the conversation." Digger snorted. "It figures."

"There's nothing I want to say to you," she replied. "Your mind is made up, no matter what I say. Just as mine is. Nothing more can be done for me in the hospital for the time being. Jordan will discuss my options whenever I make an after-stay appointment. My doctors can prescribe pain meds and sedatives for at-home use."

Now that he thought about it, Mortician understood why Meggie was so fucked up over Johnnie's gaslighting. She was still healing, medicated, and worried about her newborn, her husband, and her other kids. Johnnie fucking loved to pounce on vulnerability.

"I'm sorry I snapped at you," Mortician said at the sound of more sniffles. He intended to punch the fuck out of Digger for hurting her feelings. "As for Bailey and Harley, they love you and CJ. They're just going through it."

"They can go through whatever they wish, but they aren't targeting my son. I'm sorry if he has lied to Harley and hurt her. I promise I'll talk to him. My issue is the blame Bailey's placing on him for your absence. And, may I add, it's her fault. She should've stopped Harley immediately."

"Maybe she agree with her," Mort said with a careless shrug, fronting like a motherfucker. It crushed him to even think that, though he couldn't unthink it since that conversation.

"If she does, then shame on her," Meggie said flatly. "You aren't measurable by your bank account, but apparently she's only happy with appearances."

Very little turned Meggie into a harsh critic. Fucking with Outlaw and disparaging her children were amongst the few.

She was his president's woman and he'd taken his life in his hands enough tonight, so he let her rant and shut the fuck up.

"Maybe, she should've found a man like Johnnie: suit by day, biker by night, and idiot all the time," she fumed.

"I love Bailey, Meggie, so don't tell me we would've been better off without each other." Her words hit a nerve because Roxanne made a similar observation. Maybe, Bailey would've been happier with Finley, or whatever the fuck the little motherfucker's name was.

He would've fit her high-end office and polished image.

Meggie sighed. "I'm sorry," she said, the fight leaving her. "I'm just exhausted. Johnnie is…is volatile. He could come in and strangle me. Christopher would walk in and find my body and then his life would be destroyed."

"Stop with the melodrama," Derby growled.

If only it was melodrama, but once Johnnie had almost strangled Meggie.

"Johnnie would never do something so idiotic," Derby finished.

"Derby?"

"Hello, Meggie."

"Mortician, what are you doing with him?"

Derby glowered at the phone.

"He's at my poker table," Boy said dryly.

"Who else is at the table, listening to my private conversation?" Meggie demanded.

"Dez," Derby answered, smirking.

"Hello, Meggie," Dez said, adopting the same condescension as Derby.

"Hello, Dez." Meggie ignored the motherfucker's tone and

drew in an audible breath. "Mortician, are you okay?"

No. "What do you want me to say, Meggie girl?"

"That's my answer," she said with a sigh. "Are you going home tonight?"

"I don't have anywhere else to go, unless I decide to camp here."

"I do believe there are six houses besides yours that you could sleep at," she replied.

"Don't volunteer my house, girl," Digger said, shaking his head.

"He's your brother," Meggie retorted. "If you don't want to go home, go to the clubhouse, Mortician. I'll hang up and call Christopher to tell him you need a room at the club, so he can let Potter know in case one of the bigger rooms is occupied. It'll be vacated by the time you arrive."

"Maybe, you right," he conceded, at loose ends. Bailey or Harley seeing him in such a disparaging light would've been bad enough. Knowing both felt that way…

"Mortician, listen to me," Meggie said into the silence. "I can't make the decision for you. Returning to the club or your house is up to you. When my marriage was on shaky ground, you advised me. I'm returning the favor. You're vulnerable right now. You're a fine, upstanding man, but hurt and anger can make us do stupid things. You don't want to threaten your marriage by a moment of weakness. I'm sure there are a bunch of beautiful, naked women at your beck and call."

"Outlaw opens his fucking mouth to much," Derby said with disgust.

"Call him and tell him, Derby," Meggie ordered, then returned to her pep talk without missing a beat. "You could accidentally cheat, Mort."

Mortician grinned. "How the fuck that work?"

"If you drink too much and go to a room, a girl might come in and you have sex with her while you're under the influence."

"You do know even Rebel call fucking fucking, right, Meggie?" Digger called.

"Man, shut the fuck up," Mortician commanded.

"As a matter of fact, I do, Digger," Meggie said. "I don't care if you're frustrated, back off right now. We can talk when I get home."

"What the fuck, baby?"

Every motherfucker at the table straightened at Outlaw's question.

"I left and you was sleepin' like a motherfucker. Now, you talkin' to…?"

"Mortician," she supplied, because of course she did.

"Mort?"

"Yes, Christopher. Wait—"

"You like livin', motherfucker? Why you keepin' my woman up?"

"Christopher!"

"Ain't givin' you this fuckin' phone back, baby. Answer me, Mort…ouch! Why the fuck you dug your fuckin' nails in my fuckin' arm?"

"I called Mortician, Christopher."

"And he fuckin' answered at almost three in the fuckin' mornin' when he know he keepin' you up?"

"You're a psycho," she yelled. "You'd be angry if he didn't answer. Now, you're angry because he's keeping me awake when I called him?"

"What the fuck she want with you, Mort?"

"Christopher—"

"Hold on, baby. Ain't talkin' to you. I got to see what type of offense this is."

"The kind that'll get you locked out if you don't give me my phone."

"Can't fuck you anyway, Megan, so I'm already locked out your pussy."

She huffed. "I thought you were with Jo."

"I came to check on you. You keep fuckin' insistin' Johnnie around."

"What, er…?"

"See, Mort? Know what my ass thinkin'? Megan fuckin' callin' you cuz of that knocked out motherfucker. When you should've told me, instead of Rebel."

Meggie's groan matched Mortician's.

"Did you kill Johnnie?"

Mortician blinked at the note in Meggie's voice.

"I can, Megan. You soundin' kinda hopeful. Here, baby, talk to Mort while I go shoot Johnnie in the head."

"What?" Meggie cried.

All Mort could do was swallow. Prez was so fucking serious.

"Wait, wait, wait!"

Alarms started beeping. Her pulse and blood pressure must've skyrocketed.

"I didn't mean it, Christopher," she sobbed.

"Calm down, baby. He won't feel no pain."

"Prez, Meggie didn't call me because of Johnnie," Mortician said quickly. "It was because Bailey called her."

"Johnnie been hauntin' the fuckin' stairwell, makin' me think my woman hallucinatin' and she ain't called you over that motherfucker?"

"Everything okay in here?" an authoritative female voice said.

"Get the fuck outta here, nurse bitch," Outlaw ordered, sounding frighteningly like his old self.

"But—"

"I'm fine," Meggie swore.

"I'll check in five minutes," the woman said.

"Make it ten," Outlaw ordered.

"Can you lower my bedrails?" Meggie asked, so frantic Mort felt for her.

"You were sedated," the nurse answered.

"I'm not anymore," Meggie said impatiently. "Please?"

"There! I'll return in ten minutes."

"I don't want Johnnie to die," Meggie said a moment later. Presumably, the nurse was gone. "Think of Kendall and his children."

"Kendall not a psycho cunt no more, so we'll make sure she's okay."

"Christopher—"

"Club business, baby."

"It isn't. This is personal."

"Nope, the motherfucker used the stairwell without authorization. If there's no threat, we don't fuckin' use it and give that escape route away. It's club business."

"But he was in the stairwell to see me!"

"Megan, baby, if you trying to save that motherfucker life, you kinda makin' me want to put my hollows in and empty my clip into his fuckin' head."

Derby tugged at the neckline of his shirt; Digger looked morbidly ill all of a sudden. Even Dez shifted and sweat beaded Boy's brow.

Fuck, if Mort wouldn't be accused of disrespect, he'd hang up. But until Meggie or Prez ended the call, he couldn't.

"Save your energy for club business," Meggie begged. "If you kill Johnnie, it'll traumatize everyone."

"Club...who the fuck you been talkin' to?"

"N-no one."

She couldn't lie to save her own life. Another motherfucker was plain fucked.

"I'm countin' to three, Megan. If you don't start talkin', Ima start shootin' the first motherfucker on my list."

"Who's on your list?"

"Johnnie, Mort, Digger, Derby, Nardo Grevenberg and his fuckhead old man…"

Mort, Digger, and Derby exchanged glances.

Meggie cleared her throat. "Nardo is under eighteen."

"Don't give a fuck. He the stupid motherfucker quotin' a stupider motherfucker, and fuckin' with Mort's girl."

"Erm, if-if…how would it matter if you k-kill Mortician, Christopher?"

"He could rest in peace."

"Oh. Why do you want to kill Mort, Digger, and Derby again?"

"For fuckin' with you."

"I called Mortician, so he hasn't done anything wrong. Neither has Digger or Derby."

"You don't even like fuckin' Derby, yet you tryin' to save his fuckin' life again when he disrespected you."

"But—"

"I fuckin' heard you tell him to take whatever the fuck up with me. I also fuckin' heard you tell Digger to back off and you ain't fuckin' carin' if he frustrated."

Of course, Prez had been listening to get as much information as possible before he walked into Meggie's room and demanded answers.

"What did Mort do?" she asked after a moment.

"Answered your fuckin' call, then put you on speakerphone so your fuckin' private conversation overheard."

"What makes you think—"

'Cause Prez wasn't fucking stupid.

"Take me for a lot of fuckin' things, Megan, but I ain't a fuckin' dumbass," he snapped. "The only fuckin' way those two motherfuckers talkin' to you is because they heard what you said. They only reason you respond to them is because you talkin' to all them at once. Motherfuckers sure not passin' that fuckin' phone around so they can talk to you one by one."

"Mortician is more of a brother to you than Johnnie. Digger is Mort's brother. And Derby is one of your closest friends," she said quietly.

"A club rule is not fuckin' up bitches. I fucked up several of them cuz of you. You think I'm gonna let anyfuckinthing else stand in my way? If a motherfucker, or fuckin' bitch, fuck with you, they fuckin' die. Case fuckin' closed."

"You'd go to jail. You'd do that to us?"

"Only been to jail once when Brooks fucked me over. I'll just dissolve the motherfuckers in acid, then incinerate what's left at the funeral home to get rid of all evidence."

"Talk him down, Meggie," Digger whispered, truly afraid. He'd fucked up royally. "Please."

"Wouldn't that be dangerous?" she asked, obviously talking to Prez since neither seemed to have heard Digger. "Mixing acid and fire?"

"You right, baby. I'll incapacitate them, then toss them in the oven."

Digger steepled his hands over his mouth and nose.

"You'd break Gypsy's heart."

"She not even with Derby right now."

"She wants to go back to him."

The hope in Derby's eyes surprised Mortician. Maybe, he really did care for Gypsy.

"If you kill him, she won't be able to do that."

Prez cursed. "She need to make up her fuckin' mind, Megan. All the fuck she do, goin' back and forth, is fuck both of them up, and their kids."

"She found out the baby isn't his."

"What fuckin' baby?"

"Serina's."

"Who the fuck Serina?"

"Er, C-Cole's sister."

A moment of silence, then, "oh, that cunt. I just added fuckin' Dez to the list. He was in on those naked cunts with Derby."

Dez choked.

Outlaw sounded too focused on Meggie to notice. "How the fuck you know who that bitch's baby belong to?"

"I just do, Christopher. Gypsy has been so unhappy. She wants to go back, but Serina has been so mean to her. I hate that Derby cheats on her. However, I convinced her to leave because of Serina. She was awful. She told Gypsy that Derby never stopped cheating..."

"Why you didn't tell me, so I could tell Derby?"

"Serina was still pregnant."

"Unless that bitch a fuckin' elephant, she should've popped her kid out months ago."

Meggie giggled. "She did."

"So how you found out and when you found out?"

"Stretch helped me," she mumbled. "And a week before Thanksgiving."

"You had the club fuckin' treasurer hack medical records, huh, baby?"

"DNA results."

Derby grinned.

"So, let me get this fuckin' straight? You been hatin' on Derby for years because you know he a cheatin' motherfucker? Nod if I'm right."

"You're right."

"You know what the fuck nod mean?"

She sniffed.

"Gypsy been back and forth with the motherfucker for years."

"Mostly back, though."

"You convinced her to leave because that bitch was knocked up and she didn't know who the father was."

"Yes."

"Gypsy gone, and you decided to recruit one of my officers to get information so Gypsy could go back?"

"Yep."

"You not makin' no fuckin' sense, Megan. Furtherfuckinmore, Stretch should've asked me."

"I forbade him to," Meggie admitted.

"You not a motherfuckin' club member, baby. Advisin' Gypsy bitch shit. Recruitin' one of my motherfuckers make it club business. Shit could've gotten bad if it turned out that cunt had Derby's baby. Next time Gypsy boohoo to you, shut that bitch down."

"She's the old lady of the president of one of your support clubs. What do you want me to do? She comes to me and asks for my advice."

"Then, maybe, I need to kill her. She puttin' you in a bad position and, in turn, my club."

Derby paled.

"The line is still open, Christopher," Meggie said tiredly. "Can we hang up?"

"Nope. They need to know where the fuck to meet me so I can fuckin' shoot them."

"Why…er…w-why would they go if they know you intend to shoot them?"

"If they fuckin' don't, I'm torture them first."

Just like now.

"Just like now!" Meggie echoed in outrage. "This is psychological torture, Christopher. That would be physical—"

"Fuck, I know what the fuck it is, Megan."

"This is Johnnie's MO. Let Mortician hang up so we can talk privately."

"No." The word fell like chips of glass. "I ain't exactly knowin' who the fuck Mort letting listen to your private fuckin' conversation because he answered your fuckin' call in the middle of the fuckin' night. Derby might be listenin'. Digger definitely is—"

"It's o-only M-Mort and me, and you're allowing our private conversation to be heard."

"Ain't fuckin' private, Megan. This a fuckin' continuation of the one you was havin' with Mort and the other motherfuckers. Besides, you a lyin' lil' motherfucker. Your stutterin' give you the fuck away."

"Oh my God," Meggie groaned dramatically.

Mort grinned, along with the others, including Digger and Derby.

"Can I just say you have top tier logic?" she said sweetly.

"Thank you, baby, but I ain't fallin' for your tactics. Motherfuckers still dyin'. You sick. They need to take care of you, not stress you out."

"You're stressing me out."

"Oh fuckin' well. In the long run, you gonna be happier. No assfucks to fuck over you and hurt your feelings. It's my fuckin' job to keep you safe. If I gotta upset you to do it, Ima make it up to you cuz I only want what's best for you."

Goddamn.

"Christopher, they are your friends. I asked Stretch not to tell you because I didn't want Gypsy to find out what I was doing. I got the idea because she didn't believe Derby. The idiot refused to show her the paternity results."

Surprisingly, Derby had no reaction to Meggie's label.

"The motherfucker probably wanted her to trust him by word alone."

"I agree," Meggie said glumly. "She asked me if I would believe him."

"We all know that fuckin' answer. Bitch just wasted her fuckin' breath."

"I told her whenever she confronted Derby with concrete proof about his cheating, he always confessed. I didn't think he'd lie about the baby. If it was his, he would've told her. He's hurt her so many times, but she's so unhappy without him, Christopher. I'm so sorry for tapping Stretch, but I didn't know what else to do. Derby likes me about as much as I like him."

"What the fuck you mean? Motherfucker like you. He just annoyed at you interferin'."

"If you say so."

"Look me in the fuckin' eye and tell me he like you."

"Why?" she asked suspiciously.

"Cuz he either like you or the motherfucker lyin' and playin' my ass."

"Do you just want to kill someone?" she cried. "What is wrong with you?"

"A fuckin' lot, baby."

"Can I let Mort go? He's at a poker game. The one you should've gone to."

"I bought in six weeks ago, Megan. If you was home, I would've gone."

"Would you give me my phone?"

"Not ready to hang up."

"If you just promise me you won't kill Mortician, Digger, Dez, and Derby, I won't ask for the phone again."

"So I'm free to fuck up Johnnie?"

"What? No! Don't hurt Johnnie either. Save it for the issues in the club."

Second time she alluded to problems within the club.

Prez noticed, too. "Mort or Johnnie mentioned club business to you?"

"Does it matter?" she asked, evading the answer. "You're needed at the club."

"You need me more."

"Don't you miss being the president?"

"Fuck, yeah, but my head not straight."

"You always enjoy poker nights at Boy's club. I wanted you to go to take your mind off—"

"If you not better, I don't even remember to eat. I sure the fuck couldn't concentrate on poker."

"You forfeited your money."

"Don't matter."

"At least it was only $5000."

"It could've been five million and I still wouldn't have gone. Who the fuck came to you about club business?"

"We need to resolve one issue before we move onto the next."

"You look worn out, Megan. Get back in bed, then tell me who. I'm thinkin' about lettin' Mortician off with a warnin'."

"What about the others?"

Godspeed.

"Derby don't like you. Johnnie tormentin' you. Digger disrespectin' you. And Dez insulted you, by tryin' to get me to fuckin' cheat."

"Derby is entitled to his opinion, Christopher. Digger is concerned about you, so he's frustrated. Dez had no power to make you cheat, and you didn't. You're not thinking clearly right now."

"The fuckin' way you keep leavin' out John Boy tellin' me everyfuckinthing I need to know."

"I think there's a reason for Johnnie's behavior."

"Assfuckery."

"Besides that."

"Megan—"

"The club needs Outlaw," she said softly.

"You know how many times you almost been fucked up cuz of Outlaw? Let me count the fuckin' ways."

"That's not how that poem goes."

"Don't give a good fuck. Snake kidnapped you and Rack strapped you to a fuckin' torture table then let motherfuckers grope you. Your step fuckhead stabbed you. Cee Cee was takin' you somewhere to fuck you and cut your fuckin' head off. Spoon beat you so bad you lost our second boy and wasn't ever able to have a normal pregnancy after. The fuckin' badges humiliated you with a cavity search. Sharper sent Digger for Bailey and you were there, so one of the motherfuckers stuck his cock in your mouth then intended to throw you out the fuckin' window. Digger's cunt, Peyton, shot you and I had to watch you fuckin' drop to the ground then send you to the hospital without me. Daphne tried to make you believe I was fuckin' her. Johnnie fuckin' strangled you."

Derby started.

"Mystic took you and left CJ all alone cuz of fuckin' Kendall. I still believe Val fucked over you but I ain't even thinkin' about that. All of it because of the club. The only fuckin' time you half safe is when you filled with my kid cuz you don't go out and about but I risk losin' you another way."

"I've survived each—"

"One day you ain't," he interrupted. "So I'm fuckin' askin' again: who the fuck riskin' me losin' you by bringin' club business to you? Mort or Johnnie?"

"I love you, Christopher," she said quietly.

He sighed. "Tell me. Don't tell me. The only thing I'm gonna do is kill. I can't solve problems or pardon nobody right now."

"You should pardon, if it isn't a club offense. The only reason I'm telling you not to kill Digger, Mortician, Derby, and Dez. And, er, Johnnie, is because they are part of our family and it has to do with me, not the club."

"You don't even know motherfuckin' Dez," Outlaw snapped. "He'll treat you the way Derby will. Which, come to fuckin' think about it, is always kind of…"

Shifting in his seat, Derby swallowed. Dez turned redder than normal.

"You promised to let me fight my own battles," Meggie said.

"These are special cases."

"Mortician, are you still there?" Meggie called.

He wished the fuck he wasn't. Over the years of Meggie's various injuries and traumas, he hadn't kept a running tab. He'd just been there to help solve her dilemmas, provide coverups, and do whatever else was needed. After hearing Prez, the fucking list read like bullet points in Mort's head. "Yeah, Meggie."

"Who else?"

"The same as before," Digger answered, not outing the other motherfuckers since it was unclear if Prez realized the number in his captive audience.

"Here, baby, get back in bed. If you don't listen this time,

I'm carryin' you there and raisin' the fuckin' rails again."

"Promise me, you won't kill anyone, Christopher," she said a moment later after a flurry of movement resounded. "Your club needs Outlaw the leader, not Outlaw the killer."

"I ain't killin' Mort," he grumbled.

"No one," she insisted. "No one on our side who I bring up or have already mentioned."

"That still leave several motherfuckers since they not on our side. Your fuckin' way of sayin' family and my friends that you socialize with."

"I have no defense against Nardo and his father. Dez, however, just thought he was showing you hospitality."

Prez growled, but Mortician couldn't stop his grin. Meggie had talked Outlaw down with patience and solid arguments. Every motherfucker at the table had reason to be grateful to her. Even Boy, though he hadn't been on Prez's hit list. Yet.

"Fine, you little pain-in-the-ass-motherfucker," Outlaw said, confirming Mortician's guess. "Nofuckinbody on our fuckin' side."

"Promise me."

"I promise...fuck! I promise I ain't killin' no motherfucker on our fuckin' side, you lil' pain-in-the-fuckin-ass motherfucker."

"Brooks called me," she said without preamble. "When you went downstairs to eat with the guys."

Dead fucking silence filled with tension and rising anger. Even though Mort couldn't see Outlaw, his outrage wafted over the phone lines like a Medieval miasma.

"You fuckin' with me, baby," he barked.

"Unfortunately, I'm not."

"The club attorney called you while you in the fuckin' hospital, recoverin' from havin' Jo too early, hemorrhagin', and pre-eclampsia?"

"Um—"

"Brooks Reddin' called my fuckin' woman and intentionally involved her in club business?"

"Christopher—"

"Out of all the motherfuckers mentioned in my reminiscin', how many still alive?"

"Digger and Johnnie," she said miserably. "And Kendall."

"How many of the fucked-up motherfuckers I fucked up because they fucked with you?"

"Brooks didn't, er, fuck with me," she squeaked.

"He didn't fuck with you?" Prez demanded. "I ain't…I didn't fuck up Spoon cuz I was with you at the hospital. I left Sharper alive out of courtesy to Mort and Digger. The rest of those motherfuckers? I shot the fuck out of, includin' those two cunts. You got caught in the crosshairs of club business. Now Brooks fuckin' Reddin', a motherfucker very fuckin' lucky to still be breathin' after his bitch's bullshit, callin' you on your sick bed and tellin' you shit you don't need to fuckin' know."

"You don't have to make it sound so bad," she grumped.

"Oh, it's fuckin' bad, baby. It's fuckin' horrendous."

"You promised me."

"Don't have to kill that motherfucker to torture him. If he fuckin' die from his injuries ain't my fuckin' fault. What the fuck he wanted?"

"It could've been to check on me," she backtracked. "You don't know why he called."

"Megan—" he bellowed.

"God," she said on a groan.

"Spill, baby."

"Your brother was in Hortensia."

"And? Cuz I'm missin' some fuckin' pieces. Why the fuck Brooks callin' you when he already talked to my ass about

Bash?"

"It…it has something to do with Kendall and Mattie. And me," she added on a mumble.

"You fuckin' shittin' me."

"No," she said faintly. "Brooks said he's concerned Bash is going to do something rash."

"How the fuck you involved?"

"Don't forget Kendall and Mattie."

"I might worry about them if I gotta fuck up Johnnie. Now, answer me."

"I don't know, Christopher. At least, I don't understand. Brooks is terrified. Johnnie didn't want him to tell you. Now, he's afraid Johnnie'll kill him for disobeying, and you'll kill him for hiding information."

"First educated thought the motherfucker had."

"Christopher—"

"He fuckin' told me it had to do with the Scorched Devils. Johnnie was payin' Bash 50Gs a month to keep Dez and his brothers safe."

Dez and Derby exchanged glances.

"How the fuck that involve you?" Outlaw roared. "You not a fuckin' member of any of the fuckin' clubs. If Brooks didn't think he could talk to me, he should've called Derby."

"He mentioned Dez and Derby, but it's confusing. Brooks said Cole—the Devil you, er, that—was a former Scorpion, so Bash wanted to avenge his death. Though that doesn't make sense, since Brooks also said Cole got out bad from the Scorpions, so why would they want to avenge his death by killing me—"

A loud crash interrupted Meggie's rambling.

Mort bet his life she hadn't meant to say that.

"Don't you say those motherfuckin' words to my motherfuckin' face, Megan. You've lost your fuckin' mind, casually fucking saying that motherfucker wanna kill you after makin' me promise not to kill motherfuckin' fuckin' Brooks!"

"Sir, I'm going to have to ask you to leave," the nurse said. "You're disturbing my patient."

"Leave, please," Meggie said, and Mortician wasn't sure to whom she spoke. "Let me calm my husband down. This is a private wing. He's only disturbing me."

"I cannot. You are obviously in distress."

"Name your price," Meggie said desperately. "I'll call my bank and have them transfer any amount. Just, please go and leave Christopher alone."

"Fine. Here's my full name. I'll pick up the check later."

"I could snatch my fuckin' hand away anyfuckintime I want," Outlaw said after the nurse left. "You might've called Mort about Bailey and whatever else, but you was callin' that motherfucker to talk to him about Brooks, huh, Megan?"

"I couldn't talk to him about it with everyone listening without you knowing," she confessed. "Besides, I got distracted."

"Distracted? By what?"

"Advice to him."

"When a motherfucker want you dead, ain't nothin' else more important. And tellin' Mort before me would've put him in the line of fire."

"I wanted to tell him because Brooks wasn't making a lot of sense. I don't know if he said Bash wants me dead because of the risk to Kendall and Mattie and throwing me in is the quickest way to remove Bash from the equation. I have absolutely nothing to do with the Scorched Devils."

"A couple of Dez's brothers been taken out, Outlaw," Digger said. "If Johnnie paying Bash to keep the Devils safe, Bash not adhering to the plan. One even had his head in a pillory and his feet in stocks.”

“Rack must’ve schooled them,” Meggie said, grunting.

“You okay, baby?”

“I’m getting sleepy again.”

“No, you in fuckin’ pain. I see it.”

“You can’t see pain, Christopher.”

“On you, I see everyfuckinthing. You in pain.”

“I’m fine. Focus on Brooks and what he said, even if it wasn’t much and didn’t make a lot of sense.”

“It ain’t connectin’ in my head, either, Megan,” Prez said, suddenly sounding more tired than Meggie. “Right now...it might not ever connect.”

“It will, Christopher.”

“If you say so, baby. Just stop movin’ before you go back into a coma.”

“I wasn’t in a coma. I was sedated.”

“You wasn’t with me.”

“I need you to talk to CJ. He’s hurt Harley.”

“CJ said he’s not fuckin’ Molly, Megan. I believe him. Harley still just a lil’ kid and our boy growin’ up. They at two different places. I’m not talkin’ to him about shit him and me already discussed.”

“But—”

“Megan, CJ and Harley just friends. He paid a mint for some expensive fuckin’ ring and she said she didn’t want to go steady. The hardest part of growin’ up is learnin’ to lie in the fuckin’ beds we made. Besides, if she don’t have absolute trust in him, they’ll never be happy.”

“Bailey was really upset when she called me. I don’t appreciate her blaming CJ for her argument with Mortician. She said she has pictures showing CJ and Molly together.”

“So Bailey really did call you?”

“Yes, she did.”

"And woke you up? Or was that Brooks?"

"You won't let us hang up because you're conducting psychological torture," Meggie accused, her voice weaker. "You know they are on the edge of their seats."

"Answer the fuckin' question."

"It was Bailey, Christopher. She's upset because Mortician hasn't come home."

"Then he the motherfucker she should've called," Outlaw barked. "Don't think I haven't noticed she or Harley hasn't once visited you. Now, she's callin' you with bullshit in the middle of the fuckin' night."

"It's important to her."

"Did she say she miss Mort? Or she's worried that he's steppin' out on her? Did she say anyfuckinthing about adult shit? Gypsy might be a whiny bitch, but at fuckin' least she come to you about her marriage."

When Meggie didn't answer, Mort's heart sank. After all, Outlaw was right.

"Uh, Bailey might've mentioned something about...about, um, how much she misses Mortician."

"You're not only a lyin' lil motherfucker but you terrible at being a lyin' lil' motherfucker."

"It's okay, Meggie," Mort said. "I already know the answer."

"Talk to your woman, Mortician."

"I will, Prez."

"It isn't as if you can do Bailey anything, Christopher," Meggie complained.

"I can't, but Roxanne can. If Bailey is losin' her fuckin' mind, leave you the fuck alone or else I'm gonna have Roxanne help her to find that motherfucker. Hear me?"

"Clearly," Meggie said.

"You, Mort?"

"Yeah, Prez."

"Good. I'm callin' that nurse bitch for you, Megan."

"No, please, call Brooks—"

"I'll talk…Mort, look into what Megan talkin' about. Call Brooks. Don't let him know I know."

"Christopher, the club needs you. No offense, Mortician."

"None taken, Meggie." She was right.

"Unless Mortician is made Vice-President, Johnnie can veto anything he decides."

"I'm not askin' Mort to make a fuckin' decision, Megan. I'm askin' him to get information. Hey, Mort, Megan gotta rest. She not lookin' too good. Call Brooks and let me know."

The line disconnected just as the door opened and Mouse walked in, arm around Pepper's waist.

"You owe me $3000, motherfucker," Boy said.

Before Mouse answered, Mort stood, and Digger followed suit.

"Don't let nothing you heard go past this room," Mort warned. "Digger, go cash in your chips so we can ride out."

CHAPTER 19

Somehow, two fucking days after he was last at the Harris house, CJ found himself there again. This time, though, it was the middle of the day, instead of the evening. He wasn't there to work on the lab project. He was there to explain to Molly that her abortion was scheduled and would take place tomorrow. The doctor was already paid.

CJ had even gotten a hotel room for Molly to rest in for two days before she returned to her hellhole of a house. She didn't need to fear her father's wrath or smell her mother's farts.

When Molly opened the door after CJ knocked then texted her, she stumbled to the brown corduroy sofa and plopped on it, hanging her head, allowing her long hair to shield her features.

"Are you okay, Mo?" he asked.

She nodded. "I just can't stop being sick," she said miserably. "I usually vomit fifty-six hours a day and sleep for twenty-four."

"That's eighty hours. Over three days."

She lifted her head. She showed no sign of comprehension. Today's tank top accompanied bikini underwear and revealed her legs. "I'm hungry but I'm nauseated."

"What did you have for breakfast?"

"Nothing. Mama lost our refrigerator. I think she hid it in the woods for the wolf."

Sighing, he scrubbed a hand over his face. "When did you last eat?"

"When you sent the steak, potatoes, and salad. Daddy stole the dessert and fed it to the moon."

Daddy was a fucking asshole. "Yeah, about him. When's he coming home?"

"The troll wouldn't let him cross the bridge."

"He's the fucking troll," CJ grumbled.

Molly glared at him. "My daddy is a fine man. He only wants the best for me."

"I take it he told you that."

"He made me write it eleven-two hundred times."

No fucking way could he make sense of that. "He made you write eleven, two hundred times?"

"He made me write that he's a fine man and only wants the best for me eleven-two hundred times."

Something else had happened. She was more out there than usual.

"Two hundred eleven times?" he pressed. "He made you write praise of him two hundred eleven times?"

She looked lost; she nodded.

CJ sat next to her and put an arm around her shoulder,

dragging her closer. At first, she held herself stiff. He refused to let her go. Finally, she relaxed against him, buried her face against his chest, and sobbed.

"Mama's mad at me. She left. She saw me vomiting and asked why I didn't need tampons anymore. I didn't know she knew about that."

"She's a girl, Mo," CJ said quietly, stroking her hair, hating that she was so upset. "At some point all girls do."

"I told her you were going to help me make the baby go away. She said I was just like that bible lady. The one she told me was good."

"Lot's wife."

"Mama is my friend. She's all I have. She'll love me again when the baby goes."

CJ clenched his jaw, wanting to call his father so bad, he almost ignored the memory of how out of touch Dad was and would be no help. Uncle Mort had his own issues.

Nope, he wouldn't run down why he didn't have support. It would only depress him and, at the moment, Rebel, his brothers, and Molly needed him. Mom and Dad did, too.

"Won't she, CJ?"

"Of course," he said, afraid to tell her he didn't think so. The woman was a pathetic wretch, while Molly was barely grounded in reality.

"My cousin, Rory, and I will pick you up about ten tomorrow morning," he said once her tears stopped.

"We can't go alone?"

They could, but CJ needed moral support for himself so he could help Molly. "It'll be safer. If you aren't feeling good after the procedure, Rory will assist you while I drive you to the hotel."

She leaned back to look at him. Her brow pleated. "We'll all be able to fit on a motorcycle?"

He grinned. "No, Mo. We'll be in my dad's pickup."

Her eyes widened. "You can drive a real car? Not just a motorped?"

"It's a moped. I ride it. You don't drive motorcycles and mopeds."

"Uh-huh," she insisted. "You steer it, so you must drive it."

He smiled at her, surprised at the tenderness he felt for her. "I'm not going to argue with you."

"I have to go," he told her, gently pushing her away from him and getting to his feet.

Her eyes clouded again.

"Do you want to come to my house with me? You'll be safe there."

She shook her head. "I have to make Mama be my friend again."

Silence was the better part of valor. "I'll order more food and have it sent over."

"Okay."

"Are you sure you'll be okay? I can always call the police on your behalf—"

"No! No, please. Don't do that. Please, CJ. Daddy knows them. He knows law justice."

Biker justice was needed for that fuckhead.

"Then come with me."

"You can stay with me," she whispered.

"I can't, Molly. I hate your fucking dad and he wants to hurt me."

"He'd never. That would make him a bad man."

He was that and more.

"I love Mama and Daddy. The giant told me so when he came down the beanstalk."

"When was the last time you read a fairytale? Or Mother Goose?"

"Mother Goose took me into her book last night after I finished writing what Daddy made me write. We talked a long time, then we said my favorite prayer."

"You have a book with Mother Goose?"

She nodded.

Wishing he knew what to do, he bent and kissed her cheek, then tipped her chin up. "I will text you when I'm on my way. In the meantime, I'll order enough food for you, your mom, and motherfucker. Eat. Understand?"

She frowned. "Do you mean Daddy? Are you being mean to him?"

Not the way he wanted to be. "No, Molly. He fucks your mother. Motherfucker."

Accepting his fucked up answer, she beamed a smile at him. "I always wondered what that meant. The mice never told me after I stopped being a pumpkin."

More gibberish he couldn't understand and wouldn't try to. Molly needed extensive therapy due to trauma or extensive rehabilitation due to psychedelics or both. If Aunt Bailey didn't hate him, he'd call her for help.

"See you tomorrow, Mo."

"Bye, CJ," she said softly.

CHAPTER 20

Matilda

Pink nauseated Mattie. Once, it was her favorite color, until her father decided she was a girl who needed shielding from the world and pink was the requisite color to achieve his brainwashing.

Fine.

Good.

Whatever.

Many times, Mattie feared her father's wrath. She went out of her way to act perfect and demure. He'd never beat her. Yet, his words could be inordinately harsh. For most of her life, he'd treated her like a fragile doll, leaving her unable to show her true self.

Over the past year, though, he'd been even more severe toward her. Rebel and Harley hadn't been able to ask Daddy's criticism. He'd used their behavior to further limit Mattie's activities.

She'd been hurt, resentful, and scared. It crushed her to realize how little value he placed on Mattie's friendship with her cousins. His unyielding position embittered her and the thought of losing Rebel and Harley as her confidantes frightened her.

Mattie believed the past months were the worst of her life.

Absolutely nothing compared to her father walking out and her mother falling to pieces, however.

She blinked away her tears, fixated on the pink ceiling in her room. At least, the molding was white like her bedroom set and desk. Everything else—walls, carpeting, curtains, comforter, desk chair, and the padded bench at the foot of her bed—was pink.

Pink because girls who were fragile and perfect loved that color.

Swiping at a tear, she drew in a deep breath and touched the bridge of her nose. She still sported a bruise from the headbutt she gave Bash. Not that anyone noticed.

They were all paralyzed with fear.

Her door opened; she didn't lift her head.

"Mat?" Blade called.

She turned to her side and drew her knees to her chest. Her youngest brother ran to her bed and climbed on. Smiling, she lifted her arm and straightened, allowing him to snuggle close to her. She kissed his cheek.

At almost three, he had the same red hair as Mattie and their mother, but their father's gray eyes. Rory and JJ were the blonds, though Rory also had Daddy's eye color, while JJ's was brown.

"Hungry, Mat."

"Ella will feed you soon," she promised, regretting turning down Lolly's invitation to visit Aunt Meggie.

She had been going with Maman until three days ago. It didn't feel right going without her. Luckily, Aunt Meggie understood. Today, for the first time in days' Aunt Meggie called Mattie to check on her. If Daddy had been home, it would've been one of the best days of her life. Hopefully, it meant Aunt Meggie would be released from the hospital soon.

A high-pitched scream startled Mattie and Blade. She bolted up; Blade wailed.

Hurrying to her feet, she swept Blade into her arms and ran to the nursery.

Ella was in the middle of the room, ringing her hands. "What's happened, Mattie?"

"I don't know," she said, kissing Blade again and handing him to Ella, though he was screaming at the top of his lungs now.

"Want, Mat, El," he howled.

"I'll be back," Mattie promised, scared that something had happened to their father and her mother had just found out. Her heart racing and her pulse pounding, she ran out of the room. Downstairs, she followed the sound of her mother's sobs.

In the kitchen, Mattie skidded to a halt. "Daddy," she breathed.

He had his arms wrapped around Maman, while he whispered to her. His jaw was swollen and his left eye blackened. Other than that, he was alive and well.

And he was home.

"Dad?" JJ said from behind her. He burst into tears and flew past Mattie in a blur, flinging an arm around their father and another around their mother. "I was so scared."

Rory walked into the kitchen from the opposite side, coming in through the door that led to the dining room. Relief swept across his face, then he clenched his jaw and glowered.

Maman lifted her head, kissed Daddy, then leaned and kissed JJ's cheek. "Where've you been, Johnnie?" she sobbed. "What happened to you? You were in a fight." She leaned her head against Daddy's chest. "What happened to you? Why did you leave?"

"I don't want to talk about it, Kendall."

"But—"

"It's club business, gorgeous." Taking her face between his hands, he kissed her tenderly on the mouth. "I'm fine."

Snorting, Rory glared at Daddy, turned on his heel and stormed out.

"I've been so worried," Maman reiterated.

"I'm back, Kendall."

Mattie rocked on her heels. It sounded suspiciously like Daddy intended to ignore the pain and suffering he caused. What did that mean?

He was unyielding, unforgiving, and sometimes unbearable. However, in Mattie's memory, she'd never known him to be so callous with her mother's feelings. Usually, he went out of his way to keep her calm. There were exceptions, though never to this extreme.

"We're going to Brooks and Charlotte for dinner," Daddy announced, disentangling from Maman and JJ. "We need to make haste."

"I don't feel like going anywhere," Maman said.

"I have to talk to Brooks and we need to eat. We're going." Daddy's gaze fell on Mattie. He opened his arms. "Aren't you going to greet your father, Matilda?"

Swallowing, Mattie walked to him and stepped into his embrace. For some reason, she burst into tears, so relieved her father was alive and well she could do nothing else.

She ignored her hollowness and how very anticlimactic his return was. He was back. Life could finally get back to their normal.

CHAPTER 21

"So, yesterday, Dad waltzes back in the house like he hasn't been MIA for almost four fucking days." Rory snorted in disgust. "No explanation to any of us. You don't want to tell us? Fine. But Mom's been a fucking wreck. At the least, he owed her more than an 'I don't want to talk about it'."

"I agree," CJ said, distracted.

They were standing on the Harris porch, where they'd been for five minutes, waiting for Molly to open the door. When he'd texted her his time of arrival early this morning, she'd sent him a thumbs up. Now, he'd knocked several times, tried the door, and knocked a little more. She wasn't even answering his texts.

It was a quiet Monday morning in this older section of Hortensia, lacking the hustle and bustle of the Medical District and the new areas. This was a low-income neighborhood where the residents struggled to make ends meet even if they held down multiple jobs, which most of them did. Partnering with Molly for the science project allowed CJ a glimpse of this side of town. Sometimes, when they walked to McDonald's, she'd stop and talk to her neighbors, then fill him in on gossip. Most of the houses on this street resembled the Harris's with cracked driveways and crooked foundations.

"How's Aunt Kendall this morning?"

Rory shrugged. "I…fuck, I don't know. She plays so many fucking games, but I think she really lost her shit when Dad walked out."

"Just because Aunt Kendall twists shit sometimes, doesn't mean she doesn't love Uncle Johnnie, Ro."

"It just means she's a fucking woman."

CJ grinned. "You're being too hard on Aunt Kendall and all girls."

"No the fuck I'm not. Girls are manipulating cunts." Rory lit a cigarette and nodded to the door that stood between them and Molly. "Take Ryan's bitch. She knew we were coming. Now, she won't let us in."

"Molly's a sweet girl. Something's up, Rory. I can feel it. She wouldn't have us come over here, especially knowing why, and not let us in."

Rory huffed out smoke. "You're feeling her?"

"I like her," CJ stressed. "She's my friend."

"You can't be friends with a chick, C. You either will fuck them or want to fuck them."

CJ fired off another text to Molly.

"Any chick you fucked you want as a friend?"

"I wouldn't know, Ro, since I've never fucked."

Puffing on his cigarette, Rory squinted. "Got your cock sucked before?"

"Nope."

Ryan's arrival interrupted Rory's response.

"You boys okay?" Uncle Val called. He'd driven Aunt Zoann's Jeep to drop off Ryan.

"Fine, old man," Ryan grumbled, topping the rickety porch. "CJ has Uncle Christopher's pickup."

Rory and CJ waved Uncle Val off, while Ryan ignored his father.

"You're a fucking asshole," CJ said once Uncle Val drove away.

"Whatever. Would you get that bitch already so we can get this over with?"

Rory blew smoke in Ryan's face. "Your bitch. Your baby."

"That I only know about because she called and told me she was getting rid of it, so fuck her."

"Did you want the baby?" CJ asked in surprise.

"Does it matter? She made the fucking decision with your help."

"She made the fucking decision because she's afraid of Bash, you stupid motherfucker," CJ snarled. "And if I wasn't here to help her, I'd bang your fucking head against the sidewalk. You know that motherfucker, just like Uncle Johnnie."

This was the first time CJ had seen Ryan since confronting him after the incident at Turn Creek Bridge. He hadn't been to school because he'd been spending his days at the hospital, trying to coax his father to continue resting as much as possible and eating more regularly, making plans to help Molly, and watching over his mother. If Rory hadn't told CJ this morning that Ryan would show up, he would've started whaling on that motherfucker on sight for more than one reason. CJ also hadn't confronted Ryan about telling Molly she broke the bank because he bought her fries, and he didn't even want to think about her sucking Ryan's cock for things. The fuckhead.

"Why is Molly afraid of Bash?" Ryan asked, not denying CJ's accusation.

"Because the baby might be his," CJ shouted.

At first, Ryan stared from CJ to Rory, but Rory tossing his cigarette seemed to snap him out of his shock.

"What—"

A lock disengaging interrupted Ryan; the door cracked. Bloody fingers gripped the edge before disappearing. A sobby moan filtered up.

Alarm racing through him, CJ tried to push the door open, but something blocked him.

"Molly, move away from the door," he said.

At first, she said nothing. "It hurts," she said finally.

Ryan stood, frozen.

"He beat me," she sniffled. "And M-mama's dead."

Ryan staggered back, while Rory's eyes lit up.

Cursing and glaring at his cousins, CJ released a sharp breath. "Move away from the door, bae," he coaxed. "We have to check on you and the baby."

"There is no baby," she said in a small voice.

Anger washed over Rory's face, and he stiffened, opening his mouth to speak.

CJ held up a hand and shook his head. "Where is it?"

Silence.

Fury darkened Rory's gray eyes.

"We won't be mad at you, Mo," CJ promised. "Just tell us where the baby is?"

Her pitiful sobs tore at him. "Daddy hurt it," she admitted. "I tried to hold it in, but it kept coming out."

The memory of his mother going limp, and suddenly bleeding swirled in CJ's head, and he closed his eyes.

"Move away from the fucking door, Molly," Rory ordered in a hard voice.

CJ glared at Rory, surprised when the door opened wider.

Rory stalked into the house, followed by Ryan. Not trusting either of them, CJ went in and halted. Molly lay on the floor, naked, bruised from head-to-toe with various wounds on her body, while dried blood stained her thighs and legs.

Removing his leather bomber, CJ knelt next to her, carefully lifted her into his arms and wrapped her in his jacket.

"Help my mommy," she whispered, sounding like a small child. "He took her in the bathroom after she told him I was pregnant."

"Didn't you say she was dead?" Ryan asked woodenly.

"She's a fairy," Molly said around tears. "Fairies always come back to life, even when they grow to a hundred feet tall and are dropped from the moon."

"I'll see to her," Rory swore, heading to the bathroom once Ryan pointed to it.

Clutching Molly, CJ stood. "Call Uncle Val, Ryan. Tell him what's going on. Then, call Uncle Mort and Uncle Digger—"

"There's no helping that woman," Rory announced, staring into the bathroom from the doorway.

CJ turned toward the door. "Give her mouth to mouth. Something. At least try."

"She doesn't have a mouth to blow air into her lungs. Her head's gone."

Ryan

One day, Ryan awakened and saw his parents in a new light. His father was a weak motherfucker and his mother was an overbearing cunt full of hot air. She cowered Val and her sons, but Ryan never saw her throw down anywhere else. Even at the club, she fussed and cussed, yet opted for diplomacy. To him, his parents were frauds and his little brother a weak pussy. He wasn't sure of the exact place and time when his resentment grew to derision and hate.

Likewise, Molly. One day, he awakened, and she was no longer a stupid bitch that he fucked. She was an airhead; however, he believed she cared about him. He hated that she partnered with CJ and harbored some bitterness because of it. A part of him even believed the baby she carried belonged to his cousin, and he'd told her in no uncertain terms what a whore she was.

She could only sob and swear she'd been faithful. In his heart, he believed her. And, in his heart, he was so fucking relieved she didn't want the baby, he almost cried. Yet, his pride stung that she'd gone to CJ first.

The motherfucker still didn't have acne. He still lived in the biggest house with the best playrooms and game rooms. His siblings still looked up to him. He was still quarterback and captain of the football team.

And he was still Outlaw's son.

At Rory's announcement, CJ carried Molly to where their cousin stood just inside the bathroom and peeped in.

"Goddamn."

"I'll take her to the meatshack." Rory's breathless words floated to Ryan.

"The fuck you will. Call Uncle Mort, asshole."

"We don't have to call anyone, C. I can have my own body."

Molly shuddered.

"She's a fucking girl," CJ said in disgust, shifting Molly. "Call Uncle Mort so we can do right by her."

"CJ—"

CJ stomped toward the door. "I'm not fucking listening, Rory. Get your fucking head out of the meatshack. Ryan, watch Molly's mom to keep Rory away from her."

He left, carrying Ryan's girlfriend.

A moment later, the motor on the souped-up pickup rumbled to life.

Rory stumbled out of the bathroom, phone in hand. He looked wild. Unhinged. "Should I call?"

CJ was right. If Ryan didn't watch over Mrs. Harris, Rory would take her to the meatshack and…and…

He couldn't finish the thought. Fuck, he couldn't go near the bathroom. Just the thought of a dismembered body turned Ryan's stomach.

"Do you think the head is here?"

Ryan swallowed and shoved his hands into his pockets. "No," he pushed out.

Rory's eyes gleamed. He glanced over his shoulder and turned. His ringing phone halted him. "It's Uncle Mort." Disappointment rang in the words. "CJ must've called him."

Of course he did. The fuckhead knew how to multitask.

Staggering outside, Rory answered the phone, leaving Ryan in the house with a dead woman missing her head.

He dropped to his knees and vomited the breakfast his mother cooked. It seemed as if he'd never stop puking. When he did, he remained on his hands and knees, trembling.

He'd spent enough time in the neighborhood to know it was practically deserted at this hour. Most of the neighbors were nice, though they were pathetic assholes with a dead-end life. However, they would've invited him in and he wouldn't be stuck here without anyone.

Motherfucking Bash must be to blame for this.

Ryan dealt with Bash to bring down CJ. That didn't mean Ryan wanted Molly hurt, whether or not she was fucking CJ. He didn't want her subjected to Bash, Willard, or Wallace's cruelty.

He'd seen Willard kill two motherfuckers on his mother and father's property by beating them to death. Bash abused bitches. Otherwise, they turned into cunts like Zoann, according to Bash. But Ryan had never seen a dismembered body.

Although it was cold and frozen outside, heat invaded him and sweat beaded his brow. He dry heaved, burning from the inside out. Needing water, he crawled to the edge of the sofa and somehow lurched to his feet.

Barely able to draw air into his lungs, he panted. Molly had said her father hurt her, but from everything Willard and Wallace said about Bash, from everything Bash said about Bash, Ryan knew he had a hand in this. Tom Harris, Molly's father, didn't shit without Bash or Cleaner's permission.

If Bash was hurting Molly, that meant Harris allowed it to happen. Meaning if Bash was angry with Molly and her mother, he'd hurt them or have them hurt.

Ryan needed to talk to Bash. Stat.

On shaky legs, he pushed open the swinging door to the kitchen. The Harris refrigerator went from locked to gone. Only an old water line sticking out from a faded yellow wall remained.

Ryan walked to the sink, intending to take one of the glasses from the dish drying rack.

Instead, he met the half-closed eyes of Mrs. Harris, her mouth frozen in an o-shape, her skin gray, and her neck a bloody stump.

He fainted.

BY ANY OTHER NAME

Spine stiff and shoulders straight, Sebastian Caldwell II walked beside his father and his namesake, unable to contain his excitement. Recently, Daddy had named him the enforcer to the mother chapter of the American Scorpions. After years of working off the grid for the club, he now had an official position. Daddy promised he'd one day become the National President, and he trusted it would be so.

In his twenty years, Daddy never lied to him.

A blast of wind cut through his clothes, and he shivered. He wished they hadn't parked their bikes half a mile away in an RV lot. Within five minutes, they'd left civilization behind and traversed through frozen wilderness.

If it wasn't January, he would've been shitting himself. As far as he remembered from school, bears were in hibernation. If he would've known they were hiking backcountry, he would've worn warmer clothing.

"Goddamn it, the cold air is turning my balls blue, Daddy."

"We'll be inside soon enough, Bash," Daddy said around a

snicker, using the nickname Aunt Kimber gave to Bash.

He had vague memories of a beautiful woman with black hair and green eyes. She loved to laugh and joke and was the one person Daddy had real affection for. He still referred to himself as Cee Cee because of her, over a decade after her death.

"What the fuck is Sharper doing out here?" Daddy grumbled, stomping toward the big cabin finally within throwing distance.

They'd arrived in Whitehorse, the capital of Yukon, a couple of days ago after riding for nearly four thousand miles over five days. For the trip, they'd purchased Touring bikes.

Earlier today, Daddy had finally gotten the call he'd been waiting for. Daddy never offered answers and Bash knew better than to question him.

The door opened before Daddy climbed the first step to the wooden deck surrounding the cabin. Bash puffed his chest out a little further, comforted by the sound of Cee Cee's jingling spurs.

The moment Bash followed his father inside the place, he rubbed his hands together, welcoming the warmth rising around him. Although a fire blazed from a huge fireplace, Bash didn't think it was enough to heat the cavernous room. He saw no other source, however.

Daddy walked to the center of the room, where a long table sat, overflowing with food and alcohol on one end.

"It's about time you arrived, fuckhead."

Bash only recognized Sharper Banks because of newspaper and magazine articles he sometimes found in Daddy's office.

"You're lucky I'm here, motherfucker," Daddy growled, "considering the fucking company I'm keeping."

Bash wasn't familiar with the other six older men. There

was also a dude about his age and two boys, one white and one black.

"For once we agree," the oldest of the strangers spat. He had graying hair and gray eyes. "I could've done without ever seeing you again, Cee Cee."

Grinning without humor, Daddy touched Bash's shoulder, then nodded to a chair next to a handsome blond man with the bluest eyes Bash had ever seen.

"This is my boy," Daddy said, lighting a cigarette while Bash took his seat. "Sebastian the Second. Bash."

"Hello, Bash," the blond man said, and held out his hand. "I'm Joe."

"And I'm Joey," the little white boy said. He sat directly across from Bash between the gray-eyed man and a brown-haired, brown-eyed man who wore a Scorpion's cut. "Joe's my dad."

"Why don't we all play nice and introduce yourselves to my boy?" Daddy said.

"This summit isn't on your fucking dime," Sharper said. "I make the fucking rules."

Bash pursed his lips, surprised at the minister's harshness. "Aren't you a holy man?"

Sharper stiffened, his stare cold and malevolent. "Shut the fuck up, asshole."

Smoking his cigarette, Daddy caught Bash's eye and gave him an imperceptible shake of his head before walking behind the brown-haired man. "Hello, Fred."

Fred swallowed. "Cee Cee."

"How's my boy?"

"Christopher's fine. Almost thirteen."

"Christopher?" Bash echoed. He hadn't heard that name in years. Sometimes, he remembered a dark-haired kid that Daddy had left him in charge of named Christopher, although Bash couldn't quite put together the circumstances. He hadn't been sure if it was just his imagination. Now, he knew it wasn't. "That baby I played with when I was eight?"

"Your brother," Daddy said.

Bash had lots of brothers, so it wasn't a great earth-shattering moment to discover the boy he thought about from time to time was one as well.

"The one I put old Fred in charge of watching," Daddy continued, squeezing Fred's shoulder.

The man flinched. "I have. He's been well looked after, Cee Cee."

"I wish he would die," Joey said.

"Shut up, son," Joe snapped.

Daddy cocked his head to the side. "You want my boy to die, kid?"

Joey raised defiant eyes to Daddy. "Yes," he hissed. "I fucking hate him."

"I see." Daddy glared at Joe, then looked at Bash. "We call him Boss, son. The old motherfucker is Logan Donovan. The fat, pig-eyed fuckhead is Wally." He smiled. "Excuse me, Rack. The skinny, pig-eyed shithead is his son, Wally, Jr. The quiet, thoughtful one is Kaleb Paul. K-P. The little black kid in the suit is Roddie Banks."

"Cleaner," Boss said, leaning back and folding his arms. "He's one, clean little motherfucker."

"Look who his Daddy is," Sharper boasted, dusting the lapels of his expensive suit coat.

"Not only were you fucking your fat slut, but you've been sticking your cock in another cumrag," Logan growled.

"Jesus Christ, Vivian is Logan's wife," K-P said with disgust. "Mother to his sons. Show her that much respect."

"Dad?" Roddie said, his eyes wide and filled with fear.

"Why don't you and Joey go to the bedroom, boy?"

Sharper said.

The two little boys stood and left the table, heading for a door on the opposite side of the room.

"I should fucking shoot you for bringing that cunt up in front of my seven-year-old son," Sharper snarled, glaring at K-P.

Daddy sauntered around to Joey's vacated seat and sat next to Bash, before leaning over and dragging an ashtray closer where he discarded his cigarette. K-P had no reaction to Sharper's words, while Logan grinned.

"What's the reason for the meeting, Sharper?" Daddy asked.

"I have several things I want to discuss," Sharper admitted. "I didn't realize you were bringing Bash."

"I thought you knew Cee Cee, Sharper," Boss said with a touch of bitterness. "He'd bring Bash to rub Celia in my face."

"Don't put fucking words in my mouth, Joseph," Daddy warned. "I brought Bash because he needs to start learning to lead my fucking club. What better initiation on dealing with enemies than meeting you fuckheads."

"You took Celia after I lost Kimber, Sebastian," Boss snarled. "You knew how much I loved them both—"

Pain flittered across Daddy's face before his expression closed. "Your cock killed her, motherfucker. You escaped alive. Take the 'W' and shut the fuck up."

Boss slammed his fist on the table, slid his chair back, and got to his feet. "She bled to death, you miserable motherfucker."

Daddy stood and turned, right in Boss's face. "Giving birth to your son, fuckhead." He shoved him back. "You took the only fucking good thing I ever had. If I never saw you again, it would be too fucking soon. I fucking despise you."

When Boss shoved Daddy, Bash and everyone jumped up. He'd never seen anyone lay hands on his daddy and survive.

"Fuck you, Sebastian. I don't give a fuck how you feel about me, but you're a dickhead for taking Celia away and denying your own fucking nephew."

"I'll see that little motherfucker dead before I ever acknowledge him as Kimber's son," Cee Cee snarled.

Clenching his jaw, Boss glanced away. "He'll never know," he said quietly. "I love him, in spite of what he thinks. I love him because he's the last of Kimber. I wanted to raise your daughter, our…" He swallowed. "Kimber's niece because she loved that little girl to bits and pieces, Cee Cee."

"Maybe, if you wouldn't spend so much time with that little fucking idiot, your boy would believe you love him, Joe," Logan said.

Though his tone was kind, the words were fucked up. Although Bash wasn't sure who Logan meant, Daddy seemed to know because he stiffened.

"What the fuck does that mean?" he demanded. "If the idiot you're referring to is my boy, why is Joe looking after him when that's Fred's specific job?"

"Does it matter?" Boss said tiredly. "We're all together for the first time since Vivian's wedding."

"We weren't all together then," Sharper barked. "Logan was tied up and marked for death. If Rack hadn't told me—"

"We were in the same fucking city," K-P snapped. "Better, fuckhead?" He looked at Daddy. "You didn't even allow Joe to attend Kimber's funeral, Cee Cee. You know she wouldn't have wanted that. Your treatment of him would've broken her fucking heart."

"Who asked you, Kaleb?" Daddy demanded crossly.

"Not a motherfucker around," K-P retorted. "I fucking volunteered because what you did was bullshit."

"It's done." Suddenly, Daddy looked and sounded old and defeated. "It can't be undone." He returned to his seat. "Why are we here, Sharper?"

"My dime, my time," the minister said smugly, retaking his seat at the head of the table.

Once everyone else sat again, Daddy lit another cigarette. He rested one elbow on the table, holding the cigarette in his hand, while he slid the other hand out of view.

"I heard Christopher had a boo-boo," he started after a few moments of silence, taxed with ugly undercurrents. Lifting a brow, he looked at Fred. "What happened?"

It seemed as if Fred had just started to relax. Now, he tensed up again. Unease slid into his brown gaze and he glanced at Logan, swallowed, then looked at Daddy. "I...kids will be kids, Cee Cee."

Puffing on his cigarette, Daddy nodded. "I'd hate to fucking think that cunt I married is turning you into a brainless idiot."

Married? His daddy was married?

"Watch your fucking mouth," Logan ordered. "Talk about my daughter with respect, fucker. Or I'll see to it that you suffer the consequences."

Daddy's eyes flared in surprise. "I see."

"Not yet," Logan said with a smirk.

Finishing his second cigarette, Daddy leaned back and shoved a hand into the pocket with his switch. Bash wasn't sure if he should pull his own piece or wait for Daddy's command. He'd never been in such a situation before.

"How are your daughters, Fred?" Daddy asked.

Fred cleared his throat. "Beautiful. Ophelia will turn three in July."

"When I grow up, I'm going to marry Zoann," Wally, Jr. boasted, speaking for the first time.

Rack slapped the side of his son's head, in the same way Daddy sometimes hit Bash. "You are grown, stupid. You're nineteen. You have to wait until she grows up. Remember?"

"Are you sure about that, Pa?"

Bash frowned. "I used to call Daddy 'pa'," he said. "You made me stop."

Daddy nodded. "I didn't want you calling me what that little pighead called the big pighead."

"My boy and me have fucking names, Cee Cee," Rack said.

"Be happy you're alive for me to call you pighead, pigshit," Daddy said around a yawn.

"Enough with the fucking threats, Cee Cee," Sharper warned. "For the last time, I'm in charge."

"I'm not here to steal your thunder, Sharper," Daddy said blandly, and the hairs on Bash's nape stood.

Someone was about to die. Beside him, Boss tensed too, apparently aware Daddy's cordiality foreshadowed death.

"I get reports from time to time," he said. "A little bird told me my son's arm was once broken. He was about three. Fred took him to the ER, but he didn't call me. He told me a blatant lie, as a matter of fact."

"Cee Cee—"

Daddy held up a hand, stopping Fred. "Sharper's running the show, brother." He shrugged. "I'm just saying. When you called me last month and told me Patricia and you brought the kids over to her daddy's for Christmas and he punched my boy—"

"That filthy little dog hit me back," Logan spat, rubbing his jaw, although it showed no injury. "Patricia defended him. Made me break her fucking hand."

"You're going to be sorry one day, Logan," Boss said with disgust. "Christopher is a brilliant kid—"

"Christopher is a fucking animal—"

"Christopher is a child, fuckhead," K-P bit out. "He has more heart than you and Simon put together."

"Keep talking, Kaleb," Logan snarled. "You're digging your own fucking grave."

"If it means escaping you, kill me, motherfucker," K-P said.

"No one's forcing you to stay, Kaleb," Sharper said. "That's one reason we're here. I know you're very unhappy. I wanted to give you a chance to get out."

K-P looked at Boss, who nodded. Heaving in a breath, K-P studied Boss, then met Sharper's gaze. "I'm out then. I'll—"

Sharper held up his hand. "Not so fast, Kaleb. There are stipulations."

"Whatever they are—"

"The weekly calls to Vivian to check on her and my sons stop immediately."

"Those boys are my godsons, and I think Vivian would have something to say—"

"You want out, you're out completely," Sharper said flatly.

"Your sons and your wife aren't part of this," K-P said. "Lucas and Marcus don't know me, but I know them, and have since they were born. You can't—"

"I can, and I will." Sharper's boast grated on Bash. He really didn't like that motherfucker. "Next stipulation is your fee. You're a charter member. If you want out, the fee is death or a million dollars."

K-P turned ashen "What! I'll never see that type of money in my life, Sharper. You know—"

"And, finally," the minister continued, speaking over K-P as if no one else mattered, "you forget Joe."

"Are you out of your motherfucking mind?" Boss yelled, no longer a passive witness. "You don't get to tell me who the fuck I see and you especially can't dictate my relationship with Kaleb Paul."

"I get to tell you any fucking thing I please, motherfucker," Sharper said. "He's not happy—"

"Then I'm out, too," Joe said.

Logan's eyes widened. "There's no way—"

"Your name is on everything, Joe. The loans. The titles. The legal documents. You can't leave."

"Buy me out. I'm fucking done. You're beside yourself."

Sharper's nostrils flared. "I'm the Alpha and the Omega. It's my fucking way or else. There's only one way out for you, Joe. Death."

"No," Logan said, horror washing over his face. "I don't care what you need to do. Joe survives under all circumstances. He saved my life when no one else would."

"I'm done, Logan," Boss said. "I helped with a bunch of fucked-up shit—"

"Because of that cunt you fell in love with," Sharper snorted. "You put Kimber on a pedestal and wanted to spoil her, so you fell back in with us."

"What are you talking—"

"You're a miserable fuckhead, Sharper," K-P interrupted Daddy. "Joe loved Kimber. He struggled his fucking ass off to give her an easy life and an easy pregnancy. Your bullshit killed her!"

"Someone tell me what the fuck K-P means," Daddy demanded.

"Nothing, Cee Cee," Boss said raggedly. "Nothing at all. It won't bring her back—"

"No, Joe. No," K-P said. "If this is the last time we see each other, I want the truth. I want to know why you never answered Joe, Cee Cee. He stuck to his word. He never used your sister as a go-between. He called you. I called you. Sharper and Logan swore they called you. He wanted to discuss the club to bring in more money for his wedding to Kimber. He wanted to buy her a house. Leave this fucking life and give her and their son a better one."

Daddy lost the color in his face as Sharper roared, "goddamn you, Kaleb!"

"If you want to blame any fucking body for Kimber's death, blame Sharper and Logan," K-P continued. "They knew it was close to her due date, but insisted Joe go on a run before they paid him, and he needed that fucking money to pay for the home birth she wanted."

"Shut the fuck up, Kaleb Paul," Daddy snarled, jumping to his feet and stalking to the other man, grabbing him around the throat. "I didn't know Joe wanted to talk to me about money for my sister. I ignored both you fuckheads and when I asked Logan and Sharper if they knew what you two wanted, they said it was about her fucking baby shower."

Boss yanked Daddy away from K-P and shoved him back. "She was three months pregnant, Cee Cee. We weren't planning a fucking shower then."

Without responding, Daddy closed his expression, then walked to the other end of the table and grabbed a berry from a bowl, popping it into his mouth and chewing thoughtfully. He glanced around the cabin with the heads of elk and bear hanging on each side of the room. On the back side were wall to wall draperies, and Bash wondered if they covered windows or glass doors.

Daddy walked to the fireplace and grabbed the poker from the side, stirring the dying embers. Unable to generate a spark, he took two thick pieces of wood from the nearly empty rack and tossed them into the fire, rekindling the flame.

He heaved in a breath, staring at the burning wood. "What made you choose Whitehorse, Sharper?"

"Roddie wanted to see the Northern Lights."

"I prefer Cleaner," Daddy said.

Sharper snorted. "As if I give a fuck."

Rack chuckled, and Wally, Jr. followed suit.

"Hear that, motherfucker?" Logan taunted, glaring at Daddy's back.

Fred shifted in his seat.

Gripping the poker, Daddy prodded the wood again. "I pay you and Logan for the lives of your sons, Christopher, Johnnie, Joe, Joey, and K-P."

Eyes wide, Boss exchanged a look of surprise with K-P.

For the first time, a look of unease slid into Sharper's face. "Well, Sebastian, er, I—"

"Kimber adored Vivian," Daddy said without humor. "Knowing how you feel about her as well as what a giant motherfucker you are to those boys, I felt compelled to protect them."

"I don't need your fucking money for my grandson," Logan sneered. "I love Johnnie."

"They are all safe," Sharper inserted quickly. "And L-Logan has declined all payments for Johnnie. He kindly allows me to...to...er...put it in a trust fund for Christopher."

"That'll be the fucking day," Daddy said with a snort, back still to everyone while he held the poker in the flame. "Fred, Fred, Fred. What am I going to do with you?"

"Wh-what do you mean?"

"You've played me, motherfucker."

"What can you do?" Logan demanded. "We are all unarmed."

"Ummmm hmmmm," Daddy said.

Fred gulped. "I haven't played you, Cee Cee."

"Then you think I'm a fucking fool—"

"I-I don't—"

"Oh, but you do."

Bash wasn't quite sure what that had to do with all K-P had revealed. It seemed as if Logan and Sharper had played Daddy, but he was conveniently overlooking that. For the first time, Bash questioned Daddy's reasoning. Under any other circumstances, he would've struck by now.

Unless he was afraid...?

The idea horrified Bash. To even think Daddy a coward shamed him.

"Cee Cee, I've taken care of your son and your wife. She wants for nothing."

"She shouldn't. I send you and her enough money to live like royalty, and to raise my son so he'll want for nothing." Daddy glanced over his shoulder, in time to see Fred wince and Logan smirk. "She doesn't see her money, does she?"

Fred looked sick. "She gives it to Logan."

"Uh huh." Rocking on his heels, Daddy sniffed, then returned to stirring the fire. He got another piece of wood and threw into the flames. "Why didn't you tell me the truth?"

"A-about what, Cee Cee?"

"Oh, I don't know, Fred. Life. Sons. Motherfuckers. I talked to you a couple weeks ago and you told me about the Christmas debacle, swearing Logan had never done anything of the kind to Christopher."

"It's true," Fred said faintly.

Silence, and then wild maniacal laughter escaped Cee Cee. Seeing Fred and the others flinch comforted Bash. He wasn't the only one who almost shit himself at the sound.

"Do you think I don't know what Donovan and his cunt of a daughter is capable of? That bitch is wickeder than her old man. If she didn't love my boy, I might've fucking buried her and taken him with me."

"Shut the fuck—"

"Logan," Sharper interrupted, shaking his head.

Bash searched his memory, trying to figure out exactly when the situation turned in Daddy's favor.

"I left Hortensia to give you and Logan my club's territory, Sharper."

Sharper's hand trembled and he balled it into a fist. "I know, Cee Cee. The Death Dwellers wouldn't be what they are without you."

The words sank into Bash, and he realized Sharper was, in fact, a Death Dweller, not just a powerful and crooked mega preacher.

"I send more money to you motherfuckers than I do to anybody, friend or foe."

"Yes," Sharper agreed.

"When Rack deserted the fucking Scorpions, I didn't kill that motherfucker. He admired Donovan, so I said good riddance."

Pressing his lips together, Rack looked between Daddy and Sharper, his eye twitching.

"Bash?"

At the sound of his name, Bash jumped to his feet. "Daddy?"

"Small towns with a sagging economy and barely any infrastructure is a vital commodity."

Not understanding, Bash wrinkled his brow. "Yes, Daddy."

Turning slightly, Daddy smiled at Bash. "You're a good boy. I'm proud of you."

"Thank you, Daddy," Bash said, beaming. "I'm proud to be your son."

"Joseph?"

Boss scrubbed a hand over his face. "Yes, Sebastian?"

"Do you want out?"

"If I can't see K-P, I'll take Joey and Christopher—"

"Christopher?" Daddy asked. "Why him? And why would Pattie allow you to take our kid? Why would Fred?"

"They are busy with their daughters," Boss responded.

"What about Johnnie? I thought they were friends."

"That's between you and Logan," Boss said. "Johnnie is his."

"What about numb nuts?"

"Simon won't go against anything Logan says," Boss responded, apparently familiar with 'numb nuts'.

"Christopher won't leave Patricia, Joe," K-P said bleakly.

Boss gripped the back of the chair since he hadn't sat back down.

"In other words, if Joe leaves with you, he walks away from Christopher, Kaleb," Daddy said.

K-P nodded.

"Or you can suck it up and stay at his side," Daddy suggested. "Be his eyes and ears. His right hand man."

"No," Boss barked, shaking his head. "I can't ask him to sacrifice his dreams...No."

"Not being able to contact Vivian to find out about his godsons will be hard," Daddy conceded, "but losing touch with you will break him, Joe. And we both know you won't leave Christopher right now."

"Then help us to find a way to make it work," Boss said quietly.

"I can't, Joseph."

"You've denied my son, your fucking nephew, and now you're making me sacrifice K-P in one way or the other for your son?"

Over a life spent on the road with his father, Bash saw many sides of Sebastian "Cee Cee" Caldwell. Regret, however, was a novelty.

"I can't look at him, Joe, and not see her. If you ever tell him we're related, I'll kill him. She died, giving birth to him." His eyes misted and his voice thickened. "I never want to hear her name on his fucking lips."

"He thinks his mother is someone else entirely," Joe said after a moment. "I took your warning to heart when you saw my kid in the hospital."

"I'll stay for now," K-P said, "but one of these days, I'll leave on my fucking terms."

Daddy shrugged. "As long as you don't betray me when that day comes, I won't give a fuck."

Sharper got to his feet and walked to the food. "Another reason I wanted to talk to you all is because I have some church events coming up. I need security."

Poker in one hand and switch in the other, Daddy turned, aimed at Fred's head, and squeezed the trigger, modified from a handgun to a mini machine gun. The bullets hit Fred's cheeks, chin, nose, lips, eyes, and the center of his forehead. His neck snapped back in a mist of blood, skin, and gore.

Hatred gleaming from his eyes, Daddy rushed Logan.

"Wait, wait, wait," he cried, spattered with Fred's blood and brain, and scrambling back so fast he toppled his chair.

"Dad!" Joey screamed as he and Roddie hurried out of the bedroom, while Logan crawled away from Daddy, Sharper shook, and Rack burst into tears.

"Come on, son," Boss said, taking Joey's hand and guiding him toward the door. "Let's take a walk. K-P, Roddie, come with us."

Even as the four of them left, the chaos continued. "Please!" Logan hollered, darting away from Daddy on his hands and knees. "Please!!"

Daddy fired again, this time hitting Wally, Jr. in the upper shoulder.

"Cee Cee, no!" Rack cried. "I'm sorry!"

The boy's screams finally halted Logan. He stopped and broke into sobs. Rack used the distraction to lift his son up and rush to the bedroom where Roddie and Joey had been.

"Strip, Donovan," Daddy ordered after Rack slammed the door shut.

"God, no! No, no!"

"Cee Cee—"

"Shut the fuck up, Sharper," Daddy snarled, returning to the fireplace and sticking the poker into the blaze. "I want to kill you so fucking bad. You knew what she meant to me. You knew. And you let Joe be the scapegoat. You allowed my son to be fucked over."

Roaring in rage, he shot Sharper, although the minister fell so quickly, Bash couldn't see where the bullet landed.

"For the last fucking time, Donovan, strip."

"I'm begging you, Sebastian," Logan sniffled. "I-I-I'll suck your cock if you let me live."

Disgust dropped into Daddy's face and he yanked the poker out of the fire, stalking to Logan and swinging. If the older man hadn't scooted back at the last minute, he wouldn't be hit with the heated weapon.

Sharper groaned, capturing Daddy's attention.

"You have a blood oath, Sebastian," Logan said wildly. "You can't kill him."

Crouching, Daddy stared at Logan's exposed ankles. He wore loafers but no socks. Even though Bash knew what was coming, he still winced at the scent of burning flesh and Logan's screams.

"Take his shirt off, son," Daddy instructed.

"God, no!" Logan cried, a wet spot suddenly spreading on the front of his tan trousers.

"Cee Cee, please stop," Sharper cried. "You've made your point."

"No, I don't think I have, cousin," Daddy spat, the situation so fluid Bash could barely keep up.

He ripped Logan's shirt away as Daddy reheated the poker.

He stalked to Logan, whose screams had quieted to sniffles and prayers. "You invited me up here for either a fucking ambush or to fuck with me. I only came because I found out Joe and K-P were coming. You fuckheads would stab me in the back, but they wouldn't as much beef as we have. They have fucking honor."

He laid the poker on Logan's back. At his bloodcurdling scream, something shifted and twisted inside Bash. Logan's look of pain and the sound of agony sent a wave of lust through Bash.

"Cee Cee, please, let him live. Please!"

"If I ever see this motherfucker again, I will kill him," Daddy said, snatching the poker from Logan's back, much to Bash's disappointment. "You stole my sister, I want reparations. Your kid."

"Vivian—"

"Not the little motherfuckers you parade in front the press to suit your respectability," Cee Cee barked, stalking to the minister. "Roddie. Cleaner. Whatever the fuck his name is. He comes with me."

Sharper's tears turned into sobs. "Cee Cee—"

Daddy grabbed the switch from his pocket and aimed it at Logan. "I'm counting to three. Your kid or your cocksucker, but you're not leaving here with both."

"What will I tell Morgan? She let me take our son—"

Daddy kicked the chair. "As if I give a fuck what you tell that cunt," he screamed, spit flying from his mouth with each word he yelled. "Tell her he drowned. Bears ate him—"

"Bears?" Bash squeaked.

"He was lost in the woods," Daddy went on, ignoring Bash.

"Tell her you fucking lost him for being a stupid motherfucker. He'll be alive, Sharper. My sister's dead."

"I'm sorry. God! I'm so sorry. Joe loved her…bitches weaken strong men. It wasn't that she was your sister," he sobbed. "She was a fucking handicap. A man should never love a woman."

"She wasn't a woman!" Daddy said, completely unhinged. "She

was my fucking sister." He kicked Sharper. "She was happy. Joe made her happy. Joe was happy, motherfucker."

"Logan tried to talk him out of it, Cee Cee. He thought she was too close to you for them to have a relationship. But Joe was enamored of her and…and…he thought she'd understood him better since she was associated with the biker life through you."

"I don't give a fuck, Sharper," Daddy said, suddenly so calm Bash wasn't sure if he should run. "Your fucking schemes cost me Kimber. Bitch was the only gentle thing in my life. Now, it's time to fucking pay, motherfucker."

ACT III

ROXANNE

Roxanne Doucette's feet ached in the new pumps her mother purchased specifically for the church trip. Pearlene hadn't allowed her to take the heels out of the box. She'd even packed them in their Payless box. That's how serious it was.

At least when she'd made her debut into New Orleans' society during Mardi Gras last year, Roxy had a chance to practice in her shoes.

The congregation sat and she followed suit, ready for the end of the event. She'd never met Reverend Sharper Banks and wouldn't have made the trip to Los Angeles with other members of her church, including her pastor, if her mother didn't think it was a good opportunity for her.

Reverend Banks was internationally known and respected. Invitations to his tenth anniversary as minister of Light of the World Church were the thing.

"Do you feel it?" the Mistress of Ceremonies demanded. "Do you feel the spirit of Jesus in the building? Swooping in and wrapping His loving arms around you? We didn't come here to look cute—"

Frowning, Roxy rested her elbow on the pew arm, glad she'd secured an end spot. Otherwise, she would've been sardined amongst the overwhelming crowd.

The church resembled a stadium with a dozen rows of pews half-mooning the stage, er pulpit, and stacked stadium seating ascending into the shadows, where the dim track lights didn't reach or were purposely turned off.

"My brothers and sisters, excuse me," the MC cried, snatching a church fan from the podium on the floor in front of the stage and fanning herself.

A deaconess rushed over and handed her a glass of water.

"Thank you, Sister Frey." Sister...her said.

Roxy searched her memory but came up blank. She'd have to look at her program to find the woman's name.

"Water is the breath of life," Sister MC—wrongly—said. "Revelations 14:7 says, 'Worship him who made the heavens, the earth, the sea, and all the springs of water'."

Pursing her mouth, Roxy straightened and opened her program, waiting for her turn. Maybe then she could sneak back to the hotel.

"I've personally never met this next Woman of Christ, but I know her pastor, Reverend Arceneaux, and he tells me she's a firecracker with a bright future ahead of her."

Okay, so change in the line-up. She'd moved up five spots in the program.

"It's always a pleasure to meet a young person possessed with the Lord and all His goodness," Sister MC began.

Must she expound on every fucking thing? Goddamn.

Gritting her teeth, Roxy glanced at the ceiling, relieved not to see it collapsing for her blasphemy.

"And, you know…"

Fuck her. Sister MC droned on for another two fucking minutes. Truly, at eighteen, Roxy hadn't accomplished enough to warrant such a long fucking introduction.

"Sister Roxanne Doucette will give us greetings from Great Redeemer. Sister Doucette?"

Standing, Roxy smoothed her hands over her yellow skirt and walked down the side aisle. At the podium, the wide brim of her hat blocked out the glaring spotlights. Hopefully, it also hid her wince. Her feet hurt so fucking bad.

If she'd been allowed on the stage, the brightness would've been worse, even with her hat.

"Thank you, Sister," Roxy said, calling herself a dumb bitch for not looking at the program for the woman's name. "First giving my obedience to God, the Great Head of my life, Reverend Banks and Light of the World, my pastor, Deramey Arceneaux, ministers on the roster, and invited guests. It's my distinct pleasure to be here tonight, bearing greeting and goodwill from Great Redeemer Baptist Church, located in New Orleans, Louisiana."

She turned halfway and met Reverend Banks' gaze. It was bright and fervent. Insane.

Ignoring the chill sliding into her, she continued. "Reverend Banks, Psalms 20, verses one through nine says, May the LORD answer you when you are in distress; may the name of the God of Jacob protect you. May He send you help from the sanctuary and grant you support from Zion. May He remember all your sacrifices and accept your burnt offerings. May He give you the desire of your heart and make all your plans succeed. May we shout for joy over your victory and lift up our banners in the name of our God. May the LORD grant all your requests. Now this I know: The

LORD gives victory to his anointed. He answers him from His heavenly sanctuary with the victorious power of His right hand. God bless you, pastor. Thank you."

Glad for her wide hat brim that shielded her eyes and her expression, Roxy smiled and stepped away from the podium, all eyes on her. Unease swept into her and a heavy weight descended into her being, like a demon brushed her.

Halfway back to her pew, Sister MC called, "Sister Doucette?"

As Roxy froze, the lights in the nosebleed section flickered on. All around her, the church brightened.

"Our Healing Ceremony is taking place. Reverend Arceneaux shared your recent illness and volunteered you," Sister MC said with sympathy.

Her recent what? Roxy hadn't been ill a day in her fucking life. She came from extraordinarily strong stock.

"Please give Brother Caldwell your hat," Sister MC instructed.

Not that Roxy had a choice. Brother Caldwell removed her hat without warning. Anger rose in her and she lifted her gaze. A man with startingly green eyes and shiny black hair smirked at her. Self-preservation killed her retort. If she detected madness in Reverend Banks, Brother Caldwell seemed soulless.

He inspected every inch of her face, lingering on her mouth and touching on her hair. She'd almost worn her Bantu knots underneath her hat. At the last minute, she'd taken them down and swept her hair into a bun because she'd been undecided if she'd go to a restaurant with some of her friends after the service.

Grabbing her elbow, he ushered her toward the line of ministers.

"Where's my hat?" she asked, low. "My momma paid

fifty dollars for it and she'd have my fucking…er…uh…" She gulped. "Sorry, Brother Caldwell. Momma…I can't lose the hat."

He snickered. "After tonight, fifty fucking dollars will be chump change, slut." He walked away.

She gasped.

"Sister Doucette," the minister said, drawing her attention, unaware at how off-kilter she was by Brother Caldwell's comments. "How are you, my child?"

Fucking terrible.

The minister, an older man with gray hair, thick glasses, and a wrinkled face, smiled at her and took her hand in his.

"Every week, the calls of the weary and the cries of the sick grow louder," Reverend Banks began from his place on the stage. His initials, SB, and Light of the World were inscribed on his podium. The fine wood and intricate detail befit such a striking man. "Every month, our Healing Ceremonies, grow bigger. Require guest ministers to assist. It aggrieved me deeply when I was advised to charge my fragile lambs."

"I can't afford this." Roxy meant her words only for her minister, but he had a mic clipped to him and her voice carried over the speakers. She groaned. "Damn it!" Of course, that carried, too. "Please, Jesus, just let the ground swallow me."

Better yet, let her shut the fuck up.

At the snickering, she turned, intending to run, and not stop until she got outside. The minister didn't give her a chance. He grabbed her arm and placed a finger over her mouth. His hand smelled sour.

Recoiling, she knocked it away. Before she could do anything else, a presence loomed behind her, and the pastor placed that same crusty hand on her forehead.

"Heal her, O Lord, so she shall be healed," he prayed, eyes

heavy-lidded and suspiciously lustful.

Roxy might've been a virgin, but she wasn't a fucking dummy.

Under his breath, he spoke a few more words. Louder, he began speaking in tongues. Voices joined in. She felt like a fish out of water, struggling to comprehend the goings-on around her and not wanting to offend anyone. They didn't speak in tongues at Great Redeemer, so she didn't know the proper protocol.

A wave of gasps and groans crescendoed beside her. The minister jabbed his finger in the center of her forehead.

Roxy jerked in surprise and met his gaze. He lifted a brow. She responded in kind. What the fuck did he want her to do?

Adding a second finger, he poked her forehead again, shoving harder and snapping her head back. Laughter rose up behind her and an inkling hit her. Did this motherfucker expect her to faint?

His third thump answered her. When the heel of his palm pressed against her forehead, she flung herself backwards, worried he'd knock her the fuck out to achieve his fraudulent goal. Thankfully, she landed in a pair of strong arms. She forced her body to relax. Otherwise, she'd look like a fucking corpse as stiff as she was.

A minute later, she staggered to her feet, deciding the power of healing would weaken a fragile body.

She hadn't been the only sick soul there as she saw others lurching to their feet on each side of her. After a song, the line of ministers filed back onto the stage, and she turned to head back to the pew.

Brother Caldwell stepped into her pathway. He wore a vest with all types of patches. President. 1%er. Cee Cee. Scorpions. The American flag.

Roxy snapped her brows together. What foolishness was

this?

"Follow me."

"No."

"I'm not asking you," he warned in a tone she really didn't like. "I'm telling you."

"Roxy, Sharper has invited you to his private party," Pastor Arceneaux said from behind her. "Cee Cee will escort you there."

Or kill her and toss her in the ocean. "My feet are hurting," she sniffed, angry her pastor volunteered her for the ridiculousness she'd endured. "I don't want to go to a party. I want to go to the hotel."

"You're not getting your hat back if you don't go to the fucking party," Brother Caldwell told her.

"There are other yellow hats, motherfucker," she bit out. "Fuck you and it."

"Roxanne!" Reverend Arceneaux gritted. "We're in the House of the Lord and you're a young lady of God." He dusted off his suit. "You're here to represent me and I demand you accept Sharper's invitation."

"Deramey anticipated the invite," Brother Caldwell said. "He brought jeans, sneakers, a T-shirt and a jacket for you to change into."

"Momma didn't tell me she packed sneakers and a jacket for me." A more horrifying thought occurred to her. "I've lost them because my suitcase isn't big and I don't remember—"

"Deramey bought them himself. Your momma don't know."

That sounded beyond ominous and underhanded.

"Either you change your clothes on your own or I do it for you." Brother Caldwell's perusal of her body made her skin crawl. He'd called her a slut and that's how he saw her. "Your choice."

"I'll do it."

"Thought so." Brother Caldwell started off but halted at Pastor Arceneaux's call.

"Our bus leaves at 10AM. Make sure she's on it."

The private estate, located in the Hollywood Hills, teemed with men in vests with back patches proclaiming them Death Dwellers from Hortensia, WA. Others were revealed to be American Scorpions and listed various cities from around the country, mainly from the East Coast, most especially, Richmond, VA.

Alcohol was flowing, the scent of weed almost crossed Roxy's eyes. Nearly naked women roamed about. Tables laden with ice sculptures and champagne fountains stood on every side of the opulent room. Servers offered hot hors d'oeuvres on silver trays. Cold food was set up as a buffet. The DJ alternated between modern music and classics.

Nothing pointed to religion, and Roxy didn't lie by pretending how frightened she was. Something wasn't right. Aside from the godlessness of the world-renowned Reverend Sharper Banks, malevolence hung in the air. Worse, she had yet to see her fucking hat and doubted she'd get it or her outfit back.

At least, her current outfit was more comfortable. Her feet appreciated her black hi-top Chucks. Her black jacket was real leather that she intended to keep. Pastor was risking her fucking neck and virtue for his own means. If she survived, the outfit would be her payment.

Chewing on her lip, she searched for a welcoming face from where she sat alone. Two tables over, a young blonde woman looked as out of place as Roxy felt. If she was anything like Roxy, she needed a friend.

Roxy stood, but a man stepped into her path. He held a glass of champagne out to her. "Sharper's on the way. He's upset you haven't been partaking of the expensive vintage he chose."

"I don't drink," she lied.

"Tough, cunt. He wants you to."

"Back up," she warned, snatching the butterknife from the table. "Or I'm cutting your motherfucking ass, bitch."

Anger darkened his eyes and a muscle ticked in his jaw.

"Quincy, what the fuck is going on?" another voice demanded from behind asshole.

"Nothing, K-P," Quincy gritted. "Sharper wants—"

"Fuck Sharper," K-P snapped, shoving Quincy aside. He glared at Roxanne and snatched the knife from her. "What the fuck did you think you'd fucking do with this, babe? Even if you fucked him up, chances are high you would've been fucked up right after."

Folding her arms, Roxy lifted her chin. "I'm beginning to doubt I'm leaving alive anyway, so why not take a motherfucker with me?" At the truth of her words, nausea twisted in her.

K-P grinned at her, snatched the champagne from Quincy, and set the glass on the table behind her.

"Kaleb, Sharper wants—"

"I don't give a fuck what Sharper wants, little brother," K-P snapped. "Get the fuck away from me before I fucking stab you."

Glaring at her, Quincy stomped away.

"You're fucking gorgeous," K-P said the moment they were alone.

"I know," she retorted, "so your flattery gets you nowhere."

His grin deepened. His handsome face was kinder, gentler than Quincy or Brother Caldwell's.

Without permission, K-P sat at her table. "Sit," he instructed.

Unsure of her location, unarmed, and out of options, Roxy complied.

K-P raised his muscular arm and signaled with his large hand. A patch on his left breast said Road Captain.

"Deramey didn't warn you to wear swaths of clothing, babe? No make-up. Maybe, exhibit a little mousiness in the church."

Roxy shook her head. "Why would that be necessary?"

"Keep you off Sharper's radar."

"Er—"

"At least when Viv was alive, he had an air of respectability."

Two years ago, Vivian Banks' car crash, a block from her husband's church, had been a huge story. Sharper's grief at his wife's untimely death lured Pearlene's sympathy for the widowed father. His two young sons in tears at their mother's graveside reminded Roxy of her own father's death years before. Admittedly, she'd been excited to meet the great man. She'd even hoped to see the two little boys in person rather than in newspapers and coverage of their mother's funeral.

Now, she questioned the minister's character. Worse, once she told Pearlene about the goings-on, her mother would be so upset.

A blubbery motherfucker with a thick black beard stopped

in front of K-P and handed him a tub of beers. He grinned at her. "Story's already changed from a butterknife you picked up out of convenience to you packing your own blade." He held out a hand. "I'm Rack, by the way."

"Roxy," she said, shaking firmly and ignoring his sweaty palm. His denim vest with patches of scorpions dotting the material proclaimed him vice-president.

"Are you hungry?" Rack asked.

She was starving. "Nope."

He laughed. "Sharper's on the grounds, so I have business to see to."

After Rack walked away, K-P gave her an unopened beer. "There's also wine, champagne, and hard liquor."

She set the bottle on the table. "Thanks, but no." Fuck no!

Swigging his beer, he leaned closer. "You've got to work with me, babe," he whispered. "I can't protect you without your help."

"Protect me?" she echoed. She didn't have to ask from who. "Why should I believe that's your intentions? You don't know me."

"There's a blonde girl two tables down," he said, instead of answering her. He finished his beer and placed the empty bottle in the tub. "I was heading to her when I saw my little brother over here. Joe was coming to you."

"Who the fuck is Joe?"

"We switched," he continued, ignoring her question. "Now, he's by the blonde and I'm with you. I'm not complaining. The moment you stood and walked to the podium, you got attention, including from me. Some girls appreciate Sharper's attention. You snatching that fucking butterknife told me you wouldn't be one of them." He slid his chair so close, their denim-clad thighs touched. "Your refusal won't matter, babe. Do you get what I'm saying?"

Loud and clear. She swallowed.

"If you tell me you want to fuck him or Cee Cee or Rack, I'll step aside. But if you don't—"

"Sharper wants this cunt, Kaleb," Brother Caldwell interrupted, grabbing her arm and dragging her up.

K-P jumped to his feet and knocked Brother Caldwell's hand away. "Get the fuck away from her, fuckhead. She's mine."

Brother Caldwell glanced between the two of them. "Sharper paid a lot of money for her pussy. She's his, fuckface."

"My pussy's not for sale!" Roxy flared. "I don't have a fucking pimp."

"What's going on over here?"

The sharp question drew K-P and Brother Caldwell's attention. A gorgeous blond man glared between them.

"Nothing that concerns you, Joseph," Brother Caldwell sneered.

"Roxanne's with me, Joe," K-P stated. "Cee Cee came to fetch her for Sharper. Not fucking happening."

"How the fuck did you get to her, Kaleb?" Brother Caldwell asked. "You were headed to that mouse…never mind. Quincy, the dumb ass, drew attention to himself." He scowled at Roxanne.

Cornered, she dropped her gaze. She didn't trust any of them. Otherwise, she might've sidled closer to K-P. She'd been protected as she grew up, but not sheltered, so she knew nothing in life was free. He'd want something from her, too.

Abruptly, cries, claps, shouts, and greetings replaced the music and the three men stiffened. Joe melted away. K-P grabbed her hand and held tightly, while Brother Caldwell positioned himself at her side. Reverend Banks zeroed in on them and started their way, his entourage dogging his steps.

"Forgive me, babe," K-P said, for her ears alone.

Fear and agitation settled into her and she wanted to know what he meant, but she didn't have the chance before Reverend Banks reached them. His perusal bordered on insulting.

He was a handsome man with meticulously styled waves in his hair, a smooth brown complexion, high cheekbones, and full lips. Tall and regal, he could've been royalty or a movie star, though his polished veneer gave him the air of a politician.

But his eyes, his eyes, frightened the fuck out of her.

"Sister Doucette," he greeted, holding out his hand to her.

She stared, praying for rescue. She wanted the safety of her bedroom in her momma's house and the familiarity of her neighborhood. Her freshmen semester at SUNO began in August and—

"Don't be afraid," Reverend Banks said, dropping his hand. The diamond on his pinky ring caught a ray of light and it sparkled. "You're amongst friends. Deramey mentions you often. Says you're quite well-spoken."

"Sharper, we were about to dust your party to fuck," K-P said lazily. "I've heard New Orleans girls are wild bitches in bed."

Mortification rushed through Roxy in hot waves.

"You were getting pussy from her?" Reverend Banks asked, unashamedly crude. He gave her a severe look. "I thought you were a virgin."

She trembled.

"Speak!"

At his roar, she jumped.

Cigarette in hand, Joe placed himself next to Reverend Banks and faced her.

"Put it out," Reverend Banks ordered.

Joe blew smoke in his face and smiled. "Make me."

"One of these days—"

"One of these days, fuck all, Sharper," Brother Caldwell said coldly. "Fuck with Joe and Kaleb and you fucking die."

A sob escaped Roxy. K-P squeezed her hand. She wanted to snatch it away from him, but she had nowhere to go.

Drawing on his cigarette again, Joe gazed at her, his blue eyes inscrutable. "We all know how much you respect balls, Sharper."

Brother Caldwell hooted with laughter while K-P and Joe snickered. Reverend Banks wasn't so amused.

"Very fucking funny, motherfucker."

Joe smirked, taking another drag of his cigarette. "Figuratively, Sharper," he said innocently. "You respect women who stand up for themselves." Abandoning his humor, he gave Roxanne a pointed look. "Those that know they're every bit as good as you and can tell you to fuck off fifty fucking ways to Sunday." He snatched an ashtray from a nearby table and tamped out his cigarette. "Tell us how you really feel, babe, and don't ever let a motherfucker stifle you. Least of all, this motherfucker." He pointed to Reverend Banks.

"You're going to kill me."

"You'd already be dead," Brother Caldwell said.

"Even if that's the case," Joe added, throwing the other man a dark look, "don't die a coward. Defend yourself and your beliefs to your death."

Her mother would. Pearlene would've cursed all of them out by now.

Heart pounding, Roxy pressed closer to K-P, in spite of herself. "I want to go back to my hotel."

"We're not ready to release you," Reverend Banks stated.

"But Joe's right. I'm interested in hearing how much you enjoyed my church anniversary."

"It was nice," she said as cordially as possible.

"You're lying," he said. "I see it in your face."

Roxy drew in a deep breath. Fuck it. If she was dying, then Joe was right. She'd meet her Maker, knowing she'd told Reverend Motherfucker exactly how she felt. She fisted her hands on her hips, lifted her chin and met the preacher's eyes. "I wish I'd never come to this motherfucker. My fucking feet are still hurting. My momma paid over a hundred fifty dollars for my outfit and the hat is missing. Your Healing Ceremony was a fucking joke. Before you marched me in front of your congregation, you should've told me I needed to fucking faint. It would've saved me from almost being knocked the fuck out. Sister MC didn't know if she was the mistress of ceremonies, the fucking choir director, or the preacher, since that bitch wouldn't shut the fuck up. You, Reverend Banks, are a fucking disappointment. Momma adores you and took her hard earned money to send me on this trip. I was looking forward to meeting you, too. We both thought you were such a great man. But you're not even a good criminal! You sent stupid fucking Quincy over here to roofie my ass." She folded her arms, praying her death was quick. "And your party is fucking boring. No one's dancing. A bunch of naked girls is walking around. If I liked pussy, I'd enjoy the sight, but since I like men they do nothing for me."

Cold amusement lit Reverend Banks's face. "Deramey was right. You are a firecracker."

Wishing she could set his ass on fire, she glared at the minister.

"And Kaleb?"

"What does K-P have to do with this?" she snapped.

"K-P, huh?" Reverend Banks considered her. "He's

extraordinarily proud of his name. I'll believe what he told me if you reveal what the 'P' stands for."

"And if I don't know?" she asked, not really needing the answer because she already understood. She was fucked.

The pastor shrugged. "Find out."

Joe rocked on his heels, drawing her attention. His mouth moved but she couldn't understand him. If she had to guess, he'd said one syllable, two at most.

Paul crossed her mind. Then, Pete. Peter.

Her mind flip-flopping from Paul to Pete, she blurted, "Paul or Pete, but there's so much ganja fumes in here, my brain's foggy and I can't remember it."

Approval flickered in Joe's eyes and he winked at her.

"What songs would you like to dance to?" Reverend Banks asked.

"*Do Whatcha Wanna* by Rebirth Brass Band. *Second Line* by Stop, Inc. *Da Butt. Baby Got Back*. I have a very long list."

He gave her a last look and walked away, taking his entourage with him and leaving behind Joe, Brother Caldwell, and K-P. For the first time, she noticed the blonde woman she'd seen earlier hiding behind Joe.

"I'm disappointed you didn't include me in your critique," Brother Caldwell mocked.

"I have nothing to say about you, Brother Caldwell," she said irritably.

K-P and Joe guffawed.

"Don't call Cee Cee Brother Caldwell, babe," K-P howled, elbowing her. "Motherfucker's not a deacon."

"That's what he was called in church," Roxy protested, throwing the other woman a tentative smile. She looked so shaken. Her blue eyes flickered in every direction. "I'm Roxy," she introduced. "I saw you earlier. I was coming to talk but Quincy interrupted."

"I-I'm D-Dinah," she stammered, wrapping her fingers around Joe's wrist. "I have to return to my hotel, so I can get on the road early," she told him. "It's a long drive back to Seattle and I have to prepare my lesson plans for next week."

"You're a teacher?" Roxy asked. "I thought about going into the profession but decided I didn't have the temperament."

"It does require discipline," Dinah said crisply. "Walk me out, Joe."

"Go to the table and wait for me a moment," Joe said. "I have a couple things to take care of."

"Or you can sit with me," Roxy offered.

Dinah shook her head. "Reverend Banks might return and I have no wish to cross paths with him again." Without awaiting a response, she walked back to the table.

"Fuck, Joe, you're sure you want to deal with that prissiness?" Cee Cee asked.

"I'm not looking for a girlfriend," Joe said sharply. "I want pussy."

Cee Cee glanced at Roxy. "Yeah, well, you missed out on this hot piece. Pity for your dick."

"You're a horrible asshole," Roxy said.

"I make no apologies to you, cunt."

"Good, cocksucker, because I didn't ask your fucking ass for one."

"I like you," he proclaimed.

"Don't give a fuck, because the feeling isn't mutual."

Laughing, Cee Cee strolled away.

"I'm escorting Dinah back to her hotel," Joe announced, "to send a clear message. I should be back in a couple hours since you're determined to see your godsons in the morning." He grinned at Roxy, then leaned in and kissed her cheek. "See you around, babe."

"I'm sorry for being so disrespectful toward you," K-P said once they were seated again, and Joe had guided Dinah out the ballroom. He grabbed another beer from the bucket. The ice was now slush but it still kept the bottles cold.

Roxy thought about his earlier apology. She hadn't understood the words then. Now, she did. "You gave me a head's up, although I was so shaken it wouldn't have mattered if you hadn't. I thought I would die."

"If I hadn't been here, you might have, but hearing Cee Cee and Rack was riding this way, Joe and I decided to hit the road, and attend the party, too. Besides, it gives me a chance to spend time with Luke and Mark."

"You're the Banks' boys godfather?" Roxy asked in surprise. "You don't seem particularly fond of Reverend Banks."

"Sharper," he said flatly. "Call him Sharper. We have a long history, not particularly good. He didn't ask me to christen his sons. His wife did."

Roxy nodded. His wistful note softened her. "You sound as if you had a special relationship with her."

"She was a good girl, babe." He met her gaze. "Kind of like you."

Warmth spread through her at his gruff words. "You don't know me," she retorted.

"I know enough," he said with a charming smile; he winked. "Vivian was quite reserved, but very smart. Sharper believed her money would go to charity if she died before her boys reached their majority. Once she discovered the real Sharper, she developed amazing self-preservation."

"Why didn't she just leave?"

Even before K-P lifted a brow, Roxy knew the answer. Sharper Banks would've killed his wife before he allowed her to walk away. Death lingered in the shadows of the mansion, only kept at bay and away from Roxy because of K-P.

"Never mind," she muttered. "Although I wouldn't have faked not leaving anything to that motherfucker. It would've been for real."

K-P smiled. "She left everything to her boys. Sharper's the executor." He sighed. "Though I'm sure he'll find a way around that. The boys are safe because of Cee Cee, so…" Voice trailing, he scrubbed a hand over his face.

"What did he do?"

"Forget I said anything."

"But—"

"Forget it," he ordered, harsher. "It's in your best interest. Fuck, I'm just tired, sweetheart. Running off at the mouth is the quickest way to get us killed."

Roxy swallowed. "I won't repeat anything you've said," she swore. "Ever."

After studying her a moment, he nodded. "I believe you, babe. Now, listen to me. I stay clear of Rack, Cee Cee and Sharper, but especially Sharper. He enjoys fear and I'm so fucking glad you picked up on what Joe was telling you."

Sighing, Roxy decided against asking all the questions rolling through her head. Except she had one she needed answered. "What did he mean when he said he paid for my pussy?"

K-P's gaze flew to hers and his eyes darkened. A different sort of awareness flared in Roxy. She enjoyed flirting and kissing and teasing but had never had a serious boyfriend. She had a wide circle of friends, a big extended family, deep church roots, and a love of life. Though she wanted kids, she wasn't ready for any and without a serious boyfriend, she didn't want the responsibility of birth control.

Yet, something about the way K-P looked at her, made

her belly clench and heat rise to her cheeks. She lowered her lashes.

"When I meet good girls like you, I can't tell you how much I regret my allegiances, babe," he whispered, the intensity in his eyes holding her captive. "I'm a selfish fuck and I understand if you say no, but can I have your telephone number?"

"We'll probably never see each other again," she said. "According to the back of your vest, you live in Washington. A long way from Louisiana."

"You're right about what's on my cut. And I've always wanted to go to Jazz Fest."

"You missed this year's," she retorted, realizing he, they, referred to his vest as a cut.

"It comes every fucking year."

"I hope you enjoy it."

He grinned. "It happens the end of every April, doesn't it?"

She nodded. "And the first weekend of May."

"That gives us ten months to talk on the phone and get to know one another."

"Do you have a girlfriend?"

"Many."

She wrinkled her nose. "That's nasty."

"It's truth," he said with a shrug. "We'll be hundreds of miles apart, Roxanne. We won't be fucking. Only talking."

"I'll see."

"It's good to have friends from all different walks of life."

"Lawd, Jesus, you're a begging motherfucker, Kaleb," she said, giggling. "I'll give you my number to shut you up but I'm warning you I don't have time to talk for hours to some old dude who lives thousands of miles away."

"Ouch." He placed a hand on his heart. "You wound me. I'm thirty years old. Definitely not old."

"I'll be nineteen in a few weeks. To me, you're fucking old," she teased.

"You can be an old man's darling rather than a young man's fool."

"You're a philosopher?"

"I'm a biker, a mechanic, and a lover of the Bard. When I was young, I used to dream of having a wife with a bunch of children and we all lived in a huge fucking house. My woman and our kids would want for nothing. I'd spoil the shit out of them, and they'd never know hunger or fear or death." His smile was sad. "That's not how it turned out."

"Not so far," Roxy said, laying her hand on his hard thigh. "But don't count out tomorrow." He'd protected her when he didn't have to. He must've had his reasons for not turning his back on Sharper Banks and the rest of them, yet it wasn't her business. After tonight, she doubted she'd hear from K-P again. Right now, she wanted to return the favor he'd shown her and lighten his mood. "My favorite Shakesperean sonnet is 116. Let Me Not to The Marriage of True Minds."

His eyes flared in surprise.

"It bears out even to the end of doom," she recited from memory. "The sonnet speaks of love that doesn't end until the world does. How does it feel to love like that?"

He lifted her hand to his lips and kissed the back of it. "Instead of kicking Quincy's ass, I should probably thank that stupid motherfucker."

"Whatever, boy," she said with a little sniff.

K-P kissed her hand again. "I know you've been traumatized, but don't tell anyone what happened. It's in your best interest, babe."

Frowning, she snatched her hand away. "Are you threatening me?"

"I'm warning you. Sharper's reach is far and wide,

Roxanne. He has contact information on every motherfucker who was at his anniversary. I assure you, he'll send you a warning to keep your mouth shut. What that'll look like, I have no idea."

"Then how will I know it's directed at me?" she demanded.

"Because you will," he said flatly.

"I haven't processed every fucking thing that happened to me," she spat. "I was waiting to escape."

A week later, Sharper Banks sent his warning. Pastor Arceneaux summoned her to a meeting to discuss her behavior during the church trip to LA. Rack's presence didn't alarm her. More fool, she.

Her mother had already torn her new one for losing the clothes she'd used hard-earned money to purchase. Her pastor's berating added insult to injury, especially since he'd been the reason she lost her fucking clothes.

Midway her dressing down, Rack pulled a .357 and shot her minister three times in the head.

"Sharper sends his regard," Rack said and grinned, her last memory before she fainted.

Part Three

What These Bitches Want

CHAPTER 22

MORTICIAN

When CJ called and told Mort about the situation at the Harris household, he'd been talking to Digger over coffee at the clubhouse. Once Mort hung up and immediately called Rory, he knew he had a major fucking problem.

A dead body and a half dead girl were dire enough, but having CJ, Rory, and Ryan involved turned it critical. It left them vulnerable in several ways. If Tom Harris, the dead-motherfucker-walking-suspect returned, the boys could be injured or killed. If he stopped CJ on the road in the guise of law enforcement, then other bullshit would ensue. He could accuse CJ of hurting Molly. He could shoot CJ down and claim he was trying to escape. He could...

Fuck, he could do a lot.

Then, there was the Rory problem, and CJ's worry the little motherfucker might try to steal the corpse to practice on.

Therefore, Mort ordered Digger and a small contingent to accompany him to the Harris house. Then, he called Cash and Stretch.

"What about Johnnie?" Digger asked once they were outside and the brothers were pulling on gauntlets and helmets a few minutes later.

"Fuck him," Mortician said, for Digger's ears alone. Johnnie needed to get his act together before shit reached a boiling point. "We'll call him once we there. Right now, I don't have time for his bullshit."

He had enough bullshit to wade through. He hadn't been home since he'd walked out Saturday night. Bailey had contacted him, although she'd gotten angry when he called her out for disturbing Meggie and making her believe CJ was dead.

Cash and Stretch joined Mort and Digger.

"Where's Val?" Stretch asked.

"Already at the house," Cash responded. "He was still close by, since he'd dropped off Ryan a few minutes before the discovery. After I talked to you, I called Val and he filled me in, Mort."

"Thanks, brother," Mortician responded.

"And Johnnie?" Stretch asked.

"Leave him where he's at," Cash advised. "We don't need two chiefs. Mort's doing just fine."

Stretch jerked on a gauntlet. "Shocking coming from you, Cash. You've sided with Johnnie against Outlaw more times than not recently."

"Johnnie wants peace," Cash said flatly. "Is it so bad that I do, too?"

"Yeah, it is." With both hands gloved, Stretch snatched his helmet. "If the officers are fractured that trickles down to the membership. Factions develop and the club weakens, until we implode."

"Better we implode, then for me to one day get news you or Ophelia or one of our kids have been killed," Cash said.

"I'm going to pretend I didn't hear that, son," Mort said as casually as possible. "I haven't given most of my fucking life over to the Death Dwellers only to have it ruined because of a few scary assholes."

"So now I'm scary, motherfucker?" Cash growled.

"If the yellow belly fits, wear that motherfucker, bruh," Digger said.

"Can you really call me yellow belly when Outlaw is suffering from the same disease?" Cash shot back. "There was a time when he wouldn't have given a fuck what was voted. He acted without anyone's permission. If he's abiding by how the club votes, he wants to."

"No, it's 'cause of Meggie," Digger said.

"You're both assholes," Stretch said.

Digger shook his head. "You the asshole, bruh. Everything your man said is right. Outlaw listen to Meggie and hide behind what Johnnie says, claiming he can't act because it isn't what the club wants. It's not what his bitch wants."

"If you don't shut the fuck up, I'll silence you myself," Mortician said as more of the men he'd summoned walked out of the clubhouse and headed toward their bikes parked in various spaces in the lot. "How the fuck can Prez act like he once did if the motherfuckers he trust the most against him? Take the fucking Gnomes. When Cash, Johnnie, and the other motherfuckers voted for peace, Prez came to us. Us." He started ticking names off on his fingers. "Johnnie. Val. Cash. Stretch. Digger. Me. Us. His friends, family, and fellow officers." He pointed to Cash. "You, motherfucker, refused, along with Johnnie. Outlaw might be able to take on individual motherfuckers without our help, but a whole fucking club? You the fucking sniper, McCall. Johnnie was Jack-of-all-Torturers, good with a blade and a gat, so don't tell me Prez hiding behind what the fucking Johnnie want if you don't want me to punch you in your goddamn mouth."

"Before we start fucking up each other, let's hit the road," Digger advised, not allowing Cash a chance to respond.

"You can apologize to me later, Mortician," Cash said.

"Don't dish it if you can't take it asshole," Stretch said, turned away and walked to his bike, mounting up.

Drawing in a breath, Cash glanced away, then headed to his bike.

"Cash…Ghost?" Digger called.

Cash stopped but didn't turn.

"The last vote about moving against another club was almost two years ago. Don't let it come between you and Stretch."

"Was it really that long?" Cash responded. "It feels more recent than that, especially since we don't have a leader to hold us together while Meggie is in the hospital and Outlaw flounders."

"It won't be solved today," Mort grumbled. "Let's fucking ride."

A few minutes later, the sound of over a dozen Harleys roaring to life was loud in the still morning. Mort signaled they head out. At the gate, Mort paused to talk to the Probate on duty. He was a small, wiry man with a long beard and a bald head.

"Flea, only allow regulars to come and go. Another motherfucker better not get through the gates. Feel me?"

"Got it, Mortician."

Arriving at the Harris house, Mort found Rory sitting on the top step, smoking a cigarette, his eyes bright and burning.

Mort nodded, silently instructing the others to go into the house. Then, he sat next to Rory and lit his own cigarette.

"Hey, little dude," he said. "You okay?"

Rory puffed in silence. Mort waited him out, tuning out the movement and chatter emanating from inside the small house.

"CJ told on me," he said finally.

"CJ not a snitch, Rory."

"I know you know I wanted her body. You both think I'm a freak."

"CJ worry about you, kid. He don't think you a freak anymore than I do."

"Don't tell my dad. He'd be mad that you know."

"Don't fucking worry, Rory. I'm trying not to talk to that motherfucker. And what do I know?"

Shifting, Rory sidled a glance at Mort, then flicked his cigarette away. "I, um, I—"

"This life we lead not normal, little dude," Mort said quietly, throwing away his own cigarette and reaching a startling realization. For the first time, he wished he'd chosen a different path. Maybe, Bailey and Harley would be proud of him. Maybe, his marriage wouldn't be in trouble. "It's not for everybody."

"It's for me," Rory said without hesitation. "I-I…Dad said… I-I always wanted to be CJ's righthand. Dad wants me to be the prez."

Anger percolated in Mort, but he wouldn't express it to Rory. He could only advise him. "Johnnie your old man, so I know you want to please him. At some point, kid, you have to live for yourself. Our world brutal, Rory. If you aren't sure of the place you want to fill—can fill—then you going to be lost."

"I already am, Uncle Mort."

Mort settled an arm around Rory's shoulders. "Then I'm here, little dude. I'm here to pick you up and guide you back. I'm not here to judge you. CJ here. Val. Outlaw."

He hung his head. "I want to kill someone," he whispered. "I want to be the one to do what I've seen my dad do. I used to have nightmares. Now…now…I wanted her body so bad." He heaved in a breath. "When I heard Ryan fall and went into the kitchen, he had fainted."

"What—"

"He's okay. It was because he found her head. If I had a way to leave, I would've stolen it and brought it back to the meatshack." Tears brimmed in his eyes. "That makes me a monster, doesn't it?"

"No. No matter the reason, you didn't steal it. You a resourceful little dude, Rory. If you'd wanted her head, you would've found a way to have it."

Mort didn't truly believe that since Rory was right. If he would've lugged a bag or a box out, he would've been questioned. However, Rory needed redirection in his young life. Hopefully, this was that opportunity. If Mort said the wrong thing, though, the moment would be forever lost.

"If you want to go in the meatshack with Johnnie, do it, Rory. You go anyway. I'll talk to Outlaw. But you have to remember all the other club rules, kid. We don't hurt chicks or defile their bodies. We don't kill just to kill. Once a motherfucker commit a death worthy offense, he can die however the mood strikes you."

"I dream of being the enforcer one day, Uncle Mort."

"We don't have a crystal ball to predict who'll be where down the road. You might be the enforcer."

"Dad said I wouldn't be a real club officer."

It fucking figured. Johnnie long ago stopped seeing Mort as a "real" officer or even a friend. "Why don't you suggest to Johnnie that he introduce a motion to change that?"

Rory smiled for the first time since Mort arrived. "I never thought of that, Uncle Mort."

Removing his arm, Mort stood and dusted off the back of his jeans. "I have to get inside—"

"We need to burn this motherfucker, Mort," Digger grumbled, stomping outside carrying a trash bag. He went to Chester's Jeep that Val drove over, opened the back door and put the bag in.

Val and Ryan walked outside as Digger returned and Rory got to his feet.

"I told you not to put that fucking head in my woman's cage, fucker," Val bit out.

Hands on hips, Digger glared at the RC. "Where the fuck you want me to put the motherfucker?" he snapped. "We got to get it and the rest of her out the fucking house and yours the only fucking transport vehicle available."

Ryan looked away, his pale green countenance, sour stench, and dried vomit on his clothes, giving away how upset he was.

"I didn't have time to get back to the club," Val said. "CJ called me and told me I needed to return."

"He's not the club president," Ryan bit out. "It's bad enough you jump to your wife's every order. Now, you're listening to that arrogant motherfucker? Have you no fucking balls, old man?"

"Shut your fucking mouth, boy," Val ordered. "CJ did what he should've done. If you would've kept your fucking cock in your pants, we wouldn't be in this situation."

Ryan stiffened. "You're pathetic. Is it any wonder I don't fucking respect you?"

"Enough!" Val boomed, despite the hurt on his face. "I don't give a fuck right now, boy. Straighten the fuck up and do what I tell you. The neighborhood's quiet now. I don't know how long that's going to last and we need to clear the fuck out. Tom Harris is a fucking sheriff's deputy. We don't need to be accused of shit we didn't do."

"Shut the fuck up, Val," Ryan said after a moment of silence. "I don't take orders from you."

"Maybe, but you taking orders from me, Ryan," Mort said, tired of the bickering. "Get your fucking ass in the fucking house and start straightening shit out. Val right. Since you, CJ, and Rory involved, and I'm pretty fucking sure Tom Harris know, I don't trust the motherfucker not to try to accuse you boys of the fucking travesty that happened today."

"If I'm not listening to him, what makes you think I'll listen to you, Mortician?"

Val bowed his head. At some point, he needed to bring his fucking kid in hand. Since today wasn't that day, Mort wouldn't beat around the bush.

He smiled at Ryan, the kind he gave motherfuckers right before he fucked them up. "Well, Ryan, you want to stand up to me like a fucking grown motherfucker? I'm going to treat you like a grown motherfucker. Right now, you disobeying not only your daddy but an officer of the club. Either do what the fuck he says or I have to fucking enforce the punishment of the club."

Ryan swallowed. "She's still in there," he mumbled, turning greener. "I-I've never been alone with a corpse, Uncle Mort. Her head...she was staring at me with lifeless eyes."

Mort wasn't happy with Ryan's near hysterics, but he couldn't help thinking how different his reaction was to Rory's. If only Johnnie had allowed his son the luxury of a gore-less childhood as Val had Ryan.

Val reached out to touch Ryan. The vile little motherfucker knocked his hand away.

"Let me take Rory and Ryan home," Val said, sighing.

He looked crushed, a feeling Mort identified with because of Harley. Suddenly, he realized his hypocrisy. He was judging Val for Ryan's behavior when his own child was acting in a similar matter.

No wonder the club was turning into a fucking warzone. Nobody wanted to see their own flaws and, instead, pointed the finger at everyone else.

"I'll come back with the van."

Rory considered Ryan. "Can I hang at your place, Ry? I don't want to deal with my parents right now."

Nostrils flaring, Ryan nodded, then walked down the rickety steps. At his mother's Cherokee, he started to open the door then stopped.

Rory looked at Mortician.

"Go ahead, little dude," he encouraged.

"I'm only doing this for you, Uncle Val," Rory admitted.

Val smiled sadly. "Don't matter, boy. The fact that you're doing it at all shows the type of motherfucker you are since Ryan don't like you."

"Ryan likes no one, Uncle," Rory said. "He doesn't even like himself. Once he does, the rest of us might have a chance."

"Call Johnnie, Rory," Mortician said. "We here now, so he can't hold us up with bullshit. You call him and clue him in."

"Won't he be mad you didn't call him, Uncle Mort?"

Digger sucked his teeth. "Motherfucker stay mad, little bruh," he said, stealing the words Mort intended to say. "We can handle him."

"Yeah, boy, if you call him, he'll see you're on his side," Val added.

"Fine," Rory said with another sigh. He started down the steps. "Although there shouldn't be sides, Uncle Val."

"We're going to clear out most of the brothers, Mort," Val

said once Rory was at the Jeep. "They've collected the clothes and cleaned up the blood as much as possible. When I get back, we'll remove her body. I need to know what to do with her."

"Take her to the funeral home," Mort instructed. "On the way to the club, you call Johnnie, too. Tell him to bring his special shit. We need to wipe fingerprints. CJ and Ryan been here several times. They won't have a body or blood evidence, but motherfucker can always accuse them of taking his woman and daughter."

"What do you think we dealing with, Mort?" Digger asked.

"Much more than a fucking deputy," Mort responded.

"Fuck!" A muscle ticked in Digger's jaw. "Now what?"

"Let Meggie get home and settled in," Val suggested. "Then we tell Outlaw. I just hope…Goddamn." He closed his eyes. "I hope Ryan on the right side of this. I love that little ungrateful motherfucker and, fuck, Puff…if something happens to Ryan, Puff would never recover."

"You have to get him in hand, bruh," Digger said.

"I just…I never wanted my boys to suffer the same abuse I did," Val admitted. "Devon is a good kid. He likes to hang out with me and his momma. Somewhere along the way, I lost Ryan."

That was true. Just as Mort had lost Harley somewhere along the way.

"I'll be back as soon as I can," Val said. On the sidewalk, he turned. "Mort, you need to ride to Nevada City. I'll explain the details when I return. I'll just say Stretch informed me a bit ago that a motherfucker hasn't settled his bill with us. He needs a visit."

"I'll head out when I'm done," Mort said. Time on the road might be just what he needed to clear his head.

RORY

Wondering if he should feel any guilt because he wasn't home watching over his mother, Rory pulled a bowl of fat green grapes from Aunt Zoann's refrigerator. He hadn't eaten a thing today, and his stomach growled in anticipation of the fruit. Smiling, he snatched two out of the bunch and popped them into his mouth. He turned and met Devon's startled gaze.

"What are you doing here, Ro?"

Rory sat the bowl on the center island. Uncle Val and Aunt Zoann's entire house consisted of natural log cuts, though in the kitchen it was a combination of light and dark wood. Sometimes, he marveled at how different each house was, although he rarely visited the log cabin since he fucking hated Ryan. "I can ask you the same thing, Dev." He popped another grape into his mouth. "Why are you here?"

"Uh, I live here."

While Ryan resembled Uncle Val with the same dark hair and turquoise eyes, Devon had Aunt Zoann's whiskey-colored eyes. Nor was he stocky like his father and brother. Rory bet he was already a little taller than Uncle Val.

"I know you live here. Why aren't you at school?"

"CJ isn't, and I heard through the grapevine the Bryds might be returning soon." Devon yanked a handful of grapes. "If I knew Ryan was home, I would've taken my chances with Willard and Wallace."

Rory snapped his brows together and stared at his cousin. "Goddamn. Ryan must be a beast if you'd prefer to deal with those two motherfuckers."

"He's that and more, Rory. Which brings me back to my question. Why are you here?"

Devon chomped the grapes, his lips smacking loudly. Rory frowned.

"Your dad dropped off Ryan and me. I don't feel like going home, so I decided to chill here." It wasn't a complete lie. If he wanted to be a real motherfucker, he could tell Devon that his big brother was a loud-mouthed pussy, but he'd keep that information in reserve. It might come in handier at another time. "Ryan went upstairs to shower and I was hungry."

Devon headed toward the hall. "I'm going for a walk. If Ryan leaves with you, text me. Otherwise, I'll be at Aunt Ophelia's."

"You shouldn't let Ryan best you, Dev. You have as much right to be here as he does."

"Don't underestimate Ryan," Devon said quietly. "Mom's the only one who can keep him in line and he hates her for it. He hates Dad because she's the one person he's afraid of too. But Mom is scary. Still, she's blind to Ryan's viciousness because he's her son and she loves him. I'm just staying in my own lane and waiting for the bottom to fall out." Sadness marred his face, and he shrugged. "I'll be here for my dad, so he can be here for Mom."

He started off.

"What do you know, Dev?"

It was obvious he knew something.

"Stuff I wish I didn't, Ro. I never meant to see…if Ryan ever found out what I knew, he'd kill me."

Debatable. Ryan was a fucking coward.

"If Uncle Christopher ever finds out, Ryan's dead, Rory."

This time, Rory didn't try to stop him from leaving. Without being told, he knew Devon's secret had to do with Bash.

A few minutes later, Ryan walked into the kitchen. His hair was damp, but his clothes were clean.

Rory had lost his appetite and sat quietly on one of the stools at the breakfast bar.

"Have you talked to Bash yet?" he demanded.

"How's that your business, cuck?"

Back on familiar turf, Ryan's assholery returned.

"After this morning, it's my fucking business."

"Not. Harris killed his cunt and beat Molly."

"You fucking sure about that, dickhead? Bash wants to kill Aunt Meggie. Are you sure this wasn't his way of sending some type of message?"

Ryan clenched his jaw and glanced away. "If you think Bash is involved why didn't you tell?"

"You know why," Rory scoffed. "My dad would be as dead as you, since I'm sure he's involved with Bash."

Ryan slid into the stool across from Rory. "If I don't respect you for anything else, I respect you for putting your father ahead of fucking CJ and the slut he dropped out of."

Rory recoiled, feeling like a crybaby, and wishing he could talk to Aunt Meggie or Uncle Mort. But he wanted comfort and reassurance. He was so afraid that life would never be the same again. Even though his childhood was interrupted by visits to the meatshack, there had been an ease to his life before Dad disappeared.

"I'm not protecting my father to earn your respect, Ryan," Rory said evenly. "I've never had it, and I don't give a fuck if I ever get it. I'm protecting him because I love him, and I love my mom. If Uncle Christopher kills Dad because he's a stupid asshole, it would destroy her."

"She's a spoiled bitch just like my mother," Ryan spat. "Just like Rebel and Harley, that…"

If Rory lived to be a hundred, he could've gone his entire life without hearing how Ryan referred to Harley.

"Say that to Uncle Mort. I dare you."

"Fuck him, Rory. And you know where they got Digger from? By combining dog and—"

"Don't you fucking say that word again," Rory interrupted.

Ryan dissolved into laughter. "Fucking cuck. You're not fucking fit to be a part of my family. Logan would hate you."

"As if I give a fuck who that motherfucker hated. I know who he didn't hate, you stupid fuckhead, and that was Sharper Banks."

Snapping his mouth shut, Ryan blinked. "I don't like what the fuck you're insinuating."

"It's the fucking truth, Ryan. Some of my dad's paperwork had letters. They were lovers."

"You're a liar! Logan Donovan was a great man. He wasn't a fucking pervert. He thought more of himself than to allow Sharper Banks…No, you're a fucking liar."

"And you're a fucking jerk."

Jumping to his feet, Ryan stalked to Rory's side. "Show me the letters."

"Fuck you."

"I demand—"

Rory getting to his feet forced Ryan back. It pleased him that he was finally taller than the motherfucker. "You're not in a fucking position to demand anything, asshole. You know what I demand? Tell motherfucking Bash to back off. Whether you like her or not, Aunt Meggie is innocent. I'm so scared she's going to be hurt, but I can't sacrifice my dad. You, though? If I can see anyway that Dad will be safe, I'll sing like a fucking canary and dance in your fucking blood. I'm going home. If I have to deal with a fucking traitor, I'd prefer it to be one in my own house." Although Dad should've left by now to join Uncle Mort. "Tell Ms. Harris 'hi' when her headless corpse visits you, fuckhead."

The color dropped from Ryan's face, and Rory smirked, turned on his heel and strolled off.

"You'll be dancing in Johnnie's blood long before you do mine," Ryan called in a trembly voice.

Not having a response, Rory kept walking, damning his cousin for getting the last word.

CHAPTER 23

Harley

After a miserable weekend that she and Mommie spent sobbing and depressed, Harley trudged into the school locker room Monday afternoon, wondering if Daddy planned to come home for dinner. He hadn't been home since Saturday. Aunt Zoann and Aunt Fee dropped her, Rebel, and Mattie off at school. They were going to visit Aunt Meggie, the reason they were together.

Harley had overheard them talking about Uncle Mort sleeping in his old room at the club, and they planned to talk to Mommie and see what was up.

Rebel and Mattie had turned accusing looks on Harley. She'd flipped them off on the downlow. After that, they ignored her.

Just as they had for the entire day. CJ hadn't come to school again today, nor had Rory and Ryan. She'd texted Rory to ask if Winter Break started a week earlier for them than scheduled on the school calendar. He hadn't responded.

During her lunch break, she'd gone to rehearsals as usual. Nardo gave her the cold shoulder because she canceled their movie date. Only her brothers showed up. After that, her day passed in a blur. It seemed as if the entire world was angry at her. Everything was so off-kilter, she didn't know who was picking her up after school. Nor did she care.

Tension had seeped into cheer practice. Where, she noted, Molly was also absent. Rebel and Mattie huddled together, ignoring Harley. Jaleena and her crew whispered amongst themselves, giggling whenever they carried out Coach Ericks's directives. The way they focused on Harley told her they were making fun of her.

Sighing, she lumbered to her locker and opened it. She intended to grab her 2-in-1 shampoo and conditioner and her body wash. Except she realized voices were echoing from the showers.

"Oh my God, can you believe those three snotty bitches? It's like they're fucking royalty."

"Princesses."

"Biker princesses."

The girls laughed. Harley squinted. She was almost positive it was two juniors by the names of Ariana and Erin. She was just as certain they were discussing her, Rebel, and Mattie.

"Hey, get me a towel so I can wrap around my hair?" Erin asked. "Thanks," she said a moment later.

"Come on. Let's go and dry off, then I'll braid your hair."

Frantic, Harley darted to the last stall.

"What do you think of the new schedule, Erin? Coach Ericks wants us to try out for state championship this year."

"It's brutal. I'm all but failing World History. If I don't raise my grade, the cheer schedule won't be my problem."

"I'm failing Language Arts," Arianna admitted. "I wish

Lumbly hadn't retired or relocated or whatever. He was the easiest grade ever."

"Not for CJ," Erin said.

Harley stiffened at Erin's dreamy sigh.

"Yeah, that's what I heard. I think that's why Lumbly was fired. I wish I'd been in CJ's class. I would've protected him. Lumbly was easy to handle if you sucked up to him."

"CJ would never," Erin said with certainty. "He is…he is… oh my god, I'm so in love with him."

"Me, too," Arianna admitted with a giggle. "I even think Mrs. LeBan is crushing on him."

"She isn't that old. Like twenty-seven or something. She just looks old because she's so buttoned up."

But still a grown ass woman.

"She looks and acts like she's fifty," Arianna grouched. "She wouldn't have a chance with him. We're prettier and younger."

Growing up in a hypermasculine environment, Harley was quite familiar with outdated stereotypes about the fairer sex. She scoffed at most of them, since she and her cousins didn't fit those cliches. Just like boys, they were people with varied emotions and personality traits. But, as she heard two of her fellow cheerleaders talking shit about the princesses of the Dwellers and Mrs. LeBan, her mind couldn't help but think of one stereotype used countless times to describe women. On many occasions, the boys and men around her claimed girls are naturally catty, and often tore each other down for no reason. Right now, as she eavesdropped on Ariana and Erin's conversation, she agreed.

At the moment, it had snowballed into talking about specific cheerleaders. The first Dweller daughter to be brought up was Mattie.

"That redhead is a spoiled two-faced bitch," Ariana

sneered.

The harsh description shocked Harley.

"Rebel is the prettiest of those three hoes," Erin announced, a sentiment Harley heard often.

"I agree," Ariana said. "She's the classic all-American beauty."

Envy assaulted Harley. She'd kill to have light eyes and silky blonde hair. Her hazel eyes were more brown than green, and her black hair was curly and unruly.

"I hear her mother is stunning," Erin commented.

"I wonder if she has a violent maniacal personality like Rebel."

"That hoe is jail bound," Erin decided.

Harley wasn't pleased with either of her friends right now, but hearing these two heifers disparage them upset her. Yes, Mattie was bougie as hell and switched personalities based on whom she was speaking to. And, sure, Rebel had a temper and was quick to make threats and throw punches.

But Ariana was a mean girl and Erin was a slut. They had no room to talk about Mattie and Rebel, who, ordinarily would've accompanied Harley into the locker room. Instead, they'd chosen to talk to Jaleena and her friends.

If Mattie and Rebel were here, neither Ariana or Erin would talk such smack. The fucking cowards. If word got back to Mattie and Rebel, they'd also backtrack.

Finally, the moment Harley had been dreading arrived as they began to speak about her.

"My cousin is in the set design group for the play," Ariana started, "and she said Harley is the worst bitch ever."

Hearing how her co-stars gossiped about her humiliated Harley.

"Harley's been a diva ass bitch. She needs to fucking chill out."

"Real talk," Ariana agreed. She was mixed like Mommie. "She thinks she's all that. Bitter Black bitch."

Alliteration aside, the words sparked Harley's temper. After suffering CJ's rejection, Daddy's unnecessary behavior, and Mattie and Rebel's desertion, she'd had enough. She threw open the stall door and reveled in the look of shock on Ariana and Erin's faces.

She stormed to them and tried to mimic the scary scowl Rebel had perfected. "I'm a what now?" she snarled.

Dressed in jeans and a turtleneck sweater, Ariana started backing away.

She was a petite girl, roughly the size of Aunt Meggie, so Harley's 5'6 frame towered over her. She liked that. It gave her a confidence boost. If the confrontation turned physical, she'd undoubtedly win.

She was raised by bikers, after all, so she was well-versed in violence. And watching Rebel and Mattie fight every two seconds allowed her to learn some techniques.

Erin—a tall girl with blue eyes and long strawberry blonde waves—grabbed Harley's arm and spun her around, glaring daggers at her.

"Thank God!" Ariana cried in relief.

"Were you stalking us?" Erin demanded.

Harley laughed in her face. "This is a public space, dumb ass. If you didn't want others to overhear, you should've talked in private. Besides, I have better things to do with my time than to stalk you two bitches."

Shock flittered across Erin's face. At school—everywhere— Harley was known as the peacekeeper among her, Mattie, and Rebel. She wasn't the confrontational one, but Harley couldn't allow them to get away with such insults.

Ariana ran to Erin's side and grabbed her hand. "Let's just go, before she calls her little gangster friends."

Harley wanted to laugh. If anything, she was the most 'gangster' of the Dweller daughters. She was the only one who'd been arrested and spent a couple hours in an actual jail cell. She didn't need help to put two catty bitches in their places.

"I don't need anyone to beat your asses," Harley declared, standing straighter. Least of all, Rebel and Mattie, who treated her like a plague victim.

Erin snorted a laugh. "I can pick your ass up, bitch."

At roughly 5'11, she probably could. And being a cheerleader, she had some muscle. Still, Harley had fought boys before and she was quite athletic herself, so she wasn't scared.

"And I can dropkick you, you overgrown giraffe."

Rage settled into Erin's face.

In a moment of boldness, Ariana inserted herself between Harley and Erin. She glared at Harley. Apparently, unaware of how tiny she was, she shoved her. "Take that back, you nappy-headed hoe."

The force of Ariana's push caught Harley off-guard. Stumbling backward, she nearly fell, but managed to regain her bearings and charge Ariana. Grabbing her light brown curls, she tossed Ariana to the grimy floor. Ignoring the smaller girl's screech, Harley straddled her and continued her attack, ending with a blow to her nose.

A crack echoed around them.

Erin gasped.

Ariana's cry of pain emboldened Harley, and she punched the girl again, hurt and angry and betrayed. Blood spewed from Ariana's nostrils. The girl's once straight little button nose would now be crooked.

Harley grinned, wishing it was Molly, Rebel, or Mattie she was punching.

"You crazy bitch!" Ariana cried, holding her broken nose. Tears streamed down her honey-colored cheeks.

Before Harley could reply, or resume her attacks, she was given a taste of her own medicine.

"Get off her!" Erin shrieked, snatching a fistful of Harley's braids and yanking her off her friend.

Bad enough. Adding insult to injury, Erin threw Harley onto the floor, allowing her friend to scramble away, and proceeded to kick Harley's stomach. The breath whooshed from her lungs as pain blossomed in her abdomen. Hot tears sprang to her eyes. Instinctively, she curled into a ball and wrapped an arm around her head.

"This is what you get, cunt," Erin snarled, stomping Harley's shoulder.

She screamed, weeping harder. Pain shot through her arm. Erin paused at the sound of the door opening.

Agony blanketed Harley's body. Though Erin's foot remained on her shoulder, the blows had stopped. Closing her eyes, she rested her head on the floor, sobbing.

"What the ever-loving fuck?"

Suddenly, Erin's foot was jerked away, and she yelped.

A clank followed, then the sound of a body hitting the floor. The scream hurt Harley's head.

Afraid the attack might resume, Harley managed to maneuver into a sitting position. Rebel loomed over Erin's knocked-out form. Blood spattered her nose and lips and there was a rapidly forming bump on her forehead. Spots of blood dotted the wall near the hand dryers.

Wild-eyed, Rebel focused on Ariana.

Immediately, the girl put her hands up. "I'm sorry!"

The apology didn't make a difference to her cousin; Rebel charged anyway.

Somehow, Ariana bypassed Rebel and scurried out of

the bathroom. Rebel's rage didn't lessen when she took in Harley's condition. Instead of giving chase to Ariana, she held out her hand.

Harley quickly gripped Rebel's fingers, groaning as Rebel yanked her off the floor. Though her head was untouched, the attacks left her out of sorts. Rebel's rescue, when there'd been such hostility between them recently, didn't help. Unwanted guilt swarmed Harley as she thought back to what she said, how she rejected the advice Rebel had offered. Had Harley listened, she might not have ended up beaten on the bathroom floor.

Harley leaned against the bathroom sink, cradling her side. "Why'd you rush to my aid?"

Rebel's pretty blue eyes narrowed. "Did the bitch hit you in your head or some shit, asking a dumb question like that? You needed my help."

The rebuke made her feel weak. She scowled. "I had it handled!" she protested, an obvious lie.

She'd been able to deal with Ariana with no problem, but she hadn't counted on Erin's …brutality.

"The fuck you did. Erin was whooping your ass when I walked in!"

Harley glanced away.

"What the fuck happened, Harls?"

Harley's cheeks heated up, unsure how to say she'd bit off more than she could chew.

"Ummm…we got into a fight?" Stating the obvious delayed the inevitable.

"No shit," Rebel huffed. "I mean what the hell led up to it?"

Erin groaned.

Sighing in annoyance, Rebel stomped to Erin, straddled her and punched her temple, knocking her out again. When

Rebel stood, she glared at Harley.

"Talk, now."

Harley nodded and equipped her big-girl panties as she started to recount the events leading up to the fight. Rebel's face darkened, and she glanced at Erin's unconscious body with a look of contemplation, no doubt plotting ways to injure the girl further.

When Harley finished, Rebel's chuckle surprised her.

"Didn't know you had that shit in you, Harley," she praised, holding a hand up to high-five Harley.

Bewildered, Harley reluctantly slapped Rebel's palm. She expected a lecture for acting so out of character, not praise for her violence. Then again, Rebel was the last person who could chastise anyone for fighting.

Rebel giggled, and Harley's lips twitched into a smile. The tension lingering between them for days had ceased for the moment; it felt great.

"Mattie and I must teach you how to properly fuck a bitch up."

This time, Harley laughed. Despite her agony, bantering with one of her best friends was a serious mood booster.

"I'd like that."

The bathroom door opened again, and someone gasped.

"Fuck," Rebel muttered, standing straighter.

Ariana marched into view, followed by Mrs. LeBan.

Harley's heart dropped.

They were so dead.

Matilda

If she'd remained in the gym, talking to Jaleena and her friends, Mattie wouldn't have spotted Ariana and Mrs. LeBan trekking toward the locker room, where Rebel had gone to check on Harley.

Ariana was a fucking cunt, who hated Mattie. The feeling was more than mutual, but that was beside the point. Seeing that bitch's swelling eyes, tear-streaked bruised face, and obviously broken nose meant trouble. Worse, she'd found Mrs. LeBan, Ridge Moore's very own Nurse Ratched. A character in a movie Mattie shouldn't know if Daddy had anything to say.

Well, he did. A whole fucking lot as a matter of fact. Luckily, Maman felt differently, and whenever it was just she and Mattie in the house, they watched the movies Daddy banned for Mattie but gave free rein to the boys.

Stupidly, when Mattie saw Nurse Ratched, er, Mrs. LeBan, she didn't run the other way. Instead, she rushed behind them and walked in just as the teacher was helping Erin to her feet.

Erin was a worse cunt than Ariana, but whatever.

Ariana spotted Mattie and burst into sobs. "She hit me first," she said, pointing to Mattie.

"What are you talking about? I don't know what

happened!" Daddy had just returned home. He still hadn't recovered his full deck, but he was back, and Mattie didn't want to tip the balance. "I was in the gym with Jaleena."

"You were not!" Erin said, swaying on her feet.

"Bitch, I will fucking drag you," Rebel barked. "Tell the truth about Mattie or sleep with your fucking eyes open."

Harley remained silent. She looked absolutely petrified and in a great deal of pain. She had various cuts and bruises on her face. Her lips were busted. Her eye was swollen, and she listed to one side.

"You assaulted me, and now you're threatening me," Erin said in outrage. "Call the police, Mrs. LeBan. I want to press charges."

"You fucking cunt," Rebel snarled, rushing Erin and almost punching the fuck out of Mrs. LeBan when she stepped between the two girls.

Rushing into the fray, Mattie dragged Rebel to a bench. "Calm down, cousin," she warned. "This won't help the situation."

Rebel jumped to her feet. "Fuck help! I want that bitch to die."

"You're going to jail," Erin said in triumph as Mattie's phone dinged.

Taking it from her pocket, she saw that Lolly had sent a message to let them know she was outside.

Mattie's fingers flew over her phone's keyboard.

Come to the locker room, Lolly. Hurry. We're in trouble.

She pressed 'send', rejoining the conversation she'd momentarily tuned out.

"I should've picked you up to knock out this bitch," Rebel said to Ariana and pointed to Erin.

"Enough, Miss Caldwell," Mrs. LeBan said briskly, "Or I

will call the cops."

"Not only will I press charges, but I'm going to sue you for pain and suffering," Erin spat, ignoring Mrs. LeBan. "All of you."

"No, please!" Harley finally spoke. "Mattie wasn't involved. Rebel came to my rescue." She explained what happened.

"Liar!" Blood dripped from Ariana's nose. "You, Rebel, and Mattie were gossiping about us."

"What's going on in here?"

At the sound of Lolly's voice, Mattie sagged in relief.

They all looked toward the door. She was leaning against it. A moment later, Aunt Zoann walked in. Her whiskey-colored eyes flared in surprise.

Lolly barreled into the fray, her gaze flickering between all of them before resting on Harley as Aunt Zoann stepped next to Mattie and placed an arm around her shoulder.

Rebel barely had a scratch on her. Harley, Ariana, and Erin, however, were bruised and battered.

"I'm asking again, what's going on in here?" Lolly said. "Someone start talking now."

Before that directive was followed, the door opened again, this time bringing in Dr. Marvey and one of the school resource officers, his radio crackling with indistinguishable voices.

"Miss Caldwell, Miss Banks," Dr. Marvey began grimly, "Officer Grey will escort you to the waiting unit." He glanced from Ariana to Erin to Mattie. "You three, follow me to my office."

"They aren't going anywhere until I know what the fuck's going on," Lolly said, stepping up to the two men.

Mrs. LeBan scuttled behind Officer Grey at Lolly's ferocious glare. Dropping her arm from around Mattie, Aunt

Zoann leaned forward. "You can run but you can't hide. Answer Roxanne or answer me. Your fucking choice."

"Hey, what's up?" Jaleena asked from the doorway. Behind her, a crowd was gathering.

Mortification hit Mattie. There was no way Daddy wouldn't hear about this incident. Even though she wasn't involved, he'd find a way to accuse her of unladylike behavior.

"Get out, Miss Davis," Dr. Marvey ordered.

"Can I please explain?" Harley said once Jaleena backed out and the door closed.

"Neither me nor Dr. Marvey are interested in an explanation, Miss Banks," Officer Grey said coldly. "Tell it to the booking officer."

"Fuck, we're going through enough right now," Lolly said with keen disappointment. "If Meggie wasn't in the hospital, I'd beat your ass first, motherfucker," she said, nodding to Dr. Marvey. "And finish with you." She nodded to Officer Grey.

Aunt Zoann smirked at Mrs. LeBan. "She'll be home soon."

"I can always call in units for you two," Officer Grey snapped. He glared between Rebel and Harley. "Now get to moving!" he yelled.

Harley burst into tears.

Rebel sat and folded her arms. "Lolly, would you please call my father."

"I don't give a damn who your father is!" the officer fumed.

"So brand new," Rebel said with a merry titter as Lolly got her cell phone and dialed.

Dr. Marvey snatched the handkerchief from his lapel. "I thought Mr. Caldwell was indisposed. Mrs. Caldwell is quite ill."

"It doesn't matter," the officer said. "I'm sick and tired of having to raise other people's children—"

"Earl," Dr. Marvey cut in, looking rancidly ill.

"The reason there's so much thuggery is because parents allow their children to run wild—"

"Earl, please—"

Earl? Was the officer named Earl Grey? Did his parents not like him? Mattie bit her lip to stifle her laughter.

"The father isn't even answering!" Officer Teabag yelled. He stomped to Rebel and snatched her to her feet.

Aunt Zoann ran to them and knocked his hand away. "Don't put your fucking hands on my niece."

Before anyone responded that fucking door opened again. At this point, Mattie was ready to rip it off the hinges.

"Out—"

"Nope," Ryder said, leading Ransom and Axel in. "CJ sent us to see what was going on, after Jaleena called him."

Ransom looked at Harley, Ariana, and Erin, then grinned at Rebel. "Oh, snap! Legendary. You beat three bitches."

Aunt Zoann and Lolly laughed, while Rebel rolled her eyes. "I was on Harley's side, dummy. Why would I beat her?"

"Cuz she broke CJ's heart," Axel said, glaring at Harley. "And she was mean to Lolly and Uncle Mort."

"This is out of control." Officer Grey spoke into the radio, requesting backup. "If you little boys don't leave, you're going to jail too. You don't belong in the upper school."

"I belong wherever I damned well please, fuckface," Ransom said, folding his arms. "My momma and daddy own this school, so if you're mean to us, your bitch-ass can be fired."

Mrs. LeBan lost her color.

Dr. Marvey cleared his throat and whispered something

to the teabag, who immediately turned and spoke into that noisy ass radio, clipped to his shoulder.

"Boys," Dr. Marvey said, "your…your sister and cousins were just going to my office. They were fighting and—"

Axel roared with laughter. "You big dummy, Harley don't fight."

"Rebel does," Ryder piped in. "She beat Ryan's ass." He offered Aunt Zoann an apologetic smile. "She does have off days, like when Mattie gave her an ass whooping."

"Would you shut the fuck up!" Rebel snapped.

Not a chance. Ryder was enjoying himself too much.

"It doesn't matter who owns what," Ariana protested. "Harley threw the first punch."

"You told me Miss Caldwell and Miss Banks attacked you," Mrs. LeBan said tightly.

"Rebel might be brutal, scary, and a would-be killer, but she doesn't pick fights," Axel said with indignation. "And Harley definitely won't throw the first hit. She might try to control my brother, but she isn't a bully."

"Goddamn, boy, if you're defending Harley and Rebel, I'd hate to have you scorn them," Lolly said, half amused and half annoyed.

Ryder held up his phone. "CJ's here."

Mrs. Leban patted her bun and straightened, while Ariana and Erin forgot their numerous injuries and clutched each other.

"He skipped school to go to the hospital," Rebel said on a sigh. "You shouldn't have called him."

"CJ was with Molly, dummy," Ransom said. "I heard Bishop and Potter talking yesterday when I was visiting Momma and showing her the pictures of our tree. They said he was taking Molly to make her baby go away."

"WHAT?" the girls and women chorused as CJ walked in

and rushed to Rebel.

She'd gone pale at Ransom's news. Obviously, CJ thought she was hurt because he pulled her to her feet and hugged her.

"Are you okay, Reb?" he demanded.

"I hate you so much," Harley screamed.

"Yeah, whatever, I know. I'm tired, Harley. I don't have time—"

Aunt Zoann jerked CJ away from Rebel and punched the side of his head.

"Ow!" He started to place a hand over his injured temple, but she hit him on the other side and he stumbled back. "Ow! Fuck, Aunt Zoann."

She went for him again, but CJ dodged her hit.

"You fucked Molly! My son's, your cousin, girlfriend."

"I...what? I—" He glared at his brothers. "I'm fucking you three up!"

"We're just the messengers, bro," Ryder said, unrepentant. "You're the bozo who fucked an idiot and got her pregnant. We overheard Bishop and Potter talking about the money Dad gave you to take care of the problem."

"Jesus fucking Christ," CJ snarled. "Is nothing secret around this motherfucker? Molly's baby wasn't mine, and Ryan and Rory was with me, since you, Aunt Zoann, might've been a grandmother. Except we aren't sure since an old motherfucker has been assaulting her! Goddamn it! By the fucking way, I didn't take her for the abortion, because her father beat the baby out of her and killed her fucking mother. I've been at the hospital with her all goddamn day. Half the fucking club is at the Harris house to—" All at once he realized how much his word vomit revealed and he snapped his mouth shut. He kicked a locker. "Fuck!"

"Even my daddy is helping her?" Harley gasped.

CJ glared at her.

"I didn't know Ryan missed school," Aunt Zoann said.

CJ transferred his glare.

She sniffed. "Sorry for trying to knock you the fuck out."

"Make it up to me by knocking out Ryan again," CJ grumbled.

"What do you mean again, baby?" Lolly asked.

"Motherfucker…saw, er, something, and fainted," CJ said.

"What?" Aunt Zoann gasped. "Ryan fainted? What…?" She snapped her mouth shut and tightened her lips.

Mattie licked her lips, wanting the details, but knowing she'd never get them.

"Dad's here," Ransom said, mimicking Ryder's earlier actions and holding up his phone.

Rebel started. "He is?"

CJ dropped onto the bench closest to him. He looked exhausted. Mattie's heart went out to her cousin. After their initial greeting yesterday, her father barely spoke to her, and her mother still wasn't back to normal.

After dinner, Gramps locked himself away with Daddy, while Grandma Charlotte coddled Maman. When they returned home, Maman and Daddy went to their room. Rory stomped to the library. JJ stole chocolate ice cream he shouldn't have taken because it was way after their snack curfew. Ella carried Blade to the nursery and Mattie was left completely alone.

Lolly must've been alerted to their return because she'd called Mattie and talked to her for an hour.

Today, at school, Mattie put on her usual airs to protect herself. She was used to surviving in such a manner. On the other hand, CJ had always had a great support system. Until recently. Now, he looked so stressed and no one seemed to notice to ask about his well-being. Though she worried he'd reject her, she tipped closer to him and placed her hand on his shoulder.

"Are you okay?" she asked. "How's Molly?"

He smiled at Mattie. "I'm fine," he said softly. "Molly's hurt really bad, Mattie." He hung his head. "Worse, she doesn't have anywhere to go."

"I have more than enough room," Lolly volunteered. "As soon as we straighten this out with Harley, I'll go to the hospital."

"No!" Harley cried. "You can't take Molly in. She stole CJ from me."

"For the last fucking time, Harley, Molly is my friend!" he said, eyes blazing. "She's Ryan's girlfriend, and she cares about the dickhead when he's nice to her. She didn't steal me from you. Until Saturday, you had my fucking devotion."

Ariana and Erin, both resembling freaks from a horror show, almost swooned. Even Mrs. LeBan licked her lips and she stared at CJ.

"Lolly—"

"You brought this shit on yourself, baby," Lolly interrupted.

"You hate me, too."

"I love you," she countered. "I will always love you, but you and your momma owe me, Knox, and your daddy apologies."

In the silence, the faint sound of jingling spurs captured their attention.

The Caldwell siblings exhibited various reactions. The Terrible Triplets' faces lit up with anticipation. CJ's shoulders sagged in relief. But Rebel? She wore a combination of hope and the adoration of a girl toward her father.

As angry as her daddy made her, Mattie understood Rebel's reaction. Though she longed for her father to accept her, see her, for herself, she loved him dearly.

Uncle Christopher opened the door. Diesel and Daddy followed him in.

"What are you doing here, Matilda?" he demanded.

"Shut the fuck up, asshole," Aunt Zoann barked. "She's here to support her cousins and if you say another fucking word to her, I'm punching you."

"She has some punches still in her, Uncle Johnnie," Axel informed him gravely. "She had to stop fucking up CJ when she found out he hadn't fucked her son's bitch."

"Shut the fuck up, Axel," Uncle Chris ordered. "You not no grown motherfucker." After lighting a cigarette, he looked at Dr. Marvey, who suddenly seemed on the verge of fainting. "Badges gone. I sent them the fuck away."

Gulping, Dr. Marvey nodded.

"Me and you talkin'."

"I can explain."

Uncle Chris grinned coldly. "I bet the fuck you can, Marvey." He looked at Officer Teabag. "Get your shit and get to fuckin' steppin'. You fuckin' fired. Johnnie, take this motherfucker and work out the severance details."

"You can't—"

Daddy's smile was as chilling as the gleam in his eyes. "Oh, but he can." He stepped aside and indicated the door with a sweep of his hand. "Officer."

The teabag stomped out of the locker room.

Daddy paused at the door. "Mattie, you've had a long day. Would you like to go shopping to cheer you up?"

"Can we go to Tiffany's? I want to buy Maman and me matching bracelets for the club's Christmas party."

"Of course, sweetheart." He left.

"Bitsy, stay with Diesel. Ariana and Erin parents on the way. You can fill in the details to help him negotiate," Uncle

Chris said. "You okay, baby?" he asked Harley.

Sniffling, Harley nodded.

"I can call Mort and tell him to get his ass back here."

"Where's Daddy?"

"Volunteered to go on a run to Cali."

"Oh."

"Roxanne, take Harley home," Uncle Chris said.

Lolly nodded. "Come on, kids. We can all go—"

"Nope, my lil' motherfuckers comin' with me."

"I want to go home and clean up, Daddy," Rebel protested.

"Yeah, Dad," CJ said. "Aunt Zoann punched the fuck out of both temples because she thought I fucked Molly and got her pregnant."

"How the fuck…?" Uncle Chris's voice trailed off and he glared at Ryder, Ransom, and Axel. "You lil' motherfuckers spyin' again?"

"No, Dad," Ryder said, unperturbed.

"Then how you know your brother's business."

"A man never gives up his sources," Ransom declared.

"A man give up his sources if he ain't wantin' an ass beatin' so fuckin' bad, he can't sit the fuck down for a week."

"Yeah, Bishop and Potter was talking," Ransom blurted, "and we overheard them."

"Goddamn, twerp, you fucking rolled very quickly," Rebel said with disgust.

"You've gotten your ass beat by Dad, Reb," Ransom said. "I'm not subjecting my ass to his belt on behalf of a motherfucker who shouldn't have been talking so fucking loud."

"You still repeated shit you shouldna," Uncle Chris said.

"Now, Dad—" Ryder began.

"Shut the fuck up, son. You ain't gettin' your ass beat cuz your ma comin' home."

CHAPTER 24

CJ

Few times in CJ's life had so many things culminated at once and wore him out. He'd awakened with a singular purpose—take care of Molly's problem. It should've been as easy as picking her up and bringing her to the clinic, then getting her to the hotel. In hindsight, he realized the issues her disappearance would've caused at her house. He just hadn't appreciated the depth of Tom Harris's motherfuckery.

CJ swore he'd never make such an error again. The man had destroyed their school project. He'd shaken CJ so badly by his behavior that CJ had felt lucky escaping with his life. Yet, CJ believed the man would just accept Molly's absence. Worse, he'd left Molly and Mrs. Harris in a vulnerable position.

"You okay, boy?" Dad asked as they boarded the hospital's elevator.

They'd been silent on the ride from Ridge Moore to

Hortensia General. CJ rode shotgun while Dad drove Mom's Lexus SUV. Rebel and Rule sat in the middle seat, while the other three little fuckheads sat in the third bench seat. CJ supposed Gunner was with Aunt Fee.

Once they were all in the elevator, Rebel pressed the 'up' button and the doors closed.

"Yeah, Dad," CJ answered. "I'm fine."

Rebel glanced over her shoulder. "Are you worried about Harley?"

It shamed him to admit he'd thought about her only briefly since leaving school, although he considered her fight to be amongst the day's ills.

"You really beat both those bitches, Reb?" Ryder sounded in awe.

The elevator dinged.

"Yep," she said as the doors opened and she stepped into the hallway. "Remember that if you value your miserable life."

Ransom snorted as they started down the hallway. "There's one of you and three of us, Reb."

"What the fuck that mean, boy?" Dad asked, reaching the general sitting area for the floor. As usual, Dweller brothers swarmed. "There's three of you and one of my fuckin' ass. Hit your sister and see how that go for you."

"Don't stress yourself, Daddy," Rebel said sweetly as some of the club members began greeting them. Rule, Ryder, and Ransom were let through the locked doors, unable to wait to see Mom. "I am more than happy to fuck them up myself."

"I heard that!" Axel screeched. "Sleep with your eyes open, girl."

CJ scrubbed a hand over his face. He really wasn't in the mood to deal with any of the three little assholes.

Rebel tossed a swath of hair over her shoulder, drawing

the attention of more than a few of the younger Dwellers. Still grown ass men. Not that she paid attention. She was focused on their little brother. "I haven't done anything, Axel," she said, frowning.

"We strike you before you get us," he said.

Drawn into a conversation with Zephyr and Billy, Dad kept one eye on CJ, Rebel, and Axel.

Considering the words, Rebel pursed her lips, then nodded. "If I drag you out of your bed and hang you by your toes out of the window, remember your logic."

"Yeah?" Axel yelled. "If I die, I will haunt you to death!"

"To bring me in the afterlife with you?" she asked. "You know I'd fuck you up for the rest of eternity?"

Axel's lower lip trembled, and he glanced at CJ.

He shrugged. "Fuck with her at your own risk, big head," he said.

"Dad?" Rule called, walking back into the hallway.

All Dad's animation fled, and he turned to Rule, staring at him with a mixture of panic and expectation. "What, son? Your ma okay?"

CJ knew his father wasn't completely back to normal and added that to the list of shit flung today.

"Mom's fine," Rule said gently. "I've prayed, and I was told she'll be fine."

CJ exchanged a frown with Rebel. Seeing Axel's sudden fear, he placed his hands on his little brother's skinny shoulders and gave him a reassuring squeeze.

"She isn't ready to leave yet," Rule continued. "There was an error with her paperwork. She said it'll be at least another hour."

"I want to see Mom," Axel said.

Rule held out his hand. "Come on. I'll take you."

"Uh—"

Ignoring Axel's hesitation, Rebel shoved him toward Rule. "He won't burn you at the stake unless he finds just cause."

Axel burst into tears.

At Rule and Dad's combined glare, Rebel shrugged.

"You look like Joan of Arc," Rule said with a sniff.

CJ frowned at him. "Are you implying Rebel should be burned at the fucking stake?" he asked, appalled.

Rebel lifted a brow. "And you, my twin, remind me of Rasputin. Ya wanna know what happened to him?"

"Both of you shut the fuck up," Dad warned, hoisting Axel into his arms since the little motherfucker continued to wail. "Ain't interested in hearin' about Medieval martyrs and mad monks."

"Oh my god, Axel," Rebel groaned. "Shut the fuck up. Your little bitch screams are giving me a major fucking headache."

"Don't ever have children, Reb," CJ grumbled.

Snickers arose amongst the guys. Considering there were at least twenty Dwellers there, the silence didn't help CJ's mood. Half the guys staring at him, Dad, Rule, Axel, and especially Rebel, were between five and ten years older than CJ.

"I want to check on Molly, Dad. Is that okay while we wait for Mom's discharge papers?"

Rebel held up her phone. "Lolly's downstairs in the ER with Harley."

"Mort on the way," Dad announced. He'd called Uncle Mort before they left the school. "You can go and check on Molly, son."

"Can I come with you, CJ?"

He eyed his sister. She wasn't the most patient with Molly, and he didn't want Rebel to upset her right now. Besides, he intended to go to the ER first and see Harley.

She might not have been uppermost on his mind, but he

was concerned about her. He didn't need Rebel's judgment.

"I'll behave, CJ," she promised.

He sighed. "I'm going to the ER first."

Folding her arms, Rebel sniffed. "Give me Molly's room number and I'll wait for you there."

"You beat ass to help Harley," Dad pointed out.

"She's my cousin, Daddy. I couldn't let two raggedy heifers best her. It doesn't mean I forgive Harley's raggedy-ness toward CJ."

"First you, now Harley," Rule said. "Once Mattie goes through her great change, things can get back to normal."

"Dickface, we're not going through menopause," Rebel said tightly.

Rule stiffened and threw Rebel a dark look that only cleared away when Dad urged Rule toward the door.

"He's going to put a fucking spell on you, Reb," CJ said with a grin, once their father and brothers were out of sight.

"He'd never," Rebel said.

Her certainty pleased CJ. If Rule was his twin, he might be sobbing like Axel.

"Molly's on the third floor," he said, starting toward the elevators.

"You know Mattie will never behave the way Harley and I have," she remarked, following behind him.

"Mattie doesn't have the luxury of such spoiled behavior," CJ said as they arrived at the elevators. "She's spoiled, but she's not—"

"Daddy or Uncle Mort's daughter," Rebel said flatly. "She belongs to fuckhead." She stomped into the elevator.

Sighing, CJ stepped beside her. "Uncle Johnnie," he reprimanded as the doors closed.

"Fuck you. I refuse to call that unworthy motherfucker uncle. I refuse to claim Johnnie as a family member."

CJ's intention had been to continue to the first floor once Rebel got off on the third. However, he stalked into her pathway and glared at her. "Uncle Johnnie—"

"Save it," she spat, her eyes blazing. "I will never forgive him for what he said to Momma."

At the moment, CJ didn't have time to hear. He was exhausted. When Dad announced Mom would be released today, CJ had the briefest exhilaration and a hope that things would finally return to normal. By the time his father got behind the wheel after talking to Uncle Mort, CJ's optimism had fled. His thoughts were so jumbled, he wasn't sure if he still believed Mom would be released today or if he walked amidst a nightmare and he'd awaken to find her gone.

Swallowing, he rubbed his eyes. "I detest Uncle Johnnie, Rebel. I want to gut him. For laying hands on me. For coming between Rory and me, and you and Mattie. For what he does to Aunt Kendall."

"Basically, for existing."

CJ nodded, unable to keep his smile at bay.

"Then why are you on my ass because of how I feel about Johnnie?"

"Uncle Johnnie," CJ gritted.

Her eyes narrowed and she opened her mouth to speak.

"Whether we like it or not, there's a hierarchy. Our job isn't to like or approve of every motherfucker included. Our job is to support Dad. Disrespect sows the seeds of anarchy and we risk undermining Outlaw, Reb."

"What about John…" She scowled at his glare, "Uncle Johnnie's fucking disrespect? Isn't he sowing seeds of his own?"

"Uncle Johnnie is a master manipulator, but we can't be seen as the enemy to him. If Dad doesn't have enough authority over his own children where they'll show proper respect, how can he keep authority over the club?"

"I hate when you're logical, brother," she grumbled, sidestepping him and starting forward again.

Grinning, CJ shoved his hands in his pockets and followed her.

"Unfortunately, Daddy has more problems than Uncle Johnnie," she threw over her shoulder. "He almost fell apart when Rule came out."

"I know," he said, grim.

"Hopefully, Momma is released today. Perhaps, we can convince Momma and Daddy to have a small celebration in a week or so, marking her release. If he just acts like the old Outlaw, even if he's still fucked up, that'll be something."

A lightbulb went off in CJ's head. As soon as he knew whether his mother was leaving today, he'd rally the brothers and their old ladies to welcome her home. Mom would understand and know what to do so Dad would seem normal. "Reb, you're brilliant," he said as they entered Molly's room in the hospital's general ICU, where everyone who was in critical condition and not his mother went.

"It's about time you realized that fact, CJ," Rebel chirped, and focused on the girl in the hospital bed. "Holy fuck."

Molly was hooked up to different monitors with an IV line connected to several bags of medicine. Her face was bruised and swollen, and her nose bandaged. She looked so fragile. When she sniffled, CJ's heart broke.

Rebel glanced back at him, cleared her throat, and marched to Molly's bedside. "Hey, chick," she said gently. She snatched a couple pieces of tissue paper from the box and dabbed Molly's cheeks. "Can I keep you company?"

Molly nodded. "Are you staying too, CJ?" she asked, her tone weak and quiet.

"I have to check on Harley." Shockingly, he didn't want

to. He hated to leave Molly. "I won't be long, Mo. My mom's being discharged, so I don't know when we'll be ready to leave, and I want to sit with you a minute."

Both girls stared at him. He was fucking rambling.

"Our momma rambles when she's nervous or overwhelmed," Rebel said, sitting in the chair next to Molly's bed. "CJ inherited that from her."

"My mama visited me today," Molly said.

CJ seriously doubted that. "Molly, your mom—"

"What did she say?" Rebel interrupted, looking at CJ with meaning.

Until that moment, he hadn't realized the seismic shift Rebel had undergone after they almost lost Mom. She was still intolerant, bad-tempered, and spoiled. Yet, that one night snatched away her childishness and much of her innocence. For their entire lives death surrounded them, taunting and teasing, but kept away from Rebel. She'd never been faced with the reality of losing someone she loved.

She'd been alive when Mom was shot and kidnapped and almost died giving birth to Axel, but she hadn't been cognizant.

"Molly?"

Ryan's voice broke into CJ's thoughts, and he turned toward his cousin. Once again, CJ noted the flicker of tenderness in Ryan's eyes. Dude was a bitter little asshole, yet he seemed to truly care about Molly.

"Hey, Ryan," she said softly, a wealth of tears streaming down her face. She looked at CJ.

Ryan stiffened, balling his hands into fists. "Can I talk to my girlfriend alone?"

"Nope," Rebel sneered. "You can visit her with me while my brother checks on our cousin."

"I wasn't asking you."

"Good, because I wasn't fucking answering you," Rebel retorted. "Go, CJ. We don't know when Momma will be ready to leave and I know you want to check on Harley."

"Molly doesn't need anymore disturbance," CJ warned, glaring between Rebel and Ryan. "If you two are going to argue, take it in the hallway."

"She's my girlfriend," Ryan said.

"But not your wife," Rebel snapped.

"You don't have the right to stay in here if I've asked you to leave," he countered. "This hospital is loyal to the Death Dwellers, not merely the Caldwells. I have rights too."

"Sweet summer child," Rebel cackled. She got to her feet. "I hate to pull rank, little man, but I am a Caldwell as well as a Foy. Do you really want me to tell you who outranks who?"

"You're a fucking cu—"

"I wouldn't if I were you, Ryan," CJ warned softly. "My sister is more than capable of wrapping your fucking tongue around your head, but I'd be an awful big brother if she had to defend herself in my presence."

"I'll leave it up to Molly." Ryan glowered at her, not caring about her tears or her injuries. "Do you want to see me alone as I've requested? Me? Your boyfriend."

"Oh my god, fuckhead." Rebel fisted her hands on her hips. "You have no fucking shame. This isn't about you, twat waddle, so please spare me. And spare Molly. She's been through enough. Be careful what you say to her. Come on, CJ. I guess I have to suffer Harley to give the crybaby time alone with Molly." Throwing Ryan a dirty look, she stalked just outside the door.

"It's twat waffle!" Ryan yelled.

Really, what else could he say? CJ started to turn.

"Look," Molly said to no one in particular. "Mama's here."

He froze, exchanging a look with Ryan. Neither of them

knew how to respond.

Rebel walked back into the room and returned to Molly's bedside. She took the hand connected to the IV and held it gently. "Where is she?"

"On my cheeks, Rebel."

Ryan staggered to the other side of Molly's bed and smiled at her. He slid his hand over her head. "We don't see her."

"She's on my cheeks, Ryan," Molly insisted hoarsely. "In the tracks of my tears."

Ryan

After that asshole left him alone in the log cabin, Ryan hadn't taken long to get to the club. He wasn't sure when he'd be comfortable on his own. Maybe, tomorrow? But the images were still too fresh in his mind. When Orange told Ryan he needed to get to the hospital to relieve Slipper from duty, Ryan rode bitch. He wanted to see Molly. He'd thought once she was cleaned up, her injuries wouldn't seem as bad.

He was wrong.

She looked broken and delicate. If he could, he would marry her to give her protection. Except he was living on borrowed time. He was still months away from his seventeenth birthday, so it was entirely possible the Dwellers would think Val knew about Ryan's activities. Or even pushed him to an alliance with Bash.

Huh. There was a scenario worth considering, although that didn't solve Molly's problems now. Nor would his parents, especially that she-wolf, ever allow him to wed Molly.

Leaning over, he brushed his lips over hers. They were cracked and dry.

"Why'd Tom do this?" he asked.

Shifting away from Ryan, Molly sniffled. "Bash grew twenty-five fists and they all beat me."

Ryan squinted, sick to his stomach. "Molly, baby, don't go in your head," he pleaded. "I need you to tell me what happened." Sensibly.

Molly fixated on Ryan's face. "Bash stole her head and made me carry it," she said finally, staring at him without blinking. "I washed her hair. She sang to me. I couldn't find her neck."

Maybe, he shouldn't have mentioned her father.

"CJ?"

All Ryan's sympathy vanished, and he stiffened. Maybe, he'd regret his actions. For now, he felt justified. First, he'd call Bash, then Molly's father. After all, the man deserved to know his daughter's location.

Harley

Aching everywhere, Harley closed her eyes and rested on the gurney in the ER. Lolly sat in one of the chairs, waiting for Mommie's arrival.

At the sound of approaching footsteps, Harley opened her eyes. She knew it wasn't her mother. Whoever was coming didn't possess Mommie's confident stride.

Rebel appeared a moment before CJ strolled into view. Harley realized it was his boots she'd heard, since Rebel wore sneakers.

"Hey," Lolly greeted, her smile wide. "Meggie already called. There's an issue with her paperwork."

"Yeah," CJ said, bending and kissing Harley's grandmother as if he had the right. "Dad's with her right now."

Rebel mimicked her brother. It was only then that he looked at Harley and offered a greeting.

"How are you feeling, Harley?" he asked softly, his face unreadable when once he was an open book. "You don't have any broken bones, do you?"

"Would you care? You've been with Molly all day. Maybe, if you'd been at school, Erin and Ariana wouldn't have jumped me."

Annoyance crossed his face. "I don't go in the girl's locker room, Harley."

"You were there today," she charged.

"I was called there…" He stopped and drew in a deep breath. "I came to check on you, not argue with you."

"I don't need your pity, CJ." Angry at the world, she glared at Rebel. As long as CJ was happy, he could use and abuse her in any way he pleased, while she and Mommie were the villains. "By the way, I didn't need your interference."

"So you said earlier, Harley," Rebel said with a shrug. "My brain and your face feel otherwise."

Harley gasped. "You're making fun of my injuries?"

"No. I'm making fun of your stupidity. Next."

"Get out."

"I'm not here for you. I'm here for my brother. I'll wait outside, CJ. Don't be too long. I'm sure Molly's waiting for you."

CJ scowled at the back of his sister's head as she marched out. The amusement on Lolly's face outraged Harley, snatching away the last of her reason.

"You're a fucking liar and a snake," she snarled viciously.

"Harley," CJ started, "listen to me. I'm so exhausted from today. I didn't come here to argue with you or to hurt your feelings. I wanted to check on you."

"You left me to return to Molly's side, which is where you've been all day."

"I left you because my mother is coming home."

"I don't care! She's on the mend. I'm the injured one. If you've been with Molly, you didn't care that Aunt Meggie was being released so stop with your lying."

CJ glared at her, then bent and kissed Lolly's cheek again. "I'm going back upstairs, Lolly."

Mommie walked in and he paused long enough to greet her.

"Weren't you leaving, CJ?" Mommie asked coolly, warming Harley's heart.

He walked off without commenting.

Glowering at Lolly, Mommie took one look at Harley and burst into tears. "My baby," she wept.

CHAPTER 25

MORTICIAN

The club's rowdy giddiness seemed like a foreign world to Mortician. His earlier plans to blaze to Nevada City, an hour northeast of Sacramento, to collect a debt from a smalltime dealer who'd gotten credit from the Dwellers to expand his enterprises fell though. He was a lucky asshole. After repeated promises to pay up, the motherfucker was evading all attempts by Stretch to contact him.

Mort had intended to take his time, spend a couple days roughing it and returning to his roots. Time away would help him put shit into better perspective, instead of staring at the walls in his old room at the club. It was a constant reminder of the state of his marriage.

After finishing up at the Harris house, he'd called Bailey to tell her his plans. She'd gone silent before finally telling him to be safe. Neither of them mentioned love. Usually, he ended most of his calls with, "I love you, pretty girl."

While he'd fueled up, contacted Lou and Kaleb, who were

at lunch.

Before all the chaos began, the boys would've been eating in the upper cafeteria with Harley and the rest of the biker brood. CJ would've kept them in line with his baby girl's help. Now, everything was upside down.

"Don't go, Dad," Lou begged once Mort imparted his plans. "We don't want to stay with Mom and Harley. We want to move to the club with you."

"We'll talk about it when I get home, little bro," he promised. "In the meantime, listen to your momma. Don't give her grief."

"We're not talking to her or Harley," Lou grumbled.

Mort had grinned. "I appreciate the loyalty, son, but that's still your momma and your sister. Respect them, especially Bailey. I won't tolerate your disrespect."

"Kaleb wants to talk to you," Lou said, not commenting on Mort's order.

"I love you, boy."

"I love you, too, Dad," Lou responded glumly. "Here, Kaleb, talk quick. Dad's leaving town."

"No! Dad, don't go." Kaleb's little voice wobbled.

He and Axel had been the youngest for several years, until Bunny turned up pregnant with Cove, followed a year later by Meggie with Gunner, and then Red with Blade.

Now, there was Baby Jo.

Kaleb sniffled. "Lou and me don't want you to leave. We can't visit you at the club. Don't go, Dad. Please."

"Dad, when are you coming back home?" Lou asked, taking over the conversation again. "We miss you. We… please don't leave us."

It was because of his sons that he was still close by when Prez called and told him about Harley's fight. He'd been sitting at the burger joint he'd met CJ at to question him about his intentions toward Harley. It had been a favorite spot for him and Harley too, until she saw their waitress, Symphony, flirting with him.

Symphony still flirted with him; he continued to ignore her. By the time he arrived at the hospital, Harley was being discharged. She gave him the cold shoulder, though Bailey was so distraught she collapsed into his arms and sobbed.

Until Harley asked what had taken him so long to arrive and he'd mentioned he'd been on his way out of town.

"CJ deserted me and left me to get beat up. Now, you're leaving me, too?" Harley started to cry.

Bailey turned away from him and ran to Harley. "Hunny bunny, it's okay—"

"CJ hasn't deserted you," Roxanne said, then told Mortician how CJ, Rebel, and Mattie helped Harley.

Mort's second mistake had been praising CJ. Harley hadn't taken kindly to his happiness at the kid's intervention or that of Reb and Mattie.

"You traitor!" she cried.

"Oh, baby," Bailey said tearfully, hugging Harley when Mort felt like shaking the fuck out of her. Which was when he knew he had to leave. He'd lost his fucking mind to even consider spanking Harley. "Your daddy doesn't mean it. He knows CJ is worthless."

Mort frowned at Bailey. "That's going a step too far, baby."

His words destroyed any progress he'd made with his wife in the last few minutes, especially when Harley cried harder.

"Mortician, go outside and wait for us," Roxanne suggested. "Let me talk to these two."

After their conversation the other night after the poker game, he eyed her with suspicion. "What—"

"Make them leave, Mommie," Harley managed. "They're going to be mean to me and I'm in so much pain. I can't bear it right now."

Mort discovered Roxanne had brought his baby girl to the ER and Bailey arrived a little over an hour later, a few minutes before Mort. Harley's melodrama angered Roxanne. To keep the peace, he'd guided her outside where they waited for Bailey and Harley, then Mort hopped on his bike and led the mini caravan of two SUVs back to the club. He'd gone home to make sure Harley was comfortable but left soon after. She'd gotten Bailey firmly back on her side.

Roxanne took Lou and Kaleb to her house, so they could eat with her, Knox, and Grant. He was home from Boston for the holidays.

When Mort walked in the club house, it was crowded and loud with a mixture of brothers, probates, old ladies, hangers on, children, and the girls the club owned. It took him a minute to thread through the crowd. He intended to go to his room and drink his fucking troubles away. Instead, seeing Cash, Stretch, Val, Digger, Cameron, Johnnie, Rory, JJ, Derby, Diesel, Devon, Brooks, Knox, Grant, and Boy at or around Prez's table halted him.

"What—"

A deafening roar drowned out his words, followed by cheers, claps, and whistles. Digger and the others joined in. Turning, Mort saw Prez carrying Meggie, flanked by Rebel and CJ. As crowded as it was, everyone had parted like the Red Sea.

Mort had completely forgotten Meggie's vow to check herself out. He'd never been so happy to see someone in his entire fucking life. He joined in the whistles and catcalls.

She started wiggling in Outlaw's arms, and Mort grinned.

"Ain't puttin' you the fuck down, Megan," Prez grumbled. "Ain't wanted to stop at this motherfucker." He sat in his usual seat, and she snuggled against him.

Rule walked up to his parents and settled a blanket over Meggie, then made the sign of the cross and backed away.

Glaring, Rebel opened her mouth, but Meggie shook her head.

"The bitches at the house, Meggie," Val said, sipping his beer. "Waiting for you."

"A patient of Jordan's went into labor," Cameron Baptiste put in. "She might not make it over."

"Roxanne didn't know until she called me after she made it home from the hospital," Knox added.

Meggie bolted up and would've stood if Outlaw hadn't tightened his hold on her. "What's wrong with her?"

Axel darted up to her. "Lolly's fine. Harley got her ass beat."

"WHAT?" Meggie said. "Omigod—"

"Remember that fuckin' ass beatin you lil motherfuckers escaped?" Outlaw growled, wrapping his arms around Meggie to keep her in place. "Say one fuckin' more thing to your ma about shit that upset her and I'm fuckin' you up."

"I'll do it, Daddy," Rebel volunteered, snatching Axel and shoving him toward Ransom.

"Ow!" Axel hollered. "Sleep with your eyes opened, Rebel."

"Sleep with your body in a fucking cast, Axel," Rebel retorted.

Laughter rose around them, although Outlaw glared between Rebel and Axel.

"Welcome home, Meggie," a female voice called from the crowd.

Meggie smiled. "Thanks, Vicki," she responded. "I wanted to stop in to thank you all for your flowers, food, prayers, card, calls, and well-wishes. I'm so happy to be back home with my friends and family."

"How's Baby Jo?" Mack, one of the newer members,

asked.

"Beautiful," Meggie said with a soft smile. "She has a long road to go, but she is getting stronger every day," she said around a yawn.

Outlaw frowned. "I told you we should've gone straight home. CJ, come get the blanket Rule gave your ma."

Rule hurried from where'd he'd been standing next to CJ. "No one else can touch it but Mom and me. I've prayed over it and blessed it with holy water."

Rebel rolled her eyes. "How the fuck can you make something that's supposed to be good sound so fucked up?"

"He has a knack for it, Reb," Ryder said with a snort.

Rule's face fell. CJ placed his hands on the little motherfucker's shoulders. "Ignore Lucinda, bro."

"If I'm the devil's wife, dickhead, what is Rule?" she demanded.

Meggie sighed. "Enough—"

"You all stressing your ma out. Shut the fuck up or deal with the fuckin' consequences."

Order restored immediately.

"Bunny and the rest of the chicks cooking a cold ass dinner," Digger said, then shrugged. "Probably not Charlotte. She don't cook."

Probably not Bailey either. Mort shoved the thought aside.

"Charlotte creates excellent menus," Brooks said.

Hearing the attorney's voice reminded Mort he still hadn't talked to him like Prez ordered.

"When lil' dude called—" Digger nodded to CJ— "and told Bunny his momma was coming home, she asked me if we should welcome you back with food and a celebration."

CJ nodded to Digger, alerting Mort to behind-the-scenes shit. It was more like CJ had called Digger and told him they needed to have a get-together.

"Did either of you motherfuckers really have to ask that shit?" Outlaw snapped. "It should've been a fucking obvious answer."

Meggie kissed Outlaw's jaw. "It's fine. I'll say 'hi' to everyone, then go upstairs."

Mort walked around the table to the empty chair next to Digger. No matter where they were his brother always saved his seat.

"CJ called you, huh?" he whispered.

"Yeah, Mort. He thought you wanted to look after Harley. That's why he didn't involve you."

He did. Harley didn't want him.

"It's cool. You don't have to explain. I don't have a monopoly on the boy."

"It just felt strange. I've been riding hard against Meggie. Now, CJ calling me for help."

"Must make you feel like a lowdown asshole," Mort retorted, ignoring the laughter and comments rising around them. He picked out Diesel toasting Meggie, followed by Knox, and Boy.

It almost felt normal. If Bailey had been with him, it would have. Feeling so sorry for himself helped nothing, however.

"Now what, Mort?" Digger asked.

Mort gazed at Meggie, adoring Outlaw as she had almost from the moment they'd met. They often spoke about what would happen to Prez if Meggie...left. But had anyone ever considered if the opposite happened, especially if she lost him to a violent death.

Mort knew it crossed her mind.

What about now? When fatigue darkened her eyes and pain tightened her smile. She was enduring the evening for Prez, showing him she was fine and urging him back into the light.

Whether CJ called her or not and told her the plan, Meggie instinctively knew the role she had to play. She'd schooled her children, especially CJ and Rebel, how to pick up on the cues.

"Ever think what would've happened if we would've killed her, Mort?"

"I try not to, Digger."

"You think we'd still have a club?"

"I don't know. But I'm sure Prez wouldn't be here. He didn't expect to live to see the second anniversary of Big Joe's death."

"Does that mean he a weak motherfucker? He can't function without her."

"He not weak, son. He lucky."

Mort exchanged a glance with his brother.

"I've been thinking about Molly and her mama."

Meggie whispered to Prez, and he smiled, a real one that Mort hadn't seen in days. "About what?"

"Johnnie cut off Big Joe head, Mort, and sent it to the club. Suppose Bash somehow involved with Harris and Johnnie know? Suppose they cut Molly mama head off as a warning?"

"Fuck. Bash is Cee Cee son. That motherfucker wanted to chop off Meggie girl head to send to Prez."

"My theory make even more sense now, Mort."

"Johnnie a motherfucker, but he wouldn't be torturing Meggie to leave without a good fucking reason. Somewhere deep down, I'm sure that asshole still want to bone her."

"Man, shut the fuck up with that. We have enough bullshit cropping up. We don't need to put those fucking words in the air and rekindle his obsession."

"I know," Digger sighed. "Kendall been straight, and I like her now. When he turn into a cunt, she turn into a bitch. I'm six years away from fifty, too fucking old to deal with that bullshit."

Mort sniggered. "Fucking asshole. I'm older than you."

"I wasn't responsible for our birth order, bruh."

"So you think Johnnie in bed with Tom Harris and Bash Caldwell?"

"Bash, yeah. Harris, though, I'm not sure. Rory just happened to be there. It was a message for CJ."

"Or Ryan," Mort said, thinking out loud. "Molly his girlfriend."

"True."

"I'm going to talk to Brooks," Mort said. "You do some digging and see what you can come up with."

"Okay." Digger finished his beer, set the bottle aside and folded his arms. "I don't have nothing against her, Mort."

Mort looked at Meggie again, hanging on Outlaw's every word, completely wrapped up in him and in love. "So you say. And keep saying. Who the fuck you trying to convince? Me or yourself?"

Digger shrugged. "Sometimes, I wish we were still single."

"No, sometimes you wish I was still single. You would've been happy having your own family and me all to yourself."

Guilt crossed Digger's face.

"I'll even go so far to say you would never have gotten married if the rest of us hadn't, but especially me."

"I love Bunny."

"I never said you didn't. I just know you."

"I don't have nothing against Bailey, Mort. Besides, without her we wouldn't have Roxanne."

"Just like you don't have anything against Meggie. Prez and me looked out for you, and you were jealous of anybody that came between that."

"I resent you making me sound like a bitch-ass

motherfucker.”

“I’m making you sound exactly like you are.”

“I hate how unhappy you are, Mort,” Digger said, sounding as weary as Mort felt. “Almost as broken up as Prez whenever something going on with Meggie.”

“I appreciate your sympathy, but not your resentment. I don’t want to lose my wife. I love Bailey.”

“I don’t doubt your love.”

Mortician stiffened.

“And I don’t doubt Prez love for Meggie or hers for him. As annoying as she can be sometimes, that woman love her some Outlaw. She what ride-or-die look like.”

“Before I punch the fuck out of you—”

“No, Mort, on the real. Prez a good motherfucker to Meggie and she pay him back in kind. You not only a good brother to me, Bailey couldn’t ask for a better husband. You spoil the fuck out of that woman. If you happy with her kind of ride-or-die, then go home. You not winning with Bailey over Harley.”

Mort didn’t want to face the truth of Digger’s words. Going home meant facing their hostility for something he didn’t do and had no control over.

“As much as I bitch and complain, I’m lucky, Mort,” Digger said quietly. “Meggie influenced Bunny, not by word but by deed. Bunny see how effective it is to band together in front of the children, even if we disagree with each other. I’m not sure about Zoann and Fee, but I know Kendall like that, too. Somehow, Bailey got away from the closeness of our women. If you love her, compromise.”

“I can’t if she won’t cooperate,” Mort said tiredly.

“I’m sorry. I don’t want to bring you down. Maybe, you being here good anyway. You can scope out more information.”

That was true, a fact Mort hadn't considered. "I'm leaving tomorrow."

"Nevada City?"

He nodded.

"Want company?"

"Fuck, fool, if you want to leave your warm bed and rough it a few days, I'm not stopping you."

Digger grinned.

"What are you two talking about?" Johnnie asked, staring at Mortician.

"If they wanted us to know, they woulda spoke louder," Outlaw growled.

Johnnie threw Meggie a cold look. For a moment, Mort thought Prez would pull his piece and shoot the stupid motherfucker. Outlaw's black fury should've deterred whatever plans Johnnie had.

"Isn't Momma pretty, Daddy?" Rebel asked.

Mort hid his grin. She sounded like a sweet little kid, though she looked as angry as her father.

"Rebel—"

"Watch how you talk to my girl, Johnnie," Outlaw warned.

"Tell her to look at me with more respect, Christopher."

"How did my sister look at you, Uncle Johnnie?" CJ inquired, accepting the cigarette Outlaw handed him.

Envy hit Mort. He wished his own family was so close. Rebel traveled Harley's path first, but it didn't splinter the Caldwells. They stood together and came out stronger.

Fuck. This was crossing a goddamn line. Instead of licking his wounds, he'd go on his run and discover what he could about Bash and Johnnie. In the meantime, he'd find a way to bridge the chasm between him and his own family.

"Do you want me to tell Ophelia to bring Gunner back to our place before you get home, sweetness?" Cash asked into the silence.

Johnnie must've ran off at the fucking mouth.

"We haven't brought him to visit you in a couple days, Meggie," Stretch added, his glance at Cash barely civil. "I know he'll be so happy to see you. Perhaps, too happy?"

"Yeah, Meggie girl," Mort added, catching Stretch's drift. "He might be a little rambunctious."

"It's okay—"

"No, the fuck it ain't. Mort and Stretch right," Outlaw said. "Tell Fee to bring the lil' motherfucker back to your place, Cash."

"What are you three planning for the evening?" Mort asked, smiling between Cash and Stretch and hoping Meggie picked up on the tension. He hated to add to her burden, but they seemed to be arguing over shit that happened months ago.

"I have reports to work on," Stretch answered. "I'll be in my office."

"You also have to watch the Harris house," Cash gritted.

"No shit?" CJ said, lifting a brow. "You put in cameras?"

"Shit not adding up," Val said. "Johnnie made the suggestion."

Brooks choked, drawing everyone's attention.

Outlaw narrowed his eyes.

"Uh, Dad, Uncle Chris," Rory inserted, swallowing, "I want to suggest a bylaw that makes the enforcer officially an officer."

Johnnie scowled. "Absolutely not."

"I think it's a wonderful idea," Meggie said. "Then Mortician will finally be counted as an officer."

"You're not a fucking member, Megan," Johnnie snarled. "Keep your fucking comments to yourself."

"In a motherfuckin' minute, you not going to be

afuckinlive," Outlaw roared, somehow jumping to his feet and holding onto Meggie.

Rebel grinned. Mort knew one person who wanted Johnnie to die.

"I want to see Gunner, Christopher. And Johnnie's right. I'm not a member. I shouldn't have passed my opinion in mixed company."

"It's okay, Momma," Rebel cooed. "We know you're still under the influence of pain meds."

"Maybe, we should go home, Mom?" CJ said. "Gunner is probably tired by now. He shouldn't be too much trouble."

"You can see the lil' motherfucker tomorrow, Megan. Rule, come take the blanket, son."

Rule rushed forward and did as instructed. The mood went from celebratory to uneasy. Meggie was still pale and Outlaw was on edge as he made his way through the crowd.

"Wait, Christopher!"

He halted.

"I haven't had a chance to say 'hi' to everyone who came to welcome me home."

"Tomorrow, Megan," Prez promised.

"Have you toasted Jo's birth yet?" she pressed.

It was tradition to toast their children's births with their club brothers.

"Let CJ bring me home and you stay for a half hour to toast our baby girl."

"The lil' motherfucker might drop you."

CJ grinned, almost as tall as Mort these days. "I got your shortie, Dad. I can handle her."

"Yeah, Outlaw," Mort said, calmer now that he had a plan of action. He was even looking forward to spending time with Digger. "Meggie girl still the size of fucking Smurfette."

Prez snickered, allowing CJ to take Meggie.

"Don't worry, Daddy. If CJ drops Momma, I will stomp him."

"Bros before hoes, Reb," Ransom said. "We will stomp you if you touch CJ."

If Outlaw hadn't been within arm's reach of Rebel, she would've thrown the fist she'd balled and probably knocked Ransom out.

"Bitch!" he yelled and ran away from her, blowing out the club with the force of a tornado.

Ryder and Axel flipped her off, then took off running, too.

"Baby, leave your brothers alone. Your ma need to rest," Outlaw said.

"Okay, Daddy," she said sweetly, kissed his cheek and followed in the wake of her three bad ass little brothers.

"That was too easy," Diesel observed.

Meggie nodded. "Take me home now, son," she ordered CJ.

"Do you want the blanket, Mom?" Rule asked as CJ started toward the door.

"When we get upstairs," she said, smiling as the claps and whistles started again, drowning out the rest of her words.

CJ halted before he walked out of view. Meggie threw a kiss to Outlaw.

"One toast, baby, then I'll be home."

"I'll be waiting," she promised. She caught Mort's gaze. "Hey," she said softly.

Mort tipped his head. "Meggie girl."

"I'm crushed," Derby teased.

"You'll survive," she chirped.

"Come with us, Rory," CJ said.

"I thought you'd never ask," Rory said, smiling.

"Can I come, Ro?" JJ said.

"Of course, you can," Meggie answered. "Dev, Ryan, you're

welcomed, too.”

“What about me, Aunt Meggie?” Grant teased.

“Of course you can—”

“Megan,” Outlaw gritted, “how the fuck you going to rest if you have a trail of lil’ motherfuckers in your wake?”

“I’ll make sure she’s fine, Dad,” CJ promised, and walked out carrying his mother and leading his cousins.

For a moment, Outlaw stared at the door, so Mort decided to step up. He walked behind the bar. “Serve bottles of beer to whoever don’t have a drink,” he instructed. “I’ll settle the tab tomorrow.”

In the time it took everyone to get a drink, Outlaw seemed unhappy and distracted. Worry was written all over his face. They tried to draw him into a conversation, but he wanted to get to Meggie.

Mort knew the feeling. He would give anything to go to Bailey and iron out their differences. All that happened before Harley turned against him shouldn’t be so detrimental that their marriage ended. Digger was right, though. Bailey was in Mama Bear mode and anything he said that upset Harley would piss off Bailey.

“I would like to toast Josephine Dinah Caldwell,” Mort said, raising his bottle of beer. “Congrats on your new daughter, Prez. May she have a long and happy life.”

Outlaw smiled at the clinking of bottles and well-wishes. It seemed to ease not only him, but everyone else, too.

Although Meggie had her shortcomings, she was proficient at reminding Prez how much the club meant to him and how deeply he was needed.

CHAPTER 26

Jaleena Davis lived with her parents and two sisters in a brick and wood, two-story home on a sloping lot. Located on a cul-de-sac in a quiet subdivision, it had high ceilings, extravagant chandeliers, three fireplaces featuring elaborate Christmas decorations, and a giant basement set up as a family room.

CJ had been to the house only once before when he picked up Jaleena for the Homecoming Dance, a few weeks ago when they'd been crowned King and Queen. That night, he hadn't gone any farther than the foyer. Today, he was there to pick up his schoolwork, since he'd forgotten to get it from her yesterday in the aftermath of Harley's fight. Once Outlaw announced Mom was being released, CJ hadn't cared about much else.

He'd gone to school for the first time in days and had been utterly fucking lost. His grades were suffering. Unlike when deader-than-dead Lumbly fucked with him and failed him because he didn't like CJ, this time the bad grades were the result of not turning in his work.

His teachers were very understanding. They all knew his mother and little sister had almost died. However, he had a lot of makeup work to do if he didn't want to fail the semester.

Still, he'd left at lunchtime and went to the hospital to visit Jo and check on Molly. Afterwards, he'd called Jaleena to catch her before she left school, but she'd been on the way home.

CJ had wanted to pick up his work, then get back home in case Mom and Dad needed anything. Jaleena insisted he come in and hang out a bit.

Somehow "a bit" turned into two hours and counting. While he was enjoying himself, he was distracted for so many different reasons.

"I win," Jillian, Jaleena's ten-year-old sister, crowed.

Like his family with all the fucking 'R' names, Jaleena's had a plethora of "Js".

Smiling, CJ handed Jillian his controller and nodded. "Fair and square," he agreed.

"My turn!" thirteen-year-old Juliana said, bouncing from foot to foot. She snatched the controllers from Jillian and held out one to CJ.

"Not!" Jaleena said with a snort, grabbing the controllers from her little sister and setting them on the TV cabinet that contained a 75-inch flat screen and several game consoles, including a Nintendo Switch, CJ's favorite of all. "Go, you two. He's my friend, and I haven't had a chance to talk to him all evening."

"You see him at school every day," Jillian pointed out. "We don't. We're stuck in the Lower Hall."

"Not my problem." Jaleena nodded in the direction of the door. "Leave."

"Bye, trick," Juliana said, flipping Jaleena the bird and scooting away.

Trilling laughter, Jillian skipped behind Juliana.

"I owe you," Jaleena yelled. Jillian slammed the door in response. "Bad ass brats."

"You don't know brats until you've met my younger brothers, J. We called them the Terrible Triplets."

Jaleena grabbed his hand and tugged him to the sofa. "You have twins and triplets in your family?" she asked once they'd sat.

"Ransom is twelve, Ryder is eleven, and Axel is ten. They are just terrible little motherfuckers, especially when they put their evil little minds together." He started to grab the cigarette behind his ear, then thought better of it.

If he had to guess, the house was at least five thousand square feet. He hadn't been in all the rooms, but those he had entered didn't have a single ashtray.

He sighed.

"No smoking in the house," Jaleena said. "We can go outside if you'd like."

"And freeze my fucking balls off? Nope. I'm good."

She swept him with a look, then focused on his mouth and licked her lips.

Rebel's order that he at least kiss Molly drummed through CJ's head. To him, Molly was off-limits because of Ryan. CJ didn't want to participate in passing her from guy to guy, no matter how much he liked her or how pretty he found her.

Jaleena, however, was a different story. He was attracted to her and the spark between them had only the usual hindrance: Harley. But she'd crossed several lines that he wasn't sure they could come back from. Still, his promise to wait until she was ready, the one she constantly threw at him, served as another excuse.

"You can kiss me," Jaleena whispered. "I won't tell."

Lifting his hand, he laid it against her face. Her smooth, dark brown skin complemented her almond-shaped, midnight-colored eyes. Her full lips, high cheekbones, and broad nose gave her a regal appearance. Scooting closer, she tipped her head, inviting him to taste her mouth.

His heart pounded and he bent, pressing his lips against hers and closing his eyes. Her mouth opened and he slid his tongue in, grunting at the sensation exploding in him. She smelled like roses and tasted like peppermint. Wrapping his arms around her, he pulled her onto his lap.

Until that moment, he hadn't paid attention to her short sweater dress. Then, she straddled him, pulled her dress above her waist, and rocked against his suddenly aching cock.

A moan escaped her, absorbed by his kisses. He grabbed her firm ass and thrust up, glad for the barriers of their clothing but disappointed, too. He wanted her so badly he could barely think straight.

Then, suddenly, a face intruded. Her face. Only...only...

Fuck it all, it was the wrong fucking face. It was Molly, not Harley, and it freaked the fuck out of CJ.

Shoving Jaleena aside, he stumbled to his feet, breathing hard, wanting to fuck her. Or Molly.

And Molly?

Goddamn.

He swallowed and scrubbed a hand over his face. Squeezing his eyes shut, he tried to remind himself how important Harley was to him. He tried to make himself want her as much as he suddenly wanted Jaleena and Molly. Six weeks ago, that wouldn't have been a problem. He had loved Harley with everything in him.

But, maybe, he'd been afflicted with the same disease as her: comfort, familiarity, and expectation.

"How is she?" Jaleena asked into the heated silence, filled only by the sound of their heavy breathing. "Erin and Ariana worked her over pretty bad."

Guilt sweeping through him, CJ shrugged. He hadn't checked on Harley again after he'd visited her in the ER yesterday. Last night, he'd celebrated his mother's release with Dad, Rebel, and his brothers. Today, at school, he noted Harley's absence. Because of her many injuries he was sure. He hadn't wanted to hear her blame, so he'd ignored his urge to text her.

Jaleena cocked her head to the side. "I'm prettier than both of them, so it can't be looks."

He shoved his hands in his pockets. "Both?" he asked, suspicious. The desire in her dark eyes made his balls throb. But he didn't want to use Jaleena.

Whether he ever forgave Harley didn't take away his hurt at her behavior. And he was so worried about Molly, he almost missed school entirely. Not only was she in a bad physical state, but her mental state also wasn't good.

She had no next of kin and, as a minor, CJ couldn't demand health updates, despite how closely tied to the hospital the Dwellers were. As soon as he could, he'd ask his father for help.

"Both," Jaleena said firmly.

He didn't want to abuse Jaleena's trust by taking what she offered, then deciding it was a bad idea. She deserved better than quick sex with no promise of going steady, while he couldn't definitively say who or what he wanted.

Or, maybe, his reasoning was an excuse and he really didn't like her in that way.

"Who are you referring to?" he insisted.

"Harley and Molly," she clarified, crossing her long legs and drawing his attention to their sleekness.

"All three of you are gorgeous," he said flatly. "And Molly is my cousin's chick."

She rolled her eyes. "Morals are overestimated. Fewer people than you think value them."

CJ pretended ignorance. "What's the point of this conversation, Jaleena?"

"I like you," she confessed again. She'd admitted as much at the dance. "I wish you would like me back." She snorted, uncrossed her legs, and leaned forward. "No matter which way I go, my parents will be unhappy."

"What the fuck are you talking about?"

"You. Who you are. Mattie. Who she is and the fact that she is a she."

"Mattie? As in Matilda. My cousin? Matilda Donovan?" She nodded.

So, Rebel was right about the spark she detected between Mattie and Jaleena.

His erection had eased, so he sat next to her again. "Who are we?"

"White criminals. One is bad enough. Both are impossible."

"You were my date to the dance," he reminded her. "Weren't your parents in the stand? Didn't they see me?"

She stared at the floor. "I told them I was doing you a favor because you couldn't get a date."

CJ lifted a brow at the blatant lie.

"I don't even want to get into our differing tax brackets," she said in a small voice. "I grew up in this house. It has five bedrooms and seven bathrooms.”

She'd been in Lumbly's classroom the day his parents revealed they'd bought Ridge Moore. However, his cousins and brothers had been hard at work distracting the other students while Mom and Dad talked to that fuckhead, so Jaleena had missed the announcement. Despite Mom and Dad's ownership, there'd been no disruptions to curriculum, staff, or schedules, and his parents preferred keeping their new roles under wraps.

“You disappoint me, J.,” CJ admitted quietly. “Until today, I didn't think all that stuff mattered to you. It hasn't seemed that important until today.”

“Maybe, it's because you've hurt my feelings,” she said softly. “I've thrown myself at you two or three times and you spurn me. I'm gorgeous. I'm wealthy. I have a very sizeable trust fund. And I'm willing to overlook a lot, including my parents' anger, to be with you.”

“I'm overwhelmed by the favor,” he said with sarcasm. “Are you sure you're not afraid your parents won't disown you if you fraternized with garbage like me?”

Sitting straighter, she winced. “My parents adore us. Their anger blows over and we inevitably get what we want. Although introducing Mattie would be a different story. They are Christians and believe only a man and woman should be together.”

“What paragons.”

She stiffened. “They're my parents and I love them. They allowed me to get on birth control to protect myself against pregnancy, even though they don't believe in premarital sex.”

CJ started to rise, but Jaleena grabbed his wrist, so he stayed seated. “Don't leave. Please. I didn't mean to offend you.”

“You meant something,” he said flatly. “Otherwise, you

wouldn't have opened your fucking mouth."

"Last week, I mentioned to my parents that I was picking up work for you. The entire school knows who you are. One, you're the quarterback. Two, you were on Lumbly's bad side, and he resigned over it."

Yeah, from life. Or, maybe, his father separated him from life?

"And, yet, you did me a fucking favor by going to the dance with me? Your parents aren't that fucking gullible."

She scowled, but didn't comment, instead continuing her previous conversation. "Three, you, your sister and brothers, and your cousins are notorious because of your fathers. More than that, Dad knows how you defended me against Willard. He's very appreciative of that, but he did lecture me about the perils of dating you if that was my ultimate goal."

"If my family's so pathetic, how can my parents afford to send six of their children to Ridge Moore?"

"It's the same thing I asked my dad. He thinks your parents either have a sponsor, get financial aid, or use criminally earned money." She looked at him with expectation, awaiting a confirmation or denial. "Which is it?" she asked at his silence.

"Does it matter? You've already reached your own conclusions."

"I haven't. Not really. I just want you to like me the way I like you. Harley is a snob and undercover mean girl and Molly is an idiot."

"You don't know either Molly or Harley well enough to label them. It just makes you seem like a mean girl. Also, let me point out that insulting me and my family by calling us poor criminals isn't a way to make me want to date you."

"Can we just forget I ever said that? I didn't mean to make you feel bad."

"I don't." He got to his feet, not allowing her grabbing his wrist again to stop him this time. "I have to get home," he said, at loose ends. He'd thought Jaleena his friend. Discovering how lowly she saw him was a rude awakening. Whether she spoke out of frustration was beside the point. "Can you get my homework?"

Misery dragged down her features. "Don't be angry, CJ. I truly didn't mean to hurt you. I was just repeating what my father said to me."

"What that motherfuck…" He gnashed his teeth together. Though Mr. Davis was a dickhead, he was still her father. "What he said is bullshit. You don't know if I live in a trailer or a mansion in the middle of a forest that's four times the size of this fucking house."

"Not many people I know grew up in a seven-thousand square foot house."

"Then you know the wrong motherfuckers."

"My parents have worked hard to provide this life for my sisters and me. I have a one-million-dollar trust fund."

He glared at her.

"That's why he's worried," she pressed on. "He said people who haven't grown up in money misuse it when they suddenly get it. He's concerned you'll see me as a walking dollar sign."

"I wouldn't have known about your goddamn money, if you hadn't opened your fucking mouth," he snapped.

"This entire conversation is going off the rails. You're taking everything the wrong way. If you'd stop being so defensive, you'd hear what I'm saying, CJ."

"As long as you're fucking blind, I'll be fucking defensive."

"You're the blind one. You can have me. Not only am I arm candy, I'm brilliant, and I can buy you whatever you want. I get two hundred dollars a month as an allowance as long as I keep my room clean and bring home decent grades."

He scowled at her. "You sell yourself short. If you have to buy me to get me, I'm not worth having."

"That's sweet, but I'm a firm believer in capitalism. Money makes the world go round. If we go steady, I can split my allowance with you."

As annoyed as he was with her, he sat beside her again and hugged her tightly. "Bae, I'm telling you if a motherfucker takes your money, he's not worth having. He should shower you with gifts, not the other way around."

"That's sexist."

"That's how I feel."

"So you'd prefer to struggle...how much allowance do you get?"

The amount would blow her fucking mind. "I'd prefer not to say."

"Exactly. I'm telling you CJ, I would be an asset to you. I promise you wouldn't regret going steady with me."

He studied her mouth. "I'm sure I wouldn't, Jaleena, but I can't overcome being white and that might create a bigger issue than you realize."

Dickhead Ryan taught him that. Of course, he was a dickhead to everybody, but there was particular disrespect toward Lolly, Uncle Mort, and Uncle Digger. Although...he couldn't recall the motherfucker ever showing his contempt to their faces.

"You can overcome being a criminal, though."

"I'm not a fucking criminal!"

"The son of a criminal."

"Show my father respect or lose my fucking number."

Her eyes widened.

"Remember the issue you took when I talked about your old man? I feel the same way. Don't ever call my dad a criminal."

She stared at him. Seeing he wouldn't back down, she nodded. "Your dad's a full-time biker. He's a club president."

"And? I intend to follow in his footsteps. It's my dream to one day run the Death Dwellers."

"My father would never go for that."

"Luckily, I don't give a fuck."

"If it was Harley or Molly asking you to have goals in life and offering to pay your way, would you feel differently?"

"Harley would never do either. She understands my position."

"Her father's a biker, too, so of course she would. She probably supports your aspirations more than I ever could."

He no longer knew what Harley supported. However, explaining would take too long.

"If you got with her and she didn't encourage you to do better in life, then she isn't worth having. You'd be stuck in an endless loop of poverty."

"Harley's parents aren't poor."

"But they aren't as rich as my parents."

Ha. "Your assumptions annoy the fuck out of me."

"They aren't assumptions, CJ. I'm trying to reason with

you."

"You're trying to buy me when I'm not for sale. I don't need your fucking money, Jaleena. Keep it and buy some common sense."

She gasped. "You called me stupid."

"You sound like a fucking brainless idiot. You should hear yourself, so high and mighty looking down on the peasants and offering favors to better us."

"I'm negotiating us being together."

"Is that what you're doing?" When she lifted her chin, CJ came up with an idea. "My family has a get-together every week. Now that my mom's out of the hospital, I'll see if we're having one soon. If we do, I want you to come over, then we can talk."

"Fine," she said on a sigh. "I warn you, though, my parents might want to check the place out. If the neighborhood is too bad, I won't stay long."

CJ smiled. "No problem, bae. If they deem the place safe, they can even eat with us."

She grinned. "Bet." Leaning over, she gave him a quick kiss on the lips. "Let me get your homework so you can be on your way. A couple of the teacher's uploaded some lessons to your account, but you still have a thick folder to work through. Let me know if you need help."

In her words, "bet."

CHAPTER 27

"Are we ready for dessert?"

At Tabitha's question, everyone glanced at each other. An hour after CJ got home from Jaleena's, Tabitha surprised Diesel—everyone—with a visit and dishes of food she'd cooked at their condo, then lugged with her. Her mixed green salad, baked beans, barbequed ribs, and homemade buttermilk biscuits were surprisingly good.

CJ couldn't wait to taste her peachy apple cobbler.

Whatever the fuck that meant. Usually, they enjoyed conversation between dinner and dessert, but since Mom was upstairs and Dad with her, he didn't want to rock the boat with his sister-in-law. Rebel seemed quite receptive to her. Anything CJ might say that went against Tabitha's suggestions could change that.

When no one spoke up, she stood. Her form-fitting, turtleneck crop top barely covered her big breasts. CJ did his best to look anywhere but at her since her titties were inescapable and he still had lingering lust after his earlier encounter with Jaleena.

Rebel grabbed her water glass. "Give us a few minutes, Tabitha," she said after she took a sip. "We digest our main course before we eat dessert."

"Yo, Tabitha," Ryder said, staring at her chest. "Why don't you put us out of our misery and just show us your tits?"

"Yeah," Ransom agreed, ignoring Tabitha's outraged gasp. "You didn't have to wear a top at all since you chose one too small for those puppies."

"That's enough," Diesel gritted, with a noted lack of outrage given the level of Ryder and Ransom's disrespect.

Mom's illness coupled with Dad staying by her side 24/7 removed Ryder and Ransom's fear of reprisal for disobeying Dad's cardinal rule of never disrespecting adults. Had things been normal, CJ's brothers never would've spoken to Tabitha in such a manner. He didn't care for her and he was outraged.

"Shut the fuck up, you little assholes, before I beat your ass," he warned.

Axel folded his arms. "Bring it on, bro."

"You weren't involved," CJ pointed out. "Stay out of it if you don't want me to include you."

Ryder smirked at him. "You can try. One of you against three of us."

"I'll help CJ," Rebel announced, glaring between the three of them. "You sure you want both of us beating your asses."

"Nope," the Triplets chorused.

"Thought not," Rebel said.

Clearing her throat, Tabitha returned to her seat. "I'll ignore your bad behavior this time."

"God will shine down on you," Rule told her, staring at her

without blinking. "Your forgiveness casts a favorable light on us."

Rebel gave her twin a filthy look. Tabitha shifted uneasily.

Diesel tapped his fingers on the table.

Axel picked up his water glass, put it to his lips and tipped it, along with his head, back, allowing cold water to sluice over his face. He burst into laughter, then reached for Rule's glass. "If you don't stop staring at me like you rose from the fucking grave, I'm plucking your fucking eyes out."

As he placed the glass to his lips, Rebel jumped from her seat and thumped the side of his head, snatching the goblet from him.

"Clean that fucking mess, stupid," she ordered, slamming the glass in front of Rule with such force, CJ was surprised it didn't break. "What the fuck is wrong with you? You have water on the table and the floor."

"I was bored, Reb," he complained. "I was amusing myself."

"Amuse yourself with a mop, fuckhead," she grumbled.

"Excuse me, young lady," Tabitha inserted. "Your language is offensive." She glared at Axel. "As is yours, mister. Keep it up and neither of you will have dessert."

"Sorry." Throwing Tabitha a sullen look, Axel stood. "I'll get the mop," he mumbled, hurt. Dessert was his favorite meal.

Tabitha lifted a brow at Rebel. "Well?"

"Bitch, you're not my mother. You're barely my sister-in-law. If you fuck with me, I will drag you to the roof and throw your miserable ass off."

"Touch me and you'll have hell to pay," Tabitha sneered.

Rebel narrowed her eyes and opened her mouth, while Diesel, Ryder, and Ransom stared at her. Rule studied her, but CJ was tired of the bullshit.

"Tabitha," he said. "We appreciate the meal you brought us but check your bullshit. If you threaten my sister again, you will be barred from this house."

"Or we can offer her as a sacrifice," Rule said casually.

Tabitha started, a tentative smile curving her features. Except Rule wasn't fucking joking. CJ saw it in his eyes.

Rebel grabbed Rule's ear and twisted. Rule smiled.

"Look, you perverted little motherfucker," she snarled, "if you enjoy self-flagellation and prayers every minute of every hour, that's on you." Getting no results, she dug her nails into his jaw.

Tears rushing to his eyes, he yelped.

"If you mention blood fucking sacrifices one more fucking time, I'll murder you in your goddamn sleep."

She shoved him away, ignoring his sniffles, and glared at Tabitha. "As for you, I'm being nice to you for Diesel's sake. I suggest you don't ignore my generosity. CJ will tell Momma and she'll tell Daddy you aren't welcomed here anymore. I'll tell my father and say how you've threatened me and want to get my mother alone in the fucking woods, and he'll kill you. Problem fucking solved."

"You wouldn't dare."

"You want to test that fucking theory, bitch? I fucking hate the ground you walk on. You're a sneaky, up-to-no-good viper. The deader you are, the fucking better. Test me one more time and see who's right."

When Tabitha glanced at Diesel, he shrugged.

"Christopher, you don't need to carry me." Mom's huff floated to them a moment before she appeared in Dad's arms, a tender smile on her lips.

The interruption came at the perfect time.

"Mom!" Ryder said, perking up immediately.

Dad sat Mom in her seat to his right, then took his place

at the head of the table. He frowned at the puddle of water on the table, looked at Rule's tear-stained face, then glanced between Rebel and Tabitha.

"What the fuck's goin' on?" he demanded, firmly on the side of almost perfect speech tonight.

Rebel sat next to Mom, then leaned over and kissed her cheek. "Tabitha and me were just getting some things straight. Rule needs a blood sacrifice."

"A what?" Mom asked.

"A. Blood. Sacrifice," Ransom yelled, enunciating each word.

"Why the fuck you yellin', boy?"

"So Mom can understand."

"I'm right here, son," she said.

"Yeah, she like my fuckin' ass, wonderin' what the fuck Rule need a fuckin' sacrifice for."

Mom nodded to Rebel's water glass, since neither she nor Dad had place settings.

She took a sip as Rule said, "I sacrificed a bird and Mom got better."

Mom choked, and Dad's suddenly dark look chilled the room. Luckily, Mom's coughing distracted Dad, else Rule might've been in grave danger.

"You fuckin' up animals ain't what saved your ma, Rule," Dad growled, once Mom calmed. "Medical knowledge did."

"And prayers," Rule insisted.

"Ain't denyin' that," Dad said flatly. "But prayers would've worked without motherfuckin' blood sacrifices. That's just your fuckin' excuse to fuck up something."

"That isn't true, Dad. Leviticus chapter seventeen, verse six says, 'For the life of the flesh is in the blood, and I have given it to you on the altar to make atonement for your souls; for it is the blood by reason of the life that makes atonement'."

"You know that verse by heart?" Mom asked, brows lifted.

"He knows the whole fucking bible by heart," Rebel complained.

Dad scowled. "Don't curse the bible, baby." He focused on Rule again. "How long it took you to learn the bible?"

"I've memorized some of it over the years, then when Mom and Jo…" Tears glistened in his eyes. "I didn't know what to do. I would've done anything to save her. I-I mean them."

"What would you have done if your prayers and sacrifices didn't work, Rule?" Mom asked gently.

Even though Mom sat in her chair with her hair in a ponytail, looking more rested than she had in weeks, Dad still swallowed at the question and pain slid across his face.

CJ glanced at his empty plate, not wanting to think of that possibility.

"I don't know, Mom," Rule admitted. "I was just so scared."

"What else did you do?"

Clenching his jaw, Rule looked away.

"Burned incense, chanted, beat his own ass." Rebel sniffed. "The list is endless, Momma. He read to me for hours on end."

"What did you read, Rule?"

"What do you think, Momma?" Rebel said in exasperation. "The bible. For hours and hours and hours."

Alarm filled Mom's eyes. "You read nothing else, son?"

Rule shook his head.

Clasping his hands together, Dad leaned forward. "Did you do schoolwork?"

"Yes, Dad."

"My ass got a question, boy. If you want to be a priest, I

won't stop you. But you've crossed a line. Most clergymen are well-rounded. Well before your ma got so sick, you'd started praying a lot. What got you on such a singular track?"

"I like to draw."

Dad nodded. "I carried a couple of your drawings in my cut for years."

"I just hated being around the cousins. Ryan was always so mean to me. CJ and Rebel defended me. I still felt out of place, like I was the only one who needed protection. When I'm alone, I don't feel that way."

"So, Ryan should be fucked up for turning you into you," Rebel said with disgust.

"Baby, I know the lil' motherfucker your twin, but would you please shut the fuck up for one fuckin' minute so I can talk to him?"

Tabitha smirked at Rebel.

"Fuck off, bitch," Rebel snarled. "Daddy told me to keep quiet for him. Not you."

"Rule, after I bring your ma back upstairs, you and me talkin'. Hear, boy?"

Rule nodded.

"I came downstairs to thank you for the meal, Tabitha," Mom said, a smile pasted on her lips.

"I thought maybe you needed help with Gunner," Tabitha cooed.

"Bunny took Gunner to her house," Mom said, frowning at Axel's spot. "No one ever said why there's water on the table or where Axel might be."

"Axel was bored, Mom," CJ inserted, "so he decided to pretend to drink water."

"And poured it all over himself," Rebel added.

"Ain't I beat his lil' ass a couple times over that?" Dad asked Mom.

Giggling, she nodded, and he chuckled. For some reason, they all began laughing, and the intensity of the arguments floated away.

"Where is Axel?" Mom asked again, once the humor died down.

"He went to get a mop, Aunt Meggie," Tabitha said. "I threatened to send him to bed with no dessert for disrespecting me."

"I see." Mom gulped from Rebel's glass again. "In future, please tell me or Christopher if one of the kids misbehave. We'll dole out the punishments."

"As the only other adult woman in the house, I thought it was my job, Aunt Meggie."

"You thought wrong," Mom retorted.

"But—"

"Look, Tabitha," Dad interrupted. "Megan told you to shut the fuck up about our lil' motherfuckers. End of fuckin' story. Your arguin' is stressin' her out. If you don't want me to throw you the fuck out, shut the fuck up and accept what she said. This is her fuckin' house. She lay the rules." His look of dislike exposed his real feelings. "I enforce the motherfuckers. Underfuckinstand?"

A moment of silence followed before Mom looked at CJ. "What have you been up to, son?"

"I spent the morning with Molly, then I visited Jaleena to pick up my schoolwork."

"You and school just don't fucking mix, huh, CJ?" Ryder asked, a plastic straw hanging from one of his nostrils.

"Stick it up farther, Ry," Ransom encouraged. "You can pull a few boogers out."

Mom wrinkled her nose. Ryder didn't follow Ransom's instructions, so Ransom pulled the straw out of Ryder's nostril and inspected it.

"That's disgusting," Rebel complained as Ransom sniffed, then threw the straw on the table.

"This not table talk," Dad said. "Throw that fuckin' straw the fuck away."

"This isn't anywhere talk, Daddy," Rebel said, watching Ransom shove his chair back, grab the straw, and throw it in the small trashcan by the server. "It's barbaric."

"You're such a girl, Rebel," Ransom told her with disgust, reseating himself. "I'm glad I don't have a pussy to get grossed-out so easily."

"You don't even have a fucking brain, so why worry about your genitals?" Rebel said sweetly, studying her nails.

"You and Aunt Meggie do look a lot alike," Tabitha said, a thoughtful look on her face.

"If you just noticed, not only are you a stupid bitch, but a blind one." Rebel snapped her brows together. "A refrain in the past hour, since I do believe I pointed out the same thing a little while ago and yet you refuse to shut the fuck up."

Dad sighed and scratched his jaw. Mom patted Rebel's hand and shook her head when Rebel looked at her.

"I'm just trying to make small talk." Tabitha sounded hurt and remorseful. "I don't mean any offense." She smiled at Mom. "You still look so pale, Aunt. You've aged ten years in the last two weeks. Don't get me wrong. You're still a pretty woman."

Face reddening and eyes darkening, Dad jumped to his feet and pointed at Tabitha, so angry his finger trembled.

Mom stood, too, and rushed to Dad's side. "Christopher—"

"Diesel, if you don't get this cunt the fuck outta my fuckin' face, you bringin' pieces of her home."

Tabitha paled.

Mom tried again. "Christopher."

"I'm not listenin', baby. No bitch disrespectin' you in front of me, but especially in your own fuckin' house."

"Please!" Tabitha cried. "I just wanted to suggest a place I know for Aunt Meggie to rest."

"Let me guess," Rebel said sarcastically. "Your fucking cabin."

"It isn't my cabin. I don't have the money to own a cabin. It's a cabin of a friend's dad, where I took a break from the hustle and bustle of life. It rejuvenated me. I admit it was several years ago, so it might've been sold by now, but that was the only point I was making."

Dad studied her. "What the fuck game you playin'? This ain't the first fuckin' time you tellin' Megan to go to a goddamn cabin."

"It's no game. I swear! I'm speaking as a concerned d-daughter-in-law."

"If Megan goes, I will go with her," Dad said.

"That's all the better," Tabitha said, her smile brightening.

"What the fuck that mean?"

"Nothing, Uncle Chris," Tabitha said quickly. "I just meant you'd get much needed rest, too."

Dad stared at Diesel, who gave Tabitha a small smile.

"You'll be in the middle of nowhere with no connection to the outside world," she said. "You will feel refreshed and new when you get back to civilization."

"Let Riley check out the cabin," Ransom suggested. "If she's telling the truth, you and Mom can go."

"Check out the cabin?" Tabitha laughed. "What does that mean?"

"Fuck all," Dad snapped.

Ryder turned to Ransom and whispered to him.

"Listen up, Tabitha. Me and Megan gonna talk about goin' away, then Ima look into shit. Don't bring that motherfucker up again. Because you're Diesel's woman, I'm givin' you one fuckin' warnin'. If you're tryin' to fuck over Megan some kind of way, Diesel will kill you. Normally, I take care of those special cases, but since you're his bitch, he's with you or with us. If you even think about betrayin' my wife and I find out, either he fucks you up or I fuck up both of you."

A pause followed Dad's words, presumably to allow Tabitha a chance to respond. But she stared at him, eyes wide and face chalky. She gave the barest nod, frozen silent.

"I can fuck up Tabitha, Daddy," Rebel offered, removing the focus from Diesel's nonreaction and Tabitha's shock.

"Girls can't join the fuckin' club, Rebel."

"The club doesn't hurt women," Rebel said. "I don't have to be a club member to fuck up any bitch who gets on the wrong side of the Dwellers."

He squinted at her. "You're not eighteen. And how the fuck you know about what the fuck the club do?"

"I've been talking to some of the members," she said calmly.

"Rebel, I think I know who that might be," Mom said with disapproval. "If you don't want him killed, stop prying."

Rebel's eyes widened. "Killed? But we've only been talking. He answers my questions."

"It's club business, sweetheart," Diesel told her, finally finding his fucking voice.

She looked at CJ.

"He's right, Reb," he said softly, pitying the horror on her face. "Bishop shouldn't fuck with you at all, but he needs to keep his fucking mouth shut about anything to do with the club, past, present, or future."

"I never said it was Bishop," she said faintly.

"You call him Shop," Mom said. "It isn't hard to guess."

Dad's icy eyes concerned CJ. He liked Bishop, but the motherfucker was past stupid for entertaining Rebel.

"Don't hurt him, Christopher."

"This club business, baby."

"That has to do with our daughter. Rebel won't ever forgive herself."

"I'll talk to him, Dad," CJ volunteered.

"I'm givin' him one pass, Megan," Dad said. "Cuz you still not all better." He looked at Rebel. "I'm givin' you one warnin', baby. You my daughter. Whether you eighteen or eighty, if they fuck you, they disrespect me. They die. Don't give Bishop no fuckin' ideas that'll get him killed quicker than him openin' his fuckin' mouth about shit you don't need to know."

"I'm not a wilting flower, Daddy. CJ knows."

Dad guided Mom back to her seat, then returned to his. "When you turn eighteen, I'll think about sendin' you on special assignments, but I need to make sure you can handle it. I gotta do it in my own time."

"Putting a gun in Rebel's hand is as bad as giving Rule an aviary," Ryder said. "Both ideas are terrible. She'll fuck up anyone who angers her, and he'll sacrifice every bird he gets his hands on."

Mom squeezed the bridge of her nose.

Ryder beamed at her. "Aren't you glad to be home?" he asked. "Didn't you miss us?"

"I did," Mom agreed without hesitation, resting her elbows on the table. "I'm ecstatic to be home. I can't wait until Jo is here with us."

"Yeah, her," Ransom said with a frown. "Babies cry a lot. I watch videos online and they are so noisy."

"Her nursery's on the third floor," Rebel said, much more subdued after the sobering conversation about Bishop. "You won't hear her." She glanced over her shoulder, then at Mom. "Do you want me to check on Axel?"

"He's probably stealing some peach apple cobbler," Ransom said.

"Peachy apple cobbler," Tabitha corrected.

"That's what I said," Ransom told her.

"No—"

"Mom, Dad, is it okay if I visit Harley if she's still awake?" CJ interrupted, in no mood to hear Ransom and Tabitha's back-and-forth.

"Don't be long, boy," Dad said.

"Is everything okay, CJ?" Mom asked.

"Nope, because Harley is a petty heifer, and CJ deserves better," Rebel said.

"Can I talk, Reb?"

"I didn't want you to leave out the pertinent details, including the woeful fact that you are probably going to suck up to her."

"Rebel!" Mom said sharply. "Let CJ tell the story."

"Fine," Rebel mumbled, raising her hands. "Whatever."

"I'm not going to suck up. I just want to check on her. And I want to talk to her. Jaleena…Jaleena—" He rubbed his eyes. Jaleena what? Why was this even an issue? He'd already decided his feelings were too uncertain to involve her in his life.

"CJ!" Rebel breathed. "Tell me it's true. You're moving on from the Wicked Bitch of the Northwest."

"I can take off my sock and stuff it in Rebel's mouth, Mom," Ransom offered. "I was going to change them tonight anyway."

Mom simultaneously groaned and placed her hand on Rebel's arm.

Dad steepled his fingers. "How long the motherfuckers been on your feet, Ransom?"

"Four days. Why?"

"You haven't showered in four fuckin' days?"

"I never go over five days, Dad. That's gross."

"The entirety of your wretched little body is gross," Rebel told him.

"Daily showers are bad for your skin, Reb," Ransom said.

"But wonderful for your fuckin' nose. Smelly balls and dick not something you want."

Mom and Rebel exchanged mutually disgusted looks at Dad's admonishment.

"Does...does anything ever get settled at the table?" Tabitha asked with hesitation.

"Private family dinners are generally chaos," CJ said with a smile, since Diesel wasn't talking to his wife. "We love every moment of it." He looked at his parents again. "Speaking of...are we having another family get-together before Christmas?"

"Your ma just got home, son," Dad said. "We don't want to tire her out. She's already talkin' about the decorations that still need doin'."

"A family get-together would be fun," Mom said. "It'll be a break from all the sadness."

"Christmas is three fuckin' weeks away, Megan. Let's wait 'til the new year to start with the weekly dinners again."

Though Mom nodded, her disappointment was clear. Dad scowled at her, probably aware a get-together was suddenly imminent.

"Why do you ask, CJ?" she said.

"I want to invite Jaleena and her parents over."

Everyone looked at him in surprise.

"What the fuck I'm missin'?" Dad asked.

"I'll explain later," CJ promised.

"It probably has to do with Jaleena thinking we're nothing but piss poor criminals with no future except jail or prison,"

Rebel said with a shrug. "Her dad's a wealthy tech exec or something and her mom's a Civil Rights attorney."

Well, that explained a lot.

"Is that true, CJ?" Mom asked.

"Basically," CJ responded. "She offered to give me half her allowance. Like a hundred bucks a month just to help me out."

"You got a high school sugar mama?" Ryder said in awe. "What's your secret, bro?"

"I do not," CJ gritted. "I told her she shouldn't want me if she has to buy me. I'm not worth that. No motherfucker is."

Ransom shook his head. "You're fucking stupid. You could've had a goldmine."

"I don't need her money, little asshole."

"Whether you do or not, she offered. My life rule is never turn down money."

"You fuckin' eleven, boy. How the fuck you got a life rule?"

"I want to join the club, too, Dad," Ransom said. "I'm getting my rules together early, so motherfuckers know where I stand."

CJ got to his feet. He wouldn't be able to sleep until he talked to Harley. For whatever reason, he needed to see her one last time before he made a firm decision about anything. "I won't be long."

"You'll miss dessert," Tabitha said.

"What dessert?" Axel asked, walking into the dining room.

His timing made it seem as if he'd been hanging in the hallway, awaiting the opportune moment.

"You ate the entire cobbler, Axel?"

"No, Mom. That bitch yelled at me and told me I couldn't have any, so I threw that shit down the garbage disposal." He glared at Tabitha, turned on his heel, and stomped out.

The announcement left everyone speechless. Even Rebel

stared in shock.

Then, Ryder guffawed and pointed at Tabitha. "Burn, bitch." He jumped up and ran out of the room, shouting, "Axel, bro!"

"Goddamn Axel," Ransom said once Ryder's voice faded away. "That little motherfucker one-upped me. If I don't come up with something better, he'll never let me live it down."

CHAPTER 28

Harley

At the sound of the robotic alert of the front door opening followed by her mother's voice floating to the kitchen, Harley sat straighter in her booth seat. It was 9PM, but Daddy and the boys were at the club.

Harley had been sitting with Mommie at the kitchen table, searching online stores for new holiday outfits, while Mommie reviewed work files on her laptop. Before they'd sat, they'd prepared hot chocolate from one of Lolly's recipes, making enough for Daddy and the boys, but that had been an hour ago.

Lou and Kaleb barely spoke to Harley or Mommie, firmly on Daddy's side. Rumors of their parents' rift were circulating at the club. Without knowing the full story, the boys had chosen their allegiance.

"Hunny bunny?" Mommie said, walking into the kitchen.

Harley expected her father and brothers. Seeing CJ shocked her and immediately annoyed her. His wince when he stopped inches from her and studied her face, set her teeth on edge.

"Would you like a mug of hot chocolate, CJ?" Mommie asked.

"No. Thank you, Aunt Bailey. I won't be long. I just wanted to check on Harley and talk to her for a moment."

Brushing by CJ, Mommie picked up her silent cellphone from its spot next to her laptop. "I was just about to call Lucas."

Harley glared at CJ. "No, Mommie. Stay. Anything CJ has to say isn't a secret. Right?" she challenged.

CJ glanced away and clenched his jaw before he met her eyes and nodded. "Right, Harley."

"See?" Harley crowed. "Please stay, Mommie. I need your moral support. After all, my friend wouldn't have allowed over a day to pass before he checked on me again."

"Why should I have?" he snapped. "When all you'd do is exactly what you're doing now. Handing me a platter of bullshit."

"Don't cuss at me," she yelled, her anger exacerbating her aches and pains.

"CJ, if you don't respect Harley, I will ask you to leave and don't come back until you learn manners," Mommie said sharply.

CJ gave Mommie an incredulous look, while Harley stiffened her shoulders in triumph.

"I don't ever have to come here again, Aunt Bailey," CJ said evenly, shocking both Harley and Mommie. "The reason for my visit tonight was to clear things between Harley and me, and to see if she needed anything. But I've done nothing to either of you." He started to turn away, then halted. "I didn't want to believe our friendship was over, Harley—"

"I never said our friendship was over," she squeaked.

"You haven't," he agreed, "but I am. I'm done."

He looked from Harley to Mommie and back again, hurt flickering in his eyes. "See you around." He turned and walked away.

"Mommie, do something!"

"CJ!" Mommie called. "Harley didn't mean—"

"She meant every word, Aunt Bailey," CJ called from the hallway. "And so did you."

A moment later, the door slammed shut.

After barely sleeping last night and still in pain, Harley couldn't make it to school for a second day. However, she still needed to rehearse for the play, since it was such a major grade, and she was battling with Nardo and Mrs. Mendez to keep the play true to its original form.

At breakfast, she asked her mother if she could hang out with Nardo at his house later that day so she could practice. Unfortunately, Daddy was there to pick up more clothes to bring to the clubhouse. After deserting them to do whatever, he thought he had a right to pass his opinion.

"Fuck no," Daddy said. "I don't trust that little motherfucker."

"Nardo's my friend, Mommie," Harley cried.

"Harley, baby, he'll still be your friend if he real about it. But you can't go. I forbid it."

Mommie bristled. "This is Harley we're talking about, Lucas. Have some faith in her upbringing."

"I have faith in her, Bailey. I just don't have faith in him. You know how teenage boys be, baby."

"He's fourteen, Lucas."

"He not a eunuch! His cock work."

Lou and Kaleb giggled but shut up at Mommie's glare.

"Besides, she vulnerable right now. She got jumped at school and CJ fed up. Nardo the type to sense weakness and use that to his advantage."

"Stop stereotyping," Mommie ordered, then smiled at Harley. "If it's okay with his parents, I'll drop you off at five and pick you up at eight."

"Thank you for trusting me," Harley murmured, smirking at her father.

Daddy stood. "I'm out."

"What time will you return?" Mommie asked, the alarm on her face shocking Harley.

"A fucking time, Bailey. What the fuck do you care since I'm persona non grata?"

Mommie swallowed. "All I'm saying is we need to trust Harley."

"And all I'm saying is we don't need to trust Nardo."

"Nardo is good and kind. Much better than lying, raggedy CJ," Harley said viciously.

"You got that all fucking twisted, baby girl," Daddy said with a shake of his head.

"CJ isn't the saint you peg him," Harley spat. "You appreciate his feelings over your own children. I bet you wish he was your son rather than Lou and Kaleb. You value him over me."

"See how you've made her feel, Lucas?" Mommie demanded. "Harley, your daddy—"

"I can speak for myself, Bailey," Daddy barked. "If that's the way you feel, Harley, then I can't change your mind if my years of love and devotion to you, your momma, and your brothers don't speak for themselves."

Without another word, he walked out of the kitchen.

Lou stood. "With the way you're acting, I value CJ over you, too, Harley," he said. "Nardo's a jerk. If you like him, then you're stupid."

"Young man, there's no name calling in this house. I'll especially not allow you to disparage my daughter. Your sister."

"Harley's your daughter, Mom, but Dad's my father," he retorted. "Can I see if I can get a ride to school with one of my cousins?"

"If that's your preference," Mommie said. "I warn you, you will have meals in your room until you apologize to Harley."

He shrugged, turned on his heel, and left. Kaleb stared toward the hallway and Mommie sighed.

"Go with your brother," she said, rubbing her temple.

He didn't hesitate to leave.

Now, hours later, Harley and Nardo had just finished eating pizza and drinking sodas. They had yet to go over their lines, but it was only 6PM.

He lived with his parents and two brothers in a middle-class neighborhood in a neat three-bedroom house that was bright and airy. Since he'd opened the door and saw her bruises, he'd been solicitous and concerned, unlike CJ who sniped and griped about all her supposed wrongs against him.

Her nostrils flared.

"You too pretty to look so angry, ma," Nardo said, squeezing next to her on the couch in the den. "Why you mad-mugging?"

"Just thinking about assholes."

"Assholes not worth the time of day, Harley. They're especially not worth it if it ruins your beautiful face."

She preened at his compliments. CJ never called her beautiful. "Thank you," she said primly. "Do you really think I'm that pretty?"

Nardo planted an arm around her shoulder, and she relaxed against him.

"If you were my chick, I'd tell you you were beautiful all day long." He fisted some of her braids. "I'd be so jealous I couldn't stand you talking to another dude."

CJ didn't care. He was too busy talking to other girls. Namely, Molly. "That's so sweet, Nardo."

"I would parade you in front the world, so they could see my prize."

"You see me as a prize?" she asked, her heart pounding at the romantic words and at her imagining all the different ways she'd let CJ know she was done with him. She'd throw Nardo in his face and make him cry.

"You're a golden jewel, girl. A diamond possession. That's what my old man always tell my momma," he confessed. "He owns her, and she lets him. I always thought it was so romantic. Claiming herself as his ride-or-die and not letting no one else near her. She only listen to you."

"It is romantic," Harley agreed. "I think it's the sweetest thing a boy has ever said to me."

He pulled her onto his lap and kissed her. When they came up for air, they were both breathing hard.

Harley gloated, wishing someone could've taken pictures of her with Nardo and sent them to CJ.

Nardo nuzzled her neck and she shivered. "Let's go to my room, ma," he whispered. "I've told you what I want from you. Show me what you're willing to give."

After CJ's treatment last night and her father's meanness earlier, Harley was ready to give anything Nardo asked of her. She wanted to show CJ who was boss and she wanted to prove to her daddy he was wrong. "Okay."

By the time her mother picked her up, Harley was already regretting her decision. The pain had been almost unbearable and Nardo ordered her to stop crying. Belatedly, she remembered protection.

"Everything okay, hunny bunny?" Mommie asked when Harley got into the SUV and closed the door.

"Fine, Mommie," she said, close to tears. She felt as if she didn't have a friend in the world.

"Oh, darling, I thought spending time with Nardo would help your hurt feelings," Mommie soothed. "CJ doesn't deserve your heartache. Until he changes his ways, I think it's best he doesn't see you."

Hours ago, she would've wholeheartedly agreed. Now, she only wanted to go back and time and change what she'd done.

CHAPTER 29

Ryan

With Meggie's release from the hospital two days ago, life would return to normal sooner rather than later. Once Outlaw rested, he would start to ask questions and then Ryan would be fucked.

Meggie dying hadn't mattered one way or the other. But then fuckhead Bash came to Hortensia with his fucking games.

Ryan still hadn't recovered from finding Mrs. Harris's head. He hadn't even been home. After he left Molly's bedside, he'd gone to stay with Willard, Wallace, and their aunt and uncle...

Fuck, their mother and father, but Wallace and Willard persisted with the falsehood that they were orphans.

All the fucking lies. It didn't matter if he somehow blamed Val for his meeting Bash, Ryan was still so fucking dead, if he didn't find a way to straighten shit out. Even Willard bitching Ryan out over his nightmares didn't matter. Nor did Zoann's demands that he come home. For once, Val found his balls and told that cunt to back down, siding with Ryan and allowing him to spend Winter Break with the Byrds...the Barts.

But he was little more than a slave at that house. They all treated Ryan with derision and made him serve them. One-on-one, he could stand up to Willard. With his whole family against Ryan, his life was on the line.

He still resented a lot about his family, but he had autonomy and a little status as Val and Zoann's son. For now, the Barts allowed him to come and go as he pleased. Unfortunately, the unstable fuckheads were a danger to his safety and could revoke his freedom on a dime.

Turning, he leaned against the railing at Turn Creek Bridge. Feet below, the icy water in the creek meandered on its downstream journey to meet up with the Columbia River. Frigid air blanketed his face and the heavy clouds threatened snow again, promising a white Christmas.

The jingling spurs alerted him of Bash's arrival before he crested the bridge and came into view.

"Why are you in Hortensia, Bash?" Ryan wasn't in the mood to fuck around with hellos. His girlfriend was in the hospital, and he couldn't make heads or tails of her words. Usually, she made some sense. Worse than that, she kept asking for CJ.

Her reliance on his cousin left him even more angry. It was why he'd left a message on her father's voicemail initially, though he had yet to hear back from Tom Harris. For some reason, the man's silence relieved Ryan. As hours turned into days, he greatly regretted revealing her location. He could only hope the motherfucker was dead, incapacitated or too busy running scared to bother with Molly.

Bash halted beside him and leaned against the railing. "Why shouldn't I be here, boy? I had business to see to."

"Business?" Ryan scoffed. "You beat my girlfriend and

made her lose her baby. You fucking killed her mother!"

Bash guffawed. "Tom killed that cunt. I just relieved her of her head to show Molly what might happen to hers if she didn't shut the fuck up. I thought about killing her." He patted Ryan's back. "I allowed her to live for your sake."

"You've fucked her up." For the first time in a long time, Ryan felt something other than hate and bitterness. Remorse and helplessness settled into him. "She's a sweet girl, Bash. Stupid as a brick. You hurt her." Apparently, he'd been hurting her. "Physically. Mentally. Emotionally."

"I give a fuck how? Don't make me regret allowing her to live, boy. She told me she didn't trust CJ enough, so he couldn't read her mind, then confessed she told him she was knocked up."

Ryan turned those words over in his head. When CJ said something similar to her the day he'd stormed on the field to confront Ryan, he hadn't understood. Now, though, he was beginning to get an idea.

"I finally got it out of her that he told her that shit and she believed him. Dumb slut," Bash scoffed. "I told her don't mention she knew me or Cleaner, and she couldn't wait to open her fucking mouth."

"She never mentioned you or Cleaner to me," Ryan snapped. "That should've accounted for something. Furthermore, you know I was fucking her because I told you. I introduced you."

"There was no need, idiot. I already knew her."

"Through Willard and Wally," Ryan guessed.

"Through Tom and Nora," Bash corrected. "Nora was one of my bitches. Tom ended up liking her, so I gave her to him as long as he stayed loyal to me."

"Are you all related?" Because, so far, there were so many relations in their twisted family history, it wouldn't surprise

Ryan. "Is Tom your brother?"

Bash cuffed the side of Ryan's head. "That would make Molly my niece!" he snarled with indignation. "What kind of depraved motherfucker do you take me for?"

"A giant depraved motherfucker," Ryan bit out, rubbing the side of his head.

Snickering, Bash lit a cigarette, so Ryan did the same. They smoked in silence for a few minutes.

"It could've been my baby you beat out of her," he said finally.

"Who gives a fuck, Ryan? Fuck her until you knock her up again, if it means that much to you. Chances are, it was your baby, since I've only fucked her twice in the last six months and she wasn't that far along."

Nausea twisted through Ryan, and he lost interest in his cigarette. He threw it over the railing. "I see."

"If it makes you feel any better, Tom tied her to the bed. She didn't want me." Bash shrugged. "Not that I give a fuck. But I do like you. Wish you were my kid, so I didn't want you to think she wanted me."

Bash's words made Molly's treatment even more egregious. Besides, how the fuck did it matter? Did Bash really think those bullshit words made Ryan feel better?

"She might not want me," Bash continued, "but she wants CJ."

Ryan stiffened.

"Just saying. If you summoned me to confront me about Molly Harris, I hope you know she'd throw you over in a minute if CJ gave her a chance."

Of course, she would. All the girls loved CJ. For now, Ryan would push aside his feelings for his cousin. At least, until Molly recuperated, then he'd make her choose. If she wanted to continue as his girlfriend, then she had to forget CJ.

"She's the main reason I asked to meet with you, but not the only reason. Why are you here, asshole?"

"I don't owe you an explanation of my schedule."

"You do when you reveal yourself to my cousins and to Harley."

"She's a pretty slut."

"She's not even fifteen yet."

"She has a cunt. She's a slut."

Worst fucking logic ever. "CJ saw you."

"And his fucking little brothers pushed me in the fucking creek. I owe those motherfuckers."

"Good luck with that. Axel, Ryder, and Ransom are the Terrible Triplets. They will fuck you up and not lose sleep over it. They have none of Meggie's qualities. Not like CJ. He has a conscience. Those three don't."

"I still owe them. And they are children. From what I understand, they've never killed anyone."

Neither had CJ. Yet, he'd taken the blood at the Harris house in stride. Of course, he hadn't seen a lifeless head alone in a sink with eyes half-closed and a mouth frozen open.

Ryan drew in a sharp breath, trying to clear away the images. Back and forth about Harley or the Terrible Triplets wouldn't get to the next point. "You know Johnnie."

Bash flung his cigarette. "So, what if I do?"

"Your appearance sent him over the fucking edge, and my cousin, Rory, on a hunt for answers." Ryan explained the conversation he'd had in the cave with Rory. "Meggie's out of the hospital now, so Outlaw will take more interest in everything else. He will kill you, me, Cleaner, Tabitha, and Johnnie. Everyone connected to you."

"I don't give a fuck what he does to me, Cleaner, you, or Johnnie. If he hurts my niece, there'll be hell to pay."

"Then you shouldn't have put that bitch in a position to be hurt, asshole," Ryan snapped. "She's fucking vicious, and the women in the family hate her."

"As long as they don't hurt her—"

"They won't, Bash," Ryan promised, shook up at the venom in the man's voice. "But what can you tell me…? What can you add to all Rory discovered?"

"I'll ask the fucking questions, you arrogant little fuckhead."

"Bash—"

"Shut the fuck up." He grabbed Ryan's collar and yanked him off his feet. "You and your fucking uncle are fucking me over, protecting Christopher's cunt. I might have to take matters into my own hands. Maybe, I should start by cutting your head off."

Fear seized Ryan, and he was so sorry he'd summoned Bash without telling anyone. Who could he tell though? His cousins and his brother didn't like him, so they wouldn't care. Molly was in the hospital. The Barts were firmly on Bash's side.

"Excuse me?"

At first, Ryan thought he was imagining Rebel's voice, until Bash stilled, then jerked him away and turned. Ready to piss himself, Ryan straightened, wincing at Rebel's narrowed blue eyes.

"Bash."

The word fell from her lips like an accusation.

"Hello, Rebel. Ryan and me—" Bash started.

"Save it, motherfucker," she said in a hard voice. "As a general rule, I don't talk to assholes, and I won't start now." She glared at Ryan. "If CJ hadn't told me Daddy knew about this fuckhead, I would call you a fucking traitor and garrot your bitch ass."

Stiffening, Bash moved forward. Rebel raised her fists.

"Rebel, didn't I ask you not to curse?" Rule stepped into view and halted, blinking at the scene before him.

His arrival halted a disaster in the making. Though Rebel was tall, she was slim, and Bash was taller and muscular.

Rule covered his twin's fists with his hands and forced them down. He took in the scene. Instead of cowering in fear, he stepped in front of Rebel and faced Bash.

For the first time, Ryan felt a smidgeon of respect for the pious prick.

"You're Bash, aren't you?" Rule asked.

"I'm famous," Bash said with a smirk.

"You're a fuckhead," Rebel said flatly.

Rule raised his hand and glanced over his shoulder. "Sister, please. I can handle this." He smiled at Bash. "A prayer will calm you."

"Those words will get us killed, dummy," Rebel complained.

"No. We come in peace."

"You come in peace. I come however the fuck this motherfucker comes," Rebel responded.

Bash laughed. "Couldn't have said it better, niece."

"Don't fucking remind me," Rebel said crossly. "It's bad enough I have to claim Uncle Johnnie."

Glancing away, Ryan hid his smile.

"You wound me, princess."

"Not bad enough. You aren't bleeding." Rebel shoved Rule to her side and lasered Ryan. "It's your lucky day. I'm in the holiday spirit, fuck face. I'm not going into the complicated details of how Mattie intercepted Uncle Val's monitoring you. I swear she's going to be a fucking spy one day. Anyway, she recruited me, and I recruited Rule and Devon. Mattie's at the fucking mall with Devon."

"Where you should be with her, and Devon with me," Rule said with displeasure. "Females are delicate flowers whose virtue and innocence should be protected."

"So you've said," Rebel conceded.

"You disagree," Bash guessed.

Rebel smiled sweetly. "Obviously, I disagree. I'm here. Besides, none of the boys in my family have a normal view of women and girls." She thought for a moment and shrugged. "Except CJ. He's the best of us."

"Of course," Ryan said with distaste, offended that even CJ's sister put him on a pedestal. "Saint CJ."

"Compared to you, he is." She glared at Ryan and turned. As she marched away, she said, "Do come along, Rule and Ryan. Mattie called Uncle Mort. He's probably arriving at the mall and is ready to search for us."

Bash stared at Rebel's retreating form. "She's gorgeous."

Unease swept through Ryan. "She's a child. Younger than Molly."

"She's gorgeous," he repeated.

"Rebel is favored with beauty and brains," Rule said.

Bash frowned at him.

"As is our mother. Mom is breathtaking. They are both blessed."

"The bible's not my thing," Bash grunted.

"It wouldn't be," Ryan said dryly, "not with your love of rape, torture, and murder."

Bash moved so fast, Ryan didn't have time to attempt escape. He grabbed Ryan's throat and started to squeeze, smiling and staring into Ryan's eyes as he choked the life from him.

"Do not be overcome by evil, but overcome evil with good."

Rule's desperate voice reached Ryan through a haze. At

any moment, he'd lose consciousness. Then, Bash would throw him into the water before shooting Rule.

Without warning, Bash released Ryan and stumbled back, his eyes wide with surprise. Rule stepped in front of Ryan and headbutted Bash, who screamed and dropped to his knees. A knife protruded from his shoulder.

Making the sign of the cross, Rule kicked Bash in the head, then calmly jerked away the knife and wiped the blood on his black jeans.

"You have to tell Uncle Johnnie about this," he said, folding the blade and then stuffing it in his jacket pocket. "CJ and Bishop were talking at the club last night. The Dwellers are trying to negotiate a peace deal with the Scorpions. Bash might take offense at my tactics to save your life." He started off.

Ryan made himself catch up to his cousin. "You...you stabbed him, Rule. You. When...when...you're always... You don't like cursing. You don't fight. You don't drink. You pray."

Halting, Rule faced Ryan and nodded. "I was told to save you."

Ryan blinked.

"After Momma took ill, He has spoken at length to me of death and torture. I've practiced on birds, rodents, and forest creatures. Sacrifices are required if prayers are to be heard. That's why she's better. Now, come. We have to get to the mall before Uncle Mort arrives. Besides, it is almost time for my evening prayers."

Fuck. Him.

Speechless, Ryan stared at Rule. He searched for, and failed to find, the words to counter that entire fucked up statement.

A half-smile curved Rule's mouth. "Don't worry, Ry. I'll

never harm a pet."

Goddamn.

Uneasy—and honestly frightened—Ryan put a hand on Rule's shoulder. As if in slow motion, Rule glanced at Ryan's arm, then searched his face. The intensity in those pale green eyes alarmed Ryan and he stumbled back.

"W-w-w-what...?" Ryan paused, swallowed, and tried to gather his thoughts. He licked his lips. "We've always been friends, cuz." Better to be friends with a murderous zealot. The thought made him shake and he snapped his hands behind his back to conceal his terror. "We share...we share, er 'R' names."

"If you ask me, there are too many 'R' names, Ryan." Rule shoved his hands into his jacket pockets. "But He's whispered to me that Momma meant no harm, so I can forgive her. He's also reminded me that she had no say-so in some instances. Aunt Zoann named you Ryan Matthew, instead of Matthew Ryan, because Uncle Val was..." His voice trailed off and he shrugged.

"You'd hurt Meggie because of some stupid fucking names?"

"She's Aunt Meggie to you."

Ryan jumped at the note of cruelty in Rule's voice.

"And, no, I wouldn't. One of the commandments is 'honor your father and mother.' Do you know it?"

Fuck. He wished he did. As a child, he'd been forced to endure Mass. Now, he searched his brain but came up with nothing.

"Honor thy father and thy mother: that thy days may be long upon the land which the LORD thy God giveth thee." Rule smiled. "It is the only commandment with a promise. Do you honor your parents? Mine?"

"O-o-o-o-of course," Ryan stammered, stiffening his

muscles to stop his entire body from shaking like a leaf in a storm.

Bash groaned.

"We aren't friends, Ryan," Rule said conversationally. "You and me. It was your teasing me and calling me names that started me on my journey."

Another groan from Bash accompanied by movement. But Rule's stare pinned Ryan to his spot. Part accusation and part dislike that promised religious retribution.

"But you're family, Ryan. Do you know a bible verse about family?"

"Uh—"

"I expect that you don't." Rule sighed.

Bash sat up.

"Should I slit his throat?" Rule whispered and glanced up at the sky. "Yes, okay," he answered, as if someone had spoken, then he made the sign of the cross again, walked to Bash, and elbowed the side of his head so hard that Bash toppled over, unconscious once more.

Rule walked off without another word, his head undoubtedly filled with voices, bible verses, and blood sacrifices.

Ryan staggered behind. He'd never fucking turn his back on his cousin again. He'd warn Val to keep a close eye on Hogzilla. He'd tell Meggie...Aunt Meggie...to never name any other child with an 'R'. He'd ask Roxanne...Lolly...to choose another name.

He'd...

Goddamn.

Breathing heavily, Ryan paused. Despite how cold it was, he dripped with sweat.

The family worried about Rory's psychopathy because of Uncle Johnnie. Perhaps, though, they were concerned about the wrong motherfucker.

CHAPTER 30

Ten days before Christmas, CJ waited anxiously at the clubhouse for the arrival of Jaleena and her parents. He was so nervous he'd even cut his visits with Molly and Jo short earlier today.

The clubhouse was crowded tonight and particularly rowdy as more brothers from out-of-town chapters arrived for the annual holiday celebrations that began with Thanksgiving. After Mom's collapse, the pace of the convergence slowed to a trickle.

Each day she grew stronger, Dad returned to normal, and CJ breathed easier. He noticed small things again, like the club decorations, which hadn't been completed until a couple of days ago.

Glancing at his watch, CJ scowled. 5:53. Seven minutes until the Davises scheduled arrival.

He turned to his father. Outlaw sat at the table with Diesel, Rory, Grant, Pop, Uncle Cam, Uncle Johnnie, Uncle Digger, and Uncle Mort.

Mom had invited the entire family, but not everyone could attend. Uncle Val and Aunt Zoann had a previously scheduled date night. Ryan was a dickhead. Devon was shy. Uncle Cash and Uncle Stretch were beefing, and Aunt Ophelia decided to babysit the younger kids with Ella's help.

CJ had begged Aunt Fee to invite Rule and the Terrible Triplets over for some of her famous sloppy joes. However, by the time CJ headed to the club, he hadn't gotten an answer from her, which he took as a 'no'.

"Son, you wearin' a fuckin' hole in the floor," Dad said, taking a turn on the blunt the men were passing around. "The motherfucker gettin' too crowded. I ain't gonna be able to clear more fuckin' tables to give you room to fuckin' pace."

Uncle Johnnie grabbed the roll and inhaled. "Christopher," he started, handing Herb to Diesel, "if my nephew is going through all the trouble of impressing this young lady—he's wearing a button-down and a cable sweater—perhaps you should take care to speak better."

"Bruh," Uncle Digger said on an exhale of happy smoke, shaking his head. "The shadacity of that comment."

"Sit, little dude," Uncle Mort advised, his glare at Uncle Johnnie matching Dad's. His willingness to meet a girl CJ was interested in revealed the state of his household. "Take a few deep breaths."

"Is she that important to you?" Diesel asked, opting for Dweller chic by wearing his cut with a button-down, cashmere sweater, jeans, and loafers.

Grant grinned. "Do we need to have the talk with you?" Like his father, he was dressed in trousers and a button-down. "Safe sex is the best sex."

CJ flipped him off, though he wasn't offended, and the snickers eased him.

"Jordan can always explain what you need to know," Uncle Cam said with a straight face. He had to be joking. "She specializes in babies."

"The result of fuckin', Cam," Dad said, "not the fuckin' itself."

"She's an obstetrician and gynecologist, Outlaw," Cam said. "She knows about the reproductive system."

"For pussies, Uncle Cam," Rory said with disapproval. "CJ has a cock, so what would she know about that?"

"Besides the obvious, little bruh?" Uncle Digger said, sniggering. He nodded to Uncle Cam. "Her man got a cock, so I'd say she knows about the motherfuckers." Eyebrows lifting, he looked at Aunt Jordan's husband. "Wait, bruh, you do got a cock, don't you?"

"A very big one," Uncle Cam said with a smirk.

Uncle Digger frowned. "I didn't need to know all that."

"You brought up the motherfucker cock, assfuck," Dad grumped. He'd replaced Herb with a regular cigarette. He took it between his fingers and looked at CJ. "If you need cock covers—"

"Dad!" CJ said, overwhelmed for the first time in memory by the sex talk.

"How important is this young lady to you?" Pop asked. "I've never seen you so nervous."

CJ had never felt as anxious. His jumbled emotions left him unsure about the reasons. Either he liked Jaleena more than he wanted to admit; he wanted everything to be perfect so she'd see that he was more than just a low-classed, underprivileged criminal; or both.

He shrugged. "I'm not sure, Pop," he admitted. "I...she thinks I'm poor. She offered me half her allowance if I went steady with her."

Rory's eyes widened and he straightened. "She wanted to pay you to be her boyfriend?"

"She isn't desperate!" CJ said, ignoring the snickers. His family found jokes in the most serious situations.

"I never said she was," Rory said. "I know how she looks. I think she's gorgeous. If she wanted to pay me for dick, I wouldn't turn her down."

"A hundred bucks, Ro?" CJ demanded.

"A hundred…That's…wow…that's pitiful." Rory frowned. "She gets two hundred dollars a month?"

"Now, son," Uncle Johnnie said, following Dad's lead by lighting a regular cigarette, "don't disparage the less fortunate."

"They aren't poor, Uncle Johnnie," CJ said.

"Indeed, they aren't," Pop said. "Roxanne is good friends with Zuria, Jaleena's mom. They've co-chaired several charities, along with Jordan. Zuria's a Civil Rights attorney and Miah, her father, has a small tech company."

Uncle Johnnie lifted a brow at Rory. "Are the Davises black?"

"Yeah, Dad," Rory said testily.

"They human, Johnnie, so shut the fuck up," Dad barked.

"Because you don't see color, right, Christopher?" Uncle Johnnie demanded. "That's a crock of shit by the way. Color is the first thing you see on a person."

"As I said, shut the fuck up. Ain't my fault if you a stupid motherfucker."

"I'm stupid? Not seeing color doesn't remove your prejudices. How can you address issues if you refuse to address differences? So, yes, I take issue with your claim that you don't see color."

Unperturbed, Dad shrugged. "You take fuckin' issue with

everyfuckinthing, so it ain't surprisin'. I see color inasmuch Mort's black and I'm white—"

"That's seeing color, Christopher!"

"In fuckin' passin', Johnnie. You see it all the fuckin' time. Still not an issue, but the motherfuckin' fact you judge people because of it, is."

"Doesn't sound like you don't see color to me," Uncle Johnnie persisted, ignoring Dad's very valid point. "You pointed out Mortician is black. I never have, though he's friends with my wife and I allow my children to refer to him and Digger as 'uncle'." He used air quotations when he said the last word.

Exchanging a glance with Uncle Digger, Uncle Mort sighed and folded his arms.

Suddenly, the noisy chatter and laughter that CJ barely noticed died away. Although he hoped otherwise, he suspected the reason, confirmed a moment later when Bishop threaded his way through the throng with Jaleena and her family following behind.

Jaleena, her two sisters, Jillian and Juliana, and their mother all wore metallic dresses with uneven hemlines in various shades of green and gold. Jaleena wore light makeup, unlike her sisters who sported none, and their mother who'd gone all out. A red tie embroidered with snowmen complemented Mr. Davis's dark gray suit.

It seemed as if the entire room focused on the Davises. As Outlaw's son, CJ grew up with all eyes on him. The scrutiny didn't bother him. However, the Davises might feel differently.

Her face inscrutable, Jaleena glanced around, then offered CJ a nod. "Thank you for inviting us to your place."

CJ returned her nod with one of his own and held out his hand to her father. "Hello, sir. I'm CJ Caldwell. I'd like to introduce you to my father—"

Mr. Davis glared at CJ's hand, looking toward the table. His brows lifted. "Knox, what are you doing here? Where's your wonderful wife?"

"She's with CJ's mom, helping to prepare dinner, Jeremiah." Pop appeared at CJ's side. "Let me introduce you and—"

"Introductions can fuckin' wait," Dad said flatly, brushing past them. "Let's walk home."

Jaleena turned her back on CJ and whispered to her mother. The two of them laughed, and his ears burned in humiliation.

Shoving his hands in his pockets, he followed his father.

"You don't live here?" Juliana asked, falling into step beside CJ.

Having so many witnesses to Mr. Davis's snub and Jaleena's formality knotted CJ's stomach. "No, I live in a house, Juliana."

"Prez, you need anything?" Potter called from a barstool, since a new crop of Probates were in training, and one currently served behind the bar.

"Nope." Dad stormed outside, but held the door open until CJ leaned against it, allowing the others to file out.

"Spooky," Jillian chirped a couple minutes later as their little group paused at the edge of the forest, while Dad scanned his fingerprint to unlock the walkway gate.

In recent years, lights were installed between the club and the houses, so it wasn't nearly as eerie as it once was.

Halfway between the club and the houses, the first glimmer of the Christmas lights on their property twinkled.

"If I would've known we had to trek through the forest, I would've worn a coat," Jaleena said from directly behind him, her voice rising above the low hum of conversation between Pop and Mr. and Mrs. Davis. "You invited us to your house, CJ, not a magical mystery tour."

Since he'd done absolutely nothing to her, CJ was over her attitude. "This is the only way we can get to my fucking house, Jaleena."

The talking screeched to a halt, and CJ gritted his teeth.

"Did you just cuss at my daughter, young man?" Mr. Davis demanded.

"It's okay, Daddy," Jaleena said with a little sniff. "He is just stressed out."

"Normally, when one is invited to a home for dinner, one has access to that home's street," Mrs. Davis said.

"Normally, when a motherfucker—"

"Er, you'd get to our house the same way, JaZuria," Pop inserted, interrupting Dad.

"Ja-Who-Ria?" Uncle Digger asked. "What the made-up name is that?"

Mrs. Davis gasped.

"Shut up, fool," Uncle Mort said. "Excuse my brother, baby. He got dropped on his fucking head as a baby. That's why it's so big. Motherfucker never unswolled."

"You a cold-ass motherfucker, Mortician," Uncle Digger grumbled.

"But a truthful motherfucker," Dad said.

"I thought her name was Zuria," Uncle Digger protested.

"It is my nickname, sir," Mrs. Davis said sharply. "My name is JaZuria. My husband is Jeremiah. Our daughters are Jaleena, Juliana, and Jillian. No matter where success takes our daughters, we will always have our 'J' names in common."

"So the 'J' names more important than the fucking obvious shit, huh, girl?" Uncle Digger asked.

"I am not a girl," Mrs. Davis said.

Fuck. "Uh—"

Too late. "You got a pussy, huh?" Uncle Digger asked before CJ could form any other word. "That make you a fucking girl, girl."

"See here, sir!" Mr. Davis said.

"See here all the fuck you want, Miah," Uncle Digger said. "I thought Meggie was fucked up with her 'R' names, but you and your bitch worse. Family bonds matter, not no fucking shared alphabet."

"Digger, only reason I ain't pullin' my piece and blowin' you the fuck away is cuz my boy want to impress Jaleena and her family," Dad snarled, in Uncle Digger's face so fast he stumbled back. "Your fuckin' brain spatterin' every goddamn where might upset them."

"Meggie like me, Prez," Uncle Digger pushed out. "I'm family."

"She family too, fool," Uncle Mort said. "Stop being a fucking dickhead and act like it."

"Are you gangsters?" Jillian asked, blinking between everyone. "Jaleena's ex-boyfriend is a gangster."

"No, Lia, it's his dad," Juliana corrected. "Nardo isn't. Momma didn't have to get him out of jail."

"You dated Nardo fucking Grevenberg, Jaleena?" CJ yelled as Uncle Digger said, "who is Lia?"

"Nardo's a good guy," Jaleena huffed. "He appreciated my value."

"Nardo is a fucking asshole and—"

"Efuckinnuff!" Dad ordered. "You didn't invite her here to talk about who she used to date, CJ. You invited her here to show her where the fuck you live."

"On the grounds of a motorcycle club," Jaleena said. "A trailer park surrounded by forest?"

"That's exactly where I live," CJ said with sarcasm. "How'd

you guess, Jaleena?"

"Because I'm brilliant," she said with a straight face. "Nardo and his family lives in a nice middle-class neighborhood."

"Yeah, and you were stupid because you were giving him fifty dollars a month because they needed groceries," Juliana said.

"Enough, young lady," Mrs. Davis said. "You and Jillian have revealed enough of our personal business."

"Nardo's shiesty," Jillian complained, and smiled at CJ. "He didn't like to play video games with me. When he did, he never let me win. You're nice. I don't care if you live in a trailer park."

CJ scrubbed a hand over his face, ready to send the Davises on their way. He drew in a deep breath, preparing to cancel the evening. "This was a bad idea—"

"Come on," Dad interrupted. "We seein' this through, boy." He started off, without awaiting CJ's input.

Moments later, they cleared the forest and halted across the street from their house.

Jillian stared in awe, mouth falling open and eyes widening. Jaleena gasped. Juliana choked.

The Christmas lights were a spectacular display of mostly red, green, and white lights, spread from one end of the property to the other, entwined through the tree branches and around the trunks, woven through the fencing, lining the pathway, and rising from the ground in the forms of characters, sleds, trains, trees, and villages. A huge wreath adorned the gate, matching the ones on each entry door.

"On Christmas Eve, the lights are timed to music," CJ said with pride.

"You have a gorgeous home, Knox. We need the name of your installer," Mr. Davis said.

"They not available," Uncle Digger said. "You not a member of the club, bruh."

Dad walked across the street and paused at the gate, so he could scan his fingerprint. The gate clicked open.

"Oh, no," Jaleena squeaked.

"Oh, fuckin' yeah," Dad said, standing at the gate until everyone passed through.

The walk to the house was only broken with, "you have a moat?" from Juliana.

"A half moat," CJ responded. "The rest of it was filled in… what…?"

"About two renovations ago?" Diesel estimated.

"At least," Grant added.

"Probably," Rory said. "I was about ten when the basement was finished. Aunt Meggie redecorated the bedrooms, the den, and her office, two years later. She just finished Jo and Rebel's rooms."

"Mom still isn't finished this time," CJ said, waiting while Dad opened the double front doors. "She wants to replace the chandelier in the foyer."

For as long as he remembered he'd stepped into the entrance hall with doors on each side indicating the east and west corridors and its massive archway directly ahead that led to a central hallway with the beautiful, bifurcated staircase. Over the span of many holidays, fiberglass witches, goblins, Pilgrims, elves, reindeer, Santas and Mrs. Clauses, and Nativity scenes shared space with the console, benches, and umbrella stand. Just inside the east corridor were doors for a bathroom and a utility closet as it marched toward a turnoff that led to the kitchen and many of the family rooms. Similarly, the west corridor had doors for a coat closet and Mom's office, but not much else, though around the corner was the laundry room and another few rooms.

It was home, a place Dad insisted Mom deserved. However, watching the amazement on Jaleena and her sisters' faces, CJ remembered how privileged he was. He'd never been prouder to be the son of Christopher and Megan Caldwell, or as grateful to have them as his parents.

Dad looked toward the east hallway and smiled, his annoyance immediately clearing. Mom glided into the foyer, her eyes only for Dad, and stepped into his arms.

She wore a sleeveless dress with sequins and feathers. It was short, but loose and flowy. Usually, she paired such outfits with stilettos. Tonight, still healing from the ordeal of Jo's birth, she had on ballerinas.

When she turned and walked to Jaleena's mom with her hand outstretched, CJ grinned. She wore her diamond encrusted gold Rolex watch and a pair of vine earrings also made of diamonds and gold.

"I'm Megan Caldwell," she said with a wide smile. "Welcome to my home."

Rebel strutted into view. She should've been the picture of innocence in a winter white, belted mini dress, but her white platform heels, full face of makeup and sleek hairstyle was sexy.

She kissed Dad's cheek. "Hey, Daddy," she said, the light catching on her diamond earrings and ring.

Mom meant no one would fuck with her children, and she'd do whatever she must to underscore the point, including this bad ass power move.

"Thank you," she said with a laugh, though CJ wasn't sure who she spoke to.

"You got any Christmas nougats, Meggie?" Uncle Digger asked. "I'm hungry."

"I put some in the mancave just for you, Digger," Mom answered.

Dad's brows snapped together. "What the fuck you mean you put them in there? I only agreed to this cuz you promised you had help."

"I did, my love," Mom said. "Either Kendall or Bunny did it for me once I asked them."

"Kendall?" Uncle Johnnie asked. "My Kendall? She doesn't work for you."

"Nope, but she works with me," Mom said cheerfully. "We all work together, Johnnie."

"She has her own household—"

"Red part of the family, Johnnie," Uncle Mort said. "Roxanne got all the girls here to help Meggie with the dinner."

Mom glared at Uncle Johnnie, then she noticed Dad's attention on them, and she plastered a smile on her face. She cleared her throat. "Rebel—"

"Meggie?" Uncle Digger called. He walked to the table near the door and grabbed a handful of M&Ms, then stuffed them into his mouth. "I got a question," he said around a mouthful of candy.

"I'm all ears."

"If Prez wanted to shoot me, you wouldn't let him, would you?" he asked, crunching through the question.

Mom's eyes widened. "I beg your pardon."

"Can we talk about this some other time?" CJ asked hastily, seeing his father's eyes frosting and his entire body stiffening. "We have a crowd milling about in need of refreshments until dinner is served. And—"

"The night is important to CJ," Mom said to no one in particular, though CJ knew she was talking to Dad. "We will resolve family issues later. After the holidays...no, after the Mardi Gras Ball—"

"Too fuckin' long," Dad grumbled, "but I don't want to

stress you the fuck out, so fine, Megan."

"You and Roxanne cavort with these people, Knox?" Mr. Davis asked with distaste. "Criminals?"

"Your bitch cavort with the Grevenbergs," Uncle Digger replied. "And that little motherfucker got my niece all fucking twisted, saying her daddy—" He pointed to Uncle Mort— "My big brother, not a real 'G' because he never been in the tank. If you want to cavort with criminals, cavort with smart motherfuckers."

"Or lucky ones," Jaleena said. She gave CJ an indulgent smile. "My parents earned their money through education and hard work, CJ. We own our stuff legally. It won't ever be in jeopardy of confiscation because it was unlawfully gained."

"If this place is theirs, pumpkin," Mr. Davis said. "It might be rented."

Rebel snorted. "Even if what you said was the case, Jaleena, which it isn't, my parents, my brothers, and me can buy and sell you and your entire family a dozen times over and still have money left. But this house belongs to my mother. My father purchased it with money he legally obtained through a medical lab that my Uncle Johnnie is the CEO of. Uncle Digger and Uncle Mortician can buy and sell us a dozen times over. Their money was inherited from their parents. My Uncle Cash is the brother of Georgiana McCall Mason, and also comes from money. If you want to compare bank accounts...?" She marched to CJ and held out her hand. "Your phone."

"You don't have to do this—" CJ started.

"Oh, yes, I do," she said viciously. "Give me your phone, CJ."

None of the adults were stepping in and, honestly, CJ did want Jaleena to eat her words for the disrespect she was showing them.

He took his phone from his jacket pocket. "I'll do it—"

"Nope," Rebel said, snatching his phone from him. "You had your chance, brother. I'll take it from here."

It only took a moment for Rebel to log into her account. Smiling with the same indulgence Jaleena had bestowed on him, Rebel held the phone in front of Jaleena's face.

Jaleena squeaked.

Rebel tapped the screen. "Do you see CJ's name?"

Jaleena nodded.

"It's his allowance just because he's Christopher and Megan Caldwell's son. His debit card is directly tapped into my mother's bank account." Rebel snatched the phone away and held it out to CJ without looking at him. She grinned at Jaleena. "If it goes below a certain amount before his allowance is due, he gets more."

"Is it wrong to say how hot you look, Reb?" Rory called.

CJ frowned.

"Yes, dickhead, it is," Rebel barked. "I'm your fucking cousin—"

"Rebel, what did I tell you?"

"I didn't say one cuss word, Momma," Rebel said defensively. "Rory made me do it."

"I didn't put the words in your mouth, Reb."

"No, you just put perversion in your small little man-brain."

"No, my son is responding exactly as a boy should," Uncle Johnnie said flatly. "You are dressed in a suggestive manner and don't expect attention?"

"I take it all back, Ro," Rebel said sweetly, rolling her eyes. "You inherited your little man-brain from a little man-child."

"I am your uncle, young lady."

"Bad luck or cosmic joke," Rebel retorted.

She was eating up that self-righteous motherfucker.

"Do you have anything to say for yourself, Christopher?" Uncle Johnnie demanded.

"Nope," Dad answered. "Rebel handlin' it just fine. If I need to step in and fuck you up, I will."

"If it was Megan, you would've stepped in," Uncle Johnnie said with disgust. "It is telling that you allow a child to disrespect me."

"It's telling how you continually engage with a child, Johnnie," Mom said, losing her patience. "The entire conversation was between the kids. You didn't have to say anything."

Rebel spoke before Uncle Johnnie responded. "Jaleena, do you want to see the space my parents created for my siblings and me and our cousins and friends?"

"You've made your point, Rebel," Jaleena snapped.

"Have I?"

"You have," CJ inserted.

"Actually, I haven't," Rebel insisted.

"Actually, you have, baby girl," Mom said. "We are still standing in the foyer. Digger has almost emptied my bowl of M&Ms. And I'm sure dinner is just about ready to be plated."

"Motherfuckers good, Meggie," Uncle Digger said.

"You ain't platin' dinner, are you, baby?" Dad asked.

"No, Christopher," Mom answered. "But I would like to sit down."

Panic crept into Dad's eyes. "You not feelin' good?"

Mom smiled at him. "I'm fine."

"But—"

"Take the guys to the mancave for a drink, Christopher," she said softly.

Drawing in a deep breath, Dad nodded.

"Rebel, darling, can you bring Jaleena and her sisters to

my office to finish wrapping the gifts for everyone's goody bags? I'll send Mattie and Ava to help."

"Sure, Momma," Rebel said demurely.

Uncle Johnnie snorted. "Any excuse to spend money," he said with disgust, unwittingly helping her objective.

"It's Megan's fuckin' money, Johnnie," Dad barked, "so shut the fuck up."

"I'm just saying, Christopher."

"If you ain't asked, don't fuckin' say." Dad narrowed his eyes at someone behind CJ. "What the fuck you lookin' at?"

"Nothing, Uncle Chris," Diesel said.

Turning, CJ lifted a brow.

"I'd say Rebel," Grant said, staring at her, too. "Rory's right. She's hot. She, uh…" He took her in front head-to-toe. "Goddamn."

"Son," Pop said with disapproval.

Rebel beamed. "I'll take that as a compliment."

"Come, Zuria," Mom said, weaving her arm through the other woman's and urging her forward. "We're in the kitchen, preparing the first course. I believe you know Roxy and Jordan."

"Er, y-yes."

"I'm so interested to know about your work. My sister-in-law is an attorney…" Her words floated away as they got farther down the corridor.

"I need a drink," Diesel said, breaking away from the group and heading toward the central hallway.

"No, bro," Ransom said, racing from the west corridor and rushing to the opposite side, Ryder, and Axel hot on his heels. "You need a new wife."

"We don't like the one you have," Axel said, the last of the trio to disappear.

"Follow me," Dad grumbled, following in the direction

Diesel went.

Rebel nodded to Jaleena and her sisters. "Come on." She sauntered to the hallway that led to Mom's office.

Trancelike, Jaleena and her sisters followed.

Once again, CJ wondered why he'd invited the Davises over. So far, it hadn't gone as planned and he couldn't see the evening turning out any better.

CHAPTER 31

MEGGIE

Although Christopher's idea to host the Davises without the family was better, Meggie needed as much assistance as possible to make her point on her son's behalf. Ordinarily, six days would've been more than enough time to plan her menu, buy the food, shop for new clothes, tidy the house, and cook. But she was still healing both physically and mentally. She and Christopher visited Jo every day. While Christopher remained with their baby, Meggie normally broke away to visit Molly and receive updates on her prognosis.

Upon Meggie and Christopher's return home, Bunny had dinner prepared for the family, the kids arrived from school, and Meggie wanted rest. Soon after dinner ended, Christopher carried her upstairs, helped her to shower, then snuggled with her in bed.

With each passing day, she fell more in love with her husband. Many instances over their years together proved her importance to him and his devotion to her. Her most recent illness revealed not only his dedication but his fear of losing her. He'd always said that Meggie was his everything, and no matter what Johnnie said, she knew with her entire being that it was true.

After convincing Christopher they should have a family dinner and invite the Davises over, Meggie realized it was an opportune time to remind Johnnie of how much she and Christopher loved and needed each other, so he'd back off.

Or, maybe, it was wishful thinking. Somehow, Johnnie always knew when Christopher was downstairs. Three days ago, he'd returned to his office at the club after their visit to the hospital and stayed two or three hours, longer than the few minutes he'd allowed since her release.

Johnnie seized the opportunity to torture Meggie, playing upon all her fears. She needed her strength back. And she needed the headaches to go away, always heralded by Johnnie's calls. She was desperate for his harassment to stop, but she didn't know how to handle the situation in a way that'd allow Johnnie to remain among the living.

Hopefully, the dinner signaled a turning point. Christmas was around the corner. Molly should be released soon. Jo was thriving. Meggie had one more appointment with Jordan before the end of the year. Tonight had to lighten everyone's mood.

Her goal of sending Jaleena and her sisters with Rebel, and CJ, Christopher and the rest of the guys with Mr. Davis, while she and the women entertained JaZuria was to put everyone at ease while getting to know each other.

CJ not only wanted to impress Jaleena but her parents. Christopher thought it would be best if he guided their son through meeting Jaleena's father, while Meggie befriended her mother. Except JaZuria Davis marched next to Meggie with decided hostility. Even when Megan complimented her on her outfit, she barely spoke.

"Hey, baby," Roxy greeted as Meggie led JaZuria into the kitchen, where a beehive of activity buzzed. As usual, Roxy was calm amid the storm, dressed in a black sequined mini dress, embellished at the wrists with feathers. "How are you feeling?"

"I'm fine," Meggie mumbled, smiling at Mattie as she rushed to her and wrapped her arms around Meggie's waist.

Like Rebel, Mattie was also taller than Meggie.

"Come and sit down, Aunt Smurfette," Mattie teased.

Giggling, Meggie allowed her niece to guide her to a stool near where Kendall tore Romaine leaves. Next to her, Bunny cubed potatoes, while Roxy finished her bread pudding mixture.

"This is Ja—"

"Should I go to your office, Aunt Meggie?" Mattie asked, speaking at the same moment. "To help Rebel with the gifts?"

Meggie looked at Kendall and gave the barest shake of her head. Kendall was stunning in a strapless, bandage dress, in the same emerald shade as the bows in her Mattie's.

"No, darling," Kendall said. "I think your daddy hasn't gone to the mancave yet."

"Rebel will text you," Meggie added, then nodded to JaZuria. She stood at the far end of the counter, her gaze touching everywhere. "This is Jaleena's mom. JaZuria Davis. JaZuria, this is—"

"Mrs. JaZuria Davis," JaZuria corrected, and nodded to Roxy. "If we hadn't seen Knox, I would have been shocked into speechlessness by your presence, Mrs. Harrington."

"Mrs. Harrington?" Kendall snickered. "When has Roxy ever been so formal?"

Roxy spooned the last of the bread pudding mixture into a

glass baking dish. "When my money is involved and bitches don't know their place." She slammed the bowl onto the counter, the spoon clanking in a haphazard movement. "If Bailey keeps it up, that bitch'll call me Mrs. Harrington, too."

Pressing her lips together, JaZuria flicked her fingers over the bodice of her dress. "I meant no harm, Mrs. Harrington. I merely wanted to relieve our bartender. If I would've known you were Knox's wife, I never would've suggested you fill in."

"Even if I was just a bitch off the street attending as a paying guest, I was in a fucking evening gown, JaZuria. Like you."

JaZuria lifted her chin, but Jordan rolling in a cart stacked with Meggie's Santa Claus dishes prevented a response.

"Ava is selecting the glasses, so…JaZuria!" Jordan halted next to the woman and smiled. "You made it."

"Hi, Jordan." Offering a relieved smile, JaZuria kissed Jordan's cheek. "It's lovely to see you."

Meggie winced. Bad manners and poor hostessing wouldn't serve CJ's purpose, whatever that might be. "JaZuria, would you help with the salad? I still need the tomatoes washed and sliced."

"We waited for you before we opened a bottle of champagne," Bunny said, picking up on Meggie's cues.

"Aunt Meggie, do you think Rebel has started wrapping the presents yet?" Mattie asked. "Maman, can you text Daddy and ask where he's at?"

"Rebel will text you, darling," Kendall swore.

Over the past few days, Kendall had thrown herself into helping Meggie, especially with their daughters. The distraction seemed to have returned her equilibrium. Before Christopher and CJ arrived with the rest of their family and the Davises, Kendall led the discussion on the upcoming

Mardi Gras Ball. The plans even drew Meggie away from her worry over Christopher and Jo, her concern about Molly, and her weariness Johnnie's behavior.

"Let me retry with the introductions," Meggie said into the silence, broken only by Jordan rolling the cart closer and Roxy shoving the bread pudding into the oven. "Mrs. JaZuria Davis, this is Kendall Donovan, my sister-in-law and a lawyer like you."

"I am an attorney, Mrs. Caldwell," JaZuria said succinctly. "I can represent my clients in court and other legal matters. Your sister-in-law, a lawyer, cannot."

Kendall narrowed her smoky, kohl-lined eyes. "I—"

"My mistake, JaZuria," Meggie said evenly, interrupting Kendall. "My sister-in-law is an attorney, and a very good one, who can represent her clients in court. The mistake is mine, not Kendall's."

"We're very informal here, Zuria," Jordan said diplomatically. "Although I am Meggie's doctor, we long ago gave up formalities, so relax and enjoy yourself."

Meggie looked at Jordan, who'd opted for a more conservative knee-length dress, though she wore it wonderfully. "Thank you," she mouthed.

Jordan nodded. "We're helping Meggie out, since she was so recently released from the hospital."

"My baby is making great strides," Meggie said. "She'll soon be 30 weeks."

JaZuria didn't answer.

Swallowing her annoyance, Meggie forged on. "This is my sister-in-law, Bunny. She is a private tutor and my part-time assistant."

"Sister-in-law because of your brothers or because of your husband's brothers?" JaZuria asked.

"Kendall is the wife of Christopher's brother," Meggie

answered, relieved JaZuria offered some engagement. "Bunny is Digger's wife, but I see him and Mortician as my family."

"I don't know any of these people," JaZuria said.

"Right. We have a very big family," Meggie said. "Uh, you know Jordan and my children's grandmother, Roxy… Roxanne."

JaZuria's almond-shaped, doe brown eyes widened, then narrowed. "You aren't funny, Mrs. Caldwell. You are aware that I'm a Civil Rights attorney as well as my standing in my community. Your attempt at identifying is insulting. I have a mind to gather my husband and my daughters and leave."

"Please, get the fuck out, then," Roxy snapped. "Your fucking sadity bitchiness is working on my ass, JaZuria, more than it did when you tried to turn me into a fucking servant."

"Servant?" JaZuria screeched. "They are staff! There are no servants in our contemporary world."

Life had become so chaotic. Every dinner, every interaction, turned disordered, like the world was restless, sweeping out the status quo and ushering in a storm. For months, peace had become a poignant memory. Meggie feared what that meant. Hopefully, they were experiencing a temporary upheaval as happened from time to time.

"We are here on behalf of our children," Meggie said politely. "Not to solve problems outside the scope of an evening."

"What does your son see in my daughter? Had he been a work-in-progress, my daughter's value would have been obvious. But I refuse to have Jaleena in a subservient role to a rich boy who needs nothing."

"Leen could never be subservient to anyone, Mrs. Davis," Mattie inserted, comfortable enough to speak up without her father's looming presence.

"Who are you?" JaZuria demanded. "And my daughter's name is Ja-Leen-a. How dare you reduce her to a rapper's drug?"

Roxy snorted. "Bitch—"

"Mattie, Matilda, is my daughter," Kendall said quickly, "and Jaleena's friend, whom she was defending. Mattie wasn't reducing Jaleena in any way, shape, or form. She can't compete with the excellent job you're doing."

"How dare you!"

"Oh, I dare more than you know," Kendall retorted. "We aren't your enemy or your daughter's."

"May I also add, you're devaluing your daughter," Meggie said. "CJ doesn't want anything from her except respect and the benefit of the doubt."

"I doubt that," JaZuria said with a snort. "I know about biker clubs and their misogyny and many prejudices." She glared between Jordan and Roxy. "That is why I am shocked you two are associated with these people." She glowered at Meggie. "That is why I am highly insulted that you claim a black woman as your children's grandmother when you are clearly lily white." She scowled at Mattie. "And that is why I do not appreciate you referring to my daughter with more respect."

Kendall snapped her fingers. "I'm here, JaZuria. You have a problem with my daughter, come to me or her father. Attorney to attorney, your defamatory remarks are slanderous. Roxanne Harrington has been more of a mother to me than my own mother ever was. She is my children's grandmother. Blood or DNA or however you wish to frame it, has nothing to do with it."

"We understand your reservations," Meggie added. Her perception of biker clubs also explained her hostility. "I won't lie and tell you there is no objectification of women in the club." She thought about Johnnie and Ryan. "Or other issues—"

"In the family," Bunny said.

Meggie nodded. "But we love and respect each other—" Again, Johnnie and Ryan rose in her head, and she managed not to wince. "You're as protective of your children as we are of ours."

Sniffing, JaZuria finally sat on one of the vacant stools. Still at the far end of the counter, but it was progress. "I will be happy to cut the tomatoes," she said stiffly.

"Pass me the rolls and the butter," Meggie said once Bunny brought the bowl of tomatoes and a knife to JaZuria.

For a few minutes, they worked in silence, each on their own little segment to bring the dinner to life. Roxy opened the bottle of champagne and poured glasses for everyone except Meggie and Mattie.

Between sips, she checked on her bread pudding and texted Knox. Once Jordan finished placing the salad plates, soup bowls, dinner plates, and dessert plates into separate stacks, she stood next to Roxy and spoke in low tones.

"You really should wear that watch more often, Meggie," Bunny said after she washed the potatoes and set them to boil.

"It is a very nice watch," JaZuria agreed, draining her glass. "If you don't care about your budget."

"She don't," Roxy barked.

Setting her knife aside, JaZuria sat straighter. "Budgeting is an excellent discipline, no matter your tax bracket or professional affiliation." She coughed and patted her chest delicately. "Or, er, associations."

Meggie pasted a smile on her face. "Christopher gave me the watch for my thirtieth birthday. Mostly, he adheres to a budget, but he does celebrate milestones."

"How admirable." JaZuria smiled. "I'll turn forty in June. I want to go on a trip around the world, and Mr. Davis is taking the girls and me as my birthday present. Mr. Davis spoils us."

"You call your husband Mr. Davis?" Bunny asked in confusion.

"Of course not, madame. I expect you to call him Mr. Davis."

"In your fucking dreams," Roxy said.

"I make one mistake and you hold it against me, Mrs. Harrington," JaZuria complained. "When I looked at you, I would never have associated you with Knox."

"You aren't making me like you any better," Roxy said.

"I don't care if you like me or not."

"Then do us a favor and shut the fuck up," Roxy said. "Stop trying to explain the reason for your bullshit."

"We moved to the area years after your wedding, Mrs. Harrington. The night I met you, you were you. Loud and brash while Knox is so elegant and reserved. I thought you wore a knock off designer dress and got lost in the VIP section on your way to a purchased table. I only sought to offer extra money."

"Instead of lording it over the less fortunate, live a little and splurge on yourself," Roxy said. "Your savior complex is a pain in the fucking ass."

"Better to be savior than saved," JaZuria retorted, then smiled at Meggie again. "You do have a very beautiful house. Mr. Davis's company has been struggling recently. Luckily, we were wise enough not to purchase such a huge house. The upkeep must be incredibly expensive. Keeping up appearances for the sake of ego takes a toll."

"You're right, so I'm glad you don't have to subject yourself to such a duty," Meggie said calmly, hoping tonight's efforts weren't for naught.

If JaZuria Davis only had reservations about CJ's close ties to the MC, Meggie might be more optimistic. A little time spent with the family could ease her fears, no matter how rough around the edges they were. However, JaZuria's attitude went beyond such concerns. She was showing herself to be a snob, plain and simple.

Meggie wished to aid her son in his efforts to dispel Jaleena's misguided perception of him, but if her mother was anything to go by, that wouldn't easily happen, if at all.

In her experience, Meggie found patience and resilience were the most effective when dealing with difficult people. But her continued recovery lowered her tolerance for combative folks. As the dinner preparations continued, she prayed the rest of the Davises were more receptive to her family's overtures.

REBEL

Intending to complete the gift wrapping as quicky as possible to show Jaleena her room, Rebel led the other girl and her two sisters to Momma's office. If Jaleena wanted a dick measuring contest, Rebel was happy to engage. Her parents had instilled in them that money wasn't everything and it wasn't necessary to flaunt your net worth.

She rarely wore the jewelry Momma, Daddy, and Diesel gifted her. Most of her clothes were expensive, but not so ostentatious as to be remarkable. She chose outfits to blend in, not stand out. Her mother had luxury vehicles. However, anyone with a downpayment and decent credit could own a Lexus SUV and a Corvette.

Their house, however, revealed everything, although few outside of family and very close friends ever received invitations past the clubhouse. Molly was an exception. And, now, Jaleena.

She had Momma so up in arms, she'd chosen her very expensive Rolex watch and diamond earrings and allowed Rebel to not only dress like a grown up but to purchase an entirely new outfit. The cost of the dress, shoes, makeup, and jewelry made Rebel's eyes water, and she considered herself a professional shopper.

Momma still wasn't feeling one hundred percent, so Aunt Kendall blew out Rebel's hair, helped her with her makeup as well as the press on nails with elaborate art.

Opening the door to Momma's office, Rebel flipped open the overhead light, although the outside Christmas lights offered more than enough illumination. At Jaleena's intake of breath, she smirked.

Momma had moved her office a couple years ago from an interior room to one with three walls of windows. Her desk sat between the west facing ones, while a window seat overstuffed with pillows dominated the south facing. The wall between the north facing windows held a smaller desk. In the middle of the room, a sofa stacked with unwrapped gifts sat in front of a coffee table where gifts bags, wrapping paper, tape, and scissors were. Gifts also sat on the two chairs on each end of the coffee table.

With Momma's release from the hospital, Christmas decorations finally hung in most of the house, including the office where the scent of cinnamon and pine wafted from a bowl of potpourri on top of one of the file cabinets near the door.

"Why didn't CJ tell me?" Jaleena asked, glancing around the room.

Shrugging, Rebel went to reach for her phone, then remembered she didn't have a pocket on her expensive dress, therefore she didn't have her phone. "Why should he have to tell you anything, Jaleena?" she demanded, sharper than necessary due to frustration over her lack of phone. She wanted to text Mattie and tell her that the coast was clear. Her dickhead daddy was in the mancave. "We need to wrap the presents."

"I can start," Jillian volunteered, rushing to the sofa.

"Wrap them carefully," Juliana instructed, following behind Jillian while Jaleena stood near Momma's desk, gazing out the window, hallowed by the Christmas lights. "They have to be perfect, Lia."

"They don't have to be perfect," Rebel corrected. "They just have to be done."

Turning, Jaleena lifted her chin. "CJ should've told me. I knew he was the big man on campus, but I always thought I was one of the wealthiest."

Rebel snorted. "Does it fucking matter?"

"Yes!" she cried. "My parents worked hard to achieve their wealth and success. I searched for a boy equal to or above me but then I met Nardo, and I realized I didn't have to level-up. He was sweet and kind and poor. My father helped my mother with her college costs, and she constantly preached that it is a man's job to provide. I'm a 21st Century woman and I don't mind helping my man."

"That's up to you, Jaleena," Rebel said. "But I happen to agree with your mother. Maybe, you need to stop with your complexes and stereotypes, and you'd find a boy you deserve. At the moment, you sure the fuck don't deserve my brother."

"Why? Because your family can buy and sell mine?"

Narrowing her eyes, Rebel pursed her lips, not liking Jaleena's undertones.

"Do you know how that sounded coming from you?"

"Like I was making a fucking point? Get over yourself, Jaleena. I also said Uncle Mort and Uncle Digger can buy and sell my family. And you don't deserve CJ because he isn't a project to fix to your tastes. He's a real boy with real feelings who wanted to impress your raggedy ass because he likes you for you. At this point, I wish he would go with Molly. I wish—"

"In case you haven't realized, CJ wanted Harley and now he wants me. Molly isn't his type," Jaleena told her. "It's so telling that you're painting Harley and me in a bad light, while Molly is an angel."

"Leave Molly alone," Rebel snapped. She'd had her issues with the girl, but at the moment, she was in a bad way physically and mentally. "Your implications insult me."

"The truth hurts," Jaleena said. "Why should it matter to me if you're insulted?"

"Because you're in my fucking house and I'm five seconds from throwing you out."

"We're CJ's guests, not yours."

"He'd back me up," Rebel said with certainty, especially once he heard her reasons. "Your accusations are baseless. My feelings are the result of you and Harley having your asses on your shoulders and hurting my brother. Molly's an airhead, but at least she respects and likes CJ."

Jaleena stomped to the sofa where the presents sat untouched because the argument enraptured her sisters. "Let's just wrap the presents."

"I'm going find Mattie and Ava," Rebel grumbled, turned on her heel and stalked out, leaving the door gaping.

CHAPTER 32

CHRISTOPHER

Glancing at the clock on the wall, Christopher wondered how fucking long he'd have to deal with fucking Jeremiah Davis. Every time CJ tried to initiate conversation with that motherfucker, Jeremiah either shut CJ down or ignored him outright.

If Christopher had to guess, his woman wouldn't want him to fuck that motherfucker up, but his patience was wearing thin. He'd give credit to Knox and Cameron for attempting to draw CJ into the conversation, extol his virtues, or both, though nothing worked.

Diesel hadn't come in and Rory and Grant escaped after five minutes. Christopher was considering taking a fucking walk before he lost his fucking temper. Howfuckinever, if he spoke or moved, he might blow that motherfucker away.

"My mom has a Corvette," CJ said. "I want to drive it so bad, but Dad won't let me."

Jeremiah cleared his throat. "As I was saying, Cam, JaZuria will be shocked when we return from her birthday trip. She's wanted a Corvette since she was in college."

CJ drew in a deep breath, his shoulders slumping slightly.

"It's okay, little dude," Digger said, patting CJ's back. "An uppity motherfucker like Miah not worth your fucking time."

"To whom do you refer, sir?" Jeremiah asked.

"To whom am I fucking looking at, sir?" Digger said. "If it was left up to me, your ass wouldn't be here."

"He's here because of Jaleena, Uncle Digger," CJ said with meaning, glancing at Christopher in a silent plea for assistance.

Christopher bet his balls his boy wouldn't want the assistance he had in mind.

"You're right, young man. I'm here for my daughter. She means the world to me and I want her happy, though I'm certain you are bad news."

Christopher jumped to his feet. "Ain't puttin' up with your fuckin' disrespect of my boy a minute fuckin' longer. Get the fuck out—"

"Dad!"

"Outlaw, Jeremiah doesn't know CJ," Knox said. "Give him a chance—"

"Motherfucker ain't never knowin' my boy if he ain't fuckin' talkin' to him. I ain't wanted none of you motherfuckers here right now for a big ass dinner that my woman plannin'. She still fuckin' healin' and ain't needin' the stress. Since it happened anyfuckinway, I ain't standin' for the fuckin' disrespect."

"Meggie not even in the fucking room, Outlaw," Digger said with a noted lack of regard. "You sound like you talking about disrespect toward her, instead of little bruh."

Christopher squinted. "You fuckin' stupid or tired of

fuckin' livin'?"

"This is the reason I don't want my daughter associated with you people," Jeremiah said. "You're classless, ignorant, and violent. Jaleena is a queen, better than a two-bit criminal."

The words arrowed through Christopher. He'd gone to great lengths so he wouldn't embarrass his wife and children. And, now, he was doing exactly that.

Clenching his jaw, Christopher reseated himself.

"All my daughters are queens," Jeremiah continued haughtily. "My wife. Cam's wife. Knox's wife. Not only that, Roxanne's quite forgiving."

Knox glanced between Christopher and Jeremiah. He laughed uneasily. "Wh-what do you mean?"

"Er, I-I thought…I…she didn't tell you about the night she and JaZuria met?"

Cam whistled. "Oh, that. She told Jordan."

"No, she didn't tell me. And, if she told Jordan and you knew, Cookie, why didn't you tell me?" Knox demanded.

"I don't repeat what my woman tells me, my brother."

"Revealing pertinent information is part of the bro code," Knox said.

Mortician laughed. "The bro code, huh, Knox?"

Digger grabbed a handful of peanuts and shoved them in his mouth. "Roxanne taught you well."

When he went for another handful, Johnnie slapped his hand away. "Dinner is almost ready—"

"I don't give a fuck," Knox interrupted. "I want to know what Miah meant."

"You never thought it was odd JaZuria calls Roxanne Mrs. Harrington, Wafer?" Cam asked, his brows lifted. "You never asked her about it?"

Knox flushed. "I've learned my lesson about questioning

her."

"Ain't the fuckin' questionin', Knox," Christopher said. "It's the way you fuckin' questioned her."

"And the types of fucking questions," Mortician said. "Usually, dead ass wrong."

"Anyway, what exactly did your wife do to mine?"

"Mistook her for a commoner," Jeremiah mumbled.

Knox drew his brows together. "Uh…" He cleared his throat. "I-isn't she?" He looked at Cam. "Does she have royal blood?"

"I don't mean like that," Jeremiah said.

"How the fuck do you mean?" Digger asked. "You either common or royal. No fucking in between."

"In Society, there's the privileged and the pretenders," Jeremiah answered. "Apparently, Zuria believed Roxanne was the latter. Two minutes before you and I walked up, she, uh, she…she…she…"

"Spit it out, man! She what?"

"Knox." Jeremiah swallowed. "Over the past eighteen months, I've lost half my money in bad investments and the other quarter in loss of income from commercial real estate. I opted not to sell my company when an offer was made, and I regret the decision—"

"I don't give a fuck, Jeremiah. What did JaZuria do to Roxanne?"

"Offered her money to fill in for our bartender, then demanded she do it. When Roxanne refused, JaZuria… if we hadn't walked up when we did, she was going to call security—"

"Motherfucker, me and you visiting the meatshack," Mort said, shooting to his feet. "That's my mama-in-law your bitch insulted."

Jeremiah flinched.

"I can't believe you," Knox fumed.

"I thought you knew. Our deal to install security systems at Harrington Enterprises didn't fall through—"

"She didn't fucking tell me!"

"Don't worry, little dude," Digger said to CJ. "Roxanne probably ate that bitch alive by now. One less sadity motherfucker you have to worry about."

"JaZuria would've told me," Jeremiah said. "And…they've served…"

"Barely," Cam said. "Jordan is the peacemaker between them. The only reason JaZuria cedes to Roxanne is because of the money. But Roxanne can't stand your wife."

"JaZuria likes—"

"Nofuckinbody," Christopher said flatly. As much as he didn't want to embarrass his boy, he couldn't hold his tongue any longer. At the beginning of the year, he'd take a refresher course in Language Arts. Saddened at how royally he'd fucked up CJ's night, he forged on. "And I'm thinkin' she put a bug in your girl's ear with the way she was treatin' my boy tonight."

"I refuse to allow my daughter to give up her life on a dead-end criminal." Jeremiah glared at CJ, and Christopher wanted to pluck his fucking eyes out. "What are your prospects? What are your intentions? Sweet talking my daughter and then moving on to the next girl. You were barely on my radar. You won Homecoming King to her Queen and was her date to the dance. I didn't know how much she liked you. Then she started picking up your homework, asking permission for you to visit, talking about you constantly. I refuse to allow her to throw her life away. If you don't back off, I'll bring charges against you. Statutory rape."

"Jaleena's four months older than me," CJ protested,

ignoring Christopher's curses.

"I'll think of something!"

"You need a fuckin' brain to think," Christopher said, weighing his options since he'd never killed a motherfucker in his mancave.

"I have a very big brain."

"As soon as I blow it the fuck outcha head, Ima letcha fuckin' know."

"Do you hear this, Knox?" Jeremiah looked at Christopher. "Sir, I will have you arrested—"

When Christopher stood, CJ and everyone else did, too.

"Dad, please," CJ said.

"Sorry, boy. I know my ass embarrassin' you. Ima work on it, but the night fucked anyway—"

"You're not embarrassing me, Dad! Stop that. I don't give a good fuck what this motherfucker said. He's wrong. I…" CJ looked at Jeremiah Davis and shook his head. "I have no idea what jacked up, preconceived notions you walked in with. Maybe, we haven't shown the best of ourselves, but you arrived with your worst face on. I've never seen Jaleena act like she has. Snobbish and self-righteous. I don't want anything from your daughter but her friendship, sir. If you want to judge me because of my father and my uncles, then I'm well judged. I know no finer men. And you should be ashamed of the way Mrs. Davis treated Lolly. You should be ashamed if she treated anyone like that."

Christopher's phone beeped. If he could have, he'd go back in time and tape this disastrous meeting to save his boy's words for posterity.

Pride and love didn't begin to cover his feelings.

Puffing out his chest, he read Megan's text.

"Dinner ready."

"No, Dad. I want the Davises to go. Mom worked hard

to help me, and I won't have them ruin it. We can enjoy ourselves without them."

Grinning, Christopher barreled to Jeremiah Davis and snatched him by the collar. He wished they were on the second floor. "You heard my boy," he said, dragging him toward the door.

"Wait!" Jeremiah yelled. "Wait, please! Jaleena will be in tears if it ends this way. Can we start over? Please?"

At CJ's indecision and glimmer of hope, Christopher knew his boy still wanted to see the evening through. Maybe, he was searching for a way to forget Harley or to distract himself from his worry over Molly. Whatever the case, Christopher was stuck with these motherfuckers for another couple hours.

"Fuck." He shoved Jeremiah away. "Fine."

"I'll go find Diesel, Grant, and Rory," CJ said, and loped away, leaving Christopher to entertain a motherfucker he truly wanted to kill.

DIESEL

Before Diesel reached the mancave, he received a phone call from Tabitha, so he excused himself and returned to the main hall containing the staircase. After twenty minutes of arguing, he hung up and sat on one of the stairs, thrusting his fingers through his hair.

Tabitha was pressuring Diesel to meet with her uncle. However, she refused to reveal the man's identity. Just as she refused to tell him the location of the cabin she kept insisting Aunt Meggie needed to use as a retreat to rest and recuperate.

On the surface, it seemed legitimate. But the very thing that led him to marry her—besides her good pussy—nagged him now. She was suspicious. Her endless questions about the Death Dwellers, especially Uncle Christopher, went beyond mere curiosity.

Yet, she'd passed her background check. She had no club affiliations outside of him. All paperwork was authentic. Her previous addresses checked out. Everything except her tits and lips were genuine.

All the same, something was amiss. He knew it; he just couldn't prove it.

The clopping of heels drew his attention and he got to his feet just as Rebel walked into the cavernous space and halted at seeing him.

Clenching his jaw, he sat down again. It wasn't until Uncle Chris asked him what he was staring at had Diesel realized he'd been gawking. Rory was right, though. Rebel looked hot.

Wincing, he shoved the thought aside, hoping she continued on her way, but knowing she wouldn't.

As expected, she glided to him and climbed up two stairs, stopping in front of him. He wouldn't inventory her curves nor would he remark upon the scent of her perfume and hair.

"Hey, Dee," she said, her casual tone easing some of his tension. "What are you doing out here? Uncle Johnnie piss you off so much you had to escape or kill him?"

Diesel chuckled. "No, brat. Tabitha called."

Her nose wrinkled, calling attention to her pink lipstick and kohl-lined smoky eye. "I prefer my scenario."

"I'm sure you do." He nodded to the space next to him, and she sat. He met her gaze. "But she's my wife and you are a child. You should respect her and any other adult, including Uncle Johnnie."

"Perhaps, if I felt like a child, I'd act like one, Diesel. I don't. It's hard to explain, especially after Thanksgiving evening. I don't know if I will ever be the same again. Rule isn't," she said quietly. "Something snapped inside of him. If Daddy wasn't so consumed with fear for Momma, he might've noticed Rule's change. You, Lolly, and our aunts and uncles took up the slack as much as possible, but they were worried about Momma and Jo, too."

"Now that Aunt Meggie is home, Rule will settle," Diesel told her, wishing he wasn't so wrapped up in his own personal problems and demons.

Maybe, he would've noticed Rule's behavior.

"I'm afraid to have babies now, Diesel. What's the draw of sex is if you know you're at risk for dangerous pregnancies?"

"Not all pregnancies are dangerous," Diesel told her. "Eventually, you'll experience sex and decide for yourself if pleasure is worth the risk."

She gazed at him through her lashes. "Do you think it is?"

"I'm not fucking answering that, Rebel."

"You're not showing me your di—"

"Don't you fucking say it, Rebel," he ordered. "I refuse to listen to you talk like you're a grown woman." Especially while she fucking looked like one.

"Never mind. Shop talks to me and answers any questions I have. I think I'll give him my virginity," she announced as if she spoke of the fucking Christmas decorations.

"I intend to have a talk with that stupid motherfucker," Diesel snarled. "Talking to you about sex warrants the removal of his goddamn tongue. If he fucks you, we hack off his cock and allow him to bleed to death. Sex is a big step."

"Yeah, whatever, dickhead," she grumbled, popping to her feet, not as affected by his threat against Bishop as she had when Uncle Chris issued his warning. She must not have believed Diesel. She reached ground level and turned to him. "Maybe, I'll give it up to Grant."

He shot up and barreled to her, furious. She'd had the audacity to abandon childhood. Before long, she'd be a woman. Like Tabitha.

Like his mother.

Both untrustworthy for different reasons. The only women he truly trusted were Roxanne Harrington and Megan Caldwell. One kept it real and the other one…divided the fucking club. Megan Caldwell was either loved or loathed. Diesel had never found anyone with a gray area.

It was much the same for CJ. Sometimes, Diesel envied his little brother's position, but mostly he empathized with him. He was solidly in the camp that loved Aunt Meggie, yet Rebel was nothing like her.

Rebel was cutthroat and ruthless, ready to annihilate anyone standing in her way, no matter what she might want. "Same principle applies to Grant, Rebel. He will get beaten, castrated, killed, or all three."

She rolled her eyes. "I'm pretty sure he's on Momma's No-Kill list."

"Aunt Meggie doesn't have a No-Maim list."

"What does it matter to you, Diesel? Weren't you fucking by my age?"

"What applies to me doesn't apply to you. I was a child of

the streets. You're just a child. And children don't have sex."

"Give it up, dickhead. You're spouting double-standards that I have no interest in hearing."

"How about I tell your father?"

"You'd do that with what he's going through?"

"I'd do it to protect you."

She cocked her head to the side. "How old were you when you lost your virginity?"

"Why?" he asked, suspicious. He didn't want her to use the information against him.

"Because I want to know. Why else would I ask the question?"

He debated for a moment. "I plead the 5th amendment."

"Overruled."

"You can't overrule my plea, Rebel. You have no basis."

"You have no basis for your fucking plea, Diesel." She squinted. "Oh, but you do, huh? You were younger than me. Weren't you? So your song and dance about me being a child is a crock of shit."

Diesel gnashed his teeth together. "Hindsight is twenty-twenty. If I could go back in time, I wouldn't have had sex at thirteen. It's a big responsibility, sweetheart. As your big brother, it's up to me to protect you."

Irritation slid into her eyes. Diesel waited for her to remind him he wasn't her brother. Instead, she released a breath. "Then don't be Daddy's son, Diesel. Help me protect myself and tell me what to do. Don't snitch on Bishop or Grant or whoever. Don't look at me as your little sister."

"Sex is nothing special, Rebel."

"Make up your fucking mind," she said crossly. "It's either a big step or nothing special. It isn't both."

"Goddamn, you're the most argumentative little piece of baggage I've ever met."

"No, jackass. I'm not. But I do have my own mind and I'm not accepting bullshit excuses so you can feel better about yourself and think you're the best big brother alive."

"Remember that when Uncle Chris confronts you," Diesel said, then wished he could recall the words.

The threat might've worked on Mattie or Harley or even some of the boys.

She laughed in his face. "I will tell him exactly what I've said to you, Diesel."

"What about his worry for Aunt Meggie?"

"I'm not the one who'll tell him, am I? It's your scenario and your threat. Deal with the fucking consequences."

"They are hypotheticals."

"As are my words. Unless you open your mouth. If you do, then you will put Grant and Bishop at risk."

"Don't turn this around on me. This is all on you."

She glanced away. "What do you want from me, Diesel?" she asked quietly.

To be the little girl he'd met all those years ago. Growing up made her innately untrustworthy.

"You can't answer me, can you? When I insisted I wanted to marry you and you weren't my brother, you were angry with me. I'm confiding in you about other boys and you still aren't happy."

"Grant is twenty and Bishop is two or three years older than that. They aren't boys."

"They are closer in age to me than you."

"They won't fuck you," he barked. "They value their fucking lives."

"They will do any fucking thing I want them to," she snarled, "and you don't have a fucking thing to say about it. If you rat me out, I will deny it."

"And if you turn up pregnant?"

She shuddered. "Then I'll bleed to death like I thought Momma did or I will survive and raise my baby."

If ever he made a difference in someone's life, Diesel wanted it to be now. He hadn't realized how much Rebel was spiraling until that moment. After moving out, he'd turned away from her, then been so outraged and annoyed at her crush on him that he felt justified in ignoring her.

He tipped up her chin. "Let Aunt Meggie heal completely first. Let Jo come home, then I'll approach our parents so the four of us can talk. I'll explain everything you've shared with me and you can fill in any details I forget or fuck up. I won't mention Bishop or Grant as long as you don't follow through with you plan."

"You'll get busy and forget."

"I swear I won't, Rebel. But you need to see Aunt Meggie come through this, then you need protection."

"Fine," she said grudgingly. "Leave Bishop and Grant alone. They are my friends, and they fill in the void left by Uncle Johnnie keeping Mattie away, Harley's desertion, and your marriage."

"I'll do better."

"Grant's funny, Dee. The way you once were, then you met Tabitha. If you start checking on me regularly, I know I will have to beat that bitch to a pulp. I'm fine with Grant—"

"Did I hear my name?" Grant Harrington walked through the same door from which Diesel had come. He was tall and blond like his father, though he lacked Knox's seriousness. He smiled at Rebel. "You really are gorgeous."

"Your shock is a fucking insult," Rebel said with a sniff.

Grant's grin widened and his eyes twinkled. "You're a natural beauty. Tonight, you're just fucking hot." He rocked on his heels, ignoring Diesel's glare. "Why did Aunt Meggie allow you to look like a fucking yacht girl?"

"Asshole," Diesel gritted.

"I know what the fuck a yacht girl is, Diesel," Rebel said.

"You shouldn't," Diesel said flatly as Grant said, "I'll bet you do."

"Why are you barely dressed and entertaining two men, Rebel?"

At the sound of Rule's voice, Diesel turned toward the staircase. Rule stood on the landing where the two staircases converged, so laser focused on Rebel that a chill slithered into Diesel.

"Hey, dude," Grant greeted.

"We're in the mancave, waiting for dinner, Rule," Diesel said.

Rule ignored them. "Rebel? You're my twin. I asked you a question and expect an answer."

"You're my brother, not my father, Rule," she replied. "I don't have to answer to you."

Rule glanced toward the ceiling. "Yes, I understand," he said.

Snorting, Rebel shook her head. "I need to find Mattie and Ava. I don't have the patience to deal with you tonight, Rule."

"You're finished with the presents, Reb?" CJ asked, walking in through the same door Diesel and Grant had used. "Mom texted Dad and said the first course is almost ready."

"I haven't even started, CJ," she admitted. "I didn't have a pocket for my phone and I left it in the kitchen, so I came to get Ava and Mattie but got distracted by a conversation with Diesel."

"No! I refuse!" Rule cried.

The outburst startled Diesel. "Who are you talking to?"

"Who the fuck knows?" Rebel said tiredly.

Wildness crept into Rule's eyes, and he shot down the

stairs, shoving between Diesel and Grant so ferociously, Rebel stumbled.

"They're telling me to punch you, Rebel, and you're mocking me?"

Rebel looked at Diesel. For the briefest moments, she let her guard down and revealed her despair. Even a touch of fear. Then she drew herself up.

"I suggest you don't listen, Rule," she said coldly. "Because I will break every bone in your fucking body."

"You're a woman, a deceiver and a temptress," he said. "Like Mom. She deceived us into thinking she was healthy and tempted Dad so she could have another baby." He took a handful of Rebel's hair and let it cascade from his fingers. "Now, she's allowing you to do the same."

"Let us talk to Rule, sweetheart," Diesel said, pulling her behind him and allowing CJ to take her place.

"Yeah, Reb," he said. "I'll text Mattie and tell her to meet you in Mom's office."

Rebel didn't move.

Grant tugged her hand. "C'mon, Reb. Aunt Meggie wants the gifts wrapped."

Pulling away from Grant, she sidestepped CJ and inserted herself next to her twin. Rule was between her and Diesel, although CJ was close enough to protect her, which made Diesel feel slightly better.

"You've got to come back to me, Rule," she whispered. "Please. I miss you. I miss sharing our secrets. You're not like this. You're good and kind and gentle. Tell the voices to go away. Momma's fine! You don't need them anymore."

For a moment, Rule's face softened. Diesel hoped Rebel's words penetrated his trauma, but then his nostrils flared and his eyes hardened.

"Liar," Rule snarled, low. "Your words are a soft damsel's,

but your spirit is cold like a battle-hardened warrior. I see no tears. I hear no tenderness."

Rebel's face crumpled. Diesel thought she might cry. Instead, she straightened and lifted her chin. "I'm not required to cry or to simper because I have a pussy. I don't even understand your words anymore. You talk in riddles."

"You aren't required to understand me. You're only required to listen. Or suffer the consequences."

Sighing, Rebel studied Rule, then nodded. If Rule saw her fist coming before it landed on his jaw, Diesel couldn't say. He certainly didn't notice until flesh on flesh connected and Rule staggered back and plopped on the last stair.

"Listen up, you fucking asshole," she snarled. "Listen to fucking voices. Get help. Do rain dances. Take medicine. I don't care. If you plan on punishing me, when I heal or come to, hide, motherfucker. Hide. I will put you out of your goddamn misery and bring your body to Rory so he can chop you into little pieces." She ended her tirade with a kick to Rule's shin. Ignoring his howls, she stormed away.

Amid the chaos, Grant lit a cigarette. Now, he released the smoke and smiled at Rebel's retreating form. "CJ, I have a question, dude?"

"I told you not to fuck with Rebel, Rule," CJ said with irritation, crouching in front of his brother and pulling napkins from his pocket. He looked over his shoulder. "What, Grant?"

"Jaleena might get it that you're wealthy, but she still might not want to fuck with you."

"Where the fuck's the question?" Diesel asked. "That's a fucking statement."

Grant sucked on his cigarette before he responded. "Are you sure inviting her over was a good idea?" He nodded to Rule. "All things considered."

"Fuck, I don't know, Grant," CJ said, not flinching when Rule jerked away and took over holding the napkin to his lip and nose. "How else was she supposed to see the real me?"

"What about Harley?" Diesel asked. They were young though, when emotions were fickle.

"Harley doesn't even want to be my friend, Diesel," he answered. "She…it doesn't matter. No matter how I feel, I refuse to allow anyone to mistreat me."

"Then, maybe, you're trying to force something with Jaleena," Diesel suggested.

"We don't blame you," Grant said. "She's quite pretty."

CJ stood. "I don't know what I want," he admitted. "It hurts a lot to think about Harley, so I try not to. I like Jaleena, but I'm not sure how and I want to be fair to her. The last time we kissed, Harley's face didn't intrude. Molly's did."

After blowing a series of smoke circles, Grant squeezed the cigarette cherry and extinguished it, then shook his head. "Damn, dude, you really are fucked up."

"If Ryan discovers you've slept with his girlfriend, that little asshole will be impossible," Diesel said.

"I haven't slept with Molly, Diesel!"

"Pssssst, CJ."

Mattie's voice floated into the hall a moment before she peeked in, revealing only her head. "Where's Daddy?"

"With my dad," CJ asked. "Why? What are you hiding?"

Biting down on her glossed lip, she glanced behind her, then walked fully into view. In the scheme of things, her body con minidress with three green bows, green stockings, and green pumps, weren't as revealing as Rebel's outfit. On the other hand, Mattie's hem was shockingly high, she wore makeup, and her hair was unbound and tousled.

Rebel pulled off her outfit by her inherent confidence.

Mattie looked like a little girl playing dress up because of her apparent unease.

"Oh, goddamn," CJ said, gulping.

"Uncle Johnnie's going to flip his fucking lid," Grant added.

Diesel was inclined to agree. "Why'd you choose such an outfit?"

"Momma…Maman said I could. I've been hiding out in the kitchen waiting for Rebel. Then I texted her to see what was up and noticed her phone on the counter."

"Your outfit is very pretty, Mattie," CJ said.

"Th-thank you. It's only now that I realize Daddy's anger might ruin your party." She lowered her lashes. "But I wanted to look like Rebel and Momma and Aunt Meggie. I wanted Jaleena to think I was pretty." She met CJ's gaze, her eyes huge and vulnerable. "I'm sorry. I-I'm not trying to compete…I know you like her—"

Although Diesel was stunned into silence, CJ went to Mattie and hugged her.

"It's fine," he said. "Jaleena is my friend, but I have no claim to her."

"Do I really look pretty? I'm so scared of Daddy's reaction." Her voice shook.

"You're stunning, Matilda," Grant piped in. "Blessed with beauty and brains."

"Beauty and brains," Rule echoed. "Beauty and brains. That's what Bash said about Rebel. Beauty and brains."

"What?" CJ and Diesel chorused.

"You've met Bash?" Mattie whimpered, starting to tremble.

"Dinner's ready!"

Diesel thought Bunny yelled the announcement, but he wasn't sure. He was too busy watching Mattie.

"Bash is bad," Rule said.

"Where did you meet him, Matilda?" Diesel asked.

"I'm starving!" Ryder yelled, racing in front of the archway with Axel and Ransom close behind.

"I had to stab Bash," Rule continued, unperturbed by the noise of his younger brothers or the chaos ensuing at the call to head to the dining room. "They said not to slit his throat."

"You did what, you little asshole?" CJ demanded.

"Bash was strangling Ryan," Rule admitted. "I had to stab Bash and knock him out to save Ryan."

"Does Dad know?" CJ asked.

"They said don't tell him."

"Fuck them!" CJ yelled. "I'm telling you to 'fess up."

"Rory!"

The closeness of Uncle Johnnie's voice made an appearance imminent.

"Oh god, oh god, oh god," Mattie cried.

"Come on, Mattie." Not giving her a chance to respond, Grant hurried to Mattie and jerked her toward the entrance hall, dashing out of sight just as Uncle Johnnie walked in.

"Did I hear my princess?" he asked.

"Not in here, uncle," CJ answered.

"Have you seen Rory?"

"No," Diesel answered, reeling by Rule and Mattie's confessions. "I can call him for you."

"No. Thank you, though." He walked out, leaving through the archway that led to the entrance hall.

When there was no fury erupting, Diesel knew Grant helped Mattie elude her father.

"You're telling Dad about Bash, Rule," CJ ordered the moment they were alone. "You left him alive, didn't you?"

Rule nodded. "He could've bled out, though. I don't know."

"Fuck," Diesel said.

"Jesus Christ," CJ breathed. "You have to tell Dad as soon as possible. Maybe, ask to talk to him while we're eating salad."

"When I checked the next day, Bash was gone. I don't think he died, so I don't have to tell Dad immediately. It'll ruin dinner because he might lose his temper."

"No shit! But he has to know."

"They—"

"You also need to tell Uncle Chris the extent that, er, they talk to you," Diesel suggested.

"No, it's a secret."

"Fine," CJ said before Diesel could argue. "We'll deal with one thing at a time. Tell Dad about Bash and Ryan."

Rule thought for a moment, then nodded. "Can I come to the dinner table?"

"The night is fucked anyway," CJ grouched, "so it won't matter if you get in Rebel's crosshairs, and she decks you again."

"I'm not a freak!"

"No, just a possible fucking murderer," CJ said.

"You're making me angry, CJ," Rule cried. "And you don't want to do that."

CJ grabbed a handful of Rule's shirt and snatched him off his feet. "Listen, you little motherfucker, would you like to see what I'll do to you if you make me angry? I'm not your enemy. You need help."

"No, I need peace and prayer."

"Prayer is supposed to bring peace, but I'm not getting into a religious debate with you, Rule. Stop with your fucking threats and tell Dad what the fuck you did."

Without warning, CJ released him and folded his arms as Rule landed on the floor.

"I'll see you both at the dinner table," CJ said, and walked out.

Diesel held out a hand to Rule. "Come on, brother. Let me help you clean up your face."

"Okay, Dee," Rule said miserably, accepting Diesel's help as he got to his feet.

"I'll sit between you and Rebel tonight."

Rule touched his bleeding lip, though it was a trickle now. "She must learn chastity. If Mom can't rein her in and Rebel won't comply to me, I'll have to take matters into my hands."

CHAPTER 33

MEGGIE

"In my home, I sit at the head of table, opposite my husband," JaZuria said, halfway through their salad. She sat on the lefthand side of Christopher, directly across from Meggie. Cutting into a piece of lettuce, she nodded to Roxy. "I especially wouldn't cede my spot to another woman."

"Luckily this aintcha fuckin' table," Christopher snapped. He allowed his utensils to clank against the Santa plate as he released them. As usual, he ate the bare minimum salad to appease Meggie. "Megan put motherfuckers where the fuck she want, and if you don't like it, get to fuckin' steppin'."

All things considered, it surprised Meggie how well things seemed to have gone between Christopher, CJ, and the rest of the guys. When they came to the table, Mr. Davis, CJ, and Rory were laughing and talking.

However, Christopher barely spoke, and he seemed to have taken an extreme dislike to JaZuria. Other than the fact that Mattie had yet to make an appearance, everything else was going fine. CJ sat between Jaleena and her mother, while Diesel placed himself between Rule and Rebel.

Rule's injuries and agitation concerned Meggie, but he'd declined a private word with her, and she had her hands full with the formality of the dinner. In all her memory, she didn't think she'd ever stuck to strict social mores such as the proper placement of forks and glasses. It was more a loose interpretation rather than rigid adherence, so she'd ceded to Roxy and Kendall's knowledge.

Yet, JaZuria still found a problem.

"I think too highly of myself, Christopher," JaZuria sniffed, ignoring Christopher's darkening glower. "And it behooves me to guide any woman who doesn't know her place."

CJ laid his fork aside. "With all due respect, Mrs. Davis, only my mother, Uncle Johnnie, Aunt Ophelia, and Aunt Zoann are allowed to call Dad by his Christian name. Everyone else refers to him as Outlaw."

"That's ridiculous," JaZuria said. "I won't address him at all if—"

"Ain't no skin off my fuckin' teeth," Christopher interrupted. "You'd do my ass a fuckin' favor if I ain't ever gotta see you or your fuckin' man again."

"CJ's right, JaZuria," Meggie said diplomatically, trying to catch Christopher's eye and silently remind him, they were doing this for CJ. "It's an unwritten rule."

JaZuria took a delicate sip of her water. "What an adorable way to lay claim on your man," she purred, setting the glass aside. "It's an odd demand, but cute."

Roxy sat her wine glass on the table with unnecessary force.

"Being amongst the privileged few to call my husband 'Christopher' is charming," Meggie agreed sweetly. "But it isn't my directive. It's his."

Next to her, Mr. Davis finished his salad and dabbed his

napkin at each corner of his mouth before returning it to his lap.

Meggie smiled at him. "I hope you find everything to your liking, Mr. Davis."

"Mr. Davis?" her family chorused like a group of juvenile delinquents, though she clearly heard Christopher's outrage.

"How the fuck his bitch call my ass Christopher but you callin' this motherfucker Mr. Davis, Megan?"

"Er, JaZuria said to call him that, Christopher," Meggie said testily. "This isn't about us. It's about CJ."

"Ain't takin' that away, baby. Earlier, I was feelin' fuckin' lower than shit cuz I embarrassed him, but that was me. No motherfucker settin' foot in this fuckin' house and disrespectin' you and I don't give a good fuck if it's for your ma—"

"Dinah dead, Outlaw," Digger grumbled, though Meggie couldn't see him since he sat further down the table on her side.

She'd never used all the extensions before. It made the table so long, each end extended beyond the area rug. Without Bailey, the place settings were uneven. However, if three more guests had come, Meggie would've had to move the dinner party to the breakfast room, where their family get-togethers took place.

That would've gone over well.

"No, assfuck, ain't no ghosts in this motherfucker."

Christopher's amused tone and the rising chuckles drew Meggie back to the conversation. Hearing Mr. Davis's laughter eased her. Seeing JaZuria's scowl didn't.

"We saw Grandma walking the other night, Uncle Digger," Ryder said calmly.

"Yeah, Ryder, Grandma was holding her head under her arm," Ransom said. "The eyes were missing."

"That shit not funny—" Digger started.

"How could she see, stupid?" Axel demanded.

"She's a fucking ghost, assfuck," Ryder grumbled. "She don't need eyes! She can see ghostily."

"That's not even a word," Ransom said.

Elbows on the table, Meggie covered her face and groaned. She'd ordered all her children to behave because the night was so important to CJ.

"No, she won't take my eyes!" Axel cried. "I'm not afraid of no ghost. She'll take Uncle Digger's. He's afraid of her."

"How the fuck you sicking that bitch on me?" Digger demanded.

CJ roared with laughter. "They're fucking with you, Uncle. Grandma Dinah doesn't visit."

"I don't fuck around with ghosts, little bruh!"

"Woooooooo," Ransom said, his voice trembling. "I seeeeee you—"

Christopher grabbed his bottle of beer and swigged. "Shut the fuck up or get your ass beat."

Immediately, her sons calmed down.

CJ whispered something to Jaleena, and she giggled. JaZuria glared at her husband and lifted her eyebrow. It seemed as if they wanted their kids to disagree.

JaZuria looked up and down the table. "I think everyone is finished, Meggie. Where's your bell to alert your servers?"

Heaving in a breath, Meggie pasted a smile on her face.

JaZuria tittered. "That's right, you don't have staff for the evening and must serve your own guests. Better you than me."

"Where is Mattie?" Roxy cut in.

Either she knew Meggie was reaching her breaking point or she was at hers and changed the subject to save an eruption.

"You're right, Roxanne," Johnnie said. "Kendall, where is our daughter?"

Kendall shrugged, unperturbed. She knew as well as Meggie that Mattie was hiding. "She's in the house, Johnnie."

"She should be at the table."

"Maybe, she's not hungry, Dad," Rory said in exasperation.

"She's being rude," Johnnie said flatly. "JJ didn't want to come, so he stayed home. She attended so she should be with the family."

"Johnnie, enough. Okay?" Kendall said sharply.

A different disaster loomed if Johnnie continued down his current path. If he didn't see it, Meggie recognized that Kendall was reaching the end of her patience. Usually, anarchy followed.

"I want her at the table now, Kendall," Johnnie ordered.

Kendall gritted her teeth but nodded. "I'll text her and tell her to come to the dining room."

"Johnnie, back the fuck off Kendall," Christopher said coldly. "I fucking swear if..." He looked at CJ and drew in a deep breath. "We talkin'—"

"Kendall's my fucking wife, Christopher. Worry about your own."

"He does, Dad," Rory said, a little too calmly for Meggie's comfort. "Much more than you worry about Mom."

"Leave our family business where it belongs, son," Johnnie barked.

"He is, Uncle Johnnie," Rule said serenely.

Meggie blinked. Speaking of calm... "Er, Rule..."

Rebel tugging on Diesel's sleeve captured Meggie's attention. When he leaned his head toward her, she whispered in his ear and he smiled, genuine amusement on his face.

Meggie cocked her head to the side, watching Rebel flush

and purse her lips. All at once, she recognized a problem. Rebel hadn't stopped crushing on Diesel. She'd just changed tactics.

This was so very bad. Meggie trusted Diesel to keep his distance while Rebel was underage, but in just over three years she'd turn eighteen.

And…crap.

Swallowing, Meggie glanced at Christopher. Rebel's outmaneuvering of him and Diesel went right over his head. He was still distracted by her.

"Mom?" Rule said. "Do you need something?"

"Um, no," he head buzzing with situations.

"I'll start dishing out the soup," Bunny said, breezing by Meggie.

"I'll help," Meggie said, rising. "Rebel—"

"You're fine, Meggie," Bunny said. "Rest. I'll—"

"What are you wearing, Matilda Donovan?" Johnnie roared, shoving back from his chair and storming to his feet.

Meggie tipped her head back to better see her niece. Mattie stood in the doorway, so pretty in her dress but mortified by her father's reaction.

Kendall stood, too. "Johnnie—"

"Shut up, Kendall. She looks like a whore—"

Mattie's face crumpled.

"Dad—" Rory started.

"Look, fuckhead," Kendall snarled. "You're embarrassing my daughter. I picked the fucking dress out for her and if you have a problem with that, fuck you." She waved Mattie over. "Come, darling. You're so pretty. If your father is too much of a dickhead to remember that a girl needs her daddy approval, I apologize."

"Enough, Kendall. You're overstepping your bounds."

"Fuck you, motherfucker. You've overstepped your fucking

bounds with Mattie every fucking day for months. I adhere to your wishes. We all do, but what you aren't fucking doing is humiliating her in front of fucking guests."

"As if you aren't," Johnnie sneered.

"Fuck you and them," Kendall snapped. "Tell Mattie she's pretty, John Donovan, or I'll show you what the fuck humiliation is."

"Are you sure about that?"

"You really want to test that fucking theory, asshole?"

"Nope," Digger said, "'cause you win everyfuckintime, Kendall. You show us how crazy really look. Johnnie a novice next to you."

"Asshole," Johnnie barked. "That's my fucking wife."

"I'm on your side. And I know who the fuck she is, John Boy. Your ass forget the woman your wife and Mattie your daughter."

"Believe me, that is always uppermost on my mind," Johnnie gritted. "I want Matilda to be respectable. I don't want her to draw unwarranted attention."

Rebel whispered to Diesel again, and giggled.

"Like Rebel," Johnnie said.

Rebel blinked.

"You're not only dressed like a fucking harlot, but you're rude—"

Before Christopher grabbed the steak knife, Meggie placed her hand over his.

"Share with us what you whispered to Diesel," Johnnie continued, not knowing or not caring that his life was in danger.

"Rebel's a child, Johnnie," Kendall said with disapproval, lifting a brow at Meggie and Christopher's hand tussle.

"In years only," Johnnie replied. "We're waiting, Rebel."

"Then wait, Uncle Johnnie."

"Yeah, you're our uncle, dude," Ryder said. "You don't get to tell us what to do."

"Especially with Mom and Dad right there," Ransom said.

Christopher growled, tightened his grip on her hand, and lifted it away. Grabbing the knife, he stood.

"Can I talk to you?" Meggie said, jumping to her feet.

"No, Megan—"

"If I wanted the table at large to hear, Uncle Johnnie, I would've spoken up," Rebel snapped. "You don't get to come in here and order me around. It won't work on me. I'm not afraid of you. I don't like you. And I don't give a good fuck about your opinion, so you can huff and puff until your fucking lungs collapse, it makes no fucking difference to me. I will never forgive you for what you did to my mother while she was in the hospital, you fucking prick."

"What are you talking about?" Kendall asked.

"Tell her, Johnnie," Christopher said.

"You're making that demand in front of strangers, Christopher?" Johnnie asked. "You're not chastising your daughter?"

"You should be thanking my sister," CJ said, eyeing Johnnie with distaste. "While she was talking to you, Mom was wrestling a knife away from Dad." He smiled. "It was probably intended for your throat."

"Whatever," Johnnie barked, reseating himself.

"What did you do to Meggie, Johnnie?" Kendall asked.

"Nothing," Johnnie said. "Right, Rebel?"

Rebel glanced at Meggie.

"Right, Reb?" Meggie encouraged with a nod.

"Yeppers," Rebel said, overly bright. She leaned forward. "Yo, push down, everyone. I want Mattie to sit next to me." She smiled at Christopher as everyone did her bidding. "Sit, Daddy. Take a load off your feet."

"We talkin' later, Reb."

"I'm sure we are, Daddy."

Christopher scowled at her.

She smiled. "I love you."

"Nice try, Reb," Axel said. "Dad's still going to beat your ass. Uncle Johnnie's an adult. If we can't call him stupid, you can't."

"Daddy won't beat me. I was defending myself. That's what enforcers do. Defend themselves and everyone else."

Mortician laughed. "I'm not ready to retire yet, Reb."

"Bitches can't join the club, Rebel," Digger said. "You can't be no enforcer."

"I can be a special assignment enforcer." She shrugged. "Or I can start my own club."

"That's fucking bad ass, Reb," Grant complimented.

"Dude, you're old and pathetic," Ransom said. "First Brynn and now Rebel. You're going to be locked up yet."

Laughing, Grant flipped Ransom off. "I'm twenty, and they are my friends. Nothing more."

"Grant's like a brother to me," Rebel said. "As much as Diesel is my brother." She smiled at him.

Unaware that he was being played, Diesel returned her smile, beaming with pleasure.

"You have an interesting family," Jeremiah said.

Meggie sipped from her water glass. "I do. We're rather loud and opinionated."

"Rather is a relative term," JaZuria said.

"Umkay. Right. We're very loud and opinionated."

"Even the children," JaZuria said with distaste. "Cultural differences at work again."

"Ain't got nothin' to fuckin' do with cultural differences," Christopher said. "Rebel a lot like me when I was her age."

"Nature versus nurture, Dad?" Ryder said because every

time one of the Davises spoke, everyone listened.

"Mom, you tried," Ransom said woefully. "But it's in Rebel's nature to be a scary bitch."

Meggie scowled. "Do not call—"

"It's in my nature to beat your fucking ass too," Rebel interrupted. "You little fucking dickhead."

"Hey!" Axel cried. "Don't talk to my brother like that, heifer. I'll hog tie you, rub you with honey, and pour ants and bees all over you, then laugh while you cry and scream. Until you die."

"And I'll haunt the fuck out of you, remove my eyeballs, and shove them down your miserable little throat until you suffocate."

"Momma!" Axel cried, bursting into tears. He stood and ran to Meggie. "Rebel's ghost is going to bite off my ears and shove them up my nostrils," he said, when she stood and hugged him to her.

"Mort, you writing this shit down?" Digger asked. "They some creative little motherfuckers. Mark JB going to be so mad he missed this."

"Megan, you been workin' really hard," Christopher said. "Sit down. Axel, if you don't kill Rebel, her ghost can't fuck you up. Think about that and go back to your seat so your ma can rest."

"Aunt Meggie, I have a question," Rory said, once Meggie sat down again.

"Yes, love?"

"How does it feel to be surrounded by giants? Even the children?"

Meggie grinned, happy to hear the laughter. Rory was always so serious around Johnnie. "Not you, too, Rory," she said, giggling.

"Yes, ma'am. Me, too. I couldn't resist. Axel is just slightly shorter than you.”

“Soon, only Gunner and Jo will be shorter than Mom,” CJ said.

Jaleena placed a hand on his shoulder, and he leaned back, to hear her. It pleased Meggie that their earlier tension seemed to have disappeared. If that was true, then she’d count the evening as a success.

Rule

Blood, blood, blood.
Rebel is good, Rule.
Overlook Mom’s name fixation.
Blood, blood, blood.
We need a sacrifice.
How do I tell Dad?
Tell Dad. Tell Dad. Tell Dad.
Blood, blood, blood.
You were bad, Rule.
PAIN!

Flinching, Rule scraped the last of his bread pudding and rum sauce from his plate and shoved the spoon in his mouth. Voices were bouncing around in his head. Some, he recognized. Others were new and he was trying to make sense of what they wanted.

Blood, blood, blood.

Since Mom's collapse, those words had been a never-ending refrain and competed with the trail of blood she'd left as Dad ran with her.

She been so pale, like Death.

The Lord is my Shephard.

Ignoring the laughter and conversation around him, Rule recited the 23rd Psalm. It was almost time for his ten o'clock prayers. The Davises had been there far longer than anticipated.

You like Jaleena, Rule.

I don't like her parents.

As long as they don't hurt Mom, let them go.

Rule nodded, though no one noticed. Mom, Dad, Rebel, and CJ were the only ones who spent time with him and loved him.

You almost lost her. Never forget that.

Repent.

Why? Was her collapse my fault?

Pray, pray, pray.

Blood, blood, blood.

PAIN!

"Why?"

"Why what, son?" Mom asked, alerting Rule that the voices had jumped from his head and slid out of his mouth.

Rebel lifted a brow at him.

Pain slid into him at the memory of her punch, and he touched his mouth.

"You okay, boy?" Dad asked.

Rule remembered to nod.

Cut Rebel.

Don't cut Rebel.

I don't have a knife!

He'd taken the pocketknife specifically for the assignment to save Ryan. Unless he caught birds or rodents for his altar, he had no other use for the blade.

I love Rebel.

Rebel's scary.

Rebel's beautiful.

Rule flinched again, ashamed. He didn't want to see her or Mom as beautiful. They should be unrecognizable to him.

You almost lost your mother.

Stop!!!

Rebel thinks you're a freak!

Blood, pray, pray, blood, blood, blood, pray, pray.

Rule thrust his fingers through his hair.

"Dad, Rule has to talk to you later," CJ said.

"About what, boy?"

"Nothing we can talk about here, Dad."

"That sounds serious," Mom said, concerned.

If she'd died...

If she gets pregnant again, save her! Cut the baby out of her!

Won't that hurt her?

Do it!

"You okay, dude?" Grant asked, staring at him.

Is he judging me?

No!

The word bounced in his head like an echoing scream. When Mom collapsed, he'd screamed and screamed inside.

Mom stood. "Now that dessert is over, why don't you and the rest of the kids, show Jaleena, Jillian, and Juliana, the basement, CJ?"

Rule frowned. All Js? It made his head hurt. Lately,

everything made his head hurt.

You can forgive Megan. Kill JaZuria!

"I want to stay up here, Momma," Rebel said. "We can dance."

"CJ and Jaleena doesn't want to spend all their time with adults, Reb," Mom protested. "We can dance another time."

Rebel glanced at Diesel, then batted her eyelashes at Mom. "Pul-leaze, Momma?" She shimmied, too provocatively. "I can show off my dance moves."

She still wants Diesel.

Kill her.

Kill him.

I love them!

She can do worse.

He has Tabitha.

We hate Tabitha.

"Fine!" Mom capitulated.

CJ interfered.

He doesn't realize Rebel's game.

Neither does Outlaw.

He's gone.

Dad's here.

Outlaw isn't.

Mom, mom, mom.

Mompraybloodpraymomblood.

The words jumbled in Rule's brain.

Stop, please! Go away!

Blood. Pray. Mom. Blood. Mom. Pray.

At least the words had separated and were distinct. In a fog, he watched everyone stand. Dad placed an arm around Mom's shoulder and guided her toward the door. Everyone followed.

Rule remained seated, his heart pounding and an

abundance of warmth swirling through him. Overheated and dizzy, he prayed for silence.

"Brother?"

She loves you.

She hates you.

She placed a hand on his shoulder. "Come on," she said softly.

Tears settled into his eyes. "They won't stop, Reb."

"I love you anyway."

"You hit me."

"And I'll hit you again, if you fuck with me."

Pussy! You stabbed Bash. Kill her!

"I love you, Reb. I never want to hurt you. I...you made me cry and I don't feel much pain anymore."

"Either I have a killer punch or our connection as twins makes you more vulnerable to me." She tugged his arm. "Come on. I want to dance with you and Diesel."

Standing, Rule sighed.

She's a selfish cunt, Rule.

"Dad will kill him, Rebel. Think carefully."

"What are you talking about?" she asked, the picture of innocence. "I'm over Diesel."

She's lying.

"Do you swear, Rebel?"

Don't believe her.

"Yes."

Make her swear on the bible.

"Will you swear on a bible?"

"Will it make you happy?"

"As long as it's the truth."

"It is."

For now.

"Later, after I talk to Dad, come to my room."

She shrugged. "Whatever."

Sweeping her hair to the side, she turned and walked away.

Stab her.

Rule clapped his hands over his ears, not that it did any good.

Walking into the family room, he found Mom dancing with Uncle Johnnie to *Good Time* by Alan Jackson. She looked so happy because she loved to dance. Sometimes, when it was just Mom, Dad, Rule, and his siblings, she even convinced Dad to bust some moves. Mainly, though, it was her, CJ, and Rebel. When Diesel lived at home, he sometimes joined in.

Uncle Mort was Mom's usual male dance partner. Dad trusted him, and few other men were brave enough to approach her because they feared Outlaw.

Outlaw is gone.

Megan stole Outlaw.

Rebel dragged Diesel to where Mom and Uncle Johnnie were. Taking her cue, CJ held out his hand to Jaleena.

Rule started to back away, but Dad spotted him and beckoned him over.

Confess and prepare to face your father's wrath.

As usual, Rule had no choice but to obey.

INTERLUDE

Joey

"*Do not go gentle into that good night, Old age should burn and rave at close of day; Rage, rage against the dying of the light.*"

Fourteen-year-old Joseph "Joey" Foy II looked up from the book of poetry he'd stolen from Christopher Caldwell's room. The jack shit moved to the club a year ago and stole away the love and attention of Joey's father. While bugger head was out, Joey went into his room, saw the poetry book, swiped it, and commandeered Rack, K-P, and his father. Now, they sat at a table, while Joey read a poem by one of the most famous Welsh poets of all time.

He reread the first stanza under his breath. It didn't matter. He still didn't understand it. "What does it mean, Dad?"

Big Joe shrugged. "Don't die easily." Displeasure oozed from each word.

Feeling attacked, Joey stiffened. "If your time's up, you're going to die. You don't have a fucking choice."

Glaring, his father polished off his pint of rum.

"What'd I do now?" Joey demanded.

"Stole." The word fell from Big Joe's lips like shards of ice. "That's Christopher's book. I'd bet my fucking life he didn't lend it to you, so you went into his room without his permission."

"What if I did?" Joey challenged, refusing to confirm or deny the accusations. "He'd steal my shit without second thought."

"He wouldn't, son," Big Joe said with a sigh. "A thief is the worst motherfucker alive. You'll never have trust or respect."

"It's just a stupid book. If I don't understand it, you know he doesn't."

Rack snickered, though K-P and Big Joe glared between them.

"Why do you fucking hate me, Dad?" Joey cried. "If we didn't share the same blond hair and blue eyes, I'd think it was because I look like Momma."

Big Joe stiffened and opened his mouth.

"You don't," K-P inserted, laying a comforting hand on Joey's shoulder. "You know that."

He knocked away K-P's hand. He was up Christopher's ass, too. "It isn't my fault she left you, Dad. She left me, too. I haven't seen her in months."

Wincing, Dad looked away. K-P stared into his half empty tankard, while Rack's lips tightened.

"Read the next stanza, son," Dad ordered.

"Though wise men at their end know dark is right," Joey started as the door opened and sunlight slivered across their table, "Because their words had forked no lightning they Do not go gentle into that good night." He stared at the words, trying to make sense of them. "What does it mean?" he repeated. A chair slid, but he didn't bother to look up. "Good men, the last wave by, crying how bright Their frail deeds might have danced in a green bay, Rage, rage against the dying of the light. I don't understand it."

"Neither me," a new voice inserted.

Startled, Joey met the silver-gray eyes of Johnnie. He'd turn sixteen in two months, but he dressed like a forty-year-old banker. His golden hair and golden skin gave him the appearance of a beautiful lion. Joey didn't despise him the way he hated Christopher. Johnnie wasn't a threat.

"*Wild men who caught and sang the sun in flight, And learn, too late, they grieve it on its way, Do not go gentle into that good night,*" another added, the person Joey loathed most. "The poem mean you got to fight death, Joey," Christopher said quietly. "But, see, death come to us all, so we might put it off a little bit. It still gets us in the end. Instead of giving up, we fight to live 'til we can't no more. It's about life and death, light and dark. *Rage against the dying of the light*, so we don't slip into blackness."

Joey thought for a moment. Seeing his father's pride and K-P's smile infuriated him, and he stiffened. "You're a fucking dumb ass. You don't know anything."

Christopher snatched the book from Joey. "I know this my fuckin' book that Johnnie gave to me. I know if you go in my fuckin' room again, I'm gonna beat your fuckin' ass."

"No one's fighting anyone," Rack spat. "There are rules around here, boy. If you put your hand on Joey, you'll get your ass beat and end up back at Patricia's."

Joey smirked at Christopher but shifted at Johnnie's frown. Sometimes, the silver in his eyes swallowed the gray and gave them a chilling depthlessness.

"You like something you see in my room, ask me and

I might let you borrow it," Christopher insisted, ramrod straight and stiff. "Steal my shit and I beat your fucking ass."

"I said—"

"Shut it, Rack," Dad interrupted. "Who gives a fuck what you said about Christopher? What I say matters, and he's right." He looked at Joey. "You're lucky he's not beating your ass now. From where I sat, he extended an olive branch by explaining the poem to you and you shit on him. Steal from him again and not only will he kick your fucking ass, but I will, too."

"Dad—"

Rack caught his eyes and gave the barest shake of his head, so Joey snapped his mouth shut.

"What are you doing here, Johnnie?" K-P asked into the silence.

"Christopher and I are going to the movies. My treat."

"Can I come?" Joey said. He was a little leery of Johnnie, but the motherfucker had Logan's loyalty. Get in good with Johnnie, he'd get in good with Logan.

"Ask Christopher," Johnnie said.

"I'm asking you."

"I don't care. I told you to ask my cousin."

"He'll say no."

Johnnie smiled. "Then you have your answer, dumb ass." He looked like an angel but sounded like Logan. "Come on, Christopher. Are you ready?"

Christopher held the book out to Big Joe. "Can you hold this for me? I'll get it later tonight."

"I'm off to a party, boy," he said, not taking the book. "Put it in your room. It'll be safe."

"I want a lock for my door, Boss," Christopher said.

"No," Rack answered. "Joey doesn't have one, and he's the president's son. Who the fuck are you?"

"A good kid," Big Joe barked.

Joey's heart sank. His brief sense of triumph wilted. If Rack hadn't spoken up, Big Joe might've declined Christopher's request. No chance of that now.

"I'll get it done tomorrow," Dad said.

"I'll hold the book for you," K-P offered.

"If he gets a lock, I want one," Joey demanded, once Christopher handed K-P the book, and walked away with Johnnie in tow.

Big Joe got to his feet. "You and Christopher would make a good team, if you'd stop competing against him, son."

"You love him more than me!"

"I don't," Big Joe denied. "I love you just as much. I just wish you weren't so much like—" Snapping his mouth shut, he rubbed his eyes and stared at Rack. "Never mind."

"Like Momma!" Joey snarled. "I know that's what you were going to say!"

A sad smile touched Big Joe's mouth. "You couldn't be less like her." He started off. "I'm hitting the road."

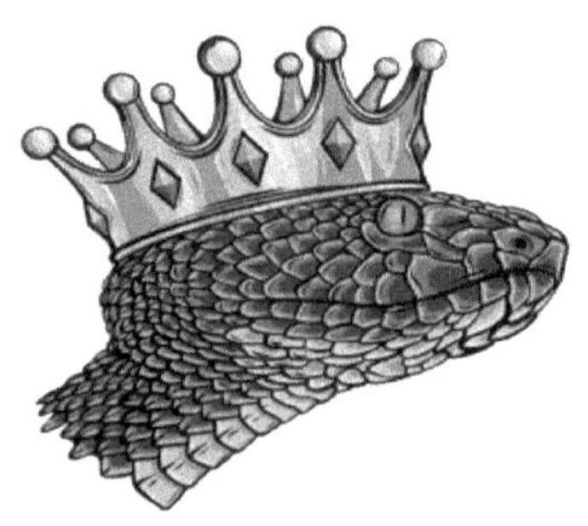

Two weeks later

"Are you ready?"

Joey nodded at Rack's question. He sat his beer on the

counter and glanced at the pool cues racked on the wall. He couldn't choose, not when anticipation crowded his thoughts. "Dad didn't forget anything, did he?"

He didn't want to act in haste and end up with his father beating his ass.

"No, boy." Rack drained his beer bottle and set it on the counter next to Joey's. Belching, he placed a hand on Joey's shoulder. "My ass is on the line, too."

With Big Joe and K-P gone, the club was quiet this evening. Still, there were spies in every corner. If a whisper of Christopher's endangerment blew in the air, Big Joe would blaze back into town and rain his wrath on all involved.

Rack flicked his gaze over the main room, then leaned closer to Joey. "Your old man would fucking kill me if he knew it was my idea."

Perhaps locking Christopher in the meatshack with a decomposing corpse was Rack's idea, but Joey was more than happy to carry it out. He hated that fuckhead, almost more than Logan. What Big Joe saw in that idiot, Joey wasn't sure. He'd shortly disabuse his father of the notion that Christopher was braver, stronger, and better. Ever since Christopher moved to the club, Big Joe forgot Joey was his only son. Fuck, his only child, and Joey meant to keep it that way, under all circumstances. Even murder.

Although Big Joe stuck his cock in more than a few cunts, he used protection. He said it was to keep his dick disease-free. Joey didn't buy it for a minute. His old man thought women were soft and gentle, in need of protection.

Joey saw it differently. Unfortunately, Christopher respected women because of the split-tails he'd grown up with. This reverence toward females won Big Joe's respect. Joey would take his father away from the Daddy-napper if it fucking killed him.

Wrapping his hand around his beer bottle, Joey shook. The cool condensation calmed him slightly. He drew in a breath, thinking of all that might go wrong.

His father was the biggest obstacle. But there was one more difficulty needing addressing.

"What about Johnnie?" he whispered. The pretty boy loved Logan, but he adored Christopher.

Before Joey drank, Rack grabbed the bottle and drained it. He released a heavy breath on a cloud of beer. "As long as he doesn't find out what you've done, you're safe from his wrath, boy."

"You're nothing but a fat, fucking coward."

Rack glared. "When I gave you the idea, I told you you'd be on your own. Big Joe would kill me for fucking with that green-eyed devil, but Cee Cee would find a way to keep me alive while he gutted me. If you don't want to take the fall, don't make the fucking leap."

At the mention of Cee Cee Caldwell, a shiver went through Joey. He cleared his throat. "He didn't gut Fred. He just shot him."

"Why, asshole?" Rack snapped.

"Those circumstances don't apply to me!"

"Why?" Rack persisted. "Tell me why, then look me in the fucking eye and swear you're not afraid to cross Cee Cee."

"Didn't you? You were a Scorpion. An officer. Now, you're a Dweller. You're still breathing."

"Logan paid my bounty."

"Dad was going to pay Fred's."

"Fred Sterling thought he could play both ends to the middle. He listened to Pattie because she has good pussy, then decided to tell Cee Cee about Logan's latest abuse of Christopher."

"It was a reasonable story."

"Told to an unreasonable lunatic about a man filled with irrational hatred. Had it been anyone other than Cee Cee, he might've bought Fred saying this was the first time he'd witnessed Logan hitting Christopher."

"We can argue all evening, Rack. You and Fred betrayed Cee Cee. Fred's been dead for four fucking years. You aren't. I can survive if I get on his bad side."

Dad had spies in the club; Joey was certain Cee Cee wasn't as vested in the Dwellers as he once was. Logan wanted Johnnie to run the Dwellers one day. Big Joe was determined to see Christopher do it. Rack wished it to be Joey; so did Joey.

But they'd take it one step at a time. First, they'd run Christopher off. Johnnie would have to die. Joey had some respect for his father's happiness. Losing asshole to death would destroy Big Joe. He liked Johnnie; he loved Christopher. However, Johnnie was by far the greater threat. With Christopher run out of Hortensia, Logan would push Big Joe to take Johnnie under his wing and teach him how to lead the Dwellers, once again sidelining Joey for a job he believed his.

"What are you about, kid?"

Krag's question drew Joey's attention to the bar. Christopher stood in the archway, a cigarette hanging from his mouth. At sixteen, he was tall and gangly. Joey hated the motherfucker, from the top of his ink black hair to the bottom of his booted feet. He despised his easy smile and sharp wit. He abhorred how all the girls flocked to him and most of the men favored him.

"Headin' to the cave," Christopher answered, loping toward the door.

"Go," Rack whispered. "He has to pass near the meatshack. Be ready." He rushed forward. "Christopher, come here."

He kept walking. "Fuck off."

"You impertinent little motherfucker. Boss and K-P not here and won't be for a fucking week. I'm in charge for the time being. Now, come the fuck here, twat face."

Christopher halted in front of the door.

For a moment, Joey wondered if he had the balls to leave anyway and suffer the consequences. But he huffed, spun around, and stomped to where Rack stood at the bar.

Joey rushed into the cold afternoon and hustled to the meatshack. Excitement made him so clumsy, he almost couldn't remove the padlock from the small, miserable shed that featured a lone window, little ventilation, and minimal light.

He threw the door open. A sickly-sweet smell of rotting meat and decaying flesh permeated the air. Joey swallowed the vomit rising in the back of his throat, controlling his need to gag just in time.

Christopher was heading down the pathway toward the edge of the property where civilization ended, and the forest began. Joey slipped on the far side of the shed, hardly able to contain his happy laughter.

Once Christopher left, Joey would be there to ease his father's disappointment. One thing Big Joe hated was cowardice. After Christopher pissed himself, screamed, and begged for rescue, Joey would finish the dismemberment. When Big Joe discovered how brave Joey was, he'd remember he didn't need Christopher as a son since he had one of his own. Dad would even overlook Joey killing a probate for the experiment, then locking Christopher in with the body, if he ever found out.

He would—

Where the fuck was Christopher? Five minutes had gone

by, if not longer. Had Joey been so lost—

A punch to the side of the face knocked Joey off his feet. Before he could scramble away, Christopher grabbed Joey's collar and dragged him up.

"What the fuck you're doin', slitherin' around like a regular snake motherfucker?"

Snake?

Keeping hold of his collar, Christopher punched Joey again. And again. Before he delivered a third hit, someone wrenched him away. In reflex, he released Joey, who crumpled to the ground.

Christopher yelped. "Rack, fuckhead!"

Groggy, Joey pulled himself to a sitting position.

"Ouch!" Rack screamed, though Joey's brain was too hit-fogged to understand what was happening. "I should fucking kill you."

"I will kill you," Christopher swore around a grunt.

"Get in there, you fucking waste of cum."

"No."

More struggles, curses, and name calling.

Joey shook his head, wanting to see the moment of Christopher's capitulation. Instead, he heard the slamming of the shed door.

"NO!" Christopher screamed. The small metal building trembled at his fierce pounding. "There's a dead man in here! Let me out!"

Satisfaction roared through Joey, and he exchanged a smirk with Rack at the sound of Christopher retching.

"Let me out, Rack," he begged a few minutes later. He sniffled. "I ain't ever did you nothin'. Let me out!"

"You're such a big man, motherfucker," Rack growled. "Cut up Holmes. If I like what I see tomorrow morning, you can come out."

Silence, then: "H-Holmes?" he squeaked. "My friend?"

Rack's eyes widened and he lifted a brow.

Joey shrugged. "I didn't want to kill one of my friends, asshole."

"How the fuck will I explain Holmes's absence to Joe, fuckwad?"

"Fuck." Joey hadn't thought of that. "I'll think of something."

The banging and screaming started again.

"If he doesn't shut the fuck up, somebody's going to hear him," Joey said, panic rising. Perhaps, he hadn't thought this out as deeply as he imagined.

Unlocking the padlock, Rack threw open the door.
The smell of death walloped Joey again. The terror on Christopher's face satisfied Joey to no end, although Rack's softening disappointed him.

"Th-thank you, Rack." Christopher started out of the meatshack. "You won't regret—"

Rack blocked him, undeterred by his height deficit, although Joey understood why. Christopher was taller. Rack was broader. "Shut the fuck up. I have a mind to kill you and bury your body in the fucking orchard."

"Do it!"

"Shut the fuck up, Joey," Rack ordered, without turning around. "You want to live, Christopher? Stop whining like a cunt. We'll let you out in the morning."

"Rack, please, don't make me stay in here with him. He was my friend."

"And he's dead because of it," Joey spat.

Christopher focused a teary gaze on Joey. His green eyes held grief and fear, but something else: hatred. Until then, Joey hadn't understood Christopher saw him as a rival, yet didn't feel one way or the other about him. It was probably why he always overlooked Joey's disdain. Christopher just hadn't given enough of a fuck to engage. Now, though…

Now…

"Kill him, Rack, or he'll kill me."

"In the morning, get your shit and leave," Rack told Christopher, ignoring Joey's order.

"I'll go home," Christopher said.

Unbelievably, Rack nodded. "When Joe returns, you'll tell him I ordered you to ready Holmes for disposal and you disobeyed me."

"But Boss won't let me patch in when I'm old enough," Christopher said on a sob.

"Stop putting on airs!" Rack snarled. "Talking all proper. Trying to sound like Johnnie. You're not him, idiot."

Joey laughed, the sound echoing in the falling dusk and drowning out Christopher's tears.

"Now, get in there like the fucking dog you are."

Rack's blow to Christopher's gut sent him reeling backward.

"In the morning, let that miserable fuckhead out," Rack instructed once the shed door was locked.

"What about Holmes?" Joey was having second thoughts about disposing of him.

"Just let Christopher out, fuckhead. Don't look in. I'll deal with Holmes myself after lunch. I'm visiting my woman."

At dawn, Joey walked a whore to the gate and let her out himself. Talbot was on gate duty, but accepted Joey's bribe to look the other way.

Instead of going back inside, he veered off down the pathway and headed to the meatshack. Once he removed the padlock, he pushed open the door. The smell walloped Joey.

"You shit on yourself?" Joey asked, sniggering and covering his nose with his hand.

Christopher staggered out. "Go in and find out."

"I'm smarter than you'll ever be. You won't get me in there and lock me in."

Instead of answering, Christopher bowed his head and started off. Joey locked the door and rushed behind Christopher, who walked to the gate and asked Talbot to let him out.

As the first rays of sun broke through dawn, Christopher shoved his hands in the pockets of his jeans, bowed his head, and started toward the main thoroughfare, a solitary figure with no friends and no home. Joey laughed in glee.

Hours later, Big Joe and K-P returned, intercepting Rack on his way to the meatshack. Unfortunately, he'd appointed Joey lookout since members were already asking about the whereabouts of both Holmes and Christopher. Rack worried if someone discovered Holmes's body, they'd assume Christopher was dead and call Big Joe first. His disappearance would be considered club business because Big Joe had taken responsibility for him.

Big Joe snatched the padlock key from Rack, handed it to K-P, and nodded toward the shed.

A moment later, K-P entered the metal structure. "Holy fuck. Joe!"

Grave blue eyes watered, and Big Joe heaved in a breath. "Christopher is missing—"

"Joe!"

Swallowing, Big Joe made his way forward. "Wait here."

Since he didn't give the order to either Rack or Joey, they both froze. When Big Joe walked out, he held a note in one hand and a head in the other. Joey might've been frightened at his father's fury, if he hadn't screamed at the sight of Holmes's head.

"Joe, I can explain—" Rack started.

Ice froze Dad's gaze. "I'd shut the fuck up if I were you, Rack."

He slammed the head against Joey's chest. Rearing back, Joey allowed it to fall to the ground. He vomited.

"Get rid of the fucking body, Joey. The pieces of the fucking body. Holmes was a good man!"

"Dad, no! Please!"

"If you don't find Christopher and get him back to the club, you'll be in smaller pieces than Holmes, Rack," Big Joe snarled, holding up the piece of paper, then shoving it in the pocket of his cut.

Smaller pieces? "Holmes's body was intact, Dad," Joey said. "What—"

Big Joe glared at him. "Let's ride out, K-P."

"You're leaving?" Joey managed, an idea forming in his head. Had Christopher actually cut up Holmes? "But where do you go every weekend?"

Dad ignored the question. "I'll deal with you both when I get back. If one hair's harmed on his head…" Voice trailing off, he snapped his mouth shut and stalked off.

"Dad!"

He kept walking, crushing Joey's soul.

"I'm a dead man," Rack said dully.

K-P smiled, but it wasn't nice. "Joe's more merciful than Cee Cee. If Christopher comes to harm…" He shrugged. "I suppose Cee Cee's forgiven your desertion, so who knows?"

Rack turned ghostie pale. "How'd you find out?"

"Talbot saw Joey head down the pathway after he walked a woman to the gate."

"That fuckhead!" Joey yelled. "I gave him $5.00 to shut up."

"You stupid little shit," Rack growled. "Talbot likes Christopher as much, or more than, Krag."

"How was I supposed to know?" Joey burst into tears. "My father will never forgive me."

K-P started off, but Joey grabbed his hand.

"Please, talk to Dad."

"Christopher already told him what happened."

"Which was?" Rack asked.

"Joey locked him in the fucking meatshack with the decomposing body of one of the few friends he had." K-P shook his head, his expression bleak. "Holmes was a good kid, and one of the few friends close to Christopher's age."

"He couldn't have felt that much for him if he…if he…" Joey swallowed.

"He's a survivor." K-P glowered between Joey and Rack. "Holmes was beyond saving, so what did you expect him to do?"

"Not that!" Joey said, his wail-snarl pathetic to his own ears. "I expected him to fall to pieces. Talk to Dad, K-P," he begged. "If not, Christopher will win."

The moment he chose to beat you and Rack at your games, you lost." K-P walked away.

For now, but Joey would not go gentle into the night.

Christopher wanted their fight to turn into war?

So be it.

ACTIV
ABC

Glancing at the clock on the wall, Dinah Fink read over her lesson plan. She'd had a long week at school, so she'd come home, prepared dinner for herself and Meggie, and taken a hot shower.

After Joe canceled their plans again this weekend, Dinah bathed her daughter, plied her with Tylenol, and put her to bed. Now, Dinah sat at the dinette table, drinking hot tea with honey and lemon and listening to a CD of country music hits.

Just as Delta Dawn by Tanya Tucker began, Dinah sat her pen down, satisfied she was finished with the lesson plan. One good thing in Joe disappointing her for a second Friday in a row. He'd arrive tomorrow morning with no explanation, but full of mischief and...and manliness.

Sometimes, she hated him, and yearned for revenge. He made her love him, then refused to do what she asked. Every time she'd visited that immoral club, those whores ignored her and crawled all over him. He'd laugh it off and swear he was hers.

Was he? He had a son! Joe wanted her to meet his boy, but she refused. She refused to care for a motherless child, even if the woman was dead.

Other times, she wondered how she'd allowed herself to get with child. She'd been so stupid! An upstanding good girl like herself who'd never had a lover before Joseph. If she'd been smart, she would demand he go to that loud black woman. Dinah was sure Joseph would've found the good time he wanted with her.

Instead, Dinah had gotten pregnant by him. Joe ultimately agreed that not only shouldn't Dinah meet his son, but the kid shouldn't know about Meggie.

As if she conjured her, her daughter stumbled into the living room and blinked. Thick, golden blonde curls tumbled about her and sleepiness reddened her bright blue eyes. At almost two-years-old, she looked like a little doll.

She toddled next to Dinah. She tugged on her sleeve and tried to scramble on her lap.

Dinah held up her hand.

"My bowel empty, Mommie, and my bottles want to come."

"How do you confuse those two words, I will never know," Dinah grumbled. Incorrect speech and grammar annoyed her beyond reason.

Meggie rubbed her eyes. She was so gorgeous, but still a living embodiment of Big Joe. Of Dinah's stupidity. She sniffled.

"Mommie cry?"

"Yes, baby," Dinah said tearfully. "But you can help Mommie to feel better if you're quiet."

"Daddy?"

Dinah stiffened. "Daddy isn't coming!" she screeched.

"Now, shut up. You're supposed to take care of me."

"Shhhh." Grinning, Meggie placed a finger over her mouth. "Quite."

"Quiet," Dinah corrected on a snarl. "Your daddy's ruined my life enough! Don't you do it, too."

When Meggie blinked again, Dinah resisted the urge to punch her in the face, opting instead for a slap across the cheek. She didn't see Meggie; she saw Joe.

Meggie yelped, so Dinah hit her again. In all her life, she'd never been so overwhelmed. She'd worked hard to earn her teaching degree. Just when she needed them most, her parents had been killed on her eighteenth birthday. An only child of only children who had no contact with their families. It was a tragedy that left Dinah alone and vulnerable to men like Joe Foy. Filthy bikers who promised her the world but surrounded themselves with sluts.

"Mommie!" Meggie sobbed, reaching her little arms up.

Dinah shoved her to the floor. When Meggie faceplanted on the carpet, she smiled in satisfaction. She wasn't sure how long she watched Joe's daughter cry and beg for her, but finally satisfied she lifted Meggie into her arms and kissed her wet face.

"I'm sorry, my love. It's your daddy's fault, but I shouldn't be mean to you. You'll love me when no one else will. You already do."

Meggie leaned against Dinah's shoulder. "Love Mommie!"

"You do," Dinah whispered, wrapping her arms around her little girl. "You always will. You'll love me more than you ever love anyone else. Isn't that right, love?"

"Yes, Mommie," Meggie sniffled, her speech almost perfect. "I want Daddy!"

"No! No, you don't," Dinah shrieked. "He's mean, Meggie. He hurts you."

"Daddy!"

Wrapping Meggie's hair around her hand, Dinah started to wrench her head back. The wringing doorbell interrupted her.

God! Joe arrived early. If Meggie told him…God!

He'd kill Dinah.

The bell rang around.

"Daddy!" Meggie called.

"Shhh, baby," Dinah soothed, desperate. Carrying Meggie, she hurried to the door. "It's okay. Don't cry anymore. I know you fell and got a boo-boo—"

"But—"

Dinah opened the door and gasped. Reverand Sharper Banks brushed past her, followed by Logan Donovan.

"Ten, twelve more years and she'll turn a good profit," he said, nodding to Meggie.

Reverand Banks glared at the man. "Shut the fuck up, Logan."

Logan stiffened, and his eyes burned with such hatred a chill slithered through Dinah. She held Meggie tighter and kissed her cheek, regretting her earlier loss of control.

"Go to your room, sweetheart." She gave her another kiss and set her on her feet. "Mommie will be in as soon as I can."

"'Kay, Mommie," she said, traces of tears lingering in her voice. She ran away, unaware of the winds of violence brewing between the two men.

"I-I called you, Reverend Banks," Dinah said with as much equanimity as possible. "You didn't inform me you were bringing a guest." Especially Logan Donovan.

The minister gave her a half-smile but didn't respond.

"Why am I here, Sharper?" Logan demanded.

Sharper's eyes gleamed. "To see Meggie. Joe's daughter."

Logan's gray eyes widened, then narrowed. "Why are you

here?”

“Dinah called me. Joe isn’t falling into line as she thought he would when she opened her pussy to him.”

Dinah gasped at the crudity. “I am not that Roxanne woman.”

“You’re not better than her, bitch,” Sharper snarled.

“Is that K-P’s cunt? The one who pushed out his half-breed?”

Sharper stiffened. “Shut the fuck up before I cut your head off and throw it in the garbage.”

“I’m just calling it as I see it,” Logan said in dismissal. He held up his hands when Sharper took a step toward him. “I’m agreeing with you, Sharper. I give her points for ferocity. I tried my fucking best to break her.” He shook his head sadly. “No matter the names I called her, what I threatened, the most I got from her were tears.”

“I can only imagine some of the names,” Sharper seethed with dislike.

“I’ll bet you can, boy,” Logan said with a laugh.

Wildness crept into Reverend Banks’s eyes, but Logan laughed harder.

“I can kill you, Logan, but then I’ll have to kill Joe’s cunts.”

“I beg your pardon?” Dinah said with as much dignity as possible, sorry she’d ever called Sharper Banks.

“Not granted,” he said coldly, sparing Dinah a brief glance before focusing on Logan again. “Shut the fuck up or you, Dinah, and Meggie are dead.”

“You’d kill Joe’s girl as much as he loves her?” Logan asked, appalled.

“He does love me,” Dinah said with meaning. “My death would—”

“Not you, stupid bitch,” Sharper snapped. “Meggie. I don’t give a fuck if he loves you or not. He adores the child.” His nostrils flared. "I still owe him for double-crossing me on my wedding day."

"Rack saved me," Logan reminded Sharper, the words mystifying Dinah. "Since you hate me now, why would you make my Joe suffer by harming his daughter?"

"You don't give a rat's ass about that little bitch. I could run a stake through her and it wouldn't matter, Logan."

Trembles assailed Dinah. "I've made a mistake! Please leave."

They ignored her.

"If anything happened to Meggie, it would destroy Joe," Logan argued.

"Meggie?" Dinah yelled. "What about me?"

"He'd survive," Sharper said with certainty.

"Get out."

"I've thought about your dilemma. How you'd like to tie Joe to your side forever."

Dinah wouldn't dignify that with an answer.

"Even for us, Joe has been getting a little hard to manage," Sharper continued. He dug in his expensive suit pocket and came up with a syringe. He held it out to Dinah.

"Drugs?"

"Drugs?" Logan echoed, thoughtful.

"It's a small amount," Sharper reassured her. "We don't want him addicted. Just manageable."

"Joe's a drug user, too," Dinah said stiffly, betrayal slicing through her. "He's a whoremonger, a criminal, and an addict."

She didn't see Logan's fist until it was a fraction from her. It slammed into her mid-section, and she crumpled to the floor. Logan dragged her to her feet then threw her against the wall. Weeping, she bounced and fell to the carpet.

"Joe's never used drugs a day in his life!" Logan roared,

looming above her. Bending, he snatched her up. "I should kill you for smearing his good name."

"No!" Dinah sobbed. "Think of Meggie."

"I am. Joe's daughter doesn't need a sniveling, self-righteous cunt to raise her."

"We can kill her and send the child to Roxanne," Sharper suggested. The syringe had disappeared.

"No!" Dinah screamed again. "No! I'll give the drugs to Joe. Shoot him up while he's asleep. We both want the same thing. I just want to make sure he comes home to me. You need him to listen to your ideas. He trusts me most of all. I'm the obvious choice for the job."

Sharper and Logan exchanged glances.

"She's right, Logan. It's only a small amount, administered every now and then."

"But what if he starts to depend on the drugs?" Dinah asked.

Sharper smiled indulgently. "He'll visit you more often, Dinah."

"Then he'd love me. Perhaps, our broken engagement might be salvaged, and we'll finally marry. I'll start this weekend."

"He's been called away for a run," Sharper said with sadness.

"That bastard," Dinah hissed. "He didn't have the decency to let let me know."

"It was last minute."

"I don't care, Reverend Banks. He keeps disappointing me and hurting me. I want him to suffer."

Logan studied every angle of her face. "Did you call Sharper for help with Joe or revenge against him because he's spurned you?"

"He hasn't spurned me! He's filthy. He wants his cock

sucked and his tongue between my legs. I'm a good girl, a God-fearing woman. I refuse to indulge his smut."

"Answer my question, Dinah."

"I don't know why I called Sharper. Maybe for help or for revenge. Reverend Banks promised if I ever needed him, he was a phone call away the day I spoke to him when he congratulated me on Meggie's birth."

"Joe doesn't like Sharper."

"As if I care! Fuck Joe," she spat. "Fuck Meggie. I hate them both. I want them to die! He left me, and so will she. She should've been a boy. If she had, Joe would love me. I hate her. She's ruined my life. I want Joe to suffer. I want to make him suffer. He made me love him, then he wouldn't do what I asked. I hate him!"

The next morning, Dinah crawled to Meggie's room and found her baby girl in bed with the covers up to her throat. Sobbing, she pulled the blankets down and felt for Meggie's pulse. It was there, but weak thanks to all the Tylenol. If Meggie pulled through, Dinah wouldn't ever be mean to her again.

In the meantime, she dragged her naked, bruised, abused body to her own bedroom and struggled into the shower. Joe had merely asked for oral sex. Logan and Sharper took that and so much more from her.

They stole a piece of her sanity. She'd never be the same again. For that alone, Joe would pay more than she'd ever meant him to when she'd called Sharper last week.

PART FOUR

Of Mice & Motherpuckers

CHAPTER 34

CHRISTOPHER

Roseburg was the timber capital of the world in southern Oregon's Umpqua River Valley. It was the county seat of Douglas and its most populous town.

Christopher didn't make a habit of visiting, though he'd passed through on his way to other places. Now, it would serve as an out-of-the way meeting point. Mort had yet to talk to Brooks because of personal issues.

Once, Christopher would've ordered him to shove the shit aside and focus on club business.

Once.

Before he'd gotten used to his life with his wife and kids. Megan had been out of the hospital for two weeks, though he took her every day to see Jo. The day after the dinner with the Davises, Rule confessed to what happened on Turn Creek Bridge.

Christopher decided to do damage control to save Rule and Ryan's miserable fucking lives and seized the first available opportunity to take care of business. The moment she reminded him of her appointment two days later, Christopher began making plans. Instead of accompanying her, which infuriated him even more, he arranged for Bunny to drive her and seized the moment to get a bead on the situation. He would find a way to make both those lil' motherfuckers pay.

"Come on, Outlaw," Derby called.

Christopher had been waiting on his idling bike in the parking lot of a bar with a closed sign on it. He had to force away his worry and fear for Megan and focus.

"You sure you want to do this?"

"Fuck, yeah." Christopher lit a smoke, killed the engine, then dismounted. "I wouldna have suggested it if I wasn't fucking sure."

The sound of motorcycles drew closer. Derby sighed. "Dez and the other Devil officers are already inside."

Puffing on his cigarette, Christopher glanced around. "Where the fuck they parked?"

"Around back. Their emblems are painted on their bikes. They don't want to leave anything to chance."

Christopher glared at Derby but didn't bother responding since five bikes turned into the parking lot. He nodded to Derby, indicating their plan was now in effect, and turned, heading into the one-story brick and concrete building.

Inside, an oversized bar, tables and chairs crowded the little place. A stage dominated the front with a door on each side, where signs indicated the men's and women's bathrooms.

Dez and his four club brothers took up all the stools in front of the bar. Four naked girls sat at a table near the stage, while two more stood behind the bar, talking to the Scorched Devil members.

Dez glanced over his shoulder and met Christopher's gaze, losing his smile, and jumping to his feet.

Christopher wasn't sure how much Derby had filled Dez in, but he didn't have time to go into detail. He walked to the bar, searching for an ashtray. Not seeing one, he squeezed the cherry to extinguish his cigarette and stuck it in his cut.

"Not all you motherfuckers might go home," he said. "I'm gonna try to get all us out alive. Follow my fuckin' cues."

Dez paled. "Outlaw—"

The door opened, and Derby led Bash in, along with four motherfuckers Christopher didn't know. Fuck, he didn't know motherfucking Bash. He knew of him, but it wasn't the same fucking thing.

Bash's spurs amused Christopher. Seeing his bandaged head didn't. A leather duster hid the evidence of a shoulder injury.

"Little brother," Bash greeted cheerfully, holding out his hand and wincing.

"Ain't here for a family fuckin' reunion, so put your motherfuckin' hand down," Christopher ordered.

A Black dude stepped next to Bash and glared at Christopher. "Show some fucking respect to your elders."

Christopher opened his mouth to speak, but the resemblance to Mortician and Digger caught his attention immediately. He narrowed his eyes.

"Cleaner," Bash said, "it's fine." He looked at the two girls behind the bar. "You two bitches, come suck Cleaner's cock—"

"No," Christopher said. "Those two for me."

Bash paused, then nodded, a slow smile spreading across his face.

"Suppose I want one of those sluts?" Cleaner sneered. "The little blonde."

Derby shifted his weight. The overhead light gleamed off his sweaty face.

"You can want who the fuck you want," Christopher said. "You get the bitches I fuckin' let you have."

"Of course," Bash's jovial words interrupted whatever Cleaner might have said.

Christopher glanced at the Devils. Dez and the other four men were no more than thirty-five. The club didn't take risks or get out of their comfort zone. They strove for neutrality, offering no benefit to anyone. It made them too weak to support the Dwellers and sitting ducks to clubs like the Scorpions.

"Dez, send your VP and RC out for food." Christopher dug in his back pocket and got his wallet, pulling out five hundred-dollar bills. "Thanks for the job last week."

Surprise marched across Dez's face. Christopher swore if the motherfucker fucked up, he'd put him out of his goddamn misery.

"I expect my cut, Dez," Derby inserted.

"O-o-okay," Dez stuttered, his ruddy complexion reddening further. He handed each of his boys a hondo. "Heath, Otis, you're on food duty."

Once the two men left, Derby played host and got everyone drinks, then introduced each of the girls. Adette was the blue-eyed blonde, taller than Megan and nowhere near as beautiful but she'd do. Sadie was the brown-eyed redhead, shorter than Kendall and nowhere as beautiful but she'd fucking do.

The others were Bea, Ava, Violet, and Dot.

Bash finished his bottle of beer in three gulps. "Three presidents, a sergeant-at-arms, and an enforcer. I'm here with only myself, my enforcer—" he nodded to Cleaner— "and three regular members. I'm wondering if I should feel threatened, Outlaw."

"Feel anymotherfuckingway you want," Christopher said, sipping his beer. "You either a bitch-ass fuckbag if you don't feel equal to other fuckin' presidents with your enforcer and Dez's enforcer."

Cleaner got to his feet and slid his hand into his cut.

Before the motherfucker moved, Christopher jumped up, piece in hand and aimed at Cleaner.

"I ain't came here to spill no fuckin' blood, son of Sharper fuckin' Banks, but you workin' on my last fuckin' nerve with your bullshit. If Bash ain't tellin' you, let my ass clue you the fuck in. You disrespect a fuckin' president, friend or foe, you disrespect the fuckin' club. I got every fuckin' right to kill you."

"What makes you think you'll get out alive?" Cleaner said, not denying that he was Sharper's son. "Only Derby seems ready to back you up. Dez and his motherfuckers are about to piss themselves."

Christopher pulled the trigger, hitting Cleaner in the shoulder, then shoving the barrel against Bash's head. "You like fuckin' livin'? Cuz I might not make it out the fuck alive, but Ima take you and fuckin' Cleaner with me."

"Cleaner, sit the fuck down and shut up," Bash ordered on a swallow, his hands up.

"And he ain't talkin' about your fuckin' moanin'."

Hand on his shoulder, Cleaner dropped into the seat, pain etched on his face.

"Tell your motherfuckers to show their pieces, Bash," Christopher said, jiggling his gun against Bash's temple.

"Fuck you, Outlaw," Cleaner said. "We're not showing you a goddamn thing."

Christopher cocked the hammer. The girls backed away and crowded on the stage.

"You fired first, Christopher," Bash said, his voice shaking. "It could've precipitated retaliation."

"I ain't here to go round and round. Neither am I here to conduct long drawn-out conversations before I fuck a motherfucker up. I don't have time for that. I did it this time in the interest of peace. What you and your motherfuckers not doing is jerkin' my fuckin' chains. I don't want to hear Cleaner afuckingain if I don't address him. Underfuckinstand?"

"Yes," Bash said. "He understands. He won't insult you again."

Christopher snatched his gun away from Bash's head, decocked it, and sat. Once, he'd allowed Megan's stepfuckhead to walk away and almost lost her. Deep down, he had the feeling he would regret not blowing Bash the fuck away. However, he had to unfuck some shit and put the word out to keep the boys safe.

First, though he needed to check something. Sometimes, he had to play defense to plan his offense.

Christopher sat. "Adette?" He sipped his beer. "Sadie?"

The blonde and redhead walked down the three steps in front of the stage and came to him. His heart pounding, he gulped more beer. Sweat coated his palms; he brushed them over his jeans. Before he changed his mind, he placed his arm around Adette and pulled her onto his lap.

However, Bash and his motherfuckers were operating on a different fucking level, so Christopher had to do the same.

It had been almost two decades since another woman...a memory of Kendall on his lap rose in his head and he scowled.

When Megan was better, he'd tell her. Hopefully, she wouldn't lock him out of her pussy too long. She...fuck...

Carefully, he tucked hair behind Adette's ear and smiled at

her. Derby's shock would've been hilarious if this wasn't so serious. Christopher tipped her chin up, made himself leer at her tits, though he only saw Megan's.

"I've always heard you were devoted to that cunt, Outlaw," Bash said casually.

Christopher pressed his lips together, adding another infraction to the motherfucker's growing list.

"Never believed them myself," Bash continued. "You, Dez?"

"Uh..." Dez gulped.

"Outlaw tries to practice monogamy," Derby said, sounding bored. "He's faithful more often than not. No man enjoys one slit for the rest of his fucking life."

Derby had already escaped with his life once for fucking with Megan. Which reminded Christopher.

"Your former brother, Cole, would've still been livin' if he hadn't fucked with Megan."

"His former...Cole was really a Scorpion?" Dez asked.

"Ain't talkin to you, motherfucker."

Dez had one fucking job—follow Christopher's cues. If Dez fucked up the instructions, Christopher would serve him his fucking ass.

"But—"

"Shut the fuck up, Dez," Derby ordered.

Dez snapped his mouth shut. However, his unexpected question removed the element of surprise, allowing Bash to realize Christopher was trying to ferret information.

"If he was a former Scorpion, his death is no affront to me," Bash said. "But back to you, your bitch, and your cock, little brother."

Christopher drew in a breath. His closest support club to help clean away blood and dump bodies was over an hour away, north of Eugene; the closest Dweller chapter was in

Medford, a few miles from the California border.

If shit went south and he was killed, he'd just disappear. Derby would do right by him if he wasn't fucked up, too.

The longer the meeting dragged on, the higher the chance blood would be spilled. Christopher needed to move forward with his plan.

Adette remained on his lap. His tactics left him repulsed. Yet to play Bash's game, he needed an even field.

Unable to bring himself to kiss Adette's lips, he skimmed her chin, then looked at Bash. If Christopher didn't know better, the motherfucker looked angry. Perhaps, he was onto Christopher's game.

He held out his hand. Sadie took it, and he pulled her to his side. He glanced at her from head to toe. Seeing her shaved pussy, he asked what was allegedly inquired of most redheads. "Your pussy hair red, too, babe?"

The other motherfuckers snickered.

Sadie stood between him and Bash, so Christopher couldn't see his expression. But, then, the uneasiness left her eyes and she glanced over her shoulder.

"A slut with a juicy ass," Bash said. "My cock can't take it."

"Get up, babe," Christopher whispered to Adette. "Grin and rub my back. When I tell you to go, don't ask questions. Derby'll get your money to you."

A smile plastered on her face, Adette slid off his lap, then shimmied behind him and began skimming her fingers over his nape.

"Sadie, come here," Christopher ordered, wanting to move Adette away when she draped her arms around his neck.

Once Sadie reached his side, he pulled her onto his lap, following the same procedure he had with Adette. To him, his actions with Adette and Sadie were a process to reach an end goal. Bash's reaction to Sadie was completely different from the one he'd had toward Adette, proving to Christopher Bash was fucking clueless. His response had been because of Adette.

That was all he needed to know.

He'd extract Derby from this powder keg. "Derby, escort these two bitches to the motel and rent them a room. I know you got to hit the road, brother. I'll call you when I get home."

Glancing away, Derby sniffed and thought for a moment. "Adette, you and Sadie Uber to the place at the edge of town," he said finally. "We'll catch up to you in a couple of hours."

Adette bent and brushed her lips over Christopher's. He restrained his recoil, then forced himself to watch her leave.

"We need more beers, Derby," he said.

He'd promised Rule he wouldn't beat his ass for stabbing Bash after the little motherfucker confessed at CJ's urging. But Christopher felt like clamping a strait jacket on him and locking him in a rubber room.

And Ryan?

Though he hadn't gone to Val or confronted Ryan yet, he wanted to kill that little assfuck. Except it would break his sister's heart.

However, even though he worried about Megan and wanted to remain at her side until she was completely better, she was out of the hospital and truly on the mend, allowing Christopher to breathe easier and think.

According to Rule, he'd gone to the mall, then decided he wanted to walk to the bridge. When he got there, he happened upon Ryan and Bash. Shit turned ugly and Bash began strangling Ryan, so Rule was forced to stab Bash in the shoulder.

Christopher had listened in silence to his son's confession, not pointing out all the fucking inconsistencies in Rule's story.

Breaking it down, he'd thought about the flawed technicalities—Rule preferred his own fucking company to a mall. He definitely wouldn't have gone just for shits and giggles. And what about the weapon? A knife? Perhaps, Christopher hadn't realized how fucking far Rule took his religious beliefs, but he did know his son didn't carry a weapon. How many times had he seen Rule check his pockets before hanging up his jackets or coats? Countless. He'd never carried a blade.

If he was going to a place where he anticipated bad shit? Then, he could see Rule selecting a blade from the gun room, where Christopher had a small cabinet of knives. Megan and their children knew the door code on the off chance the house was ever breached and they needed to defend themselves.

Finally, he'd thought about the procedurals. Camera footage had been erased and the tracking signals intercepted. That shit had Matilda, or Rebel, written all over it. Unfortunately, the overwhelming flaw in the monitoring had yet to be addressed. If those two could so easily hack their tracers, other motherfuckers could, too.

Combined, the evidence fired Christopher's suspicions. What fucking reason did Bash have to contact Ryan? He'd thought maybe it had to do with Molly. He understood a man's need to protect his girl.

Ryan was neither a man nor protective, so that shit didn't fly.

Besides, Rule discussed Bash with an odd mixture of familiarity and distaste. As if he knew, or knew of, the motherfucker.

Whatever else Christopher didn't know, he was fucking

certain: 1. Ryan already knew Bash; 2. Rule had known of Ryan's with meeting Bash in advance; 3. Bash was fucking with the kids for a reason; 4. Christopher bet it had something to do with him; 5. Bash would've struck if it was club related; he would've targeted Bitsy or Val if his beef was with them; 6. Johnnie and Brooks mentioned Megan, Kendall, and Mattie; 7. Lying motherfuckers surrounded him; 8. Bash was trying to get to Megan; 9. Bash, Johnnie, Brooks, and now Cleaner, had a fucking date with the meatshack; 10. He was counting the days to Ryan's 18th birthday, still eighteen months away, but what-the-fuck-ever.

Once the beers were replenished, Christopher made another show of good faith. His anger toward Rule and Ryan inched a little higher.

"Why don't Cleaner go see to the wound?" he suggested casually. "It was a .22, but the motherfucker still got a foreign object in him."

After the initial moaning, he'd shut the fuck up. His eyes, however, burned with hatred.

"I'm fine," Cleaner gritted.

Christopher shrugged. He'd gotten his first piece of evidence by Bash's reaction to Adette. He was lurking because he wanted something from Megan. It didn't have anything to do with Kendall or Mattie as Brooks explained. Maybe, they were being used as bait, but this had to do with his wife. Adette and Sadie weren't as gorgeous as Megan and Kendall but they resembled enough to where Bash could see his wife and sister-in-law in Derby's two strippers.

He'd already seen to a personal problem. Now, he'd insert a little club business before looping back to the two little assfucks he shared blood with.

"What issues are you havin' with the Scorched Devils?" Christopher asked.

Dez slid his chair back, angling himself slightly behind Christopher. Eugene, the road captain, and Kenny, the enforcer, looked ready to cry.

"None that concerns you, Outlaw," Bash said blandly. "They aren't a Dweller support club or under your protection."

"Not formally," Christopher said. "But they are under the protection of Derby's club, and you know the Burning Hounds is a Dweller support club."

"Do I? My club's in Salt Lake City. How do I know what's going on in your territory?"

Christopher got the cigarette he hadn't finished earlier, lit it, and enjoyed the menthol taste. "Why the Scorps moved from Virginia to Utah?"

Bash narrowed his eyes. "Because some motherfucker blew up the fucking building when most of our members were there to celebrate our 30th year. It nearly wiped us out."

Releasing smoke from his nostrils, Christopher nodded. "Wonder who the fuck that coulda been."

"I'd say the same fuckhead who killed my daddy and five of my brothers," he snapped.

"Ain't hurtin' my fuckin' feelins claimin' none of those assfucks, Bash," Christopher said. "Cee Cee fucked with Megan."

Bash shifted, fear flickering in his eyes. "Should I take this as a confession, Outlaw?"

"I don't give a fuck how the fuck you take it." He skated between the speech he'd worked so hard to learn and the one he'd grown into and felt most like himself. But he was fucking floundering, so off his game, he was like a duck out of water. He wanted to be with Megan. She hadn't looked right to him when she went downstairs to see him off.

Fuck, he was going to shake the fuck out of Rule and knock the fuck out of Ryan.

"Brooks told me," Christopher announced, tired of going around in circles and reaching no conclusion.

The color dropped from Bash's face, and he choked. "What?"

"Everything," Christopher stressed, though the motherfucker hadn't told him anything close to the fucking truth. Of that, he had no doubt.

"We'd like the details of the peace agreement," Dez inserted.

"Dez—" Derby started.

"No, Derby. Outlaw is standing up for us—"

"Shut the fuck up," Christopher snarled.

"No, brother," Dez said, thinking he was doing right when he was fucking up direly. "It isn't fair your wife, sister-in-law, and niece, are in the line of fire because Brooks and Johnnie can't reach a peace accord on our behalf."

Bash glanced from Christopher to Dez, then back at Christopher, who was so fucking furious his pulse pounded. He discarded the cigarette in the ashtray, considering how painful he'd make Dez's death.

Confusion knit Bash's brow. "I beg your pardon?"

"The peace accord, Bash," Cleaner said. "The one Johnnie and Bash visited the club for at the beginning of the year."

"Yes, I remember." Bash laughed nervously. "The visit that had to do with us backing off the Devils."

A muscle ticking in his jaw, Christopher ground his teeth together. He'd been so fucking close to the truth. Until Dez opened his fucking mouth afuckingain.

Motherfucker didn't need his fucking tongue. Or his brain.

"If your club's in Salt Lake City, why the fuck you movin' in on the Devils?" Christopher asked, mentally flipping a coin to see if he'd relieve Dez of his tongue or brain first.

Tails.

Fuck, it was the tongue.

"The Devils are a small outfit that bothers no one," Derby said, inserting himself deeper. "They are in our region, Bash. Yet, you've killed two of their members. Do you want our territory?"

Christopher leaned forward. "Or do you just want my fuckin' attention?"

"The last thing I want is your attention, Outlaw," Bash said calmly.

"Fuck you," Christopher barked, losing his patience. A little over three hours separated him and Megan. He needed to hit the road to see her and make sure she was fine. "If you ain't wantin' my fuckin' attention, why the fuck you was stranglin' my fuckin' nephew?"

The second time Bash displayed a combination of shock and fear.

"You after something, assfuck, and I'm involved some fuckin' kinda way." Christopher slammed his fist on the table. Bottles slid into each other, but none toppled. "If my boy ain't fuckin' stabbed you and knocked you the fuck out, you woulda killed my nephew." As well as Rule. "Ain't no motherfucker afraid of me if he fuckin' stalkin' my fuckin' family. That's the quickest fuckin' way to get you hurt and brought to the meatshack to be dissected."

Dez, Derby, Otis, and Kenny shifted uneasily.

Bash leaned back in his seat and studied Christopher. "I met you when you were a baby. The last time I was face-to-face with you, you were about four and I was twelve."

"You coulda been face-to-face with me last fuckin' night. Ain't changin' my position."

Bash's mouth turned down. "You don't miss a beat, do

you? Most motherfuckers would've been shocked to hear of meetings years ago with their brothers."

"Ain't most motherfuckers, Bash."

"I've always heard you were devoted to your bitch," Bash said, flipping the script, still trying to throw Christopher off-kilter. "I wonder how she'd feel if she knew you intend to fuck Adette and Sadie."

"Betrayed," Cleaner said, laughing.

Christopher had given them the ammunition, but he'd needed some of his own. "Megan Big Joe girl," he said casually, deciding to address the fucking bed he'd made for himself.

Distaste marred Bash's face and anger lit his eyes.

Christopher pulled up a photo of Megan on his phone. She wore a short red leather dress with red stilettos, showing so much of her beautiful skin that his cock hardened.

He was committing so many egregious offenses against her today. He held the picture in front of Bash's face. When he laid his phone on the table, the combination of lust and hate lighting Bash's eyes startled Christopher. Lust he'd expected and he'd seen the anger when he looked at Adette. But fucking hate?

He scrubbed a hand over his face. "Another reason I called the meeting was to tell you all contact with Ryan ends tofuckingday. Same with my boy. Rule was defendin' his cousin."

"He stabbed me and gave me a fucking concussion."

"It fuckin' ends tofuckinday," Christopher reiterated. "You got beef with my boy? Take it up with me. If you wanna retaliate, stab my fuckin' ass?"

"What?"

"The exact fuckin' spot Rule stabbed you, motherfucker. If you go deeper or fuck me up, your entire fuckin' club fucked.

Whether you motherfuckers picked off one-by-one or fucked up together, it will fuckin' go."

"They'd have to find us first," Cleaner said, still not fucking passed out.

Fuck, Christopher should've used his other gun.

"Wouldn't be fuckin' hard," Christopher said with a shrug. He knew it was in Salt Lake City. That was enough.

"Dead men can't talk," the motherfucker said. "You think we'd let these motherfuckers walk out alive? Or the bitches?"

"First of fuckin' all, I ain't knowin' exactly where the fuck your club at now, Cleaner. Second of fuckin' all, other motherfuckers know the location. Ryan. Johnnie. Brooks. You opened your fuckin' mouth and said those last two motherfuckers visited you at your fuckin' club."

Cleaner looked away.

"Daddy wanted to form an alliance with you," Bash said into the silence.

"Do you gotta refer to that motherfucker as Daddy, assfuck?" Christopher asked with a snort. "You fifty-eight. By now, he should've moved to Dad."

Bash glowered at Christopher. "Very fucking funny."

"You see me fuckin' laughin'? Listen up, Bash, I ain't givin' a good fuck if you call him Daddy Dearest, I was just askin' a fuckin' question. I'm gonna have Brooks send you an agreement between our clubs. You clearin' the fuck out of the region. You leavin' Dez, Derby, Brooks, Johnnie, Ryan, and Rule the fuck alone. I'm gonna send you a quarter rock. You sign and accept my fuckin' money, then fuck over me like you doin' Johnnie, Ima fuckin' cleave you in two with the fuckin' chainsaw, then blow your club the fuck up." Christopher sipped his beer, calmer. Maybe, he'd just cut the tip of Dez's tongue off as a warning.

"Suppose there are other motherfuckers I want revenge

on?"

Finally. They were getting to the heart of the matter. "First, I wanna know what my woman did."

Bash jumped to his feet and stared at Christopher, his mouth dropping open in shock.

"She hasn't done anything," Cleaner said.

Christopher didn't take his gaze from Bash. "According to you, Cleaner. Bash feel different."

"He's never met—"

"He saw my woman in that blonde. Adette. He wasn't angry at that bitch. He saw Megan in her."

They were all staring at him like he'd grown two fucking heads.

"Tell me I'm fuckin' wrong. I ain't the most educated motherfucker, but I ain't a stupid one."

"Outlaw—"

"Shut the fuck up, Bash. If you thinkin' about fuckin' with Megan, consider that shit very carefully. I'm fuckin' thinkin' you wanna fuck with her cuz of Big Joe."

"Jesus Christ," Bash breathed.

Christopher got to his feet and stalked to Bash. As expected, his brothers rose and flanked the motherfucker.

"Get your fucking asses over here," Derby ordered, arriving at Christopher's right side.

A moment later, Dez, Eugene, and Kenny slinked over.

"You wanna die, slow and painful?" Christopher asked. "Or you want me to shoot you like I did your fuckin' daddy? He was already fuckin' dead when I got him to the meatshack. Cuttin' him up wasn't as much fun without his fuckin' heart beatin.'"

Bash started trembling.

"Look me in the fuckin' eye, motherfucker, man-to-man, and tell me what the fuck you got against my wife? What the fuck Big Joe did to you?"

"Nothing, Outlaw," Bash whispered.

"If you fuck with Megan, you know how I'm gonna kill you? Slow. Stick an icepick in your knees. Rip out your fingernails. Slice away a hand. Maybe, a foot." He squinted. "You fuckin' hearin' me, Bash?"

"Are you declaring war, Outlaw?" Cleaner asked.

"Nope. I'm declaring my recipe to fuck up Bash if he fuck with Megan."

Bash cleared his throat. "I have nothing against your woman," he said evenly. "She, Kendall, and Mattie seemed like the perfect targets to scare Johnnie to make him continue to pay me to keep the terms of the peace agreement."

"That you fuckin' broke," Christopher pointed out. "You killed two Devils."

"I didn't realize you had such an interest in them."

"You don't have nothing against Megan?" Christopher asked.

Bash shook his head. "Not a thing."

"Fine." He returned to his seat.

Believing a lying motherfucker wasn't Christopher's style, but most of his fucking club insisted on peace. He didn't even trust Cash and Johnnie enough to clue them the fuck in on his destination. Stretch wasn't really a killer and aligning with Christopher would put him in opposition with Cash. In turn, that might hurt Fee. Val was with CJ, Rory, Ryan, and a few other sons at the mall for Christmas shopping. Mort was dealing with personal problems. And Christopher didn't trust Digger for a different reason. He was sure the motherfucker had said something to Megan the night he'd caught her on the phone with him and Mortician. She refused to say what.

It was the same fucking reason Derby was with him. As penance for that fucking night.

"I didn't mean Meggie when I referred to revenge against someone else."

Bash's familiarity didn't escape Christopher. Calling Megan Meggie and Matilda Mattie.

"Who the fuck you meant then?"

"Ryder, Axel, and Ransom," Bash announced, and yeah that shocked the fuck out of Christopher.

His eyes widened.

Bash smirked. "Those three little motherfuckers pushed me over the fucking bridge and into the water."

Christopher jerked. "Rule didn't fuckin' say his brothers were with him."

Immediately, Bash's smugness fell away, and he scratched his goatee, then pursed his lips. Shifted his weight. Sipped his beer.

Christopher narrowed his eyes. "Wait a fuckin' minute. You was there another fuckin' time?"

"I have a question, little brother."

"Answer me, assfuck!"

"How the fuck do you figure out everything?" Bash asked with irritation, giving away his dumb ass.

He had to die. Maybe not today. But soon. Case fucking closed.

"Suppose I want more than a quarter rock?" Bash asked. "Suppose I want that amount for each demand? Each infraction? Each person?"

He'd expected the counter. "You can fuckin' suppose all the fuck you want to. Ain't no fuckin' way. I am willin' to give you two rocks for everything we discussed. On one condition."

"And that is?"

"Leave Molly the fuck alone." Christopher was hoping he'd get a reaction from one of the other men, but only Bash froze. Tom Harris wasn't there. "Ain't cuttin' your cock off for what the fuck you did to her. If you fuckin' do it afuckingain, I fuckin' will. She's Ryan's bitch and CJ's friend. Most of fuckin' all, she's a fuckin' kid."

"I see."

"Do you, Bash?"

"Johnnie called me big brother. I kind of liked that."

"Do I look like motherfuckin' Johnnie to you?"

"You don't," Cleaner taunted. "But Ryder does."

"The bullet finally hurtin' you the fuck enough where you want me to put you out your fuckin' misery, huh, motherfucker? Cuz Logan was also a fuckin' blond, and since Ryder that dirty assfuck great-grandson. Megan a blonde, her old man was one, her ma was one, as well as her fuckin' brother."

"All of them are dead," Cleaner said. "Know anything about that?"

"I shot the fuck outta Big Joe and I shot the fuck outta Snake. I ain't touched Dinah. Anything else?"

"Meggie know you killed her—"

Christopher heaved in a breath. Cleaner was poking, trying to get Christopher to lose his temper. He didn't doubt if he pulled his piece again, Bash and his motherfuckers would, too.

"Megan know," he said flatly. "Either you accept my terms so we can get the fuck out of here. Or don't so we can get the fuck out of here."

"I'm not ready to leave. I want pussy," Cleaner said.

"We don't fuck Black guys," Dot said with disgust.

Christopher glanced over his shoulder. Dot was a tall, slender woman with pale skin, big blue eyes, and black hair.

She also was glaring at Cleaner, her lip curled.

"You don't want to be with me?" Cleaner asked, hurt pulling down his features.

He didn't have dreads like Mort and Digger, but he had their height and a resemblance, though he favored Sharper with darker skin, darker eyes, and a cruel mouth.

Almost like Bash's.

Christopher snapped his brow together, barely paying attention as Cleaner got to his feet and went to where Dot stood. But as he neared her, her shoulders straightened and she stood taller, thrusting her tits out. Something about Cleaner's deliberate movements made Christopher stand.

He got halfway to the stage before the other girls screamed and Cleaner backed away just in time for Christopher to see the river of blood pouring from the slit in Dot's throat and her body falling to the ground.

"What the fuck?" Derby yelled.

"Oh god, oh god, oh god, oh—" Cleaner's bullet to Kenny's head stopped him mid-sentence.

"No!" Eugene screamed. A bullet hit his temple and he fell back.

"Fuck, asshole," Bash yelled as everyone got up and pulled their weapons.

Christopher jerked his .22 from one pocket and his .9mm from the other, about to pull both triggers.

"Hold your fucking fire!" Bash cried, flailing his arms. "You want peace, Outlaw—"

"Fuck peace," Christopher snarled. "Ain't fuckin' around with women killers."

He was going to shoot Rule and Ryan. He wouldn't kill them. Just fuck them up. For Johnnie, he'd rent a freezer at a meatpacking company and hang that motherfucker from his toes.

And Brooks?

Because of them, he…fuck!

He opened fire, shooting two of Bash's motherfuckers.

"Christopher!" Bash screamed. "I accept your offer! We surrender! I accept your offer."

"I want fuckin' Cleaner, Bash."

As white as a sheet, Bash heaved in a breath and shielded Cleaner.

"We surrender," Bash said. "If Cleaner and me don't return, do you really think your sons and nephew will be safe?"

Of course fucking not. That's why he wanted to shoot

Ryan, Rule, Ryder, and Ransom. Axel was only ten. He'd get his ass beat.

Christopher shot Bash's other club member. "Now get the fuck out of my face before I change my fuckin' mind," he snarled.

Cleaner and Bash hurried out.

They had to clean up the fucking carnage, and he had to get the fuck home, knowing there was more fuckery to come.

CHAPTER 35

CJ

Perhaps, the time had come for CJ to drop out of school. Mom was home, Dad's head was clearing, yet CJ still felt lost and profoundly affected by all the turmoil.

Jaleena had apologized for her behavior at the dinner, yet she rarely texted him anymore.

Luckily, he remained busy by steadily working through the mountain of make-up lessons, but school was no longer a top priority. Since he'd found Molly, he hadn't even had the heart to continue their project. He wasn't sure when, or if, she'd return to school. Their grade fell on his shoulders. Every time he tried to make any progress, CJ couldn't do it, overwhelmed with sadness.

Molly hadn't contributed much work. Still, he missed her. Though he saw her as much as possible, she wasn't the same and he doubted she ever would be after the trauma she'd experienced.

Coach Yancy removed him from the starting line-up,

keeping him on the practice squad and placing Ryan in CJ's position, since Willard's attendance was also infrequent. The coach promised CJ could return to his place before he'd stopped caring.

Christmas was five days away. With the way the dates fell, Winter Break began in two days. Instead of going to class, CJ was at the mall with Grant, Ryder, Ransom, Rule, Rory, Ryan, and Devon. CJ drove his father's pickup with Rory riding shotgun. Uncle Val brought the others in Aunt Zoann's Jeep. One, CJ didn't want to lose his patience with his bad ass little brothers, even though it was only two of the three because Axel was sent to school for a make-up test. Besides, CJ intended to meet his mother for coffee, meaning Rory would also have to go home with Uncle Val when he picked up the boys. Aunt Bunny would drop Mom off at the coffee shop. Once they were done, CJ would drive her home, since Dad was...fuck, somewhere.

"I think I'm getting an earring," Ryan announced, surprisingly subdued, though he kept an eye on Rule. He grabbed a French fry from their mountain of potatoes sitting in the middle of the two food court tables they'd pushed together. "Maybe, one in each ear."

"Mom won't like that, Ry," Devon said, sitting on the opposite side of his brother with Ryder, Ransom, and Rule.

"Fuck that—"

Rule lifted a brow.

"I-I-I m-m-mean she can't tell me what to do." Ryan huffed. "It's my fucking ears."

CJ sincerely wished he was facing Ryan so he could see his expression, but he wouldn't give the asshole the satisfaction of showing interest. Later, he'd ask Rule what he had said to frighten the fuck out of their cousin.

"You still need her permission, bro," Grant pointed out.

"Or Uncle Val's. You're not eighteen." He grabbed a handful of fries.

"Val will do it."

Rule cleared his throat.

"Er, Pops," Ryan amended.

A small smile tipped the corner of Rule's mouth. He glanced at the beamed ceiling and nodded.

"Wh-wh-what?" Ryan screeched. "What did He say, Rule? I-I-I-I'm trying to do better."

Rule chomped a French fry. "Try harder."

"Maybe, we should bring you in to help us with Wallace, Rule," Ryder said with a sigh. "We can't come up with a plan."

"What is that supposed to mean?" Ryan demanded.

"Just what the fuck Ryder said, Ryan," Rory replied. "Wallace is fucking with Mattie in some kind of way."

"Wallace is Willard's younger brother," Ryan said.

Snatching more fries, Rule's look turned thoughtful. "I may have to go to my room for consultation and meditation." Chomp, chomp, chomp.

He calmly ate while planning fucking blood sacrifices and biblical punishments.

Ryan gasped. "What do you mean, Rule?"

Ryder rolled his eyes. "It's obvious, man! My brother's a scary motherfucker. Almost as scary as Rebel."

"Yeah," Ransom agreed. "And she don't need Jesus to scare the fuck out of us. That bitch is the devil."

CJ scowled, but Rule spoke before he could.

"My twin, our sister, is sweet and innocent, and you won't ever disparage her again or face our wrath."

Ransom and Ryder glanced at each other, then broke into peals of laughter.

"Fuck you, Rule," Ransom said around his chuckles. "I

will sacrifice you to the fucking devil or to God or to whoever if you ever fuck with me. Remember, there's one of you and three of us. Fuck with us at your own fucking risk."

Rule narrowed his eyes, but Ransom flipped him off and stood. "Come on, Ry. Let's go buy more stuff before I punch Rule in his fucking mouth."

"Ryan is Ry," Rule said. He glared at CJ. "Mom is so lucky I've been ordered to honor her. All of these 'R' names are a travesty."

CJ's eyes widened. Rule's announcement interrupted Ryder and Ransom gathering the shopping bags of shit they'd already purchased.

"Joan of Arc was burned at the stake, Rule," Ryder said. "Don't make us tie you to your fucking bed and burn you."

"Jesus Christ, would you walking representatives of the need for birth control, shut the fuck up?" CJ ordered. "Rule, if you think to hurt Mom, I will break you in two, then give you to Rory for practice. Ryder, you'd burn the fucking house down, you little asshole. Not to mention murdering your own fucking brother."

"That would be strictly self-defense, C.," Ryder defended.

"An offensive move to protect Mom," Ransom added.

"I said defense, Ryder," Ransom said.

"Don't give a fuck," Ryder said, shifting his heavy bags. The little asshole purchased more shit for himself, then gifts for the family, which was the main reason to shop today. "If you make the first move, it's offense. Ask Dad."

"Rule made a threat, prompting a preemptive strike," Ransom argued.

"You sound like an attorney," Grant said with a grin. "Do you want to study law?"

"Nah, you, Diesel, Brooks, and Aunt Kendall has that covered. I want to go into finance. White collar crimes net a lot of money."

"And a lot of fucking time behind bars," Devon pointed out.

"Mom's real good with numbers. She's teaching me…" Ransom's voice trailed off and he lowered his eyelids. "Well, she was."

"Mom's home now, Ran," Rule said softly. "She's going to be fine. I'll pray for you to have peace and faith."

"Fuck, please don't." Ransom shook his head. "Please. You might decide to try and sacrifice me after I fuck up if you've spent time praying for me."

"This isn't funny," Rule snapped. "You're blasphemers. My faith and beliefs aren't a game. I want to be a priest. Stop joking about my rituals. Stop minimizing my religion. Or else."

Ryder leaned closer to Rule and belched, polluting the air with the onions he'd had on his burger. "As long as you insist on your fucked-up threats, I will continue to fuck with you. You don't scare me, Ransom, or Axel, Rule."

Rule glared at Ryan. "Shut up. You don't know what I'm capable of."

"We're Dad's sons, too, assface," Ransom said with disgust. "The same weapons you have access to, we do as well."

"If I harm someone or ever kill someone, it'll be for the greater good. I would never hurt anyone I wasn't instructed to. And Axel is afraid of me."

"Axel's ten," Ryder said. "Easier to scare. I'm warning you, Rule, if anyone ever tells you we need to be fucked up, you risk getting yourself fucked up."

"Exactly," Ryan crowed. "Thanks for putting shit into perspective, Blondie."

Rule clenched his jaw, and CJ wondered how much of his

boasts were bravado to keep Ryan from bullying him and how much Rule actually believed.

"Didn't put nothing into perspective for you, Ryan," Ransom said with disgust. "Make no mistake. Rule hears fucking voices. We have something you don't, and if you forget that, you'll get your ass killed."

"Yeah, cuck, what the fuck is that?" Ryan sneered.

"Caldwell genes," CJ supplied. "Lifelong lessons from our dad. We're not afraid of each other. In a fight, the odds are even, but if you don't bring all you have, we can fuck you up together or individually."

"I have Donovan genes," Ryan said. "So does Rory and Dev."

"In case you forgot, so do we," CJ snapped. "Logan Donovan was our great-grandfather, too."

"He was a great man," Ryan said. "Greater than any fucking Caldwell."

"Logan Donovan was a fucking asshole, Ryan, and you know it," Rory spat, raising CJ's suspicions of a deeper meaning to the statement.

Grant dug in his shirt pocket for his pack of cigarettes and lighter. He was the only one who wore trousers, a white button-down, loafers, and a wool peacoat. Like CJ, the others donned jeans, boots, turtlenecks and leather jackets.

"Sounds like you know something we don't, Rory," Grant said as he stood. Smoking wasn't allowed in the food court.

"You shouldn't know anything," Ryan said. "You're not related to us."

"He's Lolly's son, fuckface," Ryder said. "That makes him one of us."

"Does he look like he has any of her blood?" Ryan asked. "She wishes he was hers."

"I don't like your fucking tone, Ryan," Grant said,

moving to the head of the table to better see the hateful motherfucker. "Lolly is my mother, just as much as my mom was. She stepped in when she married my dad when she didn't have to."

Forever the asshole, Ryan snorted. "If she wanted him, she did."

Grant started toward Ryan, but CJ stood and blocked Grant's path. "Beat his ass at the club. Being arrested is no fucking fun."

Anger darkening his eyes, Grant jerked away from CJ. "Ryan, don't fuck with Roxanne if you know what's good for you. It's a personal affront to me." He glared at CJ, turned, and stalked toward the exit.

Christmas music piped in through the speakers, such a fucking contrast to the tension amongst them.

Could one fucking day pass without bullshit?

Sighing, CJ sat down. Rule and Devon stood and grabbed their bags.

"We have to finish our shopping," Devon said, stuffing his hands in his pockets and not meeting anyone's gaze. "Before Dad comes back."

CJ looked at his watch. "Uncle Val is picking you up at two. You still have an hour and a half."

"Have you heard from Mom yet?" Ryder asked.

The bullshit prevented him and Ransom's departure, though they remained standing, awaiting escape.

"No, I haven't," CJ answered.

Fear and worry slid across all three of his brother's faces. He couldn't admit to either feeling and send them into a panic.

"After her appointment, she's going to spend some time with Jo," CJ reminded them, the thought comforting him, too.

"But she's okay?" Ransom asked.

"Yeah," CJ said, praying it was the truth. "Finish your shopping. If she calls before we meet back here again, I will text you."

After the four of them walked off, only CJ, Rory, and Ryan remained at the table. CJ stood and took a seat on the opposite side, to better see his two cousins.

"How's Aunt Kendall?" he asked.

"Better now that Dad's home," Rory answered.

They fell silent. The discomfort between Ryan and CJ wasn't surprising. They only had shared blood in common. On the other hand, him and Rory had been quite close at one time. As Uncle Johnnie pulled Rory to the dark side, a gulf opened between him and CJ. He wondered if they'd ever bridge it.

CJ needed a smoke, too. However, he still had several gifts he wanted to purchase, and he wasn't sure what time his mother would call.

"Rory!"

At the sound of Gypsy's voice, CJ lifted a brow at his cousin a moment before Derby's wife arrived at the table. A headband held her frizzy blonde hair in place. Ivory tit mounds drew attention to their generous size. She was a full-figured woman with generous curves and an attractive face, even with the wrinkles.

"Hey, CJ," she greeted, her smile faltering. She nodded to Ryan. "Ryan."

Ryan offered her a two-fingered salute and turned his head, a clear dismissal.

"Hey, Gypsy," CJ said, hoping his smile put her at ease.

A moment of awkward silence passed.

She cleared her throat. "Uh, Rory, can I talk to you?"

"Don't have the time today." Rory got to his feet, dug in

his pocket and pulled out some cash. He handed the bills to Gypsy. "I'll text you in a couple days."

A blush crept into her face, and she bit down on her lip.

Rory took his seat again, grabbed his phone, and focused on it.

"Er." Gypsy pressed her lips together. "Um, how's Meggie, CJ?"

"Mom's better," CJ said politely, glancing between her and Rory. "I'm waiting for her to call me, so we can meet for coffee."

"You boys are all grown up," she said nervously.

"If that helps you sleep at night, bitch," Ryan said with a smirk.

Gypsy gulped. "Bye, CJ." She turned and rushed away, soon swallowed by the crowd of holiday shoppers either passing through the food court as a shortcut to the other side of the mall or searching for a bite to eat.

CJ scrubbed a hand over his face. "When Derby kills you, I'll visit your fucking grave, Rory."

"I can introduce you to a few hot cougars, Ro," Ryan offered. "You're wasting your cock on that dried up slut."

"We don't fuck, dickhead. I give her fucking money."

CJ had enough fucking problems. He didn't have the energy to explain to Rory why giving money to Gypsy was wrong on so many different fucking levels. She should know better.

"You don't have a fucking job, Rory," Ryan said.

Rory set his phone aside. "And? I don't intend to ever have a fucking job, Ryan. Not in the sense you mean. I want to be the club's enforcer."

That was news. "What happened to VP?" CJ asked.

Shame crossed Rory's face. "I won't be good at it, CJ. I just know it. Sometimes, I think if Dad..." He glanced away. "Dad should've been the enforcer or the treasurer. If he would've focused on his strengths rather than what he felt was his right, he would be happier."

"VP wasn't only his birthright," Ryan said. "The presidency was."

"As much as it was Uncle Christopher's, Ryan," Rory said quietly, taking the words out of CJ's mouth. "But Uncle Christopher is a master of diplomacy and revenge. We saw him in action at the Scorched Devils meeting. If my dad wasn't so bitter, he could allow Uncle Mort to become the VP. Dad would be an awesome enforcer."

"You're so fucking stupid, Rice Krispie face," Ryan scoffed and stood. "You'll never be anything more than a stupid shitface. I'm the oldest of the cousins—"

"Grant's the oldest," Rory corrected.

"Diesel's the oldest," CJ said.

"They aren't members of our family. Neither are Mortician and Digger's mongrels." Ryan stalked off, losing himself in the crowd.

"I say we kill him, C.," Rory said.

"I say we don't fucking kill him, Ro."

"He's a problem."

"How much of a problem?"

"A big one, CJ." Rory sighed, rested his elbows on the table, and leaned forward. "My parents give me an allowance. I'm not sure if they split the amount or what. I do know it comes from Dad's account. He earns the bulk of his money from the club, so technically I'm already on the club's payroll."

"Skewered reasoning, but whatever. The fucking point?"

"Gypsy is helping me with something. Since the night I served as the cover for your date with Harley, I've kept in contact with Gypsy. Does she send me explicit photos? Yes.

Does it matter to me? No. I don't...I'm different, CJ," he whispered. "Some things still hurt me. I was so scared of what Mom might do when Dad left. I worry about my little sister. I cried when I thought Aunt Meggie would die. I miss you. Other than that, I'm numb inside. Even the nightmares have stopped. When I look at Gypsy, all I see is a woman. Fragile one moment and scheming the next."

"You should see a grown woman with a motherfucking husband who thinks nothing of cheating on her. However, he'd want to kill her and her lover in a reverse situation."

"Does it matter? Uncle Christopher has been involved in the club in one way or the other since he was ten. We look at him as a legend now. Do you know what he must've seen and done in the eight years before he was legal? No matter what the others want to do, you and I have always wanted to patch in. You must accept that things won't always be legal or palatable or politically correct or wrapped in a neat bow."

"I know."

"Maybe, but knowing and accepting are two different things, CJ. I knew my mom was fragile. I have memories of when she attempted suicide. I don't know what's real or what I've embellished. Until she fell apart a few days ago, I hadn't truly accepted her instability."

"You should've called me—"

"You could've visited."

CJ shook his head. "No, Rory. I didn't know when, or if, Uncle Johnnie would return. I'm tired of his punches. Sooner or later, I'm going to forget he's my uncle and give him the fight he wants."

"It's the only way Dad might ever back off," Rory said. "I'd prefer you to beat him up, then Uncle Chris to fuck him up."

"What is Gypsy helping you with?"

"I can't tell you."

"What about Logan Donovan? It sounded as if you were referring to specific incidents."

Rory evaded CJ's gaze, then he sighed and shrugged. "I'll tell you as soon as I find what I'm looking for."

"Which is?"

"I can't—"

"Is it dangerous? Does it have anything to do with Bash turning up in Hortensia?"

"Why...why do you say that?"

"Ryan knows that motherfucker and so does Uncle Johnnie," CJ gritted. "There's a fucking reason for that."

"I think so, too," he confessed. "And, yes, that's what I'm searching for. Gypsy is going to ask some of the old broads who've been associated with the Burning Hounds for decades if they know anything about Logan and Bash."

"I'd think it would be Logan and Cee Cee," CJ said. "It's a logical fucking conclusion since Bash was my grandfather's son just like my dad."

Rory stood. "I have a few more presents to buy, but I will keep you updated as soon as I find out more."

"Before I forget, that officer that was in the locker room the day of Harley's fight has been terminated."

"As in?"

CJ snickered. "Fired from his job, motherfucker. Not from life."

"Like Lumbly?"

"How..." The meatshack rose in CJ's head and he scowled. "That motherfucker didn't."

"Allow me to help dismember fuckface? Indeed, Dad did. Uncle Mort and Uncle Digger were supposed to do it the morning after. Instead, Dad took me in the middle of the night." Rory shrugged. "You should let me show you what goes on one day, CJ."

"When my dad thinks I'm ready for it, I'll take you up on your offer," he said flatly.

"Suit yourself, C." He started off, then halted. "I...thank you. No matter how different I feel, you always treat me the same and that means a lot."

CJ smiled. "I always have your back, Rory."

Rory nodded. "Same."

Alone at the table, CJ glanced at the Christmas decorations, intending to enjoy them as he decided upon the remaining gifts he needed to purchase. Before he began to prioritize his list with his dwindling time, Nardo Grevenberg sat at the table.

"What the fuck do you want?"

Nardo leaned back in the chair and folded his arms. "Talked to Harley lately?"

"Not your fucking business, so get the fuck."

"That's a no." He smirked. "She belongs to me now." He laughed. "She gave me what you wanted."

A buzzing started in CJ's head, a combination of anguish and anger. He knew exactly what Nardo meant. He'd spent the last two years in football locker rooms. Not to mention the years of conversations he'd heard at the club. "You're a lying motherfucker, Grevenberg. If you spread that fucking rumor, I'll beat your fucking ass from one end of the school to the next."

"Do it. You'll be expelled."

Possible. Not probable. That was the perks of having his parents own the fucking school. They stayed out of day-to-day administration, but they'd never allow him to be expelled.

"I'm not lying, by the way. That's just your wishful fucking thinking. Your time as big man on campus is over." Nardo stood. "I can get Harley to do whatever I want and there's nothing you can do to stop it. She don't want your cheesy ass anymore."

Losing interest in shopping, CJ stood from his seat and headed to another exit. Grant hadn't returned, so he was probably chilling outside in the interest of not killing Ryan. Whether Nardo spoke the truth, CJ was still crushed and didn't want to see anyone.

He had to get himself together for when Mom called. She had enough to worry about without concerning herself with his problems.

No matter how devastated he was.

CHAPTER 36

MEGGIE

"I won't press you now. Christmas is five days away, but after Outlaw's birthday party, we must sit down and discuss setting a date for the surgery."

Pressing her lips together, Meggie nodded at Jordan's words. Professionally, she still went by Dr. Will, but she was so much more than that. She'd delivered CJ and kept watch over Meggie during her pregnancies, even if another obstetrician served as Meggie's main caregiver.

"You don't want any more babies, Meggie," Jordan continued. "We discussed it while you were still in the hospital."

"I know."

"You still sound uncertain. We can go with option 2, until you make a firm decision. I can remove a LARC at any time, whether you want another baby or the hysterectomy."

Long-acting reversible contraception was a better choice for the time being. She needed to get her baby girl home, get help for Rule, and monitor Rebel and Diesel. Then, she could sort through Johnnie's continued bombardment of what she and Christopher did and didn't want. Then there was Molly and her withdrawal from very hard drugs; CJ and his heartache over Molly, Harley, and Jaleena. Meggie wished she'd never invited the Davises over. It seemed to have made matters worse between CJ and Jaleena.

She also had her younger sons to get in hand with Christopher's help. Her husband needed her, too. He was trying to get back to normal, so she'd never tell him how awful she was feeling because she'd had to drive herself to her appointment. Just as she and Bunny were leaving the club, Digger came in and said he needed to go on a run, so Bunny couldn't accompany Meggie and had to watch their kids since everyone else was already engaged.

Meggie knew Digger was angry with her for advising Bunny to start tutoring, but her friend seemed so wistful whenever she talked about her teaching degree. It wasn't as if Bunny had never tutored over the years. Except, this time, Digger's routine had been upended. After years of enjoying one-on-one time with Christopher at least twice a week while Meggie and Bunny worked together to cook, set the table, see to their kids, and clean the dishes, he was relegated to watching his kids.

Meggie never stopped him from joining them as he had when Bunny worked full time for her. Digger chose not to. He complained—to her—that she took Christopher away from him anyway, by asking for his help, so he opted out of coming over.

She was happy Bunny was giving up the tutoring because it was Bunny's choice. Meggie also hoped Digger would finally ease up on her now that things would return to how they had been.

"Let me reiterate my recommendation," Jordan said. "A hysterectomy."

She had to get her family right before she had the surgery. Right now, she didn't have the time. She especially wanted Jo home. Besides, according to Johnnie, her hysterectomy would break Christopher's heart. Every argument she put up, including pointing out Christopher's botched vasectomy, Johnnie shot down. She was afraid she'd die and leave the kids she'd already been blessed with; die and leave the man she loved more than life itself.

Johnnie called her a failure and a disappointment. He wanted her to go. He said she was a handicap to Christopher. Her illnesses and her inability to have more children left him saddled with her.

Until Christopher told her he didn't want her or love her, she would stay.

Jordan snapped a folder shut and leaned forward in her desk chair. Her offices were now housed a couple of miles from Hortensia General instead of in the medical building across the parking lot.

"I need you to calm down before you end up in the hospital again. This time, with a stroke. Your blood pressure was slightly elevated today, so I've sent in a prescription. Cut back on the salt and processed foods. Take it easy," she reiterated.

"Christopher wants me to hire May and Gurly as cook and housekeeper. Bunny has given up her teaching position because it has become too stressful, so she is back with me full time. I feel so…so…" What had Johnnie called her? "Useless."

Jordan studied Meggie closely. Gray sprinkled her long braids, a style she'd worn ever since Meggie had first met her when she needed an obstetrician to see her through her first pregnancy.

"You have eight surviving children, Meggie," the doctor

said kindly. "You've done your duty as Outlaw's wife and provided him with beautiful sons and daughters."

"You're right," Meggie said raggedly, unable to reveal the pressure Johnnie was putting on her to either leave or do the one thing she was good at. As he saw it, Christopher's one and only request he'd ever made of her was that she give him children. "He loves kids."

"He loves you more."

"I know, and I am tired of having babies," she confessed. "I have another girl, which I have always wanted. Admittedly, I wasn't planning for her when it happened."

"I understand. We'd discussed your options for another baby before your fortieth birthday. At which point, you intended to have your tubes tied. What's changed?"

Meggie shrugged.

"Roxy is picking up Molly from the hospital. Once you visit Jo, why don't you go home and enjoy your family. You're in a vulnerable state right now."

"I'm meeting CJ for lunch in a couple of hours. He's been so worried about me. I thought it was a good idea if we talked away from home or the club. The holidays are always a beehive of activity."

"Are you sure nothing else is on your mind?"

A lot. She cleared her throat. Right now, she wanted to think of something happier and plan for the future. Maybe, after Christopher's birthday, she'd take Tabitha's advice and go to the cabin to clear her head and get away from Johnnie. She could only be away for two days at most if Jo wasn't out of the hospital. At the thought of her baby, she hung her head, blurting the first thing that came to her mind. "When is it safe to have sex again?"

"You're healing very well but give it another two or three weeks."

Twenty minutes later, Meggie checked out. After phoning her husband with an amended truth about how she got to the appointment and how she currently felt, she went to Hortensia General and visited Jo, then called Rebel, who told her Gunner had gotten into an opened jar of Vaseline and caked it on his face and hair. Apparently, Digger was back because Bunny was at the house, still cleaning Gunner's mess, so Meggie didn't call and disturb her. Once she talked to Diesel and messaged her other sons, she texted CJ to meet her.

Christopher had a meeting hours away and wouldn't be home until late, so Meggie thought it was a good time to spend 1-on-1 time with her potato. Besides, she was evading Johnnie. If he didn't already know Christopher wasn't waiting for Meggie, he'd harass her the moment he realized it.

Somehow, she needed to convince Johnnie to back off. Before Christopher found out and killed him, which would completely destroy Kendall.

The Medical District and her favorite coffee shop were on opposite sides of town. She really needed to talk to Christopher about getting the owner to open a second shop.

Hortensia didn't have as much forested areas as it once did. The town was thriving, although the park with the creek she'd lived in when she first arrived remained untouched. She zoomed past Kendall and Brooks's law firm, sped by the street where Ridge Moore was located, and tried to force her unease and sadness away.

Meggie turned up the radio, blasting the holiday music, hoping to drown out her racing thoughts.

Ten minutes later, she arrived at the coffee shop and turned into a parking space, close to the small building, decked out in Christmas decorations straight from a

Norman Rockwell scene.

Stepping out of her Lexus, she glanced around, but didn't see Christopher's pickup.

Crap!

She'd have to give CJ a reason why she had her SUV.

Ideas running though her head, Meggie started toward the shop. The cold, bracing air invigorated her.

"Megan?"

Johnnie's call, from behind, stopped her, and she stiffened. "Go away."

He sauntered into view and blocked her path.

She started to turn. "I'm not—"

Grabbing her arm, he jerked her around. "You are," he said harshly. "You're too selfish to leave, so Christopher can be happy."

"You're out of your stupid mind! Christopher would never be happy if I left."

"You're wrong, sweetheart. Frankly, your arrogance shocks me. It's unbecoming."

"It isn't arrogance, jerk. Christopher needs me as much as I need him. We couldn't survive without each other."

"Spare me the theatrics, Megan."

"Spare me your vitriol, John Donovan," she retorted, glaring at him. "I've had it up to here with your assholery." She raised her hand above her head to demonstrate her point. "You have no place in my marriage. What I choose is a decision for me and Christopher. Not you."

She started around him, but he grabbed her arm and jerked her back, spinning her toward him and shaking her. "You've placed yourself so far above everyone, you can't see that Christopher is unhappy knowing you can't have any more children. You practically live at the hospital."

"Jo is still in the hospital," Meggie said tiredly, her small bit of peace evaporating.

"You can't fuck him. Excuse me, have sex with him. How long has it been? At least a month. Have you even sucked his cock?"

Her suddenly pounding head sent a wave of dizziness through her. "I haven't healed from Jo's birth. I can't—"

"Exactly. You can't. You can't fuck him, suck him, or give him more sons."

Meggie drew in a shaky breath. "Christopher never said he wanted more sons."

"Any way it goes, you're going to make him miserable," Johnnie persisted, disgust in his eyes. "The club is in shambles because of you. Everyone is walking around in a daze because the great Queen Megan was ill. You are Christopher's downfall. Your dysfunctional womb will complete his ruin."

A sob escaped her.

"Can you even fuck him? He's unhappy. It wouldn't surprise me if he turned to another woman. Remember Kiera? You didn't change him, Megan. He changed himself. But you're old and used up now. He needs a younger, more vibrant woman. My guess is if he hasn't already found her, he soon will."

She pressed a hand to her mouth to hold in her tears. "Christopher would never cheat on me. He'd never allow another woman anywhere near him!"

"He's broken enough," Johnnie said, ignoring her vehement faith in her husband. "Before you break him completely, why don't you prove how much you love him and go. I'll pay you ten million dollars. Take Jo with you—"

"I am not leaving my husband. And you're wrong, I can still give him children. If he wants ten more sons, I will give birth to them."

"Mom?" CJ stepped next to Johnnie and stared at her. "You're crying! What—" He stiffened and narrowed his eyes, looking for all the world like his daddy. "What did you say to her, fuckhead?"

"CJ, he's an adult."

"He's Uncle Johnnie," CJ spat. "Adulthood was long ago forfeited."

"Fuck off, nephew."

"Fuck you, uncle. I've fucking had it with you. You sent Aunt Kendall over the fucking edge. Until my dad is my dad again and can kill you, I'll protect my mom."

"None of us can protect her, CJ," Johnnie barked.

"I heard what the fuck you said," CJ snarled. "You want my mother to take my prematurely born baby sister and leave my dad."

CJ balled his fist. For a moment, Meggie thought her son would strike Johnnie. If that happened, the situation would turn dire. She didn't doubt Johnnie would strike CJ, then Meggie would have to find a rock and bash him in his stupid head.

"Let's go inside, son," she said, throwing Johnnie a dirty look. "I'm freezing."

She wasn't. She felt peculiarly warm and lightheaded.

"I swear to you, CJ, I only said what I did out of sarcasm after spending the last twenty minutes trying to talk her into having a hysterectomy. She insists she wants ten more children."

Lowering her lids, Meggie glanced at the sidewalk. It was better for CJ to believe that flaming lie for the time being. Drawing herself up, she smiled at her son. "I love babies," she mumbled.

Disapproval crossed CJ's face, then he glared at Johnnie. "That's between my parents, fuckhead. My father is her husband, not you, so get to fucking stepping and the fuck out of my mother's face."

"Megan—"

"Now, uncle." CJ nodded in the direction of the parking lot.

"This isn't over." Johnnie stormed away.

Meggie wasn't sure what game Johnnie was playing, but Christopher wasn't in a good frame of mind. He'd shoot now and regret later, since worry for her continued to consume him. Whenever she broached the subject of another baby to feel him out and see if there was any truth to Johnnie's words, Christopher insisted he wanted whatever she wanted.

Now, Johnnie was switching tactics, claiming she wanted more babies after she'd almost died having Jo and her family was traumatized.

Something was brewing and none of it was good.

Inside the coffee shop, CJ guided her to a table near a window but secluded from most of the other patrons.

Meggie's head was pounding. No matter how much she pretended otherwise, Johnnie's unreasonable words, and sudden reversal, were affecting her. She wanted to crawl into bed and stay there.

But no matter what Johnnie said, Christopher would be as devastated and inconsolable as her if they separated.

"Here, Mom."

CJ sat a medium sized coffee in front of Meggie, along with two steaming Cheese Danishes. He walked away, returning moments later with a blueberry muffin, chocolate croissant, and a slice of lemon loaf, along with a large coffee.

"Eat," he encouraged after taking his seat and scarfing down the croissant and the muffin. He gulped his coffee and started on the lemon loaf. "Dad said you didn't eat breakfast. You must be starving."

Meggie smiled. "I had a banana and juice."

"Hours ago." CJ narrowed his eyes. "Wait! Are you okay? What did Aunt Jordan say? Fuck, Mom!" He jumped to his feet. "Give me your keys. I'll rush you to the ER. Let me call Dad—"

"Son!" Meggie stood and stepped in front of her frantic boy. She placed a hand on his chest. "Calm down, potato. I'm fine. Jordan said I have to watch what I eat." She explained about her blood pressure, then nodded to CJ's chair. "Sit."

"Does Dad know?" he asked, after they were both seated again.

"Not yet," Meggie admitted. "By the time I got home, he'd have Kendall making menus for us."

"For you," CJ said, grinning. He winked at her. "We love you, Mom, but in this instance that would be your cross to bear. Aunt Kendall thinks it's good culinary skills to cook charcoal, kelp, ink, and clay."

Meggie bit into one of the Danishes. "She finds edible ingredients, potato."

"None of that is edible, Mom," CJ said with indignation.

"Squid ink is, as is activated charcoal." She bit another piece of her pastry, then sipped her coffee.

Scowling, he snatched her untouched Danish and chomped on it. She giggled.

"You had a huge breakfast, CJ," she teased.

"I'm a growing boy, ma'am. Besides, shopping is exhausting. I'm so glad Uncle Val had Bishop and Orange bring the cargo vans to transport motherfuckers and merchandise back to the club."

"Don't call your brothers and cousins motherfuckers, son."

CJ guffawed. "Don't say motherfuckers, Mom. Your propriety butchers the word."

Meggie laughed. "I haven't had lifelong practice, child of

mine."

"Nor have I. For a long time, everyone was fucka mudnas."

"It didn't matter," Meggie said with another giggle. "Your daddy was quite proud."

CJ puffed out his chest and finished the Danish. "I have a question."

Suspecting what that might be, Meggie nodded. CJ was as fiercely protective of her as Christopher. "What, son?"

"Why are you driving?"

Yep, right on target. "Digger had something to do at the least minute, so Bunny had to stay behind. We were walking out of the club. I didn't want to cancel—"

"It was more like you didn't want Dad to know."

"Digger said it was club business, CJ."

"Fine, Mom. If it was Uncle Johnnie, I'd suspect duplicity, but I know Uncle Digger adores you so I won't tell Dad."

"There's no need," Meggie said firmly. "I have a slight headache, although it has nothing to do with driving myself a month after the C-Section."

"More like two weeks after your release."

"I'm fine, CJ," Meggie stressed. "Have you seen Molly?" she asked a few minutes later, once the annoyance cleared from her son's brow. She wasn't sure if Molly willingly took drugs or if they'd been forced into her. Either way, it would devastate CJ. She'd only found out last night when Roxy called, so she hadn't talked to Christopher yet, which she wanted to do so they could tell CJ together. "I haven't had a chance to talk to her today, since Roxy had already picked her up by the time I saw Jo."

"Molly's healing physically. Mentally, not so much."

"Yesterday when I saw her, she said the Easter Bunny had moved to the North Pole to live with Mrs. Claus."

Pain slid across CJ's face. "Do you think it's her way of

escaping?"

It was a combination of factors. "Bailey is going to provide therapy for her."

"Harley gave permission for such benevolence?"

"She doesn't know, potato."

"It figures," CJ grumbled.

"Bailey wasn't going to do it, but I told her if she didn't help Molly I'd never talk to her again. She accused me of betraying Harley, a little girl I've known since before she was born." Meggie's mood plummeted and a throbbing started at the base of her skull, joining the pounding in her temples. "In moments of lucidity, Molly told me, Roxie, and your aunts, that you and she are just friends. She even said she sent the photos to make Harley jealous so Harley would be nicer to you. If Bailey sides with Harley, that's her prerogative, but she isn't making an innocent girl suffer because Harley is insecure. And she certainly isn't maligning you in the process. I believe my child. She believes hers. But she crossed a line when she called you a liar again."

Two days after the Davises dinner party, Meggie had been sorry Bailey and Harley showed up with Roxy to see Molly. Harley had been sobbing. Bailey had been screaming. And Meggie had been outraged at Bailey deeming her potato as a fucking liar, cheating motherfucker and a scheming asshole.

Bailey blamed CJ's callousness for the fight Harley had with Ariana and Erin. She'd felt Rebel defended her out of guilt. Meggie hadn't ever been as angry with Bailey.

Roxy got control of the situation, sent Harley out of the room, and made Bailey apologize. At first, Meggie hadn't accepted it since it was fake, given under duress at Roxy's threatened beat down.

Bailey had told both Roxy and Meggie to fuck themselves because they were stupid, miserable, emotional bitches and annoyed everyone.

When Bailey came to five minutes after Roxy's punch, she'd been in tears. Roxy, though, had been on a warpath.

"You've lost me, Bailey. I never thought I'd see the day that you'd turn into such a disrespectful sadity bitch. And don't come running to me when you lose Mortician. If I was him, I would've walked away from your shoddy treatment years ago. Who the fuck do you think you are? You've turned your back on him, on me, on your sisters, on your children, and on the club. Well, fuck you, girl. I hope you live a long, miserable life in your high-class office." She'd stomped off, pausing at the door to say, "Bye, Meggie. Don't expend your energy on a bitch who's not worth it."

"Momma, wait!" Bailey wailed, although her jaw was swelling.

"Girl, fuck you," Roxy snarled from the hallway, her voice wobbling.

Bailey ran to the door. "Momma, please. I'm so sorry. I didn't mean it. I'm sorry."

"You meant every motherfucking goddamn word your bitchy ass said to Meggie and me." Roxy's voice was farther down the hall. "You've been on the warpath because Harley can't see the fucking forest for the fucking trees. She wants

to be you. And you want to be any fucking body but you. Two more miserable bitches I've never fucking seen."

"Momma, you're cussing a child. For that matter, you're cussing your child."

"My child is lucky I don't fuck her up. My child called another woman's child everything but a child of God. Stop being a fucking hypocrite. It's as unbecoming as your bitchiness even if it fits."

"Momma, please, help me. I'm losing my husband. I love him so much. I just wanted him to be proud of me. I wanted to earn my own money."

Roxy stomped back into the room. Molly was awake but she was staring into space. After closing the door, Bailey stumbled to Roxy and hugged her.

"I'm so sorry. I'm sorry. Everything is spiraling out of control and I don't know how to stop it."

"First, get control of Harley. Whether you're on her side or not, she's dividing and conquering you and Mortician. In turn, it reveals the cracks in your relationship."

"I just want to support her. CJ has crushed—"

Meggie stiffened. "Please, leave my son's name out of your mouth. He isn't here to defend himself, and I'm never talking to you again."

Turning away from her mother, who hadn't returned her hug, Bailey came to Meggie. "I'm so, so sorry. It was unworthy of me."

"It was fucked up," Roxy snapped.

Bailey nodded. "If I'm honest, I'm sorry I ever took my practice out of Hortensia. I had clients willing to travel to see me."

"You also had clients who couldn't see you in Portland because they had no transportation. Not only because of transportation but the insurance you don't accept and your *increased fees."* Meggie reminded her. *"Zoann, Kendall, and me had to pool our resources to help people you left high and dry."* It hadn't been the first time that their home healthcare business came in handy for referrals and other medical needs.

"Why didn't you tell me, Meggie?" Bailey shifted her weight. *"Lucas trusts you a lot, so what did he say when I made the move?"*

"How proud he was of you," Meggie said honestly. *"How much he loved you. How lucky he was to have you as his wife and the mother of his children."*

"Have I ruined that?"

"Do you care?" Meggie retorted.

"I'm sorry for what I said about CJ," Bailey said again.

"Girl, shove your apology up your ass," Roxy snapped. *"How many fucking times have you apologized to me in the past few weeks? They don't mean shit. You slide back into bitchery."*

"Meggie, please. I swear I'm sorry. I'll do anything to prove it."

"If you ever call my son one name again, I'll never talk to you from that day on. But if you're really sorry and want me to tell you more than a 'hello', help Molly. Harley doesn't have to know. We'll find a way to help her through whatever she's dealing with. Molly has no one, though. Her mother's dead. Her father's missing. She was assaulted. She needs us, too, Bailey."

"Do you think Molly should move in with us? She can stay in Diesel's room."

Meggie considered CJ's words and studied him closely. "Do you want her to live with us?"

"I don't want Harley to be mean to her."

"Would Roxy allow that?"

CJ glanced away. "I don't know. If Ryan wasn't such a fucking dickhead, I'd ask you to talk to Aunt Zoann, but Molly deserves better than him."

Meggie smiled at her son's fierceness. "Let me know what you think is best for her, and I'll see that it gets done, potato."

"Do you think…do you think…a guy can be friends with a girl?"

"Most definitely. Mortician is your daddy's best friend, but he's also one of my closest friends. Kendall considers him a close friend. At one time, I considered Johnnie a dear friend. Val and I have had our ups and downs, but we're good friends again now, too."

"What happened between you and Uncle Johnnie?"

"A lot, son. We have a complicated history, and I'll leave it at that."

"You and Uncle Val?"

"Refer to my previous answer," Meggie said with a smile, and quickly changed the subject. "If you have feelings for Molly—"

"I don't. Not in the way you mean." He scratched his jaw. "Fuck, I wish I did. Or for Jaleena. I'm so fucking sick of Harley's bullshit. I haven't touched any girl, which is the reason Harley's accusations are so infuriating. Molly and Jaleena are so fucking pretty, but in my eyes neither of them compare to Harley, though I've flirted with both of them." He lowered his gaze. "I don't know, Mom. Maybe, Harley's right and I am a cheat."

"You aren't a liar or a cheat," Meggie said fiercely, offended on her son's behalf. "Harley is having a rough time right now, and I sympathize with her, but she can't make you miserable because she is. My suggestion to you is to have as much patience with her as possible. I think she regrets turning you down when you asked her to go steady. It's in the past and you both have to move on."

CJ looked so sad. Her heart hurt for her son.

"I think she already has, Mom," he said quietly. "Nardo Grevenberg was at the mall. We had words and he told me… he told me." CJ hung his head. "He said he had sex with Harley."

Meggie groaned inwardly.

"He was gloating so much," CJ continued miserably.

"Do you believe him?"

"I want to talk to her. I didn't even intend to tell you." He drew in a deep breath. "I have no claim on her, so if it's true that's her business. If it isn't, I'm killing Nardo."

"You are not killing anyone!" Yet. The word went unspoken, but it hung between them. Once he patched in, he couldn't avoid killing. "Tell Mortician. Let him kill Nardo."

"Uncle Mort wouldn't. Nardo won't be eighteen for sixteen

months."

"Then he can wait until then."

CJ smirked at her. "There's a nice fucking eighteenth birthday present. His scheduled execution courtesy of me and Uncle Mort."

"No, son. You're not a member of the club yet, so—"

"About that—"

"I'll talk to your daddy." CJ had long wanted to forego college and become a Dweller prospect when he turned eighteen, so she already knew what he'd say. "No promises, so focus on football and good grades for now."

"Billson has given me the option of finishing the project I started with Molly or joining another team. I think I want to finish what Molly and I started."

"And Harley?"

"She'll always be my friend, Mom. I just want her happy, and if motherfucking Nardo makes her happy, then good. But if he's lying…" he added darkly.

"You tell Mortician," Meggie said firmly.

"Dad?"

"I would like him to know. However, it's a delicate matter and I don't want Harley embarrassed, whether it's a lie or the truth. I'm going to talk to Bailey…um, Roxy. Someone needs to know either way. Roxy might be angry, but she won't immediately hunt him down."

"Like Uncle Mort?"

Meggie was sure once Roxy found out, Bailey would be informed. "Exactly."

"Okay, Mom."

"What gifts did you buy?" she asked, proud of the fine young man CJ was turning into, but missing the days of MegAnn and fucka mudna. A thought came to her. "I need to reinstate Rebel's debit card."

"I bought her a bunch of clothes and jewelry, as well as gift cards to some of her favorite stores, so she can do her own shopping. If you give her her debit card again, that'll be the best present ever. She'll be so happy."

"She's suffered enough." Meggie sighed. "We all have."

CJ glanced away and tightened his jaw. "You're getting a hysterectomy."

The order neither surprised Meggie nor annoyed her. CJ had a lot of her qualities. However, he had just as many of Christopher's.

"Dad still hasn't recovered, Mom. How would you have felt if you survived but he died from stress?"

"Neither of us died, CJ."

"Then how can you think having another baby is a good idea?"

She didn't. Instead of confessing and drawing her son into her drama, she said, "You don't understand."

CJ glared at her. "Give me some fucking credit. I'm not an imbecile. My name is CJ, not Johnnie."

The words startled a laugh from her, though she tried to hide it by coughing. "CJ, he's an adult and your uncle to boot," she said, as severe as possible. "Give him the respect he deserves."

None, but whatever.

"Then I can call him a motherfucker every day and not worry about it," CJ snapped. "He deserves no respect, and he'll get none from me. He's an asshole, an idiot, a whiner, a wimp, and a fuckhead."

"Well." Meggie shifted in her seat. "Tell me how you really feel."

"I can continue, if you're not convinced how much I loathe him."

"Johnnie's a complicated man."

"Dad's a complicated man. Uncle Mort. Uncle Val. It doesn't make Uncle Johnnie special. Without complexities, a person's a one-dimensional boor. Somehow, Uncle Johnnie manages complexity and stupidity."

"Enough, CJ. Your daddy wouldn't be happy hearing you malign one of your uncles."

"Bullshit, Mom! Dad is losing his fucking mind. I could knock Uncle Johnnie the fuck out, and all Dad would do is blink. Or say how unhappy you are."

Later, Meggie would cry. Right now, she drew in a breath, and summoned her strength. "I'm unhappy for a number of reasons, son—"

"So Uncle Johnnie was right! Of all the motherfuckers to have to agree with, you're making me side with him. You shouldn't have any more babies. We love you, Mom. We need you. You're enough for us. Please let us be enough for you." Tears glistened in his eyes, and he reached across the table and grabbed her hands. "Dad...Dad would give up his own life if you asked him. Please, Mom. If you don't do it for me or Rebel or Jo or the rest of your sons, do it for Dad."

Meggie squeezed his hands, even though they dwarfed hers. "Son, listen to me. Johnnie...I don't know...never mind. I'm tired of having babies. Jo wasn't planned, but I was happy. After all the turmoil and the early birth, I feel..." Shame slid into her and she lowered her lashes. "I don't feel a connection to her," she mumbled. "I'm still so tired." And Johnnie wouldn't leave her alone. If he'd let her heal and rest, maybe she could think more clearly. "Your daddy wants more children."

Mouth agape, CJ blinked and fell back against his chair. "You're joking."

Sniffling, she shook her head.

"Mom! Listen to this: Diesel, CJ, Patrick, Rule, Rebel,

Ryder, Ransom, Axel, Gunner, Jo. How many names?"

Meggie counted in her head. "Ten."

"Ten, Mom. Ten. Nine biological, one adopted. Nine alive, one deceased." He leaned forward. "How many fucking bedrooms in the house?"

"There were six. Now, there's eight."

"Eight bedrooms for eleven motherfuckers, if I include you and Dad, and no guest rooms, unless you spend more money to add more rooms."

"CJ, Johnnie told me Christopher wants more children. He said…he said I had a dysfunctional womb and—"

"He said what?"

"He won't leave me alone, CJ. He hid in the hospital stairwell and seemed to know when Christopher left. He'd come in my room and…and he wants me to go. He's offered me millions of dollars to leave."

Nausea curled through Meggie's insides and mild dizziness turned into an assault on her entire body. The thumping in her head threatened to burst her skull.

CJ's "fuck" was the last thing she heard before she sank into unconsciousness.

CHAPTER 37

MORTICIAN

Jamming a cigarette in the corner of his mouth, Mortician read and re-read Bailey's text. He was at a bar near where the motel Meggie once stayed at had stood. It had been demolished about three years ago. With no clear use for the land, Mort considered purchasing it to add to his portfolio. So far, his bids fell through.

For the time being, it didn't matter one way or the other. Left up to him, he'd sit on his money. He hated the idea of bankruptcy. Maybe, his frugality edged into stinginess.

Fuck, no maybe in it. He was a stingy motherfucker.

He'd lived through some very lean times. When he was seventeen, he'd spent a summer at the club. He'd gotten drunk, fought a stupid motherfucker, and been arrested. Sharper only bailed out Mort because it would make him look bad. As damage control, the press painted Mortician as a juvenile delinquent bad seed, a blight upon the great and holy Reverend Banks.

K-P and Big Joe rode to Cali, along with Outlaw, as a favor

to Mort's godmother. Or was it his godfather? Neither of who he'd ever met.

K-P, Big Joe, Outlaw, and Mort's fairy godmotherfucker changed the trajectory of his life. He might've straightened up, though he doubted it. His father was a cold-blooded, miserable fuckhead who corrupted or destroyed everybody that crossed his path.

Mort had left Cali, riding bitch with Outlaw, and not having a fucking nickel to his name.

Puffing on his cigarette and blowing out smoke, Mort smiled at the memory. He'd been like a duck out of fucking water at the club. He'd also been the only black person in a club where Lowman lurked in the shadows.

Grim, Mortician tamped out his cigarette in the ashtray in front of him. He sat in a corner at a small table. The place was quiet and nearly deserted with only one other patron and the bartender.

Logan Donovan had been a power hungry, insane fuckhead. He'd been low. But his genes were fucking strong. Those motherfuckers thrived in Johnnie and Ryan.

"Hypocritical motherfucker," he mumbled to himself.

Didn't Sharper's genes abound in him and Digger? His father's tightfistedness infused Mort and the penchant for harsh criticism lived in his brother.

He hoped they had some of their mother's fairness and awareness. She'd known what a motherfucker Sharper was. Years before she was killed in that car crash, she'd changed the terms of her will.

His mother's money had helped his father become the world famous preacher with a megachurch. It wasn't until after he'd killed Sharper did Mortician discover his father's treachery.

The safe filled with cash wasn't the only money his mother

left him and his brother. Sharper had been the executor of her estate until her boys turned thirty. He received a quarterly fee. If one of them predeceased the other, then the surviving son received everything.

Mortician finally understood why Sharper had lured Digger away, although Mortician had already been over thirty by then. Sharper's attorneys filed motions with the court claiming Mortician couldn't be found.

It was a tangled fucking web that almost cost so many innocent lives—Bailey, Meggie, Mort, Digger…

Harley.

Once he found out the house he grew up in had been in his mother's family, Mort decided to rebuild after all the dust settled and him and Digger received their inheritances from both estates.

Digger still didn't know what the fuck to do with money. Fortunately, he gave most of their quarterly payments to Bunny. She didn't save as frantically as Mort but she didn't spend as recklessly as Digger. Besides, Meggie's investments supplemented that fool, which he knew, so his resentment of her was all the more annoying.

When Mort received his quarterly payment, he gave half to Bailey for her to do whatever the fuck she pleased. But he didn't have a respectable career. He only had wealth.

Bailey: I love you so much. Please answer me.

The message fired his screen, brightening the darkness that swallowed him.

This was the first time in weeks she'd said those words to him. For that matter, she hadn't sent him an invitation to anywhere, not even to fucking hell, in days.

He almost responded to her immediately. But she'd

hurt him deeply. Shit he once overlooked now remained uppermost in his mind. Never mind her protecting Harley so fiercely. Her daughter, her decision.

However, Harley was his, too, and he was also entitled to his opinion about her behavior. Maybe, if he was a deadbeat, bitch-ass motherfucker they'd both have the right to disparage him. He wasn't. Even if everybody hadn't told him what a good husband and father he was in recent weeks, he'd just have to sit and reminisce to remind himself.

In the midst of debating if he should answer Bailey, I'm the Man by Aloe Blacc blasted from his pocket.

Mort immediately answered. "What's up, little dude?"

"Uncle Mort, Mom collapsed." CJ's voice trembled. If he wasn't crying, he sounded close to tears. "I'm following the ambulance to the hospital." He sniffled. "Her Lexus is still at the coffee shop."

The fear in CJ's tone alarmed Mort and everything else fled his head. "I'm on my way."

"I haven't called Dad yet. Right before the paramedics closed the ambulance doors, I saw her eyes open. I want him...he'll..."

Have a fucking fit. "CJ, focus on the road," Mort said as calmly as possible, jumping to his feet and rushing outside.

Ignoring the cold air blasting him, he headed to his bike, thankful that the snow had stopped. His surroundings were white and frozen, perfect for Christmas.

If only life wasn't so fucked up.

"You still there?" he asked once he mounted up.

CJ had been silent for the last minute.

"Yeah, Uncle Mort. The ambulance just got onto hospital grounds."

Relief flood Mort. "I'm not too far away. I'll be there in ten minutes."

"Should I call my dad?"

"No. If your momma bad off, Prez'll wipeout getting to her." Mort swallowed. "I'll go to him myself and drive him to her."

"Okay, I'll see you in a few minutes," CJ said, and disconnected.

Mortician arrived in eight minutes, speeding around to the ER entrance and parking at the edge of the circular driveway, right near the two ambulance bays.

The moment the hospital entrance doors slid open and Mortician walked in, he went to the intake station. "I'm looking for CJ Caldwell," he told the man behind the desk.

His badge read 'Omar Brown'. Yawning, Omar barely glanced up. "I don't have a CJ Caldwell admitted," he said after a few clicks on his keyboard and a study of his screen.

"His momma, Megan Caldwell, the patient. CJ should be in a private waiting room."

Omar's kohl-lined eyes widened; he straightened in his seat. "Yes, him. He'll be in the last room, right near the entrance for the patients transported by ambulance." He pressed the big silver button on the wall and the double doors flew open.

Mort nodded, then went into the restricted area, hoping he'd see Meggie or someone he might talk to and find out anything he could. When he reached the turnoff, he debated on continuing forward. The area for patients with the central medical station could provide answers.

Soon enough. CJ needed support, so Mort turned and walked down the short hallway to the last door, marked 'Private'. Without knocking, he opened the door and walked in. Since he intended to check on Meggie, he didn't close the door.

CJ was sitting on the sofa, elbows on his knees and his

head hung.

Decorated in burgundy, green, and gray, the room contained a sofa along one wall. On the opposite side, a loveseat stood in front of a coffee table that was flanked by two wing chairs.

The hospital's massive upgrades took place over the past decade, mainly funded by money from the club, Meggie, and Mortician. Not only was there a private wing and stairwell, but the hospital had several "safe" rooms and sitting rooms for club members. They were all soundproof and bullet proof because when motherfuckers fucked with the Dwellers, bullshit kicked off anywhere.

It was well known that most of the changes, especially that private wing, had been done with Meggie in mind. However, it was available for use by all brothers and their immediate family, as well as their support clubs if the need arose.

Mort walked forward and placed a hand on CJ's shoulder. "CJ?"

He looked up, tears brimming in his green eyes. For a moment, Mortician only saw the small boy CJ had once been, so filled with mischief and energy. All along Meggie knew Outlaw's world would draw in her son, too. She'd only borrowed him for however long she could. But by allowing him to emulate his father without judgment, CJ had grown into a confident young man.

Right now, he was scared.

"How your momma?"

"I don't know. They won't let me see her—"

"I'll find out what I can."

At the sound of Johnnie's voice, Mort started, and he glanced over his shoulder just as Johnnie walked his uninvited ass fully into the room and closed the door. Before he had a chance to ask the stupid motherfucker what the fuck he was doing there, CJ jumped to his feet and shoved Johnnie.

"Get the fuck out of here, you stupid motherfucker," he snarled. Right. In. Johnnie's. Face.

CJ's fury startled both Mort and Johnnie.

Unfortunately, Johnnie recovered before Mort tried to force CJ back.

"I should beat your fucking ass, boy," Johnnie sneered. "For putting your miserable hands on me."

"I'll fucking show how the fuck I can put my hands on you," CJ spat, grabbing Johnnie's collar and yanking him so close their noses almost touched.

Mortician's shock quickly gave way to enjoyment. He decided to see where this was going before he intervened.

"You fucking followed my mom, you miserable fuckhead." CJ tightened his hold, unconcerned at Johnnie's threats. "Telling her that fucking bullshit about leaving my dad. If anything happens to her, I'm fucking killing you."

Johnnie clipped CJ's jaw. "I take that as a fucking threat—"

"Take it however the fuck you want," CJ replied, sounding frighteningly like Prez, rubbing the place Johnnie hit. "I issue it as a promise."

"If I blow you the fuck away—"

"Johnnie," Mortician growled.

CJ punched Johnnie. The motherfucker stumbled back and grabbed his jaw, frozen in shock.

"I will never fucking forgive you, asshole," CJ said. "I can take your words as a threat, too. I don't carry a fucking gun, but I have access to an arsenal, and I can shoot your fucking ass off. If you kill me? Well, uncle, I'll see you in fucking hell because my dad will blow you the fuck away, you miserable motherfucker. Do me a fucking favor and fucking die."

"You're crossing a fucking line that you can never recover

from, CJ," Johnnie yelled. "Apologize to me. Because if you don't and you ever need me, I'll laugh in your fucking face."

"The day I need you is the day my cock falls off, fuckhead."

"We'll see who's right, won't we, nephew?" He turned. "I'm going to check on Megan."

A mad dog growl escaped CJ. The little motherfucker grew wings because he moved so fucking fast, he blurred in front of Mort and grabbed a handful of Johnnie's hair, then put him in a headlock.

Clearing his throat, Mort sat on the sofa and folded his arms. He would have to do fucking damage control anyway and CJ needed an outlet.

"I will snap your fucking neck if you go anywhere near my mom." CJ dragged Johnnie to the door.

Fearing he might bash Johnnie's fucking head into the wood, Mort called, "CJ!"

Although Johnnie was flailing and trying to pry away CJ's hold, CJ was younger, stronger, and livid. Somehow, the little motherfucker opened the door, and threw Johnnie out, then stalked back to Mort and glared. "I don't want a fucking lecture, Uncle Mort."

"I'm on your side, little dude, but I will beat your ass if you disrespect me since I haven't done anything to warrant it."

A muscle ticking in his jaw, CJ scowled.

Johnnie stormed back in, red-faced and furious, his hand at his side. He slammed the door shut.

Sighing, Mort got to his feet and placed himself in front of CJ.

"This is between my nephew and me, Mortician. This is a private family matter."

"If you touch CJ, it will become a fucking club matter, Johnnie," Mortician barked. "Either I save your fucking life now or kill you later on Prez's orders. On second thought, scratch that. He'd fuck you up himself."

"When Christopher isn't around, I'm in command," Johnnie said. "You're not a fucking officer, Mortician, so I order you to move or face repercussions."

CJ stood, in the line of fire since Johnnie's hand remained at his side, over his holstered gun. "For what? Do you really want to consider how it'll go if my dad finds out why Uncle Mort is facing the consequences of disobeying you? We can start with you telling Mom to leave Dad."

Yeah, a fact that went over Mort's head until that moment.

"Or, it can be, Uncle Mort shielding me from your intentions to shoot me. Which one, Uncle Johnnie? The latter will get you maimed. The former will get your live body fucking incinerated in the cremation oven at the funeral home."

"Leave, Mortician. I want to talk to my nephew alone."

"Man, fuck you. I'm not leaving CJ with you, especially with your hand on your fucking gun."

"If life had gone differently, CJ would be my son," Johnnie gritted, like the stupid motherfucker he was.

"What the fuck is your delusional mind cooking up now?" CJ demanded.

Johnnie opened his mouth.

"Nothing, little dude," Mort inserted. The kid was going through enough without Johnnie revealing the messy history between him and CJ's parents. "Now, sit the fuck down so I can talk to your uncle."

"I disinherit him! I don't want him as an uncle. All he's ever done is disliked me, Uncle Mort."

At that, Johnnie scowled. "You're wrong, CJ. I don't dislike you. I could never! How can you say such a thing?"

His genuine shock shouldn't have astonished Mort. Stupid motherfuckery was all-encompassing and a deranged

Donovan trait.

CJ narrowed his eyes.

Fuck.

Angry green snake eyes were a fucking Caldwell trait.

"You either hate me, my parents, or all three of us, fuckbag."

"Enough with the goddamn names, CJ. I draw the fucking line—"

"My line was drawn when my sister told me you snuck in Mom's room. You crossed my motherfucking line today when I walked up on you harassing my mom. Next."

"I'm not harassing Megan," Johnnie huffed.

Yanking his phone out of his jacket pocket, CJ smirked at Johnnie. "According to Merriam-Webster online, the definition of harassment is as follows: 1a. Exhaust, Fatigue; 1b.1 to annoy persistently;1b.2 to create an unpleasant or hostile situation for especially by uninvited and unwelcome verbal or physical conduct."

Johnnie's nostrils flared. "I know the definition of harass, you disrespectful little motherfucker."

"Of course, you do," CJ said with sarcasm. "All know-it-alls are stupider than fucking bricks."

"Do you hear how he's talking to me, Mortician?" Johnnie demanded. Not waiting for a reply, he turned his icy gaze to CJ. "The day is coming where you will need me, and I'm going to gleefully deny you."

That sounded ominous.

"Why?" CJ demanded, low. "What do you know that my dad doesn't?"

Unease swept across Johnnie's face. Forever fronting, he stiffened. "I resent that fucking question."

"I stopped caring what you fucking resent years ago, Uncle Johnnie. I'll answer for you, since you're too chickenshit to do it. You're fucking over the club with motherfucking Bash. Just like Ryan."

"CJ, enough," Mortician warned, not missing Johnnie's flinch. "This club business, and you not a fucking member. I've told you before overstepping is dangerous."

"Really, Mortician? You're calling him down for that but not for his insolence toward me?"

"I couldn't interfere with that, Johnnie," Mort said with a shrug. "Family business. It wasn't my place to say shit."

"Oh, so now it's family business? When I ordered you to stand down, you ignored me. I'm his uncle and he's turned against me. What do you think he'll do to you one day?"

"Uncle Mort's my uncle too, you worthless piece of shit," CJ fumed. "And don't ever fucking say otherwise."

"Give me a chance to talk, little dude," Mort said, schooling his features to hide how touched he was by CJ's defense of him.

"I respect you, Uncle Mort. You've always been kind and protective of me. You've always respected me—"

"Respected you?" Johnnie scoffed. "Do you know how entitled you fucking sound? You're a child. Who the fuck made you think you deserve respect? Never mind. It's Megan. She was a fucking child when she had you so of course she'd think a child should have respect, instead of discipline and a firm hand."

"How's that working out for you?" CJ said evilly. "We have to watch decapitated bodies to keep Rory from stealing them. Mattie has to hide what a lively, loyal girl she is. JJ stays in tears and Blade is rarely away from his nanny."

This was getting out of hand.

"Johnnie, go check on Meggie," Mort said.

"Uncle Mort, no—"

"Yeah, kid. Outlaw is going to wonder where she at.

Johnnie on the hospital board. He'll get answers."

"He was following her. Or watching the coffee shop, waiting for me to leave so he could harass her again. How else could he have known to come?"

"Even if that's true, little dude, we have to figure shit out now. We have to call Prez soon." He drew in a regretful breath. "What happened in here today has to be swept aside for now."

"I refuse to keep CJ's rudeness from Christopher. For you to suggest otherwise because of Megan—"

"When you got to be such a fucking asshole, son?" Mort asked crossly. "It got nothing to do with Meggie. If Outlaw shoot your ass off, he might regret it later. We got to wait until he can handle the repercussions of his actions."

Johnnie bared his teeth at Mort. Folding his arms, he lifted a brow, wondering if the motherfucker thought to intimidate him.

"Fine," Johnnie gritted. "I'll see what I can find out about Megan." He stomped out of the room and slammed the door.

"Strangle on shitty birdfeed," CJ shouted.

"The room soundproof," Mort said, in case the little motherfucker didn't know.

CJ's shoulders drooped and he sat just as another text message from Bailey came through.

Bailey: Don't leave me on read, Lucas. Respond. Please. Come to my office. Please. I'm begging you.

He sighed and dropped next to CJ.

"Is that Harley?"

"It's Bailey. She want me to come to her office party." Mortician hated to see CJ's despair returning. "Once we see how Meggie doing, maybe we can go together. It'll take your mind off shit for a little bit and you can talk to Harley."

CJ glanced away. "I have nothing to say to her, Uncle Mort. I'm the worst motherfucker alive, according to her and Aunt Bailey."

"You not? Bailey adore you—"

"No, Uncle Mort." CJ met Mort's gaze without flinching. "Whatever else that happened over the past few months, I've learned very few people actually adore me. I'm either reviled or revered with little in between for absolutely no reason. It would be fine if they actually knew me. Most people don't, so the reverence and revulsion are shallow interpretations of fucking rumors."

Mort had nothing to say to that.

"But I have something to tell you, Uncle Mort. After, I'm sure you'll hate me, too."

"Kid, I could never hate—"

"It's about Harley."

"CJ, kid, I know you're angry with her, but she has suffered, too. The boys at the club with me. Her momma and me barely speaking. She got beat up. She misses you—"

"No, she doesn't miss me." His nose reddened and the tears that had been in his eyes earlier returned. "She has Nardo."

The argument he'd had with Bailey over Harley going to that little motherfucker's house rose in Mort's mind.

"I hate that motherfucker so much, Uncle Mort." CJ's voice trembled with anger and pain. "I ran into him at the mall today, and he told me about his and Harley's private business."

Mort pressed his lips together to keep his own tears at bay.

"I don't know if he's lying. I'm hoping he is, but he was just too...too." CJ scrubbed a hand over his face, wiping away a covert tear. "I don't want Harley to turn up pregnant or with a disease."

"Goddamn." Mort sagged against the sofa. His heart, already shredded by Bailey and Harley, stuttered and then quickened. "I discussed fucking Char when I was twelve and she was fifteen. Shit hits different when it's your own baby girl."

"Who's Char?"

A bitch better left in the past. "The mama of my firstborn. Tyler. Killed—" by Sharper— "the same day Meggie was shot, and Digger kidnapped you and Bunny."

CJ didn't respond.

"Fuck, man." Resting his head on the back of the sofa, Mort stared at the ceiling. "This my fault, CJ. If I was home, this wouldn't have happened." He jumped to his feet. "Goddamn."

"It would've happened whether you were there or not, Uncle Mort. Harley doesn't think she's pretty or special. She even asked me if I had a problem with her hair. Can you believe that? While she doubts herself, she'll recklessly search for fucking validation. And…and I just can't with her anymore. I'm sorry. I've kissed other girls, but I've never had sex. I was waiting for her."

Mort felt numb. He didn't have words or advice for CJ. He couldn't even express admiration at his intelligence.

Another text message came through.

> **Bailey:** I'm selling my practice, Lucas.

Wait, now. Say what?

> **Mort:** Don't do that, Bailey. Your dream always been to have a practice in Portland. You put a lot of time and effort into it.

Bailey: No, I've been so unfair to you, and I'm so sorry. I'm going
          to call you.

Mort: Not yet, Bailey.

He pressed send immediately.

Mort: Meggie collapsed and I'm at the ER with CJ. We trying to find
          out her condition.

Bailey: Oh my god! Let me know how she is as soon as possible.

Mort: I wi

Halls of Illusion by ICP peeled from his phone, interrupting Mort's typing.

"Fuuuuuuuccccccckkkkkk."

"He was going to call eventually," CJ said glumly, knowing it was Outlaw since he'd chosen the ringtone.

Mort answered. "Hey, Prez."

"Where my woman, Mortician? Her fuckin' location at the coffee shop, but she been there for hours and she not answerin'."

"Where you at?" Mort asked cautiously.

"On my way from Roseburg with Derby."

"I'm going to call her, Prez."

"She had a doctor's appointment today, Mort. Suppose… suppose…? What if she ain't okay?"

"Then you would know." Mort winced at the lie. For now, it was the best he could do. "Give me a few minutes and I'll hit you back."

Mort disconnected and studied CJ for a few minutes.

"I think I fucked up, Uncle Mort," he said into the silence, leaning forward and returning to the position Mort found him in. "Dad would want me to take Mom's SUV, but he tracks her, so I followed the ambulance in his pickup. I took her wallet with her ID and insurance cards and stuck her phone and purse under the driver's seat." He glanced over his shoulder. Was I wrong?"

Mort smiled gently. "No, little dude. You was dead on."

The door opened and Johnnie walked in. Unlike earlier, CJ didn't lunge. He deflated, seeming too weary for one so young.

"Megan is asking for you, CJ," he announced. "The doctor is recommending she remain overnight, but she's demanding to be discharged."

CJ stood. "I'll talk to her. If she wants to leave and the doctor wants her to stay, it'll just upset her more."

"I need to call Bailey, CJ."

Mort's life was forever changed because Harley's was. At one time, he would've known what to say to her. Now, he felt like an outsider. Although Bailey seemed to have a change of heart, she had worked her ass off. Besides, he didn't want her to throw in his face what she gave up "for him" down the road. He didn't trust that she wouldn't turn against him again. Especially once he told her about Harley, though it wouldn't be tonight.

"Yeah, whatever," CJ said to Johnnie.

"Without Christopher here, it's the only way, CJ," Johnnie said. "He has the final say in these situations."

"I think Meggie checked herself out a few days ago, Johnnie," Mort pointed out. "If you saying Prez wants to make that call, even over Meggie, then his instructions wasn't followed."

"Maybe, because she was going to be released soon anyway?" Johnnie suggested.

"Fuck, if that's the truth, and Mom finds out, she's going to be madder than a motherfucker," CJ grumbled.

"Meggie girl used to Prez taking extreme measures to try and keep her safe," Mort protested.

"Fine, Uncle Johnnie. I'll let you know if the doctors deny her request so you can help her out."

Johnnie nodded and held out his hand. "Friends again, nephew?"

CJ visibly gritted his teeth, but accepted the peace offering and shook Johnnie's hand. "Friends, uncle. Stay away from my mom and that will continue." He snatched his hand away and stalked out, leaving the door wide open.

Mort snickered, then headed toward the hallway.

Johnnie's voice stopped him. "Why doesn't his privileged behavior annoy you, Mortician?"

"Let me flip that, John Boy. Why the fuck it does annoy you? When I first met you, your ass was privileged. Entitled. The golden child. Whatever the fuck you want to call it."

"I set that aside and chose loyalty to Christopher—"

"Maybe. What you forgot to leave at the fucking door was your condescension. A part of you always put yourself above us lowly motherfuckers. What you didn't have then and don't now is a natural born ability to lead. CJ and Prez got it, and your bitch ass hate them for it." Mort walked out, turning his attention to his wife.

Fuck Johnnie.

CHAPTER 38

MEGGIE

Despite the ER doctor suggesting she remain for overnight observation, Meggie insisted on going home. Christopher had left early this morning, and she'd only talked to him once when she telephoned him. She'd thought maybe he was seeing to business. However, none of his officers or, as far as she knew, any of his club members accompanied him.

Whatever it was, his silence indicated he wasn't in Hortensia. She refused to have him get into an accident after trying to get to her from miles away.

Once she received her discharge papers, she directed Mort to guide CJ to the back entrance. Whoever was on gate duty might note her arrival in Christopher's pickup, instead of her SUV.

"Call Bunny, Meggie," Mortician instructed after she strapped herself into the passenger seat and CJ was behind the wheel. "Fuck, never mind. She probably with the kids. I'll tap Digger and Val to get your Lexus back to the club."

Relaxing against the seat, Meggie closed her eyes.

"Mom?"

"Meggie?"

Meggie lifted her lids. "I trust you, Mort," she said tiredly. "It's almost six in the evening. Christopher left at dawn. He might already be home, wondering—"

"Now, Meggie, you know if Prez was around he'd be blowing up our fucking phones looking for you."

The words turned over in her head and she snapped her eyes open. "Suppose he's hurt? Do you know where he went, Mort? Oh my god, why haven't I heard from him more than once today?" Her head started pounding again.

"Mom!" CJ called. "Dad's fine. Stay calm. Otherwise, I'll take you back into the ER."

She glanced at CJ, then at Mort. As her panic increased, so did her dizziness.

"He fine, Meggie. He with Derby."

"Derby?" she asked, frowning, still terrified for Christopher's safety. "Why would he spend the day with Derby?"

"Ask him when you see him, Mom," CJ said. "You left the hospital so you wouldn't alarm him. If he gets home before us, he will be alarmed."

Meggie nodded.

"You all good, girl?" Mortician asked.

"Yes," she whispered.

Mort leaned into the pickup to look at her son. "We'll head out in two or three minutes, little dude. Once I make the call about Meggie SUV."

"Okay, Uncle Mort."

"When we pass the usual turn, slow your speed. The second turn that leads to the back forest is easy to miss. The third turn that'll bring us to the road for our houses is even harder to see."

"Do I need a code?"

Mort nodded. "I'll keep my bike in front of the sensor so you can blaze through. Prez designed it to close quick. That's why he made it wide enough for a bike and Meggie cars to fit side-by-side."

Five minutes later, their caravan of two started off. CJ drove in silence, so Meggie closed her eyes, determined to remain calm.

"Mom, we're here," CJ said, a little while later.

He opened her door, unstrapped her seatbelt and lifted her into his arms.

At first, confusion muddled Meggie's brain, then she blinked. Although her head was still hurting, some awareness seeped into her as he started walking and she relaxed against him, trusting him.

"Outlaw isn't home yet, CJ," Bunny said.

Meggie lifted her head, smiling as her friend leaned against the gate in front of her house.

"Get Meggie into bed, little dude," Mortician called, "I'll be waiting for you, so we can get Prez's pickup back to the club."

"I don't know how you're going to pull this off," Bunny said, framed against the Christmas light display in the yard. "Someone's going to realize Meggie or her Lexus hasn't come through the gate."

"Not much Prez can complain about if Meggie safe and sound in the house, Bunny," Mortician said.

Inside, the warm air circulated the scents of pine, cinnamon, and cedar. The silence surprised her.

"Where are the rest of the kids?"

"Roxanne called Rebel and asked for her help with a cake. Rule tagged along. Zoann is watching Gunner. My kids and Ryder, Ransom, and Axel are with Ophelia. Mort thought it best."

"Yeah, Mom, the less witnesses, the easier the lie," CJ said.

"Is Cash and Stretch with Christopher?" Meggie asked hopefully.

"I don't think so," Bunny answered. "Ophelia said Stretch and Cash left together at about 3 this afternoon and expect to be gone overnight."

"I see."

When they reached the third floor and her bedroom, CJ sat her on the edge of the bed.

"Are you going to be okay, Mom?" he asked, unable to hide his concern. "I-I can stay."

"I'm fine, potato," she promised, though she was anything but. She was exhausted and worried about her husband. "I want a quick shower."

"No, I don't think that's wise, Mom. Your pressure went really high and—"

"I'll be with her, bud," Bunny promised. "Help your uncles see to the cars."

Indecision tore across CJ's face. "Are you sure?"

"Positive," Meggie stressed. "If anything happens, Bunny will be right here with me, and she'll call immediately."

"I won't be long, Mom." CJ backed toward the door. "Don't go anywhere."

Meggie smiled. "I won't, son. I'll be waiting for you."

The moment he walked out, Meggie sagged. "Has Digger heard from Christopher?"

"No, babe." Bunny looked as if she hated to answer. "I'm sorry."

"God—"

"Let's get you showered, Meggie. Once you're settled in bed, I'll see if I can contact Stretch. He'll get a bead on Outlaw."

Bunny busied herself in the bathroom while Meggie took a quick shower and washed her hair. Once she finished, she took a towel from the towel warmer, wrapped it around herself and then sat at the vanity to comb and braid her wet hair. By then, Bunny had found a nightgown for her.

In two days, it would be a month since she'd collapsed and went into premature labor. Despite today's setback, she felt she was doing remarkably well.

"I pushed myself a little too much today," she said lightly, climbing into bed and settling against a stack of fluffy pillows.

"You did," Bunny agreed quietly. "I should've come with you."

"It's okay," Meggie soothed. "No harm done. I'm fine."

A 'person detected' alert resounded on Meggie's phone, and she grabbed it to watch Mortician, CJ, and her Christopher enter the front gate and head down the walkway to the door.

CHRISTOPHER

If he hadn't been so worried about Megan, he would've fucked up Derby and Dez tofuckinnight. Unfortunately, his retribution would have to wait until tomorrow.

Dez hadn't done anything more than the previous

infractions. But motherfucking Derby?

The motherfucker stood by Christopher's side and helped clean up the bodies. His assfucks weren't nearly as thorough or sophisticated as the time and attention Johnnie, Cash, Val, Digger, and Mortician gave to scenes. Beggars couldn't be fucking choosers, so Christopher took what he could get.

In the middle of the cleanup, Megan called and told him Bunny was driving her to the coffeeshop to meet CJ. All seemed on target for him to hit the road no later than one and get back to Hortensia about four.

Except…

Derby reminded Christopher he needed to get to the motel to pay Adette and Sadie.

"I'm gonna give you the bills, Derby."

"No, Outlaw, this won't take long. I need you as a cover."

"A motherfucking what?"

Grinning, Derby sped off.

He'd been solid during Christopher's encounter with Bash, so he decided to return the fucking favor.

The moment Christopher followed Derby into the motel where Adette and Sadie were, Adette had been all over him. Even when he'd shoved her away and told her to back the fuck off, the bitch hadn't backed the fuck off.

Then, he'd heard sounds of fucking.

Motherfucking Derby was sticking his cock in another bitch afuckingain.

It fucking figured.

"Come on, Outlaw," Adette cooed, grinding her naked body against him and wrapping her arms around his neck.

She really was taller than Megan. His wife could reach his neck if he leaned down or picked her up.

"You wanted me at the bar."

Christopher shoved her away, ignoring Derby's grunts and

Sadie's moans.

"I fuckin' needed you at the bar—"

She gave him a sly look. "Well, I need you now. Pay me with a pussy lick and some dick and we're even."

"I'm offerin' two fuckin' forms of payments, bitch. A fuckin' bullet or some fuckin' bills. Tell me now what the fuck you want so I can hit the road."

She blinked, then giggled, apparently not believing how imminently in danger she was placing herself by continuing to fuck with Christopher.

Closing his eyes, he thought of Megan. She wouldn't want him to indiscriminately kill, so he tried another tactic.

Of course, he had to wait until Derby and Sadie finished coming and shut the fuck up. And, of fucking course, Christopher's cock hardened.

Adette grabbed his dick through his jeans.

Christopher jerked back and shoved her away at the same time. "Adette, I gave you the fuckin' impression I wanted to fuck you. I'm fuckin' tellin' you I don't. I love my fuckin' wife. I needed your help to verify a fact. I'm gonna pay you for your time and I'm gonna apologize if I led you on."

Derby zipped his fly. Sadie laid on the bed, spread her legs, and displayed her fucked pussy, dripping with Derby's cum. Chuckling, Derby climbed on the bed and buried his face between her legs.

Christopher's hands shook. It had been a month and a day since he'd last fucked. He threw open the door, his cock beating him into the hallway. He almost made his escape.

Adette had other ideas and wrapped her arms around his waist, pulling him back into the room and closing the door. Derby stood, dragged Sadie from the bed, shoved her on her knees, and pushed his cock between her lips.

Sweat beaded Christopher's brow.

He was faithful, but he wasn't a fucking monk. However, he didn't put himself in places where other pussy could even tempt him. Today had been the exception.

Derby pumped into Sadie's mouth.

Christopher's balls throbbed. He ached for Megan.

"You can't leave unless you fuck me," Adette said. She leaned against the door and licked her lips, blocking his exit.

"If I kill you, I can fuckin' leave."

Suddenly, Derby's grunt stopped. "Outlaw—"

"Shut the fuck up, motherfucker. You been boofuckinhooin' about your bitch. You got that bitch back and you still fuckin' over her?"

"Just because I love Gypsy doesn't mean I want to be faithful. The trick is covering your tracks."

"You're a smart man, babe," Adette said. "I'm sure you can cover—"

"I love my wife. I ain't fuckin' you. I've fucked over her enough today by allowin' you two bitches on my fuckin' lap."

Hooting with laughter, Derby tucked away his cock, then patted Christopher's back. "That wasn't fucking over Meggie, Outlaw." He helped Sadie to her feet, then kissed her deeply. "Take care of him. Make him come so much his toes stay permanently curled. I swear to you this is what you need to get your head on straight, brother. I promise. You need a buffer between you and your wife. Your reward for not only surviving today but saving us is good hot cunt."

"Derby," Christopher started, attempting to squeeze past Adette when she allowed Derby to leave the room.

Growling, Christopher picked Adette up to move her aside. As he did, Sadie grabbed him from behind, giving Adette the opportunity to wrap her legs around his waist and grind her bare pussy over his jeans, marking him with her scent.

He couldn't fucking believe he was grappling with two bitches determined to fuck him on Derby's orders while ignoring what the fuck he wanted. Derby truly believed he was doing Christopher a favor.

The pipes on Derby's exhaust roared to life.

Christopher stopped fighting. Instead of trying to get away, he held Adette loosely. She rocked her pussy against him, pressing her lips against his, while Sadie nuzzled his neck. Digging into his cut, he took his .9mm in hand, pressed it against Adette's temple and pulled the fucking trigger.

Releasing her spasming body and allowing it to drop to the floor, he shot Sadie, cutting her off mid-scream. He shot each of them in the head once more, then went to the bathroom and wiped their blood off his face, hands, and arms. He hadn't noticed surveillance cameras but he still needed to call Stretch and Cash so they could try to tap into the feeds and erase any footage of his entrance and exit.

Motherfucking Derby.

By the time he got on the road again, it was close to 4PM. He'd tried Megan but the call went straight to voicemail, so he'd called Bunny, who hadn't answered. Next, he tried Mortician. Cash and Stretch had been busy trying to unfuck Christopher out of Derby's shenanigans, but he'd still called and asked if they could track Megan. They swore she hadn't left the coffee shop, although Bunny's signal indicated she was at the clubhouse. So far away, he couldn't do anything. Then, he'd had to stop in Eugene to buy another pair of black jeans, and find another shabby motel for a quick shower.

Now, as Christopher followed his boy and Mortician down the walkway, the light display calmed him. He'd survived Bash. He'd ironed out a deal. He'd escaped those two bitches who wouldn't take fucking no for an answer. And he was home, starving for a glimpse of his wife and starving for a bite to eat.

He had a lot of confessing to do to his woman, but all in all he felt like Prez again. Not just a shadow who was neither biker, father, or husband, afraid to leave Megan because he feared she'd be stolen from him.

The first thing he noticed when he walked into the house was the fucking stillness. His children were noisy lil' motherfuckers. Silence was unnatural.

"Megan?" Christopher called, closing the door behind him. He sniffed but didn't smell any food. "What did your ma cook, boy?"

Swallowing, CJ bowed his head, then shrugged. "Nothing, Dad." He shoved his fingers through his hair and yanked a handful. The lil' motherfucker needed a haircut. "We ate at the coffee shop." He glanced at Mortician.

Alarms rose in Christopher. "Where's Reb and the boys?"

CJ shrugged again. "Not here."

"Where's your ma?" he asked carefully.

"Upstairs, Dad," CJ mumbled. "In your room."

Fear seized Christopher and he took off running, rushing up the staircase, hating the daunting quietness and damning his decision to leave today.

It had been too soon. He'd ordered Mortician to talk to Brooks. Christopher should've waited.

By the time he arrived in their bedroom, he was breathless at all the scenarios running through his head. He found her propped against her pillows, her hair braided, and wearing a flowing white nightgown. Dark circles ringed her eyes and she looked...off.

Just as she had this morning. When he'd left her anyway and forced her out of his head to conduct business. She smiled groggily. Her lips were dry and cracked. He sat next to her on the edge of the bed.

"Megan," he whispered, caressing her cheek, knowing something wasn't right, but unsure what. He gathered her into his arms and inhaled the cherry blossom scent of her hair. "What's the matter, baby?"

She planted a tiny kiss on his chin. "I'm tired, Christopher."

"What did Doc Will say?"

Her head lolled against his chest. "I collapsed in the coffee shop and was brought to the hospital in an ambulance," she murmured. "My blood pressure went so high. I was so dizzy."

"What the fuck you mean, Megan? Why didn't nobody call me?"

"No one knew where you were. We didn't want you to wipe out trying to get to me if you were far away."

He had been far away. Worse, he'd been with two bitches. Willingly at first. He hadn't cheated on Megan, but he'd crossed a fucking line. Then, Derby had left him to fuck those two bitches or for those two bitches to fuck him.

Instead, he'd killed them because they didn't respect his determination to remain faithful to his wife.

Two things Megan expected him not to do, he had. While she…she'd been taken away from the coffee shop in an—

"CJ was with you?"

She nodded.

No fucking wonder his boy looked so fucking shellshocked.

"I was so worried about you. No one had heard from you all day today. I-I…" She shuddered against him.

He tightened his hold on her. "How long you been home?"

"About thirty minutes."

"But your ride and your purse showing you at the coffee shop."

"CJ left them there and followed the ambulance in your

pickup."

"To purposely throw me off?" he demanded.

"To protect you."

Christopher's anger died. Megan and CJ had been going out of their way to ensure his safety while he'd been fucking around with Bash and Adette.

How could he ever live in peace if he had to leave Megan? How could he have forgotten how fragile she still was?

Standing, he turned and laid her on the bed, tucking her in, then bending and kissing her forehead. He needed another shower before he touched her again.

"Where were you?"

"Club business."

"With Derby?"

He'd told Mort he was with Derby. "It was club business, Megan. Derby and the Burnin' Hounds one of my support clubs. We have business together."

She studied him for a moment, then turned her back on him, and curled up. "You've had business with him before. You've never been off the grid for hours when you're together."

Scowling at the back of her head, Christopher wasn't sure what to say, especially with the guilt eating at him. "Lemme get this fuckin' straight. You found proof to show Gypsy that cunt's baby wasn't his so she could reconcile with Derby, but you ain't trustin' me to be with the motherfucker for hours if I ain't contactin' you?"

"I'm tired, Christopher. And my head's hurting. Leave me alone."

"Just what the fuck are you accusin' me off?"

"You have an underlying smell of soap." Her sob tore through him. "Soap that isn't yours."

"Megan, listen to me."

"You showered while you were away." Another sob escaped her and another and another, until gut-wrenching ones wracked her.

He slid behind her into bed and tried to take her into his arms but couldn't immediately because of her fierce struggles. Her full strength hadn't returned, otherwise she would've fucked him up. However, it gave him the advantage. He waited until she tired herself out and could do nothing else except collapse in defeat.

"Megan, baby, I swear I ain't cheated on you. I swear. You ain't goin' to like what the fuck I did do, but I ain't stuck my cock in no other bitch."

"If you haven't touched another woman, why did you shower?"

"I didn't say I ain't touched another girl today. I said I ain't fucked another girl."

"What do you mean? You were still with another woman."

"For a reason, baby. Two girls sat on my lap and I had to make it seem like I intended to fuck them."

She elbowed him. "Go away. Of everything that Johnnie said today, when he told me you would find another woman, I defended you, Christopher! I told him you'd never touch another woman. If he was right about that, he must be right about everything!" She scrambled to the other side of the bed and got out, swaying on her feet.

"What the fuck you talkin' about, Megan? What the fuck Johnnie been sayin' to you after I told him to stay the fuck away from you?"

"Everything you told him—"

"I ain't told that motherfucker nothing."

She fell into the nightstand and grabbed it to steady herself.

Christopher shot to his feet and rushed around to the

other side of the bed, wrapping her in his arms. At first, she tried to push him away, then she clung to him and sobbed so pitifully Christopher's heart broke.

Earlier, he had a laundry list of motherfuckers to kill. Now, he didn't care. He just wanted Megan safe and healthy and loving him.

"You know me, Megan."

She didn't answer, so he took her face between his hands and stared into her eyes, searching for his girl, craving that look that told him all he needed to know.

"You know me. If I fucked another bitch, I would tell you."

Tears slid down her cheeks and she lowered her gaze, focusing on his shirt.

He opened his mouth to reaffirm what he thought she knew—his love for—and commitment to—her.

But she interrupted him before he uttered a word. "I believe you," she said. Her look of adoration rose in her eyes, stark and vulnerable. She swayed and leaned against him again. "Don't ever...I couldn't bear it."

He lifted her in his arms and kissed her. "I know, Megan. I ain't never cheatin' on you. You it for me. My everyfuckinthing, baby."

She pressed her forehead against him. "Just...please... please, God, make him stop. Please."

Christopher froze. Not only because Megan sounded so fucking tired, but in all their years together, she'd never begged him to make any motherfucker stop.

Especially that motherfucker. Usually, she went out of her way to prevent fucking ups.

For a long time, Johnnie had a piece of Megan's heart. It was tiny, but still fucking his.

Now, she'd finally given Christopher a chance to spill what he'd wanted since that motherfucker strangled her.

Johnnie's blood.

CHAPTER 39

Harley

"Dan, you remember my daughter?" Mommie smiled between them. "Harley, this is Dr. Daniel Stokes."

Dr. Stokes was a handsome man with bright brown eyes and thick blond hair. If Harley remembered correctly, he was older than Mommie, but younger than Daddy.

Harley smiled. "Nice to see you again, sir," she said with a shy smile.

"Likewise, Harley." He placed his hand at the small of Mommie's back.

Discomfort crossed her features and her smile dimmed. "We have a good turnout for the office party."

"Who can resist such a lovely hostess," Dr. Stokes responded.

Harley frowned. "My daddy's nickname for her is Pretty Girl."

The doctor gave her an indulgent smile. "Reductive, to say the least. Your mother is a gorgeous woman, Harley. Not just a 'pretty girl'."

Harley was tired and hurt. Her bruises and cuts were just beginning to heal from her fight. Rebel and Mattie still barely spoke to her. Lolly had picked up Molly from the hospital earlier today, ignoring Harley's protests. Daddy preferred to be with that traitor, CJ, and his family, rather than at Mommie's holiday office party.

Dr. Stokes eyed her mother. "She hasn't been a girl in some time."

"Only a jackass would say that as a compliment," Harley said with venom.

The doctor glared at her, and Mommie stiffened.

"I'm so sorry, Dan. You will apologize this instant, Harley Banks."

"Yeah. No. You're angry with me when you're in the wrong, Mommie. When Symphony flirted with Daddy and I called her out, he didn't get upset."

Her screech drew attention to their place near the window. Inside, like outside, was decorated with myriad Christmas decorations. Smartly wrapped presents ringed the balsam fir in the corner. Her mother's staff wore brightly colored clothes. Servers in black and white handed out hot cider, champagne, and hors d'oeuvres. Mommie wore a short red coat dress, heeled sandals, and fine jewelry. She looked nothing like a biker's wife.

With eyes more green than brown and silky dark hair, she barely looked like Harley's mother and Lolly's daughter.

Harley glanced around, horrified to find herself the darkest person there. She turned accusing eyes to her mother.

"Not a word," Mommie said stiffly. "You're embarrassing

me."

"Spare the rod," Dr. Stokes started.

"Enough!" Mommie said in a steely voice. "You're crossing a line, Dan. Another line. I could overlook your hands on my back, but don't let it happen again."

He raised his hands. "Fine. I just thought after our talk—"

"In which I told you how much I love my husband."

"The one who's never here," Dr. Stokes said with a disbelieving laugh, just as the door opened.

"Lucas," Mommie breathed.

Harley turned, afraid to believe her father was actually there, but he was, dressed in full leathers, his dreads queued.

"Daddy!" Bursting into tears, Harley ran to him and wrapped her arms around his waist. She'd made so many mistakes over the past few days. Most of which she wanted to change. "I didn't know you were coming."

Her father hugged her. "I told Bailey to let it be a surprise, baby," he said. "Why you crying, Harley?"

For so many reasons, but she could share none of them. "Dr. Stokes is an asshole," she mumbled against his chest.

Daddy snickered. "Flirting with Bailey, I take it."

Harley nodded, refusing to remove her head from against her father's chest.

"Lucas, my love," Mommie said into the silence.

Instead of insisting Harley move, Mommie enveloped her in the hug she gave to Daddy. Something hard pressed against Harley's back, but she dismissed it.

"I thought you weren't coming, Daddy," she said. "But I'm glad that you remembered your loyalties."

"Harley," Daddy said with disapproval. "I've had enough of your judgmental bullshit, baby."

"Your daddy's right, hunny bunny. Ease up on CJ."

Harley stiffened. The object pressing into her almost felt

like a...a gun. "What has he said to you for you to desert me?" she screeched, overwhelmed with guilt and misery. "Daddy knew about the party, but he went to CJ's house first."

Daddy released her. "I went to the fucking hospital, Harley," he growled. "Meggie collapsed and CJ called me. He didn't want Prez to fucking wipeout."

"How is she, Lucas?" Mommie asked, unable to see Harley's shock and horror, although her father could and ignored it.

"They got her pressure down, Bailey. They wanted to keep her for overnight observation, but she went home. Luckily, Prez was hours away, so me and CJ got her home and Bunny got her settled twenty minutes before Outlaw walked in."

"I'll visit her tomorrow," Mommie promised.

Glancing at Harley, Daddy nodded. "Okay, Bailey. Prez was suspicious because of the way CJ acting." He scrubbed a hand over his face and stared at Harley again. "I sat and had a long talk with him, while Outlaw went to Meggie. I didn't see him again before I left."

"It was good you spent time with CJ," Mommie said.

Harley's mouth dropped open. "Hello? What about me?"

"I've waited for you to make the announcement, Lucas," Mommie said, ignoring Harley.

Daddy followed Mommie's cue. "Bailey, I told you don't do this. I love you too much to let you throw away your dream of having a practice."

"Veni, vidi, vici," Mommie said.

"Okay, Caesar," Daddy teased as Harley worked out the words in her head.

I came. I saw. I conquered.

"Selling my practice and opening a smaller one in Hortensia is the right thing. I miss you and my children. I miss spending time with Meggie, Kendall, Zoann, Bunny, and Ophelia. I have to do this, as much for us as it is for me."

"As long as you sure, Pretty Girl—"

"I've tried to dissuade her," Dr. Stoke interrupted.

Daddy stiffened. Backing away, Mommie grabbed Harley's shoulders.

"Come with me, son," Daddy said politely. "Let me put a little bug in your ear."

"I don't need your advice. And, please, don't refer to me as 'son.'"

"I think you do." Daddy stepped closer. "My public service announcement is just for you. It might save your life. Son."

Her father put an arm around Dan and guided him toward the door. Dr. Stokes glanced over his shoulder.

Smirking, Harley gave the idiot a small wave. For the first time in weeks, she felt as if things were looking up. Unbeknownst to her, her parents had worked things out. For now, it was enough to give her a semblance of peace, though she doubted she'd ever be happy again.

Even if she didn't blame CJ for what had transpired with her and Nardo, he'd never forgive her if he found out.

On the other hand, if he hadn't betrayed her with Molly, she wouldn't have returned the favor with Nardo.

"I wonder if Lucas needs my gun."

The words sank in, and Harley spun to face her mother. "What?"

Mommie shrugged, and lifted the hem of her coat dress, revealing a lacy thigh holster with a small gun strapped to her.

Harley's eyes widened.

"Bunny and I carry guns. Meggie doesn't. She doesn't like them. Zoann was never taught to shoot, and Johnnie doesn't want Kendall packing heat." She shrugged. "Momma carries a knife and a gun." She smiled tenderly. "Let's circulate while your daddy talks to Dan."

She walked away, leaving Harley speechless and even more confused.

CHAPTER 40

MEGGIE

The next afternoon, Meggie found herself back at the coffee shop awaiting Gypsy's arrival. Once again, Christopher left in the early hours, promising to return as soon as possible. His actions both shocked her and raised her suspicions, especially after last night's confessions from each of them. Normally, after her medical crisis, he glued himself to her side.

Despite Mortician's reassurances and Christopher saying otherwise, maybe, Johnnie was right and her husband was tired of her many illnesses and difficult pregnancies. She was just so exhausted, she couldn't make sense of anything. She hadn't even made it to the hospital to see Jo. With Gypsy running late, Meggie was beginning to rethink her decision to drive herself over, but her friend had sounded so frantic.

As another ten minutes trudged by, Meggie texted Gypsy that she was going home. She tried Christopher, but didn't get an answer, so she purchased pastries for each of her kids, then headed to her Lexus.

Halfway to the SUV, a man inserted himself in front of her in a sad repeat of yesterday. However, it wasn't Johnnie.

"Meggie."

"Bash." She'd never met Cee Cee's oldest son, but Christopher had told her about him a few years ago. She couldn't remember under what context. However, the Caldwell emerald eyes, aquiline nose, and masculine jaw made his kinship unmistakable.

Unlike Christopher's beautiful full mouth, cruelty thinned Bash's lips. He was a tall, muscular man with huge hands, like his father and brother.

It didn't surprise her that he knew her. As Christopher's wife, many people were aware of her existence, even if they'd never seen her. As Bash's sister-in-law, he'd make it a point to find out about her.

"What do you want?" she demanded, oddly calm and bone tired.

"To say hello."

"Hello. Now, excuse me." She started around him, but he blocked her. She sighed. "If you have a message for Christopher, I'll relay it to him."

His nostrils flared. "Maybe, I just want a family reunion with my little brother."

"No, maybe, you want to die. Christopher isn't interested in reuniting with you."

His mouth twisted into a nasty smile. "You're so sure what he wants, you little cunt. He was with me yesterday. With my own two eyes, I watched him fuck two sluts."

Christopher said he hadn't cheated. Supposedly, he was with Derby. If her husband had dealings with Bash, an enemy, he would've had the men he trusted the most at his side. "You're a liar. My husband is faithful to me."

"According to Derby, Outlaw's mostly faithful." Bash

sniffed. "Outlaw himself said that no man's happy sticking his cock in one slit for the rest of his life."

Given her knowledge of yesterday's events, the words were like a knife twisting in her heart and she stumbled back, dropping her box of pastries. Christopher never lied to her, yet the events of yesterday, Johnnie's barrage of taunts, and now Bash's words, undermined her confidence in herself, her husband, and the state of her marriage.

Bash laughed, and the sound of motorcycle pipes barely penetrated her pain and despair.

"I'm going to fuck you before I kill you, Megan," he swore, bending close to her ear to impart those words. "I'm sick of waiting."

"Meggie!"

She thought she imagined Derby calling her name, until he was suddenly in front of her with another man who had red hair and a ruddy color.

"Derby—"

"Meggie, babe, I'm sorry I'm late," Gypsy said, rushing up to the small, little group, hot on Derby's heels. She sidled a glance at Derby and tears filled her eyes. She nodded to the other man. "Hey, Dez."

"What the fuck are you doing here, motherfucker?" Derby demanded, glaring at Bash and preventing a response from Dez. "If Outlaw finds out you're fucking with his bitch, he will fucking kill you—"

"Motherfucker had the chance to kill me," Bash snapped. "He didn't."

"I didn't come for this," Gypsy said stiffly, sniffling.

A dull ache started at the base of Meggie's skull. She needed to get home before she ended back in the emergency room. She sent an 'SOS' text.

"Outlaw is gunning for Derby, Dez, and Johnnie—"

Meggie blinked. "Gypsy, what—"

Gypsy grabbed Meggie's bloodless hands. "Listen to me—"

"Outlaw killed two of my bitches, Meggie," Derby said, jerking her to him and then shoving her back.

Gypsy released another sob. "You put their lives in danger," she cried. "You're a miserable fucking cheater and you're trying to make Outlaw one, too."

"I'm sorry, babe! I swear. Fuck, I thought he'd finally broken down. I didn't…"

"Shut up!" Gypsy snarled, swiping at the tears cascading down her cheeks.

Meggie was trying to make sense of the situation. Johnnie's taunts drummed in her head, competing with Bash's gloating. "Christopher ch-cheated." Her voice broke, so she paused, determined not to fall apart in public, especially in front of Derby and Bash. She pointed to him. "He told me what Christopher said about not wanting one woman for the rest of his life."

"Goddamn." Derby scrubbed a hand over his face. "I'm so fucking dead."

"Outlaw didn't say that, Meggie," Dez said sharply. "Derby did."

"Talk to her with respect, motherfucker," Derby ordered. Like Bash, sweat was beading Derby's face and head. "She's the only one who can save us." He glared at Bash. "Tell her the truth, if you don't want to die slowly and painfully."

"I can shoot her down and disappear," Bash said casually. "Then what?"

"Dez or me would take you down."

"You'd die for this cunt? I assure you, one or both of you would die with me." He studied Dez. "You sure you want to throw your allegiance to a sinking ship?"

Gypsy's tears and the men's arguing pounded through

Meggie's head. She sent another blanket 'SOS' and added '911', not caring who received the message, as long as someone came to her assistance.

"Who the fuck did you text?" Derby demanded.

"The club," Meggie snapped.

"Jesus fucking Christ," Bash breathed, losing his color. "Outlaw, too?"

"He's the president of the club, idiot," Meggie told him, "and my husband."

"Oh my god!" Gypsy cried, falling to her knees in front of Meggie and wrapping her arms around her waist. "Meggie, please—"

Her phone began buzzing with incoming texts, just as Christopher's ringtone blasted from her phone. It could've been anyone, but Heaven by Julia Michaels was a dead giveaway as to the caller's identity.

"He didn't cheat!" Bash said, his eyes wild with fear and crazed with anger as Derby grabbed her phone. "Not as far as I know."

Dez stepped forward and bowed his head, while Gypsy sobbed against her. Dazed, Meggie laid her hands on Gypsy's shoulders.

"I have young kids, Meggie," Dez said, close to tears himself as Christopher hung up and Mortician started calling.

"Goddamn."

The sounds of speeding Harleys rose around them and it seemed as if the earth shook.

"Go," Derby ordered Dez, then looked at Bash and nodded. "You, too, motherfucker. Outlaw don't need to shoot you down in public and go to fucking jail."

Bash and Dez wasted no time following Derby's orders.

"Meggie, please—" Derby begged as Christopher,

Mortician, Digger, Val, and so many of the club members streamed into the area, it resembled a bike rally. Notably, Johnnie was missing. "He didn't cheat. I...please...I don't want to die. I swear, I swear I'll spend the rest of my life thanking you—"

Before she could respond, Christopher grabbed her and shoved her against him.

"Fuck, Prez!" Mortician called. "We in public."

Christopher fired, and Gypsy shrieked.

"Don't knock my fuckin' hand away afuckingain—"

Meggie disentangled herself and wrapped her fingers around her husband's wrist. "Christopher!" she screamed, hoping her voice penetrated his fury. "Christopher, listen to me!"

He glared at her. "What the fuck you doin' out?"

"Gypsy wanted to meet—"

"Your bitch called my woman out her sick—"

"Christopher!" Meggie cried, desperation creeping into her. "Don't do this. Whatever Derby did isn't worth his blood."

"He disrespected you. He left those two cunts in that fuckin' room and I had to shoot them—"

"Shhh," she said, trembling. "You could've...you could've smacked them," Meggie said, trying to reason with him, although she didn't know the full story since he hadn't volunteered the minute details. "But—"

"Hit a girl?" he asked in outrage. "I ain't no woman beater, Megan."

"Fuck, Outlaw, I'm sure those bitches would prefer you knocked them the fuck out instead of fucking shooting the fuck out of them," Slipper called, milling downwind of Meggie.

The situation was the furthest thing from funny, however,

her husband's twisted logic and the stress of the past hour sent her into a fit of giggles, even as tears streamed down her face. "You're such a psycho, Christopher."

She saw the exact moment he came back to her. He smiled. "Yeah, but I'm your psycho, Megan."

"You can't kill Derby, Dez, or Johnnie."

Christopher returned his gun to his cut. "First two club business. Last motherfucker either hidin' or lucky. I been lookin' for him all fuckin' day. You can't change your mind now. You told me to make him stop."

Oh, dear God. She did. Last night. She was so distraught, though. She hadn't realized what she was saying.

"SOS not for allies, Meggie," Digger said, tossing the cigarette he'd been smoking. "It's for motherfuckers about to harm you."

"Shut the fuck up, son," Mortician warned. "Prez ain't got the bloodlust out."

Val stepped next to Mortician. "You okay, Meggie?"

"Er—"

Cash and Stretch flanked Val and stared at her.

"You want Outlaw to know anything, sweetness?" Cash asked with meaning. He must've tapped into the security cameras outside the coffee shop.

"What the fuck you talkin' about, Ghost?" Christopher demanded as Johnnie walked up.

"What's going on?" He lifted a brow at Meggie. "Are you okay, sweetheart? I came as soon as I received your 'SOS'."

Christopher growled. "Where the fuck you been, assfuck?" he roared.

"In Portland," Johnnie answered in surprise. "With Knox. We were finalizing payment for the Ball, then we stopped at a diner. They have delicious food—"

Snarling incoherently, Christopher shoved his hand into

his pocket. Meggie leaned her head against his arm and he stilled.

He drew in a deep breath. "I'm going to ask you a couple questions, baby. Hear me?"

She nodded.

"The SOS ain't had nothin' to do with Derby, huh?"

"No."

"Johnnie?"

"He was in Portland, Christopher."

"Dez?"

"Wh-what does he have to do with this?"

"Answer me!" Christopher roared.

"No," she said glumly.

His arms encircled her and he kissed her forehead, his big body tautening. "Bash?" he asked with so much hatred and venom, Meggie shook. "Tell me what the fuck you saw on the fuckin' cameras, Cash," Christopher ordered at Meggie's silence.

"Outlaw—"

"I made the same fuckin' mistake with Bash that I did with your step fuckhead, Megan. I'm beatin' Rule and killin' Ryan."

"WHAT?" Meggie screeched, bursting into tears. "What? You can't...what? Christopher—"

"Shut up, Megan. Rule stabbed motherfuckin' Bash to save Ryan."

"Outlaw—" Val started, his voice shaking as much as Meggie's entire body.

"Ain't listenin'."

"Christopher, please, think of Zoann."

"I let those two motherfuckers live to get the word out that Ryan, Rule, Ryder, Ransom, and Axel were off fuckin' limits. I was the stupid motherfucker. Ryan fuckin' with Bash a betrayal to the fuckin' club. Ain't killin' Rule yet—"

"Christopher—"

"They put you in fuckin' danger. I put you in danger. If I could fuck myfuckinself up, I would, but then I would be away from you."

"I don't know what Ryan's up to, Outlaw," Val said in a rough, raw voice, ignoring Meggie's sobs. "He don't like me much anymore, but that don't mean I don't love him. Take me to the meatshack, brother."

"Wait a minute," Johnnie started, "you met with a rival club without conferring with the brothers?"

"Johnnie, shut up!" Meggie snarled tearfully. "Christopher isn't the bad guy!"

"And you aren't a member," he barked.

"There was a time when you would've stood at his side," she said. "No matter how the membership voted. You and Digger and Mortician and Val and Cash and Stretch backed him up, and he got things done. He protected the club, sometimes without their knowledge." She swiped at her tears, wishing she could tear Johnnie apart with her bare hands. "Everything was fine, so he got the glory. You're forgetting you and Cash block him every time he wants to strike, so he gets the blame! So...fuck off, jerk, and leave my husband alone. You aren't making him out to be the scapegoat for your stupidity. And, please, for the love of God, leave me alone. I don't want you dead. I just want you stopped."

"What are you talking about, Megan?" Johnnie demanded, the picture of innocence.

"You're still gaslighting me!" she snarled around her tears. "And for what, jackass?"

Johnnie smirked at her.

Sniffling, Meggie stared at him through watery eyes.

Dizziness was swirling through her head and the base of her skull pounded. She should never have left. Now, she couldn't help but wonder if it wasn't Derby who'd sent her the text because Gypsy utilized her open invitation to visit Meggie on a regular basis.

"You can't answer me," Johnnie said, gloating. "Not only are you interfering in club business, you're making excuses for Christopher—"

"Move, Megan," Christopher ordered.

Her hope that he allowed her to fight this battle with Johnnie died. Of course, Johnnie couldn't continue to poke the bear and not strip away the agreement she had with her husband. Before things reached the point of no return, Meggie acted, shoving Johnnie with all her might. Caught off-guard, he teetered backwards and fell on his butt, unable to regain his balance. It was rare that he was in punching distance and that Christopher was there to protect her. Normally, she was fighting for her life and Johnnie didn't feel her licks.

This afternoon, the stars aligned, and she balled her fist, punching Johnnie's stupid jaw and the side of his head. One was for his insult to her Christopher and the other was for his torture of her. She would've punched him again if he hadn't jumped to his feet at the same time Christopher wrapped one arm around her waist and lifted her away and punched Johnnie in the mouth simultaneously.

Meggie struggled in Christopher's hold. "Put me down, Christopher."

"Nope."

"Yes! I will beat up Johnnie. You can't kill him. You can't kill Ryan or our sons. They are children. You can't kill Derby. You can't kill Dez."

"I can kill any fuckin' body I want, especially if they fuckin' with you. I just got back to the fuckin' club when I got that message. Do you fuckin' know what the fuck it did to me when I ain't had a fuckin' chance to dismount and I see a clubful of motherfuckers rushin' to their rides."

"Well, jackass, if you hadn't left early this morning, maybe that wouldn't have happened. You can't kill our family because you're angry for protecting our children—"

"Ryan not my child—"

"Yes, they are all our children, and our children are theirs. You will not kill them."

"They put you at risk. I put you—"

"Shut up! You didn't put me at risk. Your stupid brother did. You can't be everywhere at once."

"I should've been with you."

"If you were out hunting Johnnie, I agree, Christopher." Meggie ignored Johnnie's widening eyes. "But you have a club to run. You must run your club. I am fine. I am your ride-or-die. I promise you I will hold down our house and our family. Run the club." Glaring at Johnnie, she sniffed. "I'm not going anywhere. As for Derby, if he hadn't come I don't know what Bash would've done. Even if I had walked away, I would have left believing you'd cheated. Derby told me the truth."

"I told you the truth, Megan."

How could she tell Christopher everything Johnnie had said to play on her fears? She hadn't slept well last night, though she pretended she had. Christopher never lied to her, yet everything in her brain felt so muddled and jumbled together.

She nodded. "I know. But I...I have a lot on my mind. I'm sorry for doubting you."

"The club goin' on lockdown," Christopher said.

"We need to take a vote," Johnnie said, removing the

handkerchief pressed against his mouth to impart those words.

"Ain't listenin'—"

"I agree with Johnnie, Outlaw," Cash said quietly, flushing when Meggie threw him the evil eye.

Johnnie nodded. "The dispute with Bash sounds more like a personal problem rather than a club issue, Christopher."

"Why don't we go to the fucking club and discuss this?" Digger said. "We out in the fucking open."

"And I'm going to have to get Mutt additional money for ignoring any calls that might have gone to the station after the shots were fired," Stretch said, glowering at Cash.

Christopher put two fingers in his mouth and whistled, drawing everyone's attention. "Meet me at the fuckin' club in thirty minutes." He made the forward motion with his hand, signaling his brothers to ride out.

When the roar of the motorcycles faded, only Meggie, Christopher, Johnnie, his officers and close friends, and Gypsy and Derby remained.

"Talk to Ryan, Val," Christopher said. "If he fuckin' with the Scorps, he betrayin' the fuckin' club."

"I know, Outlaw." Val's voice shook.

A muscle ticked in Christopher's jaw, and he glanced away. "Ain't no different than what Big Joe would've done. He would've killed any of us if we fucked with the enemy."

"I don't think so," Johnnie said. "You got away with a lot, Christopher."

"And I fuckin' suffered just as much," Christopher said. "Ain't like you can talk, motherfucker, since you could've fucked all of us up and Big Joe couldna done fuck all cuz of Logan."

Johnnie snapped his mouth shut.

"I want a lockdown," Christopher said. "I need your

support, Johnnie. Yours, too, Cash."

"No." Johnnie glanced away. "I'm sorry. I really am. My life is different now, Christopher. Our lives. We'd prefer to find solutions rather than war. One of these days, we'll come out the loser."

"Bruh, if you lost your stomach for it, patch out," Digger said with sympathy. "Or step down and become a regular member."

"Fuck no! It is my god given right to be in the position. I should've been…Never mind."

"President, right, Johnnie?" Christopher said quietly. "You should've been Prez. Except you ain't ever had the patience."

"Or the diplomatic skills," Val said, looking and sounding more like himself now that Ryan was out of danger.

Meggie swore regret flared in Johnnie's eyes before it morphed into coldness.

"I had the fucking education. I had the knowledge to not sound like a fucking idiot. Even now, when everyone is behind you, you can't keep it straight. You're not a leader. You're a fucking joke, Christopher. Do us a favor and step down, take your family, and leave us in fucking peace."

"Speak for your fucking self, Johnnie," Mortician spat. "Without Prez, the club going down."

"Don't you mean without Megan?" Johnnie barked.

"Fuck you, John Boy," Stretch said. "Mort means Outlaw. I'd say Outlaw and Meggie, and I stand with them, although I'm sure Cash doesn't."

"Fuck off, Woo Woo Boy," Cash said in disgust. "You don't get to speak for me."

"And you don't get to fucking talk to me," Stretch replied. "How dare you go against Outlaw's wishes for a lockdown. The Scorpions should be dealt with once and for all."

The words floated around Meggie, but she focused on

Christopher. His pain was almost palpable. He hadn't taken his gaze off Johnnie in the last several minutes.

She took Christopher's hand in her own, brought it to her lips and kissed it, before squeezing gently. "I'm tired," she said softly.

"Okay, baby," Christopher said. "Ima…I'm gonna…I'm going to drive you home."

She kissed his hand again. "You know what I've realized, my love? When you're relaxed or angry, you say what needs to be said without bothering who you offend or any errors you might make. But when you're worried about me or vulnerable to morons, you're uncertain. We love you, Christopher. Your family don't care what words you choose as long as you're you."

"Maybe, Johnnie right, Megan," Christopher said, instead of addressing her words. "Maybe, it's time to step down. That might be the best fuckin' way to protect you."

Johnnie

Over the years, Johnnie had made questionable choices followed by questionable actions. These decisions fell into three categories. Some were by design, others by accident, and others were because he saw no other option. Usually, varying degrees of repercussions followed. Often, meted out by Christopher or Mortician.

He couldn't remember the last time he'd felt so low in his dealing with Christopher. Johnnie meant to anger Christopher, not hurt him. Take Megan on a vacation to cool off and by the time he returned, Johnnie could have Bash in hand.

Obviously, the motherfucker was running rampant if he'd not only confronted Megan but had a run-in with Ryan and Rule.

Arriving back at the club, he parked his bike in its place and dismounted. Most of the members were already back. The parking lot was overflowing.

In silence, he watched as Christopher held his hand out to Megan. She took it without hesitation and allowed her

husband to help her out of her SUV. Mortician, Val, and Stretch crowded around Christopher and Megan, while Cash and Digger headed to Johnnie.

"You were so fucking wrong, Johnnie," Cash said.

He was. At the moment, he couldn't quite remember his initial reasons for keeping Bash's bullshit away from Christopher. Now, he was running scared. For Kendall, Mattie, and Megan because of Bash, and for himself because of Christopher. The only way he could escape with his life was to double down on the pressure he put on Megan and his insistence for peace.

Anytime Christopher thought about killing Ryan, Johnnie wouldn't stand a chance. If he had to die, he wanted it to be in exchange for his wife and daughter's lives. If Christopher killed him, that wouldn't happen.

"What you said to Outlaw was foul," Cash continued. "Meggie should've punched you more than twice."

Johnnie preferred her punches to Christopher's.

Digger snickered. "However else I feel about her, Meggie stand ten toes down for Outlaw and she always have."

"What the fuck does that mean?" Cash asked.

"Yeah, you've kind of been a dick to her lately," Johnnie said."

"Bruh." Digger shook his head. "If that's not a dick calling a dick a dick. Wait…"

"Yeah, fuckhead, you just called yourself a dick," Cash said.

"I didn't mean to. All I'm saying is Johnnie been a dick, too."

He couldn't deny that. He'd been a dick to everyone. "Your point? Not that it matters. My behavior shouldn't dictate yours and vice versa."

"Meggie made a lot of sense. I always saw her as the reason Outlaw sank or swim. Fuck, bruh, we needed her when she first got here because she got his head on straight, then she got so fucking annoying, flitting through life with a fucking smile."

"You really don't like that woman, do you?" Cash said.

Digger shrugged. "I do. Most of the time. Sometimes." He scratched his jaw. "Fuck, I don't know. It's been so long since Meggie been a wild little bitch, I fucking forgot what a temper she got. The last few years, she been a spoiled, Barbie ass cunt."

"You do know the last few years she took portions of the money we found in that basement, invested it, and increased our collective wealth?" Johnnie asked.

"Of course I do! Boss was good with numbers," Digger grumbled. "Meggie should be good at something else other than fucking and sucking Outlaw and pushing his babies out."

"Are you okay?" Johnnie asked in all seriousness.

"As if you fucking care. You've been creating fucking anarchy yourself. Don't think I've forgotten how you fucking bragged about manipulating Outlaw into negotiating peace."

"I like our lives—"

"I don't," Digger interrupted. "If Bailey leave Mort or if Meggie die, maybe shit might get back to normal."

"I'm not listening to this bullshit," Johnnie said.

"Why? I don't have no old lady anymore. I got a wife. Meggie encouraged Bunny to return to tutoring, so she did. Instead of letting my woman go, she convinced her having two jobs is good. So I have to take care of our children while Bunny living her best life. All because Meggie can't keep her fucking mouth shut."

"Bunny didn't have to follow Meggie's advice," Cash pointed out. "Maybe, she's hiding behind that excuse to keep the peace between you and her."

"My woman not like that. She speak her fucking mind. Anyway, if that's the case, it just turned me against Meggie. She took Prez from us. She took Mort from me—"

"That was Bailey," Johnnie said.

"It was Meggie. It was 'cause of her my brother met Bailey. It don't matter because, now, she took my girl. Things was fine when Bunny worked for Meggie. They took care of the kids together. I went over there and ate almost every day. Outlaw talked to me about club shit while they cleaned up, then suddenly that bitch told my bitch to find a teaching position if it made her happy."

Before Cash or Johnnie responded, Christopher guided

Megan toward them, with Mortician, Val, and Stretch following behind.

"I see CJ now," she said.

Johnnie glanced toward the private gate just as CJ closed it.

"Goddamn, Prez, you spit on the little motherfucker," Mort said.

"Nope, just came real hard when I made him."

Megan groaned, shaking her head at the laughter.

"Hey, Shortie," CJ greeted, leaning down and kiss Megan on the cheek. "You're okay?"

"I'm fine."

"Hey, Dad."

"Hey, boy."

CJ nodded to everyone, although when he got to Johnnie, it was the barest movement of his head. "You need me to carry you, Mom?"

"No, son," she said with a smile. "I can walk."

"Okay." CJ settled an arm around her shoulder and guided her toward the walkway. "Let me know if that changes."

"I'll be home as soon as I can."

"Take your time, Outlaw," she called.

CJ grinned over his shoulder. "What she said, 'Law."

Watching her retreating form, Johnnie thought about the feelings he'd once had for her. They'd refused to die and he'd never understood why.

Now, he realized her strength and loyalty had always drawn him. If Bash succeeded, he wouldn't only take her from Christopher but all of them.

As they filed into the clubhouse, Johnnie knew he would go against Christopher and push for peace with Bash, though it wouldn't make a difference.

Bash wanted Meggie dead, but Johnnie wanted her safe,

and he'd do everything in his power to see that it was so.

THE END

Thank you for reading ***Restless***.
If you enjoyed it, please consider leaving a review at your point of purchase and on Goodreads. It means a lot to me to hear what you think.

CONTACT KAT

Website: https://katckelly.com
https://Deathdwellersmc.com

Email: katkelwriter@outlook.com

Snail mail: 24200 Southwest Freeway, Suite 402, Box #353,
Rosenberg, TX 77471

Amazon Author Page: https://sqr.co/Follow-Kat-on-Amazon/

Website: https://www.katckelly.com

Dedicated Series Website: https://deathdwellersmc.com

Facebook: https://www.facebook.com/kathryn.kelly.336717

Twitter: https://twitter.com/katkelwriter

Blog: http://kathrynkellyauthor.blogspot.com

Pinterest: http://www.pinterest.com/kathrynkelly336/

Goodreads: https://www.goodreads.com/author/show/7422779.
Kathryn_Kelly

Instagram: https://www.instagram.com/katkelwriter/

YouTube: https://sqr.co/Kat-on-YouTube/

BIBLIOGRAPHY

Cocky Hero Club
Savage Suit

Death Dwellers MC Legacy
Reckless, Book 1
Restless, Book 2
Relentless, Book 3
Ruthless, Book 4
Remorseless, Book 5

Death Dwellers Next Generation
(COMING SOON)

Death Dwellers MC
Misled
Misappropriate
Misunderstood
Misdeeds
Misbehavior
Misjudged
Misguided
Misalliance
Misconduct
A Very Christopher Christmas

Misfit
Mistrust
Misgivings
An Outlaw Valentine
Misrule
Death Dwellers: The Complete Set
Outlaw's Dictionary

Phoenix Rising Rock Band
Inferno
Incendiary
Scorched
Inflame

Dirty Boy Studios
Dirty Boy

Single Titles
Captivated
All My Tomorrows
The Enforcers' Revenge co-written with Emma James
Sexy Santa

Anthologies
Pink: Hot 'N Sexy for a cure: The Books for Boobies 2015 Anthology
When Clubs Collide
Desire Me
The Marriage Monologues – Forever A Dark Obsession Anthology
Sexy Santa – All I Want For Christmas Anthology
Red Stiletto – Call My Bluff Anthology Hazel & Grayson – Brothers
Grimm Fairytales: An Erotic Anthology
Barebacked – Game Player Anthology
Breakfast & Bedlam – Happily Ever After Anthology
Drifter's Vow: Red Rum MC – Vow of Protection Anthology
How Innocent My Love – Secrets of Me Anthology
Misconstrued - Forever His Ride Or Die Anthology
My One and Only – Goodbye Doesn't Mean Forever Anthology
Gods & Goddesses – Wicked Realms Anthology
Ignite - My Perfect Pleasure Anthology

Last Chance To Call You Mine
House of Secrets

Writing as Leslie Ferdinand
Wicked Allure
Picture Perfect
Forty Minutes to Disaster - Down In The Dirt Magazine

Writing as Christine Holden (Mother-Daughter Team Shirley Ferdinand and Leslie Ferdinand)
A Time For Us
Patterns of Love
Bedazzled
A Hitch In Time
Dearest Beloved
Een toegewijde dienaar - Dearest Beloved - Audax Publishing Amsterdam

Kindle Vella
Urchin of the Court
Ace of Spades - Red Rum MC

ABOUT KAT

Kathryn C. Kelly is a New Orleans native who has called southeast Texas home since 2005. She had intended to travel the world while always returning to her beloved New Orleans. Hurricane Katrina had other plans. She is the mother of three beautiful daughters and the daughter of one gorgeous mother whose footsteps she followed in by becoming a writer.

Kathryn is the former owner and editor of Inside Rose Rich Magazine. She and her mother have been published by Jove Books as Christine Holden. The books have long been out of print but they got the rights back to the five novels and have plans to re-release them soon.

Kathryn is a cancer survivor. In 2010, she felt a small lump in her breast. In 2015, at the urging of her mother, she went in for her bi-yearly mammogram and was diagnosed with Stage 2b/3a HER2 positive breast cancer. On November 30, 2016, she rang the bell. During her treatment, she was also diagnosed with Li-Fraumeni Syndrome.

In 2013, Christopher "Outlaw" Caldwell introduced himself to Kat in the most cliché way ever. He came to her in a dream. After the inauspicious meeting, he planted himself in her mind and the gentleman hasn't left yet. In what was only supposed to be one book about the fictitious Death Dwellers MC, Outlaw has become a source of amusement, a well of frustration, and a bone of contention between Kat and one of her daughters.

She is hard at work on Reckless, the book that will bridge the OGs with a new generation of Death Dwellers. Her work has been included in several anthologies and she is looking forward to other upcoming single title releases, including Savage Suit from the Cocky Hero Club World created by Vi Keeland and Penelope Ward. She is a former RWA member. She also served as Vice President for the SOLA chapter of RWA.

She is a New Orleans Saints fan, but roots for the Texans, the Rockets, and the Coogs (U of H) as long as they aren't playing any Louisiana teams. She loves champagne and sparkling wine. One day, she will try Snoop's brand. She still loves Chivas Regal but had a chance to taste Sassenach Scotch. A #lifegoal is to one day buy herself an entire bottle and keep it all for herself.

In her head, she is a biker babe with a Harley in her garage, waiting for her to hit the road. In reality, she has yet to hop on a bike and ride. She loves Cards Against Humanity, has very strong opinions that she keeps to herself, has to take her time to talk in public so nothing untoward pops out, and always strives to see the best in people and in life.

www.ingramcontent.com/pod-product-compliance
Lightning Source LLC
Chambersburg PA
CBHW040849010826
48978CB00013BA/941